A man for all seasons?

Summer Reed needs a hero, although she'd be the last one to admit it. Little does she guess that gorgeous Derek Anderson has a plan—to be her *Hero in Disguise.*

Spring Reed is ready to loosen up and live a little.And fun-loving Clay MacEntire is more than willing to offer her adventure, excitement...and *him,* her *Hero for the Asking.*

Autumn Reed's independent streak has got her into trouble one too many times. She needs somebody she can trust. And who could be more reliable—not to mention tempting—than good-looking Dr. Jeff Bradford, a true *Hero by Nature?*

HOLDING
OUT FOR
A HERO

When he cares enough to be the very best!

D0451301

Dear Reader,

When my first book, *Hero in Disguise,* was published in 1987, it was the culmination of a goal I'd had longer than I can remember—to be a published writer. And when I was able to follow my first sale with two connected books, *Hero for the Asking* and *Hero by Nature,* I thought I couldn't be any happier.

Now, several years later, I know the truth—that this writing life just keeps getting better and better. And although I have written more than fifty books for Harlequin and Silhouette, I must admit the Reed sisters will always be special to me. Not only did they launch my writing career, but through them I learned what I did best—creating stories that deal with families and falling in love, featuring real-life heroines trying to follow their hearts, and of course, the dashing men who steal them.

I hope you enjoy taking a trip down memory lane with me.

Sincerely,

Gina Wilkins

GINA WILKINS

HOLDING
OUT FOR
A HERO

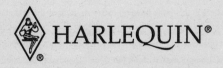

HARLEQUIN®

TORONTO • NEW YORK • LONDON
AMSTERDAM • PARIS • SYDNEY • HAMBURG
STOCKHOLM • ATHENS • TOKYO • MILAN • MADRID
PRAGUE • WARSAW • BUDAPEST • AUCKLAND

HARLEQUIN BOOKS

by Request—HOLDING OUT FOR A HERO

Copyright © 1999 by Harlequin Books S.A.

ISBN 0-373-20162-1

The publisher acknowledges the copyright holder of the individual works as follows:
HERO IN DISGUISE
Copyright © 1987 by Gina Wilkins
HERO FOR THE ASKING
Copyright © 1988 by Gina Wilkins
HERO BY NATURE
Copyright © 1988 by Gina Wilkins

This edition published by arrangement with Harlequin Books S.A.

Visit us at www.romance.net

Printed in U.S.A.

CONTENTS

He snuck into her life—
and stole her heart....

HERO IN DISGUISE

by Gina Wilkins

HERO IN DISGUISE

by Gina Wilkins

1

"OH, MY GOD, what is *he* doing here?"

Connie's distressed query drew Summer's attention away from the noisy, uninhibited party going on in their living room. She turned her eyes toward the open doorway. Her pulse gave an odd little leap at the sight of the attractive man standing there looking curiously around the crowded room. Surrounded by movement and color, he was conspicuous by his very stillness and neutrality. He looked to be in his late thirties and was dressed quite conservatively in a tan sport coat and dark brown slacks, a muted striped tie knotted at the collar of his cream shirt.

"Bill collector?" she inquired of her obviously displeased roommate.

"Worse," Connie groaned. "It's Derek."

"That's your brother?" Summer asked in surprise, her eyebrows shooting upward to disappear beneath her heavy fringe of amber-brown bangs. "What's he doing here?"

"That's what I want to know. He's lived across the bay from us for six months and he has to pick tonight, of all nights, to pay a surprise visit," Connie muttered grimly. "And I was having such a good time," she added in a wail. Squaring her shoulders beneath her brilliantly patterned, oversize sweatshirt, she tossed her unruly red hair out of her face and started across the room toward her older brother.

Summer found herself unable to look away from Derek Anderson. Because Connie and Derek had been at odds since he had settled in Sausalito six months earlier, Summer had not had the chance to meet Connie's brother be-

fore that night. He looked nothing like the mental picture
she had formed of him. Connie had always described her
older brother as average in appearance, stern of personality. Summer had expected to meet a man who looked
older than his thirty-seven years, dull and unappealing.
That was not what she saw as she stared at him. True, Derek's tobacco-brown hair was conservatively short, his
black-framed glasses quite conventional and his clothing
rather staid. But there was something about him that
didn't conform to Summer's preconceptions. Something
about the spark of streetwise intelligence in pewter-gray
eyes when they met hers for a moment from across the
room. Or the six feet of hard, lean muscle beneath the
strictly tailored clothing where there should have been
softness and perhaps a little flab. Or maybe it was something about those broad, squared shoulders.

He looked strong, solid, a little tough. Even as she
watched him conversing stiffly with his defensive sister,
Summer decided that there was more to this man than
Connie had implied. Never one to resist a challenge, Sum-
mer vowed to make an effort to find out more about Derek
Anderson—personally—at the earliest opportunity.

"Hey, Summer," someone said, drawing her attention
reluctantly away from her roommate's possibly interesting brother. "Tell Clay about the ninety-year-old dude
who tried to pick you up in the supermarket the other
day."

"Ninety?" she scoffed, her brilliant blue eyes widening
dramatically. "He was a hundred if he was a day." Then,
with great enthusiasm and liberal embellishment, she
launched into a mostly apocryphal account that soon had
her listeners bellowing with laughter. Her own laughter,
which had once been described by an infatuated and
quickly dispatched young man as "the tinkling of dozens
of fairy bells," floated frequently above the less refined
guffaws.

"What are you doing here, Derek?" Connie demanded
the moment she came to a stop in front of him.

"I wanted to meet some of your friends," her brother replied in a conciliatory voice. "I heard you mention this party to Mom last weekend and I thought this would be a good opportunity for us to interact socially."

"Did it ever occur to you to request an invitation?" Connie asked him sarcastically, her green eyes glittering. "And don't give me that stuff about interacting socially. You're just here to criticize my friends and make more cutting remarks about the way I run my life."

Derek sighed. "Would you give me a break, Connie? I'm trying to offer a truce."

"Sure you are. The same way you 'offer' advice, right?"

Derek ran his fingers through his short brown hair in frustration. "You want me to leave?"

"Suit yourself," Connie answered with a shrug. "I'm sure you'll be bored to tears. Don't expect me to entertain you. I plan to spend the evening with my friends." She placed extra emphasis on the last word.

Derek was tempted to tell his sister that she was acting like a brat but knew that comment would not help matters between them. "I'll stay for a while, then," he told her. "And I won't expect you to entertain me."

Connie shrugged again. "Whatever."

He refused to allow her to make him angry. Instead, he looked around the crowded room, pausing when his gaze clashed with a pair of vivid blue eyes. "Who's the woman on the bar stool?" he asked, hardly aware of having spoken aloud.

"That's my roommate," Connie answered coolly. "Summer Reed. You've heard me talk about her. Go introduce yourself if you want to. I'm going to mingle with my guests." She didn't add "invited guests," but then she really didn't have to. Her tone said it for her.

Not for the first time, Derek was aware of a sense of regret that his absence from the country for most of the past fifteen years had left such a rift between him and his only sibling. A rift that he was having no luck trying to repair. He'd had some vague notion of getting closer to his estranged sister by meeting some of her friends and learning more about her life-style, of which he frankly disapproved. Unfortunately, he'd made her angry again. He seemed to have a real talent for it, he thought, stifling a sigh. Connie was convinced that he was there only to criticize her.

Looking around, Derek was relieved to discover that the admittedly eccentric group of young people with whom Connie claimed friendship was not quite as unsavory as he had expected. True, alcohol was flowing freely, but no one seemed to be indulging more than the usual overly enthusiastic party guest, and Derek saw no sign of illegal substances being used. The music was too loud, the clothing decidedly strange and the humor rather twisted, but on the whole he saw nothing more detrimental than the quite obvious signs of immaturity and irresponsibility.

Derek's attention wandered back toward the battered wooden bar across the room. Specifically he focused on the young woman chatting animatedly from the only bar stool. His immediate attraction to Summer had startled him. She was too young for him, for one thing. He knew she was Connie's age—twenty-five, twelve years younger than Derek. She wasn't particularly glamorous. Her short, silky hair was golden brown, her eyes bright blue, her face lovely in a refreshingly wholesome way. She seemed to wear a permanent smile, a wide, contagious grin that displayed very even white teeth and a glimpse of pink tongue. Because he was consumed by a sudden hunger to have that smile turned upon him, Derek straightened his tie and moved deliberately toward the bar.

The floor of the large living area of the furnished apartment had been cleared for dancing—no big deal since the only furniture consisted of a sagging couch and a couple of small, worn armchairs flanked by a rickety coffee table and two mismatched end tables. Music throbbed from the stereo system in one corner. Still perched on the stool beside the functional bar, Summer sipped her liberally spiked punch, watching what promised to become a hilarious dance contest. Clay McEntire—Crazy Clay—was in rare form that night, and Summer was fully prepared to enjoy the show.

"Has the queen bee been deserted by her drones?" a dry voice inquired from her side. Though not raised above the screaming music, the words were clearly audible nonetheless.

Summer looked around with an eyebrow lifted in curiosity to find Derek Anderson leaning negligently against the bar beside her. "I beg your pardon?"

"You've been sitting here surrounded by an audience since I arrived. What are you to keep them so entertained, a stand-up comic?"

"A sit-down comic, actually," Summer replied in her soft Southern drawl, resisting the impulse to rub her right knee. "How are you, Derek? I'm Connie's roommate, Summer Reed."

"Yes, I know. I hope you don't mind that I crashed your party tonight."

"Of course not. I'm glad you're here. I've wanted to meet my all-time favorite roomie's brother. Connie's told me a lot about you."

"I'm sure she has." His voice was heavy with irony, his pewter eyes entirely too knowing. "Has she told you that 'Derek the Dictator' is a sanctimonious, interfering stuffed shirt?"

Summer grinned. "That about sums it up."

Derek's eyes slid slowly down to her smile, and Summer was rather surprised to feel a momentary self-consciousness at the intensity of his close regard. Though Derek's expression seemed admiring enough, she was under no illusion that he was bowled over by her beauty. She wasn't beautiful. Her hair, the color of clear amber honey, was cut very short in the back and left longer in the front to fall in a flirty fringe over her intensely blue eyes. The rest of her features, in Summer's opinion, were rather ordinarily pixieish—a small, tip-tilted nose, high cheekbones and a generous smile. No dimples, thank God.

She'd always thought that dimples would have made her just too "cute" to bear.

She crossed her denim-covered legs and returned Derek's unblinking look. "I've always wondered how accurate Connie's description of you was," she informed him with a suggestion of a question mark at the end of the comment. She especially wondered now, as she found herself responding to his hard strength in a decidedly physical way, if all those derogatory remarks Connie had made in the past few months had been anywhere near the truth. Summer had certainly never expected to find herself attracted to the man, yet her quickened breathing and accelerated heartbeat as he leaned closer made it impossible for her to deny that she was. "Are you really as bossy as she says?"

His breath almost brushing the soft cheek of the woman on the tall stool beside him, Derek seemed to reflect a moment, then his hard mouth twisted into a smile of sorts. "I suppose she was fairly accurate."

There was just something about him.... Summer eyed him consideringly. "I wonder."

Seeming to suddenly grow tired of the subject of himself, Derek nodded toward the writhing bodies on the makeshift dance floor. "I know why I'm not out there making an idiot of myself, but what about you? Why aren't you dancing?"

Summer shrugged, unable this time to keep herself from protectively cupping her knee. "I'm just not into dancing. Tell me about the new business you've started, Derek. Management consulting, isn't it?"

"Yes, that's right. I'm specializing in small, struggling businesses."

Though he didn't elaborate, Summer knew that Derek was already making a name for himself in his field. In spite of herself, Connie had not quite been able to hide her pride in her brother's early success. He was not yet rich from his new enterprise, nor was he known in any part of the country other than Marin County and the surrounding

San Francisco area, but Connie seemed to think it was only a matter of time. Examining the determined glint in Derek's gray eyes, Summer knew Connie was probably right. This was a man who could accomplish whatever he desired.

She peeked at Derek through her lashes as she lifted her punch and took a sip. "You must be very good at what you do."

He looked at her suspiciously. "Why?"

She returned the look innocently. "Connie tells me that you're an expert on offering advice." Connie had been quite vocal in her displeasure with Derek's heavily paternal treatment of her. She'd informed Summer that Derek offered advice to struggling businessmen during working hours and to his resentful younger sister in the little free time his career left him.

Derek winced, obviously well aware of his sister's opinion of his "advice." "I think I'll pour myself a drink."

Summer laughed softly. "Why don't you do that? Would you like some punch? It's pretty good, though God only knows what's in it."

"No, thanks. I'll pass." He reached for a bottle of Scotch, splashing a generous amount over two ice cubes in a glass that looked suspiciously like a jelly jar.

Summer exhaled dramatically. "Okay, we'll drop the subject of your present career. How about your former one? Were you truly just a government gofer, as Connie likes to say, or were you really something more exciting, like a spy?" Actually, Connie had been rather vague about what Derek had done for the fifteen years prior to settling in Sausalito, but Summer had understood that he'd worked in some sort of diplomatic capacity that had kept him on the move from one American embassy to another.

Derek answered without changing expression. "A spy, of course. But I try not to spread that around."

Delighted with his answer, since it indicated that he did possess a sense of humor, Summer smiled brightly. "Of course not. Tell me, Derek, was it terribly exciting?"

"Terribly."

"And chillingly dangerous?"

"Chillingly."

"And desperately romantic?"

"Desperately."

She laughed and leaned against the bar, cocking her head to meet his studiously grave expression with a friendly smile. "You have such a colorful way with words, Derek. Are all spies as silver-tongued as you?"

He nodded. "Just like James Bond."

"Why in the world would you leave such an exciting life to become an ordinary California businessman?" she asked tauntingly.

He shoved one hand into the pocket of his brown slacks and leaned beside her, his drink held loosely in his other hand. He continued to watch her with that oddly intense gaze as he answered lightly, "All that excitement, danger and romance gets boring after a while. I needed a change."

"How fascinating." So he was capable of returning nonsense for nonsense, Summer thought in fascination. Connie hadn't mentioned that. In fact, Summer added reflectively, her eyes straying to Derek's powerful chest and muscular thighs, there were several things about her brother that Connie had failed to mention. She decided it was time to test his reflexes. "So, Derek, Connie tells me now that you've retired from globe-trotting, you've decided to settle down and become domesticated. Looking for a wife?"

He had just taken a sip of his Scotch. For a moment Summer thought he might choke, and she watched expectantly. Instead, he swallowed, set his glass on the bar and leaned even closer so that his chest brushed her shoulder. "Perhaps," he agreed. "Are you applying for the position?"

Summer chuckled and lifted her plastic tumbler in a mock salute. "Good comeback, Derek."

She imagined that his almost imperceptible smile was reflected in his metallic eyes. "Maybe I was serious."

"I think you should know I'm not exactly good wife material."

"Why not?" he inquired, looking admirably unfazed by the personal nature of his conversation with this impish stranger.

She lifted her watermelon-painted fingertips and began to enumerate. "A respectable businessman-type such as you would want someone punctual, fond of schedules. I'm neither. I'm not particularly well educated. I dropped out of college in the second semester of my sophomore year. The only thing I'm serious about is not being serious. I'm not socially or professionally ambitious. I require a great deal of attention and I like being entertained. Connie says you're a real sports nut. The only sports I participate in are people-watching and an occasional card game—for fun, of course. Do I sound like the woman you've been looking for?"

"No," he answered genially. "You don't sound at all like the woman I've been looking for. Perhaps I've been looking for the wrong kind of woman."

Summer's smile grew even more brilliant, though she wished rather breathlessly that he would step back just a little. She was entirely too aware of the feel of him against her shoulder. "I like you, Derek Anderson," she told him candidly. "Connie forgot to mention that her brother can be charming when he chooses to be. You and I might even manage to become friends."

The suggestion of a smile faded abruptly from Derek's eyes. "I can't seem to accomplish that feat even with my own sister."

Summer caught the undercurrents of pain in his voice. "I don't think Connie knows that you *want* to be her friend," she told him carefully.

He exhaled through his straight, sharply carved nose and changed the subject. "So what kind of man are you looking for, since you've turned up your nose at respectable businessmen? Or are you looking?"

Swallowing another sip of her punch, Summer swung

one leg in time to the music pounding over their conversation and replied, "Not actively. I'm waiting for the kind of hero Bonnie Tyler describes in her song, and they seem to be in short supply."

A slight frown creased Derek's brow behind his dark-framed glasses. "What song?"

"Sorry. I should have known you aren't into rock and roll. It's called 'Holding Out For a Hero.'"

"Oh. So what special qualities must this 'hero' possess?"

A flippant grin punctuating her words, she responded lightly. "Well, for starters, he has to have a great sense of humor. And he has to be adventurous and occasionally impulsive yet always there when I need him. I'd want him to be kind and caring, strong in more than the physical sense and emotionally mature. Like I said, there aren't many of them around."

Derek studied her face. "I thought you only wanted to party. Doesn't seem like you should want anyone to be beside you in times of trouble if you don't *have* times of trouble," he pointed out.

"Everyone has times of trouble. Times when it would be nice to have someone to lean on," Summer answered, unaware that her eyes had filled with an old, distant sadness as she thought back five years to a time when she had needed someone and to a man who had not been there for her. Then, realizing that she was allowing the conversation to become too heavy, she pasted her best party-girl smile back on her animated face and added, "Even Minnie Mouse has good old Mickey."

Derek's eyes gleamed with a sudden inner smile. "You're saying your hero is Mickey Mouse?"

She laughed. "Close enough." With the conversation back on a light line she was much more comfortable, able to throw off the past.

"Maybe the problem is that you've been dating the wrong kind of men. Maybe you should try dating men who are more—"

"Like you? Thanks, but no thanks," she quipped, though she wondered what she would say if he did ask her out. She wasn't sure she'd be able to turn him down, particularly if he was standing as close to her as he was now.

"Have I just been insulted? What's wrong with men like me? I'm emotionally mature, and I'm particularly good in times of trouble."

"I'm sure you are, but you're entirely too proper and conventional. I know it drives you crazy that Connie quit school and has no career goals and that she never misses a chance to party. You just can't resist offering her advice on how to improve her life. Like Connie, I would frustrate someone like you, and I would get tired of always being expected to follow your suggestions. A real hero for me would be a cross between you and…and someone like Clay McEntire over there." She pointed to a rugged, blond jock-type who was doing a really funny impersonation of a Motown backup singer as an oldie from The Temptations played in the background.

Following the direction of her pointing finger, Derek grunted and shook his head. "I'd jump feetfirst into a tar pit before I'd make a spectacle of myself like he's doing," he admitted. "Wouldn't it bother you to put on that kind of performance?"

"Oh, I've given a few performances in my time. Sometime Clay and I will have to show you our special impression of Gladys Knight and One Pip," she answered humorously. "You can't have any fun if you're stiff and formal all the time, Derek."

"Fun," he replied thoughtfully. "You call this party fun?"

"Very much so," she answered decisively. "Do you really dislike it all that much?"

"No." He looked directly into her eyes. "Not at all."

She started to ask him to elaborate, then decided not to. His proximity was doing unusual things to her senses, and suddenly words eluded her—an odd experience for Sum-

mer Reed, who always had a ready quip on her lips. She
could smell the crisp after-shave Derek wore and see the
sheen of tanned flesh where the indirect lighting of the
room fell on his face and throat. She was also becoming inexplicably fascinated by his eyes, their color changing
from dull pewter when he was serious to a gleaming silver
when they reflected the smile that barely touched his stern
mouth. She was becoming more and more aware of his
physical attributes, which she found rather dismaying.

"Are you actually admitting that it's okay to enjoy a
party?" she asked him quickly, forcing her voice through
her tight throat.

"Occasionally," he replied. "But there's no excuse for
making it one's only purpose for living as my sister seems
to do."

Summer straightened defensively on her stool, glaring
at the man beside her without a trace of her lovely smile.
"Connie is my best friend, Derek Anderson, and she's a
terrific person. Sure she's made a few mistakes in her life,
but who hasn't? You should consider yourself lucky to
have her for a sister rather than trying to change her into
your idea of the perfect young woman."

"That's telling him, Summer." Standing just behind
Summer's shoulder, Connie applauded her roommate's
indignant speech. Her improbably red hair worn in a
shaggy semipunk style and her green eyes outlined liberally with kohl, Connie looked even younger than her
twenty-five years in her baggy sweatshirt, which hung almost to the knees of her skintight black leggings. She
could not have made a more startling contrast to her
brother's conservative attire. "I should have warned you,
Derek, my friend Summer won't be any more hesitant
about telling you off than I am. You don't intimidate
everyone, you know."

"I never tried to intimidate you, Connie."

Watching in silence, Summer thought she detected a
shade of sadness in Derek's eyes. She believed that he
truly wanted what was best for his sister, though he

couldn't seem to accept that Connie had a right to her own mistakes. She turned her eyes to Connie and recognized the wistfulness in her friend's voice when she answered. "You just refuse to believe that I'm completely happy the way I am, don't you, Derek? You won't let me forget the mess I made of my marriage to Stu, as if none of it would have happened if I had only listened to you.

"But how could I have listened to you, Derek? Where were you when I was seventeen and madly infatuated with a handsome young actor? Somewhere in Europe or Southeast Asia or the Middle East, giving advice, as usual. I never saw you, I hardly ever heard from you and yet I was supposed to conform exactly to your expectations for me. Well, forget it, Derek. I'll do just fine without your advice now, just as I always have before. And if you're disappointed with what I've become in the fifteen years since you went off in search of adventure, that's just tough."

"Connie—"

"Hey, Connie!" someone yelled from across the room. "Come on, let's dance."

"I'm on my way," Connie yelled back, then tilted her head defiantly, looking at Derek even as she called across the room, "Let's party till we drop! Who wants more punch?"

"All right! Bring on the punch!"

Spinning on one heel, Connie threw herself back into the party with what Summer sensed was a desperate act of defiance. Summer ached for her friend, whose self-confidence and self-image had been so badly damaged by her failed teenage marriage. Connie would never admit those weaknesses, just as Summer found it hard to reveal her own insecurities and vulnerabilities to others, but the buried scars were there, in both of the determinedly cheerful young women.

Summer also felt rather sorry for Derek, whose face had gone hard but whose eyes were still so sad. "Can't you just accept her the way she is, Derek?" she asked suddenly, wanting to help despite her reluctance to get involved in a family matter. "You said you wanted to be her friend. Give her a chance to show you what a wonderful person she is."

"Now who's offering advice?" he questioned her shortly, then sighed. "Sorry. Listen, I think I'll cut out now. I've had about all of this 'fun' I can take."

For some strange reason Summer was reluctant to see him leave, but no hint of that reluctance was allowed to creep into her voice as she responded. "All right. I'm glad we had the opportunity to meet tonight, Derek. Perhaps we'll see each other again soon."

Derek turned his attention away from his sister to give Summer another one of those intense, unsettling looks. "You can count on it," he told her. Then he drained the last of his Scotch and started across the room toward the door. Before he reached it, Bonnie Tyler's wonderfully sandpapery voice sounded from the speakers in the chorus of "Holding Out For a Hero." Summer had been watching his departure, so she was looking straight into his eyes when he turned, jerked his head toward the stereo to indicate that he'd recognized the words, then lifted two fingers in a kind of salute before he disappeared through the door.

Nice, Summer thought. Strong. Dependable. Too bad he was so darned proper.

"Well, what did you think of my brother?" Connie asked later. "You two certainly talked for a long time. Wasn't he just the way I described?"

"Oh, I don't know," Summer answered vaguely. "I think you might be underestimating him, Connie. He's not as stern and inflexible as you've told me he is."

"Uh-oh. Don't tell me *you've* been taken in by his embassy charm."

"I like him, Connie—for a respectable businessman-type. I think he's unhappy about the distance between you. He implied that he'd like to be your friend."

Connie snorted bitterly. "Friends accept each other the

way they are, like you and I do, Summer. They don't try to change each other."

"Maybe Derek will figure that out for himself before long. Give him a chance," Summer urged, repeating the words she'd used to Derek. "After all, he's only been back in the country for a few months after being away for most of your life. You've hardly seen him during those years, so the two of you have had to start almost as strangers."

"He still treats me as if I were ten years old," Connie complained. "I'm so tired of him telling me that I could do better for myself than what I'm doing."

"Give it time, Connie. He's trying."

"I'll try," Connie sighed. "It would please my parents if Derek and I learned to get along better," she added, as if it really didn't matter to her one way or the other. Then she rushed back into the middle of the party, obviously intending to put her brother completely out of her mind.

Summer shook her head in sympathy, never asking how two siblings could be so different. After all, her own family was a good example of the same phenomenon. Summer's two lovely sisters were as different from each other as they were from Summer.

But Summer and Connie—now *they* were a well-matched pair. Summer had liked Connie Anderson from the day she'd first met her in the accounting office where they both worked. They loved to laugh together, and their sense of humor was almost identical. They enjoyed music, parties, people and comedy clubs. They both hid any fears or doubts they might carry inside them behind quick wits and ready smiles, each having her own good reasons for doing so.

Their only major difference was their approach to men. Trying to bolster her bruised ego, Connie flitted from one man to another with all the discrimination of a starving honeybee in a field of wildflowers. Summer dated frequently and enjoyed the company of men, but few of the relationships she'd tentatively entered during the past five years had progressed beyond friendship. She maintained that she was waiting for a flawless fairy-tale hero—though she knew she would never find one—which was her method of protecting herself from the type of pain and disillusionment she had experienced five years earlier. Only to herself would she admit she wouldn't really know what to do with a fairy-tale hero if she found one. She suspected that a truly perfect man would make her all too aware of her own imperfections, as well as boring her to tears.

Other than that one relatively unimportant diversity, Summer and Connie could have hatched from the same egg. They continued to work in their uninspiring, undemanding jobs only to finance their more pleasurable pastimes, were the despair of their families and employers and the delight of their many friends. All in all, Summer reflected contentedly, fate had been very kind to allow her path to cross Connie Anderson's.

She had no idea of how fate had capriciously decided to bring Connie's brother into Summer's life, as well.

2

SUMMER CAME partially awake with a muffled groan, reached out a hand and slapped at her alarm clock. When that failed to stop the persistent chiming that had disturbed her, she groped for the telephone receiver and pulled it to her ear. "Hello? What is it?" she demanded hoarsely, then glared at the instrument when it responded to her impatient question with a monotonous dial tone. Finally waking enough to realize that the chimes were the result of a determined finger pressed to the doorbell, she muttered an unladylike curse and snatched up her light-weight robe.

"Who on earth would be ringing my doorbell at eight o'clock on a Saturday morning?" she grumbled, stumbling across the party-littered living room to the door. "Derek!" she exclaimed in surprise, throwing open the door to reveal the impatient-looking man in the hallway. "What are you doing here?" And how could anyone look so crisp and alert at this hour of the morning? she added silently.

His gray eyes leisurely surveying her tumbled hair, sleep-blurred features and bedroom attire, Derek answered, "I'm here to see Connie. Is she still sleeping?"

"I'm sure she is," Summer replied, leaning weakly against the edge of the door she held open. The slow, thorough journey of his eyes from the top of her head to her bare toes had affected her as if it had been his hand that had examined her, leaving her feeling a little shaken. God, it was too early in the morning to deal with this type of sensation. She hadn't even had her coffee yet!

"Would you mind waking her?" Derek asked quietly in

that gravelly voice that was like a sandpaper caress to her senses. "I thought I would take her out for breakfast."

Summer's habit had always been to lighten a tense moment with a wisecrack. Since Derek was making her decidedly uncomfortable with his unblinking pewter regard of her, she grinned impishly. "My goodness, is this an impulsive action?" she asked in mock astonishment, then continued without allowing him to respond. "It's very nice of you, but you'd need an airplane to get to her before lunch. Connie's in Los Angeles."

Derek looked startled, and Summer imagined that one did not often catch that particular expression on his stern face. "Los Angeles? How can that be? I left her here less than ten hours ago."

"You left the party only a couple of hours before Connie left for L.A."

Derek ran an impatient hand through his tobacco-brown hair and attempted to make sense of the conversation. "My sister left for Los Angeles at midnight?" he asked slowly.

"That's right. Please come in, Derek, and I'll make us some coffee. I find it very hard to give explanations before I've had my caffeine fix."

"I gathered there was some reason for our lack of communication," Derek commented dryly. He took a step forward. Since Summer had not yet moved aside to allow him entrance into the apartment, she found herself suddenly standing so close to his sturdy chest that she could almost feel the rise and fall of his breath. Instinct told her to move hastily backward, but her reflexes seemed to be unusually slow. She stayed right where she was, staring into Derek's unrevealing gray eyes like a paralyzed rabbit into bright headlights. Did she imagine it, or did something suddenly flicker in those silvery depths? Something dangerous and infinitely exciting.

"You are rather slow before you've had your coffee, aren't you?" Derek murmured, and Summer imagined that his voice was a little rougher than usual. She took an awkward step backward, giving him just enough room to enter the apartment, his arm brushing her as he passed. Suppressing a quiver at the momentary contact, Summer closed the door and leaned against it, watching as Derek looked around the cluttered room with a slight moue of distaste. "Connie left you with the mess, I see," he commented.

Summer cleared her throat soundlessly. "I told her I didn't mind. I had nothing better to do this morning." Her eyes wandered from his face, idly approving the lean strength beneath his crisp white shirt and sharply creased navy slacks. "Do you always dress so conservatively for a Saturday morning, or is this the proper attire for escorting one's sister to breakfast?" she asked with deceptively mild curiosity, retreating again behind a facetious remark. "Do you even own a sweatshirt or a pair of jeans?"

"You're hardly in a position to criticize *my* appearance," Derek returned, eyeing her with an enigmatic half smile. Her short golden-brown hair was wildly disarrayed, and one recalcitrant lock stood straight up at her crown. She'd made a halfhearted effort to remove her makeup before falling into bed at three o'clock that morning, but there were still faint smudges of mascara on the fair, smooth skin beneath her heavy-lidded eyes. The garishly flowered pink-and-green satin kimono she wore clashed appallingly with the silky legs of her pumpkin-colored pajamas. She was hardly dressed for seduction. Yet his entire body was taut, vibrating with a sudden surge of desire for her. He shoved his fists into his pockets to loosen the front of his snugly tailored slacks, his dark brows drawing downward in self-annoyance.

"I'll change after I've had my coffee," Summer answered with a shrug, unaware of Derek's problem. "Can you tolerate instant, or should I brew a pot?"

"I'll make the coffee. You go wash your face. You look like a panda bear. Cute but distracting." Definitely distracting. Those soft smudges made his fingers itch to smooth them away. He needed a few minutes alone to remind himself of all the logical reasons that he should not take advantage of his sister's absence to make a move on her attractive roommate.

When Summer didn't immediately respond to his suggestion, Derek reached out with a faint smile to give her a light push in the direction of her bedroom. Since she had been precariously balanced on one foot, the other crossed in front of her, his slight shove caused her to wobble. Before Derek could make a grab to steady her, she fell to one knee, gasping in pain as she made contact with the uncarpeted wood floor.

"Summer, I'm sorry." Derek was sincerely contrite as he knelt beside her to help her to her feet. "I certainly never meant to—"

"I know you didn't," she interrupted him, brushing off his apology. Clutching his arm, she rose slowly, flexing the offending knee when she was upright. "Don't worry about it, Derek. It was simply an accident. I told you I'm not at my best before my coffee."

"Are you all right? You look a little pale." He had an arm around her shoulders for support.

Much more aware of his nearness than the ache in her knee, Summer swallowed and shrugged casually out of his supportive embrace. "I'm fine. I just landed on an old war injury," she told him lightly. "Go make the coffee, Derek, while I remove my 'cute but distracting' panda mask."

Partially reassured by her airy dismissal, Derek nodded and stepped away from her, though his eyes frowned steadily at her back as she moved toward her bedroom. She had taken only three steps when his exclamation of distress stopped her. "Dammit, Summer, you're limping! I really hurt you, didn't I?" Before she could open her mouth to deny his self-recrimination, he had swept her into his arms as if she weighed nothing and was carrying her to the worn sofa, which was still shoved against one wall.

"Derek, will you put me down!" Summer gasped,

clutching at his shoulder for balance. Lord, he was strong. And so warm. His warmth scorched her through her thin nightclothes. "You did *not* hurt me. I *always* limp," she told him as evenly as she could under the circumstances.

She was completely ignored as Derek deposited her with great care in the center of the sagging couch and, holding her leg still with a hand at her ankle, began to roll up her wide pajama leg. "Derek! Stop that!" She reached down to arrest his hand, reluctant for him to see her leg, but he easily overpowered her.

"Dear God, Summer, what did you do to this knee?" Derek stared in near horror at the slender appendage, which was disfigured by a veritable spiderweb of scars from her lower thigh to two inches below her knee. The kneecap itself was unnaturally lopsided.

"If you had listened to me instead of throwing me around like a sack of potatoes, I would have told you," she answered crossly, not caring that her analogy bore little resemblance to his somewhat high-handed but unarguably gentle handling of her. She looked away from the expression on his face, not wanting to see the revulsion that usually followed the shock.

"I'm listening now."

"I was injured in a motorcycle accident five years ago. A car ran a stop sign and smashed into me. I'll walk with this limp for the rest of my life, but since I nearly had to have the leg amputated, I'm not complaining. Now are you satisfied that you did not cause me a terrible injury?"

Still holding her leg just behind the knee, Derek sat back on his heels and looked intently up at her. "How'd the guy driving the motorcycle fare?"

"*I* was driving the motorcycle, you chauvinist. And the accident wasn't my fault." She wished she could control the slight trembling of her muscles beneath his warm palm. With uncharacteristic bitterness she told herself he must not be aware that he was still holding the disfigured leg. It was hardly a sight to make him want to touch her.

"How long did it take you to get back on your feet?"

"Almost two years," Summer admitted reluctantly, desperately wishing he'd move his hand. "I spent some time in bed, then in a wheelchair, then using a walker and crutches. I skipped having to use a cane, though."

"Good for you. I have a feeling you hated being an invalid."

"Despised it. The main reason I moved to San Francisco was because it was as far west of my tender loving relatives as I could get without falling into the Pacific. I needed to stand on my own two feet again—excuse the pun." Unable to bear the bittersweet feel of his touch for another moment, she reached down toward her rolled-up pajama leg.

Derek stopped her by catching her wrist and moving her hand firmly back to her lap, obviously intending to smooth the pajamas back into place himself. He grasped the soft fabric in both hands and began to unroll it, then stopped. Shooting a quick look up at her, he shocked her by leaning over to brush the gentlest of kisses across her kneecap. Her leg jumped reflexively. Without a word Derek finished rolling the pajama leg down, smoothed the fabric from knee to ankle with excruciating slowness, then released her. In an easy, gracefully coordinated movement he turned and sat beside her on the sofa, wincing when a semiprotruding spring poked him in the posterior. "Just where *are* your tender loving relatives?" he inquired as if he hadn't just caused her heart to leap into her throat and hang there in quivering convulsions. "Obviously you're from the south. Memphis?"

Summer blinked twice and swallowed her heart back into her chest, deciding to follow Derek's lead and ignore that odd little kiss. She'd have plenty of time to think about it later—and she knew she would think about it. When she spoke, her voice was amazingly normal. "Hasn't Connie told you anything about me? I just assumed you knew that I limped and where I'm from."

Derek shook his head, his expression grim. "We haven't

talked much," he admitted. "Every time we try to have a conversation, we end up in a fight."

Summer decided not to mention that Connie had been rather more vocal with her roommate. Summer knew how disappointed Connie had been when her brother had moved back home after so many years only to treat her in very much the same heavily paternal manner that he would have shown her had she still been an adoring ten-year-old. Giving unwanted advice, criticizing her choice of jobs and lack of long-term career goals, reminding her that her impulsive nature and stubborn independence had led her into an ill-fated marriage before her eighteenth birthday. Expecting Derek to return to the States as a sophisticated, indulgent older brother with the heart of an adventurer and the fascinating stories of a seasoned world traveler, Connie had instead been faced with a determinedly conservative businessman, closemouthed about himself and intent on settling into a quietly successful routine.

Derek turned the conversation back to Summer before she had time to comment on his relationship with his sister. "All I know about you is that you've been rooming with Connie for eight months, that the two of you have a great deal in common, according to her, and that you both work in the accounting department of Pro Sporting Goods. You're, uh—" he paused, seeming to grope for the right words "—you're different than what I expected."

"In what way?" she asked curiously, wondering if his preconceptions of her had been as inaccurate as hers of him.

But he refused to enlighten her. "Just different," he replied unhelpfully. "I'd like to know more about you. So answer my question. Where are you from. Memphis?"

"You're close. I'm from Rose Bud, Arkansas."

He sighed. "Why do you insist on making fun of me when I'm only trying to talk to you? Where are you really from?"

Relieved at the change of mood, Summer laughed at

him. "I told you. Rose Bud, Arkansas. Population two hundred and two. It's just down the road from Romance, about fifty-five miles north of Little Rock, if that pinpoints it for you."

"You're serious?"

"Yep. My parents own a seed and feed store there." She waited expectantly.

He groaned, thinking of her last name. "Not, er, Reed's Seed and Feed?"

She laughed again. "That's exactly what it's called. The store was nearly blown away by a big tornado a couple of years back that wiped out about half the buildings in Rose Bud—even the pool hall. But Dad got busy and rebuilt his place and most of the other merchants did the same, and now the town looks almost new. We even got us a red brick post office." She was chattering to mask her lingering nervousness, but Derek only listened, looking at her as if he weren't quite sure whether to believe a word of what she was telling him.

When he spoke, it was in a carefully neutral voice. "I like your laugh. It sounds like…like…"

"Like the tinkling of dozens of fairy bells?" she supplied helpfully.

"Certainly not," he retorted with a look of disgust that sent her laugh pealing through the room once again. "Who told you that?"

"A very handsome young man with aspirations of becoming a poet."

"Did he succeed?"

"Not so far. The last I heard, he was selling waterless cookware."

Again Derek shot her a suspicious look before asking another question. "Do you have any sisters or brothers?"

"Two sisters. Spring's a year older than I am—she's twenty-six. She's an optometrist living in Little Rock. Autumn's about to turn twenty-four. She's an electrician."

"An electrician? That's an unusual occupation for a young— Dammit, Summer, I told you to cut the bull! Do you honestly expect me to believe that your parents named their daughters Spring, Summer and Autumn? You've been feeding me a line all along, haven't you?" He glared at her as she rocked with laughter, her sore knee forgotten.

"Oh, Derek!" she gasped. "I love that look of outrage on your face. It's so cute. And now you look outraged and appalled. I love it!" Wiping at the tears of laughter that were making streaky paths through her faint mascara rings, she shook her head, trying to control her amusement. "I swear to you that every word I told you is true. I can't help it if my life sounds like one of those phony southern television programs—*The Dukes of Hazzard* or *Gomer Pyle U.S.M.C.* or something equally stupid. That was really the way I grew up."

"You really have a sister named Spring who's an optometrist and one named Autumn who's an electrician? And your father really does own a store called Reed's Seed and Feed in Rose Bud, Arkansas?"

"I truly do and he truly does," she assured him, making a determined effort not to laugh again. Really, Derek could make some of the funniest faces. Connie hadn't been exaggerating about that, even if she had misled Summer by telling her that Derek was dull and ordinary. Summer was finding out rapidly that nothing could be further from the truth.

Derek shook his head. "No wonder you and my sister are such good friends. At least it sounds as if you fit in very well with your family. Connie swears *she* must have been given to the wrong family at the hospital. Neither my parents nor I could ever really figure her out."

Summer sobered abruptly. "You're wrong about my family. I never fit in, either. My parents might sound like nuts, but they are staid, hardworking people with very little imagination. Dad's store is called Reed's Seed and Feed because that's his name and that's what he sells. My sisters and I were named after the seasons of our births—Spring's birthday's in May, mine's in July and Autumn's is in September. My parents always complained that I laughed at them from the day I was born and they could never catch on to the joke. I love them, of course, but honestly, they can be so exasperating."

"And your sisters? Are they dull and uptight like me?" Derek inquired glumly. "Do you and Connie make jokes about them, as well?"

Summer's hand fluttered in the air as she searched for words to describe her sisters. "We're just different, that's all," she said finally. "Spring's the brainy one, the one with all the ambition. She worked her way through college, then optometry school, and now she has opened a nice practice in Little Rock. She's quite serious, though she can be fun when she loosens up. She really has a cute sense of humor; she just keeps it well hidden. She reminds me a little of you, actually. Perhaps you should meet her, Derek. Did you say something?"

"No," he answered wryly. "Go on. Tell me about Autumn." He shifted a little closer on the worn couch, lazily, as if he were only interested in hearing more about her family. His leg brushed Summer's thigh, and she backed off immediately, then mentally scolded herself for bringing a knowing smile to his eyes.

"Autumn's the liberated one," she said a little breathlessly. "Fiercely independent, determined to prove herself equal to any man. It's her way of rebelling against the small-town Southern values that were pounded into all of us while we were growing up. You know, women exist only to serve men, a woman's greatest destiny is helpmate and mother, et cetera, et cetera. When she's not on her soapbox about the oppression of women, Autumn's okay. Spring disapproves of my lack of ambition, and Autumn thinks I'm a traitor to women because I believe in fairy tales, but we get along fine as long as we don't spend extended periods of time in one another's company."

"And what is Summer like?" Derek asked unexpectedly, his eyes keen behind the polished lenses of his glasses.

One slender shoulder lifted in a shrug. "I told you all about me last night. Remember? When I listed the reasons why I didn't fulfill your requirements for wife candidate." For some reason that little joke wasn't quite as amusing this morning, nor as easy to toss out.

"I remember everything you said to me last night," Derek answered, looking at her steadily. "Did you drop out of college because of your accident?"

"Yes. I dropped out not long before I probably would have flunked out, anyway."

"You don't seem to be lacking in intelligence."

"Thank you, sir. Actually, there were a few people who suggested that my college career might have been more profitable had I ever attended classes or opened a textbook. It was a novel idea, but I was creamed by the Ford before I ever had the opportunity to try it." When Derek just looked at her, she added, "That was a joke, Derek. I *did* attend a few classes, you know."

"I'm perfectly capable of recognizing a joke when I hear one," he informed her. He stood suddenly, reaching down a hand to help her up. "Get dressed. I'm taking you out for breakfast."

She looked surprised but accepted his assistance after only a momentary hesitation. "What am I, your surrogate sister?"

"Hell, no. I'm hungry and I don't care for eating alone."

"What a gracious invitation. Thank you, Derek, I'd love to have breakfast with you." She smiled brilliantly. As long as she could laugh at him, she could keep her disturbing attraction to him under control, she told herself optimistically.

He had the grace to look sheepish. "Sorry. I'm not usually so clumsy."

"I'm sure you're not," she told him kindly. "Working for the government for so long must have made you a master of civilized diplomacy. I guess I just have a talent for bringing out the worst in you."

Derek threw her a dark look and shoved his hands into

his pockets. "Why is it that I always feel like I'm being insulted by you?"

She gave him a cheeky grin and patted his arm as she limped past him. "Because you're an astute and perceptive man, Derek Anderson. Give me twenty minutes to shower and change and I'll be ready to leave."

"I'll give you thirty," he offered magnanimously.

Reluctant to keep Derek waiting in the cluttered living room, Summer showered and washed her hair quickly. Her short, short hairdo took little time to style, and she applied only a minimum of makeup before pulling on her clothes. At random she selected a red, short-sleeved camp shirt to wear under a sleeveless yellow cotton vest. Her dirndl skirt of red-and-yellow plaid fell to midcalf, adequately concealing the ravages of her right knee. Sliding her feet into low-heeled red espadrilles, she was ready.

And then she wasted almost five minutes trying to tell herself that she was *not* on the verge of hyperventilating just because Derek Anderson was taking her to breakfast. What was it about him that made her turn into a swooning adolescent? she wondered with wry humor. What was it about his silvery eyes that made her long to see them glimmer with his smile? What was it about his strong arms that made her fantasize about having them around her? And how could one little kiss brushed lightly across her ugly, scarred knee turn her into a panting lapdog wanting only to feel his hands upon her? Disgusting, she told herself sternly, frowning at her image in the mirror.

But nice. There was something definitely nice about the feelings he brought out in her. Oh, she was going to have to be very careful.

As fast as she had been, Derek had been faster. Summer gasped when she stepped into the living room to find all the remains of last night's party cleared away. She found Derek in the kitchen, loading the last chip bowl into the dishwasher. A large plastic bag of garbage, neatly tied, rested at his feet. "Where do you take your garbage?" he asked, glancing up to find her staring at him.

"You wouldn't happen to be wearing a Superman costume under those mild-mannered businessman's clothes, would you?" she asked curiously.

His lips curved into one of his faint, dangerous smiles. "No. Would you like me to take them off and show you?"

Yes. The answer popped into her mind with such conviction that Summer blinked, telling herself that his occasional flashes of humor were definitely strange. "What I meant was," she enunciated clearly, "how did you ever get all this done so quickly?"

"Organization and efficiency." His eyes gleamed with that smile that so rarely touched his mouth. Summer was beginning to like that camouflaged smile very much. "I thought it was the least I could do after knocking you down when I arrived."

"It wasn't necessary, but thanks."

"You're welcome. You look very nice."

"Thank you again. We can leave now, unless you'd like to clean the bathroom first?"

She had injected just enough wistful hinting into the question to cause Derek's mouth to quirk into a genuine smile. "I think I'll pass on that opportunity."

Amazing what a mere curve of lips and a very brief glimpse of even white teeth could do for a rather ordinary male face, Summer thought in momentary bemusement. His rare smile made Derek look almost handsome. Downright sexy. And he was looking at her like…

"Breakfast," she said determinedly, shaking off her unsettling fascination with his facial expression and turning back toward the living room.

Derek chuckled and followed her, placing a warm palm on her back as they left her apartment. Summer tried very hard to ignore it. She failed completely.

3

DEREK TOOK HER to a restaurant in a nearby luxury hotel—a far cry from the quick Egg McMuffin that she sometimes picked up on the way to work, if she ate breakfast at all. He allowed her to make a good start on her generous meal before asking about his sister. "Why did she leave for Los Angeles at such an odd hour? And what is she doing there?"

"It was an impulsive trip," Summer explained. "Do you remember seeing Cody Pierce at the party last night? Curly red hair, plaid sport coat?"

He frowned, remembering. "Yes."

"He has aspirations of becoming a stand-up comic. Actually he's a systems analyst, but he's been performing at some local improv clubs, which led to a chance to perform at The Comedy Store in L.A. tonight. He mentioned last night that he was really nervous, and he asked Connie to go along for moral support. She accepted, threw some things in an overnight bag, and they left at midnight. For luck."

"For luck?" Derek repeated, looking confused.

"That's what they said," Summer answered cheerfully, reaching for her coffee. "Don't you ever do anything impulsive, Derek? Just for the fun of it?"

"Not very often," he answered flatly.

She nodded as if in perfect understanding. "I suppose it would be too dangerous in your former line of work."

His brows drew sharply downward. "What?"

Her eyes wide and guileless, she replied, "Why, the spy business, of course. You weren't just teasing me about that, were you, Derek?"

"Oh, that." He drained his coffee cup. "What do you think?" he asked smoothly, setting his cup back on the table and eyeing her enigmatically. "*Was* I teasing you?"

She smiled. "I don't think you quite know how to tease, Derek." He did, of course. He'd teased her delightfully about having been a spy. Was that when she'd started to like him so much? Or had it been from the moment she'd set eyes on him?

"Maybe you should teach me," he suggested smoothly. "You seem to be an expert at it."

She only shrugged and smiled weakly, still wrestling with her own mental questions.

A waitress approached quietly to refill Derek's cup. Derek waited until the woman had left before asking, "Is Connie dating this Pierce guy?"

"She's been out with him a couple of times. She's not dating anyone seriously."

Derek looked grim as he pushed away his well-cleaned breakfast plate. "One of our cousins told me that Connie's been sleeping with anything in pants since her divorce. Is that true?"

Summer dropped her fork. "What a tacky thing to ask me! As if I'd tell you the intimate details of my best friend's love life. It must have been Barbara who made that catty remark to you. Connie's told me her cousin Barbara is a self-righteous snob."

Derek looked pained. "Barbara is a very respectable woman who has raised two exceptionally well-behaved daughters. She has been genuinely concerned about Connie and was hoping I could exert my influence over my sister."

"Connie doesn't need your influence, Derek," Summer informed him flatly. "She's doing just fine. When you showed up this morning to take her to breakfast, I thought you were finally going to try to be her friend. But if you were only going to start lecturing her again, I'm glad she's out of town."

"I wasn't going to lecture her," he snapped irritably. "I

was going to tell her I was sorry about the way we parted last night. Still, she needs someone to make her see that she's wasting her life: a dead-end job, endless parties, kooky friends and a dump of an apartment furnished with junk the Salvation Army would probably reject. What kind of life is that for an attractive young woman with Connie's intelligence?"

"I'm trying very hard not to take your incredibly arrogant and condescending remarks as a personal insult," Summer said, holding on to her temper with an effort. Strange, she fumed, she didn't usually have a problem with her temper. She usually found a reason to laugh when others got angry. But she could find very little humor in Derek Anderson's reference to Connie's "wasted life." Instead, she felt vaguely hurt and disappointed, as if he'd been talking about her rather than Connie. Had she been so foolish as to begin to hope that her attraction to Derek might lead to something more? If so, his words had shown her how silly that expectation had been. Summer had lived with disapproval for most of her life; she had no intention of getting involved with any man who could not accept her—or her friends—just as they were.

"If you'll remember, I work at the same dead-end job, I go to the same endless parties, I have the same kooky friends and I live in the same dump of an apartment furnished with the same Salvation Army rejects. And I'm perfectly content, thank you—even though I don't have an older, wiser brother to exert his influence on me. Thank God."

"I wasn't trying to criticize *you*, Summer," he said hastily, visibly uncomfortable. "What you do is your business. I just hate to see Connie, well—"

"You're only going to make it worse, Derek, so I think you'd better drop it," Summer told him, trying to sound cross though her irrepressible sense of humor was already diluting her unaccustomed anger, as it had so many times in the past. She rested her elbows on the polished tabletop and tapped her fingertips against her cheek, drawing on that comfortable humor. "Unless you want me to retaliate by telling you what I think of your life?"

"You don't know anything about the way I live," he informed her. "You've done nothing but poke fun at me and look down your up-tilted little nose at me since we met last night, simply because I wear conservative clothes and think there should be more to life than parties and games."

"And Connie and I think that life is short, so we should make every effort to enjoy it," Summer retorted, thinking of how easily her own life could have ended in that accident five years ago. How a shattered knee and equally shattered dreams could have led to a life of bitterness had she not resolved then to hang on to her humor and her sense of fun, no matter what else might befall her.

"Are you telling me that you enjoy the job you're in now?" Derek asked skeptically.

"I enjoy the paycheck very much, such as it is," she answered glibly. When he didn't reply, she prodded. "That was another joke, Derek. Should I cue you when to laugh?"

"I didn't find it particularly amusing," he replied. Actually, he'd been wondering what would happen if he tried to shut her smart little mouth with a kiss. He emptied his second cup of coffee, set the cup aside and straightened his glasses with a blunt fingertip. "I think we'd better talk about something else."

And *he'd* better keep reminding himself that this infuriatingly attractive young woman was off-limits, he added to himself grimly. There seemed to be little chance of her being equally attracted to a man she found so annoying and amusing. She'd made it pretty clear that he wasn't her type. Could he convince her that she was wrong? Did he want to try?

Talk about something else? Like what? Summer almost sighed, thinking of the many differences between them. One, in particular, was weighing on her mind. "Connie told me that you're a real sports enthusiast. She says you're quite a competitor. What types of sports do you enjoy, Derek?''

He shrugged, then realized that she was trying to make innocuous conversation and answered more fully. "I'm not quite as active as I used to be, but I still try to stay in shape. Working out bores me, so I get my exercise through participation in competitive sports. And I run every morning.''

"Do you still run in marathons?''

Derek eyed her curiously. "Connie has told you a bit about me, hasn't she?''

Did he think his sister completely ignored her brother's existence? Summer wondered. "Of course she has, Derek. She talks about all of her family.''

He looked thoughtful but answered her question. "I haven't run in a marathon since I came back to this country. I don't have the time to train properly since I've been so busy establishing my business.''

"Do you miss it? Are you sorry you didn't become a professional athlete?''

"No. I'm doing exactly what I want to do. Sports are only a form of recreation for me. I get enough competition from the occasional tennis and racquetball game to satisfy my competitive urges.'' He smiled a little, knowing how Connie talked about him.

Summer toyed with her fork, remembering Connie had mentioned that Derek usually dated women who were as athletic as he was. According to his sister, a typical date with Derek usually consisted of working up a sweat on a tennis court. Connie had been sneering at the time, and Summer had laughed. She didn't find it quite so funny now that she'd actually met Derek. She thought of the woman Connie had most recently mentioned in connection with Derek.

"Connie tells me that you've been seeing Senator Payne's daughter since you've moved to Sausalito,'' she heard herself saying, surprised that she'd actually brought the subject up. "I met her at a party once. She's quite beautiful."

He lifted one eyebrow behind his glasses. "Yes, she is. I took her out a few times, but we're not seeing each other now."

Summer leaned both elbows on the table and rested her chin on her linked hands, gazing at him. "Why ever not?"

"Summer—"

"No, really, Derek, I would think she'd be exactly what you'd be looking for in a corporate wife." Her humor had resurfaced, for some strange reason, the moment he'd informed her that he was no longer seeing Joanne. She decided not to dwell on reasons as she continued to tease him.

"Summer, this is really none of your—"

Her face was all innocence when she interrupted him again. "After all, she's cultured, refined, educated, athletic. Exactly what you've tried to mold Connie into being. She has a career. I've seen her paintings, and they're quite interesting, though not exactly my style. Of course, she *is* thirty. Still, more and more women are having children after thirty these days."

"Summer?"

"Yes, Derek?"

"If I promise to stop criticizing the way you live, will you shut up?"

She laughed, inordinately pleased that the suggestion of a smile was back in his silvery-gray eyes.

"Why, yes, Derek, that sounds like a fair deal to me."

Derek kept a hand at her elbow as they left the restaurant soon afterward and walked to his tasteful gray Lincoln. A protective hand, Summer thought with resigned amusement. Of course he would be the type to want to assist the slender young woman with the bad limp—even if he *did* disapprove of her. So, as usual when something made her uncomfortable, she cracked a joke. "You know, with all its hills, San Francisco is a great place for me to live. I just keep my gimpy leg uphill and I walk almost straight. Of course, going the other direction is—"

"Don't do that," Derek cut her off sharply. "Don't make light of your injury."

Summer sighed. "Oops. I forgot to cue you again. It was a joke, Derek."

"It wasn't funny."

She sighed again, wishing once more that she wasn't so foolishly attracted to this man who seemed to disapprove of everything she did.

Derek hesitated before starting the car. "It's a beautiful day. Would you like to go for a drive with me, maybe take a stroll through Chinatown or visit Golden Gate Park?"

"Thank you, Derek, that sounds lovely, but I can't," Summer answered regretfully. "I have plans for today. I really should be getting back home."

She wondered if the brief flicker of expression that crossed his face was disappointment. She found herself hoping that it was.

At her door she thanked Derek politely for buying her breakfast and promised to have Connie call when she returned from Los Angeles the next day.

"Thanks." Derek stood awkwardly just inside the apartment. Why was he so reluctant to leave? he asked himself. What would she do if he were to kiss her? He'd been aching to taste her smile since the thought had occurred to him at breakfast. Even before that.

Summer wondered if she should offer him a cola or something. Derek seemed almost reluctant to leave, and to be honest, she wouldn't mind spending a little more time with him. She had about half an hour before Clay picked her up for their late-morning appointment at Halloran House. Giving in to temptation, she said, "Would you like to stay for a little while? We could...we could get to know each other a little better. After all, you are my best friend's brother."

"Summer—" Derek bit off whatever he'd been going to say, looked at her in silence for a long time, then reached

out to touch her cheek. A butterfly touch that elicited a
fluttery little response somewhere in the pit of her stomach. She stared at him, wide-eyed, as his head lowered
very slowly. He was going to kiss her, she thought in startled wonder. Why? Did she really want him to?

God, yes.

She felt his breath on her parted lips. And then the telephone rang.

Derek jerked his head up and around, staring at the instrument as if he'd like very much for it to explode into
oblivion. Feeling much the same way, Summer cleared her
throat and limped to the end table where one of the apartment's extensions sat. "Hello?" she asked a little hoarsely.
"When, tonight? Sure, that sounds like fun." She felt Derek move restlessly beside her. "Yeah, Clay's supposed to
pick me up in about a half hour. I'll tell you about it tonight. See you at seven. Bye."

Derek looked particularly stern when she turned uncomfortably back to him. "Uh, Derek—Well, darn," she
muttered as the telephone rang again. She looked at him
apologetically.

"Look, I'd better go. I'll see you later, okay?" Derek
ground out, heading for the door. She had men standing
in line for her, he told himself angrily. Damn.

Her hand on the telephone receiver, Summer swallowed a sigh. "All right. Thanks for breakfast, Derek."

He only nodded as he walked out of the apartment.
Summer picked up the telephone, explained that Connie
wasn't home, promised to relay a message and hung up.

Chewing on her lower lip, she walked into her bedroom, thinking that her impromptu breakfast date with
Derek had been unexpectedly nice. They got along quite
well when they weren't talking about Connie. Or Summer's limp. She wondered why her self-directed jokes
bothered him so much. Most people thought the comments were funny and admired her for being able to laugh
at life's misfortunes. Obviously, seeing her scars had bothered Derek so much that he didn't even want to discuss

them. Her hand went unconsciously to her knee. Derek wasn't the first man who'd been turned off by her scars and her limp, she reflected grimly.

She tried to divert her thoughts by remembering how easily she and Derek had conversed, almost like old friends. Then she told herself that he would probably have even more to talk about with a woman like Joanne Payne, the senator's lovely daughter. The thought made her feel depressed again.

As she gathered the things she would take with her to Halloran House, she tried to tell herself that she couldn't care less whom Derek dated. There was certainly nothing between Summer and Derek, other than their mutual involvement with Connie. Perhaps he was a little attracted to her, as she was to him, but that was all there was to it.

"It's just that I think Connie's wrong about Derek," she told the enormous Winnie the Pooh bear that sat beside her bed. "He's a pretty nice guy, even if he *is* a little stuffy and arrogant, and all he needs is to fall madly in love with someone who'd keep that lovely smile in his eyes."

Now what had put that thought into her head? "I wasn't talking about myself, of course," she assured the sympathetic bear, patting his one-eared head, her fingers lingering on the heavy stitches that repaired the gash where his other ear had once been. "I'm waiting for a hero, remember? Derek might *look* kind of heroish, but he's just too…too proper. He'd…he'd probably bore me to tears inside a week." Now why didn't she have more conviction in her voice?

And why were her thoughts lingering on the brush of his lips against her scarred knee and the look in his eyes as he'd been so close to kissing her just before the telephone had interrupted? She wondered if she felt relieved or disappointed that the phone had stopped that unwise move.

Disappointed. Definitely disappointed.

SUMMER HAD CONSIDERED going to church Sunday morning, but for some reason she hadn't been able to go to sleep until very late the night before and she overslept. In an attempt to lighten her mood, which was rarely that gloomy, she turned on her radio and dressed in a bright purple sweatshirt and her most comfortable jeans. By early afternoon she had thoroughly cleaned the apartment and was restlessly trying to think of what she wanted to do for the remainder of the day. She could call a friend and go shopping, or there was a barbecue that she'd been invited to attend. She'd gone to a movie and then out for drinks with two women friends the night before—it had been that invitation that had interrupted yesterday when Derek had been about to kiss her—and her friends had assured her that the barbecue party would be "crawling with hunks." So why didn't she want to go? She dropped onto the couch and rested her chin in her hands, wondering why none of her usual pastimes held any appeal for her that day. When the telephone rang, she lifted the receiver with a spark of optimism, hopeful that the call would provide the answer to her boredom. "Hello?"

"Summer, it's Derek."

"Derek!" She wondered at her sudden surge of excitement, then scolded herself as she realized why he was calling. "Sorry, Connie's not back yet. She probably won't be home until late."

"I wasn't calling to talk to Connie," Derek replied unexpectedly. "I wondered if you have plans for the afternoon."

"I was just trying to decide. Why?"

"Would you like to come to my house for a swim? We can throw some steaks on the grill afterward for dinner. I'd like to talk to you about Connie."

Her initial pleasure at the invitation evaporated with his explanation. "I thought I'd made myself clear about the subject of Connie, Derek. I like her, I think she's getting along fine and I refuse to help you interfere in her life."

Derek's sharp exhalation was clearly audible through the telephone line. "Summer, I'm not asking you to help me interfere in her life. Connie's my sister, and I'm tired of feeling like there's a war going on between us. You're her best friend, so I thought maybe you could help me find a way to make peace with her."

"The only way you're going to be able to do that is to accept her just as she is," Summer answered bluntly.

"I'll try. Will you come over and give me some pointers?"

She wiggled her bare feet on the coffee table in front of her and watched them with a little smile playing at the corners of her mouth. "How are you at taking advice, Derek?"

"I haven't had a great deal of experience at it," he answered ruefully, "but I can try. Shall I pick you up in an hour?"

"Sure. See you then." She hung up the phone and wriggled her toes happily. She tried to tell herself that she was suddenly in such a good mood because she now had plans for the rest of the day. She tried to tell herself that she was pleased that Derek seemed willing to try to patch things up with his sister, which should make both Anderson siblings happier. But she knew that the real reason she felt good was that she would be spending the afternoon in the company of a man she was beginning to like very much. Not an ideal hero, of course, she reminded herself rather sternly, trying to quell some of the anticipation she felt toward seeing him with her old, standard excuse for not getting involved. Still, teasing Derek had turned out to be more fun than she'd expected.

Then her smile faded. Swimming. She'd have to wear a bathing suit in front of him. Her body wasn't so bad, but there was no way to conceal her mutilated right knee in a swimsuit. After five years she'd learned to wear her maillots and occasional shorts without too much regard for what others thought of her scars, but for some reason Derek's reaction was more important to her. She told herself that she was being silly. He'd already seen the scars, hadn't he? Still, she knew that her scars and limp would only remind both of them of the many reasons there could be nothing more between Summer and Derek than friendship. He would want a woman who was more nearly perfect, physically and every other way. Summer wanted a man who could accept her, flaws and all.

So she would concentrate on making friends with him and helping him do the same with his estranged sister. And she would try very hard to avoid any more intimate scenes like that near kiss the morning before. No matter how much she might be tempted to do otherwise.

IN HIS ELEGANT SAUSALITO HOME Derek replaced his own receiver and frowned down at the telephone beneath his hand. Calling Summer with the impromptu invitation had been an impulse, just as dropping by to invite his sister to breakfast yesterday had been. Dumb move, Anderson, he told himself.

He wondered dispassionately at the urge that had made him call Summer and invite her to his home. True, he wanted very much to come to some kind of an understanding with Connie. And true, Summer was Connie's best friend and would therefore be the logical person to advise him on how best to approach Connie with a long-overdue attempt at reconciliation. But was that really the reason he'd called Summer? Or was it just an excuse to spend more time with her?

From the little Connie had told him about her roommate, he hadn't expected to like Summer Reed immediately. But he had. So much so that he'd wanted to spend more time with her. Alone. He had to ask himself if the real reason he'd wanted to ask Connie to breakfast yesterday had been so that he could see Summer again and find out if she was really as intriguing as she'd seemed at the party. She was.

He swallowed, remembering the rush of heat that had hit him at her door. He wanted to be with Summer, not only because she made him want her to the point of distraction but also because she had proved to be such damned good company. She irritated him, she amused him, she kept him on his toes. She made him feel alive again, really alive for the first time in nearly a year. He'd thought he was past thriving on risks and challenges. It seemed that he was not.

Summer was not at all the type of woman he'd expected to find himself suddenly obsessed with. And yet he was.

It was a shame she was wasting her very obvious intelligence and competence in a job that admittedly bored her and a series of parties that seemed only to fill her free hours. Of course, he had no right to criticize her. Could it be that his sister's life should be equally exempt from his well-meant interference?

He had never meant to drive Connie away from him when he'd come home. It was just that he'd had such expectations for her when she'd been a bright, spunky little girl. He couldn't help but be disappointed that she wasn't taking advantage of the opportunities she'd had to better herself. Ever since her marriage to that jerk actor when she'd been no more than a kid, she'd seemed intent on living as frivolously as possible. Was he supposed to just stand by and say nothing?

With a frown and a shake of his head he abandoned the troublesome self-debate and allowed himself—just for a moment—to contemplate Summer's visit with an unfamiliar sense of anticipation.

Catching sight of himself in a mirror on the wall in front of him, he realized he was wearing a stupid, infatuated schoolboy grin. The expression made him look like a stranger, even to himself. What was this woman doing to him to make him look like that? What was it about her that was tying him in knots, making him plot and connive for ways to convince her to spend more time with him?

He was going to have to be very careful, he told himself sternly, the grin slowly fading to be replaced by a look of wary caution.

And then he found himself whistling as he started toward his kitchen to thaw the steaks.

4

"YOU'RE AN EXCELLENT SWIMMER," Derek complimented Summer after a swimming race he'd won only with great effort.

Gasping for breath, Summer clung to the edge of the pool, tossing her wet bangs out of her eyes and smiling at him. "Thanks," she said when she'd regained her voice. "I spent hours in pools during my recuperation from my accident to strengthen my leg. I still try to swim laps three or four times a week."

Derek reached out to brush a wet strand of hair away from her eyes. "I thought you said you weren't athletic."

She wanted to turn her cheek into his hand, to drop a kiss into his palm. Instead, she casually shook his hand away and pulled herself out of the pool. "I'm not," she threw back at him, reaching for her gaily colored beach towel. "Exercising is just something I do, or I'd end up walking more like a duck than I do now." Wrapping herself in the huge towel, she dropped onto a lounge chair at the pool's edge, watching as Derek shoved himself out of the rippling blue water.

More than once during the afternoon she'd found herself tempted to ignore her resolution to keep things between them strictly platonic. There had been several incidents in the pool, when wet skin had brushed wet skin, that could have turned into something dangerous if both she and Derek hadn't been so obviously trying to remain in control. She'd known from the moment he'd picked her up that Derek was as determined as she to make an effort to ignore the unbidden attraction that had flared between them from the beginning.

Summer had fallen instantly in love with Derek's home, a good-sized house of rock, cedar and smoked glass nestled into the Sausalito hills. Though she was sure the place had been professionally decorated, Derek had opted for comfort and warmth rather than trendy style. Each room he led her into on the quick tour he'd given her upon their arrival had been beautiful, yet Summer could easily imagine a family living in the home without worrying about smudges and clutter. She could be very comfortable in such a house, she found herself thinking, then made herself stop picturing herself in residence here. Such thoughts were detrimental to her peace of mind.

She'd been in Derek's company for more than two hours now and was surprised at how well they got along. Carefully avoiding the subject of his sister, they'd kept their conversation light and impersonal, with Summer tossing out her usual quota of one-liners and Derek serving with amiable resignation as her straight man. She had yet to make him laugh outright, but the hint of a smile had flashed frequently in his pewter-gray eyes. The only quips that made him frown were the ones she made about her physical impairment.

In response to her remark about walking like a duck, he was scowling now as he draped his lean form on the chair beside his guest's. He pointedly made no reply.

Chuckling under her breath, Summer slid an oversize pair of purple-framed sunglasses onto her nose and settled comfortably in her chair to enjoy the still-warm early September sun, allowing the beach towel to fall aside to reveal her becomingly simple scarlet maillot. It was simply habit to keep the towel draped over her scarred knee when she was with people she didn't know well. She was hardly aware that she had done so this time.

Derek was lounging in a position almost identical to her own, his eyes half closed as he squinted meditatively across the pool. Since he wasn't wearing his glasses, his eyes looked smaller, his dark lashes longer. Summer took advantage of the opportunity to study his roughly carved profile and powerful, slim physique.

When he had stripped to his conservative navy swim trunks, she'd realized that her first impression at the party Friday night had been correct. His body was as solid and firm as she'd first thought, corded with hard-earned muscles and marred only by an interestingly jagged scar across his left shoulder. Thinking of their silly repartee on the night they'd met, Summer mused that Derek's body looked like that of an ex-spy's, even if his sister would have scoffed at the very idea that he could do something so daring and irresponsible.

It had been easier than she'd expected to appear before him in her own swimwear. Though his eyes had drifted down to her scarred leg, he'd managed to keep any distaste he might have felt well hidden. He neither stared at the scars nor pointedly avoided them. Funny, she'd almost forgotten her earlier misgivings.

"Why are you keeping your right leg covered with your towel?" Derek asked suddenly, as if he'd read her mind.

Summer flushed a little and looked down. "Just habit, I guess."

"Obviously you don't always keep it covered or your right leg wouldn't be as tanned as your left," Derek pointed out logically. "Your scars don't bother me, Summer. I have a few of my own, and I'm not trying to hide them."

Summer sighed and brushed the towel away from her knee. "You're right, of course. It's silly." She glanced at his shoulder. "How did you get yours?"

"Trying to prove what a hotshot jock I am," he answered, telling her nothing yet reminding her that this was a man who enjoyed sports of all kinds. Sports she would never be able to share with him, she told herself rather cruelly.

"Where were you attending college when you had your accident?" he asked suddenly.

Grateful for the distraction of Derek's question, Summer

answered. "UALR—the University of Arkansas at Little Rock."

"What was your major?"

"Theater arts."

His eyebrow lifted. "Drama?"

"Mmm. Drama, dance, music."

"Had you had any training before you entered college?"

"Yes. I took dance lessons from the time I was three years old, after one of my aunts—a frustrated ballerina—decided I showed some talent. I loved it, and though my parents thought it was basically a waste of time, they never complained about the expense involved."

"What were you planning to do when you graduated?"

Summer fluffed her drying bangs with her fingertips and answered lightly. "Oh, I had dreams of becoming the next Mary Martin or Debbie Reynolds. I thought Hollywood would revive the musical comedy movies just for me."

"Were you any good?"

"Oi was bloomin' marv'lous, oi was," she answered in a shrill Cockney accent.

Derek nodded approvingly. "You played Eliza Doolittle?"

"I beat out two dozen others for the spring production of *My Fair Lady* my sophomore year. Which was rather surprising since I only auditioned to please my boyfriend, a gorgeous senior who'd won the part of 'Enry 'Iggins."

Derek frowned at the mention of her old boyfriend but let it pass without comment. Still, he had more questions to ask. "How were your reviews?"

She sighed dramatically. "Alas, I'll never know. I was on my way to the final dress rehearsal when I had the close encounter with the motorcycle-eating Ford. My stand-in got all the rave reviews." Summer had gotten drugs to dull the agonizing pain in her shattered knee, and the news that she would never dance on stage again.

Derek sat still for a moment, studying her seemingly unregretful expression before finally asking, "Whatever happened to 'Enry 'Iggins?"

"As soon as he graduated, he headed for the bright lights of New York. He's on a daytime soap now."

"Do you ever hear from him?"

"No. He married an actress on the same soap. We broke up soon after my accident." And she'd learned that active men did not want to be slowed down by a woman with a handicap. She'd do well to keep that in mind now, she told herself.

"Was he a hero-type?"

Summer forced a laugh. "Hardly. He took one look at my mangled leg in the hospital and fainted dead away. He managed to visit me twice before he announced that he just couldn't deal with it and took off for New York. The really funny part is that he plays a doctor on the soap."

"You don't appear to be brokenhearted."

She shrugged. "It's ancient history." And broken hearts mend with time, as do broken limbs, though the scars remain for a lifetime.

"You told me that you've had several jobs since you left college. What have you done, and how did you end up in the accounting department of Pro Sporting Goods?"

"What is this, an interview?"

"You interest me. I'd like to know more about you," Derek replied candidly. "You don't have to answer if you don't want to."

"What the heck. Somehow you've managed to drag my entire life story out of me during the two times we've been together. You might as well ask about my work history, too." She shoved her sunglasses higher on her nose. "While I was recovering from the accident, I kept the books for my father's store. We were both relieved when I ditched the walker and decided to look for employment in Little Rock. There I found a job in a small credit union for a while, but it was so boring. I quit after only four months."

"Then what?"

"Well, my next job was in a ladies' dress shop, but it didn't work out."

He groaned. "Let me guess. You told the ladies exactly how they looked in the dresses they tried on."

She giggled. "How did you know? That's exactly what I did. Can you imagine how some of those, um, well-endowed women looked in dresses two sizes too small and ten years too young? I could tell I wasn't cut out to be a saleswoman, so I decided to move here and try something new."

"Why San Francisco?"

"I had a crush on Michael Douglas when I was a teenager. I watched *The Streets of San Francisco* every week, so when I decided to get out of Arkansas and started imagining all the places I could go, I automatically thought of San Francisco."

"That's a damned odd way to choose a place to pick up and move to," Derek grunted, looking at her again with that dull silver glint that told her he wasn't quite sure whether she was teasing him.

"A lot of things I do are damned odd," she replied airily.

"I wondered if you were aware of that."

"But fun," she added, swinging her legs over the side of the lounge chair. "Any further questions?" she asked as she sat up facing him.

"How many jobs have you had here?"

"Only two. The first was as a hostess in a lovely little restaurant. That didn't work out, either."

"I'm almost afraid to ask why."

"Well, every time I invited the diners to 'walk this way'—"

"Summer, that's enough of the jokes about your limp. It's sick humor, and I don't find it at all amusing."

"It's called gallows humor, and you're just too stuffy to appreciate it."

He sighed but asked one final question. "How'd you get the job with Pro Sporting Goods?"

"No one else wanted it." She stood, dropping her towel. "If the inquisition's over, I'm going back into the pool."

He waved a hand to indicate that she could do as she liked, then watched broodingly as she limped to the side of the pool and dived expertly into the cool depths. In the water her awkwardness vanished, giving way to a graceful style that was a pleasure to watch. His eyes followed her through several laps, noting the racer's turns at the ends of the pool, modified so that she was pushing off only with her strong leg. Summer was a puzzle to him. She seemed too bright, too complex, to explain her apparently shallow approach to life. But when she'd told him about her accident and the long months of recovery, the end of her career as a dancer and as a performer, the desertion of her college boyfriend and the chain of unfulfilling jobs, she'd tossed out the pieces of information as if she'd been speaking of someone else. Did she really think that her glib manner hid the pain and traces of bitterness in her eyes? Was he the only one who could see them there?

Why the hell should he care? he asked himself exasperatedly. He barely knew the woman. She was someone he was spending time with only because he wanted her to help him get closer to his sister.

Bull. Even he didn't believe that.

He narrowed his eyes as Summer stopped swimming to float lazily on her back, her eyes closed in pleasure. Her trim, sleek figure floated effortlessly in the clear water. The wet scarlet maillot hugged her taut curves caressingly. Caressingly? Now where had that word come from? His palms were itching, but that didn't necessarily mean that he was imagining the feel of Summer's skin beneath them. Dammit, he had no intention of giving in to an inexplicable attraction to a woman who would only laugh at him if he should tell her how he felt. She probably used men as unconscionably as his sister, her alleged search for the perfect hero an excuse for going through scores of potential candidates. Someone could get hurt in a relationship with the flighty young woman in his pool—and chances were it wouldn't be Summer, he told himself sternly.

He closed his eyes and tried to remember if his palms had itched even once during his pleasantly uneventful, short-term affair with Joanne Payne. He didn't remember them doing so. Damn.

The steaks were tender and perfectly grilled, the weather beautiful for eating on the terrace overlooking his pool. Everything should have been fine, yet Derek realized that things had been going downhill between him and Summer since he'd questioned her so intensely an hour or so earlier. The lazily amused friendliness she had shown him during their swim had been replaced by an unsubtle mocking attitude that he was finding increasingly annoying. She'd gibed at him throughout the meal, making fun of his life-style, his bureaucratic establishment background, even his home. And all the while she looked so temptingly touchable as she lounged across the small patio table from him that he found himself wanting to haul her inside and throw himself on her slender body— after he warmed her fanny for daring to laugh at him.

He asked himself what he'd done to cause such an abrupt change in her manner toward him, then decided that he'd gotten too close with his questions. This was her way of paying him back for digging into history and emotions that she preferred to keep hidden behind her brilliant smile.

He watched broodingly as she brushed her almost dry bangs back from her face in what he assumed was an unconsciously sexy gesture and widened those deceptively innocent blue eyes at him. "What's the matter, Derek? Something wrong with your steak?"

"No, it's fine," he answered shortly, glaring down at the expensive piece of meat that had lost its taste for him.

"Of course. You're very good with a grill. But then, you're very good at everything you do, aren't you, Derek? It must be nice to be so capable."

She made the word sound like a curse, Derek fumed,

looking resentfully at her. He could feel himself going on the defensive, and he didn't like it. "I never claimed to be perfect, Summer."

"Didn't you?" Without giving him a chance to respond to her murmured question, she turned her head and looked slowly around the lovely lawn of his home. "Such a beautiful place. Did you have Joanne in mind when you bought this house?" she inquired blandly.

"Of course not," he answered impatiently, feeling his face grow hard with his rising anger. He breathed deeply, telling himself that she was using one of his sister's tricks of getting him mad so that he would do or say something she could pounce on to mock him further. "I bought the house because I like it and it's a good investment," he added in a determinedly even tone.

"Still, it looks like a family home. You must have had marriage in mind when you purchased it. If Joanne doesn't quite meet your requirements, perhaps Connie and I could find you someone else. I personally know several cultured, refined ladies that I would be happy to introduce you to. Of course, you'd better tell me what was wrong with Joanne so I'll know what to avoid when I set you up with someone."

Derek very deliberately set his napkin on the table beside his plate. "Drop it, Summer."

She eyed the set of his jaw. "It's not that I don't think you're capable of finding your own perfect mate," she assured him briskly. "I'm just trying to offer advice."

Enough was enough. Derek decided it was definitely time for him to regain control of this situation.

She hadn't seen him move. One minute he was sitting across the table glaring at her and the next he was standing beside her chair, having hauled her to her feet, holding her there with a biting grip on her upper arms. "Is this what it takes to shut you up?" he demanded gruffly, moments before his mouth covered hers.

The gasp that couldn't escape her lips lodged in her

throat. Summer stood motionless in Derek's arms, too surprised to struggle against the angry embrace.

Actually, the bruisingly punishing kiss wasn't bad. Feeling his tongue thrusting inside to dominate her mouth, she responded tentatively, telling herself that it was only wise to humor an outraged male until he recovered his self-control. After all, it *was* her fault, sort of. And the only reason she allowed her arms to slide up and around his neck was that the sooner he was mollified, the sooner the kiss would end.

For all she knew, it could have been hours before Derek slowly lifted his mouth from hers. Sometime during the kiss the earth seemed to have tilted on its axis or something, leaving everything looking decidedly different to Summer's dazed, unfocused eyes. Even Derek's glasses looked crooked, which couldn't be the result of unrestrained passion—could it?

She thought she saw his fingers shaking a little when he reached up to straighten the dark frames but told herself that that, too, must be the result of her bemusement from the unexpectedly hypnotic kiss. "Uh, Derek—" she began tentatively, only to have him step away from her and cut her off with a sharp statement.

"Forget it, Summer."

She frowned. "What?"

"I know you find me vastly amusing and that you have thoroughly enjoyed your game of Derek-baiting during our meal, but it's going to stop right here. I'm not going to be the latest toy for your amusement."

"I don't know what you're talking about."

"The hell you don't," he returned roughly. "You told me at the party the other night that I wasn't your type and that you had no intention of becoming involved with someone like me, so all I can assume is that you've decided to entertain yourself with me. Am I that much of a novelty to you, Summer? Do you plan to laugh with Connie about how you seduced her straitlaced brother?"

"Hey!" she exclaimed abruptly. "Who kissed whom? *I* wasn't the one who initiated that little interlude."

"Do you deny that you provoked it?" he demanded.

Had she provoked it? Well, yes, she supposed she had, she admitted to herself, looking away from him for a moment. She'd been irresistibly tempted to try to shake that cool composure of his, but she'd impudently expected him to yell or kick something—preferably not her. "I suppose I did provoke you," she muttered. "I wanted to make you mad, but I never expected you to demonstrate your anger in quite that way."

Derek looked taken aback when she shot a quick look at him through her lashes. "You wanted to make me angry?"

"Yes."

"Why?"

"I was teaching you an object lesson," she told him, defiantly lifting her chin.

Derek cleared his throat and pulled at the neckline of his light blue T-shirt as if he were wearing a tie that had been knotted too tightly. "What kind of an object lesson?" he asked, forming the words with exaggerated care.

"I was trying to show you how infuriating it is for someone to interfere with your life. Who you date and why is none of my business, and you were quite correct to be annoyed by my nosy questions and comments—just as Connie has a right to be angry when you ask if she's 'sleeping with anything in pants,' as you put it. And just as I was irritated when you asked all those questions about my past and my job history, then looked so stuffy and disapproving when I answered you."

Derek leaned against the railing of the cedar deck, a thoughtful frown darkening his face. The view of the Golden Gate Bridge and its San Francisco skyline backdrop behind him was breathtakingly beautiful. But he was oblivious to the glory of his surroundings as he stared at the woman who faced him from a few feet away, her vivid blue eyes returning his look without blinking. "I think you made your point," he conceded after a time.

"Sorry about the way I went about it, but you just wouldn't listen when Connie or I tried to explain reasonably," Summer answered, straightening the red Mexican gauze sundress she'd donned over her swimsuit as she offered a tentative truce with her tone.

Derek slowly shook his head. "You made me furious," he told her softly.

She smiled faintly, still a little shell-shocked from his expression of that fury. "I know. Now you know how Connie feels when you start telling her how she ought to live and offering unwanted assistance."

For only a moment an expression of pain crossed Derek's tanned face. He turned to look out over the distant landscape, but not before Summer had seen the emotion and recognized it. She wondered if anyone else would have seen it, or whether she had become so attuned to Derek's feelings that she was almost psychic where he was concerned. She was unaware that her thoughts closely echoed the questions he had asked himself earlier about his ability to read her. Pushing her fanciful thoughts aside, she stepped closer to him and rested a small hand on his rigid arm. "Derek, it's not too late. You and Connie can still be friends, if you'd just give each other a chance. You have to accept her as she is, and she needs to learn that you're not really a humorless stuffed shirt."

He shot her a quick glance. "You don't think I am?"

"No," she answered ruefully, her most charming smile curving her unpainted mouth. "I think you're a pretty nice guy, actually. I mean, you *are* a stuffed shirt, but you're not a completely humorless stuffed shirt."

He chuckled—he actually chuckled! she thought in wonder—and then forgot to be pleased when he reached for her.

"Summer."

She stepped back so hastily that she had to clutch at the railing to maintain her precarious balance. "No, Derek. No more of that. Whatever attraction the two of us might feel for each other could only lead to homicide. Possibly double homicide. I think we'd better stick to being friends."

Her logical little speech did not seem to accomplish the purpose she had intended. Derek's eyes narrowed thoughtfully behind his glasses. "You're attracted to me?" he asked with apparent intrigue.

She gulped and attempted an answer. "Well, yes, but— No, don't!" She wasn't quite quick enough this time to evade his reaching hands. She found herself plastered against his broad chest. "Oh, Derek, this isn't wise." She sighed, even as her head tilted back to welcome his kiss.

"No," he breathed against her moist, parted lips. "Not wise at all." And then his mouth covered hers.

This time the kiss was anything but punishing. In fact, Summer wondered dazedly if she were being rewarded for doing something wonderful. If kisses could be bronzed and hung on a wall for posterity, this one should be.

She lifted her arms and curled them around his neck, her fingers seeking the short hair at the nape of his neck. His hair felt so soft, so thick, his body so solid, so hard against hers. And growing harder.

"Oh, God, Summer," he groaned, slanting his head only to kiss her from a new angle. He slid his hands under the curves of her bottom, lifting her into his pelvis to show her quite graphically that the kiss was as powerful for him as it was for her. Summer could only moan softly and press closer. Her swimsuit and thin dress became unwanted barriers between them, as were his T-shirt and swim trunks. The warmth that penetrated their clothing taunted her, making her want even more.

When the second knee-melting kiss ended, Summer somehow found the strength to break away from him. Or maybe he'd decided to release her. Whatever it was, she stood panting for breath and staring at him in a kind of awed wariness that twisted his mouth into his infrequent smile. "Don't look at me like that, Summer," he ordered indulgently. "I was only teaching you an object lesson."

"An...an object lesson?" she asked in a breathless voice

that showed an annoying tendency to squeak. "What object lesson?" she demanded, bringing her voice sternly under control.

He crossed his arms across his wide chest, looking rather pleased with himself, and leaned against the railing. "That people who teach object lessons sometimes get unexpected results," he replied quietly.

Summer blew her bangs out of her eyes and doubled her fists on her slender hips. "Look, Derek Anderson, if you and I are going to be friends—and I have serious doubts about whether that's possible—we're going to have to get something straight right now. I am *not* looking for an amusing toy to keep me entertained. I have no intention of getting involved with any man at this time, and especially not a proper, respectable businessman like you, even if you *are* an Olympic-class kisser. So let's forget this ever happened and make sure that it never happens again. Agreed?"

"Olympic-class, huh?" Derek looked disgustingly pleased with her ill-chosen adjective.

She sighed. "We were discussing your sister," she reminded him archly.

"So we were," he agreed, obviously deciding to allow her to lead the conversation—for now. "Let's carry these dishes inside and we can continue this discussion—about Connie—in the den."

5

"ABOUT CONNIE," Summer began when she and Derek had settled down with drinks in the den. She felt the need to say something since he continued to look at her in a way that made her rather nervous—as if he were ready for dessert and she were it.

"Yes?"

"D'you really think you'll be able to be her friend?"

"I can only try. Actually, I had an idea for a peace offering."

"Really? What?"

"I'm having a small cocktail party here next Saturday evening, one of those obligatory functions for my clients and potential clients. Do you think Connie would like to serve as my hostess?"

"I don't know, but you could ask her," Summer replied, pleased with the idea. "I think she'll be honored. It will make her feel like you trust her to behave herself in front of your associates."

"Can I trust her?"

"Of course you can! She knows how to act at a genteel cocktail party. She doesn't particularly like them, of course, but she would probably attend this one for your sake."

He nodded. "I'll ask her, then."

"Good." She smiled at him.

Derek shifted his weight, ending up a little closer to her on the deep, oatmeal-colored couch. Summer looked at him suspiciously, but he only said, "I'd like for you to come, too."

"Why?"

He lifted one eyebrow. "As Connie's friend, your being here might put her more at ease."

"Oh." For a moment she'd thought he was asking her simply because he wanted her to be there. She tried to tell herself that she wasn't disappointed that he was only thinking of Connie.

"Besides," he continued as if her thoughts had been audible to him, "I'd like for you to be here."

"Why?" she asked again.

"Because I enjoy your company," he replied simply.

"You do?"

"Yeah. I do." He leaned closer.

Summer backed off quickly. "I thought we'd agreed there would be no more of that."

"You agreed," he reminded her. "I agreed to no such thing."

She glared at him, trying to read his expression. Was he teasing her? The funny little smile was gleaming in his metallic eyes, but he didn't actually look as if he were teasing as he leaned even closer.

"Derek?"

"Yes, Summer?"

Intrigued by the way he'd said her name, she almost forgot what she'd been about to say. Then she remembered. "You don't approve of the way I live my life."

"Not entirely, no."

"And you're no hero."

"God, no."

"So it would be a waste of time for us to…you know."

"Perhaps."

"And you don't believe in wasting time, remember? Connie says—"

"Connie has a big mouth."

"I'm her best friend. She tells me everything." Then she remembered that she'd been about to make a point. "So do you agree that it would be best for us to remain friends?"

"You and Connie? Absolutely."

Summer growled. "No, Derek. You and I. *We* should remain friends. Nothing more."

"Yes, we probably should."

She relaxed. "Good. I'm glad that's settled." Now she had only to convince herself, she thought.

"So am I." He moved the six inches that separated them and kissed her deeply.

Her heart playing hopscotch in her throat, Summer stared at him when he pulled back. "Derek, haven't you been listening to a word I said?" she demanded. "You just agreed that we would remain friends. Friends don't sit around kissing each other."

"They don't?"

"Not…not the way you kiss."

"Olympic-class?" He still seemed rather pleased with that description.

"Well, actually, I think I should change that."

He looked disappointed. "Not Olympic-class?"

"No. I'd forgotten that all the competitors in the Olympics are amateurs. I don't think you'd qualify."

He grinned. It was the closest thing to a real grin she'd ever seen him wear. Before she could do any more than go all gooey inside in response, he was kissing her again. "You have the nicest way of asking a man to back off," he informed her when he released her mouth, keeping his face close to hers.

She cleared her throat with difficulty. "I don't think you're paying much attention."

"I don't seem to be, do I?"

Setting her half-empty wineglass pointedly on the low coffee table in front of them, Summer rose to her feet. "It's time for you to take me home now, Derek."

"All right," he agreed, standing beside her. "Will you come to my party next weekend? It's only fair, you know. I went to yours."

"I'll think about it."

"Do that."

DEREK FOUND HIMSELF actually smiling into the darkness as he climbed into bed that night. He'd stumbled onto an excellent way of dealing with Summer Reed, he decided in satisfaction. He'd wondered the other day what would happen if he silenced her teasing with a kiss. Now he knew. At first he'd merely been punishing her for her pointed little "object lesson." Then, when he'd discovered that his kisses seemed to shake her up so much that she actually forgot to laugh at him, he'd decided to continue the interesting assault. And face it, he told himself, he'd been wanting to kiss her ever since he'd first seen her sitting on that bar stool in her apartment, her lovely smile seeming to light up the dim corner in which she sat. She'd been so self-assured. So coolly amused.

Remembering her dazed expression when he'd left her at the door tonight with a kiss that could have blown all the fuses in her apartment building, he chuckled softly. He'd wondered if there was a way to penetrate her laughing composure. It seemed he had found it.

There was only one problem with his method of controlling Summer. He liked it too much. Kissing Summer could rapidly become addictive. It compared easily with the adrenaline rush that had come just before he'd gone into situations in his government work that he'd known would be highly dangerous. He could imagine only one thing more exciting than kissing her. Imagining that one thing had sent him straight home to a cold shower.

He thought of those dangerous situations that he'd faced with appalling regularity before he'd retired from the job that he'd always misrepresented as a safe, diplomatic attaché position. He wondered if his analogy of danger had been too close for comfort. Involvement in those situations could have cost him his life. Involvement with Summer could cost him...what? His peace of mind? His very soul?

The hairs on the back of his neck used to stand on end when he'd sensed that an assignment would be particularly explosive. They were standing on end at this moment. But just as he'd been unable to resist the lure of danger for fifteen years, so he seemed unable to resist it now. Derek was taking on one more assignment. He wanted Summer Reed. He intended to have her.

He'd tried to fight his attraction to her. Hadn't he?

Yes, he had. He'd lost the battle. He wanted her. She wasn't exactly the type of woman he'd thought he was looking for when he'd decided to settle down into a more normal life, but what the hell. He wasn't exactly the type of man he'd presented to the world during the past few months, either.

Oh, yes, he wanted her. Defiant, eccentric, impudent, unpredictable and vulnerable Summer. But could he make her want him? Was she so convinced that he was a dull, regimented businessman that she would refuse to acknowledge there was something exciting between them? Would she be more interested in him if he told her about what he had really done for the government?

No, dammit, he was no storybook hero, despite his past. She'd take him as he was now, or not at all.

Derek Anderson was a man of action. Quick to make decisions, quick to act on them. He went to sleep still making his plans for his campaign to win the heart and trust of Summer Reed.

"LET ME GET THIS STRAIGHT. My brother invited you over for a swim and a barbecue and you went? You spent the entire afternoon and evening with him?" Connie stared across the tiny dinette table, her green eyes wide with surprise as they focused on her roommate.

"Yep." Summer swallowed her first sip of morning coffee, her eyes closing in momentary pleasure. How she loved that first sip of coffee.

"And you had breakfast with him Saturday?"

"That's right. I'd have told you all about it last night, but you got in so late. I just couldn't wait up for you." Actually, Summer had not wanted to tell Connie everything the night before. She had needed the time to sort out her thoughts about what had happened between her and Derek yesterday. And she'd finally reached a conclusion. "Your brother is the most arrogant, high-handed, exasperating man I ever met in my life."

Connie laughed shortly. "I hear that," she muttered, using an expression she'd picked up from her Arkansan friend.

"Why didn't you tell me that he takes revenge when someone manages to get the best of him?"

"I've told you that he hates to be bested. What did you do to him, and how did he get his revenge?" Connie asked curiously.

"All I did was demonstrate how frustrating it is for someone to try to tell a person how to live his or her life," Summer explained rather obscurely, though Connie seemed to have no difficulty following the garbled explanation. "I thought I was helping you out, and you'll be glad to know that I think he finally got the message about interfering."

"If you're right, I'll owe you my eternal gratitude. But I take it you demonstrated in such a way that he felt it necessary to take revenge?"

"I'm afraid so," Summer answered glumly.

"Gulp. How'd he do it?"

"He made a heavy pass at me—several of them, actually."

Connie choked, then sputtered with laughter. "Joke, right?"

"No. Your brother assaulted me. The first time he said it was to shut me up, and after that I think he just did it because he knew I couldn't think of a thing to say in retaliation."

"He kissed you?" Connie asked in awe. "Not once but several times? And *you* were at a loss for words?"

Summer plopped her elbows on the table and cupped her cheeks in her hands. "Connie, your brother should be declared a lethal weapon. His kisses short-circuited my mental facilities. I mean, we're talking smoke out of the ears and sparks flying and hair standing on end."

"Wow!"

"You don't have to look quite so proud of him," Summer grumbled.

"It's just... Derek!" Connie shook her head, dazed. "Who'd a thought it?"

Summer sighed deeply. "He must have had a good laugh when he got home last night. I was a basket case by the time he dropped me off here, and he knew it."

"Maybe he was serious. Maybe he really is interested in you."

"Connie, the man said I have an idiotic life-style, that I have kooky friends and that the Salvation Army would turn up its nose at our apartment and its humble furnishings. He also said that I have no ambition and that I'm wasting my life. Does that sound like he's interested in me?"

"No," Connie admitted. "It sounds like something he'd say about me."

"Well, actually, he was talking about you, but it's the same difference."

"Thanks a lot."

"Anyway, he told me himself that I'm not his type. So why else would he have kissed me except to punish me for being right about him not having any right to interfere in your life?"

Connie kept her answer to herself, choosing, instead, to ask curiously, "He's a good kisser, huh?"

Summer turned soulful eyes at her amused roommate. "Connie, he's the best. It's a shame he's your brother so you can't find out for yourself."

"Hmm. I have to admit that he's earned himself a few points in my estimation of him. I would have thought he'd kiss as properly and conservatively as he does everything else."

"Hah!"

"What are you going to do now?"

"I'm going to forget it ever happened," Summer answered determinedly, wishing she believed her own words. "Maybe he will have forgotten it, too, by next weekend. Or at least he'll probably have decided to leave me alone. The joke's over."

"What's next weekend?"

"He's having a cocktail party for some of his clients. He wants you to serve as his hostess."

"Me?" Connie exclaimed in surprise, then shot her friend a stern look. "Whose idea was that?"

"His very own. He probably wanted to tell you about it himself, but I'm too annoyed with him to care."

"Well, he can just forget it. I'm not going to do it."

Summer blinked in surprise. Connie's reaction was something she hadn't expected. "You're not? Why?"

"Why should I?" Connie demanded belligerently, glaring down at her coffee. "Why should I do Derek any favors?"

For the first time Summer was conscious of a genuine surge of vexation at her roommate's attitude toward her brother. "Because he's going to ask you to. He's trying to make peace, Connie. Why won't you at least meet him halfway?"

"He's got you taken in, Summer. This is just another way to manipulate me. He's asking me to help out with his boring cocktail party to point out the contrast to the party you and I threw last week. He'll probably lose no opportunity to inform me that *his* is the proper type of social entertainment."

"I think you're overreacting. He's giving the party, anyway, whether you serve as his hostess or not," Summer pointed out logically. "He's trying to show you that he trusts you to help him out without embarrassing him. That he respects you, Connie."

"Why are you taking Derek's side in this?" Connie demanded. "Are you in some kind of conspiracy with him? Just what did the two of you say about me yesterday, anyway?"

"Connie!" Summer set down her coffee cup and glared at her roommate. "You know better than that."

Connie sighed. "You're right. I'm sorry. I've just gotten too used to having to search Derek's every action for ulterior purposes. You really think he's doing this as a peace offering?"

"Yes, I do," Summer answered flatly, not certain herself of why she was so sure of Derek's motives. She only knew that she trusted him and she had believed him when he'd said he wanted to be closer to his sister. And she knew that she wanted to help. "Will you do it?" she asked.

Connie grimaced. "I'll probably hate every minute of it, but I guess I will. But I warn you, we may all regret this."

"I don't think you will," Summer assured her, devoutly hoping she was right. "Anyway, he invited me to the party, as well," she said, hoping that fact would make Connie more enthusiastic about the event. Forgetting that only moments before she had urged Connie to trust Derek, she added in a mutter, "He probably hopes I'll do something to embarrass myself. Well, I'll show him that I can conduct myself as properly and respectably as…as Joanne Payne."

Connie looked closely at Summer's flushed face and gleaming blue eyes. "Summer, you're not actually… interested in my brother, are you?"

"Interested?" Summer tried very hard to sound incredulous. "Connie, does Derek seem like the hero-type to you?"

"Well, no…"

"I categorically refuse to give in to an attraction to a stuffy businessman. Even if he does kiss like an angel."

Again Connie remained wisely silent, though her eyes brimmed with sudden smothered laughter. "This should prove to be interesting," she murmured after a moment.

Summer glared at her and drained her coffee. "I'm going to get ready for work," she announced haughtily, rising to her full height with immense dignity.

Connie giggled and allowed herself to waste a few moments contemplating a tempestuous love affair between her sober brother and her happy-go-lucky roommate. It might definitely be interesting, she told herself gaily. Suddenly the idea of Derek's cocktail party didn't sound so bad.

"ARE YOU SURE I look all right?" Connie fretted on the doorstep of her brother's home. She smoothed the skirt of her dark green strapless cocktail dress over her well-rounded hips, then straightened the scanty bodice, which clung as if by magic to her full breasts. The auburn hair, which was usually worn in a heedless riot of curls, had been subdued into a sleek chignon at the base of her slender neck.

"Connie, you look beautiful," Summer assured her friend firmly. Summer hadn't been present when Derek had asked his sister to attend this party, so she didn't know exactly what had been said, but she assumed the conversation had been amicable enough. Connie was here. "Derek will be proud to have you as a hostess. How about me? Do I look okay?"

"More than okay," Connie replied sincerely. "You look fantastic."

Summer had chosen an interestingly draped silk jumpsuit of a rich blue that made her eyes seem more incredibly vivid than ever, reflecting the sparkle of rhinestone buckles at her shoulders and tiny waist. A cut crystal pendant glinted from the deep décolletage, and matching earrings twinkled in delicate cascades from her earlobes. A spray of white baby's breath was clipped at one side of her ultrashort hair to feminize the style for the evening, though Summer's appearance left no doubt about her gender.

Summer lifted one foot and scowled at it, eyeing the delicate straps of her silver sandals beneath the tight ankle-length hem of her jumpsuit. "If only I could wear those deadly four-inch heels like you've got on," she mourned. "There's just something dangerous about a woman in four-inch spike heels."

Connie laughed. "You would definitely be dangerous in four-inch heels, my friend. You don't walk that great in flats."

Summer's gurgle of laughter was cut short by a low growl from the door, which neither of them noticed had been opened during their mutual admiration. "That wasn't funny, Connie."

Summer rolled her eyes at her friend, adequately concealing that she was a bundle of nerves at Derek's sudden, silent appearance. Especially since he looked so damned sexy in his dark, European-cut suit. "I knew there was something we forgot, Connie," she quipped. "Cue cards."

"Cue cards?"

"Yeah. To tell Derek when to laugh. He has trouble recognizing a joke, you see."

Connie giggled. "He always has."

"Are the two of you going to stand on my doorstep and insult me all evening, or would you care to come in?" Derek inquired dryly.

Connie swept past her brother with stylish panache. "Good evening, Derek. Is everything ready?" she asked in an exaggeratedly cultured voice.

"Yes, everything's ready," he replied, watching Summer as she limped past him in Connie's wake. "Both of you look beautiful."

"Thank you, dahling," Connie returned with a regal nod of her red head. "And please take note that we are thirty minutes early, just as you dictated, er, requested."

"Connie."

"Yes, Derek?"

"Stuff it."

Connie laughed. "What did you do to Derek last weekend, Summer?" she demanded of her unusually quiet friend. "He sounds almost like a normal older brother. You must have loosened him up." She stumbled over the latter words, remembering too late how they must sound in light of what Summer had told her about the events of the previous weekend.

Summer shot eye-daggers at her roommate, but her smile was convincingly natural as she glanced at Derek, automatically noting that his eyes were gleaming almost silver. So Connie's remark had amused him, had it? Perhaps he thought that Summer would blush and stammer in confusion at the implied reminder of his devastating kisses. Well, she'd show the arrogant male that he wasn't the only one who could keep his opponent off balance. "I certainly tried my best," she murmured in answer to Connie's comment, allowing her eyes to hold Derek's for an extra moment before sliding coyly away.

"Is there anything I can do before the guests arrive, Derek?" Connie interceded hastily, though her round face was alight with suppressed laughter.

"You can make a run-through of the tables, if you like," he replied. "The caterers have everything set up, but you could just check to make sure it's all satisfactory."

"No problem." Connie walked away, admirably confident on her spike heels. She winked back at Summer just before she disappeared through the doorway into the living room.

Summer would have followed her friend, but Derek's hand on her elbow stopped her. She lifted an inquiring eyebrow at him, finding him to be making a slow, thorough examination of her from head to toe—just as he had done when she had opened her door to him early last Saturday morning. Once again she had the sensation that the examination had been more than visual. She could almost feel the warmth of his touch on her breasts, her waist, her hips. She knew the warmth was reflected in her cheeks.

"You look lovely," he said at length, lifting his eyes back to her face.

"Thank you, Derek." She would have stepped away from him, but his hand tightened on her elbow, detaining her.

"I've thought about you a great deal during the past week," he informed her, his gaze holding hers as captive as his hand held her arm.

She swallowed. "I'm sure you have," she replied coolly. Probably laughed himself to sleep every night over the way he'd shattered her composure on Sunday. "Excuse me, I'll go see if Connie needs my assistance."

"She doesn't," Derek answered bluntly. "You're not afraid to be alone with me, are you, Summer?"

Determined to keep up with him this time, she placed a beautifully manicured hand on his dark sleeve and lightly rubbed his arm through the expensive fabric. "Of course I am, Derek," she answered seductively. "You know I just don't trust myself around you."

The gleam in his eyes became more pronounced, but he didn't smile. Instead, he lowered his head to nuzzle her crystal-enhanced ear, murmuring softly, "You know what they say about playing with fire, Summer-love."

"Mmm," she replied as quietly, her heart slamming against the walls of her chest. "Sometimes you burn exactly what you intend to burn."

"Meaning me?"

"I don't know. Are you feeling warm, Derek?" she asked sweetly.

"I'm beginning to," he answered, turning his face so that his mouth grazed her cheek.

Her lids began to drift downward, then shot back up when Connie's voice interrupted from the doorway into the living room. "If you're hungry, Derek, the canapés look delicious."

"I prefer nibbling on your roommate," Derek shot back easily though he stepped away from Summer and offered her his arm. "I seem to have kept you in the foyer, Summer. Please come in."

"Why, thank you, Derek," she replied, resting her hand on his arm without a perceptible pause. Nothing about her relaxed, poised stance would indicate that her mind was reeling and her senses vibrated wildly from that intimate moment with him. Avoiding Connie's quizzical look, Summer shot a glance at Derek to find him looking back at her with a hungry expression that made her gulp. There

was definitely something different about the man tonight.
Something that made her quite nervous.

"May I get you a drink, Summer?" he offered smoothly.

"Yes, Derek, thank you." *I hope it's a strong one*, she
thought fatalistically. *Something tells me I'm going to need it.*

Summer wasn't sure if she was more nervous about the
way Derek was looking at her or the idea of mingling with
his guests tonight. She didn't care for parties where she
didn't know many people. She infinitely preferred the
loud, cheery bashes she and Connie usually attended,
where most of the guests were from their crowd and the
new ones blended in swiftly. Unless they were like Derek
Anderson, she amended, who didn't belong at those parties in the first place.

But tonight would not be like that. Tonight would be
formal and restrained, and Summer would be the one who
did not belong. She would have to make conversation
about subjects that bored her—politics, the economy, artsy
movies with subtitles—and she would have to make explanations about her limp. It always happened in encounters with strangers. Some well-meaning soul would assume she'd recently injured herself and would inquire
solicitously about her, and she would have to explain that
the limp was a permanent part of her. Then she would
have to see their pity as they told her how sorry they were.
God, she hated pity. At her parties she could make jokes
about her limp, laugh off her motorcycle-riding days, and
everyone would laugh with her. She had a feeling her
usual flip responses would be inappropriate tonight.

She took a rather desperate gulp of the champagne that
Derek had procured for her—and she didn't even like
champagne. She started to ask if he had any rum punch,
then decided against it.

"What's wrong, Summer?" Derek asked perceptively,
watching her grimace at the taste of the expensive champagne.

"Nothing," she assured him, not quite meeting his eyes.

"You're not nervous about tonight, are you?"

"Now why would I be nervous?" she bluffed.

"Some people would be a little intimidated before a gathering of people who are all strangers."

"I don't know about Summer, but I'm scared spitless," Connie threw in, draining her own champagne. "You usually couldn't drag me to one of these affairs. Hope I don't embarrass you tonight, Derek."

"You won't," he answered assuredly. "Have I remembered to tell you how much I appreciate your doing this for me, Connie? Parties seem to go much more smoothly when there is a hostess as well as a host, don't you think? The caterers will take care of everything, for the most part. All I want you to do is mingle and keep the conversation going, and keep an eye on the caterers to make sure the trays of canapés and drinks don't get empty. Easy, right?"

"Piece of cake," Connie answered glibly. When Derek turned away, she mouthed in Summer's direction, "Help!"

Summer laughed, steeling herself for the evening ahead. She recklessly swallowed the rest of her champagne, deciding that false courage was better than no courage at all.

6

THE FIRST GUESTS ARRIVED soon. Derek introduced Connie and Summer as his sister and "a very close friend." Almost from the beginning Connie and Summer seemed to take on the role of co-hostesses, both of them mingling easily with Derek's guests—more easily than Summer would have imagined earlier—and keeping a close watch on the tables. Soft music played in the background, serving as no deterrent to the subdued conversations and restrained laughter. A far cry from the party that the two spirited young women had hosted the week earlier.

Though it wasn't quite as bad as Summer had feared, she still found herself getting bored when the party was only some forty minutes along. Everything was so...so predictable. Everything except Derek. He was driving her slightly crazy.

Derek practically glued himself to Summer's side from the moment the party had begun. He included her in his conversations, frequently asked her opinion about various topics of interest and had his arm around her waist as often as not. Summer was irritably aware of the assumption being made by Derek's guests. One woman even asked how long Summer and Derek had been dating and remarked that they made a lovely couple. At first, Summer had resisted his annoying little game by trying to excuse herself whenever he approached or subtly trying to slip away from that distressingly exciting arm around her waist. But since resistance only seemed to make Derek more determined to pursue her, she soon stopped trying and willed herself to relax against him. Only Derek could have known that the sweet smiles she gave him were delivered with silent promises of retribution.

"God, I'm glad you're here tonight, Summer," Connie said with a sigh when they met in the kitchen for a quiet moment an hour after the party had begun. "I'd be going crazy if it weren't for you. This is definitely not my kind of party."

"I know," Summer commiserated. "But you're doing fine, Connie. I'm sure Derek's proud of you. Anyone who didn't know you would probably think you were a real, proper lady."

Connie snickered. "Then I'd better continue to resist the urge to turn the stereo to a loud heavy-metal station or dance on Derek's expensive coffee table. Too bad Clay's not here to liven things up, isn't it?"

Grinning, Summer nodded. "Hang in there, kid. You'll get through it. By the way, I noticed that you were fast making friends with a very attractive man with gorgeous black hair and a sexy mustache. The one in the gray suit that cost more than our combined paychecks for the past two weeks."

A mischievous smile playing at the corners of her plum-glossed mouth, Connie winked at her best friend. "Nice, isn't he? His name is Joel Tanner, and he's going to be quite wealthy, thanks to my brother. He was one of Derek's first clients."

"Married? Engaged? Gay?"

"None of the above. Those were the first three questions I asked him. I think I'll go ask him some more. Ta, darling."

An hour later they met again, this time in the rest room, where they collapsed against a marble-topped vanity table as spasms of pent-up giggles erupted from them like steam from a pressure cooker.

"Summer, I can't stand it!" Connie wailed. "I swear, if this party doesn't end soon, I'm going to scream, just to see if anyone is ill-bred enough to notice. Or maybe I'll just jump Joel's bones right there in the middle of the room. I am so totally bored."

"I thought you were going to blow it for sure when you asked that fat, stuffy banker if he'd ever considered piercing his ears and then told him he had lovely lobes," Summer commented with another giggle. "Oh, the look he gave you."

"It was nothing compared to the look my brother gave me." Connie sighed. "But I just couldn't resist. Those are absolutely the god-awfullest earlobes I ever saw. Isn't it awesome the way they wiggle back and forth when he talks? I just couldn't tear my eyes away from them."

"And I thought it was Joel you couldn't tear your eyes away from."

Connie smacked her lips expressively. "The longer this ordeal goes on, the better he looks. He asked if he could take me home when this slumber party is over. You won't mind taking a cab home alone, will you, Summer?"

"Of course not. How could I deny you your fun after you've worked so hard to please your brother?"

Connie crossed her arms in front of her and lifted a delicately arched brow at her shorter friend. "Speaking of my brother, what's with him tonight? He's placed himself constantly at your side, and when he's not with you, he's watching you from across the room."

"Tell me about it," Summer replied glumly. "I'm sure everyone here has noticed."

"What do you think it means?"

"Revenge, Connie. He's still getting back at me for daring to laugh at the great, perfect Derek Anderson. He's hoping he'll make me nervous enough that I'll do something stupid."

"Are you nervous? Nobody'd ever know to look at you."

"I just hope Derek doesn't know. He'd love it. Your brother has a weird sense of humor, Connie."

"You're telling me?" Connie chuckled.

Summer sighed and checked her appearance one more time before saying, "We have to get back to the party."

Connie groaned but obediently followed her friend from the dressing room.

"Where've you been, Summer-love?" Derek asked softly from close to Summer's ear, only minutes after she'd rejoined the party. "I missed you."

Summer shot a glare over her shoulder at his smugly bland face. "It's not going to work, Derek," she told him quietly.

"What's not going to work?" His tone was interested.

"I'm not going to lose my cool with you tonight. I know you're trying to punish me for daring to attempt to teach you a lesson about your sister, but I'm on to you now and you can just forget it. It won't work."

"I have no idea what you're babbling about."

"Yes, you do!" she argued heatedly, forgetting to hold her social smile. "The way you've been hovering over me tonight and watching me and calling me, uh…"

"Summer-love?" he supplied helpfully.

She grimaced. "Yes. You might as well stop it now, Derek. You've had your fun."

"Excuse me, darling, one of my guests looks like he's leaving, and I'd like to have a word with him first. I'll get back to you as quickly as I can."

Before Summer could make any sort of reply, Derek brushed her mouth lightly with his and walked away, leaving her staring openmouthed and fuming at his retreating back. Damn the man, didn't he know when to call it quits? she asked herself in a near rage. Did he have any idea what he was doing to her? Her nerves were so tight that, like overwound springs, they were in danger of snapping. She was almost quivering with a mixture of anger, chagrin and raw sexual excitement. She wondered almost desperately how the evening would end. Even as she glowered at the hard, lean man in the deceptively innocuous suit as he bent attentively over a bearded older man, she was admiring the breadth of Derek's shoulders and feeling again those powerful arms around her slender waist.

Had he really called her darling?

CONNIE MANAGED to remain at the party until most of the guests had departed, at which time she located her brother and explained that she was leaving with Joel Tanner, if Derek had no objections.

Derek did not look particularly pleased, but he merely thanked his sister for doing an excellent job as his hostess and told her that he would make sure Summer got home safely.

"It's really not necessary for you to take me home, Derek," Summer assured him when Connie and Joel had departed along with the final guests. "I can call a cab. I do it all the time."

"I'm taking you home tonight, Summer, and that's final." Derek had forgotten to use the velvety tone he'd affected throughout the evening when he'd spoken to Summer, and the words came out typically arrogant.

Summer smiled, much more comfortable now that the real Derek was showing through the facade he'd assumed for her benefit. "How can I resist when you ask so sweetly, Derek?" she murmured tauntingly.

His eyes narrowed as he realized that he'd been provoked once again into the high-handed behavior that Summer so enjoyed mocking. Ignoring the caterers, who were discreetly and efficiently clearing away all signs of the party, Derek stepped closer to Summer and slipped his arms around her waist, locking his hands behind her back. "Were you and my sister laughing at me and my guests when the two of you slipped off together so often tonight?"

She'd learned that protests had no effect on his behavior, so Summer made no comment at his familiarity, though her pulse leaped exasperatingly at his touch. Again her senses were vibrating, thrumming with excitement and a primitive form of fear. Silently ordering her traitorous body to behave itself, she reminded herself sternly that she had no business wanting this man. "It was a very nice party, Derek," she answered courteously, her face suspiciously bland. "Exactly the type of party I expected you to host."

"Meaning dull," he translated, though he did not seem particularly offended.

"I didn't say that," she pointed out, concentrating on their conversation in an effort to ignore the breadth of his chest so close to her tightening breasts. There seemed to be a Ping-Pong game going on inside her own chest, which was making it difficult to breathe naturally.

"Perhaps I should have arranged for dancing," he mused, his hands beginning to stroke Summer's back almost absently.

All too aware of the lazy movements of those hands, Summer pretended to give his comment serious thought. "It might have been nice," she agreed finally.

"It's not entirely too late," Derek informed her, drawing her even closer to him. "The music is still playing, and you and I are still here."

"But I don't dance," she reminded him in a voice that was too breathless for her own comfort.

"You can dance with me," he replied imperturbably. "Put your arms around me, Summer."

"No, Derek."

"Please."

She sighed in frustration. "What is this, another way to show me up? You know I—"

A smothering kiss cut the words off neatly. "I just remembered what it takes to shut you up," Derek growled when he lifted his head. "Now put your arms around me, Summer."

She did. When Derek began to move very slowly to the easy music, she moved stiffly with him at first. Then she began to relax as she realized his feet were barely moving and his strong arms were supporting her so that she was able to dance lightly on the toes of her right foot to balance her more fully extended left leg. Before long her arms were around his neck, her cheek against his shoulder, her eyes closed as she gave herself up to the joy of dancing for the first time in five long years. Derek's hands moved lower on her back to hold her in intimate contact as his cheek nestled against her silky amber-brown hair. Neither of them noticed when the sprig of baby's breath fell to the floor.

"This is nice," he murmured after a while.

"Yes," she whispered in reply. "It is."

"You really haven't danced since your accident?"

"No."

"Why not?"

"I was afraid to try," she admitted, then opened her eyes in surprise at her own words. What was she saying? Summer Reed never confessed to such weaknesses.

"Afraid of what, Summer?"

"Oh, nothing. Forget I said it."

His arms tightened around her. "Talk to me, Summer. What were you afraid of?"

She sighed. It was hard to concentrate when she was being held so closely to his powerful body, moving slowly to the strains of romantic music. It seemed easier to just answer honestly than to try to shrug off the subject with a wisecrack as she would have done with anyone else. "I was afraid of falling or looking awkward or otherwise making a fool of myself. And I miss the kind of dancing that I used to do, the tap and jazz that I studied for so long. I didn't think that slow social dancing would compare very well."

"Do you find this dance boring?"

Brilliant blue eyes smiled up at him through thick, half-lowered lashes. "No, Derek. I'm not bored."

"Good." He pulled her even closer and dropped his cheek to hers. The first song ended and another began, and still they swayed silently in the center of the living room, the glass wall behind them reflecting their images against the diamond-studded darkness outside their softly lighted private world. When the second song came to an end, Summer lifted her face to speak to him, only to forget what she'd meant to say when he took advantage of the opportunity to kiss her long and deeply.

"Derek," she breathed when she could speak. And then fell silent as words eluded her. Pressed as they were from chest to knee, she was vividly aware of the arousal that had been growing in him since that first dance, and he had to be aware of her own physical response as her swollen, hard-tipped breasts were flattened against him. Blue silk and delicate lace could not conceal that she was stimulated by his nearness, as he was by hers. "Oh, Derek." She sighed and tightened her arms around his neck to pull his head back down to hers. "Kiss me again."

"Summer," he whispered against her lips just before his mouth opened to cover hers completely. He kissed her as if he would devour her, as if he would learn all her secrets with only this all-consuming embrace, and Summer opened herself to him, holding nothing back from him.

There was no longer any pretense of dancing. Derek kissed her, drew back only to tilt his head to a new angle and kissed her again. Summer returned kiss for kiss, the need for oxygen a secondary consideration to her need for Derek.

Derek's hand moved from the small of her back to slide between them, stopping at the deeply draped bodice of her jumpsuit. His palm moved in a slow, circular rhythm over her hardened breasts, the silk fabric gliding sinuously beneath his hand. Summer gasped as her body arched instinctively toward him. His head lowered further to drop moist, hot kisses along the delicate curve of her throat.

"Oh, Derek," she moaned, her eyes tightly closed. Nothing had ever felt so right, so natural, as his arms around her, his mouth against her skin. His hardness against her softness told her how much he wanted her, and she admitted to herself that she wanted him, too.

He kissed her deeply again as her control slipped even further. Derek loosened the front of her jumpsuit just as her back touched the sofa, and she realized hazily that he had moved her to the sofa as easily as he had guided her in their dance. His breath was ragged, as was hers, clearly audible over the soft music still pouring from the hidden speakers. She could feel his breath on her skin, hot and moist, when he pressed his lips to the upper swell of one breast.

Growing impatient, she lifted herself toward him and clutched the sides of his head, needing to feel his mouth upon her. She cried out when he obliged her by taking one pointed crest between his lips.

"So beautiful. You're so beautiful," he muttered, his tongue teasing the sensitized tip he'd captured.

Summer shuddered, feeling as if there were a fire blazing between her legs. She'd never known desire so intense, need so desperate. She plucked ineffectively at his clothing, wanting to feel those sleek shoulders beneath her palms.

Their caresses escalated until they were almost out of control. With a gasp Derek tore his mouth from her heated skin. His chest heaving, he stared at her, and Summer wondered through her mist of passion when he'd removed his glasses. "I want you, Summer," she heard him mutter through the thick fog that seemed to surround her. "I've never wanted any woman this much."

"I want you, too, Derek," she whispered, knowing it wasn't necessary to tell him with words when her body had already shown him how much she wanted him.

"Ah, Summer. Sweetheart. Make love with me. Stay with me tonight."

"B-but…" she stammered, knowing there was some reason she should refuse. "The caterers!" she exclaimed. No, she thought dazedly. That wasn't it.

"The caterers left a long time ago, Summer-love," he told her tenderly. "There's no one here but us. Come, darling." His arm curled gently around her, lifting her from the sofa to support her at his side.

The movement seemed to bring her out of her stupor.

Going stiff in Derek's arms, Summer closed her eyes and took a deep breath. This wasn't going to work, she told herself regretfully. As much as she would like to have Derek carry her into his bedroom, she just couldn't do it. It simply wasn't in her nature to make love with a man only because it felt good at the time, with no chance of a future involved. Perhaps Derek had chosen to ignore their differences for now, but Summer could not. His wanting her didn't change the fact that he considered her a flighty party-girl, that he disapproved of her.

She refused to set herself up for heartbreak again. This time the wounds might never heal.

"I'm sorry, Derek, I can't," she said finally when she felt that her voice was under control.

He stiffened in resistance to her words. "What? What do you mean, you can't?"

Pulling away from his arms, Summer took a few steps away from him, her limp seeming more pronounced than usual, and turned to face him. "Maybe I phrased that wrong. I should have said I won't," she clarified. "I told you last weekend, Derek, I'm not in the market for an affair."

Taut with frustration, Derek shoved one hand in his pocket and the other through his hair. "Dammit, Summer, you said you wanted me."

She laced her fingers tightly in front of her. "I'll admit that I'm very attracted to you, Derek. But that doesn't mean I'm going to sleep with you. I'm not."

"We're good together, Summer. Admit it."

"No. We're too different."

"I don't think that we are," Derek countered, some of the tension beginning to leave his body. He had begun to recognize the fear behind the bravado in her eyes. "We have a lot in common, Summer. Similar tastes in many things. We've never had trouble talking. I like you, and I've enjoyed spending time with you."

He liked her. Why should those words hurt? Summer lifted her chin. "But you don't approve of me."

He hesitated. "I'm not crazy about some of your attitudes about things that I think are important, but I don't disapprove of you. I'm beginning to understand you. I suspect that there's a lot more to you than you allow the world to see, and underneath your glib facade is a complex, fascinating person. Look how well you fit in with the people who attended my party tonight. You looked perfectly at ease in a social situation that is hardly the type you're accustomed to."

She found that statement rather patronizing, and her narrowed eyes told him so. Derek seemed to be deluding himself that he could mold her into the type of woman he wanted Connie to be. How dare he think that Summer needed changing? Did he have some sort of compulsion to change people? And just how the hell did he plan to repair Summer's leg so that she could be as perfect as he probably wanted her to be? Some tiny inner voice told her that she was being unfair in her anger, but only through anger could she resist the hunger she still saw in his lambent gaze.

"I really don't think we need to discuss this any further, Derek," she told him coolly. "I like you, you're a nice guy, and I hope you and Connie manage to patch up your relationship. Sorry, but I'm not interested in anything else."

By all rights he should have been angry. Instead, he was incredibly gentle when he cupped her face in his hand. "Summer, I'm not going to try to force you to make love with me if you're not ready. That's not the way I want it to be between us. But don't try to tell me you're not interested."

She trembled at his touch, wanting nothing more than to throw herself into his arms. Why was he being so damned understanding? Why wasn't he snarling at her, shouting at her, anything to help her resist him? Surely he could only be contemplating an affair. He would amuse himself with her for a while, then go off in search of a woman more like himself. And Summer would be devastated.

He'd certainly never mentioned any permanent relationship with Summer. Only that he liked her and he wanted to sleep with her. Not that she should expect anything more from him after only a week, she told herself candidly. But still, the thought of making herself so vulnerable to Derek terrified her. The intensity of her feelings for him frightened her.

She'd known so much pain.

"I'm not going to bed with you, Derek," she told him bravely. "Not tonight and not ever."

He dropped a kiss on her nose, startling her into a gasp, then stepped away from her. "Don't make promises you can't keep, Summer-love," he advised her with a note of humor in his gentle, deep voice. "Now get your purse and I'll take you home. For now." He crossed his arms over his chest in a gesture that seemed to imply the debate had ended and he considered himself the victor.

Well, he's not, Summer told herself, straightening her clothes as she stalked away with as much dignity as her faltering walk would allow. *It's time someone teaches that man that he can't have everything his way,* she muttered silently. *And that someone is going to be me!*

The drive across the Golden Gate Bridge and on to Summer's apartment was made in a silence that fairly sizzled with unspoken challenges and resolutions. Summer didn't invite Derek inside but told him good-night at her door in a crisp, dismissive voice. She would have marched straight inside and closed the door in his face, but he caught her to him for a hard, searing kiss that was too brief to allow her to struggle, yet long enough to leave a lasting imprint on her senses.

"Stop doing that!" she yelled when Derek released her.

"No way," he answered imperturbably. "I'll see you tomorrow, Summer."

"No, you won't."

"Yes," he answered very softly, "I will. Sleep well, Summer-love."

"You—Ooh!" The door slammed very satisfactorily behind her when she bolted into her apartment.

"That…that man!" she fumed aloud. "That arrogant, presumptuous, pompous, swaggering, domineering—"

"You could only be talking about my brother," Connie commented, tying the sash of a slinky gray robe as she entered the living room from her bedroom. "In which case you left out regimented, despotic, egotistical, condescending and self-righteous. I've been through the same list of adjectives many times. You can find them in the thesaurus under Derek Anderson."

"What are you doing here?" Summer asked in surprise. "I thought you and Joel would—"

"He brought me straight home!" Connie interrupted incredulously. "He drank a cup of coffee, told me I was delightful and that he would like to see me again, asked me out for dinner Wednesday night and left with a kiss."

"How was the kiss?" Summer asked, wondering if it could even begin to compare to Derek's kisses.

"On a scale of one to ten—fourteen."

"Not bad. He seemed very nice, Connie."

"Yes, he is. I really go for him, you know? And I thought he felt the same way about me. But now I don't know."

"Connie, he asked you out. Obviously he does like you. For heaven's sake, not everyone jumps into bed after knowing each other for only a few hours."

"But…" Connie sank to the sagging couch, looking bewildered. "Well, all the guys I know seem to expect, well, you know."

Summer sighed and ruffled her short hair, feeling suddenly old. "I keep telling you that men care about more than sex from a woman. Not many of them, it's true, but there are a few men left who function with their brains instead of their jockstraps. Your brother is not among them, I might add," she finished darkly.

"Don't tell me Derek made another pass at you."

"Did he ever. Damn the man, Connie."

"Oh, wow." Connie shook her head, her green eyes dazed. "I can't believe this is my brother we're talking about. The man is so proper and straitlaced where I'm concerned that I've thought he should be a candidate for the priesthood. Now he's trying to seduce my roomie. Did you tell him to take a hike into the Pacific?''

"He seems to have a hearing problem," Summer answered dolefully, thinking of his patient refusal to accept her attempted rejection of him. She dropped her face into her hands. "Connie, the man is driving me crazy. What am I going to do with him?''

"Honey, I've been asking myself the same question for years. He was always kind of bossy, even when he was a teenager, but ever since he went off to Vietnam and then into that mysterious government work of his, he's been like a stranger to me. That didn't keep him from trying to run my life long-distance," she added bitterly. "God, I get so tired of trying to live up to his expectations."

Which was exactly the reason Summer was afraid to get involved with Derek. Like Connie, she was afraid she wouldn't live up to his expectations. She could see first-hand how much it hurt to love him and not be able to please him. Still, she wished that Connie and Derek could find a way to live in some sort of harmony. After all, they were family. Reaching out a tentative hand to touch Connie's shoulder, she said carefully, "Derek does love you, Con. Very much. I've seen it in his face, and I've seen how much it hurts him when the two of you fight. I don't know why he is such a perfectionist about the people he cares for, but he must have his reasons. Maybe it's a lingering result of his experience in Vietnam. It must have been horrible."

"I know. But he won't talk about it. Ever. In fact, he rarely talks about himself. Just hands out suggestions."

Summer thought about Connie's words for a moment, realizing they were true. Derek had asked a lot of questions about her past, but he had never volunteered any information about himself.

"It's like he came home with a neat list of things to do," Connie continued glumly. "Buy a house, establish a management consulting business, reform Connie."

"If it makes you feel any better, I think I've replaced you as his next project," Summer said on a sigh.

Connie thoughtfully twirled a long red curl around one fingertip. "I noticed something different about Derek at the party tonight, Summer. With you, he's different. He teased you and smiled at you, and I could have almost sworn that the Derek I knew years ago was back. He was even more relaxed with me when you were around. I think you're good for him."

Summer shook her head quickly, not wanting to hear anything that might lead to false hopes. "No, Connie, it wouldn't work. He'd start trying to change me, and I'd hate being told what to do.

"You have a point there." Connie released the curl she'd twisted into a corkscrew tangle and stared down glumly at her crimson-painted toenails. "I don't know if it's possible for him to learn when to butt out."

For a time the two young women sat in almost identical poses, faces cradled in hands, elbows propped on knees, as they contemplated the exasperating man whom both were drawn to despite their annoyance with him. Summer was the first to rouse from their mutual stupor.

"The hell with it," she announced, pushing herself off the couch. "I'm going to bed, and I suggest you do the same thing. We'll both get a good night's sleep, and tomorrow we'll wake up fresh and ready to take on one Derek Anderson."

"You're right," Connie agreed decisively, rising to stand beside her friend. "Uh, Summer?"

"Yes, Connie?" Summer paused on the way to her bedroom to look back over her shoulder.

"What *I* would really like is for Derek to just love me, without qualifications, exactly the way I am. I don't suppose you'd want the same thing from him, would you?"

Summer tossed her head. "Don't be ridiculous. I'm holding out for a hero, remember? Not a stuffed-shirt businessman." She wished she could have had just a little more conviction in her voice.

"So you've gotten immune to his kisses, huh? They didn't turn you on tonight?"

Summer sighed deeply. "No more than a current of electricity turns on a light bulb. Damn the man." She closed the door firmly on Connie's sudden laughter.

IF ONLY SHE COULD close the door as resolutely on her thoughts as she had on her roommate, Summer thought much later, tossing and turning in her bed. Derek had shaken her badly tonight, especially when he'd made her realize how much she wanted to make love with him. And he'd wanted her. Why? Why would he want a woman of whom he disapproved so strongly? What was it about her that attracted him?

Even more to the point, what was it about him that attracted her? After all, he wasn't handsome. Sexy, yes. Virilely attractive, yes. Nicely built, yes. But not handsome.

And he didn't have a great sense of humor. Well, maybe he did, judging from the way he'd teased her and the suspiciously smile-like gleam that flitted so often in his lovely pewtery eyes. But he certainly did his best to keep his sense of humor hidden.

He was arrogant and overbearing. She tried to forget the gentleness he'd shown her, first when he thought he'd hurt her last Saturday and even tonight, when he should have been angry at being so abruptly rejected. How could he have been so understanding?

He was too conventional. Yes, there was one accusation that would stick. Summer craved adventure, excitement. That was why she drifted from job to job, trying to find something to replace the thrill of dancing and acting, why she hated schedules and routines, why she'd moved to an eccentric town like San Francisco, a place as different from Rose Bud, Arkansas, as anyone could possibly imagine. Derek had put excitement and adventure behind him, choosing a quiet, settled life as a businessman over his former government career. Now his idea of adventure probably consisted of trying out a new restaurant or a new brand of toothpaste.

So what did Derek see in her? Was she his thrill of the month? Did he get some kind of kick out of the idea of taking a free-spirited, lame butterfly to his bed?

Deciding that she would never decipher Derek's motives tonight, Summer rolled over in the bed, slammed her fist into her pillow a couple of times and pulled the covers to her ears. She lay still for a long moment, deliberately concentrating on clearing her mind of all thought.

Which left it open to sensation.

Once again she could feel Derek's arms around her as soft music swirled around them, could feel his lips on hers, his hands on her back, his breath and tongue on her breasts. "Dammit!" she muttered, kicking off her covers and throwing her pillow to the floor in an unwonted temper tantrum. "Get out of my bedroom, Derek Anderson!"

She plopped onto her stomach, leaving her pillow where it had fallen, and willed herself into a restless sleep.

Across the bay Derek lay in his bed and stared up at the ceiling of his bedroom, his arms behind his head. The pieces of the puzzle that made up Summer Reed were slowly beginning to come together for him. Despite her pretense of carefree sophistication, Summer was basically a sweet, somewhat old-fashioned young woman who still believed in the values she'd been taught during her childhood in Rose Bud, Arkansas. She loved to laugh but behind the laughter were tears that she would allow no one to see. Tears of disappointment for the career she'd never had a chance to pursue, tears of frustration for the unfulfilling life she'd drifted into, tears of chagrin for the uncomfortable disability that prevented her from participating in many of the activities a healthy young woman of her age enjoyed. Dancing, sports, runs on the beach. Perhaps even limited her daily activities. Shopping, walking. He'd noticed the way her limp grew even more pronounced when she'd been standing for a long time.

He hated the thought of Summer in pain. Just the idea of her lying bloody and torn on a street after the accident made him break out in a cold sweat. Did the leg still give her pain? Of course it did. He'd seen injuries like that before, in Vietnam, and they never completely healed. But she'd never let on if she *were* in pain. She'd just make a joke about it and change the subject.

She was so very vulnerable. So afraid of being hurt again. Had she really thought he didn't know that? Did she really think he'd ever do anything to hurt her? He wasn't going to let her insecurities stand between them when something much stronger was pulling them together.

Derek was beginning to suspect exactly what it was he felt for Summer Reed, though he would wait until he was sure before applying a label to his feelings. Unlike Summer, the idea of a relationship, a permanent relationship, did not frighten him at all. She was wonderful; she was everything he'd been looking for. He wanted nothing more than to make her happy.

Derek went to sleep feeling very optimistic about his future, exhilarated by his new mission.

DEREK STOOD outside Summer and Connie's apartment at nine o'clock on Sunday morning, just in case Summer had planned to leave early to avoid seeing him. He pressed the doorbell. He knew his pursuit of Summer Reed would not be an easy one. She was going to resist him. She'd spent too many years hiding her feelings to open up to him immediately. But what the heck—he'd taken on assignments with slimmer odds and won. He had every confidence he would win this time. He pressed the bell again.

It was his sister who finally opened the door, wrapped in a gray robe and nothing else, her eyes sleepy.

"Don't you think you should ask who's ringing the bell before you open the door dressed like that?" he growled in concern.

"Give me a break, Derek, I saw you through the peephole," Connie returned crossly. "Besides, rapists don't ring doorbells. They climb through windows."

"Connie, that's ridiculous." He brushed past her. "Summer still in bed?"

"Yes, she is. And she'll probably stay there until you leave." Connie ran a hand through her tangled curls and yawned. "Why don't you leave the poor girl alone, Derek? Stick to your campaign to reform me. I *have* to put up with you. You're my brother."

"Let's you and I make a deal, Con," Derek suggested casually. "You keep out of my affair with Summer, and I'll stop giving you unwanted advice."

Connie smiled brightly. "Hallelujah. Too bad you haven't a prayer of having an affair with Summer, or I'd take you up on that very tempting offer."

"I didn't mean it quite that way, but don't write me off yet. You never know what will happen." He walked past her, moving in the direction of Summer's closed bedroom door.

Connie frowned. "Derek…"

He glanced back without pausing. "Butt out, Connie."

For the first time Connie noticed the way her brother was dressed, and her eyes widened. A brown leather bomber jacket, white knit pullover shirt, well-worn jeans and scuffed brown biker's boots. Derek had come dressed for trouble.

Derek closed Summer's door behind him and stood looking down at her for a long moment before approaching the bed. The doorbell hadn't awakened her. She lay on her stomach, her head cradled on one arm, the other arm dangling off the side of the bed. The covers were tangled at her feet, and her legs were sprawled as carelessly as a child's, the knit nightshirt she wore hiked up to reveal green-and-white-striped panties over a shapely tush. Derek fought down the impulse to jump on top of her and walked to the head of the bed, kicking aside the pillow on the floor. He knelt beside her, pushing a large stuffed bear out of the way, and examined the sleep-flushed face be-

neath the short, tousled golden-brown hair. The faintest
purple rings under her long, closed lashes indicated that
she hadn't slept well. Had her rest been disturbed by
thoughts of him?

God, she was lovely. His insides twisted with a desire so
powerful that it rocked him back on his heels. He'd never
wanted a woman this much in his life.

Very slowly he leaned forward until his lips just
brushed a down-soft cheek. She tasted good. So very
good. He touched his lips in a butterfly caress to the end of
her adorably tilted nose. Her velvety eyelid received a
fleeting salute before his roving mouth touched the corner
of her slightly parted lips. Her breath was warm and soft
against his skin, and he kissed her mouth again. She
stirred, and the beginnings of a smile touched her face.
"Derek," she murmured without opening her eyes.

A wave of emotion surged through him, so intense that
he nearly doubled over from the force of it. "Yes, Summer,
it's Derek," he whispered, his voice hoarse.

Her smile deepened, her eyelashes fluttering on her
cheeks. Blinking at the light, she squinted shyly up at him.
"Hi, Derek," she murmured, sleep still deepening her
voice.

"Oh, God, Summer." Unable to resist any longer, Derek
leaned over the bed and took her in his arms, his mouth
covering hers in a kiss that was as hungry as it was gentle.
She made a sound like a purr deep in her throat and lifted
her arms to slide them around his neck, her lips opening to
his without hesitation. Derek knew she was still half-
asleep but took full advantage of her momentary weakness as he lowered himself beside her and deepened the
kiss.

Stretching like the cat whose purr she imitated, Summer
snuggled into Derek's embrace, luxuriating in his warmth
and strength. His mouth moved against hers, his tongue
stroking hers in a kiss that was even more beautiful than
those that had haunted her dreams. Holding herself even
closer to him, she silently begged for his touch. As if she'd

moaned the request aloud, he gave her what she desired, his hand sliding across her back and around her waist to cup her breast. Summer whimpered and held him more tightly, arching into his palm. Derek lifted his head only to pull in a shuddering breath, then kissed her again. His hand moved feverishly over her scantily clad figure, discovering and stroking all her feminine secrets. Summer felt as if she were on fire. She wanted him. Oh, how she wanted him.

And then his hand moved over her hip and down her thigh, slipping behind her knee to lift her leg over his. Her right knee. She flinched as the mangled joint, always stiff in the morning, protested the movement with a twinge of pain.

Dismayed, she tore her mouth away from Derek's and pushed against his chest, fully awake. "What the hell are you doing in my bedroom?" she said on a gasp, scooting back on the bed to put a safe distance between them.

Reluctantly acknowledging that the golden moment was over, Derek made no effort to detain her but lifted himself slowly onto his elbow, looking at her with a rueful smile. "I would think the answer to that question is obvious," he told her huskily.

"You came here to seduce me?" she demanded, crossing her arms defensively over her chest. "In my own bedroom?"

Something about the outraged question struck him as funny, and he chuckled. Then, as her eyes narrowed in sudden fury, he realized that laughter was not exactly the most tactful response to this particular situation. "I only came in here to wake you," he assured her gravely, pushing himself upright to stand beside the bed, easing his hands into the pockets of his painfully tight jeans as he did so. "I'll admit that things got a little out of control, but I'm certainly not apologizing. I thought it was fantastic. You were enjoying it, too. Admit it."

"I was asleep!" she protested, pushing her bangs out of her eyes with a trembling hand.

"You knew what you were doing," he answered relentlessly. "You called me by name."

Flushing vividly, she dropped her eyes from his, frowning as she took in his casual attire. "Your clothes."

"What about them?"

"They make you look...different."

"You asked me if I own a pair of jeans. You see now that I do."

Thoroughly disoriented, Summer shook her head as if clearing the last vestiges of sleep, then glared at him. "What are you doing in my bedroom?" she asked again.

He just couldn't help it. He chuckled again. "We've already been through that, remember? You look wonderful in the mornings. Even if your hair *does* tend to stand straight up." His eyes made a lazy survey of the skimpy nightshirt that had proved so little barrier against his wandering hands. The words printed across the front of the orange knit shirt darkened his eyes: Motorcycle Mama. "That shirt is sick."

"Connie gave it to me. I think it's cute."

"You would. Get dressed. We're spending the day together."

"The hell we are."

He sighed. "Look, Summer, you can either get dressed and go out with me, or we'll spend the entire day right here in your bed. Personally, I'd prefer the latter, but something tells me that you wouldn't agree."

"You're damned right I don't agree."

"Then get dressed. I'll go find some coffee and wait for you."

"Derek, you can't just walk into my bedroom and tell me that I'm going to spend the day with you."

"I just did. See you in half an hour." He winked at her as he walked toward the door.

Summer groped for her pillow, hoping to find it in time to throw it at his retreating back. Too late she remembered that she'd thrown it to the floor the night before. With one last insolent glance back at her Derek walked out of the room, quietly closing the door behind him.

Her head buzzing with conflicting emotions, Summer took her shower. A cold shower. Even that could not quench the fires Derek had started within her. Damn him! She'd never met anyone like him. Though she'd met some single-minded, intractable, persistent males in her life, Derek should win a prize. When he set his mind on something, he intended to achieve it regardless of the consequences. Not through flashy, ostentatious, creative measures, but by steady, thorough, relentless pursuit. No grand hero, this Derek Anderson, but a man who achieved his goals quietly. Not qualities she normally admired in a man. So why did she find them so utterly fascinating in Derek? And why was she beginning to resign herself to the fact that an affair with him was fast becoming inevitable?

While she dressed in an oversize white fleece top and baggy stone-washed jeans, her rational side continued to remind her of the reasons she must resist the temptation to give in to Derek, even as her body throbbed with the remnants of passion he'd created upon awakening her. She told herself that she had taken an unusual amount of time with her makeup only to hide the aftereffects of her restless night, not to look particularly attractive for Derek. Sliding her feet into the stylish leather flats that she wore from necessity as well as fashion, she took a deep breath before heading for the door through which Derek had departed only twenty minutes earlier.

She found him in the kitchen, sharing coffee with his sister. Summer wasn't particularly surprised to discover that they were talking about Joel.

"Did you know him before he hired you to look over his business?" Connie was asking as Summer entered the room. "Joel was a little vague about how the two of you met."

"I've known him for a while," Derek answered.

"Oh, great. You're about as helpful as he was," Connie complained. "Don't you like him, Derek?"

Derek looked steadily at her. "Now how should I answer that? If I tell you that I don't like him and wish you wouldn't see him, you'll throw yourself into his arms. If I encourage you to see him because he's a decent guy and would be good for you, you'll drop him like a hot rock."

Summer swallowed a chuckle at Derek's wickedly accurate assessment. He obviously had no intention of commenting on Joel Tanner.

"Well, you should be pleased to know that your friend brought me straight home last night and told me goodnight without even making a pass."

"That must have been quite a change for you," her brother muttered into his coffee.

Connie started to bristle, but Summer interceded hastily. "Good morning, Connie. Sleep well?" she asked, ignoring Derek as she limped across the room to pull a coffee mug from the cabinet.

"Until I was so rudely awakened, yes," Connie replied. "The sugar's in the sugar bowl, Summer."

"What a unique place for it. Usually we just dip it from the sack."

"Don't look at me. Derek's the one who filled the bowl."

"I should have known."

"Stop talking about me like I'm not in the room," Derek commanded them both, rising to his feet. "Here, Summer, take my chair. I'll lean against the counter. Why the hell don't you invest in some decent furniture? Surely between the two of you, you could afford some good used furniture that isn't in danger of falling apart."

"This furniture came with the apartment. Besides, we have other ways we'd rather spend our money," Connie answered with a shrug. "It's not like either of us makes that much."

Derek sighed but resisted further comment on that particular subject. "Aren't either of you going to have breakfast?"

Again it was Connie who answered. She lifted her coffee cup. "You're looking at it, brother dear. How did you think we eat as much as we do on special occasions and still maintain our girlish figures?"

"But breakfast is—"

"The most important meal of the day. Honestly, Derek, you sound like someone's grandmother."

He only grunted.

"Isn't it amazing how much meaning he can put into that one short sound?" Connie asked Summer, smiling across the table in a conspiratorial manner.

"You're talking about me again," Derek complained.

"It's not the first time," his sister retorted.

"I'll bet," he responded resignedly. "I'd ask you to join Summer and me today, Connie, but I know you and Mother are planning to visit Barbara's newest grandchild."

"I'm only going because Mother insisted," Connie grumbled. "I dread spending even five minutes in the same room with Saint Barbara."

"Connie—"

Again Summer jumped in before the Anderson siblings came to verbal blows. "I told you earlier, Derek. I'm not spending the day with you."

"Yes, you are."

"No, I'm not. I have plans for today, and I have no intention of changing them."

He scowled. "You have a date?"

She considered using that excuse, but she wouldn't lie to him. "Well, no, not exactly a date."

His expression cleared. Rubbing his chin consideringly, he shrugged away her argument as unimportant. "Okay, I'll go with you. Where are we going?"

"You weren't invited!"

"I am now. Where are we going?"

Connie laughed. "You might as well give up, Summer. If you don't take him along, he'll just follow you."

Derek nodded genially. "That's right. Where are we going, Summer-love?"

Summer looked down at her coffee cup, her fingers twitching on the chipped handle.

Reading either her mind or her expression—Summer devoutly hoped it was the latter—Derek said softly, "I wouldn't recommend it, Summer."

Connie giggled, but Summer only glared at him. "I wouldn't dream of wasting my first cup of coffee of the day on your shirtfront," she told him loftily.

"Smart move." His mouth tilted into the grin that was making an appearance with increasing regularity, the one that made Summer want to throw herself on him and taste it.

Dismayed and even a little frightened by the strange impulses Derek aroused in her, Summer decided to go along with him without further argument. She'd let him tag along today, she determined abruptly. Later he'd be sorry he insisted. Maybe today he'd get the picture that there could be no question of a relationship between them, regardless of how brief. "I don't think I'll tell you where we're going," she told him slowly. "You're sure you don't want to back out now?"

"I'm sure." He tilted his cup, drained the contents and set the cup in the sink. "When do we start?"

"Whenever you're ready."

"I'm ready now."

She pushed herself away from the table. "Then let's go. See you later, Connie."

"Bye." Connie seemed to be holding in gales of laughter as she eyed the other two, her dancing eyes giving away the emotion she was trying to suppress. "Have fun, kids."

"Yeah," Summer muttered heavily. "You bet."

Derek assisted Summer into the passenger seat of his plush gray Lincoln—as if she needed help to climb into a car, she thought resentfully. She watched through her lashes as he slid behind the wheel. "Where to?" he asked pleasantly.

She named the nearest shopping mall.

"We're going shopping?" he asked without evidence of distaste.

"I have to buy a birthday present for Autumn," she explained. "Her birthday's next week, and I need to get the gift in the mail by tomorrow or it will never get to her on time."

He nodded. "Is that all you have planned for today?"

"No," she answered rather curtly. "I'll tell you the rest later."

"Fine." Still he didn't start the car but sat twisted in the seat, facing her as if he were waiting for something.

"Forget how to start it?" she inquired facetiously.

"Nope. But I'd really like to kiss you again before we leave. With you awake this time."

She flushed. "Forget it," she told him gruffly.

He kept his face suspiciously innocent though the corners of his mouth twitched. "Not even a little one?" he asked hopefully.

She sighed. "What is it with you and kissing, Derek? Don't you ever think of anything else?"

She knew she'd asked the wrong question as soon as the words were out of her mouth. Derek laughed. A quick, unexpected laugh that seemed to startle him almost as much as it did her. "Yes, Summer, I think of something else. I could elaborate in great detail, if you'd like."

"No, that's not necessary," she told him hastily, cheeks burning, though her heart was fluttering crazily in response to his wonderful laugh. He'd actually laughed, she told herself wonderingly, and her own lips curved into an answering smile.

"Well?" he asked humorously. "May I kiss you? Or are you only brave in your sleep?"

He shouldn't have made it sound like a challenge. Summer never could resist a challenge. "I'm not afraid to kiss you, Derek," she told him flatly. "I can control my emotions."

"Prove it."

She reached out a hand and grabbed him by the shirt collar, tugging to bring him closer. She leaned forward in her seat to meet him halfway, stopping just short of completing the embrace. When he moved no further, she swallowed. It was clearly up to her to do the kissing this time, she realized nervously. Derek was calling her bluff. Hesitating only a fraction of an inch from his firm mouth, she inhaled, then pressed her lips to his.

Surely she'd only meant to give him a brief, friendly kiss, she told herself dazedly a long time later. It surely couldn't have been her intention to extend the caress into a passionate clinch that had threatened to steam the windows of the car and melt all the plastic on the instrument panel.

It wasn't even Summer who pulled away first. Derek was breathing raggedly when he pulled back and sat her firmly in her seat, running his hand through his hair as he turned back to the steering wheel. "I think we'd better go to the mall," he said huskily, "before I think of a good use for that nice big back seat."

Summer clenched her hands in her lap and stared down at them, grateful for small favors. At least he hadn't teased her for allowing the kiss to get so wildly out of control.

If Summer had expected Derek to be disconcerted when she walked straight into a small boutique that specialized in expensive lingerie, she was destined to be disappointed. He strolled into the shop with the ease of a man who'd spent many pleasant hours in such places. Perhaps he had, Summer thought glumly. He stood quietly aside as Summer selected a luscious black nightgown for her fiery-spirited, auburn-haired sister.

"This is for the liberated sister?" he inquired with a lifted brow, examining the filmy scrap of froth.

"Yep," Summer replied cheerfully, picturing Autumn's exasperation upon opening the gift. "I like to remind her occasionally that she *is* a woman."

"Maybe you should try it on so we can get an idea of

how it would look on," Derek suggested with an exaggerated leer.

Summer firmly declined, though she had to turn her face to hide the flush that accompanied several unbidden fantasies of herself wearing such a garment for Derek.

While she was in the mall, Summer made several other purchases, items she'd waited until the weekend to stock up on. She blithely loaded Derek down with her packages.

"Is there anything else you'd like to buy before we leave the mall?" he asked her politely, his arms full. "Like a couple of dozen pairs of shoes?"

"No, thanks," Summer replied airily. "Come along, Derek."

Her charming attempt at imperiousness delighted him so much that he stopped right in the middle of the crowded mall to kiss her, earning himself a glare and another one of her rosy blushes.

"I'm hungry," she told him when they were back in the car. "Why don't we have some lunch somewhere?"

He agreed very cooperatively and took her to Fisherman's Wharf, spending the quiet time during the meal learning more about her childhood years in Arkansas. She answered his questions stiffly at first, but Derek's genuine interest in her words put her quickly at ease. Soon she was chattering away, making him smile and once even laugh with her stories of her boisterous childhood.

Summer even managed to draw Derek out enough to talk a bit about his own childhood. He admitted that he had been quite a handful, always tumbling into trouble and making frequent visits to the emergency room.

"When did you turn into such a respectable citizen?" Summer asked him with gentle mockery.

He grimaced at her but answered semiseriously. "Probably about the time Connie was born. My father told me that I had to set a proper example for my baby sister, since I was so much older."

"How did you feel about having a little sister after being an only child for so long?" Summer asked curiously.

Derek lifted one shoulder, his expression almost wistful. "I thought it was nice. She was cute, as babies go, and I used to enjoy playing with her. But then I ended up in Nam and drifted into the government job, and before I knew it, she was grown-up and practically a stranger. I don't know what happened, exactly."

Her heart twisting at the sadness in his eyes, Summer reached across the table to touch his hand. "You made a good start at repairing the damage last night, Derek. The two of you were a little more relaxed together this morning."

"Yeah, I think so, too," he answered, looking faintly pleased.

Summer released his hand, aware of her reluctance to do so. "How do you really feel about Connie dating Joel?" she asked Derek, forcing herself to keep her mind on their conversation.

To Summer's surprise Derek broke into a broad grin. "I find it very amusing," he informed her cryptically.

Summer frowned in confusion. "Why?"

But Derek only shook his head. "I'll tell you another time," he told her, refusing to say another word about it.

When the meal was over, Derek asked again, "Where to?"

She gave him a rueful smile. "I hope you're feeling rested and refreshed. Our next stop is Halloran House."

He frowned. "Halloran House?"

"It's a home for children with emotional or behavioral problems. It's Clay McEntire's pet project—he spent some time in a similar home when he was growing up, and he doesn't mind telling people that he would have ended up in prison by now if he hadn't received excellent counseling and guidance at the youth home. Anyway, the kids at Halloran House are putting on a talent show. Clay volunteered my services to them when he found out that I'd been a theater arts major. They've been rehearsing on Wednesday evenings and Saturday mornings, but they're putting on the show this coming Friday and they wanted to work in one extra rehearsal today. You can just drop me off if you don't want to stay."

"I'll stay." The words were spoken decisively. Derek was vaguely aware that he was enjoying himself more than he could have imagined. The more time he spent with Summer Reed, the more she fascinated him. And the more he wanted her. "What's the address?"

8

HALLORAN HOUSE HAD been established in a large, renovated Victorian home by a wealthy industrialist who had
lost a son to a drug overdose, Summer explained as Derek
drove. It relied on donations for its continued existence,
many of which were obtained from wealthy families
whose children had been in trouble with drugs or other serious adolescent problems. Though most of the children in
residence at Halloran House were from low-income families, there were some there from the middle and upper
classes. Mostly between the ages of eleven and sixteen,
these were kids who, either because of neglect at home or
the influence of their peers, had gotten beyond the control
of their parents and teachers, though they had not yet been
convicted of any real crimes.

Summer was greeted warmly by the Halloran House
residents, though Derek was not welcomed with open
arms. The troubled young people there did not trust adult
strangers, and they looked him over thoroughly when
Summer introduced him. Derek was grateful that he'd
chosen to dress in leather jacket and jeans that morning.
His short, almost military haircut earned him enough suspicious looks. His usual crisp white shirts and dark,
creased slacks would have put him in contempt with these
defiantly ragged youths with their too old eyes.

In the cavernous, one-time ballroom, which now served
as a recreation room, a stage had been erected and a stereo,
with huge blaring speakers, set up. Young people were
practicing all over the room, oblivious to the chaos around
them. At least half a dozen different pop songs were being
mangled simultaneously, dancers were leaping like de-

mented deer, a teenage girl dressed like Cyndi Lauper was swaying sinuously, another was twirling a baton and a group in one corner seemed to be loudly practicing a comedy skit. Summer had told Derek that there were only twenty full-time residents. Ten more attended counseling sessions there after school while living at home. Not all of those would be involved in the show, but to Derek there seemed to be hundreds of noisy adolescents in the room.

Through the confusion they heard a male voice yell "Summer!" and the rugged blond that Derek remembered from Connie and Summer's party broke away from the crowd and came quickly across the room. He greeted Summer with an enthusiastic kiss on the mouth, which brought a murderous scowl to Derek's tanned face.

"Derek, do you remember Clay McEntire?" Summer asked. "Clay, this is Connie's brother, Derek. He was at our party last weekend."

The two men shook hands—Derek with some reluctance—but before they could do more than murmur appropriate greetings, another man approached. A prematurely balding fellow of about thirty with thick glasses and a seemingly permanent grin, he was introduced by Summer as Frank Rivers, the director of Halloran House. " 'Bout time you got here, Summer. We've got a madhouse on our hands."

"No problem," Summer assured him airily, then cupped her hands and shouted, "All right, you animals, the director's here. Let's show a little respect."

Magically the chaos subsided. Laughing, the kids gathered around Summer, who ordered them to sit on the floor in front of the stage. Derek was rather astonished when they obeyed her without question. Summer dispatched him to a straight-backed chair in one corner of the room to watch the proceedings. Like the kids, he did as she told him without protest.

For the next two hours Derek watched in fascination as Summer turned the eighteen insolent delinquents attending the rehearsal into surprisingly adequate performers.

Laughing, teasing and cheerfully insulting, she had the
kids eating out of her hand, even as she managed to maintain control of the rehearsal with very little help from
Frank and Clay. She applauded each performance, offered
suggestions when needed, even walked through the
Cyndi Lauper routine with the girl, smoothing out the
rough edges of the lip-synched pantomime. Despite the
enforced awkwardness of her movements, Summer maintained a graceful fluidity that Derek knew had been developed through long grueling hours of therapy and practice.
The talent that had won her the role of Eliza Doolittle was
very much in evidence.

Later he was given a sample of her singing talent when
a shy, pretty teen with chocolaty eyes and a smooth mocha
complexion requested assistance with a song she planned
to sing, particularly with one measure that was giving her
problems. Summer glanced at the music, murmured a few
words to the woman who had been recruited to play the
piano and sang the song in a key that was much easier for
the young person to carry.

As the rehearsal concluded, Summer again walked
through the closing number with the entire cast, a simply
choreographed version of the title song from the movie
Fame. Derek frowned as he noticed that Summer's limp
was growing more and more pronounced. Searching her
face, he thought she looked tired. He was considering
dragging her off the stage and making her take a rest when
she called an end to the rehearsal.

Summer sincerely complimented the performers as they
left her, promising to see them Wednesday night for their
final rehearsal before the show on Friday evening. As she
said her goodbyes and made her last-minute remarks,
Clay approached Derek. "She's good, isn't she?"

"Yeah," Derek answered simply. "She's good."

"I knew this would be good for her, but I had a hell of a
time talking her into it."

"Oh?" Derek studied the pleasure on Summer's tired
face as she looked into the young faces turned to her. "I'd

have thought she'd jump at the chance to do something like this."

"I think she was afraid she couldn't do it," Clay explained in a low voice. "You might not have realized it, but our Summer's not quite as carefree as she lets on. We all know that she's a little sensitive about her limp, but she's brave about it, isn't she?"

Resenting Clay's thinking he might know more about Summer—Derek's Summer, not *our* Summer, he added to himself—Derek only nodded. He was a little deflated to realize that he wasn't the only one who understood the complex young woman who had come to mean so much to him in such a short time. He was also jealous as hell of anyone who had known her longer than he had. He glared at Clay as Summer approached them.

"Sorry it took so long, Derek. Are you bored out of your mind?"

He slipped a supportive and unmistakably possessive arm around her waist. "Not a bit," he assured her, his voice husky and intimate. "Tired, Summer-love?"

"Mmm. A little," she agreed, not protesting the supportive arm.

"Then let's go." He gave her little chance to say goodbye to Frank or the avidly curious Clay as he hustled her out the door and into his car.

Summer sank gratefully into the plush seat of the Lincoln, resting her head against the high back. "Weren't they wonderful?" she asked Derek huskily.

"I felt like I was watching one of those old Mickey Rooney and Judy Garland movies," he confessed. "The ones where they're always saying 'Let's have a show!'"

Summer laughed softly. "Kids haven't changed all that much over the years. They still love attention, and they need to know they have special talents that make them worthy of praise. Even the ones who can't sing or dance were able to participate in the skits or operate the lights or sound system, so they feel like an important part of the show. Basically, these kids are the ones who crave attention so desperately that they got into trouble to impress their friends or get their parents to notice them.''

Out of the corner of his eye Derek watched as Summer kneaded her right leg almost absently. He frowned. But rather than commenting on her action, he asked only, ''Who will attend the show?''

''The parents and some of the home's benefactors. Not that many people—there's not an abundance of room.'' Pulling her thoughts away from the rehearsal, she turned her attention to the route Derek was taking. ''Where are you going?''

''My place.''

She turned to look at him. ''I never said I was finished for the day. I might have other plans.''

''Tough,'' he answered succinctly. ''You need to rest. We're going to my place, and I'm going to make dinner for you.''

Summer considered her options. She could berate him for his arrogance and order him to take her home, or she could go along with his autocratic and typically domineering decree. Judging from the hard set of his jaw, she had little chance of success with the first option. He'd do what he wanted to do, anyway.

A little smile played on her tired features as she settled back more comfortably into the seat, realizing that she wanted the same thing.

SUMMER STRETCHED and opened her eyes, then gasped as she looked frantically at her watch. Sitting up on the bed in Derek's guest room, she realized that she'd been asleep for just over an hour. She had protested heatedly when he'd ordered her to lie down and rest as soon as they were in the house, but he'd stubbornly insisted that she would either lie down alone or he would join her.

She had hastily agreed to lie down alone.

She hadn't expected to be able to relax, much less sleep. A near sleepless night followed by an unusually strenuous day had caught up with her, however. Now she was a little embarrassed.

She wondered what Derek had done during the time she'd been asleep. Had he looked in on her? She didn't like the idea of being so vulnerable to his knowing eyes twice in one day.

Combing her hair with her fingers, she thought back over the past few hours. It had been wonderful having Derek by her side all day, she mused wistfully. She could easily get used to having him around all the time. She thought of his willingness to stay on the sidelines during the rehearsal, his cheerful acquiescence at the mall, his stubborn protectiveness when he'd seen that she was tired.

Oh, yes, she sighed, pushing her feet into her Loafers, she could definitely grow accustomed to his company. She'd known him only a little more than a week, and already she was dreading the idea of a weekend without him. For a woman who'd placed so much value on her independence in the past few years, the realization of how easily she could become emotionally dependent on Derek was quite daunting.

She hadn't relied on anyone but herself for her happiness in a long time. Now she was starting to shift toward Derek. She didn't care for that one bit. But it was too late to do anything about it now except to hang on fiercely to whatever willpower she had left. Which wasn't much.

Sighing, she straightened her clothes and went in search of Derek.

She found him reading a newspaper in the den. He didn't hear her at first, and she had the chance to study him for a moment. Her heart sank as her eyes hungrily devoured the sight of him, so relaxed and sexy. She could feel her shaky willpower growing weaker by the moment.

Derek looked up and smiled at her, his eyes heart-wrenchingly tender behind his glasses. "Hi. Feel better?"

"Yes," she whispered, moistening her lips. She tried to strengthen her fading voice. "I'm sorry I went to sleep for so long."

"You needed the rest. Are you hungry?"

"Yes, I am, but—"

"Good. I've got dinner ready to go under the broiler. Nothing fancy, just ham, cheese and tomato open-faced sandwiches. Sound okay?"

"Definitely okay," she agreed with a touch of shyness. Her eyes seemed to have become fixed on the open collar of his close-fitting knit shirt, fascinated by the silky dark curls nestling there. She knew how hard his body felt through his clothes. Would he feel as hard without them? she wondered dreamily. She should make every effort *not* to find out. But already her fingers were twitching to test him.

Dinner was consumed in near silence, though Summer could have sworn she could hear her own heartbeat booming through the room. A new note of intimacy had been introduced into their relationship that day, and now she was aware, as she had not been before, of being truly alone with him. She sensed every movement he made, found herself incredibly attuned to his breathing and deep voice. Though the sandwiches were good, she found she could barely taste her food. Instead, she found herself avidly watching him eating his, finding the experience amazingly erotic. She'd never really thought eating was sexy, despite the books she'd read, but now she was beginning to understand. Each time Derek's mouth closed around his sandwich, she shivered, imagining those lips on her skin.

Dammit, stop this! she told herself desperately. *Say something! Anything!*

"This is the second time you've made dinner for me, Derek," she said at last, as if he couldn't remember that vitally important fact for himself. "I'll have to return the favor sometime."

Really dumb, Reed, she scolded herself. *Why didn't you just ask the guy for a date?*

"I'm not much of a chef," Derek admitted. "I've served you my entire repertoire of dishes now. Steaks and sandwiches."

"Both of which have been excellent."

"Thank you. Do you like to cook, Summer?"

"Sometimes. Nothing fancy, though. Connie says that I cook with an Arkansas accent."

"Meaning?"

"Just that I cook like a rural Southern housewife—the way my mother cooks, to be precise. Plain meats, potatoes and gravy, vegetables boiled with pork seasoning. California nutritionists would be appalled at the amount of calories and carbohydrates and cholesterol, or whatever, but the food tastes good, and that kind of cooking has raised generations of healthy Reeds and Welches."

"Welch was your mother's maiden name?"

"Yes. Amazing what little tidbits you're finding out about me, isn't it?"

"There are still a lot of things I want to know," he replied.

Summer shook her head. "No more of my life history. I'm bored with the subject. I'd rather talk about you tonight."

"Now that's a boring subject." Derek gathered his supper dishes and carried them into the kitchen, leaving Summer to assume that the conversation had been brought to an abrupt end. She sighed in exasperation and reached for her own plate.

"How's your leg?" Derek asked when they were seated on the oatmeal-colored sofa in the den, two cups of coffee on the low table in front of them.

"Fine. Tell me about your work, Derek."

He refused to take the hint. "It's throbbing, isn't it?"

"Your work? Interesting, perhaps, but hardly—"

"Summer." He put the palm of his hand firmly over her mouth. "Your leg. Does it hurt?"

"A little," she mumbled behind his hand, glaring at him.

Derek nodded shortly and dropped his hand. "I think I prefer the other way of shutting you up," he told her, his eyes glinting silver with his smile. "With a kiss."

Summer privately decided that she preferred that method, as well, but she chose to keep that thought to herself.

Derek patted his lap. "Put your leg up here. I'll massage it for you."

"Oh, I don't—"

"Dammit, woman. Must you argue with everything I say?" he roared. "Give me the damned leg!"

Summer gave him the damned leg. "You're so bossy," she accused him resentfully.

Derek's long fingers began to work magic on her aching knee. "And you're so stubborn. Why did you push yourself so hard this afternoon? Your leg started hurting almost an hour before the rehearsal was over, didn't it?"

She sighed. "It was the Cyndi Lauper dance," she confessed. "I got a little carried away."

"Why didn't you stop? You could have rested for a few minutes."

She shrugged. "If you take a break with those kids, you're liable to lose them entirely. I didn't want to risk messing up a great rehearsal. Wasn't it terrific? There wasn't even a major fight among the performers this time. Some of the kids really show talent, don't you think?"

"They're not bad," Derek conceded, watching her face as he continued to massage the slender leg in his lap. His fingers were warm through the soft denim, and the tense muscles under them were slowly beginning to relax. "But you were the one with the talent."

Summer found herself contending with conflicting sensations. Derek's skillful massage was wonderful, the all too familiar ache in her leg receding under its effect with magical speed. Yet the movement of those long fingers on her thigh and knee were bringing another kind of ache deep in her abdomen, an ache that threatened to be infinitely more serious than the twinges of an old injury. Infinitely more dangerous. "Uh, thank you," she said, remembering that he'd complimented her. *Concentrate on the conversation,* she ordered herself sternly.

"It's really a shame that you abandoned your talent when you had the accident," Derek commented, still watching her face for a reaction.

"Oh, I think the entertainment world is surviving without me," Summer returned lightly. "Tell me about your travels with your government job, Derek. It must have been fascinating seeing all those different parts of the world."

"Hotel rooms and smoke-filled offices look pretty much the same everywhere," he replied, using the stock answer that he'd been throwing out for the past ten years or so. He had become an expert on evading questions about his former line of work simply by making it sound too dull to discuss. "You're good with kids. Have you ever thought of teaching theater arts to young people?"

"You're good with open-faced sandwiches. Have you ever thought about becoming a short-order cook?"

Summer almost flinched from the look of anger that Derek turned her way. "Will you take nothing seriously?" he demanded. "Don't you ever get tired of turning every statement into a stupid joke?"

"Don't you ever get tired of giving advice to other people about how they should conduct their lives?" she retorted evenly. "I'm not one of your clients, Derek. I haven't hired you to offer your valuable services. Save it for the businessmen who *want* to hear it."

"So you're perfectly content drifting along the way you have been, working in a job you dislike, donating a few hours of your time to good causes, wasting the rest of your life playing games and making jokes?" His fingers had ceased their soothing motion and were gripping her leg in a white-knuckled clench that clearly expressed his frustration.

"Yes!" she answered hotly. "Face it, Derek. I'm exactly the shallow, empty-headed party girl you've thought I was all along. I know you've hated admitting that you might actually be attracted to such a person and you've tried to find a frustrated career woman inside me. It's time for you to realize that she isn't there. I'm exactly what you see, and I have no desire to be anything else."

"You are a fraud, Summer Reed." Derek's voice was cold as he lifted her leg from his lap to set it with care in front of her.

She immediately scooted back to put more space between them, watching him warily. "What do you mean?"

"Just what I said. You're a fraud. A fake. An actress putting on a twenty-four-hour-a-day performance. You act like an airhead hedonist to hide the fact that you were devastated by the accident that left you lame and took away your hopes of a career in entertainment. You continue to find dead-end jobs because you know there's nothing you really want to do other than sing and dance and act. If you can't have that, you don't want anything. Right?

"You pretend that your hours with the kids at Halloran House are just a favor to your buddy Clay, not anything that brings you fulfillment. You keep avoiding serious relationships with men on the pretext of looking for a non-existent hero, when the truth is that you're scared. Because one jerk couldn't deal with your physical imperfection, you assume that no other man could, either."

"Stop it!" Summer shouted, appalled. Her eyes were a brilliant blue in a face that had gone white. "Who the hell asked for your opinion of me, Derek Anderson? What gives you the right to act like you know me so well?"

"Because I do," he answered implacably. "I've watched you, Summer. I've read the shadows in your eyes, the expressions that crossed your face when you thought no one was looking. I saw the wistfulness there when your friends abandoned you in a corner while they danced at your party. I saw the courage it took for you to circulate with the people you didn't know at my party, the tiny spasms of pain whenever one of my guests would innocently inquire about your limp. And I saw the sheer joy in your beautiful eyes this afternoon when you were working with those kids, singing and dancing and performing."

Summer clasped her hands in front of her in an exaggerated show of amazement. "Derek, that's incredible!" she jeered. "How long have you been a mind reader? You should work up a nightclub act, and I could be your assistant since I'm nurturing all these hidden desires to perform that you've told me about."

"Dammit, Summer, stop it!" he shouted, dropping his hands on her shoulders and clenching his fingers as if he'd like nothing more than to shake some sense into her. "Can't you stop joking even long enough to get mad at me? Curse at me or hit me or something, but stop hiding what you're feeling behind this idiotic clown act!"

Summer felt something break inside her head, releasing a torrent of emotions that had been safely dammed for a long time. With the flood came an outpouring of words, furious and twisted and tumbling as they flowed from her mouth almost against her will. "What do you want from me, Derek? Do you want me to fall apart and sob into your shoulder about the cruel trick life played on me? All right, dammit!

"I hated waking up in a hospital with a bloody pulp where there had once been a pretty nice-looking leg! I hated the fear I felt when the doctors told me they might have to amputate! I hated the pain that was so excruciating that I screamed and cried and begged for drugs to make me sleep so that I wouldn't feel it! I hated having the man I thought I loved look at me with pity, then tell me that he couldn't deal with an invalid!

"I hated those months in bed, and the operations that left me with more artificial parts in my leg than real ones. I hated being in a wheelchair. I hated the walker and the crutches. The exercises that hurt like hell yet were necessary if I ever wanted to walk again. And I hated knowing that for the rest of my life people will look at me with pity for the poor, crippled woman!"

Derek did shake her then, though gently. "Look at me, Summer," he commanded her, holding her only inches away from him. "Look at my face. Do you see pity there? I said *look at me!*"

Tear-washed blue eyes tentatively searched his face. She saw the remains of anger there, and a pain that she wasn't sure she understood. She ran her eyes slowly across his dark face, her gaze lingering on his emotion-darkened gray eyes. Anger, pain, desire, frustration—but not pity. Even after all she'd just told him. "No," she whispered, remembering that he'd asked her a question. "I don't see pity."

"Summer, there is so much more to you than a quick wit and a fast mouth and a lame leg. Do you really think any of your true friends care whether you walk with a limp or would think any less of you if you carried on a serious conversation without cracking jokes? I know you love to laugh, and you've probably always been a tease and a cutup, but don't hide your other nice qualities. Give people a chance to get to know the real you—fears and disappointments and insecurities and all. Nobody expects you to be perfect."

Summer looked wonderingly at him for a long moment before dropping her head to stare at her lap. "When I was little, I learned that people love to be entertained," she said quietly, almost surprising herself at what she was saying. Derek shifted on the sofa beside her but remained quiet, encouraging her to continue as if he knew that the explanation she was about to make was important to both of them.

"My older sister, Spring, was smart and serious and everyone admired her, and Autumn was the baby—beautiful and spunky and tough, which earned her respect at an early age. I could make people laugh. I could sing and dance and do imitations, and people enjoyed my performances. I thrived on the applause and the approval."

She cleared her throat. "I found out that people are uncomfortable with the pain and fears of others, but everyone loves to share a good joke. So I hid my fears and insecurities and I always had friends. Sometimes I wished that

I had someone I could cry with or tell my problems to, but I was afraid my friends wouldn't have liked me as well if I stopped making them laugh."

"It wouldn't have mattered to your real friends," he told her softly.

"Perhaps." She didn't sound convinced. She glanced up at him, then as quickly looked away. "I was quite popular in college. The other kids admired me because I didn't seem to care whether I passed or failed while they sweated through classes in fear. I did care, of course, but I didn't want anyone to know—just in case I failed. If they thought it was because I didn't care, they wouldn't think of it as failure, I thought.

"I had such big dreams. Few people knew the number of hours I spent practicing my dancing and my singing and my acting. I pictured myself as a star with constant applause and thousands of friends and fans. Then I met Lonnie."

"The boyfriend? 'Enry 'Iggins?"

She didn't smile. "Yes. He was gorgeous. And he had talent. I thought the two of us together would be a team to take the country by storm. He thought so, too. I don't know if we were in love with each other or with our mutual dreams of stardom. And then I had the accident." She swallowed. "He was so angry with me."

Derek looked startled. "Angry?"

She nodded. "For ruining everything. He never did like me taking the motorcycle out on the streets—said it was too dangerous for a dancer. When I proved him right, he wouldn't forgive me for taking the risk. He told me that a crippled girlfriend would hold him back, that he needed someone who could share his life in every way."

"Bastard."

"Yeah, well, anyway, those first few days after the accident were pretty grim. The pain and the knowledge that my dancing days were over made it hard for me to be brave. All I could do was cry. My friends didn't quite know what to do with me. They visited me, of course, but it was easy to see that they were uncomfortable and they felt sorry for me. I hated that. So I forced myself to smile and built up a repertoire of gimp jokes. Pretty soon my friends were flocking back around me, telling me how brave and wonderful I was."

"What about your family?"

Her face softened. "Bless their hearts, they were wonderful. They might not have understood me all the time. Maybe they didn't know quite how much my dancing meant to me, but they knew I was in pain and bitterly disappointed and they rallied round me. My sisters were there to let me cry into their shoulders, and my mother bullied me into doing the exercises even when they hurt, then kissed me when I cried. My father put me straight to work to give me something to concentrate on besides my problems. I had to be careful not to become too dependent on them all."

"Which is the reason you moved to San Francisco?"

"Yes. I had to prove to myself and to them that I was capable of functioning on my own. And I have. Even though they, like you, aren't all that thrilled with the way I've chosen to live."

"Perhaps they don't approve, but do they pity you?" Derek asked perceptively.

"Why, no," Summer answered, surprised that he would ask, "of course they don't pity me. They love me."

"Even though they've seen you at your lowest point, and they've heard you cry and curse and feel sorry for yourself?" he asked quietly.

She grimaced at him. "Another object lesson, Derek?"

"Merely an observation."

She squirmed uncomfortably on the couch. "I don't know why I always end up telling you my life story," she told him accusingly.

"I know you think I'm interfering and nosy, but I can't help it," Derek confessed. "I'm not usually like this outside of business."

"How did Connie and I get so lucky?" Summer asked dryly.

A touch of red darkened his high cheekbones, startling Summer. "Connie's my sister," he muttered. "I love her, and I want what's best for her. And you, well, I...I like you," he said with an uncharacteristic stammer. "It bothers me to see you hiding your pain and your feelings from the people who care for you."

Summer's own cheeks were suspiciously warm. "I've never even talked to Connie the way I just talked to you," she admitted in a very low voice, almost a whisper. "I don't know why I've been able to tell you things that I couldn't tell anyone else."

"Maybe because I've insisted," Derek suggested wryly.

She smothered a nervous giggle. "That might have something to do with it." She risked an atypically shy glance at him and found her eyes held by his. She found it hard to read the expression she saw deep in the pewter-gray depths. Had discovering her weaknesses changed the way Derek perceived her? Was he disappointed that she wasn't as strong and tough as she'd pretended? Did he...did he still want her?

Suddenly she had to know. She couldn't come right out and ask, but she could find out another way. "Would you...would you hold me, Derek?" she asked hesitantly. "Just for a little while?"

9

WITHOUT EVEN a momentary hesitation Derek took Summer into his arms. Folded against his wide, hard chest, Summer released a breath that she hadn't known she'd been holding and snuggled into his strength. She felt his heart beating steadily against her cheek through the soft knit fabric of his white pullover. In only moments she felt the heartbeat speed up, just as her own was doing. Her arms went around Derek's lean waist.

His hands moved on her back, tentatively at first, then more demandingly. Finally one hand moved up the back of her head, fingers threading through the short, silky hair there as he tilted her head back. They both felt her tremor as she turned her face up to his in mute invitation. He kissed her with a force that was surprisingly gentle, considering the fire and passion it incited in her.

"Derek. Oh, Derek." Summer pulled her arms from around his waist to throw them around his neck.

"Summer." Derek's voice was so hoarse that neither of them recognized it. "I want you so much it's driving me mad."

She believed him. Derek didn't pity her. He was not repelled by her scars or her awkward limp. He wanted her. As he pulled her rather roughly against him, she was made physically aware of just how much he wanted her. And she wanted him. Her fingers slid into the crisp hair at the back of his neck, curling there to bring his mouth down to hers.

Her eyes locked with his, she brushed her mouth across his lips, then back again. She felt the sudden stillness that gripped him, tensing his muscles against her. He waited, seemingly without breathing, as she drew back fractionally and then kissed him again, bolder now. The tip of her tongue slipped out to taste him. Derek's short, dark lashes swept downward to hide the glitter of his eyes from her for just a moment before his feverish gaze locked once again with hers. That moment was long enough for her to recognize his vulnerability. Amazingly enough, Derek seemed unsure what to do next.

It was his uncharacteristic hesitation that removed the last vestiges of her own doubt. "I want you, Derek," she whispered, her lips like wisps of smoke against his.

"Summer?" His voice was raw.

"Yes, Derek. Please."

He gave a little sound that was half groan and half exultant laugh. As if he were afraid she'd change her mind, he swept her into his arms and off the couch before she was quite aware of what was happening. She put her arms trustingly around his neck, enjoying the feeling of being carried in the arms of the man who was about to become her lover.

Her lover. The thought made her go so weak that, had she been trying to walk, she would have fallen. She had never wanted another man this much.

Depositing her carefully on the geometric-print bedspread that covered a massive king-size bed, Derek began to tug at her white fleece top even as she reached for the band of his own white knit shirt. Both felt the need to touch and explore, and it was not necessary for them to put their desire into words. They communicated with their eyes and their lips, with husky little moans and breathless laughs, and when small, soft breasts were pressed at last to broad, plated chest, their delirious sighs sounded in stereo in the shadowed room.

"God, you feel good," Derek groaned, sliding sensuously against her.

"So do you," she whispered in response, feeling her breasts tighten and harden in delicious response.

He kissed her throat, then lower, moving toward those

pebbled tips that so craved his attention. "You're protected?" he questioned suddenly, lifting his head for a moment to look at her in concern. "If not, I can—"

"It's okay, Derek," she assured him quickly, her fingers tangling in his hair. "I'm protected." Her taste for adventure did not preclude taking certain precautions, a habit for which she was now very grateful.

Derek's murmur signified his own relief that there was nothing to hold him back from finally satisfying his hunger for her. He lowered his head once more.

Summer rapidly discovered that Derek's talent at kissing was only a hint of his skill as a lover. From the short, tousled strands of her amber-brown hair to the hollows of her ears and throat, from her flushed, swollen breasts to the delicate indentation of her navel, from the silky curves of her inner thighs to the ticklish arches of her feet, he explored and pleasured so thoroughly that Summer was a writhing, moaning creature of pure sensation by the time he lost his own tenuous control.

Moments before she couldn't have imagined it was possible for the pleasure to intensify. Now, with her legs wrapped tightly around his lean hips, his fingers biting into the soft flesh of her buttocks, Summer discovered that there were heights of passion that she had never dreamed existed. Arching into his driving thrusts, she responded wholeheartedly to his every movement, drawing moans of delight from him in answer to her own.

Her head tossing on the pillow, she arched again to draw him even deeper into her. "Oh, Derek," she whispered brokenly.

"Summer. So good," he moaned, the words hot against her throat.

She tried to tell him that it was good for her, too, but the words shattered into a cry of joyous release as tiny ripples swelled into pounding waves of fulfillment. Dimly aware of the shudders that rocked Derek's body within the cradle of her arms and legs, she smiled in exhausted satisfaction, then collapsed beneath him with a long, audible sigh.

Lying heavily on top of her, Derek knew he'd have to move, but he wondered where he'd ever find the strength. It seemed to take everything he had left when he finally made himself roll to one side to relieve her slight body of his weight, though he didn't take his arms from around her. "God," he groaned after a few more moments of recovery. "I think I died."

His words provoked a breathless little laugh from the woman in his arms. "You, too?" she asked in a gasp. "I feel like I've melted into a puddle all over your lovely bedspread."

She squirmed around to face him, lifting herself on one elbow. Smiling down at him, she reached out to brush a strand of dark hair away from his forehead. Her lover, she thought again, and this time the words were fact.

He lifted one hand to touch her cheek. "I wanted you so much that I went a little crazy. I didn't hurt you, did I?"

She smiled and kissed his palm. "No, you didn't hurt me."

"How's your leg?"

"Deliriously happy."

He chuckled and pulled her down against his chest. "Lie still a moment," he ordered her indulgently. "I need some recovery time."

"Mmm." She snuggled her cheek into the hollow of his shoulder and idly caressed his chest through the swirls of dark hair. Her eyes closed in pure contentment, she allowed herself to drift, holding serious thought at bay. She was not quite ready to consider the change that had just come about in her life—and she knew the change was a momentous one. No, for now she wanted only to bask in the security of Derek's arms. Her eyes opened halfway and her gaze wandered idly around his bedroom, narrowing a little as she took in the assorted trophies and sports pictures with which he had chosen to decorate. Even that discovery was pushed quickly to the back of her mind. No thoughts of physical handicaps or other differences between them were to be allowed to intrude on her euphoria.

As if to block any further observations, her eyes closed again, firmly. She wouldn't have believed that she would be able to sleep again so soon after her nap, but the deep, even rhythm of Derek's breathing soon lulled her into a light dream state, a soft smile gracing her flushed features.

The line between dream and reality wavered and languorously dissolved. A tiny sound of pleasure flowed from Summer's slightly parted lips as she felt her heavy-limbed body being thoroughly and leisurely caressed. Arching like a lazy cat into the gently arousing strokes, she opened luminous eyes to study Derek's face, so close to her own.

His face would never look soft, but it held more warmth now than she had ever imagined seeing there. His eyes gleamed silver, his mouth had relaxed its stern lines into a semismile. Fascinated by the way his dark, disheveled hair was beginning to curl at his forehead—*so that's why he keeps it so short*, she thought in tender amusement—she drank in the sight of him. He looked approachable, she mused, reaching up to touch his lean cheek. He looked wonderful. "I take it you've recovered?" she murmured huskily.

He kissed the soft upper slope of her breast. "Umm."

She took that to be an affirmative. "Oh, good." Her drawl turned to a gasp as his tongue darted out to circle her already distended nipple, and then he was pulling the dusky peak into the liquid warmth of his mouth. Summer moaned her approval and threaded her fingers into his hair to hold him closer.

Derek's hand slid down her side, pausing to trace each rib. She squirmed, offering her other breast to his worshipful mouth. Her attention alternated between the manipulations of his lips, teeth and tongue, and his slowly descending hand, which was shaping her hips.

She stiffened fractionally when his exploring fingers slid

down her leg and touched the ridges of her scars. How could he not be repulsed by them?

Misinterpreting her tension, Derek lifted his mouth from her moistened nipple to kiss her chin. "I won't hurt you," he whispered against her lips.

"I know. It's not that," she assured him. "It's just—"

She stopped by necessity when his mouth covered hers. Even as he kissed her with a hunger that was unabated by their recent lovemaking, Derek cupped her impaired knee, his fingers tender, soothing. Uncertain of what message to read into his actions, Summer reached down to capture his wrist and pull his hand to her breast. Again she had chosen not to linger on thoughts that threatened to dim her present pleasure.

Complying with her unspoken request, Derek concentrated on rebuilding her arousal. Summer responded eagerly to his skillful attentions, her own fingers dancing across his sleek back. When his hand moved downward again, it was only as far as the damp nest of curls between her thighs, where the bud of her femininity quivered beneath his touch.

Her breath catching in ragged gasps, Summer arched again and again into his palm, her mouth seeking and finding his. He moved between her legs, and she stopped breathing entirely, anxiously awaiting the moment when he would once again make them one.

And then he murmured something that stopped her heart along with her breathing.

"I love you, Summer."

"*What?*"

His hand on his chest, Derek stared at the woman who'd leaped straight up to sit on the bed beside him and was staring openmouthed back at him. "God, Summer, you almost gave me a heart attack. Why did you shriek at me like that?"

"What did you say?"

"I said you scared the—"

"No, before that."

"Oh." His face relaxed into a smile. "I said I love you."

"Oh, my God." She covered her face with her hands.

Though his body still quivered with his arousal, Derek laughed under his breath and reached for her wrists. "I should have known your reaction wouldn't be the traditional 'I love you, too, Derek.' But I had no idea I'd have to peel you off the ceiling once my heart started beating again. Is it that much of a shock, Summer-love?"

Her hands completely limp in his, Summer gaped at him. "A shock? Yes, Derek, I guess you could call it a shock." She sounded stunned.

"Why? Couldn't you see it coming? I've suspected it for some time. I've never been in love before, but I'm not so dense that I didn't recognize the emotion when it hit me."

"How could I have seen it coming?" she asked spiritedly. "My God, Derek, we've only known each other a week."

"A week and two days. Not that it matters. I wanted you from the first moment I saw you sitting on that rickety stool in your apartment. I think I fell in love with you the first time I kissed you, though I was mad enough at that moment to strangle you."

She couldn't believe he was saying these things, not Derek. She'd known he wanted her, of course. But love? How could he tell her so calmly that he loved her, when she was certain that such an admission could not come easily to a reserved, careful man like Derek?

Searching her face, Derek stopped, his smile fading. "Maybe I've been taking too much for granted. I thought you were feeling the same way I was. Was I wrong, Summer?"

"I…" She let her voice trail off and dropped her eyes to hide her fear and confusion. "Derek, you can't be in love with me. I'm not anything like the women you've dated before."

He groaned. "Don't start that again. I was never in love with any of the women I dated before. How could I have known what kind of woman I could fall in love with before I met you? I wasn't even sure it was possible for me to fall in love. And then I fell head over heels for a smart mouth and the most beautiful blue eyes I've ever seen." Before she could form a reply, his fingers tightened around her wrist in what she could almost believe was a surge of desperation.

"Summer, I love you. I can't give you logical explanations or reasonable excuses, but I know it's true. How do you feel about me?"

Avoiding his intense scrutiny, her eyes focused painfully on a framed photograph of Derek breaking the tape in a marathon race, his arms lifted in triumph above his head, healthy legs shown to perfection beneath his brief running shorts. "Derek, we need time," she whispered. "It's too soon. You—we can't be sure."

"Oh."

The single syllable was stark enough to make her risk a quick look at his face. Derek was so good at hiding his feelings, but somehow she had learned to read him quite accurately in the past nine days. Only she could have seen that she had hurt him. She felt as if she'd plunged a knife into her own heart.

"Derek, you don't understand. I care for you, of course I do, but—"

"But I'm no hero, right?" he finished tonelessly. "I'm still just Connie's brother, Derek, the stuffed-shirt businessman who happens to kiss well enough to entice you into bed."

The knife twisted. "That's not what I was going to say."

"Listen to me, Summer Reed." He caught her chin between his thumb and forefinger, lifting her face until his stormy gray eyes were boring directly into hers. "I'll give you time if you need it, but I'm not giving up. I love you like no fairy-tale hero could ever love you, and I know you better than anyone else ever has. You don't stand a chance against me. I have a reputation for achieving my goals, and you are my priority-one goal from now on. Do you understand?"

He had barked out the words in a militarily autocratic tone that automatically stiffened her spine. "I hear you, Derek."

"Good. Believe it." He leaned over to kiss her, hard, then released her. "Do you want me to take you home now?"

She wanted him to take her into his arms and make love to her. She wanted to allow herself to believe that he really loved her and that his infatuation would not go away when he tired of her erratic humor and offbeat life-style and her inability to keep up with him physically. She wanted to believe that her heart would not be permanently shattered when he moved on to someone else. She knew better. She'd thought Lonnie had hurt her when he'd turned away from her after the accident. She suspected now that she'd never known pain as she could know it if Derek were to love her for a time and then leave her.

No. She'd had too much pain. This time she had to protect herself.

"Yes, please, Derek. Take me home."

Hurt and anger dulled the silver in his eyes, but he only nodded and reached for his scattered clothing as she did the same.

Though he walked her to the door after the painfully silent drive, carrying the packages she'd so cheerfully loaded into his arms several momentous hours earlier, Derek refused to go inside the apartment. He explained that he was not in the mood to deal with Connie just then. He transferred her packages to her arms, making a visible effort not to touch her. "When can I see you again?" he asked, the question verging on demand.

Summer looked pleadingly at him. "Please, Derek. I really think y—we need time. It's happened too fast."

His face hard, he glared immovably down at her. "When, Summer?"

She sighed. He would not make it easy for her, she thought glumly. His mind was set. She'd just have to prove to him that they were not suited to each other, no matter how desperately she wished they were. Perhaps another weekend with her would bore him, make him restless for someone who could play tennis or run with him. It would rip her heart to shreds, but perhaps he'd finally see what she was trying to tell him. "Call me later in the week," she said finally. "Maybe next weekend—"

"Fine," he cut in shortly. For a moment she thought he was going to walk away without another word. But then he reached for her, and his voice was urgent when he spoke. "It was good for us tonight, wasn't it, Summer?"

Giving in to a momentary weakness, she dropped her packages unheeded to the floor and burrowed into his arms. "Oh, yes, Derek," she breathed, looking up at him with an expression that left no doubt of her sincerity. "It was wonderful."

"Better than anything that ever happened to me before. Remember that," he told her softly. "Remember the way we've been drawn together from the beginning, despite our unimportant differences. Remember that you've been able to tell me things about yourself that you've never shared with anyone else. There's more to what we have than sexual attraction, Summer, and you're bright enough to figure that out if you'll stop fighting it. I love you."

He kissed her long and hard, with undertones of the passion they had shared in his bed. And then he was gone.

Summer was breathing raggedly when she entered the apartment. Connie was sitting on the couch, the telephone cradled on her shoulder as she painted her long nails a bright fuchsia. She smiled at Summer in greeting. Summer tried to return the smile as she passed the couch to her room, where she closed the door, threw her packages on a chair and fell in a nerveless heap on the bed.

She hadn't bothered to turn on a light, so the darkness of her bedroom closed around her as she lay huddled in a position of abject misery. It was so utterly ironic, she thought bleakly. Derek had tried to convince her that she was in love with him. Little did he know that she needed no convincing. She knew full well that she loved Derek Anderson. Blindly, desperately, hopelessly, eternally. She'd never loved like this before, she'd never love like this again.

And he had said he loved her, too. She should be deliriously happy. Instead, she wanted nothing more than to die.

"Summer?" Connie cracked open the door and peeked inside when Summer did not respond to a light knock. "Why are you lying here in the dark with all your clothes on? What's wrong?"

"Nothing," Summer answered in a voice so thick with tears that it was obvious she was lying. "Everything."

Connie promptly walked inside, crossing the room to sit on the bed beside her unhappy roommate. "Do you want to talk about it? We're friends, Summer. We should be able to share the bad times as well as the good."

Summer mopped at her face with one hand, sorely tempted to pour the whole story into Connie's shoulder. But maybe Connie wouldn't want to hear her roommate's problems, she thought. After all, Connie probably had problems of her own. For the first time in her life Summer understood that, with all the friends she had attracted over the years with her playful, carefree humor, there had never been anyone she could cry with. Derek had forced her to admit that earlier; now she realized that it was really true.

"Summer, honey, what is it?" Connie had never seen Summer cry, just as she had never allowed herself to shed tears in front of her roommate. But, rather than being uncomfortable or impatient, as Summer might have feared, Connie reacted as a true friend, with a sympathetic desire to help. She reached out and touched Summer's shoulder. "Talk to me, Summer."

Without further hesitation Summer sat up and threw her arms around her friend—her *real* friend. "Oh, Connie, I *do* want to talk about it," she moaned, the tears flowing freely.

"It's about Derek, isn't it? Believe me, I know how much his continuous criticism can hurt. I've come home and cried more than once. What did the creep say to hurt you?" Connie's voice had become more heated with each word.

Summer shook her head and swallowed a sob. "No, Connie, it wasn't that. He didn't criticize me."

Connie went still. "Oh, no." She gasped. "He didn't— Summer, did he—"

Realizing the direction of Connie's thoughts, Summer sat up straight in indignation. "Connie, he didn't hurt my physically, if that's what you're thinking. My God, he's your brother. You surely know him better than that."

Connie went limp with relief. "I thought I did," she admitted. "But where you're concerned, I don't know him at all. He's different with you."

The sob escaped. "I know," Summer whispered, covering her face with her hands. "Oh, Connie, what am I going to do?"

"You've fallen in love with him, haven't you?" Connie asked in surprise. "You've actually fallen in love with Derek."

"Yes," Summer whispered. "Are you very much surprised?"

"Maybe a little," Connie admitted with a short laugh. "I mean, you and Derek… Still, I've watched you with him. I've seen the way you treated other men during the time you and I have known each other. You wouldn't have let any of them boss you around like Derek does. And there was something in your eyes when you looked at him at his party last night, and again this morning when he came for you. It's in his eyes, too, you know."

"I know," Summer murmured.

"But if you're in love with him, I can see why you're so unhappy. I guess I've started to see that Derek's not quite the boring tyrant I've built him up to be during the past few months, but I don't know if he's capable of really loving a woman the way you'd want to be loved. He'd have to admit that he's as human as anyone else."

"Connie, he told me tonight that he loves me," Summer blurted out bravely.

Connie gazed wide-eyed at her friend. "He did?"

"Yes, he did."

"How? I mean, was he passionate and romantic and the whole bit?"

Summer chuckled despite her pain. "He was marvelous, Connie. Passionate and romantic and the whole bit."

"Wow." Connie shook her head in pleased amazement. "I knew you were good for him. So what's the problem? Why the tears?"

"That's why," Summer wailed. "He can't really be in love with me."

"Come on, Summer, Derek's not the type to lie to you just to get you into bed. One thing about my brother, he's honest. Too honest sometimes," she added with a wince. "If he says something, he means it."

"I know he thinks he's in love with me. He certainly wasn't telling me just to get me into bed. I was already there." Summer sighed. Rushing on when Connie lifted an eyebrow in interest, she continued, "I think he's been carried away with physical attraction, Connie. He's convinced himself that he's in love because it happened so fast and so intensely and he doesn't know how else to explain it. He's not giving himself enough time to be objective and look at the reasons why it just couldn't work."

"Summer, forgive me, but that's the dumbest thing I've ever heard," Connie said bluntly. "You act like he's an infatuated schoolboy. The man's pushing forty, Summer, and he has certainly had his share of women. I don't mean to offend you, my friend, but it's not like you're the type of woman who'd drive a man senseless with lust. You're cute and everything, but we're not talking Miss Universe here."

"Oh, Connie." Summer smiled through her tears.

"Don't make me laugh now. Can't you see I'm trying to be miserable?"

"I can't help it. Derek would laugh, too, if he could hear what you're saying. I think he knows lust from love."

"But how could he be in love with me? He barely knows me, and he doesn't approve of what he does know."

"You're in love with him, and the situation is the same for you," Connie pointed out. "You haven't known him any longer, and he's hardly the hero you've been looking for. Come on, Summer, if anyone had told you a couple of weeks ago that you would fall for a somewhat stuffy, ultraconservative former bureaucrat, you'd have laughed in his face. Admit it."

"Well, yes, but Derek's not really like that, Connie. He has a great sense of humor; he just expresses it subtly. And he isn't all that proper when he's after something he really wants," she added, remembering the jeans and leather jacket and the incredibly adventurous lovemaking.

"Just as there is more to you than you'll allow most people to see," Connie said succinctly. "Obviously Derek has the intelligence and good sense to see beneath your eccentric exterior to find the common ground the two of you share."

"I'll admit that both Derek and I have sides to us that we don't normally put on display," Summer conceded. "But the parts of us that *are* visible are real, Connie, not deliberate misrepresentations. Derek really is a conservative businessman to whom things like schedules and responsibilities are important. And I truly enjoy the crazy parties we throw and the nutty friends that we've made and an occasional lapse into impulsive insanity. I'm terrified that Derek would try to change me into someone more like, well, like Joanne Payne. I'm afraid we'd start to hate each other, and I couldn't bear that."

"If he'd wanted Joanne Payne, he'd have kept her around. It's called compromise, Summer. It's part of any relationship between two naturally different individuals. That's why Stu and I didn't make it—because neither of us would give an inch. But you and Derek could do it, if you try. You give in on the things that are particularly important to him, and he does the same for you. You attend his boring, business-related cocktail parties, and he learns to enjoy himself at your bashes. You live on his schedule during the week, and he keeps the weekends open for impulsive adventures."

"Maybe." Though she didn't sound entirely convinced, Summer allowed that subject to drop. "There's something else," she murmured, looking down at her clenched hands. Without looking up she explained. "Do you think Derek has really stopped to think about what it would be like to be involved with a woman who couldn't join him in all those sports he loves so much? You told me yourself when he was dating Joanne that you thought her backhand was the quality he most admired in her. I put myself on crutches for almost a month last year simply by playing a sedate game of volleyball. If Derek loves sports so much, he's going to want to continue to participate in them. And, while I wouldn't mind occasionally, I sure don't want to spend all my leisure time sitting on the sidelines. That may be selfish, but I can't help it. I'm a doer, Connie, not a watcher."

"Compromise," Connie reminded her. "You find things that you can do together. Like swimming. You've always been overly sensitive about your limp, Summer. It doesn't make that much difference to the people who care for you. Tell me, Summer, did you discuss these things with Derek tonight?"

"No," Summer admitted. "I ran. I just knew I had to give him time to be absolutely sure about his feelings for me."

"But you did tell him that you love him, didn't you?"

Summer squirmed. "No."

"Oh, great. He's probably as miserable as you are right now. Maybe he thinks you're the one who couldn't possibly love him, and you're trying to find a way to break it off gently."

I'm no hero, right? Derek had asked with pain in his deep voice. Summer winced as she realized how badly her instinctive rejection had hurt him after he'd opened up enough to tell her that he loved her. Especially after the lovemaking they'd just shared. *God, what a mess,* she moaned inwardly.

"Maybe you do need the time, Summer," Connie said gently. "Time to work out your fears. But don't shut Derek out. Talk to him like you've talked to me tonight. If you're going to work this out, you're going to have to do it together."

"Connie, when did you suddenly get so wise?" Summer asked with a watery smile. "And why are you pushing me into your brother's arms?"

Connie grinned. "Are you kidding? This is the best thing that ever happened to me. If you marry Derek, I'll have the world's greatest sister-in-law and you'll keep him so busy that he'll never find the time to rearrange my life for me. You'll be happy, Derek will be happy, my parents will be happy and I'll be happy. This is great!"

"Connie, you're dreaming, but thank you. I really needed to talk this out with someone."

"Anytime, kid."

"If you ever need a shoulder…"

Connie stood and sighed melodramatically. "Offer Wednesday night after my date with Joel. I might need it then."

"You think there's a chance that you and Joel could get serious?"

"Who knows? You and Derek are living proof that stranger things have happened."

Summer was almost surprised to hear herself laugh. "Thanks a lot, friend."

Connie paused in the doorway on her way out. "Would it hurt to call Derek and wish him sweet dreams? I hate to think of my big brother crying himself to sleep."

Summer laughed again, as she'd been meant to do, and watched Connie leave. She spent a few minutes in contemplation of true friendship before stripping off her jeans and top and pulling on a pale blue nightgown. The silky fabric felt especially sensuous against her skin still sensitized by Derek's lovemaking. The memories that flooded her mind made her tremble. She stared at the telephone on her nightstand. She reached for the receiver, pulled back, drew a deep breath and reached out again.

10

DEREK SOUNDED GUARDED when he answered his phone. He obviously knew Summer was the caller.

Now that she had him on the line, she wasn't sure what she'd wanted to say. "Derek, it's Summer," she told him after a short pause.

"I thought it might be," he answered, confirming her guess. "Are you okay?"

The concern in his voice made her blink back a rush of tears. She hadn't cried this much in five years, she told herself impatiently. "I'm fine, Derek. Are you?"

"I'm sitting here staring into a double Scotch and wondering if I should have refused to take you home tonight," he answered flatly. "I'd like to be holding you instead of this glass. What happened, Summer?"

"I panicked," she admitted softly. "I just panicked. Things got too serious, and I couldn't think of a joke to lighten the mood, so I ran."

"That's what I thought," he murmured. "Summer, why did you go to bed with me tonight?"

She couldn't speak for a moment as the words jammed in her throat, then she forced herself to answer. "That's why I called, Derek. There was something I wanted to tell you."

There was a pause, and then he spoke tonelessly, as if dreading her answer but wanting to get it over with. "What is it, Summer?"

How vulnerable he was, Summer thought in bemusement. As vulnerable as she. She had been unintentionally cruel to him tonight. "I forgot to tell you that I love you, Derek. I think I have from the beginning."

When the pause at the other end threatened to turn into minutes, she asked anxiously, "Derek, did you hear me?"

"I heard you, Summer," he finally answered. "Did you just realize this?"

"No. I knew it even before we made love. I just wouldn't admit it."

"Then why did you put me through hell tonight?" Derek demanded in frustration. "What are you doing there when you should be here, in my bed? I thought you were trying to let me down easy because you didn't love me and didn't think you ever could."

"Derek, I never knew I could love anyone like this. But I still think you need time," she added hastily.

"Me? You were giving *me* time?" he asked incredulously. "Summer, I know how I feel. I'm not confused by my feelings for you. Forgive me for being blunt, darling, but I've known physical desire before and I've never confused great sex for anything more than it was. Tonight wasn't sex, Summer. Tonight was love."

"Oh, Derek, I want so much to believe that. I still think you should take time to think about what a relationship with me would involve. It would take compromise and lots of time because we really are different in some ways. I *am* lame, and I just can't promise that I'll be on time to everything or plan my days or weeks according to some schedule or—"

"Summer." Derek interrupted her gently, his voice sounding considerably lighter than it had when he'd answered the telephone. "Do you love me?"

"Yes, Derek, I love you."

"Then we'll work it out," he told her confidently. "Dammit, Summer, why didn't you stay and talk to me instead of leaving me to think you didn't love me?"

"I'm sorry."

"You should be. I don't know if I'm going to spank you or throw you to the floor and ravish you the next time I see you."

"Do I have a choice?" she asked with an attempt at humor.

"No. I think I'll let you worry about it. You deserve it. Will I see you tomorrow?"

Summer took a deep breath. "No, Derek. I still want you to take this week to think about us. Think about everything I've said and whether it's worth it to you to make some sacrifices and compromises. If you decide that I'm not right for you after all, I'll...I'll try to understand." She'd die, she thought, but she didn't voice that glum thought.

Derek growled very distinctly into the receiver. "You are driving me slowly insane, Summer Reed. The biggest obstacle I can see between us right now is your stubborn refusal to give me a chance to convince you that we can overcome the other obstacles. I'll take the damned week if you insist, but it's not going to change a thing. I'm old enough and experienced enough to know what I'm feeling and to understand what is involved here. Dammit, woman, I love you, and I'm going to convince you of that if it kills us both."

Summer laughed softly, reluctantly. "I'm beginning to believe you."

"Good. I'm the guy who always gets what he's after, remember?"

"I love you, Derek."

"I love you, Summer. Let me prove it to you."

"I'll talk to you next weekend," she promised and hung up the phone. When she went to sleep several hours later, it was with the hope that she and Derek did have a chance.

DEREK STARED DOWN at the phone, placed his glass of Scotch very carefully on the table beside it and stood motionless for a full minute. Then he suddenly punched the air above his head with one fist. "Yeah!" he yelled.

She loved him. Summer Reed loved him. High on a burst of sheer adrenaline, he was as exhilarated as he'd ever been after winning a marathon. His heart was pounding, his chest tight. She loved him. God, he felt good!

But how could she have walked away from him tonight after the most incredible lovemaking that he'd ever experienced? She had ripped him apart when she'd turned away from him after he'd told her he loved her. Maybe he'd been an arrogant jerk to assume she loved him simply because he loved her, but he could not imagine that she could respond to him the way she did and not care for him. And then she had closed her door in his face.

It had hurt. He hadn't known anything could hurt that much. But she loved him. That knowledge erased the pain as if it had never existed. Thank God she had called.

Imagine her thinking that their unimportant diversities would keep them apart. He knew they had their differences. Did she think he was so dense he didn't realize there would be compromises and sacrifices to make? There were some adjustments to make in any relationship that was worth pursuing. He could handle it. Summer was worth anything. But how could he convince her that he knew what he was doing?

Damn that spineless, self-centered actor who had walked out on her when she'd needed him. No wonder she was afraid to trust Derek's emotions now. What was it about charming, shallow actors that his sister and Summer had both been attracted to them in their pasts? Now Derek had to repair the damage. But how? How could he convince her that they weren't all that different?

He stood in deep contemplation for a while, then snapped his fingers. The grin that split his tanned face would have astonished his sister. It was an expression of pure mischief. Derek had a plan.

THE FLOWERS ARRIVED at her desk on Monday morning, a dozen red roses in an exquisite crystal vase. As the other women in the accounting department drooled in envy and her no-nonsense supervisor, Mr. Gleason, glowered at the distraction, Summer ripped open the card with fingers that displayed a disturbing tendency to tremble.

She knew right away that the bold, slashing script belonged to Derek, though the card was not signed.

You want romance? I'll give you romance. I love you.

"Wow," Connie breathed, coming from behind her desk to reverently touch the velvety petal of one perfect rose. "Oh, wow."

Summer hesitated for a moment, then handed Connie the card. She had to share what she was feeling with someone. Connie read the card in awe, then looked up to shake her head and repeat, "Oh, wow."

Summer took a deep breath and laughed shakily. "That's exactly the way I would have put it."

"This is so romantic. I can't believe Derek did this. How can you resist this?"

"I can't. And he knows it, the rat."

Connie laughed as Summer shook her head in exasperation.

"ANDERSON." Derek's voice over the telephone was clipped.

"Derek? It's Summer."

His voice softened. "Oh, hi, sweetheart. Did you get the roses?"

"Yes, and they're beautiful. But you're not playing fair."

"Hey, we never set any conditions about this week. I promised to give you time, but I never said I'd let you forget about me."

"I hardly think I'm going to forget you, Derek."

"You're not kidding. I've gotta go, sweetheart. I love you." He hung up before she could answer.

Derek smiled down at the telephone in satisfaction. He'd mapped out a precise campaign for the upcoming week, all carefully thought out to convince Summer that he was the man of her dreams. His siege had been planned as carefully as any mission he'd ever undertaken.

Once again the thought momentarily occurred to him that he should have told Summer the truth about the past, but still there was a reluctance to risk impressing her with a distorted image of a life of danger and adventure. No, better to leave it alone for now. That would make her eventual surrender to him all the sweeter.

Thinking of the delivery he planned for her to receive the next day, Derek grinned wickedly. He'd almost forgotten how to play during the past few years, he mused. The sights he'd seen in Vietnam and in back alleys across Europe and the Middle East had been grim enough to drive the laughter out of even the most lighthearted of men. But Summer had given him back the ability to laugh and the urge to play. He could love her for that, even if he did not already adore her for her sweetness, her warmth and her kindness.

Derek pushed a button on his telephone and leaned close to the speaker. "Miss Barrett, get my travel agent on the phone for me, please."

ON TUESDAY a ragged bicycle messenger brought a thick manila envelope into the accounting department. Mr. Gleason looked more disapproving than ever when Connie immediately jumped up and rushed to Summer's desk. "Well?" she demanded. "What is it?"

"I don't know. I'm almost afraid to look." Summer carefully peeled back the flap. The envelope was filled with travel brochures. Brightly colored, glossy booklets extolling the virtues of the Bahamas, Japan, China, Australia, Southern France, Italy, India and more. A plain white card bore Derek's distinctive handwriting.

You want adventure? Tell me when you want to leave.

"I think I'm going to cry," Connie wailed when she read the card.

"Do that and Gleason will fire us on the spot," Summer protested, blinking back her own tears.

"I guess you're right. But it really is sweet, Summer."

"Yes," she whispered dreamily. "It really is sweet."

Derek wasn't playing fair at all.

ANOTHER ENVELOPE CAME on Wednesday. Mr. Gleason was heard to utter a rare curse when half the accounting department gathered around Summer's desk to watch her open it. Her heart pounding in her throat, Summer smiled tremulously at Connie and ripped open the envelope. Then shook it. Then pulled it apart and stared into it.

"It's empty," she concluded finally, looking up in bewilderment.

"It's empty?" everyone repeated in disappointed unison.

"He must have forgotten to put whatever it was in the envelope before he sealed it," Connie said slowly. "Though goodness knows that doesn't sound like Derek."

Summer pursed her lips and frowned thoughtfully at the torn package. "No," she said finally. "Derek didn't forget to put anything inside. This envelope was meant to be delivered empty. Just don't anyone ask me why. I have no idea."

"You mean," asked one of the women nearby, who had always found Summer and Connie thoroughly amusing, "some guy paid a fortune for a bicycle messenger to deliver an empty envelope?"

"I think so," Summer agreed.

The woman giggled. "Can you beat that? I always knew that you'd fall for someone as funny and unpredictable as you are, Summer."

The women went back to their desks, delighted with the unusual romance being carried on in their normally routine workdays.

Connie and Summer stared at each other for a moment, then burst into helpless laughter.

THE ROOMMATES RUSHED home from work Wednesday afternoon, both in a frenzy to get ready for their respective appointments. Munching on a peanut butter sandwich, Summer stripped out of the sweater and skirt she'd worn to the office and pulled on a purple-and-yellow-printed knit shirt and a pair of baggy yellow overalls. Then she began to look around her bedroom for the notes she'd need during the final rehearsal of the Halloran House talent show. Naturally, the papers were nowhere to be found.

"Dammit!" she muttered, heedlessly trashing the tiny writing desk in one corner of the bedroom. "Where are those notes?" Paperback romances and leather-bound classics fell into a heap on the carpet, followed by an oversize pictorial history of musical comedy movies and a *Cosmopolitan* magazine.

When the desk failed to produce the papers she needed, Summer groaned and began to go through a stack of magazines on the floor beside her bed.

"Summer! I can't find my red knit dress. Do you have any suggestions where it might be?" Connie's voice from the other room sounded frantic.

"It's at the cleaners. You asked me to take it with my things just yesterday," Summer yelled back, tossing magazines in all directions.

Connie screamed.

Summer sighed and pushed herself to her feet, going off to assist her friend.

Connie was nearly hysterical. "What am I going to wear?" she wailed. "Joel will be here in twenty minutes, and I look like Bertha the Bag Lady. Help!"

"Calm down, Connie," Summer ordered, amazed at her roommate's unprecedented behavior. Connie went on dates nearly every night of the week and more times than not did not come home until morning. Now she was having a nervous breakdown over a routine dinner date, for

Pete's sake. "Wear your gray paisley silk with the black jacket. It makes you look classy."

"You think so?" Connie asked dubiously, reaching for a dress that she'd spent half a month's salary on, to Summer's dismay at the time.

"Absolutely," Summer declared. "It's perfect. Much better than the red knit would have been."

"My gray shoes! Where are my gray shoes?"

Summer counted to ten and prayed for patience. "One of them somehow fell into San Pablo Bay, remember?"

Connie screamed again.

"God, Connie, would you stop doing that? You can borrow my gray pumps."

"They're half a size too small. My feet will kill me before the evening's over."

"So what? I have it on the best authority that women who limp are incredibly sexy. Drives men crazy."

"Judging from my brother's behavior, you may be right. Give me the pumps."

Summer went back to her room to find the missing notes, glancing anxiously at her watch. Clay was due in fifteen minutes. She stared around the room, then snapped her fingers and dived under the bed. After a few minutes of scrabbling she found the papers. "All right! Way to go, Reed!" she cheered herself aloud, clutching the scribbled notes in both hands, half of her body still under the bed.

"Is there something going on under there that I should know about?" a familiar male voice asked with interest from somewhere in the vicinity of her feet.

"Aaiii!" Summer raised instinctively and saw fireworks and stars when her head made solid contact with the underside of her bed.

"Hey! Are you all right?" Derek asked in concern, hauling her unceremoniously out from under the bed by her ankles.

Rubbing the lump that was forming beneath her silky hair, Summer stared at him as if she could not quite believe he was there. "What the hell are you doing in my bedroom?" she asked him.

Kneeling in front of her, he laughed. "Isn't that the same question you asked the last time you saw me here?"

"Probably. So answer it. Why are you here and—why are you dressed like that?" she demanded, staring at his clothes. Derek had on the most disreputable pair of jeans that she'd ever seen, complete with holes in the knees and white fringe at the bottom above his grubby once-white Adidas. Over the jeans he wore a faded yellow jersey with the letters USC peeling across his chest.

"This?" he asked innocently, glancing downward. "I'm just dressed casually."

"Derek, this is not casual. We're talking major tacky here."

"No tackier than a purple-and-yellow shirt and yellow overalls," he pointed out politely, lifting an eyebrow at her own attire. Once again he'd left off his glasses, and he managed to look so sexy that Summer was tempted to drag him under the bed with her.

"What are you doing here?" she asked again. "I have a rehearsal at Halloran House tonight. Clay's picking me up in five minutes. Would you like to go with us?"

"No, thanks," Derek declined graciously. "I'm not supposed to see you this week. I'm taking the time to think logically and seriously about our relationship without being distracted by your gorgeous body. You've got a cute butt, by the way. It was the first thing I noticed when I came into the room just now."

Summer choked on a gurgle of laughter.

"I just came by," he continued blandly, "to ask if you've been getting the gifts I've sent the past two days."

"Yes, you lunatic, and you're about to get me fired." She frowned at him. "Okay, my curiosity is getting the best of me. What was the empty envelope for?"

"That's the other reason I'm here," he answered, his expression suspiciously serious. "I had to make today's delivery in person. I didn't know how to send it by messenger without being jealous."

Then he leaned over and kissed her so thoroughly that Summer was trembling when he finally released her. "Don't let McEntire put a hand on you tonight, you hear? No friendly kisses. And don't overdo the dancing. You'll hurt your leg again. See you this weekend, Summer. I love you."

With that he left.

Summer sat in the middle of her bedroom floor, her eyes glazed, her jaw slack, until Connie came in with a curious look to announce that Clay had arrived. "What did Derek want?" she asked. "Or is it none of my business?"

"He was just bringing me the contents of that empty envelope I received this morning," Summer answered in a voice that sounded distinctly odd to both of them.

"Yeah? What was it?"

"Well, let me put it this way. Do you happen to notice this smoke coming out of my ears?"

"Oh, wow."

"Yeah. Oh, wow."

THE ACCOUNTING DEPARTMENT buzzed with excitement Thursday morning. Mr. Gleason looked grim. Everyone was expecting a delivery for Summer.

They were not to be disappointed. When an outrageously costumed clown strolled into the office at just after ten o'clock, a huge bouquet of helium balloons in one hand and a gaily wrapped package in the other, the entire department turned and looked at Summer with grins of pure joy.

"Oh, my God," Summer breathed, burying her face in her hands.

"Oh, wow," she heard from the desk behind her.

The clown delivered the balloons and the package without a word and left the office. Summer tied the balloons to the back of her chair, carefully avoiding Mr. Gleason's eyes, and untied the ribbon on the package. No one in the room made any pretense of looking anywhere but at the package as Summer ripped into it. Inside the paper was a small cardboard box, about the size of a small square tissue box. Summer pulled off the tape that sealed it shut.

Squeals and laughter echoed around the room as the box seemed to explode in Summer's hands. It had been filled with the leaping snakes that are normally found in trick peanut cans. Summer wondered for a moment if anyone in the room knew how to administer CPR and was greatly relieved when her heart started beating again on its own. Her fingers were shaking when she lifted out the card in the bottom of the box. Derek's handwriting proclaimed:

Yes, love, I know how to have fun. I only needed you to remind me. I love you.

"Miss Reed."

Summer dropped her hand from her still pounding heart. "Yes, Mr. Gleason?"

"For how much longer can we expect to be entertained by this continuous soap opera?"

Summer tried to ignore Connie's muffled giggle. "I have a strong feeling that it will end tomorrow, Mr. Gleason."

"Good. See that it does."

"Yes, sir."

Summer sat back down and dropped her forehead onto her desk, dislodging a paper snake from the top of a pile of invoices.

"Oh, wow."

DEREK HOPED the clown hadn't gotten Summer fired, though he was at the point where he honestly didn't care. She didn't much like the job, anyway. If she lost it, he'd find something else for her. She could work for him, for that matter. He'd like to see her go back to school. She was too good to waste her talent when she could be sharing it with aspiring young performers.

Instinct told him that his determined campaign was serving its intended purpose. Summer had looked so delightfully bemused when he had left her in her bedroom the night before. God knew that leaving her at that moment had been the hardest thing he'd ever had to do. He allowed his mind to dwell for a moment on exactly what he'd have liked to have done with Summer last night, but that train of thought proved entirely too painful.

Instead, he concentrated on the future.

SUMMER SIPPED her coffee very slowly Friday morning, delaying the time when she would have to leave for work. She could not help but wonder what would make its way to her desk that morning.

Connie was so excited that she could hardly contain herself. "I love this, Summer. I really love this," she told her friend. "This is the Derek I knew fifteen years ago, and then some. It's amazing."

"I think I've created a monster."

"Yes, but don't you love it? Really?"

"Fact?"

"Fact."

"I adore it."

Connie sighed deliriously. "Thank God."

"It's driving me crazy, but I do adore it," Summer elaborated.

Connie giggled. "I knew you would keep him too busy to worry about me, but I had no idea he'd get this carried away. I should have introduced you to him six months ago."

Summer thought rather wistfully of the six months that Derek had lived only a few miles away from her and she hadn't even known him. "Yes," she murmured. "Perhaps you should have."

"It's fate," Connie decided abruptly. "Definitely. That you and I met and liked each other so much right away, and then that you met Derek and the two of you tumbled right into love. It must be fate."

Summer smiled indulgently. "And Joel? Did fate have something to do with you meeting him?"

"Of course. It's all part of the same plan. If it hadn't been for you, Derek wouldn't have asked me to serve as his hostess, or even if he had, I wouldn't have accepted. So my meeting Joel at the party is all wrapped up in this. Awesome, isn't it?"

"Totally," Summer agreed gravely, pleased that Connie was so smitten with Joel. Summer liked the quiet, personable man. When she'd first met him, she'd worried a little that Joel was too gentle for Connie, that Connie would tire of him too quickly. But now she thought that perhaps Joel was just what Connie needed to rebuild her self-image and put some stability into her haphazard life without subduing her irrepressible spirit.

Perhaps it *was* fate, she mused as she washed her coffee cup and prepared to leave for work. Already she was anticipating the delivery she knew would arrive that morning.

THE HOURS PASSED with painful slowness. Even Mr. Gleason looked mildly surprised when no oddly garbed messenger had arrived with a delivery by late morning. Summer and Connie were both disappointed. They had been so sure that Derek would send one last message.

"I knew it," Summer muttered at one point. "He *is* trying to drive me crazy." He would have known, of course, that she was expecting something from him. Trust Derek not to do the expected.

At eleven Connie walked up to Summer's desk with a comical frown. "What do you suppose he's up to?" she demanded.

"I have no idea," Summer replied with complete honesty.

Connie sighed. "Oh, well. We'll find out soon enough, I

suppose. By the way, Joel's picking me up for lunch and he wants you to join us. Interested?"

"Sure, I'd love to. Unless you want me to politely de- cline," Summer teased, grateful for the distraction.

"No. I want you to get to know Joel. And he you."

"Then it's a date."

Summer enjoyed lunch very much. Joel was charming. He was thirty-five, never married, serious, but not too much so, and quite handsome with his black hair and mustache and smiling blue eyes. He was also visibly infat- uated with Summer's vivacious roommate. He didn't seem at all disturbed by Connie's less-than-circumspect past, but rather seemed to admire her for her unapologetic individuality. He made a very good foil for Connie, and Summer found herself crossing her fingers under the ta- ble, hoping that the budding relationship would flower into a serious romance.

Joel was vastly amused by Connie's tale of Derek's un- usual courtship of Summer. In fact, something about his amusement puzzled Summer. She had understood that Derek and Joel did not know each other very well, but now she was beginning to think that they knew each other quite well, indeed. She studied Joel more closely through- out the remainder of the meal, wondering if he were quite as mild-mannered and innocuous as he first appeared to be. There was something about him that reminded her faintly of Derek, though she knew better than to mention that fact to Connie.

The thought of Derek distracted her, making her forget her curiosity about Connie's newest friend. Summer couldn't quite believe that the series of deliveries was over. She continued to wonder about the delivery that had not yet been made.

Promptly at three o'clock two packages arrived. Sum- mer grinned when Connie gave a low cheer. Derek hadn't let them down. He'd just wanted to keep them on their toes. Mr. Gleason didn't even bother to scowl. He simply waited for Summer to open the packages with almost the same overt curiosity as the rest of the gaping spectators.

The larger of the two boxes was neatly marked Open First. Summer obediently opened it first. Inside was nestled a somewhat smaller box marked Weekend Survival Kit. She swallowed and tore open the taped lid. She blinked back tears as she silently examined the contents— a small alarm clock with a smashed front and a shredded calendar.

The contents needed no further explanation to Summer or to Connie, though the rest of the observers looked somewhat bewildered. Summer and Connie knew that Derek was offering his weekends to Summer to fill any way she wanted, no schedules, no itineraries.

The smaller box contained a delicate gold chain on which dangled a gold, heart-shaped pendant. Inscribed on the charm were the words I love you.

"Now I *am* going to cry," Connie announced thickly.

"Good. I'll join you," Summer replied. And did. So did half the women in the accounting department.

Mr. Gleason got up and left the room.

11

THE TALENT SHOW was going even better than Summer had anticipated. Crowded into the hallway that opened off the old ballroom, she had a clear view of the stage. In lieu of curtains, sheets had been hung between the stage and the opening to the hallway, which served as the back-stage area. The young performers of Halloran House waited restlessly in the hallway for their turn on stage, at which time Summer motioned them to walk behind the sheets and onto the plywood platform. To her relief and that of the director and staff of Halloran House, the troubled youths were exceptionally well behaved that evening, with only one fight backstage during the show and a minimum of clowning onstage.

Summer was trying very hard to concentrate on the show and her responsibilities to it. Her blue eyes focused fiercely on the performers, as if there were nothing at all on her mind but that talent show. Nothing could have been further from the truth. She hadn't been thinking clearly since the delivery she'd received that afternoon. She fingered the gold charm at her breast. She was a goner, she thought dispassionately. Derek had won. Hands down. If he asked her to tie herself to a block of concrete and throw herself off the Golden Gate Bridge, she'd probably do it. She would live on a schedule, she would start working harder at her job, she would do anything she had to do to keep this man in her life.

She loved him.

"Good show, huh?" Clay murmured in Summer's ear as he looked over her shoulder to the stage.

"Very good," she whispered, smiling back at the handsome blond. "You must be proud of your kids tonight."

"You bet," he replied with a dazzling, toothpaste-ad smile. Crazy Clay had dressed in a manner that he considered appropriate for opening night of a youth home talent show. He wore a tuxedo-printed T-shirt, black denim jeans and red, high-topped sneakers with orange laces. Though Clay was thirty-four years old, he looked younger, like a virile, carefree surf bum. Only the faintest of lines around his blue-green eyes gave any indication that there might have been problems in this man's past.

Summer had dressed a little more formally, having chosen to wear a high-collared rose silk blouse and pleated gray flannel slacks. She had wanted the youngsters to know that she considered their production worthy of respect. They were used to the way Clay dressed.

"Have you seen the audience?" Clay asked, his eyes following the movements of the two would-be actors on stage.

"Only a peek. Did Thelma's mother come?"

"Yes, thank God."

"Oh, I'm so glad. Thelma would have been devastated if her mother hadn't shown up tonight. She's been working so hard on that song."

"To be honest, I did some arm-twisting. I told Mrs. Sawyer that if she missed this program tonight, she would be missing any chance of ever reclaiming her relationship with Thelma."

"Good for you." Seeing that the skit was almost over, Summer signaled for Dodie, the fourteen-year-old Cyndi Lauper impersonator, to step behind the sheets and get ready to go onstage. "I hope you're right about this program bringing in some healthy donations," she continued to Clay. "Frank told me things have been getting tight around here."

"I think it will help," Clay replied optimistically. "We managed to draw some wealthy and influential businessmen here tonight. I see Connie brought her brother.

Maybe he'd like to make a contribution to a worthwhile charity."

Summer had been enthusiastically applauding the conclusion of the skit, but her hands fell to her sides at Clay's comment. "Derek's here?" she said with a gasp, staring up at Clay. "Connie was supposed to come with Joel."

"It was her brother she walked in with," Clay insisted.

Summer's heart began to hammer painfully in her chest. No wonder Connie had smiled mysteriously while they'd dressed for the show, she thought wildly. Summer hadn't known that Derek would be here, but obviously Connie had been in on the secret.

Now that she knew Derek was here, Summer wondered if she would be able to wait until the end of the show to see him. Derek was here! Only a few feet from where she stood! The long week was over, and the only thing that had changed was that Derek had managed to destroy any lingering resistance she had to him—and without even seeing her, other than that brief, rather weird visit to her bedroom.

"Summer, I asked if you're ready for me to get behind the curtains," a young voice repeated impatiently, and Summer realized that she'd gone into a near trance right there in the crowded hallway. Ignoring Clay's curiously amused regard, she managed to rouse herself enough to resume directing the show.

The *Fame* song and dance was an unquestionable success. At its conclusion the audience gave a good-natured standing ovation. His eyes proud behind his thick glasses, Frank Rivers then took the stage to give a little talk about the operation of Halloran House, concluding with a typical fund-raiser's plea for donations and a general invitation for cookies and punch at a "cast party" that would begin shortly.

In the hallway Summer was generous in her praise of all the performers. "You guys were terrific!" she told them, glowing with pride. She had only been involved in the home since Clay had recruited her eight weeks earlier, but she had grown to love the youths there and desperately wanted to help them find ways to work out their problems. Like Clay, she believed that a sense of self-worth was the best foundation for healthy futures for these kids, and she intended to do what she could to strengthen that foundation. "I'm so proud of all of you."

"We owe a lot of it to you, Summer," Thelma Sawyer said shyly, stepping forward with a brightly wrapped package. "We got you something to show our appreciation."

"How sweet." Surrounded by her young friends, Summer ripped into the gift. Inside the box was an engraved plaque with her name in ornate letters, the date of the performance and the words To the Best Director in the World, With Thanks from the Animals at Halloran House.

She seemed to be making a habit lately of opening gifts and choking back tears, Summer told herself mistily. "I love it. You're the best bunch of animals I ever met. Now go have your cookies and punch with your fans."

"They're crazy about you, Summer," Clay told her when the boisterous young people dashed away. He draped an arm around her shoulders. "Tell me, have you ever considered working with talented young people? With your dramatic talents and your gift of communication, you'd be a natural."

"It has been suggested to her," a deep male voice said from behind them. "McEntire, if you value that arm, you'll remove it from my woman's body."

Clay threw a cocky grin over his shoulder and lifted the arm with haste. "Since this is my favorite arm, I'll take your advice," he told Derek. "I had guessed last week that you and Summer were seeing each other, but I wasn't aware that the relationship was to the dangerous stage."

"Very dangerous," Derek answered evenly, dropping his own arm where Clay's had been. He smiled down at Summer's flushed face. "The show was great, Summerlove. You did a good job directing it."

"Thank you." Her eyes glowed at him, noting how

good he looked in his charcoal-gray suit with the pearl-gray shirt and burgundy striped tie. As sexy as he'd been in ragged jeans and tattered T-shirt. "I didn't know you were going to be here tonight," she told him, looking accusingly at Connie, who was grinning beside them.

"I just found out myself this afternoon," Connie answered apologetically. "He forbade me to tell you. Sorry."

"I'm not," Summer admitted with a smile. "It was a very nice surprise. I'm glad you're here, Derek."

"Thank you, Summer." He kissed her gently, and she could feel the tremendous effort he made to keep the kiss under control. Something about the hungry way he looked at her told her it had been a long week for him. Just as it had been for her.

Derek lifted the charm at her breast, his knuckles brushing the softness beneath as if by accident. Swallowing painfully, Summer knew there had been no accident involved.

"I see you got my latest gift."

"Yes. I think my boss would like to meet you. He would probably love for you to be present when he cans me."

"Oh, well. You didn't like that job, anyway."

"This from the man who said I should be more career-oriented?"

"Only if you're in the right career," he countered.

Summer looked at Connie, ignoring Derek's remark. "Where's Joel?"

"He had a late meeting tonight and had to skip the show. He's going to pick me up later to take me dancing," Connie explained. Dressed in a shimmery gold shirtwaist dress of raw silk, Connie glowed from her artfully arranged red curls to her gold spike-heeled sandals, and Summer was well aware that the glow was because Connie would be seeing Joel soon. Summer knew the feeling well enough to recognize it—Connie was already on the verge of falling in love with Joel Tanner. Summer prayed that this relationship would work out for Connie, who deserved happiness as much or more than anyone Summer knew.

"We'll spend a few minutes at your cast party, then take Connie home and go on to my place," Derek informed Summer, then added hastily, "If that's all right with you."

Summer smiled at him. "You're learning," she murmured.

"I'm trying, sweetheart. I'm trying."

Summer could not have said later what went on at the exuberant party in the Halloran House recreation room. She chatted and laughed and made all the correct responses when spoken to, but all she could remember later was the way Derek looked at her with the silvery smile in his eyes. She felt as if she were in some wonderful dream, as if only that could explain the way she and Derek had met and fallen almost instantly in love, as improbable as that might be. She had tried to give him time to be sure, yet here he was, his eyes telling her that she had only been wasting time. The sense of relief was overwhelming.

Derek left her side only once, to procure her a glass of punch. Clay took advantage of the opportunity to tease Summer about her dangerous lover. "How long have you been seeing the guy, anyway?" he asked.

Blushing a little, Summer replied, "Two weeks. Sort of."

"Oh." Clay nodded. "Two weeks, sort of. Very interesting."

She laughed. "It's crazy, I know, but it's also wonderful. In case you haven't noticed, I'm walking on air tonight."

"I noticed," he replied with a smile. "I'm standing here green with envy."

Summer patted his arm. "It will happen for you, Clay. When you find the right woman, you'll know exactly how I feel."

Clay shook his head, looking around the room full of young people and their parents. "It would take some special kind of woman to accept my dedication to troubled kids," he mused aloud. "I'm not even sure I have anything left over to offer. These kids are my life, Summer."

She sighed. "Now I'm the one who's envious. I'd like to know that I was making a real contribution somewhere, like you are."

"I've given you a suggestion," he reminded her. "The kids need someone like you on their side, Summer. Think about it."

"I will," she promised, and then Derek joined them, driving the conversation from her immediate thoughts as he drew her possessively to his side.

SUMMER'S EUPHORIA WAS abruptly shattered during the drive home, when all of her fears returned to threaten her relationship with Derek.

Summer on one arm and Connie on the other, Derek escorted them to his Lincoln. They all slid into the front seat, where Summer snuggled happily against Derek's side and chattered gaily about the show and the generous promises of donations it had generated afterward.

"The parents all looked so proud," she mused, then reluctantly reversed herself. "Well, most of them. I heard one father tell his son that it all seemed like a waste of time to him. That's probably the kind of comment that put the boy in Halloran House in the first place. Clay heard it, too, and I could tell that it made him angry."

"Summer, you can't expect miracles in one evening, from one little talent show," Derek pointed out with gentle logic. "Those families have long-term problems that have led to their children's need for help. The social workers and psychologists will do everything they can to help solve those problems. And the money taken in tonight will finance those therapy sessions for a while longer, so the show did bring about results of one kind."

"You're right, of course. It's just that I've seen the sweetness behind the defiance and bluster in those kids, and I want so much to help them."

"Then you should," Derek told her flatly. "Stop wasting your time in that accounting department and start working with kids."

"Uh-oh," Connie muttered. "Here it comes." She sank down into her seat.

"Derek, I can't just find a job teaching. I'd have to go back to school myself first."

"So? You're only twenty-five. You've got a few good years ahead of you, Summer."

"More helpful advice, Derek?" she grumbled, glaring up at him through her lashes.

"I was merely making a suggestion," he answered irritably.

Forgetting that only a short while earlier she'd thought herself willing to leap from the Golden Gate Bridge at his command, Summer sat up straight on the seat and scooted away from him, almost ending up in Connie's lap. "You're trying to change me!" she accused him heatedly. "Dammit, I knew this would happen. I knew you wouldn't be content to take me just the way I am."

"Would you please answer me one question?" Derek shouted, turning into the parking lot of the apartment building where Summer and Connie lived, his tires squealing as he pressed the gas pedal in frustration. "Why is it that you only smiled when Clay McEntire made the same damned suggestion, but when I said it, you blew your top and accused me of trying to change you?"

"Because you are!" Summer yelled back. "You're trying to tell me what to do, just like you do to Connie."

"Better leave me out of this," her roommate whispered.

"I only want what's best for you," Derek argued. "Both of you, dammit."

"And God gave you the knowledge of what's best for Connie and me, right?" Summer threw at him in disgust. "It must be nice to be so omniscient, Derek."

Almost growling, Derek shoved open his door and leaped from the car. "Upstairs, both of you!" he ordered furiously. "We're going to settle this issue right now, if it takes all night."

"But I've got a date with Joel!" Connie protested, crawling out of the car to stare at her brother aggrievedly.

"He can join us. Hell, we'll ask the whole damned neighborhood to join us," Derek grated between clenched teeth, already walking toward the apartment building as Summer and Connie trotted after him. "Ask them if it's so damned terrible of me to try to help the people I care about."

"It's not that we don't appreciate your intentions, Derek. It's the way you say these things," Summer puffed, clutching Connie's arm as they hurried to keep up with his angry strides. "You always sound as if your way is the only right way—for you and everyone else."

"Face it, Derek, you've been trying to tell me what to do since I was ten years old," Connie said in turn. "Even when I wouldn't see you for months or years at a time, you'd send me letters telling me to live up to my potential, to study and make something of myself. Well, I didn't want your words of wisdom. I wanted my brother!"

"Okay, so I came down too hard on you over the years," Derek answered heatedly, turning in the hallway to glare at the two gasping young women who clung to each other and faced him defiantly. "It's only because I wanted so much for you. Mom and Dad didn't seem to know how to handle you, and I thought I might have more influence with you. I knew you were capable of accomplishing anything if you put your mind on it, but I wasn't sure that I would live long enough to see it happen."

Both Summer and Connie frowned at that. "What's that supposed to mean?" Summer demanded.

Derek blinked as if he couldn't quite believe he'd said that. "As much as I traveled, anything could have happened," he explained inadequately. "Plane crashes, car accidents, whatever."

Connie and Summer shared a puzzled look that indicated that neither of them thought he was telling the whole story.

Derek exhaled loudly. "Let's not stand out here in the hall. Let's go in where we can talk rationally."

Summer nodded her agreement. It was extremely important that they settle this issue finally, she told herself anxiously. Her future with Derek hinged on the discussion that was about to take place. She had to make him understand, once and for all, that, though she was willing to make certain compromises for him, he would not be able to change her into someone else. She was just herself, and if he wasn't happy with her as she was, then they might as well give it up now. It wasn't that she wasn't willing to discuss possible career changes for her future with him, but she would not allow him to dictate those changes to her.

They were less than six feet from the door to their apartment when Derek suddenly stopped, frowning. "That wasn't there earlier," he muttered, his eyes focusing on a fresh scar near the lock on the battered wooden door.

"What wasn't there?" Summer asked him, trying to find what he was looking at so intently.

He pushed her unceremoniously toward the hallway wall, motioning Connie to follow suit. "Stand right there," he ordered them softly. "I want to check your apartment."

"But, Derek, what is it?" Summer asked again, studying his expression. The look he wore now was different from the heated anger he'd shown during their argument moments earlier. He looked hard, cool, rather daunting. She swallowed.

"Hush." He touched her arm in an absentmindedly gentle gesture that made her knees go weak despite her lingering anger with him. "Don't move until I tell you to."

The roommates watched in nervous confusion as Derek moved soundlessly to the door and tested the knob. The door wasn't locked. Easing it silently open, Derek prepared to enter. Just before he stepped inside, all three of them heard a muffled crash from inside the apartment.

Summer jumped and covered her mouth in consternation, her eyes locking with Derek's.

"My God, there's someone in there," Connie whispered, her own green eyes huge. "We should call the police."

"Just a minute," Derek whispered distractedly, looking back toward the doorway.

Summer watched as he flattened himself against the door, obviously preparing to go in. She did not miss the way his right hand slipped inside his jacket, almost as if by instinct. The hand came away empty as a look of impatience crossed his face. Then he eased the door all the way open.

"Derek, no!" Summer whispered frantically, moving impulsively to stop him from going in. He shot her a look that plastered her back against the wall, her heart in her throat. Blindly she reached for Connie's hand as Derek slipped inside the dark apartment.

Oh, Derek, be careful, Summer pleaded silently. *Oh, God, don't let anything happen to Derek.*

She had never been so frightened in her life, not even when she'd been hit by the car five years earlier. Only her life had been at stake then. This was Derek in possible danger, and she would willingly give both her legs to keep him safe.

She had known that she loved him. She was only now realizing how deeply that love had planted itself within her. How desperately she needed him. She closed her eyes and tried to calm herself enough to think of some way to help him. She was afraid to leave her position in the hallway long enough to make a call for help, terrified that something would happen to Derek if she moved.

Long moments of silence passed. And then a muffled exclamation, a grunt and a crash sounded from inside the apartment.

Connie squealed in fear and dropped Summer's icy hand. They looked at each other for a fraction of a second, then moved in mutual agreement toward the apartment door.

Summer groped for the light switch. When the light came on, she and Connie both gasped at the sight of Derek dragging a large, raggedly dressed, prostrate body from Connie's bedroom.

He dropped the intruder in the middle of the floor, then looked at Summer and Connie. He staggered as two soft forms flung themselves at him, both holding on to him as if belatedly trying to protect him from harm.

"Derek, did you kill him?" Connie breathed, staring down at the man at their feet even as she maintained her grip around her brother's neck.

"No, of course I didn't kill him," Derek answered impatiently, trying to disentangle himself from the women clinging to him. "He's just unconscious. Connie, call the police."

As if he hadn't spoken, Connie put her fists on her hips and planted herself squarely in front of him. "Derek Anderson, that was the most stupid, asinine, ridiculously macho stunt I have ever seen! Are you crazy, waltzing into an apartment where you know there's a burglar? What were you trying to do, impress your girlfriend like some show-off teenager? Why didn't you just do handstands in the parking lot? Don't you know this sleaze bag could have killed you?"

"Connie, would you please shut up and call the police?"

"No, I will not! I'm not finished with you yet! What if he had…"

As Connie continued to berate her brother, Summer stepped carefully over the unconscious body of the would-be burglar, walked to the telephone and dialed the number of the police station, a number she'd carefully memorized but had never needed before now.

When she hung up, she looked around the apartment, finding her portable television, Connie's stereo, a camera and some jewelry piled on the living room floor. "He was really going to rip us off!" she exclaimed indignantly.

"No kidding," Derek responded in exasperation, ignoring the fact that Connie was still raging on at him without even pausing for breath. "Lord, how have the two of you managed to live here for almost a year without this happening before? No security in the building, locks on your door that wouldn't keep out a five-year-old delinquent.

This guy probably had the door open in less than a minute. If I hadn't been with you, the two of you would have just walked right in on him."

"Isn't that exactly what you just did?" Connie demanded, his criticism setting her off again. "Of all the dumb, stupid, irresponsible…"

Ignoring his sister, Derek threw a dark look at Summer. "The police will be here soon. Go throw some things in a bag. You're spending the night at my place. I'll have new locks installed here tomorrow."

Summer almost bristled at his tone, but remembering how frightened she had been for him, she only nodded and turned toward her bedroom. She really didn't want to stay here tonight, anyway, she told herself logically, stuffing jeans and a shirt into an overnight bag. Even if the apartment were double-locked and guarded by Mr. T, she'd rather sleep in Derek's arms.

In the other room she heard Derek inform Connie that she, too, would be spending the night at Derek's house.

"But, Derek, Joel's going to be here in a few minutes to take me out," she heard Connie argue.

"Tell him to drive you to my place when the evening's over," Derek answered with exaggerated patience. "Unless you spend the night at his house, in which case I want you to call me."

"I am not a teenager!" Connie shouted. "And besides, our relationship is not at that stage."

"Your relationships usually reach that stage as soon as the guy's finger touches your doorbell."

"Of all the—"

"Would you two please stop it?" Summer yelled, throwing her makeup case into the overnight bag. "Haven't we had enough violence for one night? Connie, pack some clothes. I'll take them on to Derek's."

The police arrived, took a statement from Derek with brisk efficiency and hauled their dazed burglar away. "The guy was a total amateur," Derek muttered disgustedly. "Probably a junkie."

"Yeah, and what if he'd been wired and armed?" Connie demanded, his words reminding her that she was still angry at him for risking his safety.

"Very few small-time burglars carry weapons, Connie," Derek explained with strained patience. "If they get caught, the possession of a weapon makes their offense much more serious."

"But you didn't *know* he was unarmed," Connie argued. "He could have been a professional."

"In this place?" Derek gestured around the apartment. "Give me a break."

"Well, thanks a lot."

Summer suddenly laughed, drawing two pairs of eyes to her face in question. "Connie, would you listen to yourself?" she asked in unexpected amusement. "You sound just like Derek when he's giving one of his lectures. If it was him talking to you like that, you'd go into orbit."

Connie bit her lip, her green eyes beginning to sparkle. "You're right," she admitted. "I do sound like Derek." She glanced sheepishly at her brother. "I was only yelling at you because you scared me half to death," she told him. "You make me mad as hell, but you're my brother and I love you. I didn't want you to be hurt."

Derek's face softened as he looked at her. "I love you, too, Connie. Let's start over, shall we? As adults."

Connie stepped into her brother's open arms and hugged him fervently. "Yes, let's," she agreed, her voice suspiciously thick before she cleared it and stepped back.

Derek glanced over at Summer, who was smiling mistily at her best friend and her lover. "Still teaching object lessons, Summer-love?" he murmured quietly.

"I guess it's becoming a habit," she replied, meeting his look with love in her eyes. They still had things to work out between them, but at last she was fully convinced that a solution was possible for them.

The only important thing was that Derek was safe, and he loved her. And she loved him. Anything was possible.

12

DEREK INSISTED that he and Summer would stay in the apartment until Joel arrived to pick up Connie. Connie made a token protest, but it wasn't hard to see that she was rather reluctant to stay alone in the apartment with its broken lock. Derek checked the locks on the windows while they waited, grumbling the entire time about the shabby security provided by their apartment. "I'll have to have every lock in the apartment replaced," he muttered.

"Did it ever occur to you that we're quite capable of having our own locks replaced?" Connie asked sarcastically, sitting on the couch with her feet propped on the coffee table in front of her as she watched Derek take his survey.

Her brother gave her a withering look and walked into her bedroom to examine her windows, having already dismissed Summer's.

"Are you sure you want to spend the rest of your life with that man?" Connie demanded of her roommate.

Summer giggled. "Hard to imagine, isn't it? But yes, as a matter of fact, I'm sure."

"Well, all I can say is that I'm glad Joel's not the bossy type. At least *he* won't yell at me for being the innocent victim of an attempted robbery," Connie proclaimed loftily.

Joel arrived shortly afterward, his thick black hair windblown, as if he'd been in a great rush. He apologized profusely to Connie for being late, so courteous and attentive that Summer could see Connie falling even harder for him right on the spot.

"Wait until I tell you about the excitement you missed," Connie told Joel after he had greeted Summer and Derek.

"What excitement?" he asked indulgently, smiling down at her.

Connie rapidly told him about the burglar they had surprised when they'd returned from Halloran House.

"*What?*"

Connie and Summer blinked at the unexpected roar from the man who'd been so quiet and amiable until now. Summer could have sworn she heard Derek chuckle.

"Joel—" Connie began questioningly, but his words cut her off.

"You mean you would have just walked right in on the guy if Derek hadn't been here to stop you?" Joel demanded, his blue eyes flashing dangerously. "Don't you ever check your door when you return from someplace? What would you have done if the door had been standing wide open? Just come on in?"

Connie's mouth dropped open, then snapped shut. "Hey! Derek was the one who just walked right in!"

"Derek is fully capable of taking care of himself," Joel returned immediately, brushing off the implication that Derek had behaved at all unwisely. "But you and Summer are another story. Don't you know that the locks in this place wouldn't—"

"Wouldn't keep out a five-year-old delinquent," Connie quoted her brother, turning a comically resigned face toward Summer. "I've heard this speech already tonight."

"Well, you're going to hear it again," Joel promised her. "This is a big city, Connie. Two women living alone have to be careful. I'm only telling you this because I care about what happens to you."

Summer was giggling when Joel and Connie left. Connie looked so stunned as she meekly accompanied Joel out the door.

"Don't forget to let me know something about tonight," Derek threw after her.

Connie glared back at him over her shoulder.

Ah, well, Summer thought in resignation. As Derek had pointed out earlier, miracles did not happen in one night.

Still, she thought the Andersons were well on their way to redefining their relationship, even to becoming friends.

And now she and Derek had to work out their own problems. Maybe now that she was beginning to understand him a little better, the reasons behind his seemingly compulsive advice-giving...

Watching Derek wearily massaging the back of his neck with one hand, Summer suddenly frowned as a vivid memory flashed through her mind. Derek flattening himself against the door of the apartment. His hand sliding under his jacket. She'd seen that particular gesture in enough television cop shows to know what it meant.

She thought of the scar on his shoulder. The air of command that came so naturally to him.

"What is it, Summer?" Derek asked, watching her watching him.

"What exactly did you do for the government, Derek?" she questioned him in an odd voice.

He went still. "Why do you ask that now?"

Tilting her head to search his face, she thought of another question she suddenly wanted answered. "Just how did you get that scar on your shoulder?"

He sighed but replied honestly. "I was shot. Three years ago, in Beirut."

She swallowed. "Then you really weren't teasing—"

"When I told you I was a spy? No."

"My God." She was stunned. How could she not have known?

His mouth twisted. "I was really more of a courier than a spy," he explained. "I carried things—messages, money, papers, sometimes weapons—into usually hostile territory. Often there were those who wanted to, er, intercept what I carried or prevent it from reaching its destination. That's how I was shot."

"And that's what you meant by not knowing whether you would be around to see your sister grown up," Summer clarified.

"Yes." He stood very still, allowing her to absorb the new information about him in her own way.

"Connie doesn't know, does she?"

"No."

"Your parents?"

"My father knows. We decided that Mom would worry too much if she knew the truth, though I think she's always suspected. And Connie, well, Connie talks too much sometimes. It was better if she didn't know the whole story."

"And just why didn't you tell me, Derek?" Summer asked heatedly. "Just what excuse do you have for not telling me?"

He looked surprised that she was so angry. "I didn't think it was important."

"Didn't think it was important?" she repeated, her voice rising. "You made me tell you every detail of my life for the past twenty-five years, but you didn't think it was important for me to know that the man I thought was a harmless diplomatic attaché was actually a secret agent?"

"Summer, I would have told you eventually. Soon."

"You had plenty of opportunity. Dammit, we even joked about it. I can understand why you didn't tell me that first night, but why not later, after we'd become…involved?"

"All right, I didn't want to tell you," he snapped. "I didn't want you to fall for me because you thought I was a movie hero like the guy you described the night we met. If that's what you were really looking for, then I'm the wrong man because all I intend to be from now on is an ordinary businessman, just as you thought I was all along."

"In other words, you thought that I was empty-headed enough to fall head over heels in love with you just because I would have been impressed with your courage and your daring?" she asked coldly. "That I would think you were a romantic James Bond, who'd sweep me right off my feet?"

He flushed uncomfortably. "No, that's not what I

thought. Well, maybe I felt that way at first, but—dammit, Summer, I don't know why I didn't tell you, all right? But now you know. Does it really make any difference to you?"

She looked at him, long and hard, reading the anxiety in his eyes, the weariness in the lines around his mouth. And she loved him so much she ached. She sighed. "No."

His expression softened. "Summer…"

She had no intention of making it too easy for him. "I'll get my things and Connie's," she informed him, backing away from his outstretched arms. "I'm tired and I'm ready to get out of here tonight. That broken door makes me nervous."

"You don't have to be nervous while I'm here," Derek told her impatiently.

She shot him a pointed look. "I can't tell you how comforting that is," she murmured, taking great pleasure in the small revenge.

He scowled and shut up.

"WHY DON'T YOU take Connie's things on into the guest room," Derek suggested to Summer as they entered his house. "I'll pour us a drink. I have a feeling we're going to need one."

"Fine," she said, leaving her own things in the den with him. She had no intention of sharing the guest room with Connie that night, though she planned to make Derek crawl a little before she pounced on him. She figured he needed it. One thing about these hero-types, she thought smugly, they tended to be a bit overconfident.

When she returned to the den, Derek was waiting with a glass of chilled white wine in his hand. He had removed his jacket and tie, unbuttoned the top three buttons of his shirt, rolled back his sleeves and taken off his dark-framed glasses, transforming himself from the conservative businessman into the macho ex-spy. Summer wondered how she'd ever believed he'd been anyone else. She forced herself to resist reaching out to stroke one powerfully muscled arm as she took her drink, though she made herself a promise that, before the night was over, she'd test the strength of every muscle in his body.

"About your former line of work, Derek," she began when they were seated on the sofa, Derek rather stiffly, Summer completely at ease.

He sighed. "What about it?"

"Why?"

He shrugged, not pretending to misunderstand. "For the excitement, the adventure. Because I was good at it, and because I wanted to make a difference for my country."

"Why did you quit?"

"Lots of reasons. I got tired. What once looked exciting and daring began to look sordid and ugly. I was ready to trade adventure for normality. As I got older, the daily routine of the regular business world began to look pretty good to me. I've always had a certain, er, talent for giving advice, so I decided to go into the consulting business. The government provided me with the references and credentials I needed to get started."

"And you're doing very well at it."

"I've enjoyed it." He glanced over at her. "When did I give myself away? When I reached for a gun that wasn't there?"

"That was part of it."

Looking contrite, he set his half-finished drink on a table beside him and turned to her. "Summer, I really am sorry that I kept my past from you. I didn't understand that it would hurt you. It's a part of my life that I want to put behind me, a part that I wasn't sure that you would admire or respect. And I'm sorry that I didn't trust you enough to recognize that I'm no movie hero, despite my background. I didn't want you to expect something from me that's just not there."

"Oh, Derek," she breathed fondly, struck again by the vulnerability that occasionally appeared in him to surprise her. "Don't you know you're all the hero I've ever wanted? You've shown me that I never have to worry about being bored with you. That you'll play with me, yet you'll be there for me to lean on in a crisis. I had already discovered all those things about you even before I found out what you once did for a living. My only concern was that you would try too hard to change me into something I'm not, something I couldn't be."

"Summer, I don't want to change you," he rasped, stroking her cheek with one unsteady finger. "Don't you know that I think you're absolutely perfect, exactly as you are? I only want you to be happy."

"I know that now, Derek. And I promise that I'll listen to your advice and then I'll use my own judgment about my decisions, just as you'll do when I make suggestions to you."

"Of course I will."

"Think you can handle being involved with a college student?" she asked him, lifting a hand to touch his cheek.

He caught her hand in his. "You're going back to school?"

"I want to work with those kids, Derek. Full-time," she confessed. "I haven't enjoyed anything that much in five long years."

"You'll be great with them. You'll make a difference, Summer."

"I hope so. I'm a little scared. I'm not sure that I can do it. It's been a long time since I studied for a test."

"Oh, love, I have no doubt that you can do it," Derek crooned lovingly, cradling her face between large, capable hands. "And I'll always be there for you, anytime you might need me."

"I'll always need you," she whispered, looking up at him with eyes like liquid sapphires. "I love you, Derek Anderson. I'll love you for the rest of my life."

"And I love you," he grated, sweeping her into his arms, heedless of the white wine that spilled over both of them. "Let me show you how much."

"Yes, Derek. Show me. Now." She put her arms around his neck and flashed her most brilliant smile for him.

Derek's huge bed beckoned to them when he carried her into his bedroom, but rather than lowering her to it, he set her gently on her feet beside it. Then he kissed her, over and over, until both of them were trembling and gasping for breath.

Summer moaned and burrowed deeper into his arms, her silky hair brushing the underside of his chin. "Oh, God, Derek, I was so frightened for you tonight. Please don't ever frighten me like that again. I wouldn't want to live if anything happened to you."

Overwhelmed by her admission, Derek crushed her to him with a sound deep in his throat that might almost have been called a sob. "I love you, Summer. I love you so desperately," he muttered in a voice raw with need.

"Oh, Derek."

He held her for a moment longer, then stirred against her, anxious to be rid of the garments that separated them. He undressed her with loving care, sliding the rose silk blouse from her shoulders and kissing each inch of flesh that he exposed. Then he reached for the snap of her gray flannel slacks even as he tugged impatiently at his own garments. They were both nude when he finished. Threading his fingers into the hair around her face, he lowered his head to rub his lips over her eyelids and cheeks.

Luxuriating in his tender caresses, Summer sighed. She felt as if she'd known this man all her life, his thoughts, his fears, his pleasures. She pressed against his hardened thighs and smiled at the low groan of arousal her action drew from him. This was her man in her arms, she reminded herself wonderingly, and she had so much love to give him.

He needed her love, she thought happily. Incredibly, he needed her as much as she needed him.

Derek was trembling when he moved his hands to her creamy, upthrust breasts, then lowered his mouth to taste them. Summer closed her eyes and clung to him for support, her fingers curling into his shoulders as she arched into him. She swayed unsteadily as Derek moved slowly downward. Only her hands on his shoulders kept her from falling as he dropped to his knees to nuzzle her inner thighs.

"Ah, Derek," she breathed, finally sinking to the edge of the bed. "You're driving me wild."

"Good," he rasped. "I like you that way."

And then he came to her in a rush of need and desire that drove her back into the soft mattress with a cry of pleasure.

Derek stroked and tasted and nibbled every inch of her eager body until Summer was blazing like a torch for him. Not content this time to lie still beneath his ministrations, she pushed him onto his back and explored his body with the same thorough attention. Derek shuddered beneath her touch, causing her to laugh as smugly as possible in a voice that was little more than a ragged exhale.

Unable to hold back any longer, he twisted until she was beneath him again, making a place for himself between her thighs. Summer welcomed him with a murmur of encouragement.

"I love you, Summer," he whispered, even as he surged into her.

"I love you, Derek," she managed before the power of speech left her entirely.

In the lovemaking that followed, Summer found a degree of physical exhilaration such as she had never experienced before—not even before her accident. She had once thought that dancing provided the ultimate physical freedom, as close to flying as possible without leaving the ground. Then Derek led her into a dramatic climax that gave her the sensation of spinning through space, weightless, carefree, unhampered by old injuries or fears. Freedom.

Much, much later Derek stirred against the pillow, pulling Summer closer to his side as they snuggled together beneath the geometric print bedspread. "Lady, you are good," Derek murmured with gently teasing approval.

Summer smiled against his damp shoulder. "Thank you," she answered primly. "You're not bad yourself, Derek."

"Olympic-class?"

"Not amateur." She lifted her head to kiss his jaw. "Definitely not amateur."

"Well, this old pro is about to sign an exclusive contract. For life."

"That sounds nice," she told him warmly. "Very nice."

"Just don't expect many more weeks like this past one," he warned her. "I'm really a very conservative kind of guy, you understand."

"Mmm." She rubbed her cheek against his shoulder, reserving comment on his questionable statement.

And then she lifted her head with a frown as a sudden thought occurred to her. "Speaking of conservative guys, what happened to Joel tonight?" she demanded.

Derek laughed softly but feigned ignorance. "What do you mean?"

"You know damn well what I mean. Just how long have you known Joel Tanner, Derek?"

"Six or seven years," Derek replied casually.

"How did you meet him?"

"Let's just say we were business associates."

"*Joel* was a spy?" Summer gasped, falling back against the pillows.

"Courier, Summer."

She shook her head, dazed. "I can't believe it. And he seemed like such a gentle, sweet man."

"You wouldn't have called him gentle or sweet if you'd seen the way he saved my neck in Beirut three years ago," Derek informed her, absently rubbing his scarred shoulder. "Joel's got a bit of a temper, you see."

"So that's why you thought it was so funny that Connie was dating him. He's just like you!"

Derek laughed. "We're not that much alike. But Joel

won't let Connie walk all over him like that wimpy ex-husband of hers did. She needs a strong man like Joel to keep up with her. He'll treat her very well, but he'll know when—and how—to draw the line when it's necessary."

"You are a devious man, Derek Anderson."

"I didn't plan this, Summer. Joel and I got out of our government jobs at about the same time. He asked me to help him set up his accounting firm, and I did. He really was a client. I never expected him to fall for Connie at my party, but when they hit it off so well, I realized they made a good couple. Who knows, they might even decide to make it permanent, like we did."

"Did we?" Summer murmured with a secret smile, fully aware that there was one question Derek had not yet asked.

"Damn straight," he answered cheerfully. He settled her back against his shoulder and kissed the top of her head.

"How do you feel about children, Summer-love?" Derek inquired blandly after a few minutes of contented silence.

"Children," she repeated thoughtfully. "As in ours?"

"Umm. Eventually. When you finish school."

"Definitely worth consideration," she told him gravely, dropping a kiss on his jaw.

"I might even let them make their own decisions, once in a while," Derek quipped with wry self-humor.

"I'm sure they'll appreciate it," she murmured, already picturing the battles sure to take place in the Anderson home when their daughter became a teenager. Summer was enthralled with her vision of the future.

"When will you marry me?"

She smiled brightly. "I wondered when you would get around to asking me."

"So answer me. When?"

"One month."

"That long?" he asked, dismayed.

"Our families are going to be in shock as it is," she

pointed out. "We've only known each other for two weeks."

"I'd have married you last weekend if you hadn't been so damned stubborn about giving me time to think," he growled. "All right, Summer-love, you have one month. Not a day longer, you hear?"

"I hear, darling. One month."

She snuggled against him once more, then lifted her head again with a frown.

"Now what is it?" Derek asked.

"You're sure my leg doesn't bother you?"

"Dammit, Summer. Of course it bothers me. For your sake, not for mine. It tears me up to think of you bleeding and in pain, and of the sacrifices you had to make. I wish for your sake it had never happened, but it doesn't make the least bit of difference in my feelings for you. Would it matter to you if *I* were the one with the game leg?"

"No, of course not. But you love sports so much."

"I've participated in sports over the years because it was a good way to keep in shape for my work and to work off the tension that was an inherent part of my job. It also made a good cover. You can't imagine how many deliveries I made in smoke-filled arenas and sweat-rank gyms. Even at checkpoints in marathon races. But I'm not going to leave you on the sidelines now that I've found you, my love. As a matter of fact," he added, his hand straying to her breast, "I can think of several interesting sports we can take up together."

"Mmm. I like the way you think," she purred, finally allowing herself to be convinced that Derek did not see her as a burden or an object of pity.

"If it makes you feel any better, I'll even tolerate a few gimp jokes. I still don't think they're particularly funny, but I'd hate for you to go back to thinking I'm a stuffed shirt."

"Oh, Derek, I love you." She rolled on top of him to cover his face with kisses. "I'll never call you a stuffed shirt again."

He laughed and hugged her close. "Didn't I warn you once about making promises you might not be able to keep."

A sinuous wriggle was her only reply. Derek's grin faded as desire returned with breathtaking abruptness. He rolled on top of her and crushed her erotically into the pillows.

Summer murmured her pleasure and responded wholeheartedly.

When the telephone rang, Derek cursed softly and flopped onto his back, covering his eyes with his forearm. "My sister has lousy timing," he muttered.

"You're the one who demanded that she call," Summer teased breathlessly, reaching for the telephone. "Hello?"

"Hi, Summer. Did I catch you at an inconvenient moment?" Connie's voice asked hopefully.

"You might say that," Summer replied dryly. "I take it you're not spending the night here tonight?"

"You got it. Think Derek will be mad?"

Summer eyed her impatient lover. "Nope. Does this mean that Joel's not still mad at you for almost being robbed?"

Connie sighed audibly. "Can you believe it? I had no idea I was getting involved with the Incredible Hulk. Remind me to try not to make him angry very often, will you?"

"You could always stop seeing him," Summer suggested impishly.

"No way. I seem to have a weakness for bossy men. And if you tell Derek I said that, I'll swear you lied."

Summer laughed and promised to keep quiet. "Besides," she added, "I seem to have the same weakness."

"Yeah. Who'd a believed it?" Connie paused, then spoke again. "By the way, Summer, I think you and I need to have a talk with these two guys about what they used to do before they became respectable businessmen."

Summer grinned. She'd known Connie wouldn't be fooled for long. Derek had a tendency to underestimate his sister's intelligence. "We'll do that. Good night, Connie. Have fun."

Connie giggled. "You, too, kid. Bye."

Summer replaced the receiver and turned to Derek. "Connie's staying at Joel's tonight."

"That decision," Derek replied unconcernedly, "is entirely up to her."

"My, my," Summer drawled. "Is this Derek the Dictator speaking?"

"Umm. See what you've done to me?"

A tantalizing smile played around the corners of her kiss-swollen mouth as Summer looked at his tousled hair, which once again was displaying an endearing tendency to curl, his gleaming silver eyes and his almost boyish grin. She remembered the grim memories that had been in his eyes when she'd first met him, understanding now what had put them there. He had needed her in his life then, just as she had needed him. "I like what I've done to you," she told him, no longer teasing.

"So do I, Summer-love. So do I."

He pulled her down beside him and began to demonstrate quite thoroughly just how much he loved her.

"JUST LOOK AT the two of them standing there."

In response to Connie's grumble, Summer turned her head and looked across the room to where Derek and Joel stood in quiet conversation in front of the impressive glass wall of Derek's living room. All around them the room was filled with chattering, laughing guests in brightly colored garments. Derek wore a beautifully tailored suit of a light gray fabric almost exactly the color of his eyes; Joel had chosen to wear navy. They looked exactly like two respectable, dignified businessmen. Summer turned back to her former roommate, tilting her head so that she could look up at the taller woman from beneath the small, net-trimmed brim of her white hat. "They look like a couple of stuffed shirts, don't they?" she murmured with a laugh.

Connie sighed, straightening the full skirt of her emerald-green bridesmaid's dress. "That's exactly what we would have thought only a few months ago. What happened to us, Summer?"

"We were conned," Summer answered without hesitation. "Completely taken in by a couple of mild-mannered businessmen with the souls of adventurers."

"They wear their disguises well," Connie mused, turning her gaze back across the room to look lovingly at the two men who'd made such changes in her life and Summer's.

"Very well, indeed," Summer agreed. "Excuse me, Connie, my mother's trying to have a conversation with Clay. I think she might need rescuing."

Connie grinned. "Your scheme to fix Clay up with Autumn certainly bombed, didn't it?"

"Did it ever. They've been chatting like old buddies from the minute they met. No chemistry at all."

"Ah, well. Maybe you can fix him up with Spring when she's able to visit you." To everyone's disappointment Spring had come down with a minor illness that prevented her joining the rest of her family for the wedding, but she had promised to visit Summer and Derek in a few months.

Summer burst into laughter. "Now *that* would be funny." Her eyes danced as she thought of her quiet sister paired with Crazy Clay.

Derek turned in the direction of Summer's laughter, his heart warmed, as always, by the musical sound. He could feel his mouth tilting into a besotted smile at the sight of the petite, glowing woman who had been his wife for almost half an hour. She looked so beautiful in her mother's antique lace, tea-length wedding gown. Already he was counting the minutes until he could be alone with her.

"I don't know about you, but I always start to worry when the two of them laugh like that," Joel murmured at Derek's side. "What do you suppose they're planning?"

"I don't know," Derek replied with his piratical grin.

"But, whatever it is, we can handle it, my friend. Excuse me."

His long, confident strides moved him quickly through the crowded room to his wife's side. He smiled at his thoroughly charmed mother-in-law as he slipped his arm around Summer's waist. "You and Connie weren't laughing at Joel and me a few moments ago, were you, Summerlove?" he asked her softly.

She looked at him with innocent blue eyes. "Why, Derek, would we do that?"

He chuckled. "Frequently."

"So," she challenged him lovingly, "what are you going to do about it?"

With a quick glance at her mother Derek leaned over and whispered into his wife's ear exactly what he planned to do about it. His suggestion was definitely at odds with his appearance of utter respectability.

Blushing scarlet, Summer smiled in eager anticipation.

Her wish was his command....

HERO FOR THE ASKING

by Gina Wilkins

1

"SO WHAT'S THIS older sister of yours like, Summer? Am I going to fall madly in love with her?"

Summer Anderson smiled fondly at the lethally handsome blond male who'd thrown himself on the floor at her feet as she rested in an easy chair in her den. She'd found Clay McEntire on her doorstep when she'd returned home from her college class—not an unusual occurrence at her Sausalito house, where her friends often dropped by unexpectedly on Friday evenings. "Not likely," she told him. "I don't think she's your type."

"Since when do you know my type?" he demanded challengingly, grinning up at her. "So far you've tried to fix me up with about a dozen women, and none of them was my type."

"I had such hopes for you and Autumn," Summer mourned with a dramatic sigh, her eyes sparkling mischievously beneath her heavy fringe of golden-brown bangs. "You were supposed to meet her at my wedding and be knocked right onto your cute tush."

"Autumn is certainly a knockout," Clay agreed solemnly. "I liked her very much."

"You treated her like a kid sister," Summer complained.

"She *is* a kid sister."

Summer sighed gustily. "Mine, not yours, idiot."

"So tell me about Spring. God, those names. What would your parents have done if they'd had a fourth daughter born in December? Anyway, all I know about Spring is that she's an optometrist and she's a couple of years older than you."

Summer laughed. "I've always been glad that my par-

ents stopped with three kids. Can you imagine going
through life with the name Winter Reed? Sounds like a flavor of LIFE SAVERS. Anyway, about Spring. First off,
she's not a couple of years older than I am. She'll be
twenty-seven in two months—her birthday's May 14—
and I'll be twenty-six in July. She's very fair—blond hair,
violet eyes, English-rose complexion. She's taller than I
am, five-seven, and slender. Like a model. She takes after
our Scandinavian maternal grandmother."

"Don't any of you sisters look alike?" Clay asked in
amusement, remembering Autumn's earthy, auburn-
haired, green-eyed beauty. Summer's wholesomely attractive features matched her cheerfully extroverted personality—enormous blue eyes, uptilted nose, golden tan,
petite frame. From what Clay had heard of the family, it
seemed as if the Reed sisters had inherited entirely different features to match their very individual personalities.

"Not a bit," Summer replied gaily. "As far as personality goes, Spring is hard to describe. She's a little like my
Derek in some ways. Serious on the surface but with a
lively sense of humor hidden underneath. Hardworking,
ambitious, goal oriented. Punctual, conscientious, responsible."

Clay chuckled and shook his golden head as he shifted
to a more comfortable position on the plush beige carpet of
Summer's den. "She's going to hate me, right?"

"I said she wasn't your type," Summer pointed out.
"But, to be perfectly honest with you, I think Spring is
bored out of her mind. She's tired of always being responsible and mature, and just itching to do something really
crazy for a change. She'd never admit it, of course, but I
still believe it's true. I think I'll advise her to have a mad
passionate affair while she's visiting me. It would do her a
world of good."

Clay held up both hands in a gesture meant to call attention to himself. "Sounds good to me. Where do I sign up?"

Summer laughed. "With Spring."

"I can but try."

"Don't blame me if you get shot down."

He looked affronted. "Why? I'm reasonably attractive and definitely available."

"You're more than reasonably attractive and you know it, you gorgeous hunk," Summer teased. "But let's face it, Clay. Spring is going to take one look at those clothes of yours and shudder. You won't get to say a word."

"What's wrong with my clothes?" Clay demanded, shoving himself to his feet and looking down at his lean, six-foot-four length. He wore an unbuttoned purple-yellow-and-white-printed cotton shirt over a yellow T-shirt and baggy white pleated pants. A purple print bandana was knotted around his neck. His sockless feet were tied into bright yellow Reeboks with green laces in the left shoe and red in the right. For Clay, he was actually dressed quite conservatively.

"You don't really want me to answer that."

"Oh, well." He dismissed her criticism with an indolent shrug. "Just remember to tell your lovely sister that I'm willing if she decides to take you up on your advice to have a mad passionate affair. Satisfaction guaranteed."

"Oh, the ego of the man," Summer murmured, her eyes turned toward the ceiling.

"Just stating the facts, ma'am," he drawled.

Summer shook her head sadly. "When it comes right down to it, I'll have to step in and protect her from you, anyway. What I really want is to get her fixed up permanently. You know what they say about us happily married women. We can't stand it until all our friends are suitably wed."

"You'll just have to limit your matchmaking to your sisters. No woman's going to want to find herself married to me."

"Now you're going to hide again behind all those poor troubled kids you work with," Summer muttered with an audible sigh of disgust.

"It's the truth, Summer," Clay protested, more seriously than before. "You know those kids take all my time."

"Hey, don't I work with the same kids? I give many
hours to Halloran House, and I'm planning to work at it
full-time when I finish my degree, but that doesn't mean I
have to sacrifice time with my husband or the family he
and I plan to have. Face it, Clay, your work is a very convenient excuse to keep you from committing yourself. You
could make some adjustments if you tried. You just
haven't found a woman yet who made you want to compromise."

"Summer!" a woman's voice called out from the doorway. "Oh, hi, Clay. Is Spring here yet? We can't wait to
meet her."

"No, not yet. She and Derek should be here any minute," Summer answered, rising to greet the couple who'd
just entered her den. Derek's sister, Connie, with her
bright, improbably red hair and brilliantly toned trendy
clothing, made an interesting contrast to the conservatively dressed man at her side, but one had only to look at
them to know that Connie Anderson and Joel Tanner were
very much in love. The hefty diamond engagement ring
on Connie's left hand was further evidence of their commitment.

Clay watched Summer and Connie with a fond smile.
He'd known Summer since she'd moved to San Francisco
from Arkansas over two years earlier. He'd met Connie
when she and Summer had shared an apartment in San
Francisco while both of the attractive young women were
unattached and dedicated to serious partying when they
weren't working at their mutual place of employment.
Clay loved them both but had never considered himself *in*
love with either. He wondered why.

Even as he joined the conversation around him, he
found himself thinking about what Summer had said just
before Connie and Joel had entered the room. She'd accused him of using his work with troubled teenagers as an
excuse to avoid commitment. He wondered for a moment
if she was right, then hastily denied the suggestion to himself. There was no question in his mind that his dedication

to the kids was genuine and demanding. He wasn't using that as an excuse…was he?

Of course, Summer had been right about one thing. He had never found a woman who made him want to try to change the way his life was now. And it wasn't for lack of trying. At thirty-four, almost thirty-five, Clay experienced the usual healthy desires for a wife and family. He loved children, would like to have one or two of his own. *Could he make time in his life for a family if he found the right woman?*

"So, Clay, how's it going?"

Shaking off his atypical self-scrutiny, Clay grinned at Joel and threw an arm across the other man's shoulders. "Joel, my friend, have I mentioned that we're having a fund-raising drive at Halloran House this week?"

Joel and Clay were almost exactly the same height and age and made a striking picture for the woman who stood in the doorway, looking around in bewilderment. Spring Reed blinked through the glasses perched on her nose at the number of people in the room where she'd expected to find only her sister. Then she stared in feminine appreciation at the two men directly across from her. Both of them were extraordinarily handsome. One was dark-haired, blue-eyed, with a gleam of white teeth beneath a silky dark mustache. But it was the other who made Spring's pulse do an odd little skip and jump.

He was gorgeous. She could think of no other word for him. Thick, slightly shaggy golden-blond hair, classic features and a smile that could easily grace the cover of a popular magazine—*GQ* and *Esquire* came immediately to her mind. The slim but well-developed build of an athlete—baseball, she thought, or perhaps tennis. Then she noted his clothing, her disapproving gaze lingering on his mismatched shoelaces. *One of Summer's oddball friends,* she thought, almost smiling as she tried to picture her ex-boyfriend Roger in such strange attire. Of course, to Roger, leaving off one's tie was ultracasual.

California, she thought wryly, acknowledging a faint

twinge of culture shock as she looked away from the colorfully dressed man to find her sister talking to a beautiful woman with copper-red hair and a beaming expression. Her brother-in-law, Derek, placed a hand lightly in the middle of Spring's back, as if sensing her sudden attack of shyness, and she gave him a grateful smile.

An unexpected illness had prevented her from attending her sister's wedding five months earlier, so Spring hadn't met Derek until he'd picked her up at San Francisco International Airport less than an hour before. He had proven to be a little different than what she had expected. The photographs she'd seen had faithfully recorded his almost militarily short tobacco-brown hair, pewter-gray eyes that peered so intensely through dark-rimmed glasses, hard, rugged good looks. But film hadn't been able to capture the almost palpable strength that radiated from Derek Anderson's firm, lean body, nor the hint of the predator beneath the veneer of a civilized businessman.

Spring had been startled to learn that her free-spirited, nonconformist, twenty-five-year-old sister had married a respectable, seemingly average, thirty-seven-year-old management consultant. Now she suspected that there was more to Derek Anderson than met the eye—something that her perceptive sister must have noticed from the beginning. With Derek close behind her Spring moved to greet her sister, whom she hadn't seen in almost eighteen months.

Clay felt Spring's eyes on him from the moment she appeared in the doorway. He looked up and froze, forgetting Joel, forgetting his own name. It wasn't that she was the most beautiful woman he'd ever seen, though she was striking. Pretty, he thought. The word fit her perfectly. Silvery-blond hair, fine as swan's down, pinned into a loose knot on the top of her head with soft little tendrils escaping all around. Light-framed glasses perched on a short, straight nose. Through the glasses he could see her eyes— slightly almond shaped, appearing almost purple from where he stood. Her face was delicately rounded, her mouth seductively painted with a color that fell somewhere between pink and coral. A heather-pink suit clung lovingly to her beautiful body.

Spring, he thought. Yes, the name suited.

He watched her eyes widen as they met his, pleased to sense an answering attraction there. Then he saw her gaze drop to his clothes. He narrowed his eyes, wondering if he'd imagined a slight curl to her lips.

Oh, great, Clay thought ruefully, watching Derek leading her across the room to be warmly welcomed by her sister. *The most fascinating woman I've seen in ages and she turns out to be a snob.* Summer had told him that her sister was rather conservative, but he'd assumed she'd exaggerated. How could free-spirited, warmly accepting Summer be related to a woman who seemed so opposite? He wondered how long it would be until he had the opportunity to confirm his first impression, and found himself hoping he was wrong about Spring.

Spring extricated herself from her sister's enthusiastic hug and smiled into Summer's eyes. "You look so happy!" she remarked with pleasure. She couldn't remember ever seeing such a look of contentment on Summer's face, though Summer had always been one to relish life. Even before the accident over five years earlier that had left her with a permanent limp from a shattered kneecap, Summer had never looked happier to Spring than she did now. "Marriage definitely agrees with you."

"Yes, it does," Summer agreed. "Are you surprised?"

Spring only smiled.

Summer turned to the attractive redhead standing just behind her. "Spring, I want you to meet Connie."

Before Spring could do more than exchange greetings with Summer's best friend and former roommate, the gorgeous blond male she'd noticed a few moments earlier stepped close to her side. Too close, she thought, wondering why she was suddenly having trouble with her breathing. She moistened her lower lip as she smiled tentatively at him.

"So you're Summer's sister," he began in a silky voice, his blue-green eyes glinting with an expression she couldn't begin to read. He offered her his hand and gave her a smile that made her toes curl. "That's a very nice suit you're wearing, but how do you keep from choking with your blouse buttoned up to your throat that way?"

Summer groaned audibly.

"I'm Clay McEntire," the man went on, clinging to Spring's hand and ignoring Summer. "Affectionately known to our little circle of friends as 'Crazy Clay.' I can't imagine where they came up with such a nickname, but you know how those things tend to stay with you. Do you have any nicknames?"

Spring cleared her throat and tugged lightly at her hand, wondering what the man was doing. Why did she have the feeling that he was testing her in some way? What sort of reaction was he hoping to evoke from her? She thought longingly of Little Rock, where people just said "Hello" or "Nice to meet you." She'd just *known* she'd be out of place in proudly unpredictable California!

As the others smiled with fond indulgence at Clay, Spring gave him a cool smile and fibbed that it was nice to meet him, deciding to ignore his question about nicknames. She pulled a little harder at her hand, noting that his hold was anything but light. Definitely a tennis grip, she decided, hoping he couldn't feel her rapid pulse in her fingers.

"Would you like to go outside with me?" Clay offered in a low, suggestive voice. "I could show you the pool."

"I think I'll wait until later, thank you," Spring answered, wishing again that she was back in Little Rock. Who was this guy, anyway? Her eyes turned toward Summer, pleading for help.

"Later is fine," Clay said cheerfully. "Just let me know when you're ready."

"Clay, stop manhandling my sister and behave yourself," Summer scolded, interceding with a light laugh. She reached to firmly pull Spring's hand out of Clay's grasp. "Ignore him, Spring. The rest of us do."

It sounded like good advice, but Spring had a feeling that Clay McEntire was going to be hard to ignore. He was still standing so close to her that she could almost feel the heat radiating from his very nice body. She tried hard to convince herself that he was not igniting an answering flame in her.

Then she was introduced to Joel, who turned out to be Connie's fiancé, and she was relieved when he seemed perfectly normal. Thank goodness he wasn't another screwball like Clay!

"It's very nice to meet you, Spring," Joel greeted her in his pleasantly soft voice. "Everyone was disappointed when you couldn't come to California with the rest of your family for the wedding."

"Not half as disappointed as I was," Spring answered truthfully. Summer and Derek had graciously offered to postpone the wedding when Spring had become ill, but she had refused to allow it. She had no intention of ever letting anyone know that she'd cried herself to sleep on the night of the wedding, lying in her Little Rock apartment, lonely, feverish and ill.

Summer giggled. "I'm sorry," she told her sister, no regret evident in her voice. "I shouldn't laugh at you for being sick—but chicken pox! At your age!"

Spring sighed in resignation. She had expected this. "I knew you found the whole thing hysterically funny—that I missed catching chicken pox in school when you and Autumn had them, then caught them from one of my patients at the age of twenty-six. I'm sure you were sorry that I couldn't come to your wedding, but don't tell me you didn't have a laugh at my expense."

"We all know that your sister has a rather warped sense of humor," Derek murmured straight-faced, his eyes gleaming at his adored wife.

"Definitely warped," Spring agreed in amusement. She had liked her brother-in-law from the moment she'd met him at the airport. She knew now that she was going to love him like the big brother she'd always wanted.

"So, Summer, what's for dinner?" Connie asked brightly.

Summer looked at Connie with a teasingly lifted eyebrow. "Funny, I don't remember asking you to dinner."

"Oh, let her and Joel stay, Summer," Clay urged. "There's always room for two more."

"I didn't invite you, either," she returned without hesitation.

"Three more, then," he amended with his best toothpaste-ad smile. "You wouldn't deny us the opportunity to get to know your beautiful sister, would you?"

Deny him, deny him, Spring silently begged.

Summer looked straight into her sister's eyes, quite obviously read her thoughts and laughed. "Okay, you can stay," she told Clay, winking impudently at Spring. "It'll give Spring something to write in her diary."

Clay slipped an arm around Spring's stiff shoulders. "I'm very good at providing diary material," he murmured into her ear.

"I'm sure you are," Spring replied, adroitly sidestepping his loose embrace. "But I prefer to fill my diary with *non*fiction."

With one of his rare grins creasing his lean cheeks Derek punched Clay lightly on the shoulder. "You may have just met your match, my man."

Clay smiled at Spring in a way that melted her lower vertebrae. "You know, Derek, you just might be right," he answered.

"OH, SPRING, it's so good to see you." Summer hugged her sister hard, then returned to the lettuce she was shredding for a salad. "It seems like so long since we've been together."

Neatly slicing a plump tomato, Spring smiled somewhat sadly, thinking of how little time she was able to spend with her sisters now that they were all grown and could really enjoy being together. "It has been a long time. I've missed you."

"Me, too. Of course, the telephone company loves me."

Spring laughed. "We should both own stock by now. Every month I pay for calls to you in California, to Autumn in Florida and to Mom and Dad in Rose Bud. The phone bill's almost as high as my rent."

"Derek's never complained about ours, but he always takes a deep breath before he opens the envelope."

"I like him, Summer."

Summer glowed. "I'm glad. I knew you would. The two of you have a lot in common, actually. I told him that the day after I met him."

"Did you?" Spring cut the last tomato and reached for a cucumber. "I loved the letters you sent me about your, um, unusual courtship. Swept you right off your feet, didn't he?"

"I'll say," Summer agreed with a laugh. "He told me he loved me exactly one week and two days after we met. Scared me witless."

"Why?"

"I thought it was infatuation, that he'd change his mind after getting to know me better. I was already so crazy about him by then that I knew I'd be destroyed if he left. Thank God he was able to convince me that what he felt was real."

Spring sighed wistfully. "I envy you, Summer. You and Derek look so happy. So do Connie and Joel."

Summer turned and leaned back against the counter, studying her sister's face. "So what happened between you and Roger? All I know is that you were seeing him steadily for several months and then you stopped."

Spring tried to look as if she were concentrating on the cucumber in front of her. "Nothing really happened," she replied vaguely. "It just didn't work out."

"Funny, that's exactly the same thing you said when you broke up with James and then Gary."

"So what can I say?" Spring asked lightly. "None of

them worked out. I guess I'm just not cut out for permanence in my relationships."

"Don't give me that. You wouldn't envy Connie and me so much if you didn't want the same thing for yourself. I've always thought you were the type who wanted marriage and children as well as your career."

"I do," Spring confessed. "Very much. But every time I start thinking of permanence with any of the men I've dated, I begin to back out of the relationship. I must be more attached to my single state than I realize."

"Or maybe you prefer your single state over marriage to any of the men you've dated," Summer countered. "I never met Roger, but if he was anything like James and Gary, we're talking b-o-r-i-n-g."

"They weren't—Well, maybe they were a little boring, but they were all fine, respectable men."

"So maybe you don't want a fine, respectable man. Maybe what you need is a bit of a scoundrel."

"Don't be ridiculous."

"Who's being ridiculous?" Summer demanded. "This is your sister you're talking to, Spring Deborah Reed. I know who your heroes were when you were growing up. You drooled over old Clark Gable films, you kept a poster of Burt Reynolds taped to your closet door and *M*A*S*H* was your all-time favorite television program because Hawkeye Pierce made you break out in a sweat. More recently you've had a not-so-secret crush on Harrison Ford. These are not fine, respectable men, Sis. They're scoundrels."

"All very well for fantasy, but not for real life. Look at me, Summer. I'm an average, unexciting optometrist who is perfectly content to live her entire life in Little Rock, Arkansas. I'm not exactly Carole Lombard, who wouldn't have been happy with anything but a scoundrel, as you put it."

"I *am* looking at you," Summer replied seriously. "I see a beautiful blonde who's always had to be the responsible big sister, the pride and joy of the Reed family, the only one in several generations to finish college and go on to graduate work. The only one ever to earn the title Doctor."

"A term of respect. I'm not an M.D."

"But you're a damned good optometrist. You've told me so many times," Summer added with a smile. "You're also bored. Admit it."

Spring abandoned the cucumber. "Okay," she conceded, turning to face her sister. "Sometimes I get a little bored. Not with my work—I love that. But my personal life is not exactly scintillating. If I kept a diary, it would look very little different than my appointment calendar at the office. Not just nonfiction but noninteresting."

"So what are you going to do about it?"

"I have no idea. What would you suggest?"

"Fall madly in love, get married and have a houseful of kids," Summer suggested promptly.

"Sounds lovely, but since I'm not even dating anyone at this time, it's a bit impractical."

"Okay, so have an affair. A crazy, no-strings-attached, passionate affair. Clay's already volunteered, as a matter of fact."

Spring flushed vividly. "You discussed this with that…with Clay?"

"Only a little," Summer answered with mock innocence. "He thought my idea was brilliant."

"Someday, Summer Linda Reed, I am going to kill you. Slowly," Spring added, pushing irritably at her glasses, which were beginning to slide down her nose. "Besides, if I *were* going to have an affair—which I'm not—it certainly wouldn't be with Clay."

"What's wrong with Clay?"

"My God, Summer, how can you even ask? The way he's dressed, the way he acts—definitely not my type."

"Do you always judge people by appearances, Spring? When are you going to learn that a three-piece suit and a tie don't make a man? Clay's a wonderful, caring person. He loves to laugh and tease—as he did with you—and he's warm and very demonstrative in his affections. He's always got his arm around someone. As a matter of fact, Derek threatened to break that arm a few times before he realized that Clay wasn't getting too cozy with me. It's a shame there aren't more men who are as comfortable with their feelings and emotions as Clay. Yes, he dresses a bit oddly, but even that is due to his lively sense of humor. He likes making people smile."

It wasn't the first time that Spring had been chastised by her younger sister for her conservative nature—or made to feel vaguely guilty about those circumspect tendencies. "He's just not my type," she reiterated somewhat gruffly. "That man is strange, Summer."

"True," Summer agreed gravely. "But he's certainly not boring."

No, Spring didn't think Clay McEntire would ever be called boring. A lot of other things, maybe, but never boring.

"There's the doorbell," Summer said unnecessarily, sparing Spring the need to comment further on Clay McEntire. "Our pizzas are here. Connie should have the table set by now, so would you give me a hand with the salad stuff?"

"Sure." Spring turned and gathered an armful of forks and salad bowls, then found herself taking a deep breath for courage before joining the others in the dining room. She had to ask herself why she felt that she needed courage. She didn't have to answer herself, though, because the first person she saw when she entered the room was Clay. And he looked even better now than he had before, if that was possible. Damn.

2

THE DINNER WAS certainly…interesting, Spring thought some time later. She hadn't heard such snappy repartee since the last Neil Simon movie she'd seen. Summer, of course, was a compulsive cutup, and Connie was just like her. With their dry wit and subtle humor Derek and Joel made perfect counterpoints to their irrepressible mates. And Clay…

Clay. Spring wasn't sure exactly how she felt about Clay. She was definitely attracted to him; there was no question about that. And she thought that perhaps he was as attracted to her. He was funny, he was charming, he was exciting. Maybe Summer was right about Spring having a weakness for scoundrels. Of course, she also dearly loved strawberry shortcake, but she knew better than to indulge. She was allergic to strawberries.

The frivolity continued after dinner, when everyone moved to the den for a game of Trivial Pursuit. Spring found herself partnered with Clay, which gave him an excuse to sit close beside her on a cozy love seat. She tried very hard to pay attention to the game, but how could she concentrate on History or Art and Literature when there was such a gorgeous male draping himself all over her? She was, after all, only human.

When she found herself mentally counting the number of times his enticingly close chest rose and fell with his breathing, she knew she needed a few moments alone to get control of herself. Summer called an intermission so that she could make coffee and slice a chocolate cake, and Spring took advantage of the opportunity to slip down the hallway to the guest room, where Derek had carried her bags.

There she plopped down on the edge of the bed, not even noticing the lovely decor of the tastefully frilly room as she wondered what on earth was wrong with her. It was almost as if in leaving Little Rock she'd left behind the rigid code of responsible behavior that she'd lived by for as long as she could remember. She wasn't normally attracted to offbeat, probably shallow men such as Clay McEntire. In Little Rock she wouldn't have looked twice at such a man. Well, she amended, she might have looked. More than twice. But would she have found him so utterly fascinating?

She found herself wondering if he really had volunteered to have a passionate affair with her. Would he be as unpredictable in bed as he was out of it? She suspected that he would be imaginative, sensitive, considerate, and just downright good.

"Oh, my God, what am I doing?" she groaned, shaking her head to dispel any such thoughts. "I just met the man, for pete's sake." She had never indulged in casual, recreational sex, nor was she about to begin now. "I'm not," she repeated out loud for emphasis.

She stood and glared determinedly into the mirror on one wall of the bedroom. She looked the same as usual. Hair still properly pinned on top of her head, white silk blouse neatly tucked into the waistband of the straight heather-pink skirt that matched the jacket she'd discarded earlier. She hadn't changed at all since arriving in California. Nor would she.

"Right," she said, nodding crisply at her reflection. Then she stepped out of the door of her bedroom and straight into the arms of Clay McEntire.

"Sorry," he murmured, though he didn't look at all sorry to find himself standing in the hallway with his arms around her. "Are you okay?"

"I'm fine," she replied. Dammit, her voice had gone all

breathless again, she noticed in disgust. "What are you doing?" Was he following her?

His lovely blue-green eyes twinkled with mischievous amusement as he nodded toward the door beside her bedroom. "That's the bathroom," he replied. "I had planned on visiting it. Okay with you?"

She flushed, trying to disengage herself from the strong arms that had tightened around her slim waist. "You certainly don't need my permission."

"For anything?"

"Of course not," she answered curtly, squirming against him. The movement made her want to groan with the pleasure-pain it caused her.

"Oh, in that case—" He smothered his own words against her mouth as he leaned her back against the wall and kissed her with painstaking thoroughness.

Had it been possible, Spring would have gulped. As it was, she went rigid with surprise. Much later she would try to convince herself that she'd parted her lips only to protest his impertinence. But whatever the reason, her action gave him the perfect opportunity to deepen the kiss—and he did.

Her fists clenched his shoulders when his tongue swept the inside of her mouth, exploring and claiming it. At the same time his hands began an exploration of their own, sweeping from her shoulders to her hips in long, arousing strokes. Spring moaned low in her chest, her eyes closing behind the glasses that were pressed crookedly between their faces. When she found herself wishing the glasses were out of the way so that the kiss could continue more comfortably, she opened her eyes wide and renewed her struggle to free herself. She twisted her head so that the kiss was broken and shoved against him with all her strength. "What are you doing?"

He chuckled shakily, though he allowed her to put several inches between them. "This time I think the answer is obvious, sweet Spring. I'm trying to seduce you."

"You—" She stopped to swallow. "Oh."

He laughed. "Yes, oh. You're enchanting, did you know that? May I kiss you again, or do you still insist that I don't need your permission?"

"No! I mean, no, you can't kiss me again. Clay, I don't even know you!"

"*That* situation can easily be changed," he murmured meaningfully, lifting a hand to trace her slightly swollen lower lip.

"No." She shook her head emphatically. "I'm only going to be here for twelve days, Clay."

"That's plenty of time," he replied, unperturbed, his fingers stroking her cheek.

"Look, I know things are…different in California, but I'm from Arkansas and I don't, well, to be blunt, I don't sleep with just anyone I happen to find attractive. So whatever Summer may have told you, I'm not interested in a vacation affair."

"Okay, so seduction is out," Clay replied cheerfully. A little too cheerfully, Spring thought with illogical resentment. Couldn't he at least have made a token protest? "How about friendship?" he continued. "Are you interested in making a new friend on your vacation, sweet Spring?"

"It *is* possible that we could be friends," Spring agreed cautiously. "But only on one condition."

"What's that?" he inquired, his fingers moving to the vulnerable spot just behind her ear.

"Stop calling me 'sweet Spring.'"

Clay laughed. "Fair enough." He kissed her cheek, briefly, barely touching her, then moved away. "If you'll excuse me, I think I'll visit that room next door."

He paused at the doorway of the bathroom. "Oh, and, Spring?"

"Yes?"

"I don't sleep with just anyone, either. I don't happen to think Arkansans and Californians are all that different." He shut the door behind him as he entered the bathroom, leaving her standing in the hallway with her mouth open.

Moments later Spring stood once again before the mirror in her bedroom. Only this time the woman who stared back at her looked slightly different. Her neat knot of hair had loosened, allowing more tendrils to fall around her flushed face, her glasses were crooked and the white silk blouse was only halfway tucked into her skirt. Her sister had been right about one thing, she thought as she tried to straighten her appearance. Clay certainly was a toucher!

Summer had been right about something else, she added to herself in wary bemusement.

Clay certainly was *not* boring.

A short time later Spring toyed with the slice of cake her sister had served her, studiously avoiding Clay's gaze, though she could feel him watching her with laughter dancing in his eyes. Whether he was enjoying a private joke with her or simply laughing at her provincial response to his blatant pass, she didn't know. Nor did she attempt to guess. She was much too busy trying to forget the feel of his lips on hers and his arms around her.

The extension telephone hidden discreetly in a carved wooden box on a glossy end table rang, and Summer, who was closest, answered it. The others in the room lowered their conversation for her benefit, so everyone heard her say, "Frank? What's wrong?"

She listened for a moment, then exclaimed, "Oh, no! When?"

Clay straightened abruptly on the love seat beside Spring, his full attention directed to Summer. Spring noticed that her sister's eyes turned immediately in Clay's direction as she listened to the person on the other end of the line. "Yes, he's here," Summer said into the receiver. "I'll tell him. Please call me if you hear anything, Frank."

Before she'd even replaced the receiver in the box, Clay was up, standing over Summer's chair as he demanded, "What's wrong? What did Frank want?"

"Thelma Sawyer has run away again," Summer answered with a deep sigh. "She hasn't been home in a

week. Her mother just got around to contacting Frank to
ask if he's seen her."

Clay flinched visibly and shoved his hand through his
thick golden hair. "Damn. What happened?"

"Frank said she had another fight with her mother."
Summer pushed herself out of her chair and looked up at
Clay. "What will happen to her this time, Clay? Will they
let her go back to Halloran?"

"Not likely," Clay answered briefly.

Spring watched them closely, thinking that Clay looked
somehow older than he had only a few minutes earlier.
She knew that her sister worked part-time at Halloran
House, a home for troubled teenagers, while she attended
classes to obtain a degree in education so that she could
work with the young people full-time. Spring hadn't
known that Clay was in any way involved with the project.

"Clay," Summer said softly, leaning into Derek's arm as
he offered comfort to his obviously distressed wife. "What
if she gets into trouble again?"

Clay exhaled. "I don't know, Summer," he admitted.
He straightened abruptly. "I'm going out to look for her."

"I'll go with you."

"No." He shook his head at Summer's offer. "You stay
here with your guests. I'm going to check with some of
Thelma's friends and a few other sources. I'll call you if I
find out anything."

"You'd better." Summer tugged him downward so that
she could kiss his cheek. "Good luck."

"Yeah." Clay bade good-night to the others, then turned
to Spring. "I'll see you again, sweet, uh, Spring," he corrected himself with a weak facsimile of his devilish smile.

"Good night, Clay," Spring answered, surreptitiously
eyeing the lines that had suddenly appeared around his
eyes. Perhaps he wasn't as shallow as she'd first thought,
she decided, watching him leave. The news of Thelma's
disappearance had obviously shaken him badly.

"This is really a shame," Connie said as Spring turned

her attention back to the others. "Thelma can be so sweet. That mother of hers ought to be locked up for treating her daughter so badly."

"Oh, they can't do that," Summer answered bitterly. "Mrs. Sawyer doesn't physically abuse Thelma. The state chooses to ignore verbal abuse. After all, that kind doesn't leave bruises—none that show, anyway."

"This is rough on poor Clay." Connie twisted a copper-red curl around one scarlet-tipped finger, her expression sympathetic. "Thelma's always been one of his favorites, hasn't she?"

"Yes."

"Yours, too," Derek murmured to Summer, his arm tightening around her shoulders. "I'm sorry, darling. Is there anything I can do to help?"

Summer shook her head. "If anyone can find her, Clay can. I just hope he's not too late."

"How old is Thelma?" Spring asked.

"Fifteen," Summer whispered miserably. "She's only fifteen, dammit."

Spring bit her lower lip. "That's so young. I wonder where she'll go?"

Summer shrugged. "Who knows? The streets are full of runaways. They develop a talent for not being seen. She may even have left town, though she never has before. It's not the first time she's run away," she explained, "but last time she got into so much trouble that Clay almost couldn't bail her out. He was able to get her readmitted as a resident at Halloran House then, but I don't think he'll be able to now. Halloran House is only for those kids who aren't considered to be truly hard cases. Most of them are there at the insistence of their parents rather than the juvenile courts."

"What does Clay have to do with Halloran House?" Spring finally asked, unable to contain her curiosity any longer.

"Haven't I mentioned that?" Summer asked, surprised. "Clay was one of the people responsible for getting Halloran House started a few years ago. He's on the board of directors and he spends most of his spare time there, counseling the kids."

"Counseling?"

"Yes. He has a Ph.D. in adolescent psychology. He could be making a fortune in private practice, but instead, he's a counselor for a public junior-high school in San Francisco."

Spring had risen when Clay left. Now she abruptly sat back down. Clay McEntire had a doctorate in psychology? So much for appearances, she told herself wryly.

The call from Frank—whom Spring discovered to be Frank Rivers, the live-in director of Halloran House—had cast a pall over the evening, so Connie and Joel left not long after Clay departed.

"You must be tired, Spring. Would you like to turn in now?" Summer asked shortly afterward. It was past ten o'clock—past midnight, Arkansas time—and Spring *was* tired.

The two sisters chatted contentedly while Spring pulled on a lacy blue gown and brushed out her shoulder-length, silvery blond hair. They mentioned their parents back home in Rose Bud, Arkansas, and chuckled together over their fiery-tempered, ultraliberated sister Autumn. Twenty-four-year-old Autumn lived in Tampa, Florida, where she worked as an electrician, and her sisters always enjoyed swapping stories about her.

After a few minutes of pleasant conversation, Summer asked with suspicious nonchalance, "Is Connie anything like you'd pictured her?"

"She's exactly like I imagined she would be," Spring replied with a smile. "I like her."

"And Joel? Did you like him, too?"

"Yes, very much." Spring swallowed, knowing what was coming next. She was right.

"So," Summer went on casually, "what did you think of Clay, once you got past your first impression of him?"

Spring looked quickly down at the blouse she was folding, allowing her shoulder-length hair to hide her suddenly rosy face. Just the mention of Clay's name had taken her back to that interlude in the hallway. She could almost feel him next to her once more, and the sensation made her pulse react again with a crazy rhythm. "He was very, um..." Her voice trailed off for lack of words.

"Very 'um'?" Summer demanded quizzically. "What's 'um'? Sexy? Good-looking? Intriguing? Irresistible?"

"Okay, so he's about the most gorgeous thing I've ever seen off a movie screen," Spring admitted abruptly, glaring at her sister's smug grin. "But I still think he's strange."

"I tried to fix him up with Autumn. I thought they'd make a terrific couple. They got along great when she was here for my wedding, but unfortunately, there was just no chemistry. He never even made a pass at her," Summer complained.

"Clay and Autumn?" Spring repeated distastefully, hating the suggestion but refusing to acknowledge why. "What a dumb idea."

"Oh, you think so?" Summer asked innocently.

"Yes, I do."

"Well, then, how about Clay and Spring?"

"An even dumber idea," Spring muttered, her flush deepening.

"You know, I would have said the same thing yesterday. Now, well, maybe it's not such a dumb idea, after all," Summer mused with a grin.

"Good night, Summer," Spring said pointedly, nodding toward the door.

Summer laughed, then sobered. "I'm glad you're here, Spring," she said again. "I know we haven't had much in common in the past, but I love you, Sis. Besides, it's so nice to hear an Arkansas accent again—other than mine."

Spring chuckled, her mild irritation evaporating immediately. "I love you, too, Summer. I'm really looking forward to spending this time with you and Derek."

"It just might be interesting," Summer commented,

then ducked out the door before Spring could ask what she'd meant.

CLAY GROANED, rolled over and promptly fell onto the floor. Cursing under his breath, he sat up, combing his hair out of his eyes with his fingers, and tried to orient himself. He'd searched for Thelma most of the night, coming home around dawn so exhausted that he hadn't even made it to the bedroom. He'd fallen asleep on the couch, still fully dressed except for his shoes. Pushing himself painfully to his feet, he noted that he looked like an unmade bed and smelled like a horse. A glance at his watch told him that it was close to ll:00 a.m. Tugging off his wrinkled shirt, he headed for the shower.

Half an hour later he felt somewhat more human. He dressed in loose, double-pleated black slacks, a black-and-white cotton shirt in a bold geometric print and a crisp winter-white blazer, pushing the sleeves up on his forearms as he dug in the closet for shoes. The ones he selected were canvas deck shoes, the uppers printed in a black-and-white checkerboard pattern. He never considered wearing socks.

He went through the motions of dressing mechanically, hardly conscious of making decisions on what to wear. He was thinking about Spring. He had thought about Spring since the moment his abrupt contact with his living-room floor had awakened him. He hadn't stopped thinking about Spring since he'd looked up the night before and seen her standing in the doorway to Summer's den. Even when he'd walked the sleaziest back streets of San Francisco during the wee hours of the morning, doggedly searching for one frightened, defiant young black girl, he hadn't been able to rid his mind entirely of the beautiful blonde he'd kissed earlier.

His first impression of her—that she'd been a snob—just might have been wrong. By the end of the evening he'd found himself liking her. A lot. Oh, she was different from Summer; he'd grant that. Quieter, more inhibited, perhaps even a bit shy. Different, too, from the women he usually dated, but in a nice way.

There hadn't been many women in his life lately, other than friends. In fact, there hadn't been *any* special woman in his life since he'd stopped seeing Jessica Dixon some four months earlier. Jessica had been amusing, outrageous and beautiful, and he'd enjoyed being with her until she'd finally gotten tired of her undeniably second-place status in his life and had broken off with him in a rather ugly scene when he'd been called away from a party to bail one of his kids out of jail. He'd never made any pretense that their relationship was anything more than casual, nor had he apologized to her for the long hours he'd spent with the students and other young people he counseled. There had been times when he hadn't called her or seen her for days—sometimes for as long as a couple of weeks. He hadn't realized that she'd wanted more. He was rather ashamed to acknowledge that he hadn't really missed her.

But it couldn't be just an overlong period of celibacy that drew him so strongly to Spring Reed. After all, there had been other women during the past four months he'd found attractive, but he hadn't wanted any of them enough to do anything about it. And certainly none of them had interfered with his concentration while he was dealing with a crisis with one of his kids.

What was it about her that did this to him? It wasn't just her looks; he'd established that. Not just a need for a woman. So what? The slightly shy, intelligent glimmer in beguilingly uptilted eyes? The low gurgle of laughter that had escaped her so often during that lighthearted pizza dinner? The musical cadence of her Southern-accented voice? The way her rounded chin had firmed and lifted when she'd informed him that she didn't sleep around? Or maybe the way she'd responded so heatedly when he'd kissed her.

He wanted to see her again, find out more about the woman who'd intrigued him so. But right now he was going to continue his search for Thelma.

"OH, MY GOD, you've been mall hopping." Derek's voice was resigned as he took in the sizable stack of packages piled on the floor of his den.

The two sisters, both exhausted, looked up guiltily from their slumped positions in matching easy chairs. "We shopped a little," Summer admitted.

"A little?" Derek looked again at the tall, colorful mountain of packages. "I thought you were going sight-seeing."

"We did," Spring said with a tired smile. "We saw every shopping sight in San Francisco and Sausalito."

"I suppose you both have smoking plastic cards in your purses?"

"Guilty as charged, your honor," Summer quipped. "We went nuts. But I did buy you a new tie, if it makes you feel any better."

"How very generous of you," Derek murmured, passing the knee-high heap of purchases on his way to the bar.

"Yes, I thought so," Summer answered complacently. She shoved herself reluctantly out of the chair. "I suppose I really should shower before changing for dinner. You did say you were taking us out tonight, didn't you, darling?"

"Yes, I think I did say that," Derek replied, splashing ice-cold orange juice into a glass. "Choose someplace cheap, will you? There are still ten full shopping days left of your sister's vacation."

Spring smiled, watching as Summer kissed her husband lovingly. It was quite obvious that Summer could buy out all of Marin County and Derek wouldn't care in the least. It was also perfectly evident that Summer would never do anything that would truly upset Derek. Not for the first time, Spring had to fight down a surge of envy at her sister's good fortune.

"How was your racquetball game?" Summer asked her husband, watching as he thirstily downed the orange juice and reached for a refill.

"Strenuous," Derek answered with a grimace. "But I managed to make a decent showing."

Summer laughed. "Not bad, considering your propensity to pit yourself against twenty-five-year-old jocks." She kissed him again before she left the room, her limp more pronounced than usual, testimony to the strenuous shopping spree.

"She's tired," Derek commented, taking a seat close to Spring and stretching out to rest as he finished his juice.

She, too, had watched Summer limp away. "Yes, I know. I was just feeling guilty."

"Don't. It would take a bigger person than you to stop her once she decides she wants to go shopping. And she's delighted to have you here. She misses seeing her family."

Hardly aware of speaking aloud, Spring murmured, "She's changed."

"In what way?"

Spring absently pushed her glasses up on her nose and shrugged slightly. "I don't know, exactly. Grown up, I guess. I still can't help looking at her from a big sister's viewpoint."

"How do you like the way she's turned out?"

"I like it very much," Spring replied decisively. "She's happy, she has a direction to her life now that she's returned to school and she's learned to share her feelings more."

"And yet she still knows how to play," Derek added. "That's a special part of her. One that I needed very much."

Spring cocked her head back against her chair and eyed her brother-in-law. "Summer thinks you and I are a lot alike."

Derek nodded. "Yes, I know. I suppose she's right, in some ways. We're both organized and ambitious and rather serious, on the whole."

"Not necessarily admirable qualities from Summer's point of view."

"Ah, but she loves us both," Derek reminded her.

"True. You're exactly what she needed in a husband. She probably thinks I need someone exactly like *her*."

"Someone like Clay McEntire?" Derek murmured with a half smile. When Spring's eyes narrowed, he explained, "She seemed to find the idea rather intriguing after you went to bed last night."

"It's ridiculous, of course."

"Of course." Derek's voice was just a bit too innocuous. Spring shot him a suspicious look. "You wouldn't happen to agree with her, would you, Derek?"

"I make it a practice never to play matchmaker," Derek informed her solemnly, "despite what Summer and Connie refer to as my compulsive habit of offering advice. A hazard of being a business consultant, I suppose."

"Whatever, I have absolutely no interest in Clay McEntire," Spring stated categorically, even as she wondered whether she was trying to convince Derek or herself.

"I'm very sorry to hear that," said an already familiar voice from behind her. "Clay McEntire is most definitely interested in you."

3

SPRING STARTED and jerked her head toward the doorway, finding the very person she'd just named lounging there with a look of amusement on his much-too-handsome face. She realized that her sister must have let him in. She could think of absolutely nothing to say.

Taking pity on her, Derek spoke. "What's up, Clay? Heard anything about Thelma?"

"Not a thing," Clay answered, suddenly grim. "If anyone knows where she is, they're not talking."

Spring lifted her eyes from his unusual black-and-white ensemble to note that he looked tired. Tired and rather despondent. She was startled to find herself wanting to cheer him up. She missed his easy smile. "Can't you file a missing-persons report on her?" she asked curiously.

"Her mother did that last week. Thelma's run away before, though, and there are so many other missing-persons reports filed each week that the cops tend to give them low priority unless they have a real lead. I'm not too crazy about having the cops haul a kid back home, anyway, unless there is no other alternative."

"Can I get you something to drink, Clay?" Derek asked.

"No, thanks, Derek. I just wanted to tell Summer that I haven't been able to find Thelma."

Derek lifted one eyebrow but refrained from pointing out that Clay hadn't needed to drive into Sausalito when a telephone call would have suffced. Spring frowned, well aware of that herself.

"In that case," Derek asked, "would you like to join us for dinner? We're going out."

Sprawled in the easy chair Summer had abandoned,

Clay nudged the pile of packages on the floor before him with one black-and-white-clad foot. "Sure you can afford that? Or were all these purchases made with Arkansas money?" he teased, smiling at Spring.

"I bought my share," Spring admitted with a shy attempt at friendliness. She was very much aware that Clay had not yet accepted or declined Derek's invitation to join them for dinner. She wasn't sure which option she preferred him to take. Suddenly and inexplicably nervous, she stood and began to gather the much-discussed packages. "I suppose I should start freshening up for dinner."

"Let me help you with those," Clay volunteered immediately, jumping to his feet.

"Oh, that's not—"

But he'd already grabbed an armload and was headed for the hallway that led to the guest room. Spring pointedly avoided Derek's amused gaze as she followed Clay.

"Where do you want these?"

"Just throw them on the bed," she replied, walking past him to do so with hers.

He grinned tantalizingly and muttered something that she thought sounded vaguely like, "I'd like to throw *you* on the bed," but prudence kept her from asking him to repeat himself.

Instead, she waited until he'd unloaded his arms, then commented, "You look tired. Have you been searching for Thelma all day?"

"And most of last night," he admitted, running his fingers through his luxurious hair, his grin fading.

"Didn't you get any sleep at all?"

"About five hours. Why? Are you concerned?" he asked with interest.

She shrugged, toying with a button on her lavender cotton shirt to avoid looking at him.

When it was obvious that Spring wasn't going to answer his question, Clay shoved his hands into the deep pockets of his slightly wrinkled black slacks and flicked a glance around the room. "Are you enjoying your visit with your sister?"

"Yes."

"Did you have a good time on your shopping spree?"

"Yes."

"Do you want to have an affair with me?"

Spring almost choked. "No," she managed at last, hoping she looked more sincere than she felt.

"Do you like going to plays?"

The man was certifiable. Deciding that the course of least resistance was to humor him, Spring nodded slowly. "Yes."

"I have tickets for an opening Monday night. Will you go with me?"

"I, uh—"

"I'm only inviting you to a play, Spring, not an orgy," he told her with mock impatience. Then he added with a near smirk, "Although I'd be happy to arrange the latter, if you like."

"I think we'd better stick with the play," Spring answered hastily.

He grinned. "Okay, I'll pick you up at six-thirty. It starts early."

She'd just agreed to a date with him, Spring realized belatedly. She started to tell him she'd changed her mind, then stopped as she focused again on those tiny, weary lines at the corners of his eyes. Damn her softheartedness, she thought with a resigned sigh. She wouldn't change her mind. "Fine. Now if you'll excuse me, I need to freshen up for dinner."

"Okay." He dropped a kiss on her lips as he passed her. "See you Monday."

Her entire body tingling from that too-brief contact, Spring spoke before he was completely out of the room, detaining him. "Aren't you joining us for dinner?"

He looked back at her. "Not tonight. I'm going back out on the streets."

"But—" She stopped, then shrugged slightly and continued, "You look so tired. And you have to eat."

His handsome face softened and his mouth dipped into a warm smile, as if her concern pleased him. "I'll grab a sandwich. And I'll try to get more sleep tonight. But I have to find Thelma, if I can."

She nodded, aware of her acute disappointment and annoyed with herself for feeling it. "Good luck."

"Thank you, Spring." He looked at her for a moment longer, then left, closing her door behind him.

Spring stood so long staring at that closed door that she was almost late for dinner.

DEREK'S SECRETARY, who'd been on maternity leave for the past month, had her baby Saturday night. Summer and Derek felt obligated to pay a brief visit to the hospital on Sunday. They invited Spring to join them, but she begged off. She had always been a person who needed time alone occasionally, and knowing that, Summer did not press her to go. Promising to be back soon, Summer and Derek left shortly after lunch.

Spring relished the time to herself. As much as she was enjoying her visit, it felt good to kick off her shoes, stretch out on a lounge chair by the pool on this unseasonably warm March afternoon and dive into the pages of a book she'd brought with her from home. She had dressed more casually than was her habit in a long-sleeved aqua-and-white-print cotton pullover and snug, matching aqua jeans. Her hair was in its usual soft knot on top of her head, and she wore a minimum of makeup. She was comfortable, contented and relaxed.

Until a rich male voice interrupted her solitude and shattered her peaceful idyll. "Now this is a lovely picture."

Spring jumped, dropping her book, and jerked her head around. "Clay!" she exclaimed, her pulse racing—because he'd surprised her or because he looked so incredibly sexy? She didn't choose to analyze. He wore jeans, washed-soft Levi's worn almost white at the knees and seat and button fly. Red tennis shoes matched his old-fashioned red suspenders. The sleeves of a blue chambray work shirt were turned up on his forearms, and a battered tweed cap completed his outfit. "You startled me," she accused him breathlessly.

"I'm sorry," he apologized. "I didn't mean to. I thought I saw someone back here when I drove up, and when no one answered the doorbell, I decided to come around and see."

She eyed his clothing. "You look like the president of the Roy Underhill fan club," she told him.

Clay's blond eyebrows shot up in surprise. "Now how do you know who Roy Underhill is? Are you into woodworking?"

"Not really. But I am into remodeling old homes—theoretically, anyway—and Roy Underhill's *The Woodwright Shop* comes on PBS just before Bob Vila's *This Old House* on Sunday afternoons at home. So are you an Underhill fan?"

"As a matter of fact, I have both of his books at home in my workshop," Clay confessed. "I love working with wood."

"Are you any good?" she asked curiously.

"Oh, I'm good," he replied audaciously. "I'd be happy to demonstrate at any time."

She just managed not to blush at his innuendo by busying herself with swinging her legs over the side of her chair and sliding her feet into her white flats. "I'll let you know if I'm interested," she informed him coolly, her tone implying that the time would never come.

"You do that," he answered, his eyes telling her that it would—and sooner than she expected. "Summer's not home?"

"No, she and Derek went to the hospital to see his secretary's new baby. They should be back in another hour or so."

"What did she have? Boy or girl?" Clay inquired as he draped himself into the chair beside Spring's.

"Boy."

"That's nice."

Since he seemed to be settled in, Spring decided she might as well play hostess. "Can I get you something to drink, Clay?"

"No, thanks. Maybe later." He smiled at her, apparently quite content to be with her on this pleasant afternoon.

She relaxed a bit, silently admitting that she was content with his company, as well. If only she weren't so aware of how very attractive he looked in the afternoon sun, how well the soft fabric of his shirt and worn jeans defined his lean muscles. "Have you heard anything more about Thelma?" she asked to distract herself.

He shook his head. "No. I've got a lot of feelers out, but no leads so far. I'm pretty sure she's still in the area, but she's well hidden."

"I hope she's all right."

"So do I. What are you reading?" he inquired, deliberately changing the solemn subject.

"It's a new one by—" She stopped when the cordless telephone that she'd carried out with her earlier rang. Derek was expecting a business call later, and he'd asked her to take a message if it came in while he was away. She reached out to answer the phone, picking up the pencil and pad beside it. A moment later she held out the receiver to Clay. "It's for you. It's Frank."

"Thanks. Hi, Frank, what's up? *What?* When? Where is she? Yeah, I know where that is. Okay, I'm on my way. I'll call you later. Thanks."

He was on his feet immediately, dropping the phone onto the glass-topped patio table. "Frank's got a lead on Thelma. One of her friends broke down and told him where she's been staying. He thinks she may be ill. Tell Summer I'll call her later, will you?"

"Clay," Spring said suddenly, when he appeared to be on the verge of leaving. "Would you...?" She faltered when he turned to look questioningly at her.

"What is it, Spring?"

"I could go with you, if you'd like," she offered in a rush of words. When he looked surprised, she hurried to add, "I just thought I could help. If you think I'd only be in the way, I'll understand."

He smiled at her, that deep-cornered, male-model smile that made her leg bones soften. "Why, thank you, Spring. I would like for you to go with me."

"You're sure?"

"If you are. We won't be going into the nicer part of town."

She nodded, gathering her things and the cordless telephone to carry them into the house. "I didn't think we would be. Just let me leave a note for Summer."

"I'll wait for you in the car."

Even as she scribbled the note for her sister, Spring asked herself why she'd volunteered to accompany Clay. He obviously didn't need her help. Spring grudgingly suspected that the reason she'd suddenly offered to join Clay had been that she hadn't wanted to see him walk away. She had *definitely* left her common sense back home in Little Rock, she concluded, even as she grabbed her purse and locked all the doors.

Spring wasn't particularly surprised to discover that Clay's car was a fire-engine-red Mazda RX-7. It was exactly the type of car that she would have expected him to drive. Of course, she would have been no more surprised to find him in a psychedelic-painted van, circa 1968 San Francisco. Come to think of it, she mused, there wasn't much Clay McEntire could do that *would* surprise her.

"How old are you, Clay?" she asked as the powerful sports car sped them across the Golden Gate Bridge.

He shot her a sideways glance before answering the first question she'd asked since they'd left her sister's house. "I'll be thirty-five in June. How old do you think I look?"

She thought about that one for a moment before answering honestly. "Anywhere from mid-twenties to late-thirties, depending on your expression."

He grinned. "Guess I'll have to practice that mid-twenties expression."

She didn't bother to tell him that he looked equally devastating either way. She figured he already knew it. There had to be mirrors in his home. She wondered where he lived. And then she wondered with whom. Shifting in her seat, she searched her mind for an innocuous topic of conversation, something that would keep him from worrying about Thelma until they reached their destination, finally settling on his work. "Summer tells me that you have a Ph.D. in adolescent psychology."

"Yes."

"Do you enjoy counseling in public schools?"

"I wouldn't be doing it if I didn't enjoy it."

"No," she murmured. "You wouldn't, would you?" She couldn't imagine Clay doing anything he didn't enjoy. Unlike herself, who often acted from her overdeveloped sense of duty and responsibility at the price of personal pleasure. People like Clay, and like Summer, had a way of taking whatever life handed them and making it suit their own purposes. Spring wished she knew their secret.

"What about you?" Clay asked suddenly.

"What about me?"

"Do you ever get bored passing out prescriptions for reading glasses?"

"I might, if that was all I did. It's not. Only recently I had a patient—eight years old—who's been classified as mentally handicapped. His teacher recommended that the boy be placed in special classes for children with learning disabilities, despite his parents' belief that their son had an average IQ. After trying tutors and child psychologists they brought him to me. We discovered that he had a visual impairment—an inability to process the two separate images detected by his eyes, to put it simply. He's really a very bright child, considering what he's had to deal with. My job is particularly rewarding when children are involved."

"That sounds fascinating," Clay conceded, and the look

he turned to her was sincere. "And it seems that we have something in common if you enjoy dealing with childhood problems."

She lowered her chin and toyed modestly with her seat belt. "Not all my cases are like that," she admitted. "Most of the time I *do* pass out prescriptions for reading glasses. But I love my work."

He reached across the console to catch her left hand in his right one. "I wasn't trying to offend you when I asked that question. Sometimes I don't mean things exactly the way they leave my mouth."

"I understand. And there was no offense taken," she assured him.

"You're a very special person, Spring Reed," he said softly, lifting her hand to his mouth. "Are you sure you won't reconsider having an affair with me? I'm yours for the asking, you know."

She laughed lightly, genuinely amused, despite her concern at what they may find in a few minutes. "I'll let you know if I change my mind," she told him.

"You do that," he replied. Then he kissed her knuckles again and placed her hand back in her lap.

Spring turned her head to look out the window beside her, but her thoughts were not on the passing scenery. Instead, she thought of Clay. She liked him. She really liked him. She liked his melting smile, his offbeat humor and his obvious sensitivity. She liked his blue-green eyes, his golden hair and the pleasure he seemed to find in the most casual of touches. She was even beginning to like the way he dressed. Now *that* should have been frightening. Yet somehow it wasn't.

Broadway, with its strip joints and businesses catering to every prurient interest, had been Spring's least favorite part of the quick sight-seeing tour of San Francisco that Summer had given her the day before. Clay took her into an area that Summer had avoided altogether. He parked in front of a crumbling dump of a building that should have been condemned years earlier, and probably had been. The littered street was completely deserted in the bright afternoon sunlight, but Spring suspected that the shadows of evening would bring out all the human flotsam that would inhabit such a place. She shivered, thinking of a lonely fifteen-year-old girl. "This is where she is?"

Looking grim, Clay tugged at his tweed cap. "That's what I was told."

Something in his posture told her that he wasn't telling her everything he'd heard. She only hoped she would be able to help him. Following his lead, she took a deep breath and climbed from the car. She noticed that his eyes, no longer smiling, darted all around them as they entered the dark, unwelcoming building through a door that had long since ceased to lock or even close properly. Clay walked unerringly to a flight of bare metal stairs. "Up here," he told Spring.

She hesitated for only a moment. He reached out and took her hand. Strengthened by the contact, she nodded at him and walked just behind him up two flights to the third floor, the top floor of the building. Clay looked around for a moment, seemed to get his bearings, then led her down a hallway to their left, never releasing her hand, for which Spring was grateful. At the end of the hallway was a closed door. Clay stood for a moment before it, then knocked tentatively. "Thelma? It's Clay. Are you there?"

When no answer came from the other side of the door, Clay knocked louder. "Thelma? Come on, sweetheart, let me in. I only want to talk, to make sure you're okay. Can you hear me?"

Again, silence. Clay looked at Spring, then at the doorknob. Still holding her hand, he twisted the rusted metal knob. The door wasn't locked. It opened with a screech of angry hinges.

The smells struck her first. She didn't know what they were, nor did she want to. Her eyes were focused on the teenager sprawled on a filthy bare mattress that lay on the trash-covered floor. The girl wasn't moving. Spring was horribly afraid that she was dead.

Clay was already across the room, down on one knee in the dirt as he touched Thelma's face. He looked up at Spring, his face as expressionless as if carved of stone. "She's burning up with fever. She's very ill."

"Do you know what's wrong with her?"

"No. Flu, maybe, or pneumonia. God knows when she ate last. I was told by one of her friends that she wasn't well when she disappeared. Her mother was mad at her for missing a couple of days at her after-school job in a fast-food restaurant. Thelma's tiny salary is more important to her mother than Thelma is, it seems." Dull fury glinted in Clay's eyes, making them seem suddenly hard, without a trace of his usual laughter.

"I'll find a phone," Spring told him, moving backward.

"No." The harsh, flat syllable stopped her. "I don't want you out on those streets. I'll go. Do you mind staying with her?"

"Of course not."

Clay touched her shoulder in passing. She could feel the fine trembling in his fingers. He paused at the doorway. "You'll be okay? You're not frightened? I won't be long."

"I'm fine," Spring assured him. "Hurry, Clay. She looks so ill."

He ground out a curse between clenched teeth and ran.

Left alone with the unconscious teenager, Spring breathed deeply for courage, then almost gagged as the rank odors assaulted her again. She took Thelma's limp hand in hers, fingers closing around the thin brown wrist to monitor the reedy pulse. She's just a child, she thought, looking down at the vulnerable face. She'd been told Thelma was fifteen; she would never have guessed so from looking at her. Thelma's hair, which was now badly in need of washing, was cut to curl around her head. Long eyelashes lay on soft, full cheeks that would normally be a rich chocolate but were now ashen. Her mouth was a child's mouth, tender and full, open to expose even white teeth. Spring felt her heart twist in her chest. She eyed the girl's dirty sweatshirt and torn, faded jeans and blinked back tears. "Don't worry, Thelma. You're going to be just fine," she murmured, though she doubted that her words registered.

Thelma's breathing was labored and harsh, punctuated by a hacking cough, her skin hot and dry. Spring wished fervently that she had a cool, wet cloth to wash Thelma's face. Then she reached eagerly for the small handbag hanging from her shoulder and dug into it, coming up with one of the packaged moistened paper napkins provided by some fast-food establishments. For once she was grateful for her habit of saving possibly useful odds and ends. She ripped open the foil package, gratefully breathing in the lemony scent before gently placing it against Thelma's face, talking softly and soothingly. She thought she saw Thelma's eyes open once, briefly, but there was no other sign that she was aware of anything going on around her.

Clay found Spring that way, on her knees beside the mattress, heedless of the dirt being ground into her light-colored jeans, tenderly bathing the face of a sick young woman she'd never laid eyes on before. He was struck by Spring's quiet strength. A lot of women would have run shuddering from the room, afraid to be exposed to whatever germs were rampant here. But not Spring. He moved over beside her, dropping an arm around her shoulders. "I'm sure that feels good to her."

Spring looked around at him. "It was all I had."

"It'll do. The ambulance will be here soon."

"She's barely stirred. Is she…do you think she's in a coma?"

"I don't know, Spring. I don't know what—or even if—she's eaten since she disappeared nine days ago. I think she's had a friend with her some, but the other kid's even younger than Thelma and not capable of dealing with the situation. She'd promised Thelma not to tell where she was, but she got scared and broke down when Frank questioned her."

The ambulance team arrived then, bearing a stretcher.

Spring thought she'd never seen two more beautiful people in her life.

"You okay?" Clay had his arms around her as she stood weakly, watching the medical team going efficiently about its business of saving Thelma's life.

She leaned her head into his shoulder. "Yes. Clay, do you think she's going to make it?"

"I don't know, Spring. I just don't know."

The two paramedics already had Thelma on the stretcher. Together they lifted her, her slight weight giving them little resistance.

"We'll follow them to the hospital," Clay told Spring, leading her to the door with one arm still tightly around her shoulders. "I have to know that she gets there all right."

"Of course." She would have expected no less. She would have allowed no less.

Thelma made it to the hospital alive. The doctors could make no promises that she would remain that way. She was diagnosed as having a severe case of viral pneumonia, complicated by various secondary infections probably caused by exposure and malnourishment. Clay called Thelma's mother, coming back to the waiting room with his face hard and his eyes angry. Spring had never seen him angry. "We'll stay until that...woman gets here," he told her. "Then I'll have to leave. I won't be able to stay in the same hospital with her without losing my cool completely."

It wasn't long before Mrs. Sawyer arrived, loudly blaming her daughter, Clay, Thelma's friends—everyone but herself—for Thelma's problems. True to his word, Clay left the hospital almost immediately, visibly restraining himself from giving vent to his anger. In his car he sat immobile behind the steering wheel, staring out the windshield at the hospital.

"Are you all right?" Spring asked tentatively, wanting to reach out to him but not knowing how. She laced her fingers in her lap, noting impassively that they were dirty.

He inhaled deeply and turned his head to look at her. "Yeah," he answered, "but it makes me so damned mad."

"I know," she told him softly.

Not as shy as she was about reaching out, Clay took her hand, dirt and all, and squeezed it. "You were wonderful. I don't know how to thank you."

"You don't have to," she told him, flushing slightly. "I didn't do it for you."

He smiled, though weakly. "No, you didn't, did you? You did it for Thelma. A kid you don't even know."

Embarrassed by his praise, she looked away. "How long do you plan to stay in this parking lot?" she demanded a bit huskily.

In answer he started the car. Backing out of the parking space, he asked, "Okay with you if we go by my place? I'd like to clean up before I take you back to your sister's. I'm filthy."

Of course she told him that she didn't mind at all, though the thought of being alone with him in his home made her swallow hard. She'd seen a different side of Clay this afternoon, a side she found much too fascinating. And even with dirt streaked across one cheek and smeared liberally on his worn jeans, he was too damned attractive for her peace of mind.

She fell in love with his house. One of the Victorians that added to San Francisco's quaint charm, it sat regal and arrogant, wearing its bright blue paint and funny little stained-glass windows with studied nonchalance. It reminded her a lot of Clay. "It's wonderful," she told him sincerely, even as she found herself wondering how he could afford such a choice piece of San Francisco real estate. He had a doctorate degree in counseling, but he worked in the public-school system, didn't he? Then she told herself that Clay's finances were none of her business. After all, they were only passing acquaintances, she reminded herself sternly.

He smiled broadly, not bothering to hide his deep pleasure at her praise. "You're not the only one who's into restoring old homes," he commented, subtly pointing out another thing they had in common. "I've been working on the inside for a couple of years. It's almost finished."

He led her in and allowed her to look around without asking for comment. She loved it. All the clever nooks and crannies, the elegant, just slightly eccentric antique and re-production Victorian furnishings that again were so typi-cal of Clay. A shiver coursed down her spine at the strange similarity in their taste in furnishings. Clay had some pieces that were almost identical to ones that were even now residing in her apartment in Little Rock!

She loved it, she thought again. And then she made a deliberate attempt to wipe the word "love" from her mind as she turned back to the handsome blonde tagging at her heels. For some reason it made her nervous. "Beautiful," she summed up succinctly.

"Me or the house?" he demanded cockily, some of his bold self-assurance returning now that they'd put the hos-pital behind them.

"Both of you," she answered with a sigh. "You said something about cleaning up?"

He wasn't quite sure how to take her unexpected an-swer, so he ignored it. "Yes, I would like to shower and change. I'll be quick. I could dig you up something to wear if you want to shower, as well."

Spring looked down at her aqua jeans, streaked with greasy dirt from the floor in that little room where she'd knelt by Thelma. Her brow creased into a frown.

"Spring? What's wrong?"

"Are there many kids who live that way?" she whis-pered, her violet eyes huge behind her smudged glasses. "All that filth…"

Clay released a long, weary breath. "Believe it or not, I've seen worse than what we found this afternoon. The streets are full of runaways, easy prey for every sleaze bag and drug dealer in town. Teenagers with unhappy homes migrate toward California, New York and Florida by the thousands. Too many for the authorities to handle, and the shelters available are sadly inadequate."

"Do you work much with runaways?"

"Some. Mostly I deal with the kids who are having problems at home, before they run. I try to prevent them from turning to the streets."

"I can see why Summer has joined your cause," Spring murmured. "It's heart wrenching to see a child like Thelma was today, when she should be hanging out at McDonald's, laughing and flirting with nice boys her age. It makes me wish there was something *I* could do to help."

"We can always use another volunteer," Clay told her, watching her more closely than his teasing tone seemed to warrant.

She forced a weak smile. "Maybe I'll look into it when I get back to Little Rock. There may be a Halloran House there in need of an optometrist's spare time."

Clay frowned at her mention of returning to Little Rock. Why the sudden hollow feeling? he asked himself. Surely he hadn't forgotten that she was here for less than two weeks. Without stopping to think about it he reached out and pulled her into his arms, ignoring that both of them were dirty. He hugged her tightly. "I'm glad you went with me," he said huskily.

She stirred restlessly in his embrace, aware of a desire to put her arms around him and return it. "I didn't help much," she protested. "I just did what had to be done."

"Always the brave, responsible big sister," Clay murmured, thinking of things Summer had told him about Spring. "It wasn't easy being the oldest, was it?" She frowned a little, wondering what her childhood had to do with what had happened that afternoon, what was happening now. "I don't know what you mean."

He chuckled softly, reaching down to lift her chin so that he was gazing directly into her eyes through her smudged glasses. "You do what has to be done," he said simply. "You have this sense of responsibility that seems to give you strength that many people lack. Like this afternoon, you didn't panic when we found Thelma in such terrible shape. You didn't scold me for taking you into that situation or leaving you alone with her while I called an ambulance. You just calmly took care of her."

"I wasn't all that calm."

"No, but you hid your qualms long enough to do what had to be done. Thanks, love."

Love. There was that word again. She reminded herself that Clay was a demonstrative man, to whom such casual endearments were second nature.

Slowly, reluctantly, she eased herself from his embrace. "Yes, well," she faltered, not quite meeting his eyes. "Why don't you go ahead and take your shower?"

"I will. And you? My offer's still open for you to take one, too."

"No, I'll just wash up. I can shower when you take me back to Summer's. Thanks, anyway."

"Okay. The guest bath is down this hall on the left. I'll be in the bath in the master bedroom if you need anything. Or if you suddenly get an urge to wash my back," he added audaciously, wanting to see her smile again.

The smile broke loose despite her efforts to hold it back. "You're a big boy, Clay. I'm sure you can manage to wash yourself."

"Someday, Spring Reed, you are going to offer to wash my back," Clay told her, leaning over to kiss her before he pulled away and headed toward his bedroom.

"Don't hold your breath," Spring shot after him, then wished she'd come up with something more original. She heard his chuckle as he disappeared down the long, wall-papered hallway in the opposite direction of the bathroom he'd indicated for her.

4

SPRING CLEANED UP as best she could, washing her face and hands and reapplying a touch of makeup from the items she carried in her purse. She brushed out her hair and twisted it back into its customary knot. Her clothes were still soiled and disheveled, but at least she felt a bit fresher. She wouldn't have been comfortable showering or changing into anything belonging to Clay. Or were there women's clothes hanging somewhere in his house? Perhaps that's what he'd meant by offering to find her something to wear.

She tried to tell herself that she was suddenly depressed only because of all that had happened during the past few hours.

Spring was waiting in the living room when Clay joined her. She inhaled sharply at the sight of him. His hair lay in damp curls around his face, gleaming dull gold and almost crying out to be touched. His skin glowed from his hot shower, and his eyes were brighter and bluer than she'd ever seen them. He had pulled on a pale yellow cotton crewneck sweater and dark brown slacks that hugged his lean hips. Barefoot, he carried brown TOPSIDERS in one hand. "Don't you ever wear socks?" she demanded, because she had to say something and nothing else came to mind just then. Nothing she cared to say out loud, anyway.

"No, I never wear socks. Don't you ever wear your hair down?" he returned, lifting a hand to touch her neatly twisted tresses.

"Not very often. It gets in my way."

"Then why haven't you cut it short, the way Summer wears hers?"

"Because I look funny with short hair," she answered with a shrug.

He laughed softly. "Or could it be that inside that practical, responsible exterior is a secret romantic who likes long hair?"

"Don't be ridiculous," she replied, annoyed. "Would you mind taking me back to Summer's now? I would really like to change into clean clothes."

"I offered you some of mine."

"I doubt that you would have anything my size," she said, her words a challenge.

"About the best I could offer is a sweatshirt and sweatpants," he agreed. "They'd be clean, but I can't guarantee fit. Afraid I don't keep women's clothes around." His words answered her challenge.

"Yes, well, I'll be fine until I can change into my own clothes," she muttered, suddenly uncomfortable. She picked up her purse and tucked it under her arm.

"Wait a minute." Clay slid his feet into his shoes, then walked toward her, stopping only a few inches away from her. "I wanted to thank you again for what you did this afternoon."

She shifted on her feet. "You've already thanked me. Repeatedly."

"Not properly," he murmured. Very deliberately he removed her glasses, folded them and dropped them into the outside pocket of her purse as she stood watching him, making no effort to move away. "Let me thank you properly, Spring." And he lowered his mouth to hers, slowly, giving her plenty of time to draw back.

She stayed where she was, her lips parting just as his touched them. She closed her eyes, blocking out the sight of his devastating face, blocking out reason, locking in sensation. His kiss was that of an experienced lover, thorough and deep and sure. She was trembling when it ended, and he had touched her with no more than his mouth. He drew back only an inch or so, took one long look at her expression, then groaned and pulled her into his arms.

The second kiss was just as thorough, just as deep, but not quite as sure. For some reason Spring thought that Clay seemed less polished this time, guided more by passion than practice. She could feel the unsteadiness of his arms around her. It would have been hard to resist him before. It was impossible now.

Neither of them noticed when her purse hit the floor at her feet. They both noticed when her arms went around his neck, pressing her full length against him. Their moans were simultaneous, aroused. Spring allowed her head to fall back, deepening the kiss. Clay swept her slender body with his hands, learning her curves, seeking out the hollow of her spine, finally pressing inward to hold her against his thighs.

Hard. He was so hard—his arms muscled from whatever sport he regularly played, his chest solid and plated where her breasts were flattened against it. Hard where his arousal boldly made itself felt against her abdomen. Yet his mouth over hers, the golden hair at his nape where her fingers burrowed were soft. So soft. She wanted to explore every inch of him, to kiss every soft spot, stroke every hard one. She wanted him.

Emotions that were already strained from the stress of the afternoon flared into desire so hot, so intense that it shook both of them. Clay didn't know whether the shudder had been hers or his or mutual. He only knew that he wanted her, needed her, as he'd never wanted or needed before. Her fiery response to his kiss was driving him mad. How could he have known that such demanding passion smoldered beneath her proper, almost prim appearance? He was delighted with the discovery. He wanted more.

"Spring," he muttered, raising his hands to cradle her face as he continued to caress her with slanting, nibbling kisses. Nothing more. Just her name. He had needed to say it.

"Oh, Clay," she breathed without opening her eyes, her hands sliding around to rest against his chest. Her fingers splayed, then curled, kneading the taut skin beneath the soft sweater.

"Look at me, Spring."

Almost shyly her lashes fluttered upward. Even slightly blurred by her myopia, his face was so beautiful. "It's not fair," she murmured, speaking to herself.

"What's not fair, sweetheart?"

"That you should look like this," she answered incautiously, touching her fingertips to his tanned cheek. "That you should make me feel this way."

"I could say the same about you," he replied, nuzzling her cheek. "You're so lovely. And you make me crazy."

"Oh, God, what am I doing?" She dropped her hand and stepped back, crossing her arms at her waist in unconscious defensiveness. "Take me back to Sausalito, Clay."

"The only place I want to take you is upstairs to my bedroom," he told her unsteadily. "I want to make love to you for hours, until you're too weak to move. And then I want to start all over again."

Her heart pounded, her mind filled with tantalizing images, but she held tightly to reason. "No, Clay."

He exhaled gustily, shoving fingers that were still not quite steady through his rumpled hair. "Okay, we'll wait until you're ready. But the time *will* come, Spring. It's inevitable."

"No, it won't," she returned with admirable confidence. "I won't let it."

He wanted to argue, to demand her reasons for holding back when they both knew she wanted him as badly as he wanted her. He wanted to pick her up in his arms and sweep aside all her objections in a flurry of kisses. But he only reached down to retrieve her purse from where it had fallen on the tapestry carpet and hold it out to her. She had her reasons. She would share them with him when she was ready. He had to make sure she was ready soon, be-

fore she left California and the opportunity to make love
with her was lost.

He stayed only a short time at the Anderson home, just
long enough to tell Summer what had happened and thoroughly embarrass Spring with his lavish praise. He left
with the excuse that he was going to see what he could do
for Thelma. Just before he walked out, he gathered Spring
into his arms and kissed her hard, right in front of Summer
and Derek. Her face was stained a vivid scarlet when he
left her with a cocky grin and a promise to pick her up the
next evening for their date.

"*Don't* say it," Spring warned Summer the moment the
door had closed behind Clay.

"You must be hungry, Spring," Derek interceded
quickly. "I'll go put some steaks on the grill. How do you
like yours?"

"Medium," she replied, still glaring at her giggling sister.

Derek made a prudent, hasty escape.

"If you could have seen your face," Summer murmured, her blue eyes dancing. "You should know Clay
well enough by now to realize that he has no regard for
spectators."

"How long have you known that man?" Spring demanded, ignoring Summer's comment.

"I met him soon after I moved to San Francisco. I'd
found a job working as a hostess in an elegant little restaurant near Nob Hill. Not exactly my style, but it paid the
rent on the tiny apartment I'd found. I didn't know many
people and I was lonely, though I'd started to make a few
friends here and there. Then one night Clay came into the
restaurant with a date. I couldn't help but watch them. He
was so gorgeous—"

"I've noticed," Spring muttered.

Summer ignored her. "And his date was drop-dead
beautiful. Tall brunette with coal-black eyes and a figure
that would make most women want to sob."

Spring found that she really didn't want to hear Summer's description, but she continued to listen in reluctant fascination.

"Anyway, the woman bitched from the time she walked into the place. I don't know what her problem was that evening or why Clay was out with her in the first place, but she was a real honey. They had to wait to be seated because Clay had forgotten to make reservations, which didn't exactly go over with his date. I caught his eye a few times and tried to look sympathetic, and then, all of a sudden, he and I started laughing. Once we got started, it was hard to stop. The wicked witch got all huffy and walked out, refusing to let Clay take her home, though to give him credit he tried. So he stayed and had dinner alone, and by the time he left, he and I had a date for the next evening."

"You went out with him?" Spring frowned, disturbed at the thought. Was Clay still attracted to Summer, despite her being married to someone else?

"Yes, we went out. By the end of our first date, we were the best of friends and we knew that's all we'd ever be. We've been the best of friends ever since. He's a very special man, Spring."

Spring looked down at her lap, rubbing at a streak of dirt with one fingertip. "I'm sure he is. He seems very committed to his young people."

"Oh, he is. He makes a big difference in their lives. He's also a good friend, always willing to offer a shoulder or a hand when he's needed. He hasn't had an easy life, but he never lost his sense of humor."

"Why wasn't his life easy?" Spring asked curiously.

"Clay was one of those troubled kids that he works with now. A real hard case. Ran away, got into trouble, came much too close to drugs and other illegal activities. He ended up in a home for incorrigible teenagers, where—fortunately—he was able to turn himself around with help from some very good counselors."

That explained a lot about the man. Spring frowned as she thought over what Summer had told her. "Didn't his family try to help him?"

"His family was his problem. Very old-money. Snobs who cared more about having a 'perfect' child than a happy one. He was ignored when he was good, viciously criticized when he wasn't. It's no wonder he rebelled."

"He was an only child?" Spring asked, her tender heart twisting at the story. She would never have imagined that happy-go-lucky Clay had come from such an unhappy background.

"Yes. He inherited a near fortune when his parents died a few years ago. Still, he works as a school counselor and lives pretty much on his salary. Other than his weakness for his house and his sports car and his crazy clothes, Clay uses his money mostly to help the less fortunate."

"As you said, a very special man," Spring murmured.

Summer shrugged. "He's not perfect, of course, but then, he never wanted to be. He only wants to be accepted for what he is. Now about that kiss—"

"The steaks are ready," Derek announced from the doorway, much to Spring's relief. "Summer-love, why don't you bring out the salad you made earlier?"

Spring shot him a grateful smile, her mind full with everything that had happened to her and everything that she had learned that day. She excused herself to change into clean clothes before dinner, and not once did Clay McEntire leave her mind.

AFTER A LEISURELY BREAKFAST Monday morning, Derek left for his office and Summer for her college class, both encouraging Spring to make herself at home. Summer had only morning classes that day and would be home by lunch, she promised. Derek planned to come home for lunch, as well. Spring waved them off, then indulged in a lazy swim in the temperature-regulated pool. She felt almost decadent enjoying such leisure after the hard pace she'd sustained at home for so long.

After her swim she took a long, hot shower. Her skin was glowing bright pink by the time she stepped out and reached for a fluffy towel. Her reflection in a mirror caught her eye, and she paused, staring thoughtfully at her nude image. A bit too slim, she thought critically, but not bad on the whole. Would Clay find her appealing if he should see her this way?

Realizing the direction her thoughts were taking, she snatched up the towel and applied it furiously. Deep within herself she was aware of a faint sense of regret that she wasn't the type who could cheerfully indulge in a teeth-rattling vacation affair and then just walk away. If she were, Clay would definitely be the man she'd choose for her fling. As it was, he was the man she most needed to resist.

Lunch was a scrumptious seafood salad prepared by Spring. She had the food ready by the time Derek and Summer arrived, and they took their time over the meal, chatting contentedly. They'd just finished eating when the telephone rang. Derek answered, listened for a moment, laughed, then extended the receiver in Spring's direction. "For you," he told her.

She knew who it was by the glint in her brother-in-law's eyes. Taking a deep breath, she accepted the phone and pressed it to her ear. "Hello, Clay."

"Hi, sweet Spring. Oh, sorry. I'm not supposed to call you that, am I?"

"No," she answered sternly. "You're not. Aren't you supposed to be working?"

"Taking a break. I'm calling from my office."

"Oh. Have you heard anything about Thelma?"

"No change," he replied, immediately serious. "She should have been hospitalized days ago. She had to have surgery this morning to remove the fluid that has built up in her lungs. The membranes had become infected. They have her in intensive care now."

"I'm sorry."

"Yeah." He paused for a moment, then deliberately lightened his tone. "Actually, I was calling to remind you about our date tonight. You haven't forgotten, have you?"

"No, Clay, I haven't forgotten."

"Great. I'm really looking forward to it. How about you?"

She pressed her tongue firmly against her cheek, then replied with mock gravity, "I'm sure it will be quite pleasant. There's nothing interesting on television tonight, anyway."

Clay seemed to choke on the other end of the line, then growled, "Talk about damning with faint praise. I owe you for that one, sweet Spring." He tacked on the nickname with deliberate challenge.

She refused to take him up on it. "I'll see you tonight, Clay."

"Okay. Oh, and, Spring."

"Yes?"

"Dress funky."

She frowned. "Funky?"

"Yeah, funky. For you I guess that means leaving the top button of your silk blouse undone. See you tonight."

Spring stared for a moment at the buzzing receiver in her hand, then slowly replaced it on its cradle. "Your friend," she told her avidly interested sister, "is a lunatic."

Summer laughed. "Yes, I know."

"He wants me to dress funky tonight."

"So what are you going to do about it?" Summer asked, the words a dare.

Spring grinned and turned her gaze to her bemused brother-in-law. "Derek, dear, how do you feel about loaning out your clothes?" she asked blandly.

Her family would have immediately recognized the look on Spring's pretty face. She didn't often indulge her sly, subtle sense of humor, but when she did, the results were never predictable. Being a new member of the family, Derek wasn't quite sure how to interpret the gleam in Spring's violet eyes. Having twenty-five years of experience behind her, Summer identified it immediately. She suspected that her own wardrobe was about to be raided and that a quick shopping excursion might even be in order. She laughed again and looked forward to the evening, immensely pleased with the unexpected developments taking place during her sister's visit.

CLAY STOOD on the doorstep of the Anderson home and checked his appearance, as anxious as a schoolboy on his first date, he mused ruefully. He thoughtfully twisted one foot in front of him, wondering if the orange high-tops clashed too badly with his tan three-piece suit and brown-on-beige striped dress shirt. He checked the knot in the mottled brown-and-green tie that he'd tucked discreetly into his buttoned vest. He'd worn his favorite tie in Spring's honor.

He chuckled as he punched the doorbell, wondering if Spring had taken his advice about how to dress. He could almost picture her now in the neat little suit she'd probably chosen to wear like a coat of mail while with him.

Summer's giggle when she opened the door and eyed his attire tipped him off that something was up. He grinned, eagerly looking for his date. His grin widened when he found her. She *had* dressed funky.

He slowly examined her from head to toe. A gray felt fedora sat atop her light hair, which she wore in a glorious frizz to her shoulders. A loose, unstructured charcoal-gray linen jacket that Clay had helped Summer select as a gift for Derek was pushed up to Spring's elbows and hung almost to her knees. Her bright pink blouse was open at the collar so that the man's pink-and-gray spotted silk tie was knotted at about the middle of her chest. Light gray slacks were pleated baggily at her slender waist, narrowing from the knees to tightly grip her ankles. Her feet were tied into heeled black lace-up half-boots. She wore enormous turquoise-and-silver earrings, a chunky matching choker and a thick black leather belt with a gaudy silver-and-turquoise buckle. Facing him with a smile that contained equal parts of shyness and bravado, she looked beautiful.

"I am in love with this woman," he remarked aloud, almost as if he were commenting on the weather. And he knew his words were the truth. He watched in amusement as her face turned almost as pink as her shirt.

"I thought you said you were going to dress funky," Spring accused him.

He frowned down at his suit. "I *am* dressed funky."

"Spring, he's wearing a *tie*," Summer pointed out with a grin. "The only part of his outfit that's *not* funky, for Clay, is the tennis shoes."

Spring shook her head, causing her crimped curls to sway around her face. "San Francisco," she muttered, then glared at Clay. "Okay, let's go."

He couldn't resist throwing an arm around her shoulders and giving her one hard hug. "We're going to have so much fun!" he told her cheerfully.

"Yeah," she answered with a resigned sigh that he found greatly amusing. "Fun."

THE PLAY THAT CLAY TOOK her to turned out to be a junior-high-school production of *You Can't Take It With You*, which happened to be one of Spring's favorite plays. She didn't tell him so. Nor did she give in to the impulse to tease him when she noticed him squinting a bit as he read the program, though her professional mind made a note to ask him later if he'd had an eye examination recently.

Instead, she sat back and enjoyed, chuckling at the more-enthusiastic-than-talented performances from the young teenage actors. Or, rather, she appeared to enjoy the play. It wasn't easy with Clay sitting close beside her, taking advantage of every opportunity to touch her. When he wasn't patting her arm, he was squeezing her knee. As the performance went on, the squeezes moved gradually up her thigh until, at the beginning of act three, she was forced to catch his hand and return it firmly to his own lap. She tried very hard to look as if his touches annoyed her, when actually they turned her into Silly Putty.

With admirably few forgotten or blown lines Alice and Tony pledged their undying love, Grandpa Vanderhof congratulated himself on outsmarting the government,

Penelope and Paul Sycamore went on with their happy, eccentric lives and the play ended. Spring applauded warmly as the flushed young actors took their bows.

"Want to go backstage?" Clay asked, draping a casual arm around Spring's shoulders.

"You know someone in the cast?" she inquired with interest.

He nodded noncommittally and led her down the aisle, never breaking physical contact. Though she told herself that she wished he'd stop touching her, Spring was fully aware that she made no effort to pull away from him.

To say that Clay knew someone in the cast was a monumental understatement. Clay knew *everyone* in the cast. And they quite obviously idolized him. Forbidden by school policy to call him by his first name—this was the very school where he worked, Spring discovered—they called him Mr. Mac. They teased him about his unusually conservative clothing, glowed with pride when he congratulated them on the success of their performances and competed avidly for his attention. The boys all tried to emulate him. The girls were all in love with him. Watching him with the kids, Spring felt herself slipping into a similar infatuation.

When Clay introduced her to the cast, Spring was glad she'd dressed so oddly, though she'd chosen her "funky" outfit just to prove to Clay that she wasn't as prim and humorless as he'd teased her about being. The kids seemed to accept her easily as his friend, even showing their implicit approval by teasing her about her Arkansan accent.

Declaring himself to be near starvation, Clay took her out to eat when they left the school. The tiny Italian restaurant he selected was tucked away in an obscure section of the city, far from the usual tourist paths. Lulled by the pleasant evening and marvelous food, Spring found herself chattering easily, more comfortable on a date than she'd been in a long time. Clay stayed on his best behavior, seemingly fascinated with stories of her childhood in Rose Bud and her optometry practice in Little Rock. Conversation turned to mutual interests, and Clay grinned more broadly each time they found something in common—favorite books, movies, music, television programs.

"It's Kismet," he declared at one point. "Our tastes are so similar. There's absolutely no reason not to have an affair."

She shook her head reprovingly at him, taking his words as a joke. "What about our taste in clothes?"

"What about it? You look great tonight."

"But I don't look like *me* tonight. I only wore these things to surprise you."

"I know you did. But I like the way you dress when you're being yourself, too. Your prim little outfits dare a man to rip them off you."

He laughed when she blushed vividly.

"The least you could have done," she complained, struggling to keep up with him, "was to dress in your usual outrageous manner after asking me to go funky. You look so…so *normal* in that suit. And it really wasn't necessary to wear a tie to a junior-high-school play."

He looked crestfallen, though his eyes twinkled with secret amusement. "Don't you like Morgan?"

She lifted a questioning eyebrow. "Morgan?"

"My tie."

"You *named* your tie? Clay, people don't name their ties."

"I do. He's named after the friend who gave him to me."

She continued to look at him as though he were crazy—which, of course, pretty well summed up her opinion of him. Gorgeous, sexy, mesmerizing, but unquestionably crazy. "Your tie is a him?"

"Looks like a him to me," he answered reflectively, tugging the end of the tie out of his vest and smoothing it downward so that she could see its full length. "Don't you think so?"

Spring choked, then burst into laughter. "Oh, my God. Your tie is a *fish*!" Fully exposed, the mottled browns and greens became scales. The fish-shaped tie was cleverly de-

signed, the end a fish-head profile, complete with gills,
closed mouth and one glassy blue eye. "That's disgusting."

Her laughter had brought an odd light to his eyes. Smiling at her in a manner that she couldn't begin to interpret—nor did she care to try just then—he reached across
the table to take her hand. "I knew you'd appreciate Morgan."

They talked of his work, both at the school and with the
young people he continually referred to as "my kids" at
Halloran House. Spring was fascinated by his dedication
to the youth, his understanding of them and the way their
minds worked.

"Do many of them run away from home?" she asked,
thinking of Thelma.

"It happens often enough," he answered regretfully.
"I'm afraid I was a runaway myself a few times. I know
how cold and lonely it can be out on the streets." He had
told her a bit about his childhood during dinner, an abbre-
viated version of what Summer had already told her.

"I always feel so sorry for the parents. Not to know
where their children are, wondering if they're dead or
alive, and all usually because of a simple breakdown in
communications."

"It's sad for everyone concerned," Clay agreed. "Sometimes the parents couldn't care less what happens to the
kids, but I know that's not always true. Many times the
problems can be remedied through family therapy, once
they realize that they need help—not that the problems are
ever simple."

Spring thought that perhaps Clay would tend to be bi-
ased toward the young people's side in any family encounter, but considering his background and his vocation,
she supposed that was understandable. She deliberately
turned the conversation to lighter subjects, not wanting
Clay to dwell on his career just then.

She was almost disappointed when he drove her
straight back to Summer's house after dinner, though she

didn't know exactly where she'd wanted him to take her. She only knew that she wasn't ready to say good-night to him.

Clay parked the car in the driveway, snapped off the lights and turned to Spring, one arm over the back of his seat as he smiled at her. "I had fun tonight, Spring. Thanks for going with me."

She moistened her lips and returned the smile. He looked so good in the shadowy artificial light from outside. But then, he looked good in broad daylight, also. Or any kind of light. "I had fun, too. Thank you."

He chuckled, his hand stretching out to twist one of her curls. "Aren't we being polite?"

Because she was fighting the urge to catch his hand and hold it to her cheek, her own smile was a bit forced. "Yes, aren't we?"

Something in her expression must have given away her feelings, for his smile slowly faded, to be replaced by a look of hunger that matched hers. "I'd like to kiss you, Spring," he murmured, his hand sliding into the hair at her temple to cradle her face. "I think I want to kiss you now more than I've ever wanted to do anything in my life."

5

Since when had he started asking permission to kiss her? She wet her lips again, realizing nervously that he wanted more than startled acceptance this time. He wanted full cooperation. He was making an implicit demand for her to acknowledge that she was attracted to him, that she wanted the kiss as badly as he did. Even as she almost shyly removed her glasses and leaned toward him, she wondered how much more he would force her to admit.

Her lips had barely touched his before he was kissing her. The battered fedora tumbled off her head, unnoticed by either of them. His mouth slanted greedily over hers, moving with the same rough-gentle passion with which he'd kissed her the day before. And, as with the last time, she could only hold on and allow herself to be lost in him. A far distant part of her mind pondered her response to him. She'd never been like this with anyone else. She'd never relinquished control. Clay took her control, yet he seemed no more the master of his own emotions than she was of hers.

It felt only natural when his hand slipped beneath her borrowed, oversize jacket to settle with bold possessiveness on one of her breasts. Almost unconsciously she inhaled, pushing herself more fully into his touch.

"Ah, God, Spring. You feel so good in my arms." His voice was only a breath against her lips; he refused to break the contact between them.

She didn't know what to say except his name. It seemed to be enough. He kissed her again, and this time his

tongue surged between her lips to caress hers. Teasingly.
Tenderly. Lovingly.

"Kiss me back, sweetheart," he muttered, then took her
mouth again.

With no further hesitation she gave in to his half-
pleading demand and returned his kiss with all the for-
merly unknown passion within her.

After what seemed like a hot, life-altering eternity, Clay
suddenly startled her by pulling his mouth away from
hers, giving a low, husky laugh and hugging her with
such fervent enthusiasm that she thought she would have
at least a few bruises, if not broken bones, when he released her. "You never stop surprising me, Spring Reed,"
he told her with apparent delight. "We're going to be so
good together."

She swallowed hard. "We're...what?"

Cradling her face in his hands, he smiled meltingly at
her and kissed her nose. "When we make love, it's going
to be the most exquisite, most erotic, most incredible thing
that has ever happened to either of us. I can hardly wait."

That got her attention. Spring backed frantically away
from him, pressing herself uncomfortably against the door
behind her. "I've already told you, Clay, we are *not* going
to have an affair."

Flashing his most boyishly charming grin, Clay grabbed
the hand that was pushing forcefully against his chest and
kissed her knuckles. "We're already having an affair,
Spring. We just haven't made love yet."

"Nor will we," she snapped, jerking her hand out of his
and shoving it shakily through her tangled hair. Summer's
hat. She couldn't find the hat. She looked wildly around
for it, talking rapidly as she grabbed her purse and the
borrowed fedora and held them protectively against her
breasts. "What happened just now was a mistake. I can't—
I won't let it happen again."

"It will happen again." Clay spoke almost lazily as he
watched her frantic preparations for escape with visible
amusement. "Again and again and again, until you admit

that it's utterly ridiculous to try to deny this thing that's between us. You can call it love or lust or earth-shaking attraction, but it's there, and it's not going to go away."

"Then we'll just have to ignore it," she declared. *Call it love*, he had said. No. She wouldn't call it love.

"Can't you see that this won't work, Clay?" She was almost pleading now. "I'm just not the type who can handle this sort of thing. Please don't ask for something I can't give."

His face softened and took on an expression of such sweetness that it brought a lump to her throat. He touched her cheek, fleetingly, not enough to force her to draw back again. "Darling, you've already given it. You just haven't admitted it yet."

Given what? Her heart? "No, Clay," she whispered, shaking her head.

He knew when to quit—temporarily. "I'll walk you to the door."

Before she could protest, he was out of the car and at her side as she walked in awkward silence to the front door of her sister's home. She used the key that Summer had given her, then paused with one hand on the doorknob. "Clay, I—"

He silenced her with a quick kiss on her slightly swollen lips. "Good night, Spring. You'll be seeing me around in the next few days. A lot."

Threat or promise, the words held a note of determination that she had to take seriously. Without giving her a chance to reply, Clay whirled on one orange tennis shoe and left her staring after him.

THIRTY MINUTES LATER Spring stood before the mirror in her bedroom, brushing out her hair as Summer sat crosslegged on the bed, her compact body almost quivering with frustration. "Aren't you going to tell me anything about your date with Clay?" Summer demanded, her elbows on her knees as she stared at her sister's reflection.

"I told you it was nice."

Summer snorted inelegantly. *"Nice.* Yuck."

Spring set down her brush and turned, tightening the sash of her pastel flowered robe. "What's wrong with nice?"

"It's insipid. It's something you'd say about a date with your ex, Roger. Not Clay."

Spring sighed. "What do you want me to say, Summer?"

"That you had an exciting, adventurous evening. That you'll never forget a minute of it. Say something romantic and sweet that will make me believe there's still hope for you."

Shaking her head, Spring dropped to sit on the edge of the bed, stretching her bare feet out in front of her on the plush carpet. "Summer, we went to a junior-high-school play and then had dinner at a little Italian restaurant with an odd name that I've already forgotten. Does that sound like the kind of date you just described?"

"No. But then, you were with Clay McEntire. He has a way of making seemingly mundane things extraordinary."

"All right, dammit! My date with Clay *was* exciting. And adventurous. I'll never forget a single moment of it. Does that make you happy?"

Blinking at her sister's uncharacteristic show of temper, Summer leaned forward slightly. "Was it something I said?"

Spring groaned and hid her face in her hands. "God, I'm sorry. I didn't mean to jump all over you like that. It's just that…that…" Her voice trailed off.

"Clay's getting to you, right?" Summer tried to sound sympathetic but wasn't particularly successful since her brilliant blue eyes were sparkling with delighted pleasure.

Dropping her hands, Spring straightened her spine. "Okay, so maybe I am a bit…infatuated with him," she admitted carefully. "But that's all it is. He's good-looking and interesting and amusing. It's perfectly natural for me to be attracted to him. What woman wouldn't be?"

"Of course," Spring agreed gravely.

"But that doesn't mean that there's anything developing between us. Nothing lasting, I mean. There couldn't be."

"Why not?"

"Why not?" Spring repeated incredulously, jumping to her feet to restlessly pace the room. "Summer, I've only known him for three days. And I'll be leaving California in nine more days. Besides, Clay and I are entirely different. Much too different to even consider a serious relationship."

Summer shook her head vigorously. "Oh, no. That excuse won't wash with me. Remember who you're talking to, Spring. I'm the former party girl married to the ex-spy-turned-businessman, remember? It would be hard to find two people more different than Derek and me, but we love each other so much that we've learned to accept those differences."

"You and Derek aren't as different as you like to imply," Spring argued. "And at least you live in the same state."

"So? People relocate all the time. I did. Besides, logic and geography have nothing at all to do with this. We're talking about human emotions here. The way you and Clay feel about each other."

"But I don't *know* how I feel about Clay. And I certainly don't know what he feels for me."

"Are you kidding? The guy's nuts about you! He's had the look of a man who's been poleaxed ever since you walked into my den last Friday. And since Clay is not a man to hide his emotions, I'm sure he's told you exactly how he feels."

Call it love, he'd said. But she couldn't call it that. She just couldn't.

"He's told me that he's attracted to me," Spring admitted. "He's convinced we're going to have an affair."

"And would that be so awful?" Summer teased.

Spring took a deep breath and glanced at her sister,

knowing her feelings were all too clear on her face. "It just might be devastating," she whispered.

Her sister's mischievous smile faded immediately and was replaced by a look of compassion. "Spring—"

"Summer, you're not in here grilling your sister for details about her date tonight, are you?" Derek's voice inquired blandly from the open doorway.

"Why, Derek. Am I the type of person to pry into someone else's personal business?"

"Yes, you are," Derek and Spring replied in smiling, unhesitating unison.

Spring thought again how very much she liked her brother-in-law. Summer tossed her head indignantly and climbed as gracefully as she could from Spring's bed. "I won't stay here and let the two of you insult me," she announced with great dignity. "I'm going to bed."

"Good night, Summer," Spring bade her fondly. "Good night, Derek," she added as he left the room with a conspiratorial wink at her.

Summer glanced back over her shoulder as she limped from the room. "Sleep well, Sis. Try not to worry about anything, okay?"

Spring assured her sister that she would sleep like a log, but she was lying through her teeth. She wouldn't sleep a wink for thinking of Clay. Her body still tingled from the desire that he'd aroused in her, desire such as she'd never known before. What was it that he did to her?

Call it love.

No, she wouldn't call it love. Not that.

DURING THE NEXT TWO DAYS Spring discovered that Clay was a man who carried through with his promises—and threats. It seemed that every time she turned around he was there. On Tuesday night he showed up on the Andersons' doorstep and invited himself to dinner. He stayed three and a half hours. During that time he patted Spring's shoulder five times, hugged her twice, squeezed her hand nine times, kissed her cheek once and kissed her mouth twice briefly and once thoroughly. She counted.

By the time he left, she was on fire. She took a long, cold shower before going to bed, but all that did was give her goose bumps. It did absolutely nothing to dampen her newly awakened libido.

On Wednesday Clay called Summer and offered to take the three of them to dinner that evening. Being the determined matchmaker that she was, Summer cheerfully accepted. Spring tried to act annoyed, but they both knew that the scolding was only a formality. The truth was that Spring couldn't wait to see Clay again, and she and Summer both knew it.

Dressed in cream and a delectable shade of mint green, Clay was at his outrageous best from the moment the evening began. He teased the others until they laughed helplessly, then laughed good-naturedly when they teased him right back. Spring spent much of the evening capturing his wandering hands and returning them firmly to him, her stern looks not very adequately concealing what those daring touches did to her.

She could have gladly strangled him when he introduced her to their waiter—who turned out to be a former student of his—as the woman he would like to have an affair with. Eyeing her vivid blush, the young waiter grinned, congratulated Clay on his excellent taste and provided a bottle of champagne to further the cause.

"You," Spring told Clay through clenched teeth, "are going to die."

"Have an affair with me," he retorted, "and I'll die happy."

Summer and Derek laughed, greatly enjoying the entertainment provided by the other couple.

"Walk me to my car, Spring," Clay ordered some time later after nightcaps in the Andersons' den. "I've got to go."

"I'm sure you can find your way to the driveway," Spring replied blandly, not moving from her chair.

"Aw, c'mon," he whined boyishly. "There's something I want to show you."

"That's exactly what I'm worried about," Spring retorted, much to Summer's and Derek's amusement. They all knew that the "something" he wanted to show her was nothing more than a ploy to get her alone. Still, she stood, with a great show of reluctance, and walked out with him.

It was a dream of a night. Cool, fragrant, inhabited by dancing fog wraiths and twinkling diamond lights spreading out for miles around them. Spring closed her eyes and inhaled, then opened them to survey the glory around her. "Beautiful, isn't it?" she murmured to Clay.

He turned and leaned against his low sports car, catching her forearms to pull her into a loose embrace. "I used to think so."

"You used to?" Almost without thinking about it, she rested her hands on his shoulders, her lower body settling lightly against his. "What happened?"

"I met you." His arms tightened around her. "Now I compare everything I see to your beauty. Nothing else measures up."

It should have sounded trite, corny. It did, of course, she assured herself, but it still made her knees go weak. She tried to sound annoyed, but her voice came out all breathless. "That's dumb. Besides, I'm not beautiful."

He lowered his mouth to within an inch of hers. "Yes, you are," he murmured.

"No, I'm—" She stopped, swallowed, then finally moaned. "Oh, Clay, please kiss me."

"Thank you," he said unexpectedly, then took her lips with the familiar hunger that was more overwhelming each time he kissed her.

Spring slipped her arms around his neck and pressed closer, her mouth opening eagerly under his. His hands were warm and searching over the lightweight sweater she wore, stroking her curves and contours with open palms. A tiny whimper lodged itself in her throat when his fingertips slid between the hem of her sweater and the waistband of her skirt to trace the soft skin there, then moved around and upward to cup one of her small breasts through the fabric of her bra.

"You *are* beautiful, Spring," he muttered against her mouth. "And I want you so much." He rocked her gently against his lower body, against the proof of his wanting. "I need you."

"Clay, I—" She caught her breath when he rolled her hardened nipple between thumb and forefinger, the sensation shooting from her breast to some deep, yearning part of her. "Oh, Clay."

He kissed her again, his tongue surging between her slightly swollen lips to stroke hers, withdrawing, then sliding back in. The sensual imagery made her weak with desire, and she arched against him in an unconscious plea for the ultimate intimacy. His hands fell to her hips, holding her almost painfully against his straining manhood for a moment before moving her a few inches away from him. His voice was raw with his need. "God, Spring. Much more of this and we'll end up making love right here in your sister's driveway."

She groaned in chagrin and dropped her hot face to his shoulder, pulling in a painfully ragged breath. "What do you do to me, Clay McEntire?" she breathed. "At home I'm so sensible, so firmly in control. With you I'm like a stranger. Impulsive and impetuous and even a little wild. I don't know how you do it."

"Don't you like what I do to you, Spring?" he asked whimsically, his own breathing returning slowly to normal.

"Yes, dammit. But it won't last, Clay. I'll go back to Little Rock next week and I'll be myself again. I'm... comfortable with my life there."

He was silent for a long moment, his cheek resting against her hair, which she'd worn straight and loose to her shoulders. Finally he spoke, almost reluctantly. "Is there someone special at home, Spring? Are you involved with anyone?"

"Not anymore."

He digested that, along with her tone. "Tell me about him."

"His name is Roger, and he's an attorney. Very attractive, very pleasant. We dated for almost six months. We had a lot in common, wanted the same things in life. Successful careers, marriage, family. A few months ago we realized that we didn't want those things with each other, so we said goodbye."

"Sounds sad," he said thoughtfully.

"It was, in a way. I cried when our relationship ended, but I think the tears were due more to the end of a pleasant fantasy than to the loss of Roger."

Clay raised his arms to cup her face between his hands, his eyes intense in the artificial light. "I don't ever want to make you cry, Spring. I never want to hurt you."

Was he warning her not to start wanting the same things from him that she'd thought she'd wanted from Roger? He didn't need to. Spring had known all along that Clay wasn't the type who would be content with someone like her. Perhaps he was intrigued with her now, but it wouldn't last. Clay thrived on excitement, new experiences, adventures. She wasn't the type who could provide such things for him on a regular basis. Nor did she want to try. She just wanted a normal, happy life. She wouldn't mind occasional adventures, some excitement, but she needed sanity, as well. She needed to be loved by a man who needed only her, who would want no woman but her.

And she really wished that man could be Clay.

"I'd better go in," she said at last, a note of weariness creeping into her voice.

"Yes. I'll see you tomorrow."

"Tomorrow?"

He nodded. "There's an open-house reception at Halloran House tomorrow night. Part of our fund-raising drive going on this week. I'd like for you to come with Summer and Derek."

"I'd love to. I'm curious to see this place that you and Summer are so devoted to."

"It's interesting." He dropped a kiss on her lips, a mere ghost of the kisses that had gone before, and set her away from him. "Good night, Spring."

"Good night, Clay."

She slipped into the house, then walked quietly toward the den, deep in thought. Her steps halted abruptly at the doorway. Derek and Summer stood before the room's spectacular glass wall, locked in a passionate embrace. Derek's head was bent protectively over his petite wife as he kissed her with familiar intimacy, her arms clenched around his neck.

Spring turned silently and headed for her room, wondering why she suddenly found herself blinking back tears.

CLAY BENT over the bed, his lips touching soft, cool skin as his hand stroked a headful of crisp black curls. "Hi, beautiful."

Liquid brown eyes smiled into his tender blue-green ones. "Hi."

"How're you feeling?"

"Not so great," Thelma whispered, turning her head restlessly on the flat pillow of her intensive-care bed. "My chest hurts like crazy."

"I'm sorry. Is there anything I can do to help?"

"No, but thanks, anyway. What time is it? I lose track in here."

"It's seven-thirty a.m.," he answered. "Thursday," he added, in case she'd also lost track of the days.

"How'd you get in here? I thought only family was allowed in. Not that I'm complaining. I'm so glad to see someone besides my loving mother." She added a bitter twist to the last two words that wrenched Clay's heart.

"I sweet-talked a nurse," he told her, deliberately maintaining his easy smile. "Told her I was your brother."

Thelma laughed weakly, lifting their clenched hands

and eyeing the contrast between her brown and his fair skin. "And she bought it, right? You're slick, man."

"Thanks. I try." He glanced at all the tubes and wires attached to her, trying not to frown. Thelma remained a very sick young woman. The doctors still hesitated to predict whether her recovery would be complete, continuing to worry about permanent lung damage—the delicate membranes had been so badly scarred by her neglect of her condition. Clay refused even to consider the possibility that Thelma could still die. "I talked to Frank this morning. He said that you're going to Chicago to live with your aunt when you leave the hospital."

Thelma nodded. "That's right. I been begging to go live with Aunt Diane for a long time, but my mother refused to let me. She's finally given in."

"Think you'll be happy in Chicago?"

The shrug she gave was heartbreakingly old for her age. "Who knows? But it couldn't be any worse than here. And Aunt Diane seems to want me with her. First time anyone's wanted me around in a long time."

"That's not quite true, Thelma. I've always wanted you around."

"Yeah, but we both know that you're a bleeding heart. Always have been, always will be."

"You got it," Clay admitted, winking at her.

"Well, you can stop bleeding over me. I've decided to get it together in Chicago. Aunt Diane says if I'll straighten up and really try to do better, she'll see that I get the money to go to college when I finish high school, major in music, like I've always wanted to do. The doctors won't tell me whether I'll be able to sing worth a damn, uh—" she paused, knowing how Clay felt about "his kids" cursing, then continued "—halfway good after this thing with my lungs, but I'm going to do it, one way or another. If I can't sing, I've always got my piano. I'm pretty good, you know."

"I've always been your number one fan, haven't I?"

"Yeah. You have. Thanks. Sorry I keep screwing up."

"Everyone screws up sometimes, Thel. Now you've just got to put the past behind you and try again. You can do it."

She sighed wearily and closed her eyes for a moment, her lashes delicate against youthful cheeks. Then her eyes opened again, and there was a sheen of tears. "I haven't thanked you for saving my life."

"It's okay. You don't have to."

"I really didn't care if I died, you know."

Clay's throat tightened. "I know. But I cared. And Frank and Summer cared. And your Aunt Diane cares. We love you, Thelma, and we're going to save your life and your future even if we have to kick your butt to get you to listen to us."

She chuckled faintly. "All right. I said I'd try." She paused again, and Clay could see that she was tiring. He moved as if to leave, but her hand tightened on his. "Don't go yet. Please. It gets lonely in here."

"All right. I've got a few more minutes before the nurse kicks me out."

"That woman who was with you when you found me…who was she?"

Startled, Clay tilted his head. "Her name is Spring Reed. Summer's sister. Do you remember her?"

"I think so. It's real fuzzy, but I sort of remember a pretty lady with blond hair washing my face and talking to me in a nice, friendly voice. I remember how good it felt. I was so hot."

"Spring will be glad to hear that. She's been worried about you. She's another bleeding heart, like Summer and me," he added, using Thelma's own words to tease her.

"Are you in love with her?" Thelma asked unexpectedly, reading something in his voice or his expression as she watched him closely.

He blinked, then grinned rather sheepishly. "Yeah. Yeah, I am."

"Going to marry her?"

"Haven't thought about it. I'm not really the marrying kind, you know."

"Bull."

He raised one eyebrow, questioningly. "I beg your pardon?"

"I said bull. You act crazy, but everyone knows you're just Joe Normal underneath. You'd be happy as a clam with a wife and a bunch of kids and *you* know it. So don't try to con me, McEntire."

"Think so, huh?"

"Know so." Her lashes fell again. "I'm getting sleepy. Sorry."

"That's okay. You need your rest, and it's time for me to get to school. I stopped by here on the way to work, and I'd better go or I'll be late. But I'll be back."

"Promise?"

"Promise. And you'd better write to me when you're in Chicago, or I'll come after you, you hear?"

"Yeah?" She looked inordinately pleased. "Will you write me back?"

"You can count on it." He kissed her cheek, then straightened. "I'll see you tomorrow."

"Okay." She stopped him at the entrance to her glass cubicle. "Clay?"

"Yeah?"

"You're dressed kinda boring today, aren't you?"

He grinned, looking down at his lime-green T-shirt, worn Levi's and white Reeboks. "I dressed in a hurry this morning. I'll try to do better next time."

"You do that. This place is dull enough. Bye, Clay."

He left with his grin still in place, though inside he was praying fervently that the teenager would recover. She deserved a break.

EXHALE. CLAY LOWERED his chin almost to the floor, his forearms straining under his weight. *Inhale.* He pushed himself up so that his body was on a slant, mentally counting, *forty-nine.*

Exhale. He lowered himself again, sweat dripping down his forehead. *Inhale. Fifty.*

With a grunt he abruptly threw himself onto his back, crossing his hands on his bare, sweat-slick chest. He really hated exercising, he thought ruefully. That's why he never did it. Good thing he stayed in shape through his usual frenetic activity.

So why was he trying to turn himself into melting Jell-O with push-ups? Good question. And he knew the answer. He was trying not to think of Spring. He'd been trying not to think of her all day, since his early-morning visit with Thelma. He'd tried not to think about her during his hours at work, during lunch with his friend Frank from Halloran House, during seventy-five sit-ups and fifty push-ups.

It wasn't working. It seemed as if she'd been on his mind since the moment he'd set eyes on her.

Okay, so he was in love with her. He'd known before Thelma had made him admit it that morning; had, in fact, known since he'd seen her in her "funky" outfit Monday evening. And it was going to hurt when she left next Wednesday. It was going to hurt bad.

He'd never felt quite like this before. The few times he'd flirted with love in the past had usually been pleasant, sometimes passionate, but never permanent. And he'd never particularly regretted that fact. He'd always put his work first. Something told him he wouldn't get over Spring as easily. The same something that told him that his work wouldn't be quite enough when she was hundreds of miles away from him. He almost resented her for that.

Six days. She was flying out of his life in six days. His stomach clenched with dread.

He'd known a lot of emotions in his thirty-four-plus years. Despair, disillusion, hopelessness, rage. Later he'd discovered fulfillment, hope, love and happiness. He'd rarely known fear. But he was scared now. He'd tried so hard to make his life work, to fill the emptiness that had yawned inside him through the lonely, unhappy years of

his youth. He lived alone now, but he hadn't consciously
been lonely. He was pretty damned sure that he would be
lonely in seven days. And in ten, and maybe even in one
hundred, and more. Lonely for Spring.

He'd never loved this way before; he couldn't imagine
loving like this again. Couldn't imagine himself making
love to any woman but Spring. It had never been like this
before.

Maybe he should back off a bit. Start preparing himself
for being without her. Stop thinking about her all the time,
counting the hours until he saw her again. Stop wondering what it would take to make her stay with him in six
days.

Grinding a rare curse between clenched teeth, he
flipped onto his stomach and flattened his palms on his
bedroom carpet. His arm muscles bulged.

Inhale. Exhale. Fifty-one.
Six more days.
Inhale. Exhale. Fifty-two.

6

HALLORAN HOUSE WAS a fascinating place, Spring decided. The twenty-odd residents were young, between the ages of eleven and sixteen, had been in trouble, but not too serious trouble yet, and wore defiant expressions that seemed to refuse intimacy yet pleaded for love all at the same time. Clay informed Spring that because the home, which had been established by a wealthy industrialist who had lost a son to a drug overdose, was funded primarily by donations, several major fund-raising events took place each year. The residents had put on a talent show last fall, which was how Summer had gotten involved. Clay had drafted her to direct the show.

The current effort was an open-house reception for patrons and potential patrons. An informal buffet had been set up in the former ballroom-turned-recreation room, and a presentation was made to outline the home's purpose. Dressed all in white—shirt, coat, vest, pants, shoes and, yes, a white tie—Clay was a highly visible participant in the program. Spring couldn't take her eyes off him, but her fascination with him had little, if anything, to do with his clothing. Instead, she watched the way the light played on the golden highlights in his blond hair, the way his laughter made his eyes sparkle, the flashing dimples that appeared as deep grooves at the side of his mouth when he smiled. It seemed that every time she saw him, he was even more beautiful.

"What do you think of my kids?" he asked Spring at one point as he snatched a moment of semiprivacy with her by crowding her into a corner.

Spring turned her head to look past him. Many of the

guests had gone by that time, leaving mostly staff and residents gathered in small clusters in the recreation room. "Some of them look pretty tough," she remarked. "And impressively big for their ages. Do you ever have trouble with them?"

"Sure, sometimes. Fights, threats, whatever. We've learned to deal with it."

"How does Summer deal with it?"

"Very well." Clay's lips quirked upward. "Not that she has that much trouble. The kids think she's really 'hot,' in their vernacular. They tease with her, but they're actually quite respectful to her. Protective, even. And then they have one little extra incentive to be nice to her."

"What's that?"

Leaning against the wall behind him, he caught her hand and laced his fingers through hers. "A couple of months ago we were having some real problems with one of our larger, more troubled kids. He's fifteen, and big. Anyway, Summer directs some drama classes, improv, readings, and so on, because we feel it's good for the kids to express themselves creatively. Most of them like it; some don't. This guy started making trouble during one session, making fun of the smaller kids until he finally had one of them crying. Then he made fun of him for being a crybaby. Summer got mad and told the guy off. He decided to show everyone how bad he could be, so he gave her a shove."

Spring frowned, instantly the protective big sister. "Did he hurt her? Was he punished? He's not still here, is he?"

Clay laughed, his hand tightening reassuringly around hers. "It's okay. The kid made a bit of a mistake. Derek happened to walk into the room just as the guy pushed Summer down."

A slight smile crept across Spring's face. "Oh. That *was* a mistake, wasn't it?" she mused, thinking of her businessman brother-in-law and the toughness she'd sensed in him from the beginning.

"You got it. I'd come into the room right behind Derek,

and I thought he was going to tear the kid apart. The kid thought so, too. He got off with nothing more than a deadly soft warning. He's treated Summer like fine porcelain ever since. He was dealt with officially here, of course, but it was Derek's threat that kept him straight from then on.''

Spring tilted her head. "I'd be willing to bet that Summer got mad at Derek for interfering.''

"Know her well, don't you? She did, as a matter of fact. Said she was perfectly capable of handling the situation herself.''

"She probably could have.''

"I've no doubt of it. But Derek never apologized to her. He just sat quietly while she chewed him out, then told her in that silky voice of his that he'll do exactly the same thing if the situation ever comes up again. And that he's fully prepared to carry through on his threats if necessary.''

"Mr. Macho.'' Spring sighed, shaking her head. She'd left her hair down that evening and it fell in a silvery blond curtain to curl at her shoulders, where it swayed against her peach silk dress at her movement.

Clay reached out with his free hand to catch a soft strand, rubbing it between his fingers as he murmured, "I suddenly see Derek's point. It's amazing how protective a man can feel about his woman.'' He met her eyes. "I know how I'd react if I found some guy shoving you to the floor.''

She blinked. *Make it a joke*, she told herself in a desperate attempt to lighten a suddenly heavy moment. "My, my. I do believe there's a bit of macho even in you, Clay.''

He grinned and allowed her to ease the tension with her teasing. "What can I say? I'm a mere male, after all.''

"Pity,'' she murmured, tugging her hand from his and stepping back. "I believe I'll have some more of that punch.''

She sipped her punch slowly, thinking that she was almost sorry she'd backed away from Clay a moment before. Oddly enough, when he'd taken her hand, it had

been the first time he'd really touched her all evening.
He'd been acting rather strangely since she'd arrived with
Summer and Derek earlier. Though he'd carried on in his
usual offbeat manner, there'd been something different in
his manner toward her. It was almost as if he'd withdrawn
from her in some way.

She couldn't help thinking of their conversation the
night before. He'd offered to back away from her, but
she'd weakly asked him not to. So why was he?

She frowned as a sudden thought occurred to her. What
if he'd been put off by her telling him about Roger? In her
moment of vulnerability she'd told Clay that she fanta-
sized about marriage and family. Was he afraid that she'd
start considering him as potential-husband material, as
she'd admitted to doing with Roger? Was he backing off,
as he'd said he would, in a subtle attempt to warn her not
to get too involved with him? It made sense, but she
wasn't sure. After all, he'd just implicitly called her his
woman, hadn't he? Or had he?

No one had ever confused her the way Clay did, she
thought, her mind growing weary from trying to understand him. And no one had ever made her want so very
badly to understand him.

She watched him across the room, clowning around
with a group of his kids. He loved them so much. She suspected that love, for him, would be an obsession. What
would it be like to be loved that way by him?

She'd like to find out, she thought wistfully.

She swallowed hard and set her punch cup on a table.
What was she thinking? What did she hope would happen? Could she even imagine leaving the successful practice she'd built for herself in Little Rock to move to California, where the competition would be so fierce? She
loved Arkansas. Unlike her sisters, she was perfectly
happy to remain in the state where she'd been born.

She tried to make herself stop thinking along those lines.
She was being ridiculous. There was nothing serious between her and Clay. Nor did he appear to want anything

more than a temporary alliance between them. He was a confirmed bachelor who dated women her own sister had described as drop-dead beautiful. He probably liked his life just the way it was—one beautiful woman after another, no strings, no messy entanglements. Nothing to offer a woman like her, who wanted…who needed so much more.

"Spring, I'd like you to meet Katie," Summer said, appearing suddenly at her sister's side. "She's a real sweetheart. You'll like her."

Fervently grateful for the distraction, Spring obediently followed Summer across the room.

Though he was talking heartily, appearing to be completely involved in his conversation, Clay knew every move Spring made across the room from him. It seemed that he was aware of each breath she took, though they were separated by several yards. It was no use, he decided fatalistically, even as he gave a lighthearted reply to a question that had just been thrown at him. He wasn't going to be able to insulate himself from her, no matter how hard he might try.

And he had tried. All evening he'd attempted to look at her and see just another pretty, interesting woman. Nothing special. Right?

Wrong. She was beautiful, more so each time he saw her. She was fascinating. And he was in love with her.

And she was going to be with him for only six more days.

Okay, so he was going to miss her when she left. Okay, so it would hurt. What was he going to do about it?

Only one thing to do, he decided abruptly. He'd take advantage of every moment of the next six days that he could spend with her. He'd make love to her as soon as he could persuade her, and if that didn't satisfy his appetite for her, he'd make love to her again. And again. And again, until she was as steeped in him as he was in her.

Maybe then she would stay.

IT WAS WITH MIXED FEELINGS that Spring accompanied Summer, Derek and Clay to a party in the home that Connie Anderson shared with Joel Tanner. She wasn't overly excited about attending a party where she knew only five other people, but it *was* another excuse to be with Clay. Summer had even stopped teasing her about seeing so much of Clay, and Derek, in his placid way, seemed to accept Clay's constant presence as inevitable while Spring was around. Spring was beginning to feel like one of a couple. She liked the feeling. She was going to miss it when it ended in five days.

Connie had moved in with Joel a month earlier, in February. They planned to be married in May, when Connie and Derek's parents returned from a leisurely, long-planned cruise, but they saw no need to wait that long to live together. This was Connie's first real party in her new home. It was cheerful, loud, eccentric. Good clean fun, Summer assured her sister.

"It's not Derek's and Joel's kind of thing, either, but they'll have a good time," she added as she helped Spring select a casual outfit consisting of a peach cotton blouse and comfortably full peach-and-cream plaid skirt.

"It's *your* kind of thing, though, isn't it?" Spring asked thoughtfully. "And Clay's."

"Sure, I love parties. So does Clay. He gets to perform."

"Perform?"

Summer only smiled mysteriously. "You'll see."

Yes, Spring thought glumly. She was afraid that she *would* see. She'd see, again, how very different she and Clay were. And, worse, he'd see the same thing. She wondered if any of his beautiful women would be there.

They were. From the moment Clay entered the room, Spring at his side, he was deluged by affectionate welcomes. Women—redheads, blondes, brunettes, all disgustingly beautiful—greeted him with kisses and hugs, teasing him about things that Spring didn't know about, illustrating so clearly how far apart their lives were. The women were dressed casually, for the most part, but with daring style that made Spring feel very provincial and un-sophisticated next to them.

The music was loud, classic rock and roll mostly. Spring liked rock and roll, but it did make conversation rather difficult. She smiled a lot.

When Bob Seger's recorded voice burst out with "Old Time Rock 'n Roll," everyone laughed and tried to talk Clay into stripping down to his shirt and briefs and doing the lip-sync routine that Tom Cruise had made famous in the movie *Risky Business*. Clay declined with a laugh, but Spring got the impression that he wouldn't always have turned down the challenge. It seemed that he had done that particular routine at several other parties. He only laughed and shrugged when she turned a questioning glance on him.

Spring managed to have a good time at the party, de-spite her initial feeling that she was terribly out of place, until a striking brunette joined the party halfway through the evening. She was dressed in Chinese red, red silk blouse and matching slacks that looked as if she'd been poured into them, and she was on the arm of an attractive auburn-haired man everyone called Ace. Spring sensed immediately that Connie and Summer hadn't known the woman would be there as Ace's date. She caught the quick, startled glances the former roommates exchanged before greeting the woman with somewhat stilted polite-ness.

Clay hadn't known the woman would be at the party, either, Spring realized a few moments later. She just hap-pened to be watching his face when he caught sight of the brunette. His eyes narrowed, and a muscle twitched in his jaw. His expression was hard to read, but Spring thought she detected chagrin. Then he glanced at her, caught her watching him and smiled, his face revealing nothing of his thoughts.

Who was she and what was she, or what had she been, to Clay? Spring asked herself the question with a fierce surge of jealousy that left her dismayed and wary. She couldn't allow herself to go on this way, she tried to tell herself sternly. She must *not* fall in love with Clay Mc-Entire!

It was all she could do not to demand an explanation from Clay when he placed his arm lightly around her shoulders and asked if she wanted a drink from the bar. "A club soda sounds nice," she said, then wondered if she should have asked for something stronger. Though she rarely drank, this night might be a good time for it.

The woman cornered them before he could even reply. It was as if she'd homed in on Clay the moment she entered the room and had barely paused on her way to him. "Hello, Clay."

"Hello, Jessica," he returned, a hint of resignation in his voice. His arm tightened around Spring's shoulders, just a little, as if the movement had been nothing more than reflex.

"Surprised to see me here?"

"Yes, I am a bit. I thought you'd left San Francisco."

She nodded, her rather slanted green eyes sparkling with feminine amusement, deep red mouth quirked into a slightly feline smile. "I did. I'm back."

"So I see."

"I wasn't at all surprised to see you. I knew you'd be at this party since you used to take me to all of Connie and Summer's parties."

"How clever of you." He managed to sound amazed and sarcastic all at once.

Her long lashes flicking in apparent annoyance, she eyed him slowly, her gaze lingering intimately on the tight black pants below his blousy, full-sleeved white shirt. Spring felt her hands curling into claws even as the woman drawled, "What is this, your Errol Flynn look? Love those knee-high boots. Quite dashing."

"Thanks." As if he'd just remembered his manners, Clay tightened his arm around Spring again and glanced down at her with a vaguely apologetic smile. "Sorry, sweetheart. This is Jessica Dixon, an old friend. Jess, meet Spring Reed, Summer's sister."

Jessica hadn't liked being called an "old" friend any more than Spring had liked his familiar shortening of the other woman's name. "It's very nice to meet you, Spring," she said in a voice that said it wasn't really all that nice. She'd barely looked Spring's way before she turned back to Clay. "Clay, darling, you haven't even kissed me hello. Surely that's not too much to expect after all we've been to each other."

That did it. Spring decided she didn't need to stand around and let the woman rub her face in the fact that Jessica and Clay had been lovers. "Clay, I think Joel is signaling for you," she said firmly. "Don't you think we should go see what he wants?"

"Yes, Spring, I think we should do just that," he replied gravely, his eyes and voice ripe with amusement. "See you later, Jess."

They were all the way across the room—nowhere near Joel and making no pretense to find him—before Spring spoke to Clay. "Could I ask just one question?"

Warily he nodded. "Of course."

"Was that the same woman you were with the night you met Summer?"

He grinned. "No."

She lifted an imperious eyebrow behind her glasses, trying to sound regal and condescending. "You have a thing for bitchy brunettes?" she asked distastefully.

"I suppose I did at one time," he answered thoughtfully, looking rather surprised at his own answer. Then he winked at her. "Guess I knew they were safe enough to hang around with until I found a particularly sweet blond."

She tossed her head. "Just don't feed me any lines right now, will you, Clay?"

Unable to resist, he hugged her. "Why, Spring Reed, I do believe you're jealous."

She glared at him. "Yes, dammit, I am. And I know full

well that it's stupid and illogical and totally unjustified, so just don't start with me, McEntire, or I'll...I'll...I'll walk out of here and leave you to that barracuda!"

"Oh, please, not that!" he murmured, laughing softly. On his face was a look of such wholly masculine satisfaction that Spring wanted to hit him. She really did.

"I want a drink," she told him flatly. "And I *don't* want club soda."

"Anything you desire, sweetheart," he answered her with mock subservience. "If you're tipsy, it will be all the easier to seduce you later."

She refused to respond to that in any way.

She wasn't tipsy, but he came close to seducing her, anyway. They had left the party not long after the encounter with Jessica. Clay claimed that he had a headache. The other guests actually believed him; it seemed that he'd been exceptionally well behaved that evening. Summer went so far as to call him "dull." Spring knew good and well that the headache was nothing more than a fabrication, but when he innocuously asked if he could stop by his place for an aspirin before taking her back to Sausalito, she told him she didn't mind.

"I can't believe you're stopping this now," Clay complained later in a ragged voice, looming over her on the deep terra-cotta-colored sofa. "We were doing so well."

About half an hour had passed since they'd entered Clay's house. Spring's blouse was open to the waist, her hair completely free of the pins that had once held it, and she was panting and flushed with passion. Clay wasn't in any better condition, his shirt open rakishly to the button of his now indecently tight pants, his hair rumpled boyishly around his face, his eyes unnaturally bright.

She inhaled deeply, tugged her blouse across her straining, well-kissed breasts and shook her head against the sofa cushion. "You promised you'd stop whenever I asked you to," she reminded him huskily.

"Yes, I know. But I kinda wish you'd asked a bit sooner,

if you just had to ask." He sighed, running a hand through his hair as he reluctantly sat up.

She chewed guiltily on her lower lip. "I'm sorry. I didn't mean to—It's just that, well, I got a little carried away."

He pulled her into his arms, nuzzling his cheek against hers. "You liked what we were doing, didn't you, Spring?"

She almost moaned at the renewal of feelings she'd just barely gotten under control. "You must know that I did."

"So why are we stopping? I want you, Spring, and I think you want me. You do, don't you?"

Buttoning her blouse, she glanced upward through lowered lashes. "Yes. I want you. But I can't make love with you tonight. The timing's all wrong."

He looked puzzled. "Why?"

Struggling to explain, even to understand herself, she twisted her hands in the lap of her wrinkled plaid skirt. "It's because of that woman."

He didn't have to ask which woman. "Spring, whatever was between Jessica and me was over a long time ago."

"I'm sure that's true. But the point is that I was jealous of her tonight. And I'm afraid that if I made love with you now, it would be because I was competing with her in some way. That's not what I want. I want to be sure I know what I'm doing, and why I'm doing it, before I make such an important decision. I don't take things like this lightly, Clay."

He dropped his forehead to rest it against hers. "Darling Spring, I love everything about you, I really do, but that convoluted mind of yours is driving me insane."

He loved everything about her? She savored the words for a moment. They were a bit like saying he loved her, weren't they? But still not enough. She was so close to loving him. She wouldn't be able to stop herself if they made love now. Maybe it was already too late, but surely she had to try. She had only five more days with him.

BY SATURDAY AFTERNOON Spring knew she'd made a mistake. Hours had passed since she'd last seen or heard from

Clay and still her body throbbed with frustration. She wanted him in a way that was all new to her. She'd been stupid to stop him when he'd been making such beautiful love to her, she decided morosely. She wouldn't blame him if he wrote her off as neurotic and stayed completely away from her for the next four days. But how she hoped that he wouldn't!

She and Summer spent the morning roaming through some of the tiny shops of artsy-craftsy novelties for which Sausalito was famous. They examined paintings, pottery, sculpture, handcrafted clothing and accessories...and all the time Spring wondered where Clay was, what he was doing. Was he thinking of her? She even wondered irrationally if he was with Jessica.

Stupid, stupid, stupid, she berated herself furiously, staring at a romantic painting of a lovely Victorian home surrounded by vivid flowers. The painting was stylish, beautiful and so very San Francisco. The colors would look wonderful in her apartment, but she couldn't bring herself to purchase it. It would remind her too much of Clay. Something told her she would think of him enough without having such poignant reminders hanging on her wall. *You have to stop this, Spring Reed. You have to stop this... this—*

"Moping," Summer said from behind her.

Spring jumped and jerked her head toward her sister. "What?"

"I said, what's with all the moping? You've been off in another world all day. And it doesn't look like such a pleasant world, from the expression on your face. What's wrong, Spring?"

"Nothing. I was just admiring this painting. Lovely, isn't it?"

Summer allowed herself to be distracted, though not without a long, searching look at her sister's face.

Clay called later that afternoon. "I think it's time I introduced you to my cooking," he informed Spring with a wicked chuckle.

"I'm not sure I'm up to this," Spring bantered, though her knuckles were white around the plastic receiver as she gripped it in sheer relief. He hadn't given up. "Are Summer and Derek invited to this culinary experiment?'

"Not this time, sweetheart. This time it's just you and me. No sister, no brother-in-law and no ex-girlfriends. How does that sound?"

She knew what he was asking. And it had very little to do with dinner. "That sounds very nice," she answered him, wondering if he could hear the whispery thread of a voice that came from her throat.

He did. "Good," he said, and his own voice had deepened. "I'll pick you up at seven. Dress sexy." With that he hung up.

Spring stood holding the receiver to her chest, staring into space, until Summer walked into the room and politely inquired if Spring was having an out-of-body experience.

It took her over an hour to get ready for her date. Though she berated herself the entire time for being silly, she was dithered over her selection of clothing. After all, she reasoned nervously, it wasn't as if her date were going to show up in an average suit and tie. Who knew what Clay would choose to wear? Not that she could compete with his flashy style, but she would like him to admire the way she dressed. She settled finally on a slinky jacquard silk dress in a pale mint green. Showing tantalizing hints of cleavage and leg when she moved, the surplice wrap dress was fastened with a wide matching belt that emphasized her small waist. The belt was the only thing holding the garment together. She'd bought the dress on impulse on that first shopping excursion with Summer. She wondered now if, even then, she'd had Clay in mind when she purchased the sexy garment.

She left her hair loose, skillfully applied pastel makeup and clipped on pearl earrings. She was ready. And her hands were trembling so hard she had to clench them in front of her to try to keep them steady. She'd heard the doorbell a few minutes earlier. She knew that Clay was waiting for her.

"You look beautiful, Spring," Derek told her sincerely when she finally came out of her room.

She gave him a grateful smile.

Summer opened her mouth to say something, noticed the expression on her older sister's face and changed her teasing to a quick compliment.

Clay took one look at her, pulled her into his arms and kissed her, deeply and passionately. She wouldn't have minded at all if her sister and brother-in-law hadn't been standing beside them.

"Clay!" she said, gasping, when he finally released her.

"God, you're beautiful," he told her with a grin, then turned to Summer. "I'm so glad you and Derek are staying home tonight."

Summer giggled. "Thanks a lot, friend. Maybe I should come along to chaperone this date."

"You'll never make it out of the house alive, pilgrim," Clay returned in his best John Wayne voice—mitigated somewhat by the unlined pink blazer and matching slacks he wore with a black-and-pink patterned shirt. Spring couldn't picture John Wayne ever wearing pink.

"You have to be the most uninhibited person I've ever met," she told him on the way to his house, thinking of that kiss in front of her sister and brother-in-law.

Clay chuckled. "I have to admit I'm not particularly dismayed by an audience," he agreed.

She thought of the things she'd learned about his childhood. "Is that why you dress so funny?" she asked curiously. "For attention?"

"Who dresses funny?" he demanded with mock indignation.

He obviously had no intention of allowing the conversation to get too serious, so Spring followed his lead and began to tease him about the unusual outfits he'd worn since she'd arrived.

They'd barely stepped into his house before Clay had her in his arms again. "You're so beautiful tonight," he murmured between brief, nipping kisses, his hands gliding over her silk dress. "I love this dress. Why don't you take it off?"

Her momentary attack of nerves disappeared in her sputter of laughter. "Clay! I thought you were going to serve dinner."

"I am," he assured her, removing her smudged glasses and slipping them into the breast pocket of his jacket. He brushed back a strand of her hair, tucking it behind her ear. "It'll be about an hour before it's ready."

She frowned suspiciously at him. "Then why am I here so early?"

He brushed his lips against her cheek, then dropped his head to nibble at her neck while he toyed with her belt. "For appetizers."

She was going weak and there wasn't a thing she could do about it but close her eyes and cling to him as his warm breath teased her ear. "I suppose…you consider this an appetizer?" she asked, her voice reedy.

"Mmm." His tongue darted out to taste the soft spot just below her ear, making her shiver with helpless pleasure. "I want you, Spring. It seems like I've been wanting you all my life."

She'd never had much willpower where this man was concerned. What little she'd started out with finally slipped away, unmissed, as her arms went around his neck. "I want you, Clay. I guess I have ever since the first time you kissed me," she confessed huskily. "I couldn't bear to leave California without ever knowing what it was like to have you make love to me. Please love me now."

Something she'd said made him go rigid, almost as if in pain, and she wondered if she'd spoiled the moment. But then he lowered his head and covered her mouth with his and she knew that everything would be all right. More

than all right. Every feminine instinct within her told her
that making love with Clay would be the most beautiful
experience of her life, a memory to treasure for as long as
she drew breath. The thought brought a frisson of fear,
even as she trembled with excited anticipation. She suspected that nothing in the future would ever compare to
Clay's lovemaking.

Clay released her mouth only to sweep her into his
arms, holding her high against his chest. She clung trustingly to him as he moved toward his bedroom with long,
confident strides. Spring was embarking on a fantastic adventure, and for the first time in her cautious, conservative
life she didn't care about consequences or repercussions.

7

CLAY SET HER on her feet beside his bed, gently, as if she were tiny and frail and, oh, so delicate, rather than tall and firm and healthy. He took her face between his hands—his trembling hands, she noted in wonder—and kissed her with such tender beauty that she almost cried. His abrupt change from passion to sweetness made her head spin. She would never know what to expect from him, nor would she want him to be more predictable. He was Clay, and just by being Clay, he made her weak with wanting him.

Her mouth was moist and soft under his, her lips parting in mute invitation. Clay moaned and touched the tip of his tongue to hers, savoring the taste of her. Had any woman ever felt as good? He couldn't remember. He knew no woman had ever made him shudder. He shuddered when Spring's hands parted his blazer to stroke his chest through his thin cotton shirt. If her touch could do this to him through fabric, how would he react to her hands on his bare skin? He couldn't wait to find out, and yet—

"I think I'm nervous," he murmured, his lips quirking into an almost sheepish smile against hers.

Her hands curled at his shoulders as she leaned back fractionally to look up at him in surprise, her violet eyes luminous in the glow of a bedside lamp. "I can't imagine you ever being nervous about anything," she told him. "You always seem so sure of yourself."

"Not with you." He moved his lips to her cheek, then to her temple. "I'm a basket case right now."

"Why?" Her question was only a whisper as she tilted

her face to encourage his ministrations, her eyelids fluttering heavily.

"Because I want to make everything perfect for you. I
want to be the perfect lover, say all the right things, touch
you in all the right ways. I want to make you forget any
other man you've ever known, satisfy you so well that no
other man will ever compare to me. I'm not usually a possessive man, but you make me want to possess you, body
and soul, heart and mind."

"Clay…" She squirmed a little in his arms, as if unsure
of how to interpret his low-voiced words, how to respond.

Suddenly uncomfortable himself with the intensity of
the moment, he spared her the necessity of response by
capturing her lips, the kiss deep and consuming. Still lost
in the kiss, he tumbled with her to the bed, reaching for the
buckle of her wide belt as they fell. The belt fell away and
the dress opened, giving him access to the skin bared by
her lacy bra and panty hose. He touched the upper curve
of her small breasts, then the silky slope of her flat stomach, fingertips sliding beneath the waistband of her panty
hose to tease the quivering area just below her navel. He
wanted to reach lower, but he restrained himself, determined to draw their lovemaking out as long as possible.

Her hands tugged at his clothing, making him wonder
just how long his noble willpower would last. He
shrugged out of his jacket, tossing it to the floor, then
tugged his shirt from his slacks. With her eager assistance
he freed both of them from everything but his narrow
black briefs and her satin-and-lace panties.

"So beautiful. You're so very beautiful." Clay's breath
was hot on one of her breasts, his hands restlessly stroking
every inch of her that he could reach.

Spring arched into his avid mouth, her fingers deep in
his golden hair to hold him closer. His muttered words
pleased her. He found her beautiful. Rationally she knew
she was pretty, at best. Yet Clay made her feel beautiful.
She moaned as he drew the straining, hardened tip of her
breast deep into his mouth. Had he really been worried

that he wouldn't satisfy her? How silly. Couldn't he tell that he affected her as no man ever had before?

She remembered another time when he had kissed her and she had sensed uncertainty in him. Just as she was attracted to his usual cocky self-confidence, she was fascinated by those glimpses of his vulnerabilities.

Call it love, he'd told her. And though she had fought it, she was beginning to believe that he'd chosen the right word.

Clay lifted his head for a moment to look tenderly down into her passion-flushed face. "Are you protected, sweetheart? If not, I can—"

"No, it's okay. I'm protected," she whispered, touched by his concern. Though there had been no one else since her breakup with Roger, she'd continued to take her birth-control pills, primarily from force of habit. She was glad now that she had.

Smiling his pleasure, Clay continued to caress her breasts with lips and tongue and teeth as his hand stroked downward, moving with tantalizing leisure toward the satin-and-lace triangle that was her only covering. Once there he taunted her further, his fingertips gliding over the fabric so lightly that she wondered if she'd imagined his touch. Gasping, she arched her hips upward, her thighs parting involuntarily as she silently begged him to deepen the caress. Still he teased her with butterfly touches and hot, biting kisses until she cried out and reached for him, pulling him on top of her.

Laughing throatily, he hugged her hard, burying his face in her hair. She locked her arms around his neck, pressing upward so that she could feel every inch of his damp, warm skin next to hers: her breasts flattening against his chest with its light covering of hair; her long, slender legs twining with his solid, rough ones; his heart pounding against her; his breath raw and ragged in her ear. The signs of his arousal heightened her own, and she whispered his name, telling him how badly she wanted him.

Still he tormented her, thrusting against her, hard and virile and throbbingly aroused. Only the fabric of their underwear kept him from entering her. Her head tossed on the pillow. "Please, Clay, please," she moaned, clutching at his waist.

"I will, sweetheart," he promised her, sliding up and down against her to create a sensual friction that soon had her panting and bucking wildly.

"Clay, *please*!" Was this really her, this mindless creature begging for completion? She'd never lost control like this, never wanted like this. Never ached like this. Was he deliberately trying to drive her out of her mind? "Damn you, Clay," she muttered when he thrust against her again in frustrating simulation of that ultimate intimacy.

Using all her strength, she shoved at his shoulders, rolling him to his side. And then she attacked him, her mouth and hands all over his body as she made him ache for her the same way he'd made her ache for him. She nibbled and sucked at the taut cords of his neck, then licked swirling patterns in the golden hair around his flat brown nipples, finally moving downward to draw long, low groans from him with her bold caresses. He didn't attempt to stop her, seemed incapable of making the effort, even when she jerked his black briefs away to bare him to more intimacies.

No, this couldn't be Spring Reed, this sexy, insatiable, uninhibited woman exploring Clay's body so wantonly. Taking such unholy pleasure in the soft, guttural cry torn from his throat when her lips and tongue stroked him. "Spring! Ah, God, Spring, *yes*!"

And then he was over her and all barriers were gone and he was plunging inside her to a level so deeply buried within her that she hadn't even known it existed. Moving feverishly, he carried her with him on a mind-shattering journey to a place she'd never been before, never imagined. And he took her there so fast and so hard that, in all the mental replays that would come afterward, she'd never exactly remember the details—only the explosive, climactic conclusion.

"Clay!" His name began as a scream but left her lips a mere whisper as she shuddered again and again beneath the shock waves that followed.

"Spring! Ah, love." And he, too, trembled in the aftermath of a climax so powerful, so unique, that it shocked them both.

He didn't let go of her, only rolled to his side to relieve her of his weight. He pulled her close to him, his arms around her as he snuggled against her back. Their position allowed him to soothingly stroke her breasts and stomach as he pressed his lips to the back of her neck. She closed her eyes and rested, her heart rate slowing, her breathing returning to normal. Even after their incredible lovemaking she gloried in the feel of him. The damp softness against the back of her thigh was satisfying evidence that Clay, too, had found pleasure with her, as if she needed proof.

They lay quiet and still for a long time, satisfied to be together. After a while a deeply contented sigh left her lips, causing Clay to stir and chuckle behind her. He nuzzled into the curve of her shoulder. "Are you sorry?"

"About what? Making love with you?"

"Yes."

She nestled back against him, pulling his arms more tightly around her. "No. I'm not sorry."

"I'm glad. So very glad."

Spring smiled ruefully. "I wasn't going to let this happen, you know. I told myself right from the beginning that I wasn't going to sleep with you."

"You haven't slept with me. You've made love with me, but you haven't slept with me."

She sighed again. "You know what I mean."

"Yes, sweetheart, I know what you mean. And I'm glad you changed your mind."

"I couldn't resist you," she answered, dramatically mournful. "Your fatal charm got to me."

He laughed softly. "Is that what did it?"

"Either that or your fish tie. I'm not sure which one."

"I can see where that would be a hard choice," he agreed solemnly, and then bit her on the back of the neck, making her laughingly chastise him. He lay still for another moment, then asked hesitantly, "I don't suppose I could talk you into staying the night?"

She chewed her lip. "No. I'm sorry, Clay, I can't. I wouldn't feel comfortable with that at all."

"It's okay. I understand. But, God, I'd love to wake up with you in my arms. Spring, I—"

And then he swallowed whatever he had intended to say and kissed her nape, his hand caressing one of her breasts as he did so. Her eyes opened in surprise when her body began to respond to his lazy fondling. Surely he couldn't expect her to…?

But he was still soft against her thigh, and she relaxed, her eyelids closing again. Her nipples were hard and swollen when finally his talented fingers left them to drift downward. "Clay?" she whispered uncertainly, squirming a little when his fingertips slipped into blond curls to trace damp folds.

"Shh, Spring. Just let me love you," he murmured, his cheek against hers as he deepened the caress, stroking over and inside her, slowly increasing the pressure until her breath was catching in tiny sobs of pleasure. "That's it, sweetheart," he encouraged her. "Let me make you feel good."

And he did make her feel good, his fingers taking her just to the edge of fulfillment. By then he was no longer soft but as fully aroused as she. Spring cried out in pleasure when he lifted her leg over his and entered her, his fingers never leaving that damp nest of curls. Then cried out again as she was overcome by spasms of ecstasy so intense that she wanted them never to stop, to go on for an eternity. An eternity with Clay.

She hadn't known she was crying until he rolled her onto her back and leaned over her, gently wiping the tears from her cheek. "I hope these are tears of pleasure," he murmured.

"Yes," she whispered, lifting a trembling hand to lightly stroke her thumb below one of his beautiful eyes. "Are these?"

"Oh, yes." The words held a note of awe, as if he, too, were having trouble believing what had taken place between them, not once but twice. And then he pulled her onto his chest and wrapped her close, and the gesture was so lovingly protective that she almost cried again.

Swallowing hard, she snuggled into the hollow of his shoulder and wondered almost dispassionately what the future held for her. Pain, most certainly, when her time with Clay ended. He'd said nothing about making their relationship permanent, had spoken no words of love. He'd told her only that he wanted her, and desire alone was not enough. Yet the future would also hold such beautiful memories. How could she regret what they'd done? She could only be profoundly grateful that she'd known such joy at least once in her life. She would never have believed that anything could have been so wonderful, had she not experienced it herself.

He must have felt her smile against his skin. "What are you thinking?"

She chuckled. "I was remembering the night I met you. I tried then to imagine what you must be like in bed."

"Did you?" He sounded delighted. "Why, Spring, I'm shocked."

"You mean you didn't wonder the same thing about me?" She tried to sound insulted.

She could hear his grin in his answer. "Of course not. And if you believe that, there's this bridge a few miles from here that I'd like to sell you."

He paused for a moment, then asked curiously, "So what did you think I'd be like in bed?"

"Imaginative, sensitive, considerate, and downright good," she replied humorously, recalling her exact thoughts.

"Mmm. And how *was* I?"

"Feeling insecure, Clay?"

"Come on Spring, I can't stand it! What's your opinion?"

Propping herself on her elbow, she relented and smiled down at him. "That you're imaginative, sensitive, considerate, and downright good."

His smile seemed to light the shadowy corners of the room. "Thank you."

"Believe me, it was entirely my pleasure," she answered with heartfelt fervency.

Then she frowned, suddenly overcome by feminine curiosity. "Well?"

He feigned innocence. "Well, what?"

"How was I?"

"Honestly, Spring, postmortems are so tacky," he drawled, then choked dramatically when her hand enclosed his throat. "Okay, okay, I'll tell."

She released his windpipe and smiled sweetly. "Well? Was I what you expected?"

"No."

"No?" Dismayed, she repeated his answer questioningly.

Laughing at her expression, he shook his head. "No. I thought you would be prim and proper and just a bit inhibited. Not that I wasn't looking forward to it, anyway, you understand. But had I known how passionate and responsive you really are, I'd have thrown you over my shoulder and hauled you into my bed that first night."

She shook her head. "It's showing again."

Lifting an eyebrow, he glanced downward along his long, perspiration-sheened body. "I beg your pardon?"

She just managed not to laugh. "I mean, that streak of macho in you is showing again."

"Oh, that."

"Idiot." The word came out an endearment. She toyed with the sparse hair on his chest for a while, then peeked through her lashes at his contented face. "Speaking of food…"

"Were we?"

"Yes. Don't you think dinner should be ready by now?"

He made a production of checking the time on his watch. "Why, yes, I do believe it is. Are you hungry, sweet Spring?"

"As a matter of fact, I am. I seem to have worked up quite an appetite since we arrived."

He climbed out of the bed and stood unself-consciously nude, looking down at her. She almost grabbed him and pulled him back into bed, but she decided that she wouldn't survive another session of lovemaking without sustenance. She laughed when he offered her his robe. The heavy brocade garment was straight out of a Noel Coward movie—velvet lapels, cuffs, one deep pocket. It trailed a foot behind her when she walked. She pushed the voluminous sleeves up on her forearms and scowled at him when he tied himself into a thigh-length white terry robe. "Maybe we should trade."

"I kind of like you in that one," he returned teasingly. "It's interesting for *you* to be the one dressed funny for a change."

"So you admit that you dress funny!"

He only laughed.

She frowned at him, struck by a sudden unpleasant thought. "This robe wasn't a present from a woman, was it?"

"Well, yes, it was," he answered thoughtfully.

She immediately began to untie it. His hand covered hers on the sash. "Summer gave it to me for a Christmas present. She said it reminded her of me, for some strange reason."

She had the grace to look sheepish. "Oh. I was being unreasonably jealous again, wasn't I?"

"Yes, you were." He turned to walk out of the room, then tossed her a cheeky grin. "*This* is the robe that was a present from an old girlfriend," he informed her, straightening his white terry lapels as he walked out.

The shoe she threw after him missed him by mere inches.

The gourmet dinner Clay had offered turned out to be a deli picnic, neatly packed into a basket on the kitchen counter.

"I thought you said you were cooking," Spring accused him, watching him unpack the tempting delicacies onto a round oak kitchen table.

"I said I was going to introduce you to my cooking," he corrected her imperturbably. "This is the way I cook."

"You're a fraud and a scoundrel, Clay McEntire, and I—" She stopped short, then continued lightly, "I really should be angry with you, but I'm just too hungry."

She avoided his eyes as she took her seat across the table from him.

She'd almost told him that she loved him. She wasn't sure exactly when she'd realized it, but she knew now. And, for the life of her, she didn't know what she was going to do about it.

He'd almost told her he loved her while they were in bed. It would have been so natural, so easy. And so true. God, how he'd wanted to tell her. But he couldn't. He didn't think she wanted to hear it. And, for the life of him, he didn't know what he'd have said afterward.

Clay kept his gaze on the plate in front of him and concentrated on his dinner. They were both unusually quiet while they ate.

HOLDING HER PRESSED AGAINST Summer's front door, Clay kissed Spring good-night. He could never get enough of the taste of her, he decided, lingering over the embrace. No matter how many times he had her, he would never stop wanting her. "It's very late. Are you tired?" he murmured, stroking the faintest of violet shadows under her eyes. She'd kept her glasses in her purse on the way home, anticipating his kiss, he hoped.

"Mmm. Pleasantly so." She tilted her head back against his arm to smile at him in a way that brought an almost painful lump to his throat. He could almost imagine that she loved him when she smiled at him that way. It hurt, he discovered.

"I suppose I should let you go in." He made no attempt to mask his reluctance to release her.

"I suppose so." She sounded no more enthused about the idea.

"I've got things to do tomorrow at Halloran House, so I may not see you."

She bit her lip in visible dismay, then made an effort to sound only politely interested. "That's okay."

"I'll call you."

"Please do."

He kissed her again. "Tonight was..." He paused, laughed briefly and shook his shaggy blond head. "I don't know what tonight was. I have nothing to compare it to. Let's just say that it was the most exciting, miraculous, wonderful night of my life."

"Mine, too. I'll never forget it, Clay." She kissed his chin. "You've given me a lovely memory to take home with me."

He felt as if a fist had just slammed into his gut. He just managed not to grunt with the pain. How could she talk about leaving him after all they'd shared so recently? She couldn't, he decided, not if she loved him. He was suddenly glad that he hadn't voiced his own feelings. He'd dealt with enough rejection in his life. He didn't need to go looking for it.

"Yeah, well..." He inhaled deeply and forced himself to step back from her. "I'll call you tomorrow."

He drove home, walked straight to the rarely touched bar and poured himself a drink, hoping it would help him forget that the woman he loved was leaving him in four days.

Spring climbed wearily into her bed, grateful that her sister hadn't waited up for her this time, buried her face in her pillow and fell asleep. She woke the next morning with traces of tears on her cheeks, though she couldn't remember crying in her sleep.

"ARE YOU GOING TO TELL ME about it or not?" Summer demanded, her voice carrying clearly. "Did you go to bed with Clay?"

"Summer!" Spring flushed and hastily looked up and down the supermarket produce aisle, hoping that no one had overheard her outspoken sister. "Honestly."

Summer sighed but lowered her voice. "Well? Want to explain that dreamy look that's been in your eyes all day?"

"You know that this is absolutely none of your business."

"Yes, I know."

"And that it's rude and insensitive for you to even ask."

"I know that, too." Summer waited expectantly, her hand hovering over the kiwifruit.

Spring exhaled in a gust of exasperation and shook her head. The truth was, she found herself *wanting* to talk about Clay, about her feelings for him. She thought it just might help her clarify those feelings for herself if she could discuss them with someone loving and sympathetic. Like her sister. "All right, we'll talk about it," she said. "But not in a supermarket! Over lunch."

"Fine."

"So let's talk about you and Clay," Summer demanded as soon as they'd seated themselves at the cozy kitchen table for lunch. Derek was playing golf that afternoon with Joel, giving the sisters a chance to spend time with each other. "Something's going on, I can tell."

With little evidence of success Spring fought the wave of color that flooded her fair cheeks. "Well, we, uh—"

Summer nodded solemnly. "And?"

"And...it was, um—"

"I see. So now what?"

"I wish I knew." Spring sighed, shaking her head.

"This is such an enlightening conversation." Summer

grinned as she absently stabbed at her fruit salad. "Are you in love with Clay?"

"I strongly suspect that I am."

"Want to try saying that with a smile?"

"I don't think I can. And stop looking so happy, Summer! This is dreadful!"

"Spring, if you're in love with Clay, which you are, and he's in love with you, which I'm sure he is, there's nothing dreadful about it! People in love find ways to work out the obstacles and be together. Derek and I did, Joel and Connie did, and you and Clay will. Be happy, Sis. Falling in love is wonderful, especially when it's the happily-ever-after kind. Believe me, I'm speaking from experience."

"I hope you're right." Spring pushed aside her barely touched plate, knowing how much longing must be written on her face. "I don't know if this is the happily-ever-after kind, but I do know it's permanent. It's not something that's going to go away when I get home."

"Good. Now you know why your other relationships never lasted. You weren't in love."

"No, not like this." Spring smiled ruefully. "Though God knows why I've chosen to fall in love—really in love, for the first time in my life—with Clay McEntire, of all people. I always thought I wanted a nice *normal* person. You know, one from the same planet?"

Summer chuckled, her blue eyes dancing with pleasure. "It has to be the way he dresses," she managed brokenly. "You just couldn't resist the pink suit."

That did it. Both of them fell back in their chairs and laughed hysterically at Clay's expense. And Spring felt much better when they'd finished. She found herself clinging to a foolish hope that she and Clay were going to be together long past the end of her vacation.

IT WASN'T going to work, Clay had decided by Monday morning. He shoved his fingers through his already disordered hair and stared glumly at the stacks of papers on his desk. His relationship with Spring wasn't going to work. He might as well acknowledge that now and start trying to accept it. Actually, he'd started accepting it yesterday, when he'd been away from her long enough to clear his love-clouded mind and take a long look at the situation. He was angry with himself because he hadn't even called her, as he'd promised. But he couldn't be objective when he was with her or even talking to her on the phone.

Spring loved her home state. She was happy there, happy with her career, her friends, having her parents within visiting distance. She'd made a success of her practice, and she'd worked hard to do it. She wouldn't be interested in giving it up and moving to San Francisco, where she'd have to start from scratch.

Besides, he asked himself honestly, leaning back in his comfortably worn desk chair and staring at the Mickey Mouse poster on his office wall, what did he have to offer her? He wasn't the most stable, settled person. He liked taking life one day at a time, living impulsively. He was unofficially on call at all hours for any troubled teenager who needed him; it wasn't unusual for him to receive calls in the middle of the night that had him jumping out of bed and running to help. His love and his energy were spent on his kids, and he wasn't sure how much was left over. Hadn't that been his reason for staying single all along? How did he know what kind of husband he'd make, assuming that he decided he wanted to marry Spring or she him?

He leaned his elbows on his desk and dropped his face into his hands. He loved her so much. He'd never imagined loving anyone this much. She was going to rip a part of him away when she left on Wednesday. But there was nothing he could do about it. He didn't feel right about asking her to stay, asking her to risk her future on him.

Another thought hit him, making him lift his head and rest his chin on his fists, frowning fiercely at old Mickey, as if the cartoon mouse had made the suggestion. Go with her? To Little Rock, Arkansas? He was California born and bred, quite comfortable with the fast lane. What was there for him in Little Rock? He wouldn't even be able to communicate with the kids there, much less help them. Would he? And what made him think she'd want him to go with her? She'd never said that she loved him, only that she was attracted to him. And that wasn't enough.

No. He slowly shook his head at Mickey, whom he fancied was beginning to wear a look of sympathy. Mick knew it wasn't going to work, too, he decided, trying to find his always present sense of humor. Even that didn't help. He didn't feel like laughing or even smiling. He felt like crying. Or going after Spring, kidnapping her to a desert island somewhere and making love to her thirty times a day until they both succumbed to exhaustion. Since he wasn't going to do either of those things, he decided to get back to work.

It was a long day. Students were in and out of his office in a steady stream. He'd heard from those who claimed their teachers picked on them, those whose parents didn't understand them, those madly in love and wanting advice or approval. Only now that school had been dismissed for the afternoon did he have some time alone to clear his desk. He pulled a file folder in front of him and began to go over the records of a recent transfer to the school, a boy who'd been in trouble at his former school in Oregon. And for the first time in years Clay found another person's problems having to compete with his own for his full attention.

8

SPRING HAD JUST PULLED the hem of her soft blue sweater over her slacks Monday night, in preparation for an evening at Connie's and Joel's, when her sister knocked, then peeked cautiously around the bedroom door. "Spring, Clay's here," Summer said almost hesitantly, knowing that Spring was upset because she hadn't heard from Clay since the wee hours of Sunday morning. "To be honest, he seems to be in a lousy mood."

He was in a bad mood? Spring was the one who was annoyed—with him, for the mixed signals that were so hard for her to understand, and with herself, for allowing things to become so awkward. Her heart curled up and whimpered, afraid it was about to be kicked. "Okay, I'm ready," she said impassively, hoping that her cool expression hid her anxiety.

Clay was waiting for her in the den. Summer and Derek had tactfully disappeared. Clay's smile was a bit strained when Spring entered the room. She clenched her hands in the pockets of her pleated slacks, hiding their trembling. "Hello, Clay."

"Hi, Spring." Even his voice sounded different somehow.

Only then did she notice what he was wearing, a bright turquoise leather bomber jacket over a baggy, multipocketed air-force-styled jumpsuit in neon yellow. Odd, she mused absently, how she noticed his clothing now only as an afterthought. She stood where she was, unsmiling, watching him. She had no intention of making things easier for him.

Clay made a sharp, impatient gesture, and then he was

across the room and she was in his arms. "I'm sorry," he murmured into her hair, holding her so tightly that it hurt.

She didn't complain but burrowed into his shoulder, her hands clutching his back beneath the buttery-soft jacket. "Sorry about what?"

"For not calling you yesterday."

She shook her head against him. "You don't owe me explanations."

"I promised I'd call," he replied flatly. "At the very least, I owe you an apology."

She wanted so badly to ask why he hadn't called, but she couldn't, and he didn't volunteer the information. It wasn't as if he owed her anything or didn't deserve time away from her, she told herself. But he'd promised he'd call.

He kissed her rather roughly and set her a few inches away from him. "I thought you and I could follow Derek and Summer in my car to Connie's tonight, if that's okay with you," he said with obviously forced airiness.

Why are you acting so strangely? "Of course that's all right with me."

He nodded and turned to stare out the huge window of the den. He seemed distant, as if his thoughts were turned so deeply inward that he was having to make an effort to concentrate on anything going on around him. He'd been so open with her until now. It hurt to be shut out.

"Did you see Thelma today?" she asked him, struggling to make conversation.

He nodded. "Yes. They're moving her into a regular room tomorrow."

"That's good, isn't it? It means she's better." *Talk to me, Clay. Tell me what's bothering you.*

"Yes, she's much better. The doctors seem quite pleased with her progress."

"How is she emotionally?"

"She's okay. Her mother's no help, but her aunt Diane is here now, and she's very nice. I think she'll be able to help Thelma a great deal."

"I'm glad." And that was all she could think of to say. *If it's not Thelma, then what is it? Are you tired of me already? I'll only be here for two more days.* "I'll go see if Summer and Derek are ready."

Clay nodded, not even looking around at her as she left the room.

They were in the library-styled room that Derek used as an office at home, Summer leafing through a magazine as her husband glanced through some files at an enormous rolltop desk. She looked up curiously when Spring entered. "You and Clay ready to go? Tonight should be fun."

Spring nodded doubtfully. "I hope so."

"Uh-oh. He's still in a bad mood?"

"He's in an odd mood. A bit withdrawn."

Summer placed the magazine on a low table, looking thoughtful. "He gets that way sometimes. Usually when he's worried about something."

Spring thought wistfully of how little she actually knew about Clay. Summer knew him much better, even though Spring had made love with him. Why had she thought that the physical closeness they'd shared would bring them closer together emotionally, as well? Obviously she'd been wrong.

Clay paced the den, waiting for the others to join him. He knew that he'd confused Spring earlier, but he didn't know how else to act with her. He'd never been at such a loss. He loved her, he'd shared something with her that surpassed any experience he'd ever had with a woman, and yet there was still nothing more between them than...than a vacation affair, he thought sadly. She still planned to leave him in a couple of days, and he saw nothing for them beyond that time. *Dammit, how am I supposed to act?*

He looked up as Spring came back into the room and mentally flinched at the wary look on her pretty face. *Don't look at me like that, Spring. Don't you know I only want to hold you, love you? Can't you see that you're tearing me apart?*

He'd thought it would be easier in a larger group of people to ignore the panic that was steadily building within him and act naturally. Instead, being with Summer and Derek and Joel and Connie during the dinner that Connie and Joel had prepared for them was unexpectedly painful. The other couples were so happy, so comfortable in their relationships. Clay found himself noting each loving look and intimate touch that passed between them. He, on the other hand, was carefully avoiding meeting Spring's eyes or touching her more than necessary because he wasn't sure how well he could control his emotions. He supposed there was some ironic humor in the situation—a natural toucher such as himself envying others for being able to touch the ones they loved. Too bad he didn't feel like laughing. And why did he find himself getting so angry?

"So you'll be back in Little Rock by Wednesday evening," Joel was saying to Spring when Clay forced his attention to the conversation going on around him. "When do you go back to work?"

"Not until Monday," Spring answered. "I have some things I want to do around the house, so I took a full two weeks off—first time since I opened my practice almost two years ago."

"You're going to be busy when you get back," Summer commented. "I'll bet your patients will be lined up at the door Monday morning."

Spring smiled. "Well, actually, my appointment book is full for the next few weeks. But I'm not complaining about business being good."

"I thought we were going to watch a movie," Clay blurted out suddenly and not particularly graciously. He couldn't sit quietly and listen to them talk about Spring leaving. He winced at the wide-eyed looks of surprise turned his way and tried to make a joke. "I'm not allowed to stay up past ten on school nights."

"Sure, Clay. We really believe that," Connie retorted, but she stood and inserted the cassette into the VCR. With surreptitious glances at Clay that he didn't miss, the others settled back in their seats to watch the movie.

Spring's attention remained on Clay. He looked up to find her watching him with an expression that he couldn't read. Disgusted with himself for acting like a jerk, he reached out to take her hand, unable to resist raising it to his lips. Her skin was soft beneath his mouth, and he felt her pulse racing in her slender wrist at the caress. His own body responded. He wanted her. He remembered his earlier fantasy of picking her up, throwing her over his shoulder and carrying her off to an isolated spot. It still sounded good. And just as impossible.

He lowered their linked hands to his thigh and turned his gaze toward the big-screen television, trying to pay attention to the recently released comedy that he'd wanted to see at one time. Now he couldn't care less about the movie.

Anger. The doctor of psychology in him recognized the emotion as reaction to his upcoming loss, his dread of rejection. The neglected little boy still buried deep inside him was unable to rationalize the inappropriate emotion away. He was hurting, and it made him want to lash out at the cause of his pain—Spring.

What is wrong with him? Spring asked herself for the…well, she'd lost track of the number of times. *Why is he treating me this way? Almost like a stranger.*

She hadn't thought he'd be the type of man to lose interest once he'd made another conquest. Maybe she'd misjudged him.

He'd barely touched her this evening. After all the touching he'd done from the moment they'd met, now he seemed to have no problem at all keeping his hands to himself. He was holding her hand now, but it seemed almost an afterthought to him, almost as if he were doing her a favor, she thought resentfully.

Was Saturday night your idea of a favor, Clay? Were you just going along with Summer's brilliant idea of providing some excitement for her bored older sister? She uncurled her fingers from his and clenched her hands in her lap. *Don't do me any more favors, Clay.*

The catalyst for seething emotion came after the movie, when the three couples were talking over nightcaps before breaking up for the evening. The talk had turned, as it so often did, to Halloran House and its residents. Summer had spent part of the afternoon there and was telling the others about something that had happened to upset some of the young people. It seemed that a fourteen-year-old friend of theirs had run away from home after a quarrel with his parents. The parents had sent the police after him. They'd found him in a bus station, preparing to leave town.

"The kids were really upset because the police made a very public thing out of dragging Tony out of the bus station. It was all terribly humiliating for him," Summer added.

Clay scowled. "I hadn't heard about that." Great. He'd been so wrapped up in Spring that he hadn't even known that one of his kids had been in trouble. *Thanks a lot, Spring.*

"The kids are all furious with Tony's parents," Summer told him, fluffing her long bangs, a habitual gesture.

Spring shifted in her seat. "What else could the parents have done? It wasn't their fault that the police were overly enthusiastic in carrying out their jobs."

"They could have gone after their son themselves, rather than sending the cops," Clay answered, standing and looking down at her as if she weren't very bright, she thought resentfully. "Or they could have called Frank or me. We could have found him."

"I only know that if my son had run away, I'd do exactly what Tony's parents did. After all, if the police had been able to find Thelma earlier, she wouldn't have been so close to death by the time you got to her."

"And if her mother had called me sooner, I'd have found her earlier," Clay argued. "The cops never would have found her at all, the way they were going. It was probably just an accident that they found Tony."

"You mean everyone in San Francisco should call you when their kids run away?" Was he really so arrogant?

He flushed at the derision in her tone, shoving his hands in his pockets. "Not everyone, of course. But if I happen to know the kids and work with them, as I have with Thelma and Tony, it would seem only logical to give me a chance to help. Hell, I didn't even know Tony had run away until just now." His tone clearly implied that it was Spring's fault that he hadn't known—quite unfairly, she thought, piqued.

"Maybe they decided to try something new, if you've been working with him and he still ran away." *Oops, wrong choice of words. I might as well have come right out and accused Clay of failing with Tony,* she realized when his face hardened. She opened her mouth to clarify the statement, but Summer jumped in hastily to change the subject, obviously hoping to avoid the confrontation that was building between Spring and Clay.

"It's getting late," Clay said abruptly, still glaring at Spring. "Are you ready to go?"

She nodded. "Yes. I'm ready."

Spring was rather surprised when Clay told Derek and Summer that he'd take her home later. After their near quarrel she expected him to take her straight back to Sausalito. Instead, she found herself walking on a beach with him about half an hour after leaving the others, huddling into the windbreaker she'd worn with her slacks and sweater as the damp, cool, salted breeze tossed her hair and reddened her cheeks.

Clay kicked at a broken shell, then bent to pick it up and toss it into the waves breaking nearby. "Tonight wasn't much fun for you, was it?"

She took a deep breath and stopped walking, turning to face him squarely. "You didn't seem to be enjoying yourself, either."

"No, I guess I wasn't." His face was deeply shadowed in the fog-diffused moonlight. "I'm sorry."

Her chest hurt. She thought it might be because her heart was being thoroughly pummeled. "What's wrong, Clay?" she finally found the courage to ask. *Please talk to me.*

"What's wrong?" He shoved his fingers through his windblown hair, staring impassively at her as he appeared to debate his reply. When he finally spoke, his voice was raw. "I'm going to miss you, Spring. I'll miss you very much."

She let her head drop forward. "I'll miss you, too, Clay," she whispered. But he hadn't asked her to stay, nor would she be the one to suggest it. How could she, when she wasn't at all sure that she wanted to stay in San Francisco? As much as she'd enjoyed her visit, she was already homesick. As much as she dreaded leaving Clay, she still rather looked forward to getting back to work on Monday. God, what a mess she'd made of everything! "Oh, Clay."

He caught her in his arms and held her tightly. "Dammit, Spring. Don't you know that you've disrupted my entire life? I haven't been able to think about anything but you since you arrived. My kids, my job, my friends—I forget them all when you're around. That's never happened to me before."

"I haven't tried to come between you and your work," she murmured, clinging tightly to him.

"I know that. I haven't forgotten that I practically had to kidnap you to go out with me." Even that was said with resentment. Spring blinked back tears.

"Clay, what do you want from me?" she asked at last, tilting her head back to look up at him. "I don't know what you want me to do or say."

"No." And this time his voice was sad. "You don't know me, do you? You don't even know how much I—" he stopped, swallowed, then went on a little too smoothly "—how much I care for you."

She didn't know what to say, so she remained quiet,

clinging to him. His turquoise leather jacket was damp and smooth beneath her cheek, his arms hard and strong around her. And despite his current moodiness making him almost a stranger to her, she loved him.

Clay pressed his mouth to her temple. "Kiss me, Spring."

She lifted her head, her hands going up to pull his mouth down to hers. It seemed like so long since he'd kissed her. He brushed his lips lingeringly across hers, then deepened the kiss. He groaned thickly when her lips parted to invite him inside, his hands tightening to lift her against him. "Spring," he muttered into the depths of her mouth. "Oh, God, Spring, I...I want you so much."

"Then what are we doing on this beach?" she asked huskily, straining to press closer—a physical impossibility with the barrier of clothing between them.

He shuddered when she arched her lower body suggestively into his, then set her firmly away from him. "It's late," he said, his voice hoarse. "I'd better take you home."

She blinked in dismay at the abrupt end of the caress. She'd thought the kiss was leading to something further, that he'd take her back to his house and make love to her again. Why wasn't he? Not because he didn't want her— they'd been in much too close proximity for him to hide his desire for her. She'd never been the instigator of love-making, but she wanted Clay so much. She had so little time left with him. "I hope you mean your home," she blurted out bravely.

"No. I mean your sister's home." He half turned away from her, his hands going into the pockets of his neon-yellow jumpsuit. "It *is* getting late, and I have to work to-morrow."

He might as well have slapped her. Spring lowered her head so that her hair fell forward to hide her face and walked slowly beside him, back to his car. Her eyes smarted with tears, but she refused to shed them. They'd parted so sweetly during the wee hours of Sunday morn-ing. She hadn't expected such awkwardness and confusion their next time together. *Damn you, Clay, why are you punishing me? What have I done, other than fall in love with you?*

Neither of them made even a pretense of talking on the drive back to Summer's house. Clay probably would have just walked her to the door and driven away had not Summer and Derek driven up at almost the same time. "We stopped for cherry cheesecake and coffee," Summer explained as the four of them walked toward the front door together. "I didn't think you'd be home until much later," she added to Spring, her eyebrow arching questioningly at their strained expressions.

"Clay has to work tomorrow," Spring replied, using Clay's own excuse. It sounded just as hollow coming from her, she decided wearily.

"Clay, I forgot to give you the proposal you asked for on doing a theatrical production with the Halloran House kids. I have it ready," Summer told him. "Want to come in and let me get it?"

Though he looked anxious to leave, Clay agreed to come in only long enough for Summer to retrieve the papers. The telephone was ringing when they entered; the call was for Derek, a late business call that he decided to take in his study.

"I was hoping that Tony would take a part in the play," Summer said before going off to look for the proposal for Clay. "He's been so interested in the drama classes we've done at Halloran House. Now I don't know if he'll be able to stay with us."

"Thanks to his parents calling in the cops," Clay muttered, darting an eloquent look at Spring as Summer left the room with a promise to hurry back.

Spring lifted her chin defiantly, still seething at his rejection on the beach and annoyed with his persistence in arguing with her viewpoint about this boy she'd never even met. *What does this have to do with us, anyway?* she asked herself, even as she felt compelled to respond to his challenge. "If they hadn't called the police, he still wouldn't be in your play," she pointed out coolly. "Who knows where he would be by now?"

"You still think they did the right thing, don't you? Even after I explained my viewpoint."

"Yes, I do," she insisted. "I realize that you are an expert in this field, *Dr.* McEntire, but even you are not infallible."

Clay stiffened, his eyes kindling with the smoldering anger that had seemed just below the surface all evening. "I never said I was infallible."

"No, just that you're always right, is that it?" Spring snapped. She glared fiercely at the man who'd turned her inside out over the past few days. "It's easy for you to say what parents should do or how they should raise their children. It's always easy for people who don't have children to tell others how to raise them."

"I suppose you know better?" he demanded, almost in a yell. "Hell, you've never even *been* a child! You were born being the responsible older sister, weren't you, *Dr.* Reed?"

Spring went cold with fury. How *dare* this...this perpetual adolescent criticize her? *She* certainly wasn't the one acting like an unreasonable stranger! "I like to think that I'm a responsible person. When I make promises, I try to keep them. I know, for example, that if I promised to call someone, I would certainly do so." *Now talk to me, Clay. Tell me why you didn't call. Why you're angry tonight. Ask me to stay in San Francisco.*

"My not calling you has absolutely nothing to do with this!" Clay protested heatedly, though he'd flushed at her pointed accusation. "We're talking about a young man's dignity here."

"And of course you're the expert on dignity." Spring eyed his fluorescent clothing as she voiced the disdainful comment, lashing out at him from the depths of hurt and confusion and heartsick love. She was sorry almost immediately, but something kept her apology inside her. She only stared at him, knowing that she had just destroyed anything that might have remained between them.

Clay's face went white. "Maybe you're right," he replied rather hoarsely. "I'm not the one who tries to live according to everyone else's rules of duty and responsibility and propriety. You've believed from the beginning that I was too much of a nonconformist for you, haven't you? An irresponsible, immature playboy who dresses funny— does that sum up your opinion of me, *Dr.* Reed? Fine. If that's what you want to believe, go ahead. I'm quite content with my life and the accomplishments I've made and will make in the future. You can go back to your Rogers in their plain ties and suits and socks and see if they can make you happy. Personally, I don't think you will be because you'll never find a man who quite measures up to your idea of mature, responsible perfection!"

And with that final, softly spoken, heart-slashing pronouncement he turned and walked with undeniable dignity out of the room. Even from the den Spring heard the front door slam behind him.

"Spring, what in the world happened? I've never seen Clay look so furious!" With Derek following just behind her, Summer entered the room and rushed to her sister's side, her lovely, expressive face creased with concern.

"I don't want to talk about it, Summer."

"But—"

Spring whirled on her younger sister with barely suppressed violence. "I said I *don't* want to talk about it!"

Derek stepped in quickly to prevent the sibling confrontation that threatened. "I think it would be best if you let it drop, Summer," he said gently. "Spring can tell you about it when she calms down, if she wants to then."

Feeling numb and clinging desperately to that blessed numbness, Spring forced a smile. "Thank you, Derek. Now if you'll excuse me, I think I'll turn in."

She felt the anxious eyes of her sister and brother-in-law on her as she left the room, but she kept her shoulders straight, her pace unhurried. And her mind blank.

CLAY STORMED into his house, walked to his bar for the second time in two days and, for the first time since he'd been in college, deliberately set out to get drunk. Unfortunately, it didn't work. He kept replaying his fight with Spring and forgetting his drink until finally he set the barely touched tumbler on the bar and began to restlessly pace the room.

He might as well admit that he'd been spoiling for a fight tonight. He just hadn't known it at the time. And, from all appearances, Spring had been just as eager to lash out at him.

Of course, all she'd said was that she would have called the police if it had been her son who'd run away. She couldn't know how Tony must have felt, couldn't understand the kinds of pressures and torments that would make a young man feel compelled to leave the safety of his home and face the streets alone. It was a degrading, humiliating experience being treated like a mindless child, forced to face the problems he'd run away from whether he was ready to do so or not.

But, dammit, how dare she argue with him about one of his kids? Couldn't she at least have given him credit to know his own field? He had a goddamned doctorate in adolescent psychology, he thought bleakly, and she had accused him of knowing nothing about kids simply because he hadn't fathered any!

Maybe it was best just to let it end this way. He hoped that his friendship with Summer wouldn't be affected after Spring left. He was going to need that friendship now more than he ever had before.

Yes, best to let it end. Before they hurt each other even more than they already had.

He dropped his chin to his chest. *Oh, God, Spring. Don't leave me.*

SPRING FOLDED the last item of clothing and placed it neatly in her suitcase, then closed the lid and firmly snapped the locks. Another suitcase sat at her feet and beside it a third, borrowed from Summer. She was taking home quite a bit more than she'd arrived with, thanks to those pleasant shopping trips she and her sister had made during her visit. She only wished she'd spent more time with her sister and less time with the man who'd managed to break her heart, she thought sorrowfully, then immediately called herself a liar. No matter how deep the pain of her loss, and it was agonizingly deep, she couldn't bring herself to regret one moment of the time she'd spent with Clay.

"I have one more thing for you to take home with you," Summer announced from the doorway, entering the room with her oddly graceful limp. In her arms she bore a large, battered Winnie the Pooh.

Spring smiled in surprise. "Pooh Bear! Gosh, I haven't seen him in years."

"Still looks great, doesn't he?" Summer asked, fondly eyeing the badly bedraggled stuffed toy. "Considering that he was yours, then mine, then Autumn's, it's a miracle that he's still in one piece. Well, mostly in one piece."

"Yes, he's still missing an ear, thanks to our fiery-tempered baby sister. How did he end up in California?"

"Autumn gave him back to me when I left Arkansas. She didn't want me to be lonely. Now I want you to take him back to Arkansas for the same reason. He's a great friend."

Spring had determined right after her quarrel with Clay that she wouldn't cry in front of her sister, but she found herself forcing back tears at Summer's gesture. "All right, I'll take him," she said softly. "Thanks."

Summer nodded. "Derek's ready to leave for the airport anytime you are. Sure you don't want me to go along?"

"No, you have your class late this afternoon, and there's no need for you to miss it. You've skipped enough classes while I've been here."

"None that really mattered."

"Still, it's better this way. I hate airport goodbyes."

"Me, too," Summer confessed. "You'll call?"

"I'll call. And write."

"You'd better." Summer reached out and hugged her sister fiercely. "I love you, Sis. I'm so glad you came."

"Me, too." Spring returned the hug with equal vehemence. "Your husband is a terrific guy, Summer Anderson. I'm very happy for you both."

"Spring…" Summer hesitated, then spoke bravely. "Why don't you call him?"

Spring immediately shook her head. "No."

"Are you still that angry with him?"

"No." It was true; she wasn't. She knew how deeply he cared about his kids. She still thought she'd been entitled to her own opinion, but she saw Clay's point, too. And, she added sadly, if he'd wanted to talk to her, he would have called. "No, I'm not angry. But it's better this way."

And it was, she tried to convince herself on the way to the airport. The relationship between her and Clay had been ill-fated from the beginning. She'd known from her first glance at him that, though he was attractive and fascinating, he wasn't for her. But, God, it hurt.

"You're really going to hold that bear all the way to Little Rock?" Derek asked doubtfully as Spring prepared to board her plane. She'd checked her other luggage, but she clung to Pooh with gentle determination.

"Yes. We'll be fine, Derek."

"Sure?" His raw, deep voice was gentle, as were his searching pewter-gray eyes.

"Yes, I'm sure."

"Spring." He took her forearms in his large hands and looked down at her. "I just want you to know that I think you and Clay are being a couple of first-class idiots. I know when two people are in love, and you and Clay are. Don't let pride stand between you."

She winced. "Derek, I know you're only trying to help, but you're wrong. Clay and I just don't work together. We're not right for each other. I'm not what he needs, and he's not— He's…" But that was one lie she couldn't voice. "Please, Derek," she said finally on a sigh.

"All right." He kissed her fondly on the cheek. "You keep in touch."

"I will. And I'll see you when you bring Summer home for Christmas. Remember, you promised."

"Right. See you then. If not before," he added somewhat mysteriously.

Spring turned for one last, lingering look around the crowded terminal before boarding her plane, ostensibly as a last glance at San Francisco. If she'd secretly hoped to spot a shaggy blond head or a man dressed in outrageous style, she tried not to acknowledge it, even to herself.

"DON'T DROP THE PIZZA!" Kelsey Rayford, Spring's office manager and best friend, cried out in teasing warning as Spring balanced the enormous white box while unlocking the door to her apartment.

"I've got the pizza, you hang on to the wine," Spring returned with a grin, triumphantly swinging open the door to her roomy west Little Rock town-house apartment. Offering a cheerful greeting to the small yellow-and-white cat that had dashed to greet her, she crossed immediately to a round oak table and deposited the fragrant, still warm box on it, then dropped her purse on a chair and turned to her friend.

Tiny, black-haired, brown-eyed Kelsey laughed as she juggled a large bottle of wine, an enormous handbag and a sizable, gaily wrapped package. "I'm losing the wine. Grab it!"

Spring grabbed, catching the bottle just as it would have plunged to the floor. "If you wouldn't insist on carrying a purse that would hold half the contents of our office filing cabinets, you wouldn't have this problem," she lectured primly.

"Oh, stuff it," her friend replied inelegantly, dropping the maligned purse to the floor. "Just because you're older than me doesn't mean you can start giving lectures."

"Hey, I'm not that much older! Three days doesn't count."

Grinning at Spring's protest, Kelsey shook her head. "Sorry. For the next three days you're twenty-seven and I'm a mere twenty-six. I intend to point that out at every opportunity."

"Somehow I knew you would," Spring retorted, rummaging in her cabinets for plates and wineglasses.

The doorbell chimed and Spring turned over the duty of setting the table to Kelsey. Her neighbor, Mrs. English, stood on the doorstep, arms loaded with packages. "You had a few deliveries today, Spring."

"I can see that." Spring smiled and took the load. "Would you like to come in for a while, Mrs. English?"

"No, thanks, hon. Tom will be home for his dinner shortly. Hope you have a happy birthday."

"Thank you."

"Oh, goody, presents," Kelsey crooned when Mrs. English had gone. "And such nice big ones."

"I can't believe they all arrived on my birthday." Spring eyed the three brown-paper-wrapped parcels with interest. Trust her family to make sure she had birthday presents, she thought fondly.

"Well, are you going to open them?" Kelsey demanded impatiently. Kelsey was always impatient.

Spring shook her head. "After dinner. Our pizza will get cold if we don't eat it now."

Sighing, Kelsey reached for a plate. "I don't know how you can stand it. I'd have ripped into them the minute I got them."

"Yes, but you've never understood the pleasure to be found in deferred gratification," Spring pointed out indulgently, seating herself across the table from her friend.

"Oh, God, now you're talking like my shrink." The animated brunette stared soulfully over a half-eaten triangle of pizza. "You'd think you were a psychologist rather than an optometrist."

Psychologist. Even the word made Spring wince. "Eat your pizza, Kelsey."

Spring chatted gaily during the casual dinner—but then, she'd become an expert on hiding her feelings behind airy chatter during the past two months. She and Kelsey talked about the office, about the volunteer work that Spring had recently taken on at a local resident treatment home for troubled young people, about the gorgeous-but-just-not-real-bright man that Kelsey had dated a couple of times recently. And though Spring mentioned her sisters frequently and occasionally referred to her trip to California, she never once spoke of a tall, golden-haired man with blue-green eyes and a brilliant white smile. She had not spoken Clay's name since she'd returned to Little Rock.

"I don't know how you do it," Kelsey murmured as they finished the pizza and lingered over a last glass of wine.

"Do what?" Spring asked lazily, feeding a tiny bite of pizza crust to Missy, her cat.

"Stay so busy all the time. You were a workaholic before your vacation, but since you've been back, you're going all the time. To be honest, I'm starting to worry about you."

Few people would have been able to tell that Spring's smile was forced. She devoutly hoped that Kelsey wasn't one of those people. "Why in the world would you worry about me? I'm doing fine."

Rich brown eyes studied her face with an intensity that almost made Spring squirm. "I don't know what it is," Kelsey said finally, "but something's been different about you ever since you got back from visiting your sister. I've asked you repeatedly if anything happened while you were away, but you always shrug off my questions. Are you sure you don't want to talk to me about anything?"

"Kelsey, when did you become such a worrier? Haven't I always been able to take care of myself?"

"You're not going to talk about it, are you?"

Deliberately avoiding those searching eyes, Spring shrugged. "I don't know about you, but I'm ready to see what's in those packages. Deferred gratification is all very well, but it's time for birthday presents."

"You can be a real pain sometimes, Spring Reed," Kelsey muttered, but her attention had already strayed to the tantalizing birthday presents. She might be close to twenty-seven, but Kelsey Rayford did love presents—

even if they were someone else's, as Spring knew very well.

"I'll open yours first." Spring reached for the colorful package that Kelsey had brought in earlier and tugged at the ribbon. The box opened to reveal a sheer, lace-trimmed nightgown in swirls of pastels. "Kelsey, thank you. It's lovely."

"It'll look great on you. I'm hoping it'll give you the incentive to find someone special to wear it for."

Avoiding her friend's mischievous grin, Spring began to open the box from Florida. She reflected somberly that it was a good thing she enjoyed wearing pretty nightgowns just for herself; she had no plans to wear the garment for anyone else. She couldn't imagine being that close again to any man but—

No. She wouldn't even think about him. She ripped the paper from Autumn's gift with unnecessary force, then laughed when she opened it and saw a heavy-duty lavender plastic case fitted with a set of tools—hammer, screwdrivers, pliers, wrenches, tape measure. A woman's tool kit. How typically Autumn. Defiantly functional, yet somehow feminine. "Now this will come in handy."

"You must have told Autumn that you're thinking of buying a house. You won't have a manager then to take care of repairs for you."

"I've discussed it with her. She agreed that it would be a good investment."

Kelsey looked around Spring's rose-and-cream apartment, carefully decorated with Victorian antiques and reproductions, and sighed. "I don't know how you could even think of giving up this place. It's so beautiful and you don't have to worry about lawns and plumbing and peeling paint."

Spring shrugged. "I like it here, but I've always wanted to own my own house. Don't ask why; it's just a personal whim. Besides, these furnishings are mine. My house would look a lot like this."

"True. Open the others."

Amused at Kelsey's childlike excitement, Spring obliged, tearing the paper off a package from the West Coast to reveal a large, flat box. Her breath caught in her throat when she lifted layers of tissue paper to reveal a painting. *The* painting. The one she'd seen in the boutique in Sausalito of the intricately depicted Victorian house surrounded by flowers, with just a suggestion of San Francisco Bay in the background.

Oh, Summer, why?

"Spring, it's beautiful! It goes perfectly with all your things. Gosh, look at the detail of that house. It's—Spring, what's the matter? Don't you like it?"

Spring cleared her throat and blinked, pushing her glasses up onto the bridge of her nose as she pasted on a smile and looked at Kelsey. "Of course I like it. I saw it in an art gallery in Sausalito and fell in love with it then. I was just...touched that Summer and Derek bought it for me."

"Oh." Kelsey frowned, still watching Spring closely, obviously suspecting that she hadn't been told the entire story.

Spring hadn't cried since she'd returned from California. Not that she hadn't wanted to, but she couldn't. The pain was too deep for tears. She refused to cry now. Tossing her head, she lifted the smaller package, barely looking at it as she fought to hold on to her enthusiasm for her birthday presents. She pushed at her glasses again and smoothed back a curl that had escaped from her prim roll of hair. She'd worn her hair up every day for the past two months.

"Oh!" The delicate gold bracelet was exquisite, engraved with an old-fashioned pattern of birds and flowers. It could have come straight from the early 1800s. It suited her perfectly. From her parents? Spring lifted the small white card enclosed in the box, read the four words written on it and dropped it with a strangled cry.

Happy birthday, sweet Spring.

"Oh, no," she whispered, her body curling inward and her eyes closing with the pain. "Oh, Clay, why?"

She'd tried so hard not to think of him. She'd stayed busy, kept her mind occupied. And it had worked—during the days, at least. Only during the nights had he haunted her. Endless, empty nights filled with laughing eyes, lazy, bright smiles, thick golden hair. A deep breath, and she could imagine herself in his arms, held close to his pounding heart as he loved her with a hungry tenderness that had surpassed any fantasy she'd ever had. And then she'd open her eyes and she'd be alone. But she hadn't cried.

She still regretted their quarrel. Though she could understand now that the argument had been the result of their precarious emotions regarding their impending separation, she wished they could have parted on better terms. They'd said some terrible, hurtful things to each other. She hoped that someday he could forgive her, as she had already forgiven him. And it seemed that he had. But it still hurt.

If only she knew how to get over him. Would there ever come a time when she could think about him without this horrible pain? When spotting a tall blond male in a crowd would not cause her heart to stop? When she'd stop thinking of amusing incidents she'd like to share with him? She had tried; God, she had tried. And she still loved him. Just as she always would.

"Spring? Spring, are you all right?" Kelsey's voice came from unexpected proximity.

Spring opened her eyes to find her friend kneeling in front of her, brown eyes huge with concern. "Spring, what's wrong?" Kelsey asked again.

Spring wet her lips, took a deep breath and sat up straight. "It's…nothing, Kelsey. I…" She stopped and buried her face in her hands, unable to lie. "Everything's wrong," she wailed, the tears finally beginning to flow.

"Only a man could cause this kind of heartache," Kelsey pronounced confidently, her hand on her friend's shoulder. "I'm speaking from experience. Who is he, Spring? Not Roger. You never looked like this over him."

Shaking her head, Spring dropped her hands. "No, not Roger."

"Ready to talk about it?"

"His name is Clay McEntire. He's…" How did one describe Clay? "He's tall and blond and has blue-green eyes and a beautiful smile. He's a junior-high-school counselor who loves kids and tears himself up over their problems. He wears funny clothes and likes to tease and shows his affection for his friends through hugs and touches. He had a lot of problems when he was young, but he overcame them. He's sometimes moody and…and he needs reading glasses, but I don't think he knows it," she finished with a sob.

Kelsey was staring at her in unmistakable astonishment. "He, um, he sounds fascinating. Not your usual type, though."

Spring choked on a humorless laugh. "No. Not my usual type."

"But you're in love with him."

"Completely. Forever."

"And?"

"And nothing. He's in San Francisco and I'm in Little Rock."

"Is he in love with you?"

"I don't know," Spring answered slowly, twisting the lovely gold bracelet between shaking hands. "I just don't know. There were times when I thought he might be. When he— When we— Well, he made me feel very special. But, for all I know, that may be the way he treats every woman in his life."

"So this is why you've been driving yourself like a madwoman ever since you got back." Kelsey shook her head in reproval. "I can't believe you've been carrying this around inside you without even telling me about it."

"I just couldn't talk about it. It still hurts too much."

"What do you think the bracelet means?"

"I don't know. Maybe it's just his way of apologizing for the quarrel we had before I left."

"Are you going to keep it?"

She hadn't thought that far ahead. Of course the logical thing to do would be to return it. It was, after all, much too expensive a gift and would only serve as a painful reminder of an incident best forgotten, she told herself. Her fingers tightened around the bangle almost in protest at the thought of sending it back. Clay had chosen this gift for her. Sending it back would almost be like saying goodbye again. "I don't know."

"When it comes to this guy, you don't know much, do you, Spring?" Kelsey asked with sympathetic amusement. "I think you should keep it."

"You do? Why?"

"Because he obviously wanted you to have it. And because he sounds like a great guy."

"He is." Spring brushed another wave of tears off her cheeks. "Oh, Kelsey, he is."

"Tell you what we're going to do." Kelsey pushed herself to her feet, rising to her entire four feet eleven inches. "We're going to drag out everything fattening in your kitchen, cover it all with whipped cream and pig out while you tell me every detail of your vacation in California— and this time you're not leaving out a guy named Clay McEntire, you hear?"

"Oh, Kelsey, I don't think—"

"Spring, trust me. Talking about it will help. Keeping it all in will only rot your insides."

Spring gave an unwilling smile, already feeling a little better. Kelsey had always had this effect on her, ever since the two had attended the same church as kids. Kelsey had grown up in Romance, Arkansas, just down the road from Spring's hometown of Rose Bud. They'd considered themselves quite cosmopolitan when they'd moved fifty-five miles south to the big city of Little Rock—population 194,000 at last count—Spring, after her graduation from optometry college almost two years earlier, and Kelsey, af-

ter her divorce a year before that. Kelsey had quit a good
job to work for Spring, and the relationship had proven
quite satisfying, both personally and professionally.

Spring left out no detail of the brief affair with Clay.
From that first kiss in the hallway on the night they'd met
to the scathing quarrel in Summer's den on that last Monday night, Spring poured out the entire story to her
warmly sympathetic, if rather startled, friend. Kelsey had
been right. It *did* feel good to talk about it.

"And that's the end of the story," she concluded, toying
with a last bite of a sinfully gooey chocolate-fudge
brownie sans whipped cream.

Kelsey looked thoughtful as she licked a bit of chocolate
from her scarlet-tipped finger. "Somehow I don't think it
is."

"What do you mean?"

"I don't happen to think the story's over. From what
you've told me, Clay is as deeply involved in this relationship as you are. And he sent you that bracelet. I don't think
he's going to let you go that easily."

"Let me go? Kelsey, he did everything but drive me to
the airport and throw me on the plane."

"Mmm. We'll see."

"It's over, Kel."

Kelsey only shook her dark head. "Want to bet?"

"The last time I made a bet with you, you took my
grandmother's earrings from me."

"I warned you not to bet them, didn't I? But you just
wouldn't believe that you and Roger would break up in
less than six months."

"Okay, so you were right about Roger."

"I'm right about this, too. I think I'll give you your
grandmother's earrings as a wedding present."

Spring flinched. "Kelsey, don't, please. It did help to
talk to you, but I can't joke about that."

Kelsey smiled sweetly. "I wasn't joking, Spring."

She left soon afterward since both of them had to work
the next day. When she was alone, Spring hung the paint-

ing from Summer and Derek in a place of honor in her living room, telling herself that someday she'd be able to look at it without fighting tears. Then she folded the nightgown from Kelsey into a dresser drawer and stored the tool kit from Autumn in the kitchen pantry. Only then did she allow herself to pick up the bracelet again. Very slowly she clasped it around her wrist. It fit as if it had been made for her.

Holding her wrist to her cheek, she closed tear-flooded eyes and admitted to herself that she would not return the gift to its sender. She supposed she'd known that all along. She would wear the bracelet always, and every time she looked at it she would remember a very special man in California. The man who'd taught her how to love.

The telephone rang just as she was about to go to bed, hoping that she would be able to sleep. It was Summer, calling to wish her happy birthday, the last of her family to call that day.

"The painting is beautiful," Spring told her honestly. "I love it. Thank you."

"You're welcome. I could tell you really liked it when you saw it. I wanted you to have it. It's perfect for you."

Yes, it was perfect for her. Even though it made her cry. "How are you, Summer? And Derek?"

"We're fine. Connie and Joel were married last weekend, you know. It was a small ceremony, very sweet. Connie and I cried all the way through it. Derek acted like we were being very silly, but I saw him wipe his eyes once. He's denied it ever since, but I know what I saw."

"I'm very…happy for them," Spring managed, though there was a break in her voice.

"Clay was there, too."

"Oh." *Don't, Summer. Please.*

"I don't see him as much now as I did before. He's staying very busy these days."

"Is he?"

"Oh, Spring, you're miserable, aren't you? And I know

he is, too. If only you'd seen his face during that wedding. He looked so unhappy."

"Summer, he knows where I am, how to get in touch with me. If…if he wanted a relationship with me, he would call." Instead, he'd sent her a bracelet and a card that only wished her a happy birthday. Nothing more.

"I think he's scared of the way you made him feel."

"Maybe he was. But whatever the reason, he's the one who ended it. I'm not going to chase after him, Summer. I can't. And, please, don't say anything to him. Please."

"I won't. He wouldn't let me, anyway. Like you, he refuses to talk about it. I'm so sorry, Spring."

"So am I. But I'll get over it." Maybe. Like when she was too old to remember.

"Happy birthday, Sis."

"Thanks for calling, Summer."

She hung up the phone and buried her face in her hands, her shoulders shaking with the force of her sobs.

Happy birthday, sweet Spring.

IT HADN'T BEEN ONE of her better days. It was ninety-seven degrees on this second Monday in July, the humidity was hovering at eighty-three percent and the air conditioner in Spring's offices had gone out. A frantic call had been put in to the repairman, but he hadn't shown up yet. Thanks to one woman who'd insisted on telling Spring her entire history of eye problems, covering some sixty-five years, Spring was running a bit late with her appointments. There were people sweltering in the waiting room, a small child was crying lustily as he waited for his brother to be fitted for glasses and the telephone hadn't stopped ringing all day.

Kelsey's dark hair was damp around her flushed face as she scrambled to keep up with calls and appointments. Spring's assistant, Andi, was dashing from one examining room to the other and Spring was trying to convince a very vain young woman that her particular vision problem did not lend itself to contact lenses. The woman left in a huff, informing Spring that she would get a second opinion.

"She'll find someone who'll fit her for contacts, you know," Andi predicted glumly.

"Yes, I know. And she'll be sorry later." Spring sighed as she swept a damp tendril of limp silvery hair back from her own glasses, which were causing her face to sweat. At times like this she considered getting contact lenses herself. The main reason she hadn't was because she thought they were just too much trouble. "Is the repairman here yet?"

"Yes, he just walked in. Kelsey took him straight to the compressor and told him she'd chain him to it if he didn't have it working in half an hour or less."

Spring laughed tiredly. "Sounds like Kelsey. How many more do we have?"

Andi checked the clipboard she held. "Mrs. Gray is in Room One. Needs a new prescription for her reading glasses. I just took Danny Gipson into Two. His glasses are in; you just need to fit them. We've got one more waiting in the lobby—a woman in her twenties who's been having headaches. Oh, and there's one last appointment due later, but he's not here yet."

"Maybe he'll be running late, too, and he won't have to wait in this heat. Do you have Mrs. Gray's file with you?"

Twenty minutes later Spring sat back on her stool, smiling with satisfaction at the seven-year-old boy grinning back at her, two of his front teeth notably absent. His freckled face was now enhanced by a stylish pair of glasses, through which his green eyes sparkled. "I see good through these, Dr. Reed," he informed her.

"That's great, Danny. Now you'll start making home runs every time you're up to bat, I'll bet."

He chuckled in pleasure. "Well, sometimes, maybe. I sure was glad to find out I'm not a klutz. Just blind."

Spring wrinkled her nose at him and affectionately ruffled his sandy hair, causing the gold bracelet on her wrist to sparkle in the bright office lighting. "You're not blind,

Danny. You're just a little nearsighted. It happens to the best of us." She tapped her own plastic frames.

"Am I done now, Dr. Reed?"

"Yes, you are. What's your hurry?"

"I gotta go beat up Bobby Clary."

Spring's eyes widened in surprise. "Why would you want to beat up Bobby Clary?" she demanded.

"'Cause he's gonna call me 'Four Eyes,'" Danny replied happily. "See ya, Dr. Reed," he added, scrambling out of the examining chair.

"Don't break those glasses, Danny!" she called after him. Something told her she'd be seeing quite a bit of Danny.

The repairman had worked some kind of magic with the air conditioner, and already the offices were feeling cooler. Spring sighed in relief as she stepped into her office half an hour later after seeing her next-to-last patient. "Did our final appointment ever arrive?" she asked Andi.

"He's in Room Two." Andi rolled her expressive blue eyes. "And is he something! Kelsey's already given him her phone number."

Spring groaned dramatically and straightened her glasses. "What am I going to have to do to keep her from chasing after my patients?" she asked teasingly, glad to know that Kelsey's flirtatiousness remained within the bounds of good taste—while in the office, anyway. "What's this guy's name?"

Andi checked her clipboard. "Mr. Crowe. He's dressed kind of loud, but he's totally hot. Wait until you see him. Need any help?"

"I think I can manage, thank you." Spring's smile had faded a bit at the description of the man's clothing. Tiny reminders like that hurt, even after four months. Clay was still as firmly entrenched in her mind and heart as he'd been the night they'd made love, even though she hadn't heard another thing from him since the arrival of the bracelet she'd worn every day since her birthday.

Spring checked her appearance in a wall mirror before

going in for her final appointment of the trying day. Her hair was still pinned up, though the tendrils that had escaped had frizzed a bit from the humid heat. Her makeup had long since faded from perspiration. The white lab coat she wore as a uniform over her plum cotton shirtdress was badly wrinkled. She looked as if she'd just put in a long, hard day. Oh, well, she thought in rueful resignation, it was just as well that she wasn't interested in the "hot" man waiting in Room Two. Kelsey could have him.

Donning her most professional smile, Spring strode briskly into Room Two, then stopped short, staring at the man in the examining chair. "Oh, my God."

"Awed reverence isn't necessary," her patient responded gravely, watching her with warm blue-green eyes. "You can just call me Clay."

Over a bright blue T-shirt he was wearing the wildest tropical print shirt she'd ever seen—huge parrots and oleanders in red, yellow, blue, hot pink and white—with red drawstring-waist slacks and red canvas deck shoes. He'd knotted a yellow kerchief around his right knee—for no particular reason that she could tell. He looked wonderful. Exactly as she remembered him—except, perhaps, for the small lines around his eyes. They seemed deeper, more prominent than they'd appeared before, making him look almost his age. "What are you doing here, Clay?"

"I need my eyes checked," he replied casually, leaning back in the chair and examining the equipment around him with interest. "Do you really know how to use all this stuff?"

"You came all the way from San Francisco to have your eyes examined?" Spring repeated sceptically, ignoring his question.

"Only the best for these baby blues," he replied, batting his eyelashes at her audaciously.

"Your eyes are not baby blue, they're somewhere between blue and green." Spring twisted her hands in front of her, her heart pounding beneath the wrinkled white lab coat. She was fighting two impulses, both equally inappropriate. The first was to run screaming from the room, protecting herself from any further pain at this man's hands. The second was to throw herself on his colorfully clad body and ravish him, keeping him chained to the chair until she grew tired of him. She figured that fifty or sixty years ought to do it.

"So you went to optometry college in Memphis?" Clay asked, reading the diploma on the wall.

"Yes. Clay—"

"See, I read that. No problem, right?"

Spring moistened her lips, still staring at him from the spot that she seemed to have been frozen to. She wouldn't ask him again why he was here, she decided. Her voice seemed to have left her, anyway.

Clay looked at her, smiled and held out his hand. "Come here."

It took her a second to propel herself across the room. And then she was in his lap and his arms were around her and he was kissing her. There were tears on her face, tears on his, and they were both apologizing between kisses.

"Spring, I'm so sorry."

"Oh, Clay, I never should have said—"

"God, I've missed you."

"I've missed you, too. And you *do* have dignity."

"And I'm sorry I called you a snob. You're—"

Spring leaned backward, frowning. "You didn't call me a snob."

"I didn't?"

"No."

"Oh." He kissed her again, then smiled. "Then I'm sorry I thought about calling you a snob."

She cupped his face in her hands and stared fiercely into his eyes. "Clay, *why* are you here?"

"To get my eyes checked, Spring. And to see you."

She laughed, happier than she'd been in four long months. "You really want me to examine your eyes?"

"You bet. You can handle it, can't you?"

"I can handle it." She leaned forward and planted her mouth firmly on his, her arms going around his neck.

"Dr. Reed, there's a tele— Oh, excuse me."

Flushing vividly, Spring looked around to find her assistant staring at her in wide-eyed astonishment. "Oh, Andi. What is it?"

"You have a telephone call."

Feeling Clay vibrating with suppressed laughter beneath her, Spring planted her hands on his chest and pushed herself out of his lap. "All right, I'll take it. And then," she added to Clay, "I'm going to test your vision. Actually, I've been wanting to do so ever since I caught you playing slide trombone with the play program on our first date."

Clay frowned. "You're not really planning to put me in glasses, are you?"

"We'll see," she replied mysteriously, throwing him a laughing glance over her shoulder as she left the room. She decided to take the call in the business office that looked out on the empty reception area.

"Want me to go keep our patient happy while you take this call?" Kelsey asked hopefully when Spring reached for the phone on Kelsey's desk.

Spring held the receiver, her finger hovering over the hold button. Now she knew why she'd chosen to use this particular telephone. "Did you really give him your phone number?"

"You bet. Isn't he gorgeous?"

Spring leaned her hip on Kelsey's desk and gave her friend a hard stare. "I want your phone number changed. Immediately."

With a sputter of startled laughter Kelsey dropped her pencil and stared back at Spring. "Does this mean you're over that Clay guy in California?"

"This means he *is* that Clay guy. And he's not in California, he's in my examining room!"

Kelsey's mouth fell open comically. "That's him? No kidding?" At Spring's happy nod she sighed gustily.

"Wouldn't you know it. I fall in love at first sight, and the guy's already taken. Besides that, I think I've just lost your grandmother's earrings!"

Her heart jumping, Spring took a deep breath and took her call, trying to sound professional when all she wanted to do was sing with joy.

Clay had come for her!

10

"SPRING, ARE YOU quite sure I need glasses?"

"Clay, I've told you that they're only for reading. You'll be much more comfortable with your school paperwork when your eyes are under less strain."

"What did you call what I have again?"

Spring smiled indulgently and unlocked the door to her apartment. "Hyperopia. You're slightly farsighted, Clay, and you have a touch of astigmatism. I explained all that in my office." She pushed open the door and stepped in, her stomach tightening nervously now that she and Clay were actually going to be alone for the first time in four months.

"Yes, I know, but...glasses! Just think how everyone will tease me."

He reminded her of Danny ready to beat up Bobby Clary for calling him "Four Eyes." She had to laugh. "They certainly would tease you if I'd let you choose those frames you tried on. Honestly, Clay, they made you look like...like Elton John, in one of his flashier concert outfits."

"Hey, you're the one who carries them in stock."

"Yes, but I never sell them to adults. Only to very strange teenagers."

"And I qualify on only one of those counts, right?" Clay walked around the living room into which she'd led him, trailing his fingers along a particularly nice Louis Philippe reproduction table. "You seem to be very good at your job. Very thorough."

"The exam doesn't normally take quite that long. But then, most of my patients don't pull me onto their laps or pinch me in various places when I look into their eyes."

He grinned. "I have to admit that I haven't enjoyed an examination so much in a long time." Without waiting for her response he looked once more around what he could see of her apartment. "This is nice. Very nice."

Pleased, she smiled at him. "Somehow I thought you'd like it."

"Odd, isn't it? This could almost be my place." He shot her a look that made her skin tingle, then glanced at the painting above her mantel. "I was with Summer when she bought this. She said you'd seen it and liked it."

"Yes." She didn't tell him why she hadn't bought it for herself. Nor did she tell him how many times in the past weeks she'd stared at it and cried. "I haven't thanked you yet for the bracelet."

"Yes, you did. You sent me a very proper little note thanking me and telling me that I shouldn't have sent it." A note he hadn't answered. Stopping beside her, he caught her hand in his and lifted it, admiring the bracelet on her wrist. "Thank you for not sending it back. I wanted you to have it."

"Why?" she asked, the word a mere whisper.

He pressed a kiss into her palm. "I wanted you to wear it and think of me."

She swallowed. "I didn't need a bracelet for that."

"Did you think of me, sweet Spring?" He pulled her closer, his hands sliding around her waist as he asked the question.

"Yes," she murmured through suddenly dry lips.

"A lot?"

"Yes."

"Good," he muttered into her hair. "Because I haven't stopped thinking of you since you left. Or missing you. Or wanting you."

"Oh, Clay." She didn't consciously place her arms around his neck, but suddenly they were there, and she was crowding close to him with all the hunger that had built up in the months since she'd seen him. He groaned and gathered her into his arms, holding her as if he'd never let her go again. She prayed that he wouldn't.

"Spring, there's so much I want to say to you, but all I can think about right now is making love to you. God, it's been so long."

"Yes, Clay, please. We can talk later." Trembling in anticipation, she pressed dozens of little kisses on his jaw, his neck, his cheek, anywhere she could reach.

His hand removed her glasses and placed them on a nearby table, then went to her hair, scattering pins across her cream-colored carpet. "You're wearing it up again," he complained.

"There's been no one to wear it down for," she answered, shaking her head slowly so that the tresses he'd loosened fell in a tumble around her shoulders.

"Thank God." He lifted her into his arms, swinging her in a full circle before stopping to kiss her. "Where's your bedroom?" he demanded when he released her mouth.

"Upstairs, first door on the left," she answered, snuggling into his shoulder.

"Too far." He lowered her to the carpet, following immediately to capture her mouth again. Before the kiss ended, he had her plum cotton shirtdress unbuttoned and halfway off. She cooperated eagerly, as anxious as he to be rid of the barriers between them. When her clothing was gone, they both began on his, tossing the colorful garments into a careless heap beside them. "Come here," he muttered, when nothing was left to separate them.

He pulled her into his arms, then rolled so that she was stretched on top of him, her hair falling around their faces. "This is what I've needed for the past four months," he told her, his fingers sliding slowly down her back to cup her bottom and hold her to him. "Nothing between us. No miles, no arguments, no clothing. Just you and me."

She lowered her head to nibble on his lower lip, wriggling a little to settle herself more comfortably against him. He was hard and hot against her, eliciting a warm, throbbing response from deep within her. "What took you

so long to get here?'' she asked, amazed at the sultry sen-
suality of her own voice. She was so different with Clay.
Sexy and uninhibited and playful. She loved the way he
made her feel. She loved him, but she wasn't ready to tell
him. Not until he gave her some indication of his own feelings.

God, he loved her. He pulled her mouth firmly to his,
kissing her as if to make up for four months of depriva-
tion. She felt so good on top of him. Holding her, he
twisted onto his side. She felt so good beside him. He
rolled again. She felt so good beneath him.

''You feel good everywhere,'' he told her huskily, relishing the little laugh he received in response. ''Am I too
heavy for you?''

''No,'' she answered, looking up at him with an adoring
expression that made him want to shout in masculine triumph. Or cry. He kissed her instead.

''Love me, Clay. Please love me.''

''I will, Spring. I do. I love you so much.'' And then he
was moving, slipping inside her to lose himself in the dark
velvet depths of her, and she was curling around him to
hold him and he thought he'd never felt such pleasure in
his entire life. Or at least, he amended on one last, rational
fragment of thought, not since the last time he'd been inside her.

Then he couldn't think at all but could only close his
eyes and let instinct drive him, shuddering as she lifted to
meet each deep, desperate thrust. He'd wanted to take it
slowly this first time after their separation, to savor each
moment, but his needs had flared out of his control. He
struggled fiercely to ensure that Spring found her own
pleasure before he gave in to the need for release, deeply
satisfied when she convulsed beneath him, crying out brokenly. Only then did he let go, her name leaving his lips in
a gasp as he went rigid for a long, pulsing moment, then
collapsed heavily on top of her.

Almost immediately he rolled to his side to relieve her

of his weight. But he refused to let her go. He'd never willingly let her go again.

Spring took a deep breath and then another, willing her
heartbeat to slow, her thoughts to clear. She found it almost hard to believe that she was lying on her living-room
floor, that it was a Monday evening after a fairly typical
day at her office. All comprehension of time and place had
left her while Clay had made love with her, and now she
was forced to entirely reorient herself. She hadn't really
been to paradise.

Or had she? Had Clay really told her he loved her?

She wrapped her arms around him and held him
tightly. "I can't believe you're actually here. I'm afraid I'll
wake up and you'll be gone again."

"No, sweetheart. I'm here. I can't believe I stayed away
so long."

She wanted to ask why he had, but she didn't know if
she was ready yet to spoil the mood by bringing up that
stupid fight they'd had. Instead, she toyed lazily with one
of the few golden curls scattered across his chest and
asked, "Why did you tell Andi and Kelsey that your name
was Mr. Crowe?"

He chuckled, his hand moving in idle patterns on her
shoulder. "I thought you'd figure that out. Crow is the en-
trée on my menu for tonight's dinner." He sobered
abruptly. "I'm sorry, Spring. For everything that happened between us that last night in California. I was spoiling for a fight when I saw you that night, and I all but
leaped on the first difference of opinion that came up."

"All right, I accept your apology. And I'm sorry, too."

He shook his head against the carpet, then pushed himself upright, helping her up to sit beside him, her long legs
tucked beside her. "No, Spring. Don't just shrug it off. We
need to talk about it so you'll understand what happened."

She sighed. "I guess you're right. I just hate to bring it
up now, after everything has been so nice."

"We're not going to argue again. I promise. I just want to explain."

She reached for her blouse. "All right. I suppose it *is* time for us to talk. Past time."

He reached out to still her hand. "What are you doing?"

"I'm getting dressed."

"No, don't. You're beautiful exactly the way you are."

She flushed, squirming a bit under his lambent regard. "I feel strange sitting here without any clothes on."

"You'll get used to it." He grinned, deliberately distracting her from her modest self-consciousness. "Surely you're not still accusing me of being dressed funny? This time my ego really *would* be hurt."

She laughed, as he'd intended, and shook her head. "You are a beautiful man, Clay McEntire. A perfect specimen. Well, almost perfect. There's that scar on your stomach. But even that looks good on you. What caused it?" she asked because she was genuinely curious about the thin white line that was a bit too crooked to be caused by a surgeon's blade and because she was still trying to delay their talk about the quarrel.

"A switchblade," he answered calmly, and somehow she knew that the talk had already begun.

"You were knifed?" she whispered in horror. "By one of your kids?"

He shook his head. "In a fight, when I was sixteen. I was carrying a knife, too, Spring. I just wasn't as good with mine as the other guy was with his."

"Oh, Clay." She reached out to touch his cheek. He was so beautiful, so wholesome and happy looking that she tended to forget the darker side of his past.

He caught her hand in his, kissed it, then lowered it to his bare thigh. "I've told you about my past, Spring. It wasn't so nice. My parents were cold, demanding people, and I could never live up to their expectations. Appearances meant everything to them and very little to me. I wanted so much to love them, as every child wants to love his parents, but their continuous emotional rejection made me angry. I took my rage out on them and everyone else around me, even myself. And that's why I was mad at you that night in California."

"But, Clay, I hadn't rejected you," she protested, her forehead creasing with a frown as she tried to understand. "Just the opposite, in fact. We'd made love."

He captured her other hand, leaning forward as he gripped her fingers in his. "Don't you see, sweetheart? I was anticipating your rejection. I was angry with you before the fact because I was so certain it was going to happen. Stupid, I know, but don't forget that I'd had several years of experience with rejection and it's not always easy to put the past behind me. You kept talking about returning home, and I knew how much it would hurt me when you left, so I took the initiative, I guess, and hurt you before you could hurt me."

"You were so angry with me for agreeing with Tony's parents."

"Another scar from the past," he confessed. "I was dragged home by the cops a couple of times when I'd had enough and decided to leave. It's a humiliating and pride-destroying experience, especially if you get a couple of thick-skulled cops who couldn't care less about kids and get their kicks by treating them like dirt. I work very closely with the police at times now, and I've developed a great deal of respect for most of them, but I'll never forget how it felt."

"And that's why you identified so closely with Tony."

"Yes. But you were entitled to your opinion, Spring. I could have told you how I felt and why, instead of shouting at you for expressing your own thoughts. I'm sorry."

"I was scared, too, Clay," she admitted quietly, her eyes dropping to their clasped hands. "You seemed so happy with your life, and I didn't think I fit in. I'm not adventurous and impulsive and outgoing, like Summer and your other friends. And I'm not exotic and beautiful, like the women in your past. I was becoming so deeply involved with you, but I thought you only wanted a fling with me

because of a fleeting attraction. Your odd behavior the
night we quarreled only seemed to confirm that suspicion."

Clay sighed deeply and raised her hands to his mouth,
pressing his lips to her knuckles before lowering them
again. "My beautiful, fascinating Spring. *Why* are you so
determined to put yourself down? What makes you think
that you're so uninteresting, and what will it take for me to
convince you that you're dead wrong?"

She shrugged a little, embarrassed. "I guess my behavior is shaped by my past, just like yours. I'm so used to being compared to my extroverted, exuberant younger sisters. When we were little, Summer was always clowning
around, performing, making people laugh with her imper-
sonations and her songs and dances. And Autumn was a
scrapper, a beautiful redheaded tomboy who impressed
everyone with her fiery personality and her athletic prow-
ess. I was known as the quiet one, the studious one, the
shy one. My mother was always talking about the mischief
Summer and Autumn got into, telling her friends the latest
thing one or the other had done, like she was complaining
but secretly amused by them. When she mentioned me, it
was only to say what a good girl I was.

"I'm not saying she didn't love me as much as she loved
my sisters," she added hastily. "I'm sure she did. And she
was—*is* very proud of me. But I just got used to being on
the sidelines, unable to compete for attention the way my
sisters did. It wasn't bad. I liked being out of the limelight.
I wasn't comfortable with too much attention."

"Poor love," Clay crooned, smiling tenderly at her. "It
must have been as hard for you to always live up to the label of good girl as it was for me to live up to the label of
bad boy."

She smiled faintly and bit her lip. "Oh, I used to rebel
sometimes, in my own quiet, unobtrusive ways. I'd play
practical jokes and never tell anyone who did them. People used to blame them on Summer and Autumn and
think it was all hilariously funny. Or I'd unexpectedly ac-

cept a dare when no one thought I would. I broke my arm once climbing a tree that everyone knew was rotten, just because Tommy Trenton dared me to. My family was shocked, but I was secretly quite proud of that cast."

"Just like I dared you to dress funky the night we went to the play at my school," he remembered with an appreciative grin.

"Mmm. And I've lived the life of a modern single woman since I left home," she added thoughtfully. "There haven't been many men in my life, but I doubt that my mother would have approved of all my actions. She's probably quite convinced that Autumn and I are still virgins simply because we're not married yet and that Summer was an innocent bride. She's very old-fashioned in that way."

Clay chuckled. "You don't think you're underestimating your mother a bit?"

"Oh, no." Spring laughed softly and shook her head. "No matter what she might suspect, she'd never admit it, even to herself. She prefers blissful ignorance—like all mothers, I suppose."

"You'll probably be the same way with our...with your children." Clay stumbled over the Freudian slip, then sobered immediately. "About the future, Spring..."

Still dazed by the thought of having children with him, Spring tensed, a bit nervous about what he was going to say. "What...what about it?"

"Let's delay it awhile, shall we? What we have together is still so new, so wonderfully mind-boggling, that I'd like to savor it before we move on to the next step. We have a lot of decisions to make, a lot to discuss, and I fully intend to do so soon, but how about if we take a couple of weeks just to get to know each other better?"

That sounded fine to her—on one condition. "Are you staying here during those couple of weeks?"

"If you'll have me," he replied with a winsome smile. "I'm taking a vacation. It's my turn."

"I'll have you," she told him, a bit too fervently, she thought immediately. She backtracked a little. "I can't take off work, though. My appointment calendar's full, and I can't take off again so soon."

"That's okay. I didn't expect you to."

"What will you do with yourself during working hours?" she asked, concerned that he would be bored.

"I could stand around your office and watch you work," he suggested teasingly. "No? In that case, I'll play tourist. I've never been to Arkansas. Maybe I'll find some barefoot hillbillies, if I look hard enough."

Spring scowled ferociously at him. "Are you daring to insult my state?"

He released her hands to hold both of his up, palm outward, in a gesture of conciliation. "Of course not! I was only teasing."

"Good. You just might be surprised at what you find in Arkansas," she told him smugly.

"I've already found something in Arkansas that's the best thing I've ever discovered. You."

She melted. "Thank you."

"This time together will also give you a chance to see what it's like to live with me," Clay pointed out, only half-teasingly. "I'm not your most normal guy, you know. And I do tend to get moody occasionally. Not very often, you understand. But I don't leave my dirty socks lying around," he added with a bit of boyish boasting.

"You don't wear socks, Clay," Spring informed him sweetly.

"That's right, I don't." He looked abashed for a moment, then grinned. "Maybe I should buy some and not leave them lying around."

"I don't think that will be necessary. I'm sure we can find another virtue in you if we look hard enough."

He seemed to consider that for a moment, then shot her a challenging look. "You're too far away. If you're going to find a virtue in me, you're going to have to look closely."

"Is that right?" Her brow lifted at the dare, as he'd known it would. "You know, the light in here is a bit dim. There's a better light in the bathroom."

He looked intrigued. "The bathroom?"

"Mmm. I thought I'd take a shower. I worked up quite a sweat today—at work," she added saucily. Then, remembering another challenge he'd once made her, she tilted her head and looked at him through her lashes. "I'd be happy to wash your back, Clay."

He, too, remembered telling her that one day she would offer to wash his back. His eyes gleamed with pleasure as he stood and held out his hand to her. "Only if you'll allow me to return the favor."

"I think that can be arranged."

The shower took a very long time. The water had run quite cold by the time it finally ended. By then they had soaped each other from head to toe, Spring had discovered two more tiny scars on Clay's body, and he'd gleefully located a shallow, round, nine-month-old chickenpox scar on her left breast, just to the side of her turgid pink nipple. Twisting the chilly water off, he covered the small imperfection with his mouth, which led to a painstaking exploration of the rest of her body, supposedly to find other reminders of the childhood disease she'd contracted so recently. He didn't find any, but by the time he'd concluded his search, neither of them remembered what he'd been looking for.

After they'd languorously dried each other with huge, fluffy towels, Spring took Clay's hand and led him into her bedroom, reminding him that she was supposed to be looking for his virtues. With a boldness that was new to her—and delightful to him—she made love to him. Slowly. Thoroughly. Imaginatively. He loved every minute of it, and he managed to tell her so in broken gasps and strangled groans.

Afterward they both fell asleep, exhausted but deeply content. They hadn't eaten dinner, but they'd satisfied their hunger in other ways. Sometime during the night

they raided the refrigerator for sandwiches, then made
love again. Clay went back to sleep almost immediately.
Spring lay awake for a short time, wondering about the future they'd been reluctant to discuss, but then she decided
to adopt Clay's live-for-the-moment attitude and she, too,
fell asleep, cradled close in his arms.

SO THAT CLAY COULD USE her car, Spring called Kelsey the
next morning and asked for a ride. She left for work with
her hair a bit mussed, her lips slightly swollen, and with
just barely enough time to get to her office before her first
appointment. But her violet eyes sparkled with love, her
cheeks glowed with happiness and she couldn't seem to
stop smiling. If she still worried about the future, she managed to hide it—even from herself. She was in love, and
Clay was here, and she intended to relish every moment.

"I would say that you had a very…interesting night,"
Kelsey commented after taking one look at her friend's
face.

Blushing rosily, Spring straightened her breeze-tossed
hair, which she'd left down that morning. "It was…nice."

"Nice." Kelsey sounded a lot like Summer when she repeated the word with disdain. "Sure."

"Okay, it was fabulous. What do you want, play-by-
play reporting?"

Grinning, Kelsey nodded avidly.

Spring laughed and shook her head. "Forget it. I
wouldn't have time, anyway. Mr. Abernathy is due at the
office in less than fifteen minutes."

"Hey, you're the one who was five minutes late coming
down to the parking lot."

Spring blushed again. "I know."

"Did he ask you to marry him?"

"Mr. Abernathy?" Spring inquired, being deliberately
obtuse.

Kelsey sighed gustily. "No. Clay Crowe McEntire. Did
he ask you?"

"No, Kelsey."

"Did he tell you that he loves you?"

Spring hesitated, then shrugged. "In a way."

"In a way? What's that supposed to mean?"

"Kelsey, really. I don't have time for this, and I'm not sure that I'd want to go into it if I did. It's awfully personal."

Kelsey smiled ruefully and nodded her dark head. "I know. It's just that I can't help worrying about you a little. I can't forget the way you looked on your birthday when you opened that gift from him. You were so devastated. This man has such power to hurt you."

Spring moistened her lips and tucked a strand of hair behind the earpiece of her glasses. "Kelsey, I know you're only concerned because you care about me, but I really don't want to talk about this just now, okay? Clay and I agreed to spend some time together before we discuss the future, and I think it was a good idea. I don't want to rush into anything at this point, nor do I want to spoil my enjoyment of being with him by worrying about what may or may not happen."

"I understand," Kelsey told her, though her dark eyes were still concerned. "Be happy, Spring. You deserve it." She parked the car in her parking space, then hesitated and turned to her friend, smiling as if she were worried that she might have put a damper on Spring's good spirits. "By the way, if you get tired of having the guy around, I'd be willing to put up with him for a few hours."

Spring laughed. "I'll just bet you would. Sorry, Kel, no chance. I'm hanging on to this one."

"I don't blame you."

"Thanks for the concern, Kelsey," Spring added quickly before climbing out of the small car. She was anxious to stay busy, knowing that the time until she was with Clay again would pass too slowly if she gave herself a chance to think about it.

She'd half expected Clay to call her sometime during the day, but he didn't. Nor did he show up at lunchtime. She wondered what he was doing with himself. She wondered if he'd like what he saw of her home state. And, finally, she wondered what was going to happen between them. It seemed that no amount of determination on her part could stop her from worrying about the future when she found herself with half an hour between appointments late that afternoon, due to a last-minute cancellation. She loved her city, her state and the practice she'd built, but she loved Clay so much more. If he asked—as she suspected that he would—could she leave the rest behind for him?

It wouldn't be easy, starting over. It scared her witless to think about it. Maybe she'd be content just to be Clay's wife—assuming he asked her to marry him, she added hastily, staring sightlessly at a patient's file. She could keep his home for him, have his children, wait patiently in his lovely house until he finished with his job and his volunteer work. It wouldn't be so bad.

It would be awful. She'd worked so hard for her degree. She loved her work. She'd go crazy with nothing to do but clean house and cook meals. Even if she had children, they would start school eventually, and then where would she be? Perhaps she would choose to take off a couple of years if she had a baby, but the operative word was "choose." She didn't like the idea of giving up her career just because she was afraid to start over in a new place.

No, she told herself bravely, she wouldn't give up her work. If Clay wanted her to go back with him to San Francisco, she'd do it, but she'd have to find a job there in her field. Perhaps she couldn't start her own practice again immediately, but maybe she could enter a partnership in an existing clinic. It wasn't that she didn't like San Francisco. She did. She thought it was a beautiful city. But, oh, how she'd miss Arkansas.

She wouldn't miss it nearly as much as she'd missed Clay during the past four months, she reminded herself. She couldn't even bring herself to consider how she would feel if she was separated from him now, after being given another glimpse of happiness with him. Even the thought was painful enough to cause her to flinch.

She quickly busied herself with work, pulling her thoughts away from the future, unwilling to dwell on the uncertainties just then.

"I MISSED YOU."

"I missed you, too. What did you do with yourself today?" Spring asked, her voice rather muffled since her head was buried deep within Clay's shoulder.

"I looked around, checked out Little Rock." He held her slightly away from him, giving her a proud-of-himself smile. "Did you know that this city has a symphony orchestra, two opera companies, a couple of community theaters, a ballet company, some very nice golf courses, hundreds of acres of beautiful parks, a zoo, a—"

"Clay, I know all that!" She laughed and clapped her hand over his mouth. "I've lived in this area all my life. Why are you telling me about it?"

"Just showing off what I've learned today," he informed her after removing her hand. "It's a fascinating town. The chamber of commerce was happy to give me all kinds of information."

"You visited the chamber of commerce?"

"Sure. It's the best place to start when you're learning a new city."

Why was he going to so much trouble to learn about Little Rock? The question puzzled her until his lips distracted her by making a little trail down her throat toward the open neck of her summery dress. "What are you doing, Clay?"

"Can't you guess?" He unfastened one button, his lips following the downward path of his fingers.

"What about dinner?"

"I can wait awhile. How about you?"

She closed her eyes and moaned softly when he found her breasts with fingers and lips. "I'm getting hungrier—but not for dinner."

He laughed softly and caught her up in his arms. "We may both lose weight during these next few weeks."

"So we'll be fashionably thin," she replied, smiling as she put her arms around his neck.

"You don't need to lose any weight," he murmured, his long strides carrying them quickly to her bedroom. "I promise to feed you well tonight. Later."

"Yes." She reached upward for his kiss as he lowered her to the bed. "Much later."

11

"Ahem."

"Just a minute, sweetheart, let me finish this article. It's about a psychologist here in town who has an interesting new method for treating emotionally disturbed teenagers." Clay held the paper a bit farther away from him, focusing with interest on the article that had grabbed his attention.

Spring sighed and walked up to his chair, sliding his stylish new glasses onto his nose. "*Now* you can finish your article," she informed him, then turned and went back to her own chair, where she'd been reading a professional journal when she noticed that Clay wasn't wearing his glasses. She'd gotten them for him on Wednesday morning and it was now Thursday evening, and he was still having trouble remembering to wear them when he read.

Clay gave her a sheepish grin, then went back to his article, swinging his leg over the arm of the easy chair in which he'd sprawled—the chair he'd claimed as his own during the four days since his arrival in Little Rock. Spring ignored the journal in her lap to admire her lover for a moment. His hair was mussed, he was barefoot, he was wearing a vivid green polo shirt with blue-purple-and-jade madras-plaid cuffed pants, and he wore her cat draped around his neck like a muffler. He looked wonderful. The glasses, with their thin metal frames, were very attractive on him. She couldn't tear her gaze away from him.

She had never been happier in her life. She'd always thought it would be difficult for her to adjust to living with someone after being on her own for so long, but she loved

living with Clay. They were completely compatible, in bed
and out, and she couldn't bear the thought of living without him now. In four days he had implanted himself so
firmly in her life and her heart that she knew he had become a vital part of her.

He was still spending his days, as far as she knew, roaming the local area, exploring anything that caught his interest. In the evenings he took her with him, showing her
parts of the city that she'd never seen, even as long as
she'd lived there. Only the night before they had taken a
ride on a paddleboat down the Arkansas River, which ran
right alongside downtown Little Rock. He was impressed
by Little Rock's cosmopolitan development and the small-
town atmosphere that somehow remained. He was
amused by the fanatic loyalty to the University of Arkansas football team, the Razorbacks, as evidenced by the
snorting red hogs depicted on signs, bumper stickers,
clothing, household articles, billboards—just about everywhere he looked, he'd informed Spring.

"And this is summertime," she'd told him with a laugh.
"You should see us during football season!" And then
she'd fallen silent, wondering where he—where *they*—
would be come fall. She only hoped that, wherever they
were, they'd be together.

Clay had expressed an avid interest in seeing other parts
of the state, naming off several places he'd like to see and
things he wanted to do. Spring had accused him of being a
compulsive tourist, but she'd made a reservation at a popular lakeside hotel in nearby Hot Springs National Park
for the weekend, eager to show him as much as she could
of her state while she had the chance. She was delighted by
his complimentary attitude and hoped he wasn't just saying what he thought she wanted to hear. They'd decided
to wait until the following weekend to visit her family in
Rose Bud, though neither would admit aloud that they
didn't want to spend time with her family until their future was somewhat more settled.

"You know, I think I'll give this guy a call next week,"

Clay mused, breaking in on Spring's thoughts as he looked up from his newspaper to find her gaze on him. "I'd like to meet him and discuss his new treatment method. It sounds interesting."

Spring smiled, knowing that Clay would probably be fast friends with the other man by the end of their meeting. He seemed to have a talent for making friends. Her neighbor, Mr. English, a man old enough to be Clay's father, had already become a friend, just from a chance meeting outside the apartments, and Clay had promised to go fishing with the other man one afternoon during the next week.

The telephone rang and Spring got up to answer it. Clay followed her into the kitchen and poured himself a soft drink while she talked to Kelsey. Spring looked up at him. "Kelsey wants to know if we're interested in a pool party-cookout tomorrow at six. A friend of ours has just decided he wants to have a party at his house tomorrow."

"Sounds like fun. Come to think of it, I've never seen you in a bathing suit." He gave her a teasing leer, his eyebrows wiggling. "Or Kelsey," he added thoughtfully, earning himself a punch on the arm. "Hey! You almost made me spill my Coke!"

"Clay likes the idea," Spring reported to her friend on the phone. "And, Kelsey, wear your navy-blue swimsuit, will you? You know, the one with the turtleneck and the patch on the right knee." When she hung up, Kelsey was still laughing.

Spring extended one hand in Clay's direction, trying to hold on to a fierce scowl. "Okay, buster, hand it over."

"Hand what over? My drink?"

"No, Kelsey's phone number. I forgot about it until now."

Clay laughed and shook his head. "Sorry, don't have it."

"She said she gave it to you." She knew her eyes were dancing with laughter, but she managed not to grin as she teased him. "Give."

"I really don't have it," he insisted humorously. "I tossed it in the wastebasket in your examining room when Andi ushered me in."

"You did?"

"Yep. I didn't know she was your best friend, but I knew I wasn't interested in any other woman's phone number. There hasn't been another woman for me since I looked up one Friday evening in March and saw a beautiful blonde standing in a doorway looking down her nose at my clothing."

Spring gave in to her smile and looped her arms around his neck. "Good. You just passed one test."

"I didn't know I was being tested." He set his soft drink down on the table, out of danger, and crossed his arms around her waist.

"Women always test men, didn't you know that?"

"How am I doing?"

"You did very well on the one about leaving your dirty socks lying around. You don't squeeze your toothpaste from the middle, you don't snore, you pick up after yourself and you don't keep other women's phone numbers—that's a big one, by the way."

Clay smiled smugly, dropping a kiss on the end of her nose. "Darn near perfect, aren't I?"

"Oh, you have a few flaws," she retorted, not wanting all that praise to go to his already swelling head.

"Such as?"

"You forget to wear your new glasses."

"I'll work on that one."

"And you get the newspaper all out of order before I read it."

"Oh. Sorry."

"You're a terrible cook."

"I suppose I could learn."

"And you've stolen my cat's affections. Missy thinks you're the greatest thing since catnip."

"And what do *you* think?"

"I think you're the greatest thing since catnip."

He grinned and dropped his head to kiss her, laughing when they bumped glasses. "I can tell that this is going to take practice."

Her own smile faded a bit as she fought to keep from telling him that she was willing to practice for a lifetime. He still hadn't brought up their future, and she wouldn't be the one to break their agreement, even though the subject had been weighing more heavily on her mind with each passing day. "We could take them off," she offered instead.

"Among other things," he added, tugging suggestively at the collar of her knit top.

"Yes," she agreed. She wanted to tell him she loved him, she thought wistfully as they walked side by side to the bedroom. She need to tell him. But that subject, too, was one that hadn't come up since Monday, when Clay had told her he loved her in a surge of passion. He hadn't told her since then, and she wasn't sure why. Was it because he wasn't sure himself? If so, she wouldn't pressure him by telling him her own feelings.

But, oh, how she loved him.

"THAT MAN OF YOURS is beautiful enough to make a grown woman weep, Spring," Kelsey said with a deep sigh, her eyes trained on Clay as he piled a plate high with a steaming grilled hamburger, pickles and chips. In his tropical-print surfing shorts that he'd chosen to wear with striped suspenders and a red sleeveless T-shirt, Clay wouldn't have been hard to spot in the crowd even if he hadn't been so tall and so very handsome. The early-evening sun, still bright and hot at this time of day in July, glinted off his hair, turning it to pure gold.

"Yes, I know," Spring agreed complacently, loving the proprietary feeling Kelsey's words had given her. Sitting cross-legged on a blanket, she took a big bite of her own burger—Clay was on his second—and watched him as he talked with a heavyset man in the line beside him. Gordon, the man Clay was talking to, owned the sprawling ranch-style house on fifty acres only a ten-minute drive out of Little Rock and frequently hosted these impromptu parties. Self-employed, he was able both financially and timewise to do so. Kelsey had met him just after she'd moved to Little Rock, and she was responsible for bringing Spring into Gordon's huge, heterogeneous circle. Clay had wasted no time getting acquainted with Spring's friends, mixing in as if he'd known everyone for years.

"And he's such a snappy dresser," Kelsey added with a grin.

Spring choked on her dinner and giggled.

"Something tells me you're laughing at me again," Clay complained as he joined them on the blanket, slipping off his red huaraches to tuck his bare feet under him. He winked at Kelsey as he looped a lazy arm around Spring's neck and hugged her. "She's got this crazy idea that I have strange taste in clothing," he explained.

Kelsey widened her eyes dramatically. "No! Why would she think that?"

"Beats me." Clay released Spring to attack his second hamburger as Kelsey's date, Wade, rejoined them after having fetched another mug of draft beer for himself and Kelsey.

"Thanks, Wade." Kelsey smiled at the solidly built ex-Razorback-turned-insurance salesman, then turned her attention back to Clay. "Spring told me that the two of you are leaving for Hot Springs in the morning. You'll like it. It's a beautiful area. Be sure and go up in the new observation tower on Hot Springs Mountain. It's over two hundred feet tall, and you can see the Ouachita Mountains and Lake Ouachita and Hamilton Lake and all of Hot Springs. It's gorgeous. Oh, and don't forget the Mid-America Museum and the Wax Museum and…"

Seeing that Clay was following Kelsey's every word with avid interest, Spring laughed and interrupted. "Kelsey, give us a break. We're only going to be there Saturday and Sunday, and Clay's already a compulsive tourist. Believe me, if it's there, he'll find it."

Clay only grinned and popped another chip into his mouth.

Half an hour later Clay and Kelsey and Wade were working off calories in a Hacky Sack circle while Spring, who'd never mastered that particular game, watched and laughed at them. Her eyes lingered on Clay as he adroitly fielded the small, leather-covered foot bag with his knee, then kicked it with the side of his foot to Wade, who expertly bounced the little ball off his own knee to Kelsey.

"Hello, Spring. You're looking very well," a familiar male voice said from behind her.

She turned her head to smile at the attractive man with neatly trimmed brown hair and rather serious green eyes, finding herself thinking in some amusement that his sharply creased jeans and Izod knit shirt looked atypically casual. "Hello, Roger. When did you get here?"

"Just a few minutes ago." He leaned down a bit awkwardly to kiss her cheek. "How pretty you look." Spring had worn a peacock-blue romper, brighter than her usual pastels, with white sandals. She'd left her hair down to tumble in loose curls at her shoulders and had stowed her glasses in their case in her purse. She knew she looked more relaxed and casual than Roger was accustomed to seeing her. Probably happier, too.

"Thank you, Roger." Come to think of it, Roger had a new glow in his own eyes. "Are you here with someone?"

His smile was just a bit shy—something else new for him. "Yes." He nodded toward a young woman engaged in a laughing conversation with Gordon. "Her name is Cathy Fleetwood. We're, uh, we're engaged."

Her eyes widening in surprise, Spring examined Roger's fiancée more closely. The tall, slender woman was strikingly attractive—and cheerfully flamboyant. In her mid-twenties, she wore her golden-brown hair in thick, wavy layers to her shoulders. Her huge blue eyes were dramatically highlighted with makeup, she wore enormous earrings that swayed with each movement of her head and her summer gauze jumpsuit was striped in hot pink, turquoise and blinding white. She looked like a feminine version of Clay. Summer couldn't help laughing, then quickly explained when Roger looked offended. "I'm just happy for you. She looks very nice."

He relaxed only marginally, still uncertain why she had laughed. "Thank you. I am happy. We're going to be married next month."

An obviously possessive arm went around Spring's waist and Clay loomed over her. "Did you miss me, sweetheart?"

"Of course I did, Clay." She smiled indulgently up at him, realizing that he must have seen Roger kiss her cheek. And he wasn't too happy about it. "Clay McEntire, this is Roger Nichols."

Recognizing Roger's name, Clay scowled for just a moment before holding out his hand.

Roger shook the proffered hand warmly, casting a glance at Clay's clothing before turning a ruefully amused look on Spring. Now he knew why she'd laughed, she realized. Both she and Roger had fallen in love with people diametrically different from themselves, and they knew it. No wonder they hadn't been able to hold on to their own relationship. Neither of them had been what the other needed. She smiled brilliantly at her former lover, silently wishing him happiness. His eyes returned the blessing before he walked away to join his fiancée and their host.

"Just what was that all about?" Clay demanded, bristling with masculine aggressiveness.

"What?"

"That look you gave each other. I thought you said everything was over between you and Roger."

"It is. Completely over." She turned in his arms, locking her hands behind his back and smiling up at him. "Clay, are you actually jealous?"

"Yes," he answered, looking stricken. "Dammit, Spring, I've never been jealous in my life!"

"Don't be, Clay. Roger's engaged and very happily so. And even if he weren't, you wouldn't have to worry.

Don't you know how much I—'' Her smile faded as she stopped herself, then she lifted her chin and finished the sentence. ''Don't you know how much I love you, Clay McEntire?''

There. She had said it. She was tired of hiding her feelings.

''And I love you,'' Clay whispered, lowering his head to hers. ''Oh, God, how I love you!'' And forgetting that they were not alone—or, more likely, not caring that they had an audience—he kissed her with all the love and need inside him.

Too happy to be embarrassed, Spring returned the kiss. She stayed very close to his side—and he to hers—for the remainder of the party.

''I LOVE YOU, SPRING.''

''I love you, too. Why didn't you tell me sooner?''

''I did. I told you Monday.''

''But you haven't said it since.''

''That's because I was waiting for you to say it.''

Spring giggled. ''God, we sound like teenagers.''

He moved sinuously on top of her, bare skin sliding against bare skin as they lay in her bed. ''Funny, I don't feel like a teenager.''

Her eyes darkened and grew heavy. ''No. No, you certainly don't. Oh, Clay.''

CLAY LAUGHED SOFTLY, the movement vibrating his damp chest below her cheek. She lifted her head and looked at him curiously, her body gradually recovering from their intense, mind-shattering lovemaking. ''What's so funny?''

''I was just thinking that I finally understand why Derek kept threatening to break my arm every time I put it around Summer when he first fell in love with her. It really brings out the caveman in a guy to see his woman looking so cozy with another man.''

Remembering Clay's possessive reaction to Roger,

Spring smiled and shook her head. "Derek's gotten over those jealous urges. You will, too."

"I suppose. But I still don't like other guys kissing you," he warned her semiseriously. "Especially old boyfriends."

"Now you know how I felt when Jessica started checking out the fit of your tight pants at Connie's party."

That piqued his interest. "Is that right?"

"I wanted to scratch her eyes out. And that's the first time in my life I ever wanted to do physical injury to another person. Other than you, of course."

"Of course." He cuddled her closer, his hand making lazy circles on her back. "These feelings between men and women are very complicated, aren't they? Overwhelming. Even scary sometimes."

"You're the psychologist. You should understand them," she replied, trying to keep the conversation light.

He shook his head. "It's different reading cases in books and actually experiencing the situations oneself. A few months ago I would have said that jealousy was counterproductive and unhealthy, that rational, clear-thinking adults did not waste time indulging in such negative emotions. I still believe that, and yet I wanted to rip off Roger's lips when they touched your face. So much for all that training."

"You're human, Clay. You managed to overcome your impulse and behave quite properly. You even had a very nice conversation with Roger before we left tonight."

"Well, he's not such a bad guy. A little dull, maybe, but Cathy will liven him up a bit. He wouldn't have been right for you, Spring."

"I know, darling. You're the one who's right for me. Exactly right for me."

"I love you."

"I love you, Clay."

He twisted until he was leaning over her. "Feel up to showing me again? I find myself still in need of reassurance."

She opened her arms to him, eager to find her own reassurance in his arms. Their future was still uncertain, but at least she knew now that he did love her. Surely their love could overcome any other obstacles that might lie ahead for them.

"C'MON, SPRING. Rise and shine. We're wasting sight-seeing time."

Spring opened one eye, looked at the clock, noted that it was just seven in the morning and closed the eye with a loud groan. "Go away."

"No, really, sweetheart. By the time you shower and we have breakfast, it will be eight. You told me that it takes about forty minutes to get to Hot Springs, which will make it almost nine o'clock. We'll do some of the outdoor sights this morning before it gets too hot—God, it gets hot in Ar-kansas in July!—then we'll do indoor things until it cools off a bit. Museums, bathhouse tours, and so on. Spring, are you listening?"

"I'm sleeping."

"Don't make me have to tickle you, my love."

She opened that eye again, looking warily at him. "You wouldn't."

He held his hand over her bare side, fingers wiggling in mock threat. "Wouldn't I?"

She sighed and rolled over. "You win. I'll get up. Oh, God, you even look like a tourist. All you need is a camera slung around your neck."

"It's waiting in the living room," he replied happily, glancing down at his green T-shirt emblazoned with the words Arkansas Is A Natural, his khaki hiking shorts and his white tennis shoes.

"How come when I made my first visit to California, all I did was shop and visit my sister, and you come to Arkan-sas and try to memorize the state?"

"You just haven't learned the fine art of touristry," he answered with a grin. "Up, up, up. I'll be studying the his-tory of the hot springs while you're showering. Did you know that they were used in healing rituals by the Indians and that Al Capone and Bugsy Siegel used to take the baths there on a regular basis?"

"No, but I'm sure I'll know all that and more by the end of the weekend." Spring climbed out of bed and brushed her hair out of her face, yawning. After getting so little sleep during their particularly active night, she was having a hard time keeping up with her exuberant lover. Not that she minded. She thought he was cute when he was in tourist mode.

She hummed in the shower, taking her time despite Clay's schedule. She intended to enjoy every moment of the weekend with him. Dressed in white shorts and a lemon-yellow top, she tossed a few things into an overnight bag and was ready for the weekend. All she had to do was drop Missy off with Mrs. English, who'd taken care of the cat while Spring was in California and was very fond of the pet.

Still humming softly, she went off in search of Clay. She found him in the living room, talking on the telephone. She paused in the doorway, realizing that he hadn't heard her approach. She didn't intend to eavesdrop, but she didn't want to disturb him, so she stood quietly for a moment, thinking he would notice her at any time.

"Okay, Frank," he was saying, his back still turned to her. "Gather it all up and hang on to it for me. I'll look it over when I get back. When? Oh, the week after next. Monday or Tuesday, at the latest. Yeah, I'm having fun. See you in a week, Frank."

Spring was back in her room before he'd cradled the receiver, her hand pressed to her stomach as if that would help the pain. She hadn't expected to hear him calmly making plans to return to California. He hadn't said a word to her about it. Sure, he'd told her when he'd arrived that he was here for a couple of weeks, but that had been before he'd told her that he loved her. She'd thought that he would ask her to go with him when he decided to leave.

Pacing blindly around the room, she stumbled, then picked up the stuffed bear that had gotten under her feet.

Holding him cradled to her chest, she stood in one spot, rocking slightly as she tried to tell herself that she wasn't breaking into pieces.

Be realistic, Spring. You knew he was only here on vacation. It was ironic, she thought with bitter humor, that their relationship had begun with a vacation fling—hers—and seemed to be ending with a vacation fling—his. No wonder he hadn't wanted to talk about their future. He didn't foresee one. At least not together.

Maybe he would still ask her to go with him, she thought on a surge of hope. And then shook her head in answer to her own thoughts. No. He surely would have said something to her before calmly making plans to leave.

Maybe he wasn't planning to end their relationship when he left. Perhaps he envisioned a long-distance affair—phone calls, letters, an occasional vacation together in California or Arkansas. Of course she knew where that would lead. Heartbreak. She didn't want to be separated from him. She didn't want to lie alone at night wondering whom he was with, what he was doing. She wanted to be his wife. She wanted to have his children. She wanted him!

"I'm having fun," he'd told Frank. *Fun?* He considered a full-scale love affair fun? Fine. She'd keep it that way for him. She'd told him goodbye before; she could do it again. She could live with a functioning machine where her heart was now. Because he would surely take her heart with him when he left.

It hurt. It hurt so much. But she wouldn't let him know. She refused to part badly with him again. She had him for another week, and she intended to create a lot of memories with him during that time. She would need them later.

"Spring, aren't you ready yet? Oh, there you are." Clay paused in the doorway and eyed her quizzically. "You planning to take the bear? It's fine with me, but I don't know if he's up to all the walking I plan to do. He looks kind of old."

She straightened her shoulders and forced a smile, setting Pooh back in his new spot on her bedroom floor. "I was just telling him to behave himself while we're gone. Is breakfast ready?''

"Yep. You have a choice of Raisin Bran and toast or Frosted Mini Wheats and toast."

"I'll have the Mini Wheats." She started past him, only to be stopped by his hand on her arm.

"Spring, are you all right?" he asked her, intently searching her face. "You look kind of funny."

She lifted an eyebrow. "Did you just call me funny looking?" she asked him in teasing challenge, hoping her smile would fool him.

He chuckled. "Of course not. I just wondered if anything was bothering you."

"I'm always like this when I'm roused from my bed at dawn after a strenuous night to face a breakfast of cold cereal and toast," she assured him airily. "To be followed by a long weekend of sight-seeing with the quintessential tourist."

"We're going to have a great time today," he assured her, looping his arm around her neck. "Trust me."

Trust him? The man who could—and probably would—break her heart? Okay, she'd trust him. For one more week, anyway.

"I love you, Spring," he murmured as they entered the kitchen.

"I love you, too, Clay." She was quite proud that she adequately hid the fact that her heart had already started to break as she spoke.

DURING THE WEEKEND Spring discovered that she was actually grateful for Clay's fascination with discovering new sights. He kept her much too busy to worry about the following week. They walked and played, climbed and explored, dined and danced until they were both barely able to crawl into bed Saturday evening, too tired even to make love. Though she'd expected to have a perfectly miserable day, she had a wonderful time, finding the fortitude somehow to push her problems to the back of her mind. She was with the man she loved; he was enjoying himself immensely. She couldn't be sad under those conditions. She even slept soundly and dreamlessly, waking to Clay's hand on her thigh, his mouth on her breast. She returned his lovemaking fiercely, determined to wring every ounce of satisfaction from her time with him.

"Spring, are you quite sure there's nothing wrong?" Clay asked her when he'd recovered part of his strength.

"I'm sure," she lied solemnly, kissing his shoulder.

He knew her too well to accept the words so easily, but he seemed to sense her wish for him to drop the subject. Perhaps he, too, wanted to make the most of the remaining week.

"In that case, let's get with it. I want to spend today at Magic Springs Amusement Park," he informed her breezily, climbing out of bed and heading for the shower.

Spring surreptitiously wiped away the tears she hadn't allowed him to see and ordered her mouth to smile. She decided that Summer wasn't the only Reed sister who'd been blessed with dramatic talent.

"Spring?"

"Okay, I'm hurrying," she assured her impatient lover, rushing to join him in the shower.

12

"So what's Clay doing today? Memorizing the history of central Arkansas? Following the De Soto Trail along the Saline River through Benton? Counting the number of C-130 transport planes on the Little Rock Air Force Base in Jacksonville?" Kelsey grinned as she listed the possibilities on Tuesday afternoon in Spring's office.

Spring shook her head. "He's meeting with a local psychologist he read about in the paper last week. A man who works with troubled kids in their own homes. Clay called him yesterday and they talked for a long time, then set up this meeting for today."

"Got a real talent for meeting people, doesn't he? I couldn't believe how well he fit in at Gordon's on Friday. It was like he'd known the gang for years."

"Yes, he's very good with people." Spring completed a report, signed it and handed it to Kelsey. "There you go. All finished."

"Okay, I'll take care of it." Kelsey paused, frowning a bit, then asked carefully, "Is anything wrong, Spring?"

"No, why do you ask?" The lie was coming easier all the time.

"No reason. It's just that you've looked, I don't know, kind of sad since you came in yesterday morning after your weekend in Hot Springs. I hope you're not having problems with Clay. The two of you seem so good together."

"No, Kelsey, we're not having problems." And they weren't. They were getting along fine. But Clay still hadn't bothered to mention that he was leaving in only a few days. Her hope had slowly dwindled and finally fizzled out completely. If he'd been planning to ask her to marry him and move with him to California, he would surely have done so by now. He was leaving in less than a week.

And still she'd managed to hide her pain from him. She must be a much better actress than she'd ever suspected.

CLAY WAS on the telephone again when she walked into her apartment after work. Again she had the impression that he was talking to Frank. He saw her this time as soon as she entered the room, stopped whatever he was saying in midsentence, then went on with a few vague, general remarks that could mean anything before hanging up.

"Just checking on things in San Francisco," he explained.

"How are things in San Francisco?" Maybe now he would tell her his plans, she thought.

"Oh, just fine," he answered uninformatively. "Hey, did I tell you I heard from Thelma a couple of weeks ago?"

"No, you didn't. How is she?" He was putting her off again. Why?

"She's doing great. She's crazy about her aunt and she's being tutored this summer so that she'll be ready for tenth grade this fall. She's in music classes and she's made a couple of friends—and she assures me they're nice kids who won't lead her into more trouble. I've got a lot of hope for that kid."

"She owes a great deal to you, Clay."

He flushed unexpectedly and shrugged. "Just doing my job."

His job? He'd never made a penny from his work at Halloran House, where he'd met Thelma, and she knew it. She smiled at his modesty.

"You haven't even kissed me yet," Clay told her suddenly. "C'mere."

After the kiss her arms remained around him, tightening compulsively as she held him. She never wanted to let him go.

Clay returned the hug with enthusiasm, then held her away from him. "What did I do to deserve that?"

"I love you," she told him, unable to smile.

"I love you, too." He kissed her again, then laughed and turned her toward the kitchen, keeping his arm snugly around her waist. "Let's find something to eat before we get distracted and miss dinner again. I'm starving."

Slipping into the determinedly lighthearted mood that she was rapidly becoming an expert at assuming, she matched her steps to his. "How did your meeting with Dr. Random go today? Are you still intrigued by his new method?"

"Very much so. I had a few suggestions to make that he seemed to like, and we had an informal consultation on a couple of kids he's been treating lately—no names, of course. We managed to preserve his confidentiality. We're having lunch tomorrow."

She looked up at him in surprise. "You must really be interested in this man's work."

"Of course I am. It's the same work as mine," he answered logically, smiling as he released her to open the refrigerator door and peer hopefully inside.

He must be missing his work very much, Spring thought sadly, if he was spending so much time just talking about another man's job. He must be looking forward to getting home.

Oh, good, Spring. Why don't you twist the knife a little harder? she asked herself impatiently. Deciding abruptly to make some iced tea, she reached into the cabinet for tea bags, groaning when her sudden move bumped her elbow into the sugar bowl on the counter. Sugar spilled across the counter and onto the tile floor at her feet in a glistening white stream. "Damn."

Without pausing a beat Clay leaped into the puddle of sugar on the floor and began to do a soft-shoe routine, whistling "Tea for Two" as he slid the toe of his sneaker through the white powder. Spring had to laugh as she pulled out the broom and dustpan, shaking her head at his antics. God, she was going to miss him!

KELSEY ACTED ODDLY on Thursday. Spring asked twice if her friend was ill or troubled about something, but Kelsey only looked mysterious and shook her dark head, her brown eyes twinkling with mischief. Even Andi kept eyeing Spring with a secretive smile that was making her decidedly nervous. What was going on, anyway?

She found out right after lunch. She'd just finished with a patient and walked out into the hallway to find Clay waiting for her. He grabbed her and kissed her, right in front of Kelsey and Andi, before she could speak.

When he released her, she frowned at the expressions on the three faces grinning at her. "What's going on? What are you doing here, Clay?"

"I'm kidnapping you for the afternoon," he informed her. "Get your purse."

She sighed. "Clay, I have appointments this afternoon. I can't just leave."

"Wrong," Andi told her. "You're quite free this afternoon."

"Are you crazy? I looked at the calendar this morning. The afternoon was booked."

"All the appointments have been rescheduled to the patients' satisfaction," Kelsey informed her smugly. "You're going to be working a few extra hours tomorrow and Monday to make up for it, but you're off for the rest of the day. Enjoy."

Spring narrowed her eyes at Clay, who was looking innocently back at her. He was wearing disreputable jeans and a Mickey Mouse T-shirt, and even the mouse looked blandly conspiratorial to her suspicious eyes. "Clay, what are you planning?"

"Sight-seeing," he told her succinctly. "Get your purse."

Groaning, she tugged off her white lab coat and got her purse.

"Well?" she asked him when they were in her car and on their way. "Where are we going?"

"I've found something really interesting. Ever heard of the Quapaw Quarter?"

"You're taking me to see the Quapaw Quarter?" she asked in bewilderment.

"Yes. It's an area of downtown Little Rock full of old homes ranging in architectural style from the pre-1836 Territorial Period to the 1940s. Many of them are Victorian mansions or large cottages, and some have been completely restored to their former magnificence. About five hundred homes and buildings in the six-square-mile area have been renovated or fixed up, with a total investment of some twenty million dollars. There are—"

"Clay!" Spring loudly interrupted. What *was* going on? Clay always liked to talk, but now he was positively chattering!

"Yes?"

"*What* are you quoting?"

He looked sheepish. "A publication that I picked up from the Quapaw Quarter Association. Did you know that there are a thousand members of the Quapaw Quarter Associ—"

"Clay, I know about the Quapaw Quarter. They have tours of some of the restored old homes every Christmas and every spring, which I've been on several times. *This* is why you kidnapped me from my office?"

"Just wait, Spring," he told her mysteriously.

Thoroughly confused, she leaned back against her seat and waited, noting in surprise that he was holding the steering wheel in a white-knuckled grip.

Clay drove slowly down Broadway, pointing out some of the restored homes, such as the Bankston House, the Thompson House and the Foster-Robinson House. He turned on Twenty-first, taking them over to Spring Street, a name he pointed out gleefully.

"I was well aware it was here," Spring told him, but he ignored her, chatting away like a tour guide to a true foreigner. She frowned when he pulled into the drive of a gray frame Victorian cottage on Spring Street. "Why are you stopping?"

He dangled a key in front of her, his eyes not quite meeting hers. "Private tour."

"We're going inside?"

"Yep. The realtor is holding my Rolex, all my credit cards and my firstborn child hostage until I return the key."

"Why?"

"So I won't take the key and run, I guess. I thought it was kind of silly. After all, the key's not worth that much, and it would be pretty hard to steal the house—"

"Clay, why are we going into this house?" she asked, holding on to her patience with an effort.

"You and I are both interested in restoring old homes, and this one is really nice. Restoration was begun a couple of years ago. Then the couple who'd started had to sell and move away, so nothing much has been done since, but it has a lot of potential. Wait until you see the gingerbread trim inside. Wonderful!"

Her heart had started to pound, but she told herself not to read too much into this odd private tour. For all she knew, Clay could just be sight-seeing, as he'd told her.

He kept up a running commentary as he led her onto the front porch, with its quaintly delicate columns, and to the door, a heavy wooden one with a lead-glass fanlight above it. "This house and most of the others in the Quarter have been researched and the information kept on file by the QQA, the Quapaw Quarter Association. They also keep a library of books on the art of restoration and preservation of historic houses, hoping to encourage more people to take on these homes as family projects."

Though part of her mind followed his words, another part of her noted in growing fascination that there was a nervous edge to his voice and that his hand was shaking so hard he had trouble fitting the key into the lock. Her own hands began to tremble. In fact, she was trembling all over as she followed him inside.

"Look at that staircase. Isn't it fantastic? And these floors. They need sanding and refinishing, of course, but they're—"

His voice broke. Shoving his shaking hands into the pockets of his jeans, he went still, staring at her with eyes that were shadowed by deep emotion.

"Clay?" she whispered, unable to look away from his face to notice any of the features of the house. "What is it?"

He took a deep breath and looked down at his sneakers. "Did you ever want something so very much that you thought you'd die if you didn't get it? Want it so much that you were afraid to even ask for it for fear of being turned down?"

"Yes," she answered, her voice raw. "Yes, I've wanted that much." *You, Clay. I want you that much. And I'm so afraid to hope.*

"I need you so much, Spring." He shot her a quick glance, looked away, then slowly turned his eyes back to her. "All my life I've wanted to be loved. The kids love me and my friends love me, and for the past few years I've thought that was enough. Until I met you. I almost died after you left, Spring. For four long months I lived in misery, so lonely that I felt like there was a gaping hole inside me. It scared me to realize that you were the only one who could fill that void. And I resented you for a while for making me need like that again, after considering myself satisfied for so long."

"Clay, I—"

"No, wait, sweetheart, let me finish." He laughed, a bit weakly, and shrugged. "I've been practicing this speech for a long time."

She nodded and blinked against a sudden rush of tears as he continued.

"I didn't want to say anything right away because I wanted you to get used to having me around all the time. In California there were always other people with us or around us, but here it's been pretty much just the two of us. I thought you'd know by now whether you wanted to have me around full-time. And I've been checking out Little Rock and the surrounding area because I wasn't sure at first if I'd be happy here, but now I know that it's a great place to live and…and raise a family.''

His voice had cracked again, sending the tears in a fresh cascade down Spring's pale cheeks. She had to bite her lower lip to keep from interrupting him before he was finished.

''There are some excellent counseling facilities for adolescents here, most of which I visited last week. And Gil— Dr. Random—has asked if I might be interested in going into partnership with him. He seems to think that the two of us could make a real difference around here, maybe publish some material that could be applied nationwide. I told him I would certainly think about it. I have to admit I'm tempted to take him up on it.

''We wouldn't have to live here, of course. Your apartment is very nice, or there are many beautiful newer homes in west Little Rock, closer to your office than this. I'd be happy anywhere if you were there with me.''

He took one more deep breath, then blurted out, ''What I'm trying to say, Spring, is…will you marry me? Please say you will, Spring.''

''Yes,'' she whispered, and then said it again, louder, throwing herself against him. ''Yes, yes, yes!''

Staggering, he caught her and spun her around in a joyous circle. ''You will? Oh, God, Spring, you don't know how happy you've just made me!''

Laughing and crying all at once, she cupped his face between her hands and kissed him. ''How could you possibly be so surprised? Didn't you know I would marry you?''

''Oh, sweetheart, I'm not that self-confident. Ever since last weekend you've been acting a bit distracted and I was starting to get scared that you were growing tired of me.

That you were ready for me to go back to San Francisco and let you get back to your sane, normal life."

"You idiot," she told him lovingly. "I was distracted because *I* was scared. I heard you talking to Frank on Saturday about returning home in about a week, and I was afraid that you were planning to leave without me."

He laughed softly and held her close. "God, we're so insecure when it comes to each other. That's exactly the way I reacted four months ago when I thought you were calmly making plans to return to Little Rock without a backward look at me. It's going to take a legal, binding, double-ring ceremony for me to get over my fear of losing you, Spring. When will you marry me?"

"Whenever you want," she answered simply. "And you don't have to live in Arkansas if you really don't want to, Clay. I decided four months ago that I would move to San Francisco if you wanted me to."

"You'd be willing to give up your friends, the practice that you've worked so hard to build?" he asked, seemingly stunned by her offer.

"Of course. Aren't you offering to do the same thing for me?"

He kissed her thoroughly, then drew back to smile down at her. "Thank you. But I like it here. I'm perfectly happy to move. It'll take me some time to get everything settled, but most of it can be done long-distance. I've already been talking to Frank about setting up a foundation for long-range money management so that Halloran House can be run without my day-to-day help, or interference, as some people might call it. And I can sell my house easily enough."

"Don't sell it yet," Spring urged him suddenly, her fingers gripping his T-shirt. "Lease it for a year."

He frowned, puzzled. "Why?"

"Because I want you to be very sure when you do sever that connection to San Francisco. If, at the end of a year, you're not as happy here as you were in California, I want you to tell me. We'll move—there, or anywhere else you want to go. As long as we're together, I don't care where we live."

"That's not necessary, darling. I know what I'm doing."

"Please, Clay. For me."

"All right, Spring. I'll lease the house. But at the end of one year I'll be selling it. I've found my home here, with you."

"I love you, Clay."

"I love you," he murmured against her lips, and then his mouth took hers in newly confirmed possession, his tongue touching hers in a mating dance that made the upcoming ceremony a mere formality. In their minds and hearts they had already made their lifetime commitment to each other.

His body growing taut with desire, Clay smiled down at her with an expression she recognized, her body responding quite physically to the silent invitation. "I haven't shown you around the house yet, have I? Particularly the bedroom."

"No, you haven't. Show me our house, Clay."

"Our house? You like it?"

"I love it. I can't wait to put on jeans and a work shirt and start remodeling with you. How are you at hanging wallpaper?"

"I'm hell on wheels at wallpaper. It's going to be a lot of work, Spring."

"It's something I've always wanted to do. I even have my own set of tools, thanks to my sister Autumn."

He had to stop to hug her again. "You are terrific, did you know that?"

"I'm perfectly willing to be convinced."

"Oh, I intend to convince you, darling. If it takes a lifetime."

"I suspect that it will."

There was another surprise waiting for her in the large, almost completely renovated master bedroom. In front of the native-stone fireplace—a mate to the one in the living room—a handmade quilt had been spread invitingly. A silver ice bucket held a bottle of champagne, and two crystal glasses with beribboned stems waited for a toast. A dozen red roses in a tall crystal vase perfumed the room, masking the faint dustiness of the empty house.

"Oh, Clay." She turned to him, her eyes filling again at the blatant sentimentality of his gesture. "What would you have done if I'd said no?"

"Poured the champagne over your head, thrown you onto the quilt and made love to you until you were too weak to argue with me," he returned promptly, holding out his hand. "Come here, sweetheart. Let's toast our very brief engagement."

"How brief?" she asked with interest, placing her hand in his and allowing him to lead her across the room and seat her on the quilt.

"As brief as your practice and my settling of affairs will allow," he replied, popping the cork and pouring two bubbling glasses of champagne. "To a long and happy life together, my love."

She touched her glass to his and lifted it to her lips, unable even to taste the expensive wine in her excitement and joy.

Clay took only one swallow from his glass, equally oblivious to the taste, his gaze fastened on the flushed, happy face of his future wife. His nerves, which had been tight with anxiety earlier, began to thrum with another type of anticipation. Still having trouble believing in his good fortune, he wanted to further seal their commitment in the most basic manner of all. He wanted to make love to her, to bury himself deep inside her and remind himself over and over that he had every right to be there, that she was his and he was hers and he would never be lonely again.

Her eyes met his, and he watched her read the message he was sending her, watched her eyelids grow heavy, her lips soften and glisten as she moistened them with just the tip of her tongue. A groan started deep in his chest and forced its way through his throat. He set his drink down abruptly and reached for her, barely giving her time to set her own glass safely out of the way.

And then he was kissing her and holding her, and she was holding him, loving him, needing him, filling that life-long void inside him. Filling it so perfectly that it would never open again. And because he'd craved that feeling for so long, he felt his eyes filling with tears of happiness and gratitude. Spring kissed away his tears, even as he did hers, and then sweetness turned to passion and tenderness to hunger and they were tossing aside clothes and reaching for each other. His thrust took him deep, deep inside her, and her arch forced him even deeper until neither of them could tell where one left off and the other began. They were one, and they would have settled for nothing less.

The words he muttered into her ear as he rocked against her, inside her, were disjointed and not particularly clever, punctuated by ragged gasps and broken sighs, but she knew what he was telling her and her clenched hands and sinuous movements answered him in kind. By the time they shuddered together and cried out their fulfillment, there was no further doubt of their love or commitment.

It seemed like a very long time later when Spring stirred, sighed and lifted her head to smile at Clay. "I hope no one else decides to check out this house in the next few minutes," she told him, lying nude alongside him on the rumpled blanket.

He chuckled. "Good point. Though the realtor assured me that I had the only key, I guess there's no need to press our luck. Maybe we should get dressed."

"I love this bedroom." She looked around the room with pleasure, anticipating many happy times there with Clay.

"There are two other bedrooms you haven't seen yet. Think we can come up with a use for them?" Clay asked hopefully.

"I'm sure we'll think of something," she answered, picturing two blond children with blue-green eyes and beautiful smiles and unusual taste in clothing.

"Someone once told me that I'll be better with kids once I've had some of my own."

She winced as she remembered their quarrel. "That someone sounds like an idiot. You're already great with kids."

"I'd still like to have a family with you. A boy and a girl. Or two boys. Or two girls. Or three or four of each."

She laughed and shook her head firmly. "Two sounds like plenty."

"Just think—we can all wear matching outfits!"

She groaned and hid her face in his shoulder. By the time she came up for air, he had grown serious, looking steadily at her, as he spoke. "I'm not going to be all that easy to live with, Spring. I get so wrapped up in young people's problems sometimes that I tend to ignore everything else, and I can't promise you that won't ever happen with you. It's a part of me that I can't seem to change, and I don't know that I even want to try."

"I don't want you to change, Clay. I love you exactly the way you are. You are a caring, loving, sensitive man, and your concern for young people is one of the reasons I fell in love with you. I care about them, too. I'd like to help you, if I can. I won't feel neglected if I'm involved, too."

"That sounds wonderful," he told her with a smile. "I promise, though, that I'll always be there for you and our children when you need me. All you have to do is ask and I'll drop everything else. Got that?"

"Got it. And I believe you, darling. You're already giving up so much to move here to be with me."

"I'm not giving up a fraction as much as I'm gaining," he returned firmly. "Remember that, will you?"

"Just keep reminding me, darling." She gave him a brilliant smile as she reached for her clothes.

"I intend to." He reached out and caught her hand, tugging her back down in a sprawl across his chest. "Believe me, sweetheart. I intend to."

Epilogue

HER MOTHER'S antique lace gown fell in soft folds to strike Spring at midcalf—it had fallen almost to Summer's ankles when Summer had worn it for her wedding ten months earlier. Fortunately, the sisters were almost the same size except in height, so the dress hadn't needed altering. A white hat and her grandmother's pearl earrings—returned to her earlier that day by Kelsey—completed her wedding outfit. Spring checked her appearance one last time in the full-length mirror in the bedroom that had been hers while growing up. In only a few minutes her wedding would begin.

As Spring had wished, it was to be a relatively small, informal affair on her mother's beautifully kept, flower-decorated back lawn. They'd waited until early evening so that the August heat would have dissipated a bit, though it was still very warm. Her parents, relatives and close friends—some fifty people in all—would make up the audience. Summer and Autumn were to serve as bridesmaids, while Derek and Dr. Gil Random, Clay's new partner, would stand beside the groom.

"Are you nervous, honey?" Lila Reed asked softly, faded violet eyes focused on her eldest daughter's serene face.

"A little. But I don't have one doubt that I'm doing the right thing," Spring assured her mother. "Clay is the best thing that ever happened to me, Mom."

"Just be happy, Spring." Lila hugged her daughter, then stepped back, surreptitiously wiping her eyes.

"I will be." Spring picked up the bouquet of colorful flowers that Clay had provided for her—a beautiful but unusual mixture, of course—and turned toward the door. "I'm ready. Is Daddy waiting in the hall?"

"Yes, and he's ready to get this over with. He's just as nervous this time as he was when he gave Summer away."

"Tell him to take heart. Autumn swears she'll never go through this 'archaic and obsolete ceremony,' so maybe this will be his last time."

"Autumn's young yet. We'll see how she feels when she meets someone as special as your Clay and Summer's Derek."

"Speaking of my Clay, what *is* he wearing, Mom? I can't stand the suspense." Spring had cheerfully given Clay free rein to wear whatever he wanted to their wedding, but he had refused to tell her what he'd chosen. She hadn't seen him since he'd gone off to change for the ceremony an hour earlier.

Lila shook her gray head, smiling girlishly. "He made me promise that I wouldn't tell you. That boy is sure going to liven up our lives, honey. I'm glad ya'll decided to settle in Little Rock so your dad and I can see you often."

"So am I, Mom. Okay, let's get on with this."

Her hand tucked into the crook of her father's work-muscled arm, the fabric of his favorite brown suit crisp under her fingers, Spring walked down the aisle formed by rows of folding metal chairs, her eyes sparkling with happiness and amusement. Flanked by Autumn and Summer in their jewel-toned summery dresses and Derek and Gil in their conservative suits, Clay fit in surprisingly well. His suit was dark blue, hand tailored, European cut. His shirt was white, his tie a muted stripe. He looked as breathtakingly handsome in his conservative attire as he did in tropical-print shorts. Spring's heart swelled with love for him.

He stepped forward to meet her, catching her hand in his as his eyes glowed warmly into hers.

"A blue suit, Clay?" she murmured.

"In honor of this serious occasion, my love," he replied softly.

"Clay, I told you that I didn't want you to change for me. I love you exactly the way you are."

He stared down at her for a moment, then gave her a smile that competed with the August sun in intensity. "I love you, Spring," he murmured, then caught her to him for a long, passionate kiss, much to the amusement of their small audience.

"You're supposed to wait until *after* the ceremony, Clay," Derek pointed out from his position as best man.

Clay chuckled and released her, though he directed her attention downward as he lifted the hem of his beautifully cut pants. "I haven't changed, Spring. I'm still the man who loves you more than life itself. Just wait until you see what I have on under the suit."

Glancing at his bare ankles, Spring smiled and turned with him toward the perplexed minister, toward their future. The next time Clay kissed her, they were husband and wife.

A hero's got to do,
what a hero's got to do....

HERO BY NATURE

by Gina Wilkins

1

AUTUMN REED HOPPED nimbly out of the cab of the pickup, tugging the brim of her battered brown baseball cap low over her oversized sunglasses to shade her face from the afternoon sun. Her auburn hair was looped into a French braid, which had loosened over the course of the day so that it bobbed behind her as she strode briskly toward the front door of the impressively sized ranch-style house to which she'd been dispatched. To anyone reading body language, her movements were indicative of her personality—quick, restless, energetic, no-nonsense. She punched the doorbell with a slender, short-nailed finger, then waited impatiently for a response.

"Well, hell," she muttered when there was no sound of a chime inside to announce her arrival. The electricity was out. What was she doing ringing the bell? She knocked loudly, imperatively.

While she waited for the door to open, she looked around. The house was gorgeous, the lawn beautifully landscaped. But then it had to be, in this Tampa, Florida neighborhood of equally gorgeous homes, equally beautiful lawns.

The door opened, bringing her shaded green eyes back around. The man in the doorway was as beautiful as his home, she thought with detached amusement. Young, probably early thirties. Coal-black hair brushed casually back from a tanned, classically handsome face. Perfectly arched black brows over deep blue eyes, perfectly straight nose, perfectly even white teeth exposed by a mouth shaped for fantasies. Smooth, dimpled cheeks, square jaw, six feet plus of body that could serve as an advertisement for a health spa. He was one of your finer examples of the human male, and Autumn was woman enough to react quite physically. Mentally she knew that there had to be more to a man than a pretty face to make him worth her interest.

"I'm with Brothers Electrical Company. You called for an electrician?" she asked in her direct, unceremonious manner.

"Well, yes, but..." He paused, looking at her with a doubtful frown.

She sighed resignedly. Damn. One of those. "I am a licensed electrician," she assured him in a bored voice. "If you need to check me out, call the office. Of course, I charge by the hour and you're wasting time."

"I'm sorry," the attractive man answered, visibly flustered. "I wasn't questioning your competence. I was simply surprised that you're a..." His voice trailed off again.

"Woman." A very nice voice, Autumn thought automatically, even as she supplied the word for him. Low, rich, unapologetically Southern. Classy, too. Like someone who was intelligent and well educated but didn't feel the need to make a big deal out of it. She had a habit of summing people up within a few minutes of making their acquaintance. She typed this guy as a successful professional with impeccable manners and a deeply ingrained woman's-place-is-in-the-kitchen-and-bedroom mentality. Too bad. "What's your problem?" she asked briskly.

"I beg your— Oh, you mean why did I call an electrician," he stammered, his eyes never leaving her face, or at least that part of it visible beneath her cap and huge sunglasses. Autumn wondered if she had overestimated his intelligence. "It's the box on the side of the house, the one by the electric meter," he told her finally, after clearing his throat. "A limb blew down during the thunderstorm last night and knocked it almost completely off. The electric company disconnected my power but told me I'd have to call an electrician to reinstall the service."

Autumn nodded. "No problem. I'll get my tools, then

you can show me where it is." She whirled and headed back to the black Ford Ranger with the magnetic signs advertising the name of the company she worked for. Her belt was in the cab, and she retrieved that first. She strapped the tools around her slender waist, over her khaki jumpsuit, seemingly oblivious to the fact that the heavy tool pouch added almost fifteen pounds to her usual one hundred and ten. Then she reached into the bed of the truck for her ladder and toolbox, only to stop short when a long, tanned arm reached past hers.

"I'll carry those for you," the dark-haired man offered, muscles rippling as he lifted out the heavy red metal toolbox as if it weighed practically nothing.

Begrudging him his superior strength, Autumn tried to protest when he reached back in for the fiberglass ladder. "I can get it. I'm used to carrying my own tools."

"No trouble at all," the man assured her, already moving away, toolbox in one hand and ladder balanced over his other shoulder, giving her a very nice view of his muscular back and lean hips. "This way, Miss...?"

She exhaled impatiently and followed him. "Just call me Autumn," she told him.

"Autumn," he repeated solemnly, smiling around at her. "That's a very pretty name."

"Thanks," she answered briskly, uncomfortable with the compliment.

"I'm Jeff Bradford. And here's the reason I called you."

Autumn raised one dark eyebrow at the sight he indicated. He hadn't exaggerated. His service entrance was almost completely torn off the house, though fortunately it hadn't been badly damaged. That would save her a trip after a new box. She pulled a screwdriver out of her pouch. "This is going to take a couple of hours," she informed him. "I'll try to have your electricity back on by late afternoon."

"I'd appreciate it," he responded with a charming smile.

Autumn swallowed and turned to her ladder. Lord, but he was attractive! Distracting, as well. "I'll let you know when I'm finished," she told him in what she hoped was a dismissive tone.

"I think I'll watch, if you don't mind," he replied diffidently. "It's, uh, it's dark in the house, and I've nothing better to do."

She shrugged, determined not to show him that his magnificent presence was in any way disconcerting. "Suit yourself." She tossed out the words and set to work with grim concentration.

Jeff shoved his fingertips into the pockets of his gray denim jeans and leaned one shoulder against the side of his house as he watched her climb three rungs of the ladder. The siding was rough through his thin cotton knit shirt, but he spared the sensation little thought as he mentally castigated himself. He was acting like a tongue-tied idiot, he told himself with disgust. What on earth had gotten into him? Fifteen minutes earlier he'd been a fairly bright, reasonably urbane kind of guy, and then he'd opened his door to this woman and lost whatever intelligence he may have possessed. He hadn't said anything worth listening to since she'd first spoken to him in that low, husky voice.

And the hell of it was, he wasn't even sure if he found her all that attractive. Her hair was a pretty color, kind of a dark red as best he could tell from the functional braid. Her face was almost completely hidden by that beat-up baseball cap and those ridiculous sunglasses. What he could see was very nice. Small nose, squarish cheeks, soft, sensually shaped mouth that did not owe its rosy color to cosmetic aid. She was small, the top of her head coming just to his chin—about five, five he guessed. As for her figure, it might be good, but who could tell with that loose-fitting jumpsuit and bulky tool pouch? And even if a woman like this would deign to enter a beauty pageant, she certainly wouldn't win the prize for Miss Congeniality. So why had he suddenly developed a tendency to stutter?

He reached up automatically to take the metal box she'd

just disconnected, noting the slight twist of her mouth as he did so. She wasn't overly pleased about him helping her. One of those rabid feminists who entered a vocation normally filled by men, then found it necessary to continually justify her choice, he decided. Well, he was sure she was a fine electrician and he couldn't care less if she chose to spend her time twisting wires, though he couldn't imagine why anyone would want to do so. Personally, he preferred women who were softer, more feminine, whatever their chosen careers. Less antagonistic.

Then she tugged off her sunglasses and shoved them into the breast pocket of her jumpsuit, glancing down at him as she did so. Jeff froze, staring at her like the tongue-tied idiot he'd just accused himself of being.

He'd always heard that one could tell a sorceress by her eyes.

Green. The truest green he'd ever seen, with deep, hot flames, carefully banked, in their depths. Evidence of a fiery temper, he was sure. He found himself wondering if her passion was as volatile. He would be willing to bet it was. Her long eyelashes and boldly shaped eyebrows were unusually dark in combination with her auburn hair.

She was beautiful. He'd suspected that she was attractive, but he hadn't guessed that there was a rare, earthy beauty hidden behind those god-awful dark glasses. And he was standing there like a tourist gazing in awe at the Statue of Liberty.

Make conversation. "How long have you been an electrician?" he asked abruptly. *Oh, terrific line. Straight out of* How to Win Friends and Influence People, he thought with a mental groan.

Autumn glanced down from her work, intending to let him know that if he was going to stand there, she would appreciate it if he'd be quiet and let her work. Instead, she found herself staring at a generous, warm smile that only a coldhearted puppy hater could ignore. "Almost five years," she answered, her voice more friendly than she'd originally intended. She looked back at the mess of wires in front of her, trying to concentrate on what she was doing.

"Do you enjoy it?"

"Beats sitting behind a typewriter," she replied as she pulled a pair of side-cutting pliers from her pouch.

Her action drew Jeff's eyes back down to her waist, which was just below his eye level. He was suddenly fascinated by the roll of black electrician's tape that dangled from a chain on her belt, swaying against her hip as she moved. He cleared his throat and turned his eyes sternly upward. "You're not from Florida originally, are you?" he asked.

"No, Arkansas. Hand me that set of cable cutters out of my toolbox, will you?" Autumn decided that keeping him busy might just keep his mouth shut, though she doubted it. She thought he had a very nice voice, but it was definitely distracting.

Jeff frowned into the open toolbox, staring at the assortment of tools there. The only thing he recognized was a big screwdriver. He'd never been much of a handyman—by choice. He preferred to pay people to do that sort of thing. Now he wished he hadn't chosen extra science classes over shop. Using a rapid process of elimination, he grabbed something big and heavy and held it up. "You mean this?"

"Yeah, thanks," she said casually, taking the tool from him and turning back to the service.

He just managed not to say "whew" and wipe his brow. He didn't know why he was suddenly trying to impress this woman, but he felt as if he'd just earned himself a few points.

"Now would you hand me—"

Jeff tensed, glaring back down at the toolbox. *What now?*

"The hacksaw?" Autumn finished.

Thank goodness. Jeff snatched up the vaguely familiar instrument and offered it upward, grinning broadly.

Autumn took the saw, wondering why Jeff was suddenly looking so pleased with himself. Strange guy, she mused. Gorgeous but strange.

A particularly vigorous movement on her part shook the ladder beneath her, but Autumn wasn't concerned as she steadied herself on the wall in front of her. After all, her feet were barely three feet off the ground. She'd fallen farther.

Jeff, however, was not so unconcerned. He reached out at the first shimmy of the ladder and steadied her, one hand on the ladder, one on the back of her leg, a scant few inches below the slender curve of her hip.

"You okay?" he asked.

Impatient, she sighed and looked down. "Yes, I'm…fine." Her voice faded as she looked down into the face turned up to hers, their gazes locking. She was suddenly vividly aware of that warm hand on the back of her thigh. She cleared her throat soundlessly, "You want to, uh…"

"Do I want to what?" Jeff asked eagerly.

"You want to move your hand?" she continued more forcefully.

His mouth tilting into a one-sided smile that she secretly found devastating, he looked down the length of her body to the hand in question. "No, not particularly," he informed her.

"Well, do it, anyway," Autumn snapped. "I'm trying to work here."

"Sorry," he murmured, looking back up at her with sparkling blue eyes that showed not the faintest apology. He moved the hand but took his time about it.

Autumn tightened her jaw and turned curtly back to the job before her, telling herself that she was *not* blushing. Dammit, she hadn't blushed since junior-high school! What was with this guy, changing from a rather sweet, shy, awkward type to a practiced flirt in the blink of an eye?

Rebuilding Jeff Bradford's meter loop should have been a routine, if painstaking, job, requiring little more than

perfunctory concentration on Autumn's part. In reality, it
became a test of her skill and professionalism as she struggled grimly to perform her job while her uninvited
"helper" hovered beneath her, making cheerful conversation, offering assistance when none was needed, occasionally handing her a tool in response to a grudging request.
Autumn had to ask herself more than once why she was
being so patient with him. She had been less patient with
other pesky males, customer or not, and had even been
known to lose her formidable temper with a few. But Jeff
continued to be so relentlessly nice and courteous that she
would have felt like a complete shrew had she been anything less than tolerant of him, though her tolerance may
have been a bit forced.

"Do you know that you have the most beautiful eyes
I've ever seen?" he asked her at one point, gazing earnestly up at her. "Are they naturally that green, or do you
wear contacts?"

Autumn swallowed and dropped the stripping knife
she'd been using, relieved that it fell nowhere near her uninvited assistant. "Jeff, do you suppose you could bring
me a glass of water?" she asked with hidden desperation,
unaware that she'd casually called him by his first name.
"It's, uh, it's really hot out here."

He grinned, as aware as she that the moist, late-October
breeze around them was quite comfortable. "Sure, Autumn," he answered without further comment. "I'll be
right back."

"Don't hurry," she called after him.

The next four and a half minutes were the most peaceful
time she'd managed since Jeff Bradford had answered her
knock on his door. So why did she catch herself smiling
when he returned with the requested water?

"Almost finished now," she announced a short while
later, relieved that she'd done a creditable job despite her
uncharacteristic clumsiness. "I just have to connect these
grounding wires to the back of the box and—"

Because her attention was more on the man beside her

than on what she was doing, she awkwardly allowed the screwdriver she was using to slip out of the groove of the screw, the forward momentum of her hand causing her knuckles to smash painfully into the side of the metal box. Autumn swore colorfully under her breath, jerking her abused hand out of the box. She was particularly chagrined that she had done this in front of Jeff, although it was a common occurrence in her job.

As she would have expected, he reacted with sympathy and concern. "Are you okay?" he demanded for the second time that afternoon. "Let me see your hand."

"It's fine, Jeff, really. I just—" Her words died in a resigned sigh as he took her slender hand in his bigger ones, probing and massaging with the skill of an expert.

"Nothing broken, but you're going to have some interesting bruises," Jeff told her with relief. "It will be sore. You really should wrap it in ice."

"Really, Jeff, it's okay. I've done this before. More often than I like to remember," she assured him, embarrassed. "Occupational hazard."

His thumb traced the delicate bones in her hand. "You've broken a couple of these bones, haven't you?" he asked, feeling the almost imperceptible ridges beneath her surprisingly soft skin.

"Yeah, I broke a couple of bones in an accident once. What are you...a doctor?"

"Pediatrician," he admitted.

She hadn't really thought he was a doctor. She'd only been asking to divert his attention from her hand. For some reason she was suddenly self-conscious, though she couldn't have explained why. "If you'll let go of my hand, I'll finish this up," she told him rather briskly.

"You're always asking me to let go just when I'd like to hold on," Jeff complained good-naturedly, though he released her hand.

Autumn made a concerted effort to ignore him as she rapidly completed her job and climbed down the ladder— with Jeff's help, of course. She figured that his mother

must have taken him to classes in Southern gallantry from
the time he could walk. She tried to tell herself that his studious politeness annoyed her, even as she found herself
thanking him for his assistance. What on earth was wrong
with her?

Her tools packed neatly into the truck, she turned to him
with a work order on a clipboard. "Just sign right here, Dr.
Bradford, and you'll be billed for the service. You can call
the electric company now and have your power turned
back on."

"Dr. Bradford?" he quizzed her as he signed the work
order in an illegible scrawl that befitted his occupation.
Autumn had never met a doctor who could write anything
readable. "You called me Jeff earlier."

"Did I?" she murmured vaguely. "Well, goodbye.
Thank you for calling Brothers Electrical Company. Give
us a call if you need anything else." Her customary reci-
tation concluded, she turned to the truck, intending to
leave without further delay.

Jeff, however, had different intentions. "Will you have
dinner with me this evening?" he asked her, surprising
them both. He hadn't intended to ask quite so abruptly—
he wasn't even free that evening, he remembered wryly—
but when she'd started walking away with such finality,
he'd spoken almost without thinking. Now he decided
that if she accepted, he'd just call Julian, his partner and
buddy, and cancel out on the poker game. Julian would
understand. Jeff really wanted a chance to get to know this
interesting woman. There was just something about her
that he found fascinating.

Autumn wasn't particularly surprised that he'd asked.
Not after the past couple of hours. What *did* surprise her
was that she found herself suddenly tempted to accept.
Not that she had any intention of doing so. Something
about Dr. Jeff Bradford made her nervous, somewhat unsure of herself, and Autumn Reed wasn't accustomed to
such feelings. Above all, she liked being firmly in control
of herself. No, Jeff was too overwhelmingly attractive, too

unpredictably charming, too…well, too something. Besides, she already had a date that evening with a man who was amusing, attractive in a less spectacular way, and much more manageable. "Thank you for asking, but I already have plans," she told him after a brief pause, keeping her voice deliberately distant.

Jeff shrugged almost imperceptibly and backed off. "Maybe I'll see you around sometime," he told her.

"Maybe," Autumn agreed, climbing into the cab of the pickup. Her tone was not encouraging.

"Goodbye, Autumn."

"Bye, Jeff." She closed her door with a snap and drove away.

Some fifteen minutes later Jeff replaced the telephone in its cradle, having been assured that his power would be turned back on within the hour. He roamed aimlessly into his den, dropping moodily onto the heavy wood-framed couch, its deep cushions sinking beneath his weight. *So you struck out,* he told himself, disgruntled. It wasn't a first, though he couldn't actually remember the last time. Jeff was no womanizing playboy, but then, he'd never had much trouble getting a date, either. Of course, he rarely came across like a thick-skulled, inarticulate chauvinist, he added with an audible groan, sinking deeper into the couch cushions. No wonder Autumn had turned him down.

For all he knew, she was heavily involved with someone. She could even be married, though she hadn't worn a ring. But then, she hadn't worn any jewelry at all. *Forget her, Bradford,* he ordered himself sternly. *She's just not interested.*

He shoved himself off the couch, determined to do just that.

JEFF WASN'T GRINNING when he opened his door two weeks later, but Autumn suspected that he was holding it back only with tremendous effort. "You called for an electrician?" she asked him coolly, eyeing him with suspicion.

"As a matter of fact, I did," he replied, just a bit smugly. "Please come in."

Her suspicions increased. "First tell me what you need done so I'll know what tools to bring."

"I need an additional outlet in my den," he informed her.

She repressed a sigh and nodded. "Okay. Hang on a minute." She turned abruptly and headed back to her truck.

Jeff followed, of course, and had her toolbox out before she could even reach for it. She totally ignored him. Outwardly, at least. Inwardly, she was vitally aware of every inch of him in his thin blue sweater, which hugged his torso and made his eyes look even bluer, and his slim-cut jeans that left little to her imagination. She hadn't forgotten the effect he had on her. Which was why she intended to stay well over an arm's length away from him while she finished this job in record time.

Autumn tried not to look impressed by the interior of Jeff's house, but it wasn't easy. It was beautiful. Professionally decorated, she was sure, but comfortable and inviting. He'd chosen to ignore the usual wicker-and-palm-tree or pseudo-Spanish styles popular in the area and had decorated in a rustic Southwestern theme. Autumn recognized the many examples of Seminole artwork scattered with studied casualness throughout the house. The Seminole Culture Center on Orient Road had been one of the first sights she'd visited after moving to Tampa almost a year earlier.

"This is where I'd like the outlet," Jeff told her, indicating a section of white-painted Sheetrock wall in his den.

She studied the wall. "No problem, but you have a receptacle just a few feet away from there," she pointed out.

"It's not convenient. To plug in the vacuum cleaner I have to crawl behind that chair," he replied.

Plug in the vacuum cleaner? She wondered how often he performed that particular operation himself. "You could move the chair."

"I like it where it is," he answered with a bland smile. "Do you want the job or not, Autumn?"

She shrugged. "It's your money." Frowning, she examined the grin that had finally broken across his gorgeous face. "I suppose you want to watch me work?"

"If you don't mind."

As if it mattered whether she minded or not. She sighed and tried one more ploy to get him a bit farther away from her. "Don't you doctors ever work?"

"Thursday's my day off," he answered genially.

"Then your meter loop was blown off on a convenient day, wasn't it?" she murmured, remembering that she had met him on a Thursday. Two weeks ago today, she thought. She refused to dwell on how often she had thought of him during those two weeks.

He shrugged, an obvious imitation of her. Autumn glared at him and started to work.

It was the last time all over again. Jeff hovered around her, helping whenever she'd let him, chatting with her whenever she'd bother to answer. It was apparent that he was going out of his way to charm her. And, dammit, she thought glumly, after he'd unexpectedly made her laugh out loud at one of his quips, he was doing it. She found she had a definite weakness for Dr. Jeff Bradford, a weakness that she had no intention of indulging. Despite his many attractions, she had learned her lesson about getting involved with charming, old-fashioned males. Five years earlier she'd broken her engagement to a very nice man who had tried and failed to break her rebellious spirit. She'd never regretted that decision.

"Almost finished," she announced, tightening the screws on the plastic outlet plate.

"This is going to be very handy. Thanks."

"You paid for it." She stashed the screwdriver in her pouch as she stood and pulled the hem of her jeans from behind the tab at the heel of her gray nylon-and-suede jogging shoes.

"How was your date?" Jeff asked unexpectedly.

Autumn lifted one dark eyebrow. "What date?"

"The one you turned me down for two weeks ago," he reminded her, watching her closely.

"Oh." She'd almost forgotten that date. It had been quite forgettable. She'd thought about Jeff all evening, which had not put her in the best of moods for the amusing, attractive and manageable man she'd been with. "It was fine."

"Will you go out with me tonight?" Jeff asked immediately.

She'd been expecting an invitation this time and had decided in advance that she was going to turn him down. But doing so was even harder than it had been the first time. Deep inside she liked Jeff Bradford. She knew she'd have a good time if she went out with him. She also knew that it would only take a touch from him to smash her normally formidable willpower into quivering blobs. And *that* was a dangerous, sobering realization. "I'm sorry. I can't."

"Tomorrow night?"

When had he moved so close to her? Autumn looked straight up into his eyes as she declined again. "No, I..." Since when had her voice ever been breathless and fluttery? she asked herself in disgust. She cleared her throat and spoke more firmly. "I can't."

He took another step forward. "Saturday?"

There seemed to be a short developing in her breathing apparatus. Her breath was coming in uneven little jerks, growing worse in direct proportion to Jeff's increasing proximity. She swallowed and stepped back, only to find herself backed against the arm of the massive chair they had discussed earlier. "No, thank you," she managed.

"Should I keep asking?" he inquired gently, lifting his hands to take her by the forearms, steadying her when she would have stumbled against the chair.

"No, you...you needn't bother," Autumn answered with a firmness she found somewhere deep inside her. Finding his bright blue eyes too mesmerizing, she dropped her own gaze to his chest, only to find herself staring in admiration at the glistening V of tanned skin exposed by the neckline of his sweater. A nest of dark curls lay there, looking soft and all too tempting.

"Is there someone else?" Jeff persisted, bringing her face back up to his by way of a gently insistent hand beneath her chin.

Becoming annoyed, she lifted her chin further to avoid his hand. "There's not anyone else specifically. I'm just not interested in going out with you, Jeff."

"Mind telling me why?"

"You don't take rejection very well, do you?" she asked irritably. His Southern-gentleman image was slipping. "The truth is that I'm not attracted to you," she lied, almost expecting lightning to zap through the ceiling. "Now will you let go of my arms?"

"In a minute." His hand returned to her chin, tilting her head back further. "First I want to check something out."

She parted her lips to answer, only to find them covered firmly with his.

She had known it would be like this. Had known, and had tried hard to avoid it. The kiss was explosive, his touch the catalyst. Match to fuse. Gasoline to flame. Man to woman.

His tongue swept the inside of her mouth. Autumn moaned, but she could not have said whether the sound was one of pleasure or protest. She was afraid she knew, especially after he lifted his head to draw a deep breath, then lowered it again without one ounce of resistance from her.

The second kiss was just as powerful. Pressed closely together from chest to knees, Autumn was as aware of her own physical response as she was of Jeff's. Things were getting entirely out of control, she thought with some distant, still-sane portion of her brain, even as her recalcitrant hands flattened hard against his back. His image of polite gentleman had definitely altered.

It was Jeff who finally broke the kiss with obvious reluc-

tance. He stepped back a few inches, his chest rising and
falling rapidly, face slightly flushed, hands still gripping
her arms through her long-sleeved knit shirt. "You want
to try again?" he asked, his voice husky, his blue eyes
glinting with what looked suspiciously like amusement
and something else that Autumn had no need to analyze.

"Do I...what?" she asked, her own voice raw.

"You said you weren't attracted to me. Now we both
know that's a lie, so I wondered if you wanted to try another excuse for not going out with me," he elucidated.

Autumn stared at him for a moment, her temper rising,
then jerked herself out of his grasp, almost falling over the
armchair behind her before catching her balance and
whirling away. "You...you egotistical *male*," she hissed,
snatching her cap up from the floor where it had fallen. "I
said I don't want to go out with you and I meant it. I don't
need an excuse."

"No, I don't suppose you do," he murmured.

Autumn glared at him through narrowed eyes, deciding
that if he let loose the smile that he was obviously struggling to hold back, she'd throw something at him. How
dare he laugh at her loss of temper? She took a deep
breath, hid behind a facade of icy professionalism and
grabbed her clipboard, holding it out to him in a curt gesture. "Sign this," she ordered, making no effort to be
pleasant.

"Yes, ma'am," he murmured, lips twitching as he
scrawled Dr. E. Jefferson Bradford across the bottom of the
work order.

"I'll be seeing you around, Autumn," he called out to
her as she climbed angrily into the cab of her pickup moments later.

"Not if I can help it," she muttered, slamming the door.
She was well aware that he stood in his driveway watching her until she was completely out of his sight.

2

"Okay, Jeff, who is she?"

Jeff blinked and frowned questioningly at the woman who stood before him, determination written on her impish face as she faced him with her hands on her well-rounded hips. "Who's who?" he asked.

"The woman you've been mooning over all evening," Dr. Pamela Cochran answered flatly. In a chair across the room her husband, Bob, chuckled as he rocked his infant daughter to sleep.

Jeff glared at Bob and turned a melodramatically fierce scowl on his partner. "I have no idea what you're talking about," he told her haughtily.

Pam laughed in disbelief. "Sure you don't. Come on, Jeff, I know you. Who's the woman, and what did she do?"

"Okay, I got shot down when I asked a woman out. Twice," Jeff answered resignedly. "There, are you happy?"

Bob made a loud choking sound, startling the tiny bundle dozing in his arms. "*You* struck out?" he demanded avidly. "Will wonders never cease!"

Jeff flushed, his frown deepening as he glared at his two best friends. "Knock it off, Bob. It's not like it's the first time someone turned me down." The discussion was strangely reminiscent of his one-sided conversation two weeks earlier, after Autumn had turned him down the first time.

"Yeah? So when was the last time?" Bob inquired perceptively.

Jeff muttered the answer he'd finally come up with after asking himself the same question that other time.

"What was that? I didn't hear you," Bob insisted.

"Eleventh grade, all right?"

Bob laughed. "That's about what I thought."

Pam shook her head repressively at her husband. "And we all know that one explanation is that the man doesn't ask enough to face the usual percentage of rejection," she summed up concisely. "We're talking about the man Julian likes to call Dr. Monk."

"Most men are monks compared to Julian," Bob muttered when Jeff only snorted. "Jeff's just more concerned with quality than quantity, aren't you, buddy?"

"Since when are you two so interested in my love life?" Jeff asked them with rueful exasperation.

"Since you barely touched my special shrimp with snow peas, which happens to be your favorite Chinese dish," Pam retorted. "Only a woman could make you lose interest in shrimp with snow peas. So who is she? Do I know her?"

Jeff shook his head. "I just met her a couple of weeks ago. Her name is Autumn."

"Autumn what?"

He shrugged. "I don't know."

"Oh," Pam said slowly. "You don't know." She sat beside Jeff on her couch, staring at him with round brown eyes. "How'd you meet her?"

"She was the electrician who worked on my house when the storm knocked my service out. She came back yesterday to install an outlet in my den. I requested her specially yesterday, for all the good it did."

There was a moment of silence, and then Bob asked, "You asked your electrician out for a date?"

"Yeah. But as I said, she turned me down. Flat."

"And to think while I was trying to take care of my patients at the clinic, you were flirting with a pretty electrician," Pam complained, her eyes sparkling with the enjoyment of teasing her co-worker. "Serves you right that she turned you down."

"I acted like an idiot the first time I met her," Jeff moaned, touching his hand to his forehead. "Stuttered, stared, generally acted the fool. I wasn't much better yesterday, though I did manage not to stutter." He decided not to mention those kisses that had been almost as unexpected for him as for her. "She probably thinks I'm a not-very-bright chauvinistic jerk."

"Chauvinist? You? Hardly," Pam denied indignantly. "You're old-fashioned in some ways, but only the nicest ways," she added. "What was she...one of those women who gets insulted if a man simply opens a door for her?"

"Your Georgia accent is getting heavier, darling," Bob murmured, not quite successfully hiding his smile.

"I'll bet that's it. She was a Yankee, right?" Pam inquired. "Used to Northern men who walk out of elevators first and open doors only for themselves."

Jeff chuckled, his bad mood slipping away. "She's from Arkansas, Pam. No need to drag out your Rebel flag. She just isn't interested in going out with me."

"Then she has no taste," Pam proclaimed loftily. "Or she's involved with someone else. Did you ask?"

"Yes. She said there wasn't anyone else in particular."

"Then what *was* her problem?"

"Give me a break, Pam. The whole ordeal was bad enough for my ego without rehashing it. Couldn't we change the subject?"

Pam tugged thoughtfully at a curl of her frizzy brown hair. "Did I mention that we've got several fluorescent lights acting up in the clinic?" she asked finally, referring to the relatively small stucco structure the three young doctors had purchased when they'd first gone into partnership. There were advantages to owning their own building, but there were also many responsibilities—maintenance among them. "I think we need to call an electrician."

"Pamela," Jeff drawled warningly.

She widened her eyes in feigned innocence. "Well, we do," she insisted. "We can't take proper care of our patients with the lights blinking on and off."

"So call someone. But not Autumn. I don't think I could take rejection three times in a row." He sighed exaggeratedly, knowing he would make her laugh.

He was right. "Poor baby," Pam crooned when the laughter had died away. "Would a big slice of my cherry cheesecake make you feel better?"

Jeff grinned. "I'm sure it would," he said eagerly.

"Hey, I could use some cheering up myself," Bob added quickly.

"Put the baby to bed and I'll cut you a slice," Pam replied. She patted Jeff's head maternally as she stood, though she was only two years older than his thirty-three. "Don't you worry about a thing, Jeff, honey. Pam will take care of it."

"Now *that* makes me worry," Jeff answered hastily. Anytime her Georgia accent got so heavy that she called him "Jay-uff" and herself "Pay-um," he could bet that she had some kind of scheme floating around in her brilliant head. "Pamela, promise me you won't…" His voice faded as he followed her into the kitchen, knowing as he spoke that he was being ignored.

"DAMN THAT MAN," Autumn muttered when she realized she'd been staring at her mouth in the mirror for a good three minutes after she'd finished brushing her teeth. It had been four days since Jeff Bradford had kissed her—assaulted her, she amended vindictively—and still she had the oddest tingling sensation in her lips whenever she thought of him. Unfortunately, she thought of him much too often. Like about a thousand times a day, she added glumly, sighing as she turned off the bathroom light.

Her huge Cincinnati Reds T-shirt flapped around her bare legs as she padded across the room and climbed into her narrow white iron bed. It was barely ten o'clock, but she'd had a particularly strenuous day at work, and she was tired. She wanted nothing more than to be asleep by the time her head hit the pillow. "Good night, Babs," she told the fuzzy white miniature poodle who'd curled up beside her.

Twenty minutes had passed before Autumn finally acknowledged that she wasn't going to fall instantly asleep. She wondered wearily why she'd thought tonight would be any different from the last three. Every time she closed her eyes in the darkness, she imagined herself being held once again in the arms of a dark-haired man with the smile of an angel and the kiss of a charming devil.

It might be easier to forget him if there was even the slightest doubt that she would ever see him again, she decided. There wasn't. Dr. Jeff Bradford wouldn't disappear easily from her life now that he had unexpectedly entered it. Her luck just didn't run that way. She would see him again. And he would ask her out again. And it would be even harder to turn him down the next time. Because her lips still tingled four days after he'd kissed her. Damn.

If only she could have stayed angry with him for kissing her, for refusing to take her at her word when she'd refused to go out with him. Unfortunately, she suspected that she'd never really been angry with him in the first place but rather with herself for responding to him so dramatically.

She had to keep reminding herself why she should not go out with him. Those tingling lips were part of the reason. Never had she reacted to any man's kiss in quite that manner. It wouldn't take many of those kisses to have her dragging him off to bed. And conservative, reluctantly conventional woman that she was in some ways, she'd end up wanting more than sex from him. Before she knew it, she'd be sorting his socks and dyeing his underwear pink with her haphazard laundry habits. She could say goodbye to blissful independence, unconcernedly irregular hours, gourmet frozen dinners. Hello to slow, deadly suffocation. She'd been there before.

Steven had been blond, rugged and attentive. His slow

smiles and practiced caresses had awakened Autumn's teenage body to its first taste of desire. The fiery-tempered tomboy had changed into a passionate young woman madly infatuated for the first time. Despite the budding ideas of women's liberation gained from her avid reading about "life in the outside world," her small-town Arkansas Baptist upbringing had led her to consider it only fitting that back-seat experimentation should lead to an engagement ring given the night she graduated from high school.

Steven had been attending agricultural college at Arkansas State University, and Autumn had been content to do office work for a small electrical service in her hometown of Rose Bud while waiting for Steven to graduate. Or at least she had tried to be content, despite the ever-increasing surges of pure panic that assailed her whenever she allowed herself to contemplate a future in Rose Bud with two or three kids and a husband whose destiny was to take over the family farm and raise soybeans and grain. She kept reading—*Cosmopolitan*, *Ms.*, other magazines targeted at young, single career women—kept fantasizing about doing something on her own, finding out what it might be like to build a life for herself. And kept trying to pretend she was happy.

Autumn wasn't sure when the occasional bouts of panic had turned to outright rebellion. She remembered watching with growing envy as the electricians she worked for went off on jobs, patting her on the head and calling her "honey" as they passed her on their way out. She remembered the resentment that had begun to build when Steven had casually asked her to bring him a beer or fix him a plate at dinner, his attempts to tame her temper and natural independence. She remembered how hard it had been each morning to slide on that miniature diamond ring that felt heavier all the time. And she remembered the desperation she'd felt when both of her sisters had moved out, Spring to college in Memphis, Summer to college in Little

Rock, leaving Autumn at home in Rose Bud feeling as if she'd never be able to escape.

She hadn't eased gracefully out of the engagement. She hadn't even been conscious of making the decision to end it. One summer evening just before her twentieth birthday, she'd attended a family gathering at Steven's home. The evening had been intolerable, rampant with Southern farmer sexism and probing questions about Steven and Autumn's plans for the future. Autumn had prepared Steven's plate for him—just as all the other women had done for their men—and later had helped clean the kitchen while Steven had joined the other males in front of the television. The second time Steven had called for a beer, Autumn had obediently carried it to him. And then kept walking, straight out the front door and out of sexy Steven's life for good. Two months later she'd been living in Little Rock, attending electrician's classes one night a week at a vo-tech school while working as an apprentice during the day.

It had been five years since she'd broken up with Steven. Since that time she'd earned her journeyman's license and had developed her independence to an art. She liked living in Florida, enjoyed working for Brothers Electrical while putting in the two years required between obtaining her journeyman's license and taking the test that would earn her master's license. Someday she would like to start her own electrical contracting company. Sure she was lonely sometimes, but not enough to jeopardize the life she'd built for herself.

She tried to tell herself that she was making too big an issue out of two brief meetings with an admittedly attractive man. She argued with herself that she could even go out with the guy without destroying her treasured self-sufficiency. After all, she barely knew him. Running from him in blind panic at this point was nothing more than hysterical overreaction. She went out with other guys, didn't she? She'd maintained a healthy, normal social life during the past five years, though she'd never really de-

veloped a taste for casual sex. She was being an idiot to lie
awake worrying about going out with a man she had only
just met, may never hear from again. If she had any sense,
she'd put him completely out of her mind, decide what to
do when—or *if* he asked her out again.

And yet her lips still tingled.

She groaned and pulled the sheets over her head, completely covering both herself and her disgruntled dog.

AUTUMN WORE a rueful smile as she pushed open the sparkling glass door of the Tampa Pediatrics Clinic and
stepped into the colorfully decorated lobby. The waiting
area was crowded with mothers and children, even
though it was the day after Thanksgiving—perhaps because of it, she thought whimsically, wondering how
many of the children had overdosed on turkey and pump-
kin pie. She hadn't been at all surprised to see Dr. E. Jefferson Bradford's name printed in gold letters on the outside
of the building, along with the names of two other doctors.
But then, she'd been expecting to see his name since she'd
been informed that the customer had specifically requested her services for this job. Dodging an active toddler
on her way to the reception desk, Autumn told herself that
she admired Jeff's persistence almost as much as his nice
bod.

She still had not come to a conclusion about what to do
when he asked her out this time. Part of her wanted to accept, the same part of her that had been so relieved that he
had not given up on her, though it had been three weeks
and one day since she'd heard from him. The same part
that tried to tell her that she was being ridiculous to keep
turning him down simply because she was afraid of her
powerful attraction to him. Another part of her was terrified of that same attraction.

The pretty brunette receptionist nodded when Autumn
gave her name and company. "Oh, yes, Dr. Cochran said
she wanted to see you when you arrived. She's just finish-
ing up with a patient, so you can go into her office and

she'll be right with you." She gave Autumn directions to the office, then turned to greet a woman holding a feverish-looking child in her arms.

Autumn frowned a little as she walked down the hallway, pausing at an open door stenciled with the name Dr. Pamela Cochran. She'd expected to be taken directly to Jeff. Who was Pamela Cochran?

The office was cluttered in a rather organized way. The wall held diplomas and certificates, bookshelves overflowed with technical-looking volumes and file folders were piled haphazardly on the desk. A gold frame held a photograph of a smiling, dimpled baby. One of the fluorescent lights above the desk was out.

"Oh, hello," came a melodic, very Southern voice from the doorway. "You must be Autumn."

Autumn turned her head as a pleasantly plain woman with dancing brown eyes and frizzy brown hair entered the office. The woman—Dr. Cochran, Autumn assumed from the white lab coat worn over a blue cotton dress, a stethoscope dangling from a deep side pocket—was looking back at Autumn with a broad smile. And something else. Speculation? Curiosity? Autumn returned the smile automatically, wondering if Jeff had said anything to this woman about his two previous encounters with Autumn. "Yes, I'm Autumn Reed. You're Dr. Cochran?"

"Sure am," Dr. Cochran replied cheerfully. "I hear you're a marvelous electrician—"

Autumn hid a grin at the number of syllables the woman managed to work into those two words. And she'd thought *her* Southern accent was heavy!

"So I asked for you specifically when I called your company. I wasn't sure you'd be working on the day after a holiday."

Autumn blinked. Dr. Cochran had called her? "Yes, I'm taking extra time at Christmas, so I chose to work today," she explained, speaking without really thinking because she was still trying to decide why Jeff had not called himself.

"Lucky for us," the doctor commented. "We're having some trouble with some of our lights. Some of them are out, like the one above my desk, and then there are a couple that are blinking and making the most irritating buzzing noise." She reeled off the entire sentence without once pronouncing a *G*.

Autumn had to smile at the woman then. "The ballasts need changing," she explained, instinctively liking Dr. Pamela Cochran. "It won't take long. I'll try to stay out of the way while I work, unless you'd rather I'd take care of it after the clinic closes for the day."

"No, that's okay," the other woman assured her. "I'll have Kelly, one of our assistants, show you around. She'll let you know which examining rooms are being used. We'll all work around each other." She gave Autumn a friendly, conspiratorial wink. "That way the clinic won't have to pay time and a half for your services."

"Very practical," Autumn murmured. She definitely liked Dr. Cochran.

"Pam, I need you in room three. I've got a patient who's going to need surgery and—Autumn!" Jeff stopped abruptly halfway through the doorway, staring at the young woman in the plaid cotton blouse and khaki pants, the ever-present baseball cap tugged over her auburn braid.

He hadn't known she was coming. He had given up on her after all. Autumn swallowed her disappointment and tried to look nonchalant, though her heart was beating wildly in her chest. Lord, he looked good in his white coat, which he wore over a pearl-gray shirt with a maroon tie and charcoal slacks. She'd only seen him in casual clothes before. Now, with his crisp black hair neatly combed and his beautiful biceps hidden beneath the uniform of his profession, he looked...different. Dr. E. Jefferson Bradford. Autumn suddenly felt self-conscious, awkward.

And then he smiled, his delectable mouth parting to show his even white teeth and deeply slashed dimples, his blue eyes crinkling a little at the corners, and he was the

Jeff Bradford she'd met at his house. Ridiculously young looking, sinfully handsome, even a bit shy. She smiled back. "Hi, Jeff."

"Here to work on the lights?" he asked, and even his voice had changed. It had been harried, brisk, when he'd spoken to Pam as he'd entered; now it was husky, slightly intimate.

Cursing her light complexion, Autumn felt the color staining her cheeks. "Yes."

"I'm afraid I won't be able to help you this time," he told her with a grin. "I'm rather busy."

"I'll manage," she answered dryly.

"I'm sure you will," he returned softly. He glanced back at Pam, who was watching them with unconcealed, avid interest. "Got time for a consultation?" he asked her, trying to sound stern.

"Of course," Pam replied, unintimidated.

"Come on, then." He glanced back at Autumn. "Don't leave without saying goodbye," he said, the words phrased like an order but sounding like a request. Particularly when he added, "Please."

She nodded. He was giving her warning, she thought desperately. He was going to ask her out again. Why couldn't she make a decision about whether or not to accept?

With Kelly as her helper, Autumn went about her job. Though she stayed discreetly out of his way, Autumn was able to observe Jeff at work, struck again by the change in him when he assumed the mien of physician. He was great with children, naturally. Gentle, patient, indulgent. He should have children of his own, she thought fleetingly, then deliberately blanked her mind as she tried to concentrate on her work.

When she'd finished and had carried her tools and ladder out to the truck, Autumn hesitated before seeking Jeff. As it turned out, it wasn't necessary. He found her. "All done?" he inquired.

She nodded, fidgeting with her clipboard as she waited

for him to issue the invitation she expected. She was *not* nervous, she told herself firmly. After all, even if she accepted, it would only be a dinner date. Pleasant, unthreatening, completely innocuous. She surreptitiously wiped her damp palms on the legs of her khaki pants, looking up at Jeff through her lashes.

Jeff had been watching her closely, suppressing an urge to chuckle when he realized that she was actually showing signs of agitation. He hadn't thought it possible that there was any shyness at all within this supremely self-confident young feminist. Suddenly all trace of his own uncertainty disappeared. Would she be shy if she weren't attracted to him at least a little? he asked himself hopefully.

She was so obviously expecting him to ask her out again. He had intended to do just that. He wondered what her answer would be this time. And then he wondered what her reaction would be when he didn't ask. He had just changed his strategy.

"Did you have a nice Thanksgiving?" he asked, pleased when she gave a little start at the sound of his voice. She *was* nervous.

Autumn nodded. "Yes, thank you." She and Babs had indulged in a frozen turkey breast and steamed fresh vegetables while watching a football game together on television. She had also talked by telephone to her parents and to her two married sisters, one of whom lived in California, the other in Arkansas. It *had* been a nice day, she told herself, ignoring the slight sense of loneliness that remained.

"So did I. Spent the day with my folks in Sarasota. Actually, though, I wanted to talk to you about something else."

Here it comes. Autumn tried to make a snap decision, failing miserably. "What?"

"I'm considering installing new outdoor lighting, particularly around the pool. What would you recommend?"

Outdoor lighting? Was he serious? "I would have to see

it before I could make a recommendation," she answered slowly. "I haven't seen your pool."

He nodded. "Of course. I'll call your company and try to schedule time with you next Thursday, if you're not already booked up."

"Fine." She waited, but he said nothing more. He seemed to be waiting for her to say something. But what? "I, um, I guess I'll see you later, then."

"I'll walk you out."

Autumn carefully avoided looking at him as they walked together down the long, bright hallway. If his purpose was to confuse her, he had certainly done it. At the door she glanced up at him to find him looking back at her with a broad smile. "Goodbye, Autumn."

"Bye, Jeff." She stepped through the door he was holding for her, then paused when he said her name.

"Autumn?"

"Yes?"

"This could go on a long time. Until I run out of electrical ideas. Or money," he added thoughtfully. Before she could answer, he had closed the door quietly in her face.

She stared blankly at that door for a long moment, then started to laugh. He was challenging her! He had just subtly let her know that he was going to keep calling her until she agreed to go out with him. He hadn't given up on her!

Oh, Lord, she shouldn't be feeling this giddy sense of relief. She shouldn't be fighting the urge to dance back to the truck or to burst into song.

"Autumn, you are such a fool," she groaned, tugging down the bill of her cap as she settled behind the wheel of the truck.

"THIS IS RIDICULOUS," Autumn muttered some five hours later, after she'd changed the channel on the television set for the fourth time in a half hour. Nothing on the small screen interested her, and neither did the thick mystery novel she'd purchased only the day before. She was trying

not to think about Jeff Bradford, but her progress so far
was lousy.

With a gusty sigh she snapped off the television and
roamed into the kitchen of her duplex apartment, remembering that she hadn't yet gotten around to eating dinner.
She burrowed in the cabinets and refrigerator, but nothing
looked overly appealing. She finally settled on a sandwich
made from the remains of the frozen turkey breast and a
handful of frosted animal cookies.

Having finished the sandwich without enthusiasm, she
carried the cookies into the modern burgundy-and-dark-
green living room, where she dropped onto the boldly
flowered chintz sofa and finally allowed herself to think
about Jeff.

She curled her bare feet under her and munched on a
pink lion, deep in thought until a gentle whine turned her
attention to the floor beside her. "Sorry, Babs, did you
want a cookie?" she asked the poodle, who was looking
hopefully up at her. The dog yipped a reply.

"Elephant or rhinoceros?" Autumn inquired.

Babs yipped again.

"Elephant it is." Autumn tossed the cookie to the dog,
smiling a little as Babs caught it deftly and began to eat
with delicate nibbles.

Her gaze on her pet's amusing greed, Autumn finally
gave in to the need to think seriously about the subject
preying so heavily on her mind. E. Jefferson Bradford.
She'd never reacted to any man this way. He had only to
look at her, much less give her one of those smiles of his, to
turn her to Jell-O, a new experience for Autumn Reed.

Her cookie eaten, Babs hopped into Autumn's lap and,
standing on her hind legs, planted a wet kiss on Autumn's
chin. Autumn hugged the squirming little body and
chuckled. "So what do you think I should do about him,
Babs?" she asked whimsically.

Babs wiggled and made a playful growling sound low
in her throat.

"Go out with him, huh? Sounds easy enough, but I have

a feeling that I'd be getting into something I don't know how to handle. For one thing, what could we talk about?''

Autumn cocked an eyebrow at the dog. ''That's all very well for you to say,'' she muttered as if Babs had actually made a suggestion. ''But if we spend an evening *not* talking, I'll be in even worse trouble.''

The dog barked sharply. Autumn sighed. ''He's turning me into a basket case. I'm actually sitting here having a conversation with a dog.''

Babs looked hurt.

''Oh, sorry, Babs. I didn't mean anything personal.''

Babs jumped down to the floor, stopping by the telephone table to scratch her ear on her way to the doggie door in the kitchen that gave her access to the small, fenced backyard of Autumn's half of the duplex. Taking that as a hint, Autumn sighed and walked slowly to the telephone. ''You're right, Babs. I can't go on like this. It's time to take action.''

Jeff's number was listed in the telephone book. Autumn hung up twice before she could make herself dial it. It wasn't that she'd never called a man for a date, but she had never called Dr. E. Jefferson Bradford. What was it about him that was so different from other men?

Finally she dialed the number and waited for the ring. She told herself that he probably wasn't home. After all, it *was* Friday night. And if he was out, fine. It wasn't meant to be.

''Hello?''

Well, hell, he was home. ''Um, Jeff?''

''Autumn?''

She supposed she should be flattered that he immediately recognized her voice. ''Yes. I hope I'm not disturbing you.'' *Dumb thing to say,* she told herself immediately. *He'll think I'm asking if he's alone.* She continued quickly. ''I was just wondering…do you really want new lighting outside your house?''

3

JEFF PAUSED FOR A MOMENT, then chuckled. "Well, I have to admit it was a spur-of-the-moment suggestion on my part, but I suppose I could think of something else for you to do if you'd rather."

"Look, why don't we just forget the games," Autumn told him impatiently. "We both know you're only doing the lights so you can ask me out again, right?"

"I have no intention of asking you out again," Jeff replied decisively.

She narrowed her eyes, fingers tightening on the dark red plastic receiver. "You don't?" she asked, her disbelief obvious in her voice.

"No, ma'am. A man can only take so much rejection," he drawled.

Oh, Lord. First a Southern gentleman, now an Old West cowhand. "Are you doing anything tomorrow night?" she asked bluntly.

"That depends. Why are you asking?"

She thought seriously about slamming the phone down in his ear but controlled herself. "Would you like to go out to dinner with me? Maybe we could go dancing or something afterward."

"Gee, I don't know. This is so sudden."

Autumn tried very hard not to be amused. "Dammit, Jeff, yes or no?"

He laughed, the sound warming her even through the telephone line. "I really need to study your technique for asking for a date," he told her. "Such charm. Such tact."

"Jeff..." Her voice informed him quite clearly that he was about to find himself talking to a dial tone.

"Okay, you've talked me into it. What time are you picking me up?"

"How's seven grab you?"

"Seven grabs me just fine. Thanks for asking."

Autumn did hang up then, and none too gently.

"I hope you're happy," she told Babs, glaring at the innocent-looking animal who'd just come back into the room, happily wagging her tail as she looked up at Autumn. "I just made a first-class fool out of myself. Why do I let him do that to me?"

Babs gave a poodle equivalent of a shrug and settled herself into a lazy curl on the carpet, signifying her desire for a nap. Autumn sighed and picked up her book again. The sad part was, she decided as she unenthusiastically opened it, that she really had wanted to ask Jeff if he was alone.

JEFF LAUGHED when the phone went abruptly dead. Autumn Reed was really something, he mused as he replaced his own receiver, more gently than she had. Although he'd chewed Pam out but good earlier for interfering, he was actually glad that she'd taken the initiative to call Autumn to the clinic. If she hadn't, Jeff would have eventually. Besides, if Pam hadn't told him, he still wouldn't know Autumn's last name.

He was doubly glad now that he hadn't asked Autumn out at the clinic. By doing the unexpected and leaving it up to her, he had stumbled upon exactly the right strategy for the stubborn, defiant woman. He had to pause for a moment to ask himself exactly what it was about her that attracted him so strongly, but the answer wasn't hard to come by. He was enthralled with her. He'd never met anyone quite like her.

She tried so hard to be tough, invulnerable. She probably even believed she succeeded. But Jeff had seen her wet her lips in an unconscious gesture of nerves, had felt her tremble in his arms, had seen the color stain her cheeks when she was embarrassed. She wasn't so tough. She'd been nervous during that phone call, despite her snippy manner. He wondered who had hurt her so badly that she'd felt it necessary to erect such a brittle shell around her inner softness.

He'd dated a few women who had really been hard, who had completely eliminated that inner softness. Autumn wasn't one of them, thank God, no matter how she might try to appear to be. Those wide green eyes of hers gave her away. She was a witch, a sorceress, but there was vulnerability behind her skillful spells. Jeff intended to find that vulnerability.

Though she wouldn't appreciate it one bit, something about her brought out the protective instincts within him. He was caught in her spell—so well trapped that he had no desire to free himself. Perhaps this was only infatuation that he felt for her, nothing more than fascinated desire, but it was a powerful emotion. Like nothing he'd ever felt before. How could he turn away without finding out exactly what it was that possessed him?

When he pursued, she ran.

It seemed that he was going to have to be the pursued.

Jeff grinned and tugged his gray sweatshirt over his head, moving toward the bedroom. The sooner he went to bed, the sooner the next day would come. And the sooner he would be with Autumn again.

GRINDING A CURSE OUT between clenched teeth, Autumn jerked the striped dress over her head and threw it on her bed, where it landed in a slither of color on top of a pile of similarly discarded garments. "Stupid, stupid, stupid!" she wailed, shoving her hands through her auburn mane as she stared into her closet.

She should call and cancel, she decided. She could tell Jeff she was sick. Or in jail. She wouldn't tell him the truth—that just over an hour before their date, she'd regressed to adolescence. She had somehow been transformed from a modern, competent woman to a silly, dithering teenager, and damned if she could figure out a way to change back. She didn't know what to wear, she wasn't sure what to say or do when she saw him, she was even starting to worry about the good-night kiss. "Maybe it's a regressive brain disease," she mused aloud, causing Babs to look at her with interest. It just had to be biological. Surely a simple Saturday-night dinner date wouldn't do this to her!

Her doorbell distracted her, and she frowned as she wrapped herself in a terry robe. She wasn't expecting anyone. She decided it must be her neighbor, Emily, with whom she had become friends during the three months that Emily and her son, Ryan, had occupied the other half of the large duplex. Crossing her living room, she glanced perfunctorily out the peephole and groaned. "What are you doing here, Webb?" she asked as she opened the door.

"Thanks, Autumn, I'd love to come in." Webb Brothers grinned lazily at her as he strolled past her, hands in the pockets of his jeans. Tall, lanky, sandy-haired Webb was the son of Autumn's boss, Floyd Brothers, owner of Brothers Electrical Company. It had been Webb who'd convinced his skeptical, traditional father to give a woman electrician—Autumn—a chance to prove herself. Webb had been her champion, her co-worker and her friend ever since. He also took great pleasure in teasing her, and it was that particular trait that had her eyeing him warily now. She was determined to hide her current emotional state from his all-too-perceptive eyes. He'd never let her live it down.

"So, my love, you want to take in a movie tonight?" he asked, tilting his light brown head in a stance he'd carefully copied from Robert Redford because someone had once told him he resembled the attractive actor. Autumn thought he looked a bit like the young Redford, but she would never tell him so. Webb was in no need of ego strokes.

"I'm not your love, and I can't go to a movie with you tonight. I have a date." In barely an hour. And she still didn't know what she was going to wear. Swallowing a moan, she narrowed her green eyes at him. "What are you doing free on a Saturday night, anyway? Don't tell me that Webb Brothers couldn't get a date!"

He grimaced at her and dropped into a burgundy-and-dark-green striped armchair. "Maybe I just wanted to do something with you."

"If you'd wanted to do something with me, you'd have mentioned it at work yesterday," she pointed out, perching on the edge of the sofa and trying to hide her impatience to get back to her dressing trauma.

Webb scooped an eager Babs into his arms and began to scratch behind her long fluffy ears, apparently in no hurry to leave. "Okay, so my date canceled out," he admitted. "She was called out of town on a business crisis. I thought since I was free, I'd see what you were doing."

"Ever heard of the telephone, Brothers?"

He shrugged good-naturedly. "This is more fun. I can watch you dress." He gave her a suggestive leer, part of the teasing flirting that had developed between them over their year-long friendship.

"Wrong."

"Then I'll wait and check out your date when he gets here."

"Wrong again. I'm picking him up."

"Well, hell, Reed. You take all the fun out of everything."

"Sorry." She wasn't, of course, and her smile told him so.

"So who are you going out with tonight? Terry? Rick? Dwayne?" he asked, naming her three most common escorts, men she liked and whose company she enjoyed, though her relationship with each of them was light and platonic.

"None of the above."

"Oh?" Autumn fancied that Webb's ears perked up with interest, as Babs's did when she heard an unusual noise. "Someone new?"

"Yeah."

"Do I know him?"

"I doubt it."

Webb sighed loudly. "This is like pulling teeth. What's his name, Autumn?"

"His name's Jeff Bradford," Autumn returned in resignation, even the sound of Jeff's name making her shiver. Lord, she was still doing it!

"Jeff Bradford, the doctor?" Webb asked with a lifted eyebrow.

Oh, no, not a friend of Webb's, Autumn thought with a mental groan. "Yes. Do you know him?"

"Yeah, I've known him a few years. We belong to the same health club, and we're in the same Jaycees chapter, though he's not quite as active in it as I am. His work keeps him too busy."

She shouldn't be surprised that Webb knew Jeff. Tampa wasn't that large a city, and Webb got around. Still, Autumn wished that he and Jeff were total strangers. If she was going to make a fool of herself over Jeff Bradford—and she pessimistically suspected that she was—she preferred to do it in total privacy. She had toyed with the idea of throwing herself into a crazy affair with the attractive young doctor until she'd worked out her foolish infatuation with him, at which time she would cheerfully tell him goodbye and return to her sane, carefully controlled life, with no one the wiser but her and Jeff. Now she had an audience. The smartest thing to do was to keep Webb from finding out the strange effect that Dr. Jeff Bradford had had on her from the moment she'd met him.

"So how'd you meet Jeff, anyway?" Webb asked curiously.

Autumn explained briefly, then tried to change the subject by adding, "I'll be glad when you and the rest of the crew finish up that shopping mall remodel. I'm getting all the small, one-person jobs these days."

Her diversion seemed to work. "That reminds me," Webb commented, setting Babs on the floor, "you'll be

working with us for the next couple of weeks. Chuck's going to take over the stuff you've been doing."

"How come?"

Webb shrugged and made a face. "He can't seem to get
along with the property manager who's supervising the
remodel. The guy's a jerk, but Chuck needs to learn when
to keep his mouth shut. Okay with you?"

"Sure. Uh, Webb, I really need to start getting ready for
my date now," she hinted broadly, hating to bring up the
subject again but anxious to get dressed—if she could ever
decide what she was going to wear.

"Don't mind me. I think I'll have a beer." Webb pushed
himself out of the chair and headed for the kitchen.

Autumn sighed. "Just make yourself at home," she
muttered.

He threw her a grin over his shoulder. "I'll do that."

Shaking her head in exasperation, she walked into her
bedroom. She hadn't closed the door yet when Webb appeared behind her. "I forgot to ask," he said, "do you
want one, too?"

"No, thanks," she answered quickly, turning to hustle
him out of the room.

Too late. He was standing in exaggerated openmouthed
astonishment, staring at the pile of clothing strewn across
her bed. "If I didn't know better, I would swear this is my
sister's room prior to a date with one of her college jocks,"
he marveled. He looked at Autumn with a questioning
frown. "Tell me that you haven't been trying on everything in your wardrobe for the past half hour."

She exhaled slowly. "So I'm having a little trouble deciding what to wear," she admitted belligerently. "What
of it?"

Webb leaned back against the doorjamb and laughed.
Heartily. "This," he said when he could speak, "from the
woman who wore a baseball cap and sweatshirt to a wedding shower? Who considers herself really dressed up if
her jeans have a name on the back pocket?"

Autumn glared at him. "Okay, so I'm not on the best-dressed list. Most of the time I wear jeans and shirts because I work at a blue-collar job and I like to be comfortable. I think women who spend a fortune on clothing and follow every fleeting dictate of fashion are in bad need of something productive to do. But I still want to look halfway decent on a date, and I don't see anything to laugh about!"

Webb shook his brownish-blond head in amusement. "I'm not laughing because you want to look nice. To me, you always look nice. You dress casually, but you've got a style of your own. I was laughing because you look so harried and nervous. That's not like you, Autumn. Don't tell me that you've fallen for Jeff Bradford."

"Don't be ridiculous! I hardly know him."

"Mmm. So how come you're blushing?"

"I am *not* blushing!" She threw her hands up to cover cheeks that felt suspiciously hot. "Oh, hell, I *am* blushing."

Webb laughed again. "Kind of like the guy, huh?"

She sighed. "Yeah, I like him. But," she added quickly, "that doesn't mean there's any big romance developing between us or anything like that."

"Of course not," Webb agreed gravely. "I know your policy about serious relationships—if there's the slightest fragrance of orange blossoms or hint of wedding bells in the air, you head for the hills. Figuratively speaking, of course."

"Isn't that very similar to your own policy?" Autumn inquired crossly, knowing that Webb was every bit as anti-marriage as she.

"Of course it is. That's why you and I are such good friends. And why I've never tried to put the moves on you."

She eyed him suspiciously. "The reason you've never tried to 'put the moves' on me is because I'm not your type. We've always been just friends."

He shook his head, brown eyes dancing teasingly at her. "The reason I've kept us 'just friends' is that you're marriage bait if I've ever seen it. You can talk all you want to about staying footloose and single, but when you fall in love, you'll be heading down that aisle just like your two sisters did during the past year. I was just making sure that I wasn't the guy waiting at the altar for you, lovely though you are."

"You're an arrogant, conceited creep, Brothers. I wouldn't have seriously dated you if you'd asked," she told him flatly, irritated at his accusation. "*You're* the one who's marriage bait!"

He looked startled. "You're crazy!"

"Yeah? I don't think you'd deny it so furiously if you didn't think you were susceptible to the weakness. Every time you start to get close to a woman, you turn pale and run. How come, huh?"

"I *like* being single," her thirty-one-year-old friend answered earnestly. "I like not answering to anyone, not worrying about mortgages and bills, not saving for college funds or second honeymoons. I like going out with a redhead one night, a blonde the next and a brunette the night after that."

"You can talk all you want about staying footloose and single, but when you fall in love, you'll be heading down that aisle just like your brother did last month," Autumn paraphrased primly, tossing her head so that her hair flew out, then settled in a thick, cinnamon curtain around her shoulders. "Now would you get out of here?" she demanded before he could voice the argument that she could see on his face. "I have to get dressed and I still don't know what to wear."

"Where are you going?"

"Dinner and dancing."

"Wear that gold thing."

Autumn looked doubtful. "You think so?"

"Trust me. I know so."

The gold thing. Autumn chewed on her lower lip, wondering if that choice would be at all wise. She shot a suspicious look at Webb, who was grinning from ear to ear. She was just about to speak when the doorbell rang again.

"What is this tonight…the gathering place for all of Tampa?" she asked her bedroom wall, tossing up her hands at this new interruption. "I don't even have my makeup on!"

"Autumn, I'm sorry to bother you, but do you have any milk? Can you believe I've run out?" Emily Hinson, Autumn's neighbor, stood on the doorstep, her fifteen-month-old son, Ryan, on her hip holding his favorite stuffed dog. Divorced since shortly after Ryan's birth, twenty-three-year-old Emily was Autumn's opposite in almost every way. She was delicate in appearance, if not in actuality, petite and blond with enormous china-blue eyes. She enjoyed her work as a secretary, loved cooking and needlework and all other things domestic, and made it no secret that she would like to be married again despite the failure of her first marriage. And yet the two women had become friends from almost the moment they'd met outside their duplex when Emily had moved in.

"There's milk in the refrigerator. Help yourself, I'm dressing for a date," Autumn told her, patting Ryan's chubby cheek as he grinned wetly at her.

Emily started in, then paused at the sight of Webb. "Oh, I'm sorry. I didn't know your date was already here."

"Oh, that's not my date. That's just Webb." Autumn was already halfway through the door to her bedroom. "Introduce yourself, Webb. I *have* to get ready!"

Thirty minutes later she took a deep breath and checked her appearance in the mirror. Even she could admit that she looked good. She wondered what Jeff would think.

Webb, Emily and Ryan looked up and blinked when Autumn came out of her bedroom to join them in the living room. Autumn hadn't realized that Emily was still there. It appeared that Emily and Webb had been talking easily for the past half hour while Autumn had dressed, Ryan playing with his toy on the carpet at their feet. "Autumn, you look beautiful!" Emily breathed, staring at the metamorphosis.

Webb shook his sandy head and grinned. "I told you the gold thing would be the right choice," he said smugly.

Autumn grimaced. "I hope it's not too much."

"It's not too much. Believe me," Webb answered solemnly, turning a smile to Emily. "What do you think, Emily?"

"I think it's gorgeous. And I truly wish it were my size so I could borrow it for a date sometime," Emily added with a light laugh. "Not that it would do for me what it does for Autumn."

Webb looked startled. "A date? Oh, you mean with your husband."

"Oh, I'm not married," Emily corrected him, looking a bit surprised that he didn't already know. "I've been divorced for a year."

Webb swallowed, looked at her again, then all but leaped to his feet. "Well, I have to go," he announced a bit too loudly. "Have a good time on your date, Autumn. Tell Bradford I said hello. Nice to meet you, Emily. Bye, Ryan." And then he was gone.

Emily frowned at the door that had closed behind him, then turned her bewildered gaze to Autumn. "Was it something I said?"

Autumn only laughed.

JEFF SHRUGGED into the jacket of his charcoal-gray pin-striped suit, adjusted his yellow silk tie and glanced at the thin gold watch on his wrist. Five minutes until seven. Five minutes until he saw Autumn. He took a deep breath, trying to calm his nervous stomach. Lord, he hadn't been so nervous before a date since…since…well, he'd never been this nervous before a date.

She was so skittish. All his instincts told him that one wrong move, one wrong word, on his part, would cause her to take flight, right out of his life. He wondered again who had hurt her, what she was afraid of and whether he would have a chance to explore his budding feelings for her without driving her away. He wasn't interested in an affair, had never been interested in empty affairs. He wanted a future, a relationship, something meaningful and enriching and nurturing. He wanted what Pam and Bob had. He'd always suspected that when he met the right woman, he would know immediately. The moment Autumn Reed had taken off her sunglasses and looked at him with those bewitching green eyes, he'd known.

Now if only he could convince her to give them a chance.

He hoped he hadn't overdressed. He'd wanted to look nice, but then Autumn seemed to be the casual type. Of course, he'd only seen her on the job so far. But then again, he thought with his one-sided smile, if she looked any more beautiful than she had the last three times he'd seen her, he might not be able to control himself.

His doorbell chimed. Jeff's heart jerked convulsively, and he swallowed, rather stunned by his own reactions. He looked in wonder at his hands. His palms were damp! Shaking his head in astonishment, he went to answer his door.

He had to make a conscious effort to keep his jaw from dropping at the vision on his doorstep.

She was the most exquisite thing he'd ever seen. Soft auburn curls glowing red in the evening sun, tumbling around her shoulders and begging for his hands. Artfully applied makeup enhancing emerald eyes and glistening lips. And that dress.

He gulped. God, that dress. Shaped like an inverted triangle with padded shoulders and bat-wing sleeves, it clung lovingly to her full breasts, then hugged the feminine curves of her hips and thighs to fall to the middle of her knees. It was made of some slinky material that looked gold at one moment, black at the next. He blinked to clear his eyes, only then realizing that the fabric was black shot with thousands of glittering gold threads.

She was beautiful, sexy, tempting. And looking at him in a defiant manner that dared him to say a word, much less follow his immediate impulse to reach out and grab her. "Would you…" He had to stop to clear his throat. "Would you like to come in for a drink?"

Was that relief he saw cross her face? Had she been so anxious about his reaction to her transformation from work clothes to evening clothes? She had good reason to be. He shoved his hands into the pockets of his suit pants, fighting all kinds of primitive urges that were as surprising to him as they would have been to her, had he followed through on them.

And then she walked past him, and he had to swallow a moan. The dress had no back. From the button at the top of her shoulders to the top of the skirt, there was nothing but silky bare skin and the delicate ridges of her spine. The skirt was split in the center to allow glimpses of the backs of her knees as she walked.

He turned his eyes heavenward as he closed the front door. "This is some kind of test, right?" he murmured beneath his breath. He remembered all his earlier resolutions about watching his step with her, being careful not to frighten her off, and he felt himself on the verge of hysterical laughter. How could he possibly have known that she would show up looking like…like *this*?

"Did you say something?" Autumn asked curiously, turning to look at him.

"Just praying," he answered, then before she could comment, "What would you like to drink?"

She looked at him rather oddly, then moistened her lower lip with the tip of her tongue. Jeff closed his eyes for a moment. This was *definitely* a test.

"I don't believe I want anything, thanks," Autumn was saying when he opened his eyes again.

Come to think of it, neither did he. The one thing he did *not* need just now was anything that might possibly weaken his control. Autumn was intoxicating enough. "Then I suppose we're ready to go."

She nodded, twisting her hands in front of her. "Yes, I'm ready."

This might turn out to be a very long evening, Jeff

thought wryly as he held the door for her to pass him. Without really thinking about it, he started to place a hand on her back, then jerked the hand away when he encountered bare flesh. A *very* long evening.

Resigning himself to always acting like a thick-skulled, not-really-bright clod in this woman's presence, he followed her to her sporty black Fiero, knowing better than to offer to drive—or to open her door for her.

4

AUTUMN CAREFULLY AVOIDED Jeff's eyes as she started her car, though she was all too conscious of him within the confines of her small Fiero. Her hand was only inches from his thigh when she reached out to shift into reverse. Unable to resist, she glanced at that thigh, so solid and powerful beneath the fabric of his gray suit, and then her gaze drifted upward to his lap. She gulped and turned her eyes firmly forward, away from the tempting territory of his masculinity.

It was going to be a long evening. She'd regretted her choice of clothing ever since he'd opened the door and immediately looked like a man who'd been kicked in the gut by the Karate Kid. She'd worn the dress only once before, to a party she'd attended with Webb. After a night of being pawed by strangers, she'd decided never to wear it again. So why had she let Webb talk her into it tonight? she asked herself in disgust.

Trust me, he'd said. She should have known right then to choose something else. Though some perverse feminine part of her was secretly pleased by Jeff's unspoken appreciation, a more rational part of her was cautious of the sparks that were so obviously flying between them. It had never been like this for her before. Never.

The silence in the car was growing deafening. She glanced sideways at Jeff, finding him watching her with a faint, enigmatic smile, as if he were waiting for her to say something. She was fully aware that she'd barely spoken to him since she'd picked him up, but she didn't know what to say. What she really wanted to do was stop, turn in her seat and just stare at him for about an hour. No man should be that good-looking. It simply wasn't fair. It was nature's way of keeping liberated women on their toes, she decided. Give a guy thick black hair, deep blue eyes and a smile that could melt the gold tips on the toes of her black shoes and watch Autumn turn to oatmeal.

When the silence began to sizzle with tension, she reached out almost desperately and pushed a cassette into the player on the dash, not even noticing what she'd chosen. She smiled wryly when the music swelled out at the high level she generally preferred. Simple Minds. Appropriate choice of bands.

She didn't know why she was behaving this way, why she was on the defensive. She only knew that Jeff Bradford was the most dangerous man she'd ever met and that she would have to stay on the defensive to survive him with heart and pride intact.

She should have worn a different dress.

Jeff tolerated the loud music for a time, then reached out and firmly turned down the volume. Autumn threw him a startled look. "You don't like rock music?" she demanded as if he'd be confessing to all sorts of terrible crimes if he did not.

"I like rock music," he answered. "I like Simple Minds," he added to point out that he had recognized the group. "But I also like to converse with my date."

"Oh."

He fought a grin without much success. She was cute when she was being insecure, he decided, though he had no intention of telling her so. Something told him that "cute" would definitely be an unsavory four-letter word to Autumn Reed.

She was so beautiful. And so uncomfortable with that beauty. She had been much more confident in her work clothes and cap than she was now in this ultrafeminine dress. An unusual woman. And yet so very fascinating.

"Pull over for a minute, will you, Autumn?" he asked on a sudden impulse.

She glanced at him with a frown. "What?" she asked as if she hadn't heard him clearly.

"Pull over. Just for a minute," he repeated.

Her frown remained, but she gave a slight shrug and signaled a lane change, turning into the Saturday-deserted parking lot of an office building. Shifting into park, she turned slightly in her seat to face him. "Okay. Now what?"

"I just want to tell you that you're the most beautiful woman I've ever seen, your dress is fabulous and I'd like nothing more than to slowly peel it off you. But," he added as a wave of scarlet tinged her fair cheeks, "I'll settle for this for now."

He caught her face in his hands and brought his mouth firmly down on hers, kissing her as he'd wanted to do since he'd opened his door to find her standing there daring him to touch her.

Autumn stiffened for a moment—only a moment—and then leaned into him, her hands settling on his shoulders. Her lips parted beneath his, an invitation he accepted with alacrity. And then she was a wholehearted participant in the kiss, and Jeff moaned softly at the pleasure of it. His pulse was roaring in his ears, his heart pounding against the walls of his chest when he finally drew back. He blinked rapidly a time or two, cleared his throat, took a deep breath, then nodded. "Okay. Now that's out of the way and we can enjoy ourselves. Where are we going for dinner?"

Autumn's eyes drifted slowly open, and the dazed expression in their green depths almost had him reaching out for her again. And then she gave a slight shake of her head, wet her lips and glared at him. "Why did you do that?" she demanded aggressively, her tone almost making him laugh. Now *this* was the Autumn he'd met three times before—arrogant, annoyed, regally self-assured. He liked her this way. He strongly suspected that he was beginning to love her this way.

"I wanted to," he answered her question, tongue in cheek as he prepared himself for her blistering response.

Instead, she turned sharply back to the steering wheel, slamming the car into drive and muttering something that sounded a lot like "obnoxious, conceited male." He did laugh then, earning himself a fulminating glance and a toss of auburn hair. But he had accomplished what he'd wanted, because she loosened up and began to reply when he made innocuous conversation. By the time they reached the popular, expensive restaurant where she'd been fortunate enough to obtain reservations for the evening, they were chatting away in relative ease. She'd been expecting him to pounce on her, he had, and now they could get on with the evening. Jeff was quite proud of himself for handling that particular situation so deftly.

Except his hands were still shaking in the aftermath of the most powerful kiss in his entire life.

"Tell me about yourself," he encouraged her when they'd ordered their dinners.

"Like what?" she asked, immediately looking wary.

He wondered what it was that could turn such a simple request into a threat to her. Why should she immediately go on the defensive just because he wanted to get to know her? "Anything," he answered simply. "Where you were born and when, whether you have any brothers and sisters, how you decided to become an electrician, when you moved to Florida, what flavor of ice cream you like, what you wear to bed."

The last suggestion made her blink, then glare at him before speaking quickly. "I was born twenty-five years ago in Rose Bud, Arkansas. My parents had three daughters in just over three years—I'm the youngest. I moved to Little Rock when I was twenty, started working to become an electrician immediately because it looked interesting and I like working with my hands. I moved to Tampa almost a year ago. I like chocolate mint ice cream and I sleep in large T-shirts. Any other questions?"

Delighted, he grinned and nodded. "Thousands."

She sighed deeply, propped her elbows on the table and looked at him with exaggerated patience. "Shoot."

He laughed. "You're certainly being accommodating."

"You're the one who said you like to converse with your dates. Converse."

"Okay. What are yout sister's names, where do they live, what do they do and are they married? Are you an aunt?"

She shook her head, looking a bit dizzy. "Whatever happened to one question at a time?"

"Takes too long. Besides, you fielded the last series so well I thought I'd give it another shot."

"Fair enough. My oldest sister is Spring McEntire. She's an optometrist in Little Rock, Arkansas, and she's married to a psychologist named Clay."

Jeff nodded gravely. "Okay. Go on."

"My other sister, Summer Anderson, is twenty-six. She and her husband, Derek, live in Sausalito, California, where she's studying to teach theater arts, and he's a business consultant. Did I answer them all?"

Laughing, Jeff shook his head. "No, you missed one. Are you an aunt?"

"Not yet. Summer and Derek had their first wedding anniversary last month, and Spring and Clay were married three months ago. I think both couples want children, though, when they decide the time is right."

"Do you?"

"Do I what?" she asked absently, toying with a bread stick because she knew what he was asking.

"Do you want children?"

She shrugged. "It's not high on my list of priorities."

"What is?"

Again a shrug preceded an answer that was just a bit too flip. "Independence. Self-sufficiency. Pride."

"Interesting answers."

"Yes, aren't they? Good thing you're a pediatrician instead of a shrink or you'd be busy trying to find out what makes me tick, wouldn't you?"

His gaze held hers. "I've been doing that from the moment we met, Autumn Reed."

She lowered her eyes, staring hard at the tablecloth. "Don't. I don't like being analyzed."

She was grateful that their dinners arrived just then. By the time they'd been served, Jeff had changed the subject, as if sensing that he'd better keep the conversation fairly impersonal if he wanted her to participate. Still, he continued to ask about things that related to her, unwilling to abandon his efforts to find out more about her. "Spring, Summer and Autumn. Pretty names, but you must have been teased quite a bit when you and your sisters were growing up."

She grimaced good-naturedly. "Did we ever. To make it worse, our father owns Reed's Seed and Feed Store in Rose Bud. Name games became our personal peeves. For a while we tried to change over to our middle names, Deborah, Linda and Sarah, but it never seemed to take. We were already firmly established as Spring, Summer and Autumn by that time."

"Autumn suits you," Jeff commented quietly, his gaze lingering on her red-brown hair, green eyes and gold-dusted dress.

She didn't quite know what to say to that, so she deftly turned the conversation back to him. "My turn to ask questions?"

He spread his hands in a go-ahead gesture.

"Where were you born and when, do you have any brothers and sisters, why did you decide to become a doctor, what's your favorite flavor of ice cream and what do you sleep in?" Autumn asked boldly.

He chuckled, then made an effort to answer in the correct order. "Born in Sarasota thirty-three years ago in July. No brothers or sisters. I wanted to be a doctor because it looked interesting and I like working with my hands." This was a teasing paraphrase from her. "My favorite flavor of ice cream is cherry vanilla, and I sleep in cotton pajamas."

Autumn choked on a sip of wine and looked suspiciously at him. "You really sleep in cotton pajamas?"

"Mmm. Want to find out for yourself?" he inquired mildly.

"I'll take your word for it," she muttered, though she was disconcerted to find herself flashing a mental image of unbuttoning the top to a set of cotton pajamas, a set being worn by a handsome, dark-haired doctor. *Behave yourself,* she crossly told her overactive imagination. "Has anyone ever told you that you're just a little too good to be true?" she casually asked the handsome, dark-haired doctor of her fantasy.

Jeff looked startled—and not altogether pleased. "What do you mean by that?"

Even to her, her smile was a bit feline. "You're a good-looking, single young doctor living in the nicest part of town in an immaculately kept home that you vacuum yourself. You're kind to children and electricians, you're every mother's dream of a polite gentleman, you have no vices that I've noticed—" he'd even turned down wine in favor of iced tea for dinner "—you don't mind if a woman asks you out or picks you up for a date, and you don't sleep in your underwear. You're darned near perfect, Jefferson Bradford."

She'd managed to make him blush, a fact she noted with a certain malicious pleasure. After all, she'd blushed a few times over him, and she hadn't liked it a bit!

"I'm hardly perfect, Autumn," he protested, still visibly embarrassed.

"Oh, yeah? Name a fault, then," she challenged him, beginning to enjoy this new game.

"I've been wanting to take you to bed since the moment I saw you, and it was all I could do not to throw you over my shoulder and haul you to my bedroom when I saw you in that dress tonight." His tone was brisk, answering her challenge in kind.

Proudly *not* blushing, she waved a hand in dismissal. "That's not a fault, it's a genetic weakness. You're a male, after all, and some things you can't help. Like breathing, eating and thinking with your hormones at times. What else?"

If he'd hoped to disconcert her, he was disappointed, but he made a valiant effort to prove himself imperfect. "I don't like cats."

She shook her head. "Lots of people don't like cats," she returned. "That doesn't count, either. What else?"

He exhaled gustily. "I was hoping I wouldn't have to tell you this."

Crossing her hands in front of her, she leaned forward, her lips curving into an avid smile. "Tell. Tell."

He looked one way and then the other, furtively, obviously checking for eavesdroppers. And then, very quietly, "I'm an addict."

He'd spoken so seriously that Autumn was taken aback. An addict? She'd read about doctors who took advantage of their access to drugs, but Jeff? No way. "You are not."

He nodded gravely. "Yes, I am. It started in medical school, and now I can't stop. I'm truly hooked."

"On *what*?" she demanded, beginning to get concerned.

"*Dr. Wilson's World*," he replied mournfully, looking deeply ashamed.

Autumn relaxed muscles that she hadn't deliberately tensed and semiseriously considered decorating his pinstriped suit with the remains of her dinner. "A soap opera? You're hooked on a soap?"

Still looking as if he'd confessed to a string of heinous crimes, he nodded. "For years. I tape it every day and watch it before bedtime or on weekends. I can't help it. When I miss it, I start wondering what's happening to Paul or Melanie or Dan or Misty or poor old Dr. Wilson, and I'm not satisfied until I find out."

"That's appalling."

"I know." He hung his head in shame.

"You know it will rot your brain."

He nodded, chin sinking even lower. Then he risked an upward glance at her though his lush dark lashes—much too lush for a man, she thought enviously—and his blue eyes were dancing with humor. "Now will you believe I'm not perfect?"

"I suppose I'll have to. Anyone who watches *Dr. Wilson's World* every day is seriously flawed."

"I can't help it," he repeated, looking quite pleased with himself. "I'm compulsive."

"I'm terribly disillusioned. So tell me, who do you think is the father of Misty's baby? Dan? Running Wolf? Or old Dr. Wilson?"

Jeff shouted with laughter, not at all concerned that dozens of eyes immediately turned his way. "You watch it, too!" he accused her in what could only be termed unholy glee.

She lifted her chin disdainfully. "Not very often, but when I do, it's for a good reason."

"Oh, yeah? What?"

"I like to watch Dr. Noble suffer."

Jeff eyed her questioningly, obviously confused by her pleasure in the many tribulations suffered by the serial's unfortunate heartthrob hero, one of the more popular actors on daytime TV. "You mean you're a fan of his?"

"Nope," she answered cheerfully. "I keep hoping he'll die in a horrible soap opera accident and fade into television oblivion. No such luck so far, but hope lives on."

"I don't suppose you want to explain?"

"Nope," she replied, deciding not to tell him that the actor who played Dr. Noble was a Little Rock native who'd painfully jilted her sister, Summer, after her permanently damaging motorcycle accident. "But I *am* glad you have a weakness. I have so many myself that you were making me feel inferior."

"Name a few."

She shook her head firmly. "Subject closed. Tell me about doctoring."

So they talked about him for a while, about the grueling course of study in medical school, the exhausting hours of internship and residency, the occasional heartbreak and more frequent rewards, the demands on time and energy. And Autumn listened in fascination, feeling herself growing more and more attracted to him—if that were possible—as the evening went on. And then they were talking about her again, and she was telling him funny stories about her work and discussing favorite books and movies and television programs, and too soon their dinner was over.

Dancing seemed to be the natural continuation of their evening, a physical confirmation of the intimacy that had begun when they'd both confessed to watching the same soap opera. While they were dancing, she discovered the small electronic pager attached to his belt, reminding her of his demanding profession. "Are you on call?" she asked.

"No. I always carry the beeper in case Pam or Julian need to contact me. They know I want to be notified if anything serious happens to one of my patients, even though whoever is on call is perfectly capable of taking care of any situation."

A dedicated man. A very special man. How could she possibly resist him?

Autumn loved to dance, and Jeff was the perfect partner. She could have quite happily remained in his arms for days, their feet moving in easy synchronization, their conversation light and low-voiced, his hand warm on her bare back.

"I love this dress," Jeff informed her, as if reading her thoughts.

"Thank you. I'm glad Webb made me wear it," she murmured, drifting along in some wonderful fantasy, barely conscious of what she'd said.

But Jeff heard her, and he stiffened. "Webb?" he asked, a bit too casually.

"Webb." She lifted her head from Jeff's shoulder and smiled up at him. "Webb's one of my best friends. You know him—Webb Brothers. He says you go to the same health club."

"Sure, I know him. Nice guy. In fact, he's the reason I called your company when I needed an electrician. I like to do business with my friends when I can. Are you and he, uh…?"

"Friends," she supplied firmly, choosing to leave it at that. After all, she didn't owe Jeff any explanations.

"Are you involved with anyone else? Seriously, I mean," Jeff asked cautiously.

She shouldn't really answer. She wouldn't. He shouldn't even have asked. But then her mouth opened, and the words came out on their own. "No, I'm not involved with anyone. And I like it that way."

"I'm not, either," he told her, returning the courtesy, even though she hadn't asked. "But I don't know that I like it that way. It's just the way things are right now."

He was a man who would want a wife and a family, a man who was probably looking for those things now that he'd established his career as a doctor. Autumn dropped her eyes to the knot in his tie, reminding herself once again that she had no business being out with this man, feeling these feelings for this man. She was single servings, irregular hours and haphazard housekeeping; he was dinner at eight, family outings and socks in the hamper. She belonged to a union and a bowler's league; he joined community service organizations and health clubs. They were opposite ends of the spectrum, day and night, apples and oranges.

And his hand on her back was turning her into marshmallow.

She stifled a sigh and swayed to the strains of romantic music, memorizing the feel of his chest pressed lightly against her breasts, his thighs brushing hers, his arms around her, his breath on her forehead. No, she couldn't allow herself to become too deeply involved with him. It wouldn't work. He deserved someone who could give more, who wanted to give more.

But, Lord, she wanted him! The sensual side of herself that she'd sternly repressed for the past few years responded to him in a way that she'd responded to no man before him, not even Steven. She was tormented by images, images that had formed in her mind the moment she'd met him. His head bent to hers, his hand on her thigh, his mouth at her breast. Her hands buried deep in his luxurious ebony hair, her lips tasting the firm, glistening skin of his chest. She groaned softly.

"Did you say something?" Jeff asked, still moving in a slow, tantalizing dance.

"No," she assured him without looking up.

An affair. The modern, sophisticated thing to do would be to have an affair with him. An affair that she controlled—taken at her own speed, ended when she was ready. The ultimate in liberation. She wanted him, he'd indicated that he wanted her. Why not? She'd learned years before that sex and marriage—even sex and love—did not necessarily have to go together. Consenting adults did it every day—met, acknowledged mutual attraction, slept together and parted, unscarred by the experience. She was twenty-five, no longer an innocent small-town girl in the throes of infatuation. She could handle it.

Couldn't she?

Of course she could.

The music ended. Jeff stepped back and smiled at her. Her heart jumped into her throat.

Then again, maybe she couldn't.

"WOULD YOU LIKE to come in?"

"Um, I don't think so. It's late." Autumn had the oddest sense of postponing the inevitable as she declined Jeff's invitation, but she still felt compelled to try.

"Could you spare just a minute? I'd like your advice on something."

She looked at him suspiciously, finding his expression blandly innocent in the murky light inside her car. "What?"

"Pool lights, remember?" He sounded surprised that

she hadn't known. "I told you that I'd like your advice on redoing them."

"At—" she squinted at the lighted clock on her dashboard "—one o'clock in the morning?"

He lifted one shoulder in a half shrug. "If you're too tired, it's okay. I understand. We'll do it another time."

With an inward sigh at her own lack of judgment, Autumn reached for her door handle. "All right, I'll look at it," she told him, swinging her legs out from under the steering wheel. Of course she didn't believe that Jeff had invited her in only to look at his pool, but then, that wasn't her purpose for going in with him, either.

It might be the dumbest thing she'd ever done, she decided, but the past couple of hours spent dancing in Jeff's arms had left her hungry for more of him. She'd made her token protest to salve her own conscience later; now she was giving in to desire and curiosity. After five years of caution and control she figured she owed herself one evening of impulsive pleasure.

Without speaking, Jeff led her straight through his house—as immaculate as she remembered it—and then through double glass doors to the screened-in patio containing his pool. Glancing almost indifferently around her, Autumn briefly noted the romantically subdued lighting, tastefully contemporary patio furniture and lush profusion of tropical plants before turning immediately back to Jeff. At that moment she had no interest in anything but him.

Jeff stared back at her, his hands in his pockets, his face carefully shuttered, but his eyes glowing with what could only be interpreted as hunger. A hunger to equal hers. Autumn locked suddenly icy fingers in front of her, her heart beginning to pound.

"So, uh—" he strengthened his voice with a visible effort "—what do you think?"

"About what?" she asked in little more than a whisper. Even that small sound seemed to reverberate in the mid-

dle-of-the-night stillness surrounding them, isolating
them.

"The lights." He gestured awkwardly with one hand,
the movement meant to include the entire patio.

"I think they're perfect." For just this little while, Autumn thought, everything was perfect. The evening, the
setting, the mood. The man. She ached for him to touch
her.

His gaze holding hers, Jeff took a slow step forward.
And then another. And then she was in his arms, and finally he was kissing her as she'd longed for him to kiss
her, as she'd dreaded for him to kiss her. Even as she gave
herself up to the devastating effects of the embrace, she
tried to convince herself that one kiss could not change her
entire life.

Jeff swallowed a groan as his hold tightened convulsively around the beautiful woman in his arms. He told
himself that her passionate response shouldn't come as a
surprise, but it did. He hadn't expected such glorious enthusiasm.

Her arms were around his neck, her full breasts crushed
against his chest. Her bare back was warm and yielding
beneath his eager palms, making him ravenous for more
of her. He swept the depths of her mouth, savoring the
sweet taste of her. Her tongue welcomed his, and this time
he couldn't hold back his groan of pleasure.

Desire had never come so swiftly, need so powerfully.
Jeff wanted her so desperately that he thought he would
shatter into dust if he couldn't have her. He ached, he
throbbed with desire for her. Inside his head, his chest. His
arms, his legs. The painfully swollen part of him that was
even now pressing into her stomach. He groaned again
when she moved closer, her body undulating sinuously
against him.

"Autumn," he muttered against her lips, needing to say
her name. It felt so good on his tongue that he said it again.
"Autumn."

Her fingers toyed with the hair at the back of his neck.

He shivered, burying his face in her softly scented throat, tasting the glistening skin there. She arched her neck for him, allowing him freer access. He pressed another kiss to her throat, then lifted his head, wanting to look at her.

God, she was so beautiful. Her fair skin was flushed with passion, her hair tousled and shining in the golden patio lighting. Lips kiss-darkened, eyes closed, lashes lying softly against her cheeks. Everything in her pose and expression told him that she was more than willing to increase the intimacy of their embraces. All he had to do was lead her inside, unfasten the button of that stunning dress and he could have her. At last.

5

JEFF BROKE into a cold sweat, his body tensing in protest at what he had to do. Somehow, from somewhere, he had to find the strength to step away from her. For he knew without a doubt that if he took her now, he would lose her.

She was offering her body, her passion. An affair, glorious though temporary. He wanted her love. Her future. Everything she had to give. He wanted to offer the same. But she wasn't ready to give or receive love. Only passion. And, God help him, that wasn't enough. He'd thought it would be, but it wasn't.

Taking a deep breath that burned its way into his lungs, he reached up with trembling hands and removed her arms from around his neck. Reluctantly he stepped back toward the glass doors that led into his house. Unaware that he was bringing the evening to an end, Autumn gave him a sultry smile that went straight to his clenched stomach. She spread her slender fingers across his chest, then leaned forward to plant a butterfly kiss on his jaw.

Jeff almost whimpered. But then he brought himself sternly under control and took her wrists in his hands, turning to walk inside with her. He didn't pause in the den but kept walking, straight to the front door. "I had a wonderful time tonight, Autumn," he told her, unable to make his voice sound completely normal. "Thank you."

Her expression stunned, Autumn blinked and looked up at him as if she couldn't quite believe she was hearing him correctly. "I had a good time, too," she said finally, "but—"

Jeff reached for the doorknob, avoiding her eyes. "Drive carefully, okay? After all, it *is* late."

"It's not *that* late," she replied curtly, and he could see confusion turning to annoyance in her emerald eyes. He could deal with her anger later, he assured himself, resisting an urge to cross his fingers.

"It's after one. And I'm on call tomorrow," he told her, deliberately casual. He dropped a light kiss on her unresponsive lips, smiled brightly, bade her good-night and politely closed the door in her astonished face.

He leaned weakly against that door for a moment before turning abruptly and heading back to the pool, shedding his clothes as he went and leaving them strewn behind him. He was halfway into his first lap before the sound of Autumn's Fiero faded into the distance. He lost count of the laps long before he crawled out of the pool, quivering with exhaustion but still taut with frustration.

AUTUMN STARED at Jeff's front door for a full minute before closing her mouth, spinning on one high heel and stalking to her car. She slid behind the wheel and slammed the door but could not bring herself to start the engine immediately. Instead, she sat in dazed silence, trying to decide what had just happened.

Jeff had thrown her out! First he'd kissed her like she'd never been kissed before, made her want him like she'd never wanted anyone, then he'd thrown her out! Slammed the door in her face, left her standing on the doorstep like...like a cat he was putting out for the night, she thought indignantly. A person could get whiplash from that abrupt a reversal!

Wouldn't you know it, she thought glumly, eventually reaching out to turn the key in the ignition. *I finally decide I'm mature enough and sophisticated enough to handle a brief affair, and I have to choose a genuine, old-time Southern gentleman who won't take a woman to bed on the first date.*

At least she assumed that Jeff had considered he was being courteous by ending their intimate interlude so unsatisfactorily. She would never believe that he hadn't wanted her as badly as she wanted him. After all, she'd been pressed as closely against him as possible while they were still wearing clothes. The man had definitely been interested. Remembering the solid, heavy feel of him, she shivered with another ripple of desire. How could he leave her this way? she wailed silently, shifting uncomfortably on the vinyl seat.

It was during the cold shower she took before turning in that she decided she wanted Jeff Bradford, dammit, and she was going to have him! How dare he think that he was the one responsible for deciding how far their relationship would go, and at what rate it would proceed! She was a woman of the eighties, fully capable of deciding for herself whom she would sleep with and when. And though she had no intention of becoming seriously involved with Jeff, she would admit to being very attracted to him and willing, if not eager, to pursue that attraction to its logical conclusion. One night, a few weeks, perhaps even a few months, and they could go their own ways, Jeff to continue his search for a suitable doctor's wife and Autumn to continue to work toward owning her own company.

Curled on the bed beside Babs a few minutes later, Autumn closed her eyes and tried to will herself to sleep. But memories of being held in Jeff's arms, being kissed and caressed by him, continued to plague her until she groaned and buried her face in her pillow. She would make him pay for this, she thought vengefully. And she'd make him enjoy every minute of his punishment. Just as she would.

JEFF LIFTED the feverish toddler from the examining table and snuggled him for a moment against his shoulder. "Poor little fella," he murmured for his tiny patient's ears. "You really feel rotten, don't you? Well, that medicine I just prescribed is going to make you feel better almost immediately, so just don't you worry about it, you hear?"

With one last pat on the lethargic little boy's diapered bottom, he passed the child to his mother, who smiled sweetly at him. "You are so wonderful with children, Dr.

Bradford," she told him gratefully. "You really should have some of your own."

"I'm working on it, Mrs. Evans," he replied cheerfully as he escorted her to the door, a hazy image of a child with red hair and emerald eyes flitting through his mind. Then he mentally laughed at himself for being an incurable optimist. At this point he'd be lucky to get another date with Autumn, and here he was fantasizing about having children with her!

Still thinking of Autumn, he sat behind the massive desk in his office and reached for his tape recorder to dictate diagnosis and treatment for the file of the child he'd just examined. He'd just snapped the recorder on when he was interrupted by Pam's appearance in the doorway. "Well?" she demanded, crossing her arms over her chest and leaning against his desk.

Jeff turned the recorder off. "Well, what?"

Pam sighed impatiently. "Have you called her yet?"

He knew who she meant, of course, but he couldn't help teasing her a bit longer. Pam was so teasable. "Have I called who yet?"

"Darn it, Jeff, you know who! Autumn! Now tell me, have you?"

"No, Pam, I haven't called her," he answered, relenting.

"Well, why not? This is Friday! If you're going to ask her out for this weekend, you'd better get busy. She's probably got plans already. Or are you waiting for her to call you?"

"I'll call her as soon as I get home this evening," Jeff assured his partner, throwing an arm over the back of his desk chair as he smiled at her. "Now are you satisfied?"

She shook her head, her brown curls bobbing with the motion. "I still don't understand why you waited so long to call her when I can tell you've been just dying to do so all week. What do you want to bet she's already got a date for tomorrow night?"

"Then I'll ask her out for another night," he answered logically. "Believe me, Pam, I have my reasons."

"Yes, you told me your reasons. Some garbage about her having to chase after you if you're going to catch her. That's not the way things were done in my day! Back then it was the men who did the chasing and the women loved it."

Jeff laughed, eyeing the indignant surgeon with fond amusement. Having put herself through medical school, graduating at the top of her class, Pam was hardly the unassuming Southern belle she was imitating. He wondered what had gotten into her lately. "Pamela, you sound like a little old lady. In your day, indeed. You've only been married for two years, remember? And according to Bob, you did a bit of chasing yourself. Weren't you the one who rammed your car into his once when you were dating so he couldn't leave having the last word in an argument?"

"That's different," Pam returned dismissively, waving one hand in the air.

"I thought you'd think so," Jeff murmured.

"Dr. Bradford, your next patient is here. And Dr. Cochran, you have a telephone call. It's Dr. Neville from Tampa General."

"Thanks, Sheila. I'll take it in my office." With one last frowning look at Jeff Pam turned and marched out of the room, leaving him grinning and shaking his head as he pushed himself away from his desk and went off to take care of his next patient.

He hoped he was doing the right thing by treating Autumn so casually. Every day for the past week he'd fought the urge to call her, reminding himself over and over that she wouldn't appreciate his chasing her too fervently. He'd told himself that he would be the pursued, he thought as he entered the examining room in which his patient was waiting. He only hoped the attraction between them was strong enough for Autumn to remain interested.

"So," EMILY ASKED with suspicious nonchalance, "have you heard from your friend lately?"

Thinking that Emily could only be referring to Jeff, Au-

tumn shook her head and glared down at her dinner plate.
"No. Not since our date last Saturday."

"Oh, I didn't mean Jeff," Emily corrected her quickly,
dabbing at Ryan's mouth with a napkin to remove a smear
of the broccoli he was happily eating with his fingers. "I
meant your friend Webb."

Autumn arched an eyebrow and looked across her dining table at her neighbor, who had joined Autumn for an
early dinner followed by a television special they both
wanted to see. So Emily was interested in Webb, was she?
Autumn grinned, remembering that Webb had casually
inquired about Emily on at least three different occasions
during the past week since he'd met her. "Of course I've
heard from Webb, Emily. I work with him, remember? I
see him every day."

"Oh, of course." Emily flushed a bit and focused her
china-blue eyes on the broiled fish fillet in front of her.
"How silly of me."

Autumn chuckled. "Emily, if you're interested in Webb,
just come out and say so. What would you like to know
about him?"

Blushing deeper, Emily smiled sheepishly and looked at
Autumn. "Everything. I thought he was nice. And so
handsome! I'm surprised that you're not dating him yourself."

"Webb and I are just friends. We're too much alike to be
anything else," Autumn explained. "He's a great guy, but
he's been known to break a few hearts. He claims to be allergic to commitment."

"It does sound like the two of you are a lot alike," Emily
agreed in amusement. "Ryan, don't rub your Jell-O in
your hair!"

Laughing at Ryan's antics, Autumn turned back to her
dinner. As she finished, she told Emily how she'd met
Webb, then shared some funny stories of escapades she
and Webb had been involved in during the past months.
Privately she thought that Emily and Webb would make a
good couple. She suspected that Emily would be the type

who'd adore and admire the man she loved, and Webb was one of those males who'd enjoy the adulation and return it in full measure once he'd accepted the inevitable. He loved kids, so Ryan wouldn't be a problem.

If only the man weren't so shy of serious involvement, Autumn mused, not finding it at all strange that she was in favor of marriage for Webb when she was so wary of the institution for herself. It wasn't marriage itself that she opposed, but the fear of losing herself within the bonds of such a union. Others seemed to handle the responsibilities just fine—her own two sisters were embarrassingly happy in their wedded states. But Autumn's too-close encounter had left her decidedly marriage-shy.

Thoughts of Jeff Bradford tried to creep into her mind, but she firmly closed a mental door against them, telling herself that there was absolutely no connection between her reflections on marriage and the man who'd shattered her peace of mind in the six weeks since she'd met him. She'd been expecting Jeff to call all week. Not that she'd made any special effort to stay close to her phone because of that, she assured herself. She'd simply had several things to do that had kept her home every night that week.

"Webb sure left in a hurry when I told him that I was divorced," Emily said with a sigh as they stood to carry their plates into the kitchen. "Has he got something against divorcées?"

Bringing her thoughts back to their conversation with an effort, Autumn shook her head at Emily's question. "No. He only runs like that when he meets a woman who could become a threat to his bachelorhood."

Emily frowned at that, then slowly smiled. "Oh. I see."

Autumn returned the smile. "I thought you would. Maybe I'll ask him over one night next week. I could use some help with the bookcase that I want to move from the living room to my bedroom."

"I think that sounds like an excellent idea," Emily agreed, her eyes dancing. "Oh, Autumn, I'm glad I met you. I've been lonely since Earl and I divorced. He'd pretty

well alienated all our friends with his drinking by the tim
we split up, and I've been reluctant to get back in touc
with them. It's nice to have a friend again."

Autumn reached into a cabinet for a cookie for Ryan'
dessert, pleased by Emily's words. "I'm glad we met, too,
she admitted. "Until you came along, I hadn't realize
that almost all my friends in Tampa are men that I wor
with. It's nice to have a woman to talk to again."

Emily started to say something, then paused as the tele
phone rang. "Maybe that's Jeff," she said eagerly, confirm
ing Autumn's suspicion that Emily knew how much Au
tumn had been hoping he'd call, even though Autumn
had said very little about Jeff to Emily.

Though her heart had begun to pound—as it had eac
time the telephone had rung during the past week, to Au
tumn's disgust—she tried to sound as if she didn't reall
care that Jeff might be the caller. "Could be. Excuse m
Emily."

She picked up the receiver of the yellow kitchen wal
phone. "Hello?"

"Hello, Autumn."

Jeff. "Hi," she said a little too breathlessly, then nodde
at Emily to confirm that it was, indeed, him. "If you wan
to go ahead and get comfortable in the living room, I'll joi
you in a few minutes," she told her grinning friend befor
turning her full attention back to the telephone call. "Hov
are you, Jeff?"

"You have company?" he asked without answering he
perfunctory question. "I can call back another time if it'
not convenient now."

Noting the displeasure in his voice with mixed feeling
Autumn wound the telephone cord around her finge
"No, it's okay. I can talk for a few minutes. Emily an
Ryan had dinner with me, and we're going to watch a tele
vision special together."

"Emily and Ryan?"

"My neighbor and her fifteen-month-old son. I though
I'd mentioned them at dinner last week."

"Yeah, I think you did," Jeff agreed, his voice suddenly sounding brighter. "What television program are you going to watch?" he inquired, obviously reluctant to end the call.

"The magician Jeremy Kane has his first TV special on tonight. The television guide said he was going to do some pretty spectacular illusions."

"You like magic?"

"Yes. And Jeremy Kane is one of my favorite magicians. I'd love to see him perform in person someday."

"I'll keep that in mind. Actually, though, I called to see if you'd like to go out with me tomorrow night. Unless you have other plans, of course."

The awkwardness of the invitation was somehow endearing. Autumn tried to steel herself against the softness he brought out in her even as she accepted. "No, I don't have any other plans for tomorrow night. I'd like to go out with you."

"Great." He didn't try to hide his pleasure. "I thought we'd do something casual this time, so don't dress up, okay?"

"Fine. Sounds like fun." She noted absently that the end of her finger was turning purple as the tightly wound telephone cord cut off her circulation.

"Seven o'clock?"

"All right."

"Autumn?"

"Yes, Jeff?"

"I need your address."

"Oh, of course." She gave it to him, listened as he carefully repeated the numbers, then hung up when he did. Unwrapping her purple finger, she stood absently rubbing it, her gaze unseeingly on the telephone. Funny, she thought, she hadn't even hesitated to accept the date. After a week of indecision, alternating between never wanting to see him again and fighting the urge to chase him down and drag him into bed, she'd meekly accepted his invitation when he'd finally gotten around to calling her. And she'd quickly explained who was with her when she could sense that he thought he'd interrupted a more intimate evening. If she wasn't careful, she thought with a weak attempt at humor, Jeff Bradford was going to have her involved with him before she even knew it.

Only the thought wasn't at all funny. That was exactly what she was worried about.

"Hello in there." Emily's voice held amusement as she broke into Autumn's deep reverie.

Autumn looked sheepishly at the doorway where Emily watched her with a smile. "Uh, that was Jeff."

"I know. Did he ask you out again?"

"Yes. Tomorrow night."

"You *are* going, aren't you?"

"Yes, I'm going."

"Good." Emily's smile broadened. "I think this man is good for you."

"No." Autumn shook her head emphatically. "He's all wrong for me. Exactly the opposite of the kind of man I usually date."

"That's what I meant. He's good for you." With that smug comment Emily turned toward the living room. "Jeremy Kane's about to come on. We don't want to miss his opening illusion."

Pulling two canned soft drinks out of the refrigerator, Autumn followed her friend, knowing as she did so that it was going to be hard to lose herself in the performer's illusions when her mind would be so fully filled with memories of Jeff. She was beginning to believe that Jeff Bradford possessed a few magic powers of his own. She could only assume that she had been bewitched.

AUTUMN SPENT quite a bit less time worrying about clothes for her second date with Jeff than she had for her first. After all, if "that gold thing"—the most powerful weapon in her wardrobe arsenal—hadn't overcome Jeff's strong willpower, no garment would. Still, she took pains to look her best in a vividly patterned, short-sleeved camp shirt and pleated khaki slacks, her thick, curling hair confined at the back of her head with a banana clip. Bold plastic earrings, a heavy matching bracelet and bright green flats completed her colorful outfit. She had just finished applying her makeup when her doorbell rang, some fifteen minutes before seven. Either Jeff was early or...

"Webb." She sighed as she opened her door. "What are you doing here?"

He grinned in pure enjoyment. "Making trouble."

"So what else is new? Go away, Webb."

"Nope." Looking as attractive as always in a fashionably casual shirt and slacks, he strolled past her and dropped onto her couch, draping himself comfortably across the pillows as if he were prepared to stay for a while. Absently patting Babs when she jumped up to greet him, he looked at Autumn. "What time's Bradford supposed to be here?"

"How do you know I've got a date with Jeff?" Autumn demanded in frustration.

"Call it a lucky guess. I was right, wasn't I?"

"Yes, you were right. Now will you go away? He's supposed to be here in fifteen minutes."

"I thought I'd say hello. I haven't seen him in a while. Got a beer?"

Autumn started to tell him exactly what he could do with himself—an anatomical impossibility—but then she paused as a mischievous thought crossed her mind. She'd teach Webb not to play games with her, she decided abruptly. He *deserved* to find himself waiting at the altar. But not with her. "Sure, I've got a beer. I'll get you one," she told him, smiling sweetly as she headed for the kitchen.

Webb straightened on the couch, watching her leave with a frown at her suspicious acquiescence. "What are you planning, Autumn?"

"I'm not planning anything, Webb," she assured him over her shoulder. "I just know when to accept the inevitable. You're not going to disappear until Jeff gets here, are you?''

''Nope.''

''So I won't waste my time pleading with you. Don't you have a date tonight?'' she asked, raising her voice to be heard in the other room as she rummaged in the refrigerator for a beer.

''Not tonight,'' Webb called back. ''Thought I'd head over to Charlie's later and check out the scenery.'' Charlie's was a popular singles' bar that Webb liked to frequent. Autumn hated the place she always called the ''meat market.''

She picked up the phone and quickly punched in her neighbor's number. ''Emily? Hi, it's Autumn. Can you come over for a minute? Yeah, right now. Make up an excuse, will you? Webb's here, and Jeff's supposed to arrive any minute. If you're here, too, Webb just might behave himself.'' The conversation was brief and low-voiced. Autumn was smiling when she hung up.

Webb had barely popped the top of his beer when the doorbell rang. He lifted his eyebrows in a devilish expression. ''Lover-boy's here.''

''Webb, why do you find it so amusing that I'm going out with Jeff?'' Autumn asked curiously, knowing who was at the door.

He lifted one shoulder, grinning unrepentantly. ''Maybe it's because I didn't think there was anyone who could rattle that tough, cool exterior of yours. I'm pleased to know that Ms Autumn Reed has a few insecurities like the rest of us mere mortals.''

Shaking her head in exasperation, Autumn opened the door, winking at Emily. ''Hello, Emily. Hi, Ryan,'' she said clearly, amused as Webb coughed on a sip of beer behind her. ''Come in.''

''Thanks. I brought the sweater you wanted to borrow.'' Her blue eyes twinkling with suppressed laughter, Emily held out a thin red oversized sweater that Autumn had once admired.

Grateful that the sweater just happened to match the outfit she'd chosen to wear, Autumn draped it over her arm. "Thanks, Emily. I'd heard a cold front was supposed to come through later and I didn't have a thing to wear with this blouse. You remember Webb, don't you?"

Autumn hadn't realized that her neighbor had any talent in the dramatic arts, but Emily's look of pleased surprise was superb. "Of course I do. Hello, Webb. How nice to see you again."

Immediately on his feet, Webb managed a smile, trying very hard to keep his eyes on Emily's lovely face instead of the creamy cleavage revealed by her scoop-necked ice-blue sweater. He wasn't entirely successful, Autumn noted with malicious pleasure. "Hello, Emily," he said faintly.

From his usual position on his mother's hip, Ryan smiled happily at Webb and held out his chubby hands, babbling a welcome in his mostly incomprehensible toddler dialect. "I think he remembers you," Emily remarked, giving Webb one of her guaranteed-to-daze-any-red-blooded-male smiles.

Predictably dazed, Webb lifted Ryan into his arms and grinned besottedly down at the sandy-haired imp. "Yeah, I think he does. How's it going, buddy?"

"He's been active lately," Emily told him with a smile. "He's practicing his climbing. He's made it to the top of the bookcase twice now."

Webb laughed, his eyes drifting back to Emily's face…and the rest of her. "I'll bet he keeps you busy."

"Oh, he does. But I'm not complaining. He's a sweetheart."

"Does, uh, does he see his father very often?" Webb asked hesitantly, his gaze turning back to the child.

Emily's smile faded. "No. My ex-husband wasn't fond of children. Ryan was an accident. After the divorce Earl decided to write both of us off as mistakes. I haven't seen him or heard from him in a year."

Webb frowned. "What a jerk. How could any man walk

away from his own son? Or from you?" he added slowly, looking once more at the beautiful young woman in front of him.

As Emily flushed in pleasure and retrieved her son, Autumn resisted the impulse to laugh out loud. *Oh, Webb, my friend, you're in big trouble,* she thought gleefully. *That'll teach you to make fun of me for being rattled by Jeff Bradford.* And then her amusement faded as she wondered if she wore the same expression around Jeff that Webb was currently wearing as he looked at Emily.

Bewitched, she thought again. *Maybe we're both bewitched.* A shiver of something very near fear coursed down her spine, and she was suddenly sorry that she'd found such amusement in almost throwing Emily at Webb. Was she to be paid back in kind?

When the doorbell rang again she jumped, earning herself a delighted grin from Webb, who was obviously not quite as distracted as Autumn had hoped.

Glaring at him, Autumn took a deep breath and opened the door, then promptly lost the breath in a soft whoosh as she took in the man smiling at her from the doorstep. He was dressed in a pale yellow crewneck sweater and light gray slacks, looking as devastatingly attractive as he had in his expensive suit the week before. Surely it wasn't possible that he grew more good-looking each time she saw him, she thought despairingly. His hair couldn't really have grown darker and thicker, his eyes bluer and warmer, his shoulders broader and more muscular. God, he was gorgeous!

"Hi, Jeff." Oh, hell. She'd sounded breathless again. Probably because she was.

"Hi, Autumn." His own voice was low, caressing, sending hot tremors through every inch of her body.

Clinging to the door, Autumn invited him in, waiting until he'd passed her to shut the door and lean weakly against it. "Jeff, you know Webb. And this is my neighbor, Emily Hinson, and her son, Ryan. Emily, this is Dr. Jeff Bradford."

Nodding a greeting at Webb, Jeff smiled at Emily. "Hi. Nice to meet you."

"You're a doctor?" Emily shot a reproving look at her friend. "Autumn didn't mention that."

"Jeff's a pediatrician," Autumn explained.

Emily looked interested. "You are? Where's your office? Ryan and I just moved here from St. Pete three months ago, and I haven't found a pediatrician for him in Tampa yet."

Jeff named his clinic and gave the address, adding that he had two partners. "Julian's a very good doctor, and Pam's a skilled surgeon," he explained. "We'd be happy to take care of this guy. Not that he doesn't look perfectly healthy." He grinned at Ryan, reaching out to ruffle the toddler's sandy hair. "Hello, Ryan. Aren't you a fine-looking fellow?"

Well, he just won Emily over, Autumn thought ruefully. She tried not to acknowledge that she was pleased that Jeff showed no signs of interest in Ryan's mother, other than polite friendliness. She would not admit that she'd been at all worried that Jeff might have exhibited the same weakness for Emily's delicate blond beauty that Webb had displayed.

Webb offered a hand to Jeff. "How's it going, Jeff? Haven't seen you in ages."

"It's good to see you again, Webb. Now that the clinic's open late on the same evenings the Jaycees meet, I don't have much chance to be active in the chapter."

"We appreciated your contribution last month to the project for handicapped kids. You were very generous." Webb waited until Jeff had modestly shrugged off the praise before shooting a mischievous look at Autumn. "So you're interested in Autumn, are you? Good luck, my friend. You've got nerve, I'll say that for you."

"Webb…" Autumn murmured threateningly as Jeff grinned at the other man.

"Can't say I blame you for trying, of course," Webb continued bravely. "But be warned, Bradford. She has the devil's own temper."

Autumn was showing signs of that temper as Emily stepped in quickly to defuse the situation. "I guess we'd better be going. It was nice to meet you, Dr. Bradford. See you tomorrow, Autumn." She turned a shamelessly limpid look at Webb. "Bye, Webb. Maybe I'll see you again sometime."

Immediately forgetting Autumn and Jeff, Webb seemed to struggle inwardly for about half a minute before blurting out, "Why don't we take Ryan out for ice cream, Emily? He *can* eat ice cream, can't he?"

"He loves ice cream," Emily replied happily. "Are you sure you didn't have any other plans for the evening?"

Perjuring himself without hesitation, Webb denied any plans for that evening. Autumn swallowed a chuckle as her friend deliberately chose an ice-cream parlor over Tampa's hottest night spot. She managed not to laugh until Webb had departed with Emily and Ryan, though she had no intention of keeping quiet about his choice next time she saw him.

"What's so funny?" Jeff asked quizzically, looking up from where he'd knelt to pat Babs.

Autumn decided not to enlighten him. Instead, she introduced him to Babs and went to get her purse so they could leave, suddenly conscious that the two of them were alone. The nervousness that had faded in her amusement at Webb's reluctant interest in Emily returned full force.

6

ANY NERVOUSNESS that Autumn may have experienced when the date began was long gone by the time she and Jeff had dined on hamburgers, chuckled through a new comedy film and then spent an hour in an arcade in friendly competition. It was as if Jeff deliberately made the date as unthreatening as possible to put her at ease. If so, his strategy worked. She had a marvelous time, laughing until her sides ached.

"Okay, lady, you asked for it. I'm breaking through your defenses this time, and there's nothing you can do to stop me." Jeff's threat was uttered in a growl, blue eyes narrowed with intent.

Autumn tensed in reaction, her own eyes returning the challenge. "Would you like to make a small wager on that?"

"I," he informed her loftily, "never bet on a sure thing. You may as well prepare to surrender."

"I," she returned haughtily, "never surrender. Give it your best shot, Bradford."

"Don't say I didn't warn you," he told her softly, then exploded into action. His arm swept in a powerful arc, the paddle in his hand sending the air hockey puck skimming across the table between them, heading straight for Autumn's goal.

Skillfully Autumn deflected the puck with a snap of her wrist, turning it back toward Jeff's goal. Over and over they returned the volley, each intent on scoring the winning point. And then Autumn happened to glance up at Jeff, taking her eyes away from the table to admire him with his face flushed, eyes bright, hair disheveled, dimples flashing—and promptly lost the game.

"All right!" Jeff leaped straight into the air, one arm waving above his head as he celebrated his victory, one of the few he'd managed since he and Autumn had wandered into the arcade over an hour ago.

"Don't gloat, Jeff. It's not becoming."

He grinned and looped an arm around her neck. "Oh, yeah? Who was gloating a few minutes ago after winning three straight games of Galactic Shoot-out? Who pointed out that she destroyed all my spaceships in the first ninety seconds of the first game? Who won the most tickets playing Skee-Ball? Who—"

"Okay, okay," Autumn interrupted, laughing. "So I gloated. Now it's your turn. Go ahead."

"I'm much too good a sport to gloat," Jeff answered with immense dignity, then added in a stage whisper, "Loser."

Autumn giggled and punched him in the ribs. Then she swallowed a moan as she realized that she had, indeed, giggled. Oh, God, she thought dolefully. She'd regressed to girlhood. It must be a recurring condition. One that affected her anytime Jeff Bradford was around.

Holding his free hand to his abused ribs with an exaggerated wince, Jeff kept his other arm around her shoulders as they left the arcade in unspoken consent. "How about some ice cream? I've been craving ice cream ever since Webb mentioned it earlier."

"Sounds good," Autumn agreed, matching her steps to his as they walked down the sidewalk. She wondered briefly how Webb's evening with Emily and Ryan had gone, then dismissed them from her mind. She was enjoying her own date with Jeff too much to concentrate on anyone else just then. She allowed her arm to slide around his waist, linking them as they strolled. Sometimes it was nice to feel like a schoolgirl, she reflected wryly.

"Chocolate mint for the lady," Jeff told the teenager behind the Christmas-decorated counter of the ice-cream store, smiling into Autumn's eyes as he spoke.

She returned the smile. "And cherry vanilla for the gentleman," she murmured, remembering their conversation from the restaurant the previous Saturday.

Grinning at the total self-absorption of the couple, the teenager obligingly scooped generous helpings of the ice cream into waffle cones. Jeff paid for the ice cream, then winked at the kid, who laughed and gave Jeff a thumbs-up gesture of approval.

"What was that all about?" Autumn demanded curiously as they left the store.

"Male bonding," Jeff answered flippantly, taking her hand to lead her off the sidewalk and onto the nearly deserted beach that stretched before them.

"You're all hopeless." Autumn sighed, curling her fingers around his as she licked her ice cream. She'd pulled Emily's red sweater over her head just before they'd gone into the ice-cream store, and now she was grateful for its light protection as a cool breeze blew moistly off the bay, catching strands of hair loosened from her banana clip and wafting them around her face. The predicted cold front had arrived, dropping the temperature to a cool—for Tampa—fifty degrees. The moon shone brightly in the clear early-December sky above them, and the waters of the bay glittered in its light. She couldn't remember ever seeing a more beautiful night—but then, she'd never spent a night like this with Jeff. Something told her that it wouldn't have seemed quite so perfect without him.

"Beautiful night," Jeff murmured, seeming to read her thoughts.

"Mmm. A lot different from Arkansas at this time of year."

"Is that right?" Jeff asked gravely, swiping his tongue over his ice cream.

Watching him, Autumn shivered, but the tremor had little to do with the weather. Swallowing hard, she nibbled at her ice cream and nodded. "I'll, uh, I'll have to pack warm clothing when I go home for Christmas in a couple of weeks. I've gotten spoiled by Florida winters, even though I've only been through one so far."

Jeff was watching her as she chattered, his eyes warmly amused. A dribble of cherry vanilla ice cream slid down one side of his cone, and he slowly licked it clean.

Autumn felt a moan forming in her chest and hastily repressed it. When had this happened? she wondered frantically. *How* had this happened? One minute they'd been laughing and playing, as comfortable together as kids, and in the next she found herself wanting to pull him to the damp sand and have her wicked way with him. *Bewitched.*

"How's your ice cream?" Jeff inquired, his voice a low rumble meant for her ears alone.

"It's...it's fine. How's yours?"

"Very good. Want a taste?"

"Um, no, thanks."

"Mind if I taste yours?"

"Go ahead." She held her cone out to him.

Ignoring it, he turned and lowered his mouth to hers, kissing her for the first time that evening. Autumn closed her eyes and clung to him with her free hand, feeling as if she were melting faster than the ice cream still clutched in her other hand. Chocolate mint and cherry vanilla combined in the most exotically erotic taste she'd ever experienced as Jeff deepened the kiss. "Mmm," he murmured when he finally released her mouth. "Delicious."

It took her a full minute to catch her breath. By that time Jeff had already turned her in the crook of his arm and begun to walk again. Spotting a trash can, Autumn tossed the remains of her ice-cream cone into it. It seemed to have lost its flavor. Without a word Jeff followed her example. She looked up to find him staring down at her. Her head tilted back, her eyelids closed, and he was kissing her again, thoroughly, hungrily, as if he'd been wanting to do so for hours, for days, for a week.

Jeff tightened his arms around her, his body hardening, his mind beginning to whirl. He'd long since accepted that kissing her had these effects on him; each time was more wondrous, more necessary than the last. He dimly realized that he'd held off kissing her earlier because he'd known he wouldn't want to stop when he did. The past week had been hell, wanting to be with her, wanting to hold her. The past few hours had been heaven, touching her, laughing with her.

Six weeks earlier he'd looked into emerald green eyes and fallen in love. Now he acknowledged that his love was real, lasting, deep. Forever. He'd found his mate, the other half of himself, and he would do whatever he had to do to make her his. Fight whatever battles were necessary. Even if Autumn herself were the opponent. And she would be.

Tearing his mouth from hers, he gasped for breath and buried his face in her throat. "I want you," he muttered. "I didn't know it was possible to want anyone this much."

"Shouldn't we go someplace more private?" Autumn asked softly, her voice a husky siren's lure.

"Yes," he whispered in response, raising his head to look down at her. He could read her desire for him in her eyes and he shuddered. She wanted him. She didn't love him—yet—but she wanted him. Maybe—just for tonight—that would be enough. Maybe.

They talked little during the drive. Jeff guided his silver BMW with one hand, keeping Autumn's hand in the other. Occasionally he raised her hand to brush her knuckles with his lips. By the time he pulled into her driveway, she was trembling with need for him.

She didn't have to ask him in. Without a word he opened his door and climbed out of the car, meeting her on the other side. She could feel the slight unsteadiness in his arm when it slipped around her waist, the hint of vulnerability increasing her own uncharacteristic shyness. It took her three tries to fit the key into the lock of her front door.

The door had barely closed behind them before she was in his arms again, his mouth slanting hungrily over hers.

Rising on her tiptoes to press closer against him, Autumn abandoned herself wholly to sensation, shutting off all thought of consequences. She wanted him. And this time she was going to have him.

Jeff's first impulse was to lift her into his arms and carry her into the bedroom. A soft chuckle left his throat as he realized that his fiery love probably wouldn't appreciate such a gesture. She'd want to walk beside him, if not actually lead him.

Autumn tilted her head back to look up at him, her eyes quizzical. "You're laughing?" she inquired curiously, her voice disturbed.

"I'm happy," he answered simply, smiling down at her. He wanted so desperately to add that he loved her. But he couldn't. Not yet. His smile dimmed.

Autumn lifted a hand to his cheek, her own smile misty. "So am I," she told him softly. "It's been a wonderful evening."

He caught her hand in his fiercely, gripped by needs too powerful to control. He ached for her, the desire all too close to pain. He could lose himself in her, pretend that she was his for eternity. But, dammit, he didn't want to have to pretend. He wanted it to be true. "I need you," he whispered rawly, turning his face into her palm. "God, I need you."

As he'd known she would, she interpreted his words to mean that he wanted to make love with her. She could not—or would not—read the deeper meaning hidden within them. Her full red lips curving into a smile that no man could resist, she twined her fingers around his and turned to guide him to her bedroom.

She snapped on a small bedside lamp, illuminating the room with soft golden light. Jeff's eyes turned swiftly to examine her bedroom and what he saw made him smile. Like Autumn, her room was an intriguing combination of the defiantly modern and the sweetly old-fashioned. It was perfect for her. Just as she was perfect for him. He turned back to her in time to watch her sweep the borrowed red sweater over her head. Her sultry gaze holding his, she removed the clip from her hair, allowing the wind-tangled auburn tresses to fall around her shoulders. He swallowed hard.

No one else in the world would have known she was nervous as she reached for the top button of her blouse, Jeff thought in a sudden surge of fierce possessiveness. Surely no one else could have seen beyond that cool, seductive exterior to find the trace of uncertainty in her eyes, in the almost imperceptible tremor of her fingers as they loosened that button and then the next. He took the two steps that separated them and caught her hands in his, raising them tenderly to his lips. And then he finished unbuttoning her blouse, sliding the crisp fabric off her shoulders to expose full, creamy breasts spilling over the lacy top of a scrap of a bra. He groaned and lowered his lips to the tempting, gold-dusted flesh.

Autumn quivered when his mouth touched her skin. Glorying in her response, Jeff lowered her to the bed, following to stretch out beside her. Still without removing her bra, he cupped one swollen breast in his hand, his lips and teeth tracing the line of lace that covered her. "You're so beautiful. So very beautiful." He barely recognized his own voice.

"Jeff," she whispered, arching up to him.

His name on her lips was the most erotic sound he'd ever heard. He had to taste it. "My name," he muttered roughly. "Say it again."

"Jeff," she moaned as his fingers found her straining nipple through thin lace. "Je—"

And then his mouth was on hers, his tongue deep inside to claim the sound. Rolling to lie on top of her, he arched into her softness, the clothing between them unwanted barriers to total intimacy. Burying his hands deep in her hair, he kissed her with all the unleashed passion inside him, his control almost completely shattered. And she kissed him back with a heat that equaled his, her silky, work-strong arms going around him to clutch him to her.

Her pant-clad legs tangled with his, the feminine juncture of her thighs willingly cradling his straining hardness.

"How do you do this to me, Autumn Reed?" he whispered between hot, stinging kisses. "What kind of a spell have you cast on me with those green sorceress eyes?"

Her laugh was thin, breathless. "And I thought I was the one who'd been bewitched," she accused him, her hands stroking the strong line of his back.

Holding her still beneath him, Jeff lifted his head and stared down at her. "Tell me you want me, Autumn. I need to hear it."

"I want you, Jeff," she answered without hesitation.

He groaned and kissed her again, his hand seeking the clasp of her bra. It was enough, he told himself thickly. I was enough—for now. It had to be.

And then he groaned again when a high-pitched beeping penetrated the thick fog of desire inside his head. Cursing beneath his breath, he forced himself to roll away from her, his hand going to the small plastic box clipped to his belt. "I'm sorry."

Her breathing as ragged as his, Autumn struggled upright, pushing her hair out of her face with an unsteady hand. "Don't apologize. It's not your fault."

Checking the telephone number displayed on the tiny screen of the pager, Jeff nodded toward the extension phone on her bedside table. "May I?"

"Of course." Autumn reached self-consciously for her blouse. *So this is what it's like to date a doctor*, she thought, with an attempt at humor that she didn't at all feel.

She couldn't help hearing Jeff's end of the conversation as she buttoned her blouse. "What's up, Julian?" he asked, his voice still husky with passion. "She is? Tonight? Damn. I was hoping she'd make it through Christmas. No, I'm glad you called. I want to be with her mother when it happens. Hang around, will you? I'll be there soon. Thanks, Julian."

Running his hands through his tousled hair, Jeff turned to Autumn when he'd replaced the receiver, and there wa sadness in his eyes. "I've got to go," he told her. "I'm losing a patient tonight, a little girl with cystic fibrosis. I want to be there for her mother."

"I understand. I'm sorry." She wanted to reach out to him, to ease the pain she read in him, but she didn't know how.

"I'm sorry, too. For everything." His awkward gesture at the rumpled bed said as much as his words.

Autumn shrugged, feeling her face grow hot. "I know."

Jeff started to turn toward the bedroom door, then he stopped suddenly, as if on impulse, and turned back to her. "Maybe it's best that this happened tonight. Before we made love."

Puzzled, she tilted her head to one side and looked up at him. "Why?"

Again he ran his hand through his hair, an atypically nervous gesture from him. "Because I'm not sure I could ever walk away from you if we make love," he blurted out at length. "Because once we've taken that step, I couldn't bear the thought of another man being with you, touching you. Hell, I can't bear that thought now. It's already too late for me. But you've been given a reprieve, Autumn. Another chance."

"Another chance for what?" she asked warily, moistening suddenly dry lips.

Moving abruptly, he cradled her face in both his hands, gently forcing her to look up at him. "Another chance to back away from the relationship developing between us before we lose control of it. I'm not talking about sex, Autumn. I won't deny that I want you, that I want to make love to you more than I've ever wanted another woman, but that's only a part of what I feel for you. I want a future, a commitment. And making love with you will only strengthen those feelings."

Her heart pounded in her chest, her hands trembled, and she recognized the symptoms of pure fear. This was what she'd tried to avoid from the beginning. Somehow she'd known that Jeff wouldn't meekly participate in the no-strings-attached affair she'd tried to convince herself she wanted with him. "Then maybe we'd better end it, Jeff. Because I'm *not* looking for a commitment right now. Believe me, it wouldn't work. I'm not the right woman for you. For an affair, maybe, some good times. But not for anything more lasting."

"You're wrong," he told her, his eyes blazing. "You're exactly the right woman for me. I've known from the moment I saw you. And don't try to convince me that you make a habit of indulging in a string of affairs. I won't believe you."

She lifted her chin in an instinctively defensive gesture at his too-close accusation. "You don't know that. You couldn't know."

"I know," he answered simply.

She jerked away from him, stepping back to put space between them. "Hadn't you better go to the hospital?"

"Yes. I wish I could stay so we could talk about this some more, but I can't. I'll call you tomorrow."

"No," she said quickly. "Don't."

"Autumn…"

"Please, Jeff. I need time. I'm not ready for this now."

He sighed and nodded. "All right. I shouldn't have brought up my feelings like this, knowing I didn't have time to stay and talk it out. But I didn't want to leave you thinking that all I want from you is an affair."

He closed the distance between them again and dropped a brief kiss on her still-swollen lips. "Think about us, Autumn. Think about the feelings that have been there between us from the beginning. More than passion, more than desire. Don't be afraid of those feelings, honey."

Honey. She'd always disliked that endearment, considered it demeaning. So why did the word make her knees go weak when spoken so softly by Jeff? "I…" She what? Wordlessly she stared at him.

"It's your move again, Autumn. I'll be waiting when you're ready to make it. Good night." He turned and moved away from her, his long strides quickly crossing the living room to the front door.

Some impulse made her run after him. "Jeff!"

He paused, holding the door open. "What is it, Autumn?"

Stopping only inches from him, she touched his cheek fleetingly. "I'm very sorry about the little girl. I know it hurts you."

He caught her hand and pressed a warm kiss into her palm. "Thank you," he whispered roughly. "Good night, Autumn."

"Good night, Jeff."

"Damn. Damn, damn, damn." Autumn dropped onto the couch and buried her face in hands. She'd known. She'd *known* to stay away from him! And it was her own fault that she hadn't. She'd called *him* for that first date.

From the beginning she'd known the kind of man he was. Warm, sensitive, honorable. Modern in some ways, but not when it came to relationships. The man wanted a wife, a family, and now he'd decided Autumn was the woman he'd been looking for.

He was so very wrong.

Her eyes stung with hot tears she refused to shed. She didn't want to hurt Jeff. She didn't want to be hurt. Yet both seemed inevitable now: How could she have deluded herself into thinking there was any other possible ending to this thing between them?

He needed someone to cherish, someone to protect. She needed to take care of herself. He would be the kind of man to love with his entire heart, to center his life on that love. She was terrified of being smothered by that type of love. He needed someone to be there for him when he hurt, someone to come home to when he'd lost one of the patients he cared so deeply about. She didn't know how to offer that kind of support. She couldn't even help him tonight when she could see him suffering in front of her. Dammit, she didn't know how!

A damp, cold nose pressed against her cheek, and Au-

tumn automatically gathered the small white dog into her
arms. "Oh, Babs, I've made such a mess of everything,"
she whispered sadly. "Such a terrible mess."

LONG HOURS LATER Jeff stepped out of his shower and
rubbed a towel over his dripping hair. A weary sigh escaped him as he walked nude to his bed after patting most
of the water from his body. He was so damn tired. He
crawled into the bed and stretched out on his stomach, one
arm draped around his pillow. He desperately needed
sleep, but it was slow in coming. Part of his mind was still
at the hospital, with the little girl who'd died and the family whose grief was so devastating despite the efforts
they'd made to prepare themselves for this inevitable
event. Yet another part of his mind was with Autumn,
hoping that he hadn't ruined everything with the impulsive declaration of his feelings.

He didn't regret telling her that he wanted more from
her than an affair. He'd never intended to pretend differ-
ently. He only hoped he hadn't frightened her away with
the ill-timed admission.

Drawing in a long, ragged breath, he burrowed more
deeply into the pillow and allowed himself to drift into a
pleasant fantasy in which Autumn was lying beside him,
her fingers stroking his hair, her skin pressed warmly to
his. The merest hint of a smile touched his lips at the
thought. Someday, he promised himself as consciousness
slipped away from him, someday it would happen. Surely
he couldn't need her this much and never be allowed to
have her.

AUTUMN SPENT the next two weeks working until she was
nearly exhausted in an attempt to convince herself that she
didn't miss Jeff, didn't think of him every waking moment. She succeeded only in losing five pounds she hadn't
tried to lose and developing purple circles under her eyes
from too many restless nights. As she'd requested, Jeff
didn't call, but she knew that he was waiting for her to call

him. A dozen times she found herself standing with her hand on the telephone. She would always stop herself at the last moment from calling him, remembering the intensity in his voice when he'd told her that he wanted more from her than an affair.

She welcomed the beginning of her Christmas vacation. She had planned to leave Babs in a kennel during her visit to Arkansas, but Emily insisted on keeping the dog. Since Babs knew and liked both Emily and Ryan, Autumn was comfortable with the arrangement, and she left Tampa with a sense of optimism. Surely it would be easier not to think of Jeff when several hundred miles separated them, she thought as she boarded the plane for Little Rock Regional Airport. She hoped to return to Tampa in two weeks completely cured of her infatuation for one nearly irresistible doctor.

She arrived in Little Rock just after noon on Friday, the week before Christmas, expecting Spring to meet her at the airport as they'd arranged. Instead, she was met by a veritable welcoming committee—Spring, Clay, Summer and Derek. Laughing happily, the three sisters exchanged fervent hugs, all trying to talk at once.

"What are you all doing here?"

"We came to meet you, Sis. What else?" Summer replied cheerfully, her brilliant blue eyes dancing with mischief beneath her fringe of honey-brown bangs. "Derek and I arrived yesterday and we spent the night at Spring and Clay's house. We thought we'd all drive to Rose Bud together this afternoon. Spring's closed her office for the rest of the day, and she and Clay can spend the whole weekend with the rest of us in Rose Bud, though she has to work Monday."

"But I'll be back in Rose Bud on the evening of the twenty-third," Spring put in, a smile in the violet eyes that regarded Autumn through light-framed glasses. "Clay and I have both announced that we're closing our offices from the twenty-fourth through the twenty-sixth, so we'll have those three days to spend together, too."

"This is great," Autumn enthused. "Summer, I'm so glad you could make it home this year. We missed you last year."

"Derek made sure that nothing kept us away this year. Poor thing's worked himself half to death during the past few weeks to arrange it."

Autumn smiled at the man behind Summer, eyeing his lean yet muscular six-foot frame and dark tan. "You look pretty healthy to me, Derek."

Derek Anderson smiled in return, leaning over to kiss her cheek. "You know how Summer exaggerates."

"My turn," another male voice insisted, and then Autumn found herself caught in a hearty embrace and thoroughly kissed.

"Hi, Clay," she managed to say when he released her amid the laughter of the others. "I see you haven't changed a bit."

"Nope," the six-four, sinfully handsome blonde replied cheerfully. "Why try to alter perfection?"

Spring groaned and rolled her eyes at her husband's immodest quip.

"It'll take us a little over an hour to get to Rose Bud," Clay mused, glancing at his colorful Swatch watch. Then he grinned boyishly at Autumn as they walked toward the parking lot. "That'll give you plenty of time to tell us all about the new man in your life."

Autumn stopped in her tracks, appalled to feel herself blushing—again, dammit. As the others stared at her, she realized that it was the first time her sisters had seen her blush in years. "What..." She stopped and cleared her throat, glaring at Clay. "What new man?"

"The one who can make you blush," Summer added avidly, taking her sister's arm. "Okay, Autumn, who is he?"

Groaning, Autumn allowed herself to be hustled along, though she was determined to change the subject the minute the five of them were settled in Spring's car. She had no intention of discussing Jeff Bradford with two happily married couples!

Were her confused feelings for him really so obvious that her family had noticed a change in her that quickly? she wondered ruefully. Maybe it wouldn't be quite so easy to put him out of her mind during the next two weeks after all.

7

"ARE YOU SURE you're warm enough, Spring? Do you want me to bring your sweater?"

"No, thank you, Clay, I'm fine."

"Well, how about something to eat? D'you want a sandwich or something? You have to keep up your strength."

"Clay!" Spring protested, making Autumn smile at the exasperated look on her older sister's face. "Isn't Gil waiting for you?"

Clay bit his lower lip thoughtfully. "Yeah, he is, but I can stay home if you need me. I don't have to watch football with Gil."

"Please go," Spring said firmly. "This is my last chance to visit with Autumn before she returns to Florida, and you promised Gil and me that you'd spend a couple of hours with him. Now go."

"Don't worry, Clay, I'll take care of her," Autumn promised gravely, trying not to laugh. She was spending New Year's Day, the last day of her vacation in Arkansas, at Spring and Clay's lovely nearly renovated older Victorian home in Little Rock. Clay would drive her to the airport the next morning to catch her flight back to Tampa. She'd enjoyed her visit very much, but she was ready to go home. She tried to tell herself that Babs and her job were the main reasons she was in such a hurry to get back.

Clay looked sheepish but smiled at Autumn in gratitude. "Thanks. You know where I can be reached if you need me." He leaned over to give his wife a long, passionate kiss before allowing himself to be shooed out of the room.

The sisters waited until the front door had closed behind him and the sound of his car engine had faded before giving in to the gales of laughter they'd been holding back. Reclining comfortably on her couch, her dainty yellow-and-white cat curled in her lap, Spring rolled her eyes in mock dismay. "Seven more months of this! Maybe I shouldn't have told him about the baby until closer to the due date."

"Spring, I think he would have noticed," Autumn remarked dryly, swinging her foot in front of her as she lounged in a large wing chair.

"It seemed like such a nice idea to tell him on Christmas Eve—kind of like an extra Christmas present. I should have known that he would overreact."

"Oh, I don't know. I think he's kind of sweet. I particularly liked it when he refused to allow you to open your own presents in case you got a paper cut or something."

Spring groaned and buried her face in her hands. "Oh, God. I'll never survive this pregnancy."

Pregnancy. Autumn shook her head slowly, trying to comprehend the reality of the word. In just seven short months Spring would be a mother. Autumn would be an aunt. Her parents would be grandparents. It was mind-boggling, thinking of the new generation beginning in her family.

Spring had made her announcement to the family on Christmas Day, to the general delight of the Reed clan. It had been a wonderful holiday, and Autumn had enjoyed being with her family again. She'd been a bit concerned that, as the only sister left unmarried, her family would show an even greater tendency than usual to treat her as the "baby," something that had always frustrated Autumn. Yet, for the first time, she felt this year that she'd been treated as an adult, a capable, intelligent career woman.

Maybe it was because she'd been on her own for several years now, or maybe because the two newest family members, Derek and Clay, had never known her as the "cute little tomboy" and therefore didn't treat her as such.

Whatever the reason, Autumn was grateful. Though various members of the family had commented that Autumn seemed to have changed in some way since her last visit home, Autumn had managed to change the subject each time. She was fully aware that she had displayed an uncharacteristic tendency to drift off into her thoughts during her holiday, particularly since Spring had made her announcement. She was also aware that, rather than putting Jeff out of her mind on this vacation away from him, he was as much a part of her thoughts as before.

Autumn had been reexamining her goals in life during the past two weeks, finding contradictions within herself that she hadn't realized were there. Until she'd met Jeff, she'd thought she wanted nothing more out of life than a fulfilling career, a company of her own that would bring her financial security and a satisfying degree of responsibility. When she'd thought of marriage at all, it had been as a nebulous possibility, perhaps when she was fully established, well into her thirties.

Now she found herself wondering what it would be like to be married, sharing her life with a man full-time. Wondering if a mother who drove a pickup truck and strapped on a tool pouch could make a nice home for a dark-haired, blue-eyed child. No, she wouldn't allow herself to get that specific in her wondering. This was strictly hypothetical curiosity on her part.

"Aren't you terrified?" The words left her mouth without conscious thought.

Spring looked a bit surprised for a moment, then smiled understandingly at the younger sister who'd always been so intense about life's roles and responsibilities. "I guess I am, a little," she admitted. "It's not like the baby's going to arrive with an owner's manual. Like any first-time mother, I'll be playing it by ear a lot. But I already love this baby so much. And Clay will be a wonderful father."

"What about your career? Will you be able to dedicate as much time and energy to your practice after the baby arrives?"

"I'll certainly have to make some changes, and I haven't worked them all out yet. I don't know how long I'll be able to take off for maternity leave, for example. I'll have to work with my patients as much as possible so they won't be forced to go elsewhere. Fortunately, there aren't that many emergencies in optometry, so we should be able to work around the four to six weeks that I'm off."

"And after the baby's born?"

"I'll start talking to other working mothers soon about the different types of child care available in the area. I know attorneys, retailers, bankers and doctors who also happen to be mothers. Good mothers. I'm sure they'll be more than happy to offer advice. My baby will be well cared for, Autumn."

Autumn smiled. "You don't have to convince me of that. I happen to think my niece or nephew is very lucky to have you and Clay for parents."

"Thanks."

Autumn twisted a curl of auburn hair around one finger, wondering how to word her next question, but feeling the need to ask. "Isn't it driving you crazy? The way you're being treated now, I mean? Like you've suddenly become a delicate, emotional creature that people have to tiptoe around. Mother hovered over you, Daddy kept patting your cheek, and Clay—Lord!"

Spring laughed. "Yes, it drives me crazy. But I guess that's just part of it. I understand that, as I get bigger, all people will focus on is my belly. My attorney friend said it was terribly frustrating when the jury kept smiling at her stomach instead of frowning thoughtfully into her eyes as she wanted them to do. She had to work twice as hard to be taken seriously while she was pregnant. No one ever said it was going to be easy, Autumn. But becoming an optometrist wasn't easy, either. I had to work for it. It was worth it.

"As for Clay…well, he's just Clay. Part of his solicitude is teasing, the other part is his way of being involved in a phase of parenthood during which the father has very little to do. Fathers feel terribly left out during pregnancy. I plan to keep him very busy for the next seven months."

Suddenly restless, Autumn sprang to her feet and began to pace around the impeccably decorated room. "You and Summer make it look so easy. You have careers, goals, plans—and yet you still make time for your husbands and look forward to having children. How do you do it?"

"Autumn, it's not easy. It's not. But it's what we want."

"But how do you *know*?" Autumn turned to look at her sister, the frustration building inside her as she tried to understand the other woman's serenity. "Neither you nor Summer seemed all that anxious to get married before you met Clay and Derek. You were busy with your practice, and Summer was having too much fun partying with her nutty San Francisco friends to care about settling down. Then you meet these guys, and suddenly you're buying homes and making babies. Was it really that simple?"

"Simple?" Spring repeated incredulously, her eyes widening. "Autumn, it was terrifying! You've heard us talk about how insecure and uncertain we were in the early stages of our romances."

She paused for a moment, her expression dreamy with her memories, then she smiled at her intently listening sister. "It wasn't simple, Autumn. I don't think it's ever simple to suddenly have another person become such an important part of your life. I only know that I feel so fulfilled now. I'm still my own person with my own goals and career, but I always have Clay when I need someone to share my thoughts and dreams and disappointments, and he has me for the same type of moral support."

She shot Autumn a sly glance, turning the conversation abruptly in a new direction. "I think that you would thrive within a happy marriage, just as Summer and I have. Maybe it's the way we were raised, with our parents setting such a good example of two people whose lives are better for being shared with the ones they love."

Autumn swallowed and started to pace again. "We weren't talking about me," she said gruffly.

"Weren't we?" Spring inquired gently. "Then why is it suddenly so important for you to understand how Summer and I justified marriage?"

Autumn moistened her lips and avoided her sister's knowing eyes. "I was just curious."

"Want to tell me about him?"

"About who?"

"The man Clay asked you about the day you arrived, the man who made you blush," Spring teased. "The man who has you asking yourself if marriage is such a terrible thing after all."

"That's ridiculous," Autumn blustered, her arms crossing defensively over her chest. "You know how I feel about marriage. I came close once, remember? I thought I was in love with Steven, but I couldn't marry him. Just the thought made me panic."

"You *thought* you were in love with Steven," Spring repeated. "You weren't. You were infatuated with his good looks and football-hero image. And you were much too young five years ago to be thinking about marriage. You've made a life for yourself now, accomplished things that you couldn't have done if you'd married then. That doesn't mean you couldn't have it all now." She paused for only a moment before asking again, "So want to tell me about this new man?"

"There's nothing to tell," Autumn answered, then had to be honest. "Well, not much. I've only known him for a couple of months, and we've only had two dates. But he's... He makes me... He... Oh, hell, Spring, I don't know. I seem to be obsessed with the man, but I don't know if it's something serious or if it's just a bad case of lust."

Spring laughed delightedly. "Oh, does this sound familiar!"

"So what am I supposed to do?" Autumn demanded, shoving her hands into the pockets of her jeans and glaring at her amused sister. "Jeff's a very traditional kind of

man. One who's looking for permanence, commitment.
don't know if that's what I want. What if it isn't?''

"What if it is?" Spring asked in return. "How will you
know unless you give it a chance?''

"I don't want to hurt him. And I don't want to be hurt,'
Autumn murmured, finally putting into words the fears
that had plagued her for the past few weeks.

"There's always that risk," Spring agreed. "But you've
never been a coward, Autumn. Far from it. You've always
willingly taken on every challenge that faced you. I can'
give you advice because I don't know Jeff or anything
about him, but I do believe that you can accomplish anything you set your mind to—a career, a marriage, a family
I always knew that when you fell in love, you'd fall hard
You've never done anything halfway."

In love? Was she in love with Jeff? Autumn frowned
going cold at the suggestion. Was this how her sisters had
felt? If so, then "terrified" seemed suddenly too tame a
word. Autumn was scared spitless.

Spring set Missy, her cat, onto the floor and rose to her
feet, assuming the stance of a concerned older sister
"Would I approve of Jeff, Autumn?"

With a reluctant laugh Autumn grimaced. "You'd adore
him. He's almost too handsome to be real, he loves kids
and animals, his manners are straight out of an old hand
book for Southern gentlemen, and yet he's modern
enough to clean up after himself and not be threatened
when a woman asks him out. I think he'd be a bit overpro
tective of the woman in his life, but he doesn't seem to be
bothered by the idea of being involved with a working
woman. And he's got a smile that could melt granite."

Intrigued, Spring straightened her glasses and peered
thoughtfully at her sister. "What does he do?"

"He's a pediatrician."

"Marry the man."

Autumn laughed at Spring's flat statement. "I should
have known that's what you'd say."

"I'm not kidding. He sounds perfect!"

"Not perfect, but damn close." Autumn ran her fingers through her hair and winced. "And that's what scares the hell out of me. I think he deserves a whole lot more than what I can give him."

"You *are* in love!" Spring exclaimed. "You're worried about whether you're good enough for him! Believe me, Autumn, you are. He'd be lucky to have you."

"And *you're* just a bit prejudiced," Autumn answered fondly. "You're family."

"True. And I love you. I'll bet Jeff does, too. I can't wait to meet him."

"Could we talk about something else for a while?" Autumn asked weakly. "This conversation is making me nervous."

Spring chuckled. "Come into my room, Sis. I've got something to give you."

Curious, Autumn followed her sister from the room, still uncertain about her feelings for Jeff but somehow comforted by having shared her concerns with Spring.

"STOP LOOKING AT ME like that, Babs. I told you I missed you. Believe me, you wouldn't have enjoyed Arkansas this time. You'd have frozen your fuzzy little tail off." Autumn kept up a running conversation with the dog tagging at her heels as she unpacked, neatly putting away her clothing and Christmas presents. "Besides, Emily told me that you had a great time visiting her and Ryan. I'll bet you're spoiled rotten now."

Closing the last drawer of her bedroom chest, she stretched and looked contentedly around the room. It was good to be home. She chuckled as she glanced at the pillows of her bed, where a large, ragged stuffed bear reclined regally, appearing quite pleased with himself, although his orange fur was a bit mangy-looking and he was missing one ear. Winnie the Pooh had been the "something" that Spring had given Autumn the day before after their conversation about Jeff. The bear had belonged to Spring as a child, then had been passed down to

Summer and Autumn in turn. Autumn had been quite attached to the bear, dragging him around for years by the now-missing ear. On a whim, she'd given the stuffed toy to Summer when Summer had moved to San Francisco. Summer had declared her intention of moving to a city where she knew absolutely no one as a means of recovering her self-sufficiency after her accident, and Autumn sent Pooh along to keep her sister company.

Spring had received the bear at the end of her twelve-day visit to California in March. Knowing that Spring was leaving with a broken heart after a quarrel with Clay, Summer had impulsively sent Pooh home with her older sister. And now Spring had completed the cycle again, returning the old toy to the youngest Reed sister.

"I think he brings good luck," Spring had said gravely, though her violet eyes had sparkled with amusement at the whimsical ceremony. "And he makes a great confidant."

The gesture had appealed to Autumn's sense of humor and she'd obligingly brought the bear home with her. Besides, she thought, patting the worn fuzzy head, she'd missed old Pooh. Babs tended to get restless if squeezed too tightly, though she was definitely the better conversationalist.

Smiling to herself, Autumn realized that her visit home had been good for her. She had her sense of humor back, she was well rested and she had finally come to a decision about Jeff. She was going to make the move that he was waiting for her to make. She'd never be comfortable leaving the situation between them unresolved. Keeping some distance between them for a few weeks had put her attraction for him back in perspective, she thought confidently. He was handsome, entertaining, amusing. There was no reason at all for her to avoid him when both of them wanted to be together—for now.

She glanced at the telephone, then quickly decided to wait a few hours before calling him. "Coward," she accused herself under her breath as she wandered into her kitchen to see if there was anything in the cabinets that she could have for dinner.

She had just closed the door to her discouragingly empty refrigerator—she'd cleaned it out before leaving—when her doorbell chimed.

"Jeff!" She really hadn't expected to find him on her doorstep. The last she'd heard, it had been her move. And suddenly she wasn't sure she was ready to make it. Oh, God, he looked wonderful, she thought on a silent wail. All her brave resolutions about keeping her attraction to him in perspective shattered into mental fragments, leaving her defenseless against him. All she could do was look at him, so tall and tanned and strong in the porch light, and fight the urge to throw herself into his arms and beg him to make love with her.

"Hi." Jeff turned one of his heart-stopping smiles on her, his eyes just a bit wary as they watched her so intently. His hands were in the pockets of the denim jacket he wore with a white Oxford shirt and jeans, his feet spread apart as if he were prepared for anything. She wondered if he were that uncertain of his reception. "I know I should have called first, but when I drove by and saw your lights on, I couldn't resist stopping."

"Come in, Jeff," Autumn invited him, moving back to give him room to pass her. She glanced down quickly at her own green sweater and gray slacks, relieved to see that they had traveled well. She resisted the impulse to lift a hand to her hair, knowing that her French braid was still quite neat. "You, uh, you just happened to be passing by?" she asked skeptically, leaning back against the door.

His mouth twisted into a self-mocking smile. "Every day for the past week," he answered quietly. "I wasn't sure when you'd be back." He paused for a moment, then added, "I missed you, Autumn."

"I, uh…" She swallowed. "Sit down, Jeff. Can I get you anything? I haven't been to the grocery store yet, but I can make coffee."

"No, thanks." Still watching her closely, he took a step

toward her and then another, until he stood only inches away from her. "Did you have a nice vacation?"

"Yes." Her voice was little more than a whisper as her body reacted to his proximity by jumping into overdrive, heart pounding, breath quickening, palms dampening. She tried to keep the conversation polite and unthreatening, though she felt as if she were fighting a losing battle. "Did you enjoy the holidays?"

Jeff lifted a hand to her face, fingertips tracing the line of her jaw from ear to chin. "As much as possible without having you with me," he replied softly, so close now that she could almost feel his breath on her flushed skin. "I thought of you constantly. I wanted you with me at Christmas, singing carols and opening presents. And I wanted to kiss you at midnight to welcome in the New Year. Did you think of me while you were gone, Autumn?"

She was unable to answer with less than complete honesty. "I thought of you. A lot."

He raised his other hand so that her face was cupped tenderly within his palms. "And?" he prompted.

"And I missed you." She sighed, her gaze locked with his. "I didn't come to any great decision about us, Jeff. I'm still not ready to make promises or commitments, but I know that I don't want to stop seeing you. Not yet."

A flicker of emotion in his eyes told her that he wasn't quite satisfied with her answer, but he suppressed it almost immediately. He touched his lips to her forehead. "I guess that'll have to do for now. It's enough—almost— that you did miss me during these past few weeks. They've been the longest weeks of my life, Autumn. I told you I'd let you make the next move, but I couldn't stay away any longer."

"I did miss you, Jeff." She let her hands go hesitantly to his waist, then creep around to stroke his back. "I would have called you tonight. I wanted to see you."

"I'm glad." His lips moved downward, touching the tip of her nose before hovering over her mouth. "I've been saving this kiss for forty-three hours. Happy New Year, Autumn."

He gave her no opportunity to respond verbally. His mouth slanted over hers with a hunger that overwhelmed her, drawing an immediate and equal response from her. His arms tightened around her, pulling her hard against him. Her own arms went up to circle his neck, fitting them perfectly together. So perfectly that she felt bereft when at length he released her mouth and stepped backward to put a few inches between them.

"Have you eaten?" he asked.

She honestly couldn't remember for a moment. Then she shook her head. "No. Not since lunch."

"Have dinner with me?"

"Yes." And anything else he wanted, she told him with her eyes.

He caught his breath and looked quickly down at his shoes, forcibly clearing his throat. "I…" He paused, then started again. "I almost forgot. I brought you a Christmas present." He reached inside his denim jacket.

Autumn watched him with a smile, finding his momentary uncertainty rather endearing. "I don't have one for you."

"Don't you?" He gave her a quick grin, then held out two thin cardboard rectangles.

Curious, Autumn looked down at the tickets he pressed into her hand. "Jeremy Kane!" she said with a delighted gasp. "He's performing in St. Petersburg next month? I didn't even know."

"The tickets don't go on sale until Monday," Jeff informed her a bit smugly. "I pulled a few strings. You'll notice I gave you two of them. You can take anyone you like with you, but don't forget who made the effort to get them for you."

Autumn laughed, knowing he fully intended for one of the tickets to be used by him. Even as her laughter faded, she wondered if they would still be seeing each other when the popular magician made his appearance in seven more weeks. Jeff obviously thought they would be. Still, it had been incredibly nice of him to go to so much trouble to get her tickets to the performance that would certainly be a sellout, simply because she'd once mentioned that she wanted to see Jeremy Kane in person.

"Thank you, Jeff," she told him. For the first time since she'd known him, she made a completely spontaneous gesture toward him, rising on her tiptoes to place a lingering kiss on his beautifully shaped mouth.

Jeff's response was instantaneous, recently banked fires flaming again at her touch. The softness in her face just before she'd lifted her lips to his had proved his undoing. He'd thought he'd be able to restrain himself until after dinner at least, but he was shaken by a wave of desire that shattered any control he had managed to retain earlier. There had been no other woman for him since he'd first set eyes on Autumn just over two months before—for some months before that, actually—and he had wanted to make love to her from that very first moment. He'd told himself before that desire wasn't enough. He still wanted more—much more—from her, but he loved her so much that he couldn't wait any longer. Couldn't find the strength to resist what she was so sweetly offering.

"Autumn," he moaned into her mouth, "I want you so much. I don't think I can walk away from you this time."

"Good," she whispered in return, her arms going around him. "I don't think I can let you walk away this time."

He hesitated only a moment before sweeping her off her feet and into his arms, turning rapidly for her bedroom.

Momentarily startled, Autumn glanced up at him with a fleeting frown. "You do understand that I'm quite capable of making this walk on my own?"

"Yes." He smiled down at her without slowing his long, smooth strides.

She sighed and relaxed, allowing herself to luxuriate in his strength. "Just so you know," she murmured, snuggling into his shoulder.

He held her more tightly, blinking rapidly at the trusting gesture. He was in danger of worshiping this woman in his arms, he thought as he lowered her tenderly to her bed. He loved her when she was prickly and defensive and independent, he adored her when she was sweet and responsive and passionate. And yet, knowing how much of him she already possessed, he could only offer more of himself. His heart, his soul, his future. Whatever she would take.

"How do you get more beautiful each time I see you?" he asked softly, his hands going to her hair to loosen the intricate braid. Fascinated by the soft, dark red curls he set free, he threaded his fingers through the thick mass and then buried his face in it. "Ah, Autumn, you feel so good."

"So do you," she whispered, her hands sliding slowly down his back, palms flattened against the rough denim of his jacket. "But you have on so many clothes."

The sound he made was half laugh, half moan. He shrugged out of the jacket, tossing it to the floor before pulling his shirt over his head. He never took his eyes from her as his hands went to the buckle of his leather belt, nor did she look away. Instead, she lay still, her approval of the body being revealed to her evident on her face. He loved knowing that she found him attractive. He planned to demonstrate quite thoroughly how beautiful she was to him.

Only when his own clothes were lying in a careless heap on her rug did he reach for the hem of her soft green sweater. Moments later the sweater, her gray slacks and her lacy undergarments had joined his things on the floor, and finally they were as he'd longed for them to be. Skin to skin. Heart to heart. As close as a man and woman could be—almost. He held off from that final joining, determined that she would need to have him inside her as desperately as he needed to be there by the time he entered her.

He wanted to make their lovemaking perfect for her. And that included making sure there would be no un-

planned consequences. "Autumn, if you're not protected,
I can—"

"No, it's okay," she assured him huskily, not bothering
to mention that she'd given in to the inevitable and visited
her gynecologist soon after meeting Jeff.

Her breasts were full and straining when he cupped
them in his hands. Her skin was soft, moist, lightly dusted
with golden freckles. He reveled in the feel of it, the scent
of it, the taste of it. Her rosy nipples pouted for his attention, and he flicked them with the tip of his tongue, causing her to gasp and arch upward. She cried out softly,
burying her hands in his hair when he opened his mouth
to draw her deeply inside.

Her stomach was flat, taut, quivering. He caressed the
silken slope, his palm sliding downward, tactually memorizing every inch of her. The auburn curls below were
crisp, springy, guarding her deepest, softest, most vulnerable part. He intimately explored the hidden folds as he
continued to pleasure her breasts with his lips and tongue.
He was hanging on to his control by the weakest of
threads, his entire body throbbing, clamoring for release.
Still he lingered, trembling with need, drawing out the
pleasure-pain for as long as humanly possible.

"Jeff. I need you now," Autumn breathed raggedly, her
hips arching into his touch. "I want you so much it hurts."

"I know, darling. Believe me, I know." His mouth took
hers, tongue thrusting inside to join hers in a wild dance
even as his fingers probed deeper. Autumn shuddered
and writhed beneath him, her hands moving demandingly over him, no longer content to let him guide their
pace. When she took him in her hand, her fingers sliding
boldly over pulsing, swollen flesh, his tenuous control
snapped.

"Oh, Jeff, *yes*!" she cried when he settled forcefully between her welcoming legs. And then she was arching upward, taking him deep inside, and all rational thought
fled, leaving him lost in a maelstrom of sensation. Feelings
too intense, too new to be described by words. Harsh

breathing and hoarse murmurings. Not knowing whether the strangled sounds came from him or her or both of them.

And then she was shivering beneath him, her release triggering his, and Jeff thought he'd die from pure pleasure. Surely no man could experience such shattering joy and live.

I love you. I love you. Dear God, I love you. The words echoed over and over in his mind as he slipped into an oblivious gray aftermath, not caring whether he'd said them aloud or only in his thoughts. *I love you.*

8

IT WAS A VERY LONG TIME before Autumn summoned the strength to move. Jeff was lying beside her, his eyes closed, one arm draped across her breasts, but she knew that he was awake. Like her, he was making a very slow recovery from their lovemaking.

There were no words to describe what had happened between them. Nothing in her experience, not even in her fantasies, had prepared her. She would not have believed herself capable of losing control so completely, of being so thoroughly mesmerized by another person. It was as if their minds, as well as their bodies, had been joined, so that there was no separation between them. She would never have allowed anyone else that much power over her.

No, that sounded as if she'd had some choice in the matter. She hadn't. Jeff had touched her, and she'd lost herself in him. That simply.

Swallowing hard, she glanced swiftly around the deeply shadowed bedroom, illuminated only by the light spilling in from the living room. Everything looked the same. Bemused, she realized that the world had literally fallen away while Jeff had loved her. She had truly lost all sense of time and place and identity. Nothing had existed for her but him. The realization was daunting.

Jeff stirred at her side, and her gaze returned to him. A swath of light fell over him from the open doorway, creating interesting highlights and shadows on his golden skin. He was truly a beautiful man. Shoulders wide, buttocks tight, legs taut and long. Though he was lying on his stomach, she could clearly picture his chest, broad and tanned, lightly furred, angling down to a flat stomach and hard thighs. The rest of him was impressively proportioned, as well. To her utter amazement, her pulse quickened as the memories assailed her. Moments before she'd been exhaustedly satiated. How could she want him again so soon?

Jeff's dark eyelashes fluttered, then lifted. "Hi," he murmured as their gazes met.

"Hi."

"Are you okay?"

She smiled. "I'm fine."

He shifted his weight, settling himself more comfortably beside her, then lifted an eyebrow and reached behind him. They'd been so impatient that they hadn't even stopped to turn back the bedspread but had made love diagonally on the bed. Now he chuckled as he pulled the stuffed toy from beneath his shoulder. "Who's this?"

"That's Pooh. An old friend," she answered lightly, brushing a lock of dark hair away from his forehead, enjoying the intimacy of the gesture.

"A teddy bear? I hadn't expected such frivolity from you, Autumn."

Lifting her head in mock indignation, she scowled at him. "I'll have you to know that I'm as capable of frivolity as anyone. Besides, it's not a teddy bear. It's Winnie the Pooh."

"You do realize that he's missing an ear?"

"Mmm. I'm afraid I'm responsible for that."

"How'd you do it?"

"Summer tried to take him away from me once when she was five and I was four. I had a good grip on his ear, but she had the rest of him."

Jeff chuckled. "I can imagine you as a willful little girl, fighting with your sisters. You must have been adorable."

"I was a holy terror. It's a wonder I survived."

He pulled her head onto his shoulder and wrapped his arms around her. "You turned out quite nicely."

"Thank you. I'll bet you were a well-behaved little boy. Nice manners, clean clothes, an apple for teacher."

"Are you daring to call me perfect again?"

"Would I do that?"

"You would," he answered sternly. "As a matter of fact, I *was* a well behaved little boy."

"I knew it."

"Unless I lost my temper," he continued, ignoring her comment.

"You don't have a temper."

He laughed. "I'm afraid there are those who would gladly contradict you. I'll admit that I don't lose my temper very often, but when I do, I have a hard time controlling it. I'm not at all proud of that fact, you understand."

"You don't sound particularly ashamed of it, either."

"Only because you seem to like me better with flaws."

"I explained that. I start feeling insecure when you seem too perfect. But I think I can accept you with a temper and a soap-opera addiction."

His arms tightened fractionally around her bare shoulders. "If not, I'll gladly come up with some more vices." He sounded just a bit too serious to be entirely teasing.

Autumn quickly changed the subject. "Didn't I hear you mention dinner earlier this evening?"

Jeff went still, then laughed contritely. "Oh, honey, I'm sorry. You must be starved. It completely slipped my mind."

He'd called her "honey" again. She really should mention to him that she didn't like being called "honey." Or at least she hadn't liked it until she'd heard it said in his deep voice.

"Why don't we order a pizza?" she suggested, reluctant to go out again that evening.

"Good idea. Make it a large one with everything. My treat."

"No, mine. It was my idea, after all."

"I asked you for dinner, remember? It was my fault that we got distracted before we could eat."

"I had something to do with that distraction. And I—"

Jeff laughed and tugged her head to his to silence her with a kiss. "Forget it. You can buy the pizza. But next time I'm buying. Deal?"

"Deal." She grinned at him, well aware, as he was, that she hadn't cared less who paid for the pizza. She just liked arguing with him.

Still laughing, Jeff pushed himself onto one elbow and looked down at her, his hand cupping her cheek. "I can tell that our relationship will never be dull. You're going to keep me on my toes, aren't you?"

Unwilling to define their tentative relationship just then, Autumn rolled away from him and pulled on her robe. "I'll order the pizza."

Jeff reached for his pants. "Tell them to make it snappy, will you? I seem to have worked up quite an appetite."

"Babs, you're going to make yourself sick. Don't you know that pizza isn't good for dogs?"

Autumn smiled at Jeff's serious tone of voice. "Don't tell her that, Jeff. She doesn't know."

He glanced laughingly at her. "What? That pizza's not good for dogs?"

"No. That she *is* a dog."

"Oh. Here, Babs, have another slice of pizza. Want a beer?"

Autumn laughed at his foolishness and munched on her own dinner, her eyes lingering on the lock of dark hair that had again fallen boyishly over Jeff's forehead. She couldn't seem to look away from him. She tried to tell herself a modern woman indulging in a modern, no-strings-attached affair shouldn't be having these giddy, tender feelings, but there didn't seem to be much she could do about it just then. She shrugged those stern thoughts away, telling herself that she was sure she'd be more herself the next day, after the wonder of Jeff's lovemaking had worn off.

Jeff stayed all night, falling asleep only to make love to

her again when they woke. If Autumn had thought that the mindless ecstasy she'd felt the first time they'd made love had been a one-time experience, she was proven wrong. It was just as incredible, just as spectacular, the second time. And the third. He left, reluctantly, with long, lingering kisses and murmured promises to see her later.

And then Autumn Sarah Reed, the tough, independent, self-sufficient, liberated woman who never cried, found herself standing in the tub, a steady stream of hot tears mingling with the water from the shower. Because Jeff had made her so very happy. And being that happy terrified her. She could all too easily become addicted to being with Jeff Bradford. And she didn't believe that such happiness could last. There would come a time when she'd have to pay for her pleasure—and the price just might be higher than anything she'd ever given in the past.

"AUTUMN, ARE YOU SURE this isn't too much of an inconvenience?"

"Emily, I'm sure. You said the baby-sitter would be here in half a hour, right? And I'm not due at the wedding until half an hour after that. That gives me plenty of time. Besides, I can get ready with Ryan here. He's no trouble."

"I really hate to ask this, but I promised Mr. Dawson I'd work tonight to finish up those reports."

"Emily, stop it. You've never asked me to baby-sit before, and I've told you several times that I'd be happy to do so. I think I can manage for half an hour. We'll be fine, won't we, Ryan?" Autumn smiled at the child in her arms, receiving a broad grin in return. "Tell Mommy bye-bye."

"Bye-bye," Ryan echoed obediently.

When Emily had gone, Autumn set Ryan on the floor of her bedroom with a cookie and a toddler's spillproof cup of juice, keeping an eye on him as she applied her makeup for the evening. A friend from work was being married that evening, and she felt obligated to go, even though she'd never been too excited about going to weddings.

"Babs, get away from Ryan's cookie," Autumn warned

automatically, her mind still occupied with her plans for the evening. For some reason she was really dreading this particular wedding. Why was she so sure that she would be haunted by thoughts of Jeff during the solemn ceremony?

She hadn't seen Jeff all week. And he wasn't at all happy about it. He'd called every day, only to have her make excuses for why she couldn't see him for another few days. The truth was she was trying to allow enough time to pass for her to get over the lingering aftereffects of their lovemaking on the night she'd returned to Tampa. Finding herself crying in the shower had been such a shock that she'd decided she'd better wait awhile before seeing him again. Make sure that she had firmly reconstructed the emotional barriers between them that he'd so effectively shattered that night. She would *not* fall in love with him, she told herself for the thousandth time. She would *not* allow herself to need him.

She added an extra layer of foundation beneath her eyes to hide the circles that testified to her atypical sleeplessness during the past week. Unfortunately, her body was not as cooperative as her mind in denying her longing for Jeff. Nor was her subconscious. When she'd slept at all, it had only been to dream of him, to replay the most incredible night of her life, to reexperience the feel of him against her, inside her. She cursed under her breath as those thoughts made her hand tremble, smudging her mascara.

She jumped when the telephone rang. She'd told Jeff her plans when he'd called last night to ask her for dinner this evening. He'd responded with growing impatience, demanding to know when he could see her again. Was he calling again already?

Ryan was still working on the cookie as Autumn passed him to answer the extension phone on her bedside table. She patted his sandy head and lifted the receiver. "Hello? Oh, hi, Webb. No, I didn't think you were Jeff," she lied. "My voice was *not* breathless! Stop being such a jerk,

Brothers, or you're going to find yourself sitting alone at this wedding. Right, it starts at—Ryan, no!"

Autumn threw the receiver down and made a lunge for the curious child, moments too late to stop him from pulling her curling iron off her dressing table by the cord and picking it up in one chubby fist—by the wrong end. Ryan screamed and dropped the hot appliance, bursting into tears of pain.

Her stomach contracting, Autumn dropped to her knees on the floor beside him. "Let me see, Ryan." She spread his clenched fingers and swallowed. The tiny palms and fingers were an angry red, already beginning to blister. "Oh, you poor baby. God, that must hurt." She pulled the crying child into her arms and rocked him against her shoulder, her own eyes filling with tears of sympathy.

Swiftly unplugging the curling iron, she looked around for her shoes, grateful that she still had on jeans and a T-shirt rather than her robe. Her gaze fell on the telephone receiver lying on the floor, and she snatched it up. Webb was yelling her name, trying to find out what had happened.

"Webb, Ryan's burned his hand," Autumn told him, raising her voice to be heard over the child's noisy sobs. "I'm going to take him to Jeff. Wait for me here, okay?"

Almost sick with guilt and concern, Autumn rushed Ryan out to her car. She didn't have a car seat, of course, but she managed to fasten the seat belt around him, hoping it would be safe enough. He cried most of the way to the clinic, calling for his mother, his hiccuping little sobs wrenching Autumn's heart.

Ryan stopped crying as Autumn took him out of the car. He placed his arms tightly around her neck and buried his face in her shoulder when she paused in front of the clinic reception desk. "Is Jeff here?" Autumn asked the receptionist. "Dr. Bradford, I mean."

"Dr. Bradford is just about to leave for the day. Can someone else help you?"

"Autumn?" Jeff stepped out from the shelves of files behind the reception desk. "I thought I heard your voice. What happened?"

"Oh, Jeff." She'd never been so glad to see anyone in her life. "Ryan burned his hand on my curling iron. It's badly blistered, and I know it's painful."

"Bring him around," Jeff told her, assuming his professional mien, though his tone was still the quiet, deep one that he seemed to reserve for her. "Sheila, call Kelly and ask her to give me a hand."

Autumn had seen Jeff at work before, when she'd worked on the clinic lights, but she was struck anew by his gentleness and patience when he treated Ryan. He talked softly to the child as he spread a thick white cream over the burned skin and then wrapped the entire hand, fingers and all, in soft gauze. Ryan took immediate exception to the latter procedure and didn't hesitate to inform everyone within about a half-mile radius.

"It doesn't hurt much now," Jeff assured Autumn with a half smile, glancing up at her pale face. "He's just mad. Aren't you, pal?" he asked the screaming toddler.

"There," Jeff said a few minutes later. "All done." He picked Ryan up and patted his back, pleased when Ryan stopped crying to curiously investigate the stethoscope dangling from Jeff's pocket, the bandage already forgotten for the moment. Jeff winked at Autumn as he handed the stethoscope over for inspection. "See? He's already forgiven me."

"What did you put on it?" Autumn asked curiously.

"Silvadene Cream. It's practically a miracle drug with burns. Soothes the pain and promotes healing. In a week to ten days the blisters will be gone and Ryan won't even have a scar."

Autumn was preparing to ask another question when she was interrupted by the arrival of Webb and Emily, escorted into the examining room by the young nurse who'd assisted Jeff in treating Ryan. "Is Ryan okay?" Emily asked immediately, rushing to Jeff's side to examine her son. Ryan dove into his mother's arms, contentedly submitting himself for her inspection.

"He's fine," Jeff assured her, explaining again what he had done and telling her how to care for the hand until the burns were fully healed.

"I'm really sorry this happened, Emily." Autumn twisted her hands in front of her, feeling terrible about the entire situation. "One minute he was quietly eating a cookie, and the next he was pulling the curling iron off my dressing table. I didn't even see him move."

"Believe me, Autumn, I understand," Emily replied reassuringly. "Now you know why I've been running myself ragged ever since he learned to walk. He's so darned fast!"

"They all are," Jeff agreed with a chuckle. "Take it from an expert in treating bumps and cuts while listening to distraught mothers saying they just took their eyes off the little darlings for a minute."

"You scared the hell out of me," Webb informed Autumn with a hand pressed dramatically to the area near his heart. "When you screamed and threw the phone down, I nearly had a heart attack."

"Thanks again for coming after me, Webb," Emily told him, giving him a smile that brought a flush to his tanned cheeks. "I know it's not serious, but you were right about me wanting to be here with Ryan. Mr. Dawson said I could finish the reports tomorrow. He's very understanding about my obligations to Ryan."

Autumn didn't ask how Webb had known where to find Emily. She'd suspected that the two had been in close touch for the past few weeks, though neither had been overly talkative on the developing relationship.

"Want to skip the wedding tonight, Autumn?" Webb suggested, glancing down at his casual clothes and her jeans and T-shirt. "We don't really have time to change now, anyway. I'm sure Carl will understand when we explain what happened."

Autumn agreed heartily, welcoming the excuse. Webb

and Emily took Ryan home a few minutes later, leaving Autumn alone in the examining room with Jeff. She swallowed a lump in her throat and gave him a shaky smile. "Thanks, Jeff."

"No problem." He stepped closer to her, dropping his hands on her shoulders. "How are *you*? You were so pale earlier that I thought I was going to have to treat you as well as Ryan."

She grimaced. "I just felt so terrible about him hurting himself while I was supposed to be watching him."

Jeff pulled her the few inches remaining between them and wrapped his arms comfortingly around her. "It wasn't your fault, honey. I wasn't exaggerating when I said that accidents like this happen all the time. Actually, you were quite efficient and resourceful. You brought him straight to me without panicking, and you had him calmed down so that we could treat him easily. Until we had to wrap his fingers, of course."

Autumn managed a chuckle. "He hated that, didn't he?"

"They all do. Kids don't like having any part of themselves bound. Too restricting."

She leaned back in his arms and smiled up at him. "You're a very good doctor, Jeff Bradford. If I had kids, I'd want you to be the one taking care of them."

His eyes darkened dramatically. "I fully intend to be the one taking care of your kids, Autumn Reed." He kissed her before she could respond, the embrace starting out light and comforting but quickly turning to searing passion.

Mindful of their surroundings, she gulped and pushed herself hastily out of his arms, refusing to consider the message he'd not so subtly sent her. "I know you were about to leave," she told him, preventing herself from babbling only with a great effort, "so I won't keep you."

"You don't really think I'm going to let you go that easily, do you?" he inquired, watching her with amused understanding. "Now that your other plans have been canceled, you have no excuse for not having dinner with me."

She tried, anyway. "I'm not really dressed to go out." Her hand swept the air between them, indicating the contrast between her jeans and T-shirt and his dress slacks, shirt and tie.

"We'll go to my place," he offered immediately. "I'll put some steaks on the grill."

"I'm not sure that's a good idea," she demurred, knowing what would happen if they were alone at his house.

"Autumn, I'm offering dinner. I won't ravish you." His eyes glinted suddenly with mischief. "Unless you want to be ravished, of course," he added.

She stifled a sigh, knowing she was going to accept. She'd been such an intelligent person before she'd met Jeff Bradford, she thought. Whatever happened to all that common sense she'd once prided herself on possessing?

Jeff drove his BMW home, and Autumn followed in her Fiero. She talked to him as he started the grill and put the steaks on, explaining that Emily's baby-sitter had called earlier to say she'd been detained, which was why Autumn had been in charge of Ryan when he'd burned himself. While the steaks were cooking, Jeff excused himself to change out of his work clothes and into jeans. Autumn sat by the pool and sipped a cool drink while he changed. She'd love to swim in that pool, she thought wistfully, but of course she didn't have a suit with her. She was musing over tantalizing images of skinny-dipping there with Jeff when he rejoined her. If he noticed her heightened color, he wisely made no comment.

After dinner they watched the episode of Jeff's soap opera that he'd taped earlier that day. Autumn teased him about his absorption in the story, though she secretly found his weakness appealing. Of course, she found everything about him appealing, she admitted reluctantly. And that was the problem.

"I know you don't like Dr. Noble, but you have to admit the guy's a pretty good actor," Jeff was saying when he regained her attention. "I don't know what his real name is, but he seems ready for feature films to me, though he's still young."

"His name's Lonnie O'Neal, and he's twenty-nine," Autumn replied without thinking. "And you can bet he's got his eye on Hollywood. He'll jump at the right role when it's offered. He's intended to be a star for years, and he hasn't let anything stand in his way so far. I doubt that he's changed since I knew him."

"Since you knew him?" Jeff repeated, turning on the couch to stare at her. "You never told me you knew him."

She realized what she'd done. Her thoughts had been so caught up in her confused feelings about Jeff that she'd talked without considering her words. "I knew him," she admitted. "Quite well, actually."

Jeff's brows drew sharply downward. "You mean you and he were—"

She shook her head quickly. "Oh, no, not me. Summer. Lonnie and Summer were engaged six years ago. She was crazy about him, though I always thought he was shallow and vain. They were both theater arts majors at UALR— the University of Arkansas at Little Rock—and they planned to become stars together. Then Summer had a motorcycle accident, and Lonnie walked out on her before she even got out of the hospital."

"He did *what*?"

"Dumped her," Autumn answered coldly, surprised that so much anger could remain after such a long time. "Took off for New York while she was still stuck in a wheelchair. Of course, in the long run it was the best thing that ever happened to her. She loves Derek much more than she ever loved Lonnie."

Jeff reached for the remote control and snapped off the television. "I don't think I'll ever watch that show again."

Autumn shrugged. "You don't have to go that far. As you said, Lonnie *is* a very good actor. I'm sure he'll make a big name for himself in the next few years. He's already quite popular with the daytime viewers."

Jeff shook his head emphatically. "I'll never like him now. I can't imagine any man walking out on a woman he claims to love when she needs him the most."

Autumn looked away, knowing full well that Jeff would never walk out on the woman he loved. He would be there by her side, caring for her, encouraging her, supporting her through the hard times. And the woman who loved him would grow to depend on him, need him. Lose herself in him.

"Is that the problem, Autumn?" he asked suddenly, bringing her eyes rapidly back to his face.

"What problem?" she asked, genuinely confused.

"Your fear of commitment. The reason you're so determinedly independent. Was your sister's broken engagement so distressing for you that you decided to avoid the same type of risk yourself?"

"No, Jeff," Autumn answered firmly, though she wondered if she *had* been affected more deeply by Summer's pain than she'd realized. It had been barely a year later that Autumn had broken her own long-standing engagement. "I was engaged once myself. It didn't work out because I'm not the type to make that kind of commitment. I started feeling threatened, smothered by the relationship. I have to be in full control of my own life, not answerable to anyone else. I like it that way."

"You didn't love him." There was no question in Jeff's statement. He looked at her with narrowed eyes, daring her to argue with him.

She shrugged. "I don't know," she confessed. "I thought I did at the time, but I was so young. I tried to change for him, be the kind of clinging, dependent woman that he wanted, but I couldn't do it. He couldn't understand why a woman would want to be an electrician, why I was fascinated by wiring and meters and cables, when he thought I should be reading recipes and attending Tupperware parties. The day after I broke our engagement was the day I felt free, really free, for the first time in my life. I haven't allowed myself to be trapped like that again."

"Love isn't a trap, Autumn," Jeff argued quietly. "And a man who truly loves you wouldn't ask you to change."

"How did we get on this subject, anyway?" She all but jumped to her feet and pushed her hands into her pockets. "You know, after all that's happened today, I'm suddenly exhausted. Thanks for dinner, Jeff, but I think I'll go on home and rest now."

"Don't run from me, Autumn." He rose smoothly and caught her face between his hands, staring intently down at her. "Haven't you understood yet that I don't want to change you or tie you down? I love you, Autumn. I want to share my life with you. I want you to share your life with me. I would never ask you to sacrifice your happiness for me."

"Don't, Jeff. Please." She tensed in pure panic at his words, though she'd been expecting them since the night they'd made love. Which was exactly why she'd been avoiding him ever since.

His hands dropped to her waist, holding her against him. "Autumn, I know you're not ready for vows and commitments. But I won't pretend that all I want from you is a temporary fling. I want forever. I think you've known that from the beginning. I think that's why you've been fighting me every step of the way. You're scared, aren't you, honey?"

"Yes, dammit, I'm scared!" She pulled away from him and walked three quick steps backward, her arms crossed defensively at her waist. "You want too much, Jeff. I can't give you forever."

"Then what *are* you willing to give?" he challenged her.

"An affair. That's all we have, Jeff. An affair. I'm attracted to you, you know that, and I enjoy being with you. But that's all it is."

He shook his head slowly, his eyes almost sad. "You're even running from yourself, aren't you? You won't admit even to yourself that you might possibly need someone."

"I *don't* need anyone!" she answered sharply. "I'm perfectly content to live alone."

"You don't live alone," he pointed out. "You have Babs to keep you from getting too lonely. You even sleep with her." He knew that from experience, having spent a night with Babs curled at his feet in Autumn's bed.

"She's a pet. Lots of people have pets."

"Yes," Jeff agreed. "Loving, caring people who enjoy sharing themselves with others." He lifted his hand in a gesture almost of appeal. "You needed me today, Autumn. And I was there for you. Was it really so bad?"

Her eyes widened, her heart jerking with a kind of shock. She immediately denied his words. "I didn't need you. I needed a doctor, and you're the only one I happen to know personally."

"Autumn, if you'd just needed a doctor, you'd have taken Ryan to the emergency room at Tampa General. It's closer to your place, after all. But you didn't even consider that, did you? You came straight to me. You asked for me at the desk."

"Jeff, you're reading entirely too much into that. I told you, I came to you because you're the only pediatrician I know."

Jeff sighed deeply. "I'm not going to give up, Autumn. You see, I happen to need *you* very badly. And I'm not afraid to admit it. You're the best thing that's ever happened to me. Our night together was the most beautiful night I've ever known. Don't expect me to walk away from that."

"Jeff, what do you want from me?" she cried, her throat tight with suppressed emotion.

"Just give us a chance, Autumn. That's all I'm asking. I won't push you, I won't pressure you, I won't even tell you how much I love you until you're ready to hear it. But don't ask me not to see you again. Please."

She closed her eyes for a moment. "I wish I *could* ask that, Jeff," she admitted at last. "But I can't because I can't stand the thought of not seeing you again. But—" she added quickly, holding up her hand as he took an impetuous step forward "—that doesn't mean I'm ready for more than the affair I've already offered. I'm not."

His eyes were glowing with hope—and the love he didn't try to hide from her. "I don't want an affair. That's not right for me, and we both know it's not right for you, whether you'll admit it or not. So until you're ready to take what I'm offering, we'll see each other as friends, give you a chance to learn that I'm no threat to you. I'm willing to settle for that. For now."

She eyed him skeptically. A platonic friendship? She would have laughed if she hadn't lost her sense of humor sometime during the past half hour. She and Jeff could hardly be in the same room without attacking each other. It had been that way from the moment they'd met. What made him think they could keep their hands off each other now, particularly since they'd already been lovers and knew how good it could be between them? Even now she was quivering with longing for him to touch her. "We can try it, I suppose," she offered doubtfully.

He laughed at the look on her face. "I never said it would be easy, honey. But it'll be worth it when you realize that I'm right about us."

Inhaling deeply, Autumn pushed an unsteady hand through her hair. "For the past five years I've known exactly what I wanted from life, exactly how I intended to accomplish my goals. You confuse me, Jeff. I don't know what I feel or what I want when I'm with you. I can't say that I like being that way. I don't."

"I'll give you time to work out your feelings, Autumn," Jeff promised again. "All the time you need. Because I have faith that when you stop running and give yourself a chance to look without fear at what we have, you'll know we belong together. Not for an affair, but for a lifetime."

9

AUTUMN HAD NEVER been courted before. Her engagement to Steven had come about quite casually, primarily because it seemed to be expected of them. If asked, she would have said she didn't *want* to be courted in the old-fashioned sense of the word. Demeaning, she would have said. Sexist.

For the next few weeks Jeff courted her in true Southern tradition, with flowers and chocolates and patience. He took her to dinner, he called her, he brought her whimsical little gifts wrapped in silver paper. He talked to her, sharing stories of his childhood, his dreams, his hopes. His pain. He came to her after losing one of his favorite little patients in a car accident, and he wasn't ashamed for her to see his tears. She held him in her arms and ached for him, wanting so desperately to take away the pain. She would have made love to him that night—just as she would have any of the nights in the preceding weeks—but again he left her with kisses that short-circuited her brain and a growing frustration that was making sleep impossible and her temper increasingly quick.

And no amount of arguing with herself could convince her that she wasn't loving every minute of his courtship, despite the frustration. She was undoubtedly a fool, she told herself every night before going to bed, but she woke every morning with a sense of anticipation, knowing that she would see or hear from Jeff that day. She stopped accepting dates from anyone else, though she refused to dwell on the implications of that. Outside work she saw only Emily, Ryan and Webb when she wasn't with Jeff.

Jeff's work was, of course, very demanding. More than

once during those weeks their dates were interrupted by the demands of his job. She heard him talking patiently on the telephone to hysterical mothers, discussing complicated medical treatments with his partners, discoursing heatedly on parents who abused or neglected their offspring. He was a doctor, first and foremost, a healer, a defender of children. She was a little in awe of that part of him.

He was also a man in love, and he made no effort to hide it. He didn't actually say the words because he'd promised her he wouldn't until she was ready to hear them, but they were in his eyes every time he looked at her, in his touch when he held her or kissed her. She never questioned his sincerity. For some crazy, incomprehensible reason Dr. E. Jefferson Bradford loved Autumn Sarah Reed, electrician, and he fully intended to spend the rest of his life with her.

As time passed, her denials of his intentions grew less forceful. In her weaker moments—and they were coming all too often now—she found herself wondering if Jeff might be right about their future.

And then she'd wake in the night, rigid with dread, unable to breathe, desperately frightened of her growing feelings for him and the heavy sense of inevitability that something would go wrong. She would dream of losing him, and even in her dreams the pain was almost too much to bear. She was beginning to need him, she thought in panic. No, she couldn't allow herself to need him.

And she'd add another emotional brick to the wall she'd built between them.

"You're doing it again." Jeff's words were uttered on a resigned sigh.

Lying in his arms on her couch, she frowned at him in bewilderment, her heart still pounding, breath still ragged from the hungry kisses they'd just shared. "Doing what?" she asked, her voice husky with passion.

"You're pulling away from me."

She looked pointedly down at their intimately entwined bodies, their clothing loosened and disheveled. He was hard and aroused against her; she was trembling with the force of her own desire. "Hardly."

He shook his head, ruffling the lock of hair that had fallen onto his forehead. "Not physically. Emotionally."

She knew now what he meant. He'd been whispering words that were all too close to an outright declaration of his love for her, and she'd found herself coming perilously close to responding in kind. She'd swallowed the words and shut a mental door on her feelings for him, attempting to abandon herself wholly to sensation. How had he known? Was he now adding mind reading to his other talents?

Jeff dropped a quick kiss on her swollen, pouting mouth and pushed himself upright. "It's getting late. Guess I'd better go."

The notorious temper that had been building for the past few weeks, exacerbated by doubts and uncertainties and sheer sexual frustration, finally broke loose. Without even thinking about it, Autumn snatched up a throw pillow that had fallen to the floor earlier and swung it at him. Hard. "You arrogant, obnoxious, unscrupulous jerk!"

Jeff choked on a startled laugh, caught her hand before she could hit him again and stared down at her as she half sat, half lay on the end of the couch. "Want to tell me what that was about?" he inquired mildly.

"Don't you dare laugh at me!" she shouted, leaping to her feet and angrily straightening her sweater and slacks. "I've had it with you, Bradford, do you hear? What gives you the right to do this to me?"

"What am I doing to you, Autumn?" He leaned back against the cushions, arms stretched out along the back of the couch, his eyes kindling with amusement though he managed not to smile. He knew exactly why she was angry, she thought furiously. *Damn* the man!

"You're driving me crazy, that's what you're doing. And you know it! Spending all your free time with me, kissing me, making me want you and then leaving me on the doorstep with a kiss on the forehead. I won't be black-mailed this way, Jeff."

He wasn't amused now. "I'm not trying to blackmail you, Autumn."

She tossed her head scornfully. "Aren't you? Aren't you using sex to make me say what you want to hear? Don't you think if you tantalize me a little longer I'll say any-thing to have you make love with me? I hadn't expected such conceit from you, Jeff."

He rose smoothly, stepped up to her and took her shoul-ders in his hands. He wasn't exactly angry—she'd never seen him angry, she thought fleetingly—but he was defi-nitely annoyed. "That's absurd and you know it. Do you think this past month has been easy for me?"

"I haven't noticed you having any trouble leaving at night," she replied defiantly.

He jerked her against his still-aroused body, his hands falling to her hips to hold her almost painfully against him. "You couldn't be more wrong. Walking away from you has been the hardest thing I've ever had to do. I've taken so many cold showers that I've developed perma-nent goose bumps and I still wake up at night drenched with sweat and shaking with need for you. God, it's gotten to where it even hurts to kiss you, but when I'm with you, I can't help it. Don't accuse me of trying to make you suf-fer, Autumn. I'm torturing myself!"

"But *why*?"

He stepped away from her, shoving his hands into the pockets of his navy slacks. "Because I love you," he an-swered flatly. "And because casual sex with you would hurt much more than none at all."

"It's not casual sex when two people care for each other!" she argued heatedly. "It's called…making love." She said the last words haltingly, her heart stopping at the flame that had suddenly flared in his eyes.

His hands fell again on her shoulders, his grip tight with emotion, though she didn't protest the near pain. "*Do* we care for each other, Autumn?" he asked softly, his words almost a plea.

"Yes," she whispered, unable to lie to him or herself any longer. "Yes, we care for each other. But—"

"Hush," he ordered roughly, pulling her into his arms. "Don't say any more. I told you I was willing to take whatever you were ready to give. As long as you'll admit that what we have is more than physical."

She buried her face in his shoulder, clinging to his shirt. "Don't leave me tonight, Jeff. I…I want you so much." She'd almost said "need." She *wouldn't* say need!

"And I want you, honey. I *need* you," Jeff retorted meaningfully, obviously reading her again. "Just don't accuse me of blackmailing you into making love with me. Please."

She shook her head against him. "No." She knew now that he hadn't been trying to coerce her into saying more than she was ready to say. He'd simply needed reassurance that he was more to her than a good lay. She was continually surprised by this man's vulnerability. And his strength.

She stepped back and took his hand in hers, noting his trembling with a surge of tenderness that took her by surprise. She knew her smile was shaky when she looked up at him, turning to walk with him to her bedroom.

Jeff seemed determined to compensate them both for the weeks of frustration. He made love to her with agonizing slowness, caressing and touching every inch of her— her temples, her throat, her breasts, her stomach, her inner thighs, her ankles. Then he turned her over and explored her back with equal thoroughness, tracing her spine, nibbling at her firm, round cheeks, licking the backs of her knees.

Autumn was shuddering, mindless with need, when he finally gave in to her strangled pleas and ended the torment. He entered her in one smooth thrust, and she rose eagerly to meet him, her knees clasping his hips with all the strength in her healthy young body. His ragged breath and muffled groans were the most beautiful sounds she'd ever heard, and her own soft cries mingled with them in an ancient, wordless duet.

Harder and faster he drove them until neither could hold out any longer against the need for release. Jeff's name was on her lips when Autumn reached that peak, and her own name echoed in her mind after his husky cry. He kept saying it, over and over, as he held her tightly during the descent to sanity. For the first time in twenty-five years she decided she had an absolutely beautiful name. Jeff's voice made it beautiful.

A long time later Autumn stretched, propped herself on one elbow and glared down at his relaxed, contented face. "You sadist."

He chuckled. "Now what have I done?"

"First you make me suffer from abstinence for a month and then you torment me by making love to me so slowly that I lose my mind."

Grinning, he caught her hand and pulled it to his lips. "I suffered from abstinence just as long as you did, you know."

"Your choice."

"No. Not my choice."

She decided not to go into that again. She was feeling too good for a serious discussion just then. Her eyes drifted slowly down his nude length, relishing every gorgeous inch of him. "Then I guess I'll have to make love to you until you lose *your* mind. That'll make us even."

He spread his arms in a gesture of total submission. "Feel free."

Her smile was utterly wicked. "I believe I will."

And she did.

VALENTINE'S DAY CAME a week later. Somehow Autumn had known that Jeff would go all out for that particularly romantic day. She was right. He gave her flowers *and* chocolates *and* an enameled heart pendant on a fine gold chain, and then he took her to dinner at one of the most ex-

pensive, exclusive and romantic restaurants in the area. I
a whimsically feminist gesture Autumn was waiting wit
flowers, chocolates and a gold keychain for him when h
picked her up for their date.

"I've never had a woman give me flowers and chocc
lates before," he mused later as he sat across the seclude
candle-lit dinner table from her.

Autumn grinned impudently at him. "Did it threate
your masculinity?" she asked.

"Are you kidding? I love flowers. *And* chocolates."

She laughed and shook her head. "I should hav
known."

"Admit it, Autumn. You're crazy about me," he accuse
lightly, though his eyes glittered intently in the flickerin
candlelight.

"I think I'm just crazy," she said with a sigh, implicitl
confirming the accusation.

To her relief, Jeff changed the subject. "I can't wait unt
we dance together after dinner. I love dancing with yo
when you're wearing that gold thing."

"So that's why you requested that I wear this tonigh
You wanted to cop a feel on the dance floor."

Jeff laughed. "You have such a delicate way wit
words, Autumn."

Her laughter blended with his, and she felt herself slip
ping even further under his spell. The word "love" hov
ered in her mind. She could deal with that word, sh
mused consideringly. Love wasn't nearly as threatening a
need. She practiced saying "I love you" in her mind, he
eyes dwelling on Jeff's face as he told her a funny stor
about something Pam had done earlier that day. Sh
wasn't certain when—or if—she'd have the courage to sa
it aloud, but the words came surprisingly easy to he
mind.

She reached across the table and caught his hand, liftin
it to her lips in an uncharacteristic display of affection. Je
ended his story in midsentence, his eyes darkening at th

look on her face. "I don't know if we'll make it through an entire dance," he told her hoarsely.

Rubbing her cheek against his knuckles, she smiled at him. "I don't mind if you don't."

And they didn't.

AUTUMN'S DOORBELL CHIMED at just after six on the following Wednesday evening. Stifling a moan, she started to rise to answer the door, but Webb stopped her with a firm hand pressed to her shoulder. "Don't you move," he ordered her sternly. "I'll get it."

"Webb, you're driving me insane. Why don't you go away?" she asked petulantly.

"This is the thanks I get for taking care of you when you're wounded?" Webb demanded indignantly, throwing her an exaggeratedly insulted look over his shoulder as he turned the doorknob. "Oh, it's you, Jeff."

From the angle at which she was lying on her couch, Autumn could see Jeff quite clearly. She watched his eyes narrow at the man who opened Autumn's door. "Are you here again, Webb? I think you and I are going to have to talk."

Autumn blinked at the very male tone and lifted her head from the pillow Webb had insisted on fetching for her a few minutes earlier. It had been a hellish day. All she needed now was for Jeff, of all people, to turn macho on her. Though she'd talked to him several times on the telephone, this was the first time she'd seen him since their Valentine's Day date, a night that had been pure magic from dinner to the hours of lovemaking that had followed. Usually he called before coming over. *Wouldn't you know he'd drop by unexpectedly on this of all evenings?* she thought ruefully.

"Why don't we save it for another time?" Webb said smoothly, his tone acknowledging the challenge in the other man's voice. "Autumn's been hurt, and I—"

"*What?*" Jeff pushed abruptly past Webb to swiftly

cross the room and drop to his knees beside the couch "Autumn, are you all right? What happened?"

"Jeff, it's nothing. Really. Just a stupid little accident. She stopped with a sigh as she realized that she was wasting her breath. Jeff had gone into doctor mode, already examining the ugly bruise on her forehead and the ragged three-inch-long cut on her left forearm that had been neatly closed by a half-dozen or so stitches. "Jeff, I've seen a doctor," she protested when he automatically checked her pupils. "Webb took me to the emergency room a Tampa General. I don't have a concussion."

"What happened?" he repeated, and she was amazed to realize that he'd gone pale beneath his tan.

She attempted a light, soothing tone. "I bumped my head and cut my arm at work this afternoon. It wasn't serious, so don't—"

"She almost killed herself," Webb broke in curtly, dropping into a chair and watching the couple in front of him with interest. "If her reflexes weren't so fast, she would have been at least badly injured."

Thoroughly irritated, particularly when she noted that Jeff's eyes had widened considerably, Autumn glared at Webb. "Shut up, Webb, and let me tell him."

Ignoring Autumn, Jeff turned to Webb. "No, you tell me. What happened?" he asked for the third time, growing visibly less patient by the moment.

Paying no attention to Autumn's attempt to interrupt Webb explained succinctly. "She was running conduit in the mall we're working on, standing on scaffolding twenty feet off the floor. She needed to reach out a little farther than her safety belt would allow her to go, so she unsnapped it." He gave Autumn a stern glance and continued. "She turned too quickly, bumped her head on a metal beam and lost her balance, cutting her arm on an air conditioning duct when she reached out to grab something to hold on to. She managed to catch herself just as one of the guys got to her to help her down, but she came so damn close to falling that my heart stopped."

"My God." Jeff inhaled sharply and rested his forehead against Autumn's for a moment before raising his head to look at her intently. "You're sure you're okay?"

"I'm sure," she answered steadily, deciding not to mention that she was in a great deal of pain from her arm and her pounding head. The shot she'd been given earlier was wearing off, and her arm felt as if it was on fire.

She should have known she couldn't fool a doctor—this doctor, in particular. His blue eyes narrowed, and she suspected that he was taking complete inventory of the circles under her eyes, her pallor and the slight sheen of moisture on her forehead. "What did they give you for pain?" he demanded.

Again Webb answered. "The pain medication is on the coffee table. She refused to take it when I tried to give it to her a few minutes ago."

"Webb, would you go home?" Autumn exploded wrathfully, her small tantrum sending painful fireworks off in her head. "Thank you for everything, but please go away."

With a deep, soulful sigh Webb unfolded himself from his chair and rose, crossing the room to drop a light kiss on Autumn's forehead. "Okay, I'm going. You've got a genuine doctor here to take care of you now, so I can leave with a clear conscience. Don't let me see you at work until at least Monday, you hear?"

"I hear," Autumn muttered, her head moving restlessly on the pillow. Jeff had disappeared into her kitchen, quite probably after a glass of water. It seemed she'd be taking the pain pills after all. Why wouldn't everyone go away and let her die in peace? she bemoaned silently as Webb let himself out the front door.

"Not a very gracious patient, are you, honey?" Jeff's voice was amused as he sat carefully on the edge of the couch at her side.

"No, I'm not a gracious patient," Autumn grumbled, glaring at him. "I'm ill-tempered and foulmouthed and horrible. I refuse to do what anyone tells me, and I don't want those pills because they'll make me loopy and I hate being that way. And I don't like being called honey!"

To her surprise, Jeff laughed softly and leaned over to place a soft kiss on her sullen mouth. "Trying to scare me away, Autumn?"

"Yes," she answered recklessly. "If you had any sense at all, you'd admit that I'm totally wrong for you, take to your heels and never see me again."

"And if *you* had any sense at all, you'd realize that you are exactly right for me. I'm not going anywhere. But I will stop calling you honey. I didn't know you disliked it. You should have told me long before this."

She bit her lip, closing her eyes and trying to fight down a surge of disappointment at the thought of never hearing him call her honey again. Lord, what was the matter with her?

"Take the pills, Autumn."

"Not now, Jeff. I'll take them later."

"Now, Autumn."

Her eyes flew open at his tone. When and how had sweet, smiling young Dr. Bradford learned to inject pure steel into his voice? His gaze met hers, and her mouth opened automatically to take the small pills he was holding to her lips.

"That was sneaky and underhanded," she complained when she'd swallowed the pills with a sip of the water he'd brought her.

"What was?" The steel was gone now, replaced by the familiar gentle amusement.

"I didn't know that you could sound like that."

"It comes in handy with stubborn patients." He set the glass on the coffee table and brushed a stray curl away from her forehead. "You'll feel better in a few minutes. You have to expect pain from a cut like this, but there's no need to suffer unnecessarily."

"So you think I'm acting like one of your patients, do you? Are you calling me a child?"

Jeff chuckled. "You're determined to pick a fight, aren't you, hon—uh, Autumn? It won't work, you know."

She sighed and closed her eyes. "I am perfectly capable of taking care of myself. I thought you and Webb understood that. So how come you've both been treating me like a helpless airhead?"

"Autumn, we care about you and you're hurt. It has nothing to do with your capability or intelligence. Now why don't you come down off that feminist soapbox and admit that you'd do the same for Webb—or me, I hope—if the tables were turned. You would, wouldn't you?"

Autumn immediately had a mental picture of Jeff hurt and in pain, and she admitted to herself that she would, indeed, do whatever she could to help him. Webb, too, she added in a quick afterthought. And, dammit, she *was* acting like a whining child. She sighed again and looked apologetically up at him. "Yes, I would. I'm sorry I've been so grouchy."

"S'okay. I'm a lousy patient myself. All doctors are, you know."

Slowly relaxing, she settled more comfortably against the pillow. "I wasn't expecting to see you tonight."

"I know. I was going to call first, but I couldn't wait that long. I wanted to see you."

"As you can see, I'm not very good company tonight."

"That's okay. Just lie back and let me take care of you. Are you hungry? Would you like for me to make you a bowl of soup?"

"Thanks, but that's not necessary. I'm not very hungry."

"Actually, I am. I'll make us a light supper, and maybe you can eat just a little."

"Jeff, really, you don't have to stay."

"I know I don't have to stay," he answered gently. "But I want to. Do you honestly want me to leave?"

She should say yes. She didn't like being taken care of, as he well knew. If she asked, he would leave and she would be alone. Wishing he were still there. "No," she whispered reluctantly. "I don't want you to leave. Not…if you really want to stay for a while."

He kissed her, not quite as gently as before, though she sensed that he was exerting quite a bit of restraint to hold back even that much. "Thank you," he told her, his voice rough. "I'll go make that soup now."

She closed her eyes wearily, listening to him moving around in the other room, his deep voice speaking softly to Babs. And she was suddenly fiercely glad that he was there, that her cross mood hadn't driven him away. Still very much aware of his presence, she allowed herself to drift into sleep.

JEFF SWALLOWED the last bite of the sandwich he'd made to go with his soup and reached for his canned cola, his eyes never leaving Autumn's face. She was sleeping restlessly, obviously in pain despite the pills he'd insisted she take. She'd be more comfortable in bed, he decided, setting the can on a coaster and rising to carry his soup bowl into the kitchen. She was liable to bite his head off if she woke up and found him tucking her in, but the thought didn't particularly disturb him. He grinned, thinking of her obvious surprise that her irritability hadn't sent him running earlier. How many men had she frightened away with her fiery temper? And didn't she know by now that he wasn't intimidated by it?

So cautious, he thought, kneeling at her side again and pressing the lightest of kisses to her moist forehead. So wary. So terribly afraid of getting involved or admitting that she might occasionally need someone. Someday, he vowed as he slipped his arms beneath her to lift her, she was going to freely admit that she needed someone. Him.

She didn't rouse when he carried her into the bedroom. He couldn't help comparing this time to the first night he'd made love to her, when she'd snuggled into his shoulder—after making sure that he knew she was doing so by her choice—and given herself up to passion. He felt his body hardening in reaction to the breathtaking memories and regretfully shook his head. There would be no such pleasure on this night. But he intended to sleep beside her, anyway. There was no way he was leaving her alone tonight.

He rummaged in her dresser drawers, looking for something more comfortable for sleeping than the shirt and jeans she was wearing. His brow lifted with interest when he came across a slinky black satin-and-lace nightgown among the more practical T-shirts. Not Autumn's usual style, he thought, an unexpected surge of jealousy rippling through him for the second time that evening. He hadn't liked having Autumn's door opened by Webb, but he absolutely hated the idea of Autumn's wearing this filmy garment for anyone but him. Then his eye caught the tag hanging from the back of the nightgown and he relaxed. She'd never worn it.

Smiling broadly, he folded the gown back into the drawer and pulled out an oversized white T-shirt. She would wear the black gown for him soon, but he wanted her fully conscious when he took it off her, he thought cockily.

He undressed her with great care, conscious of the tenderness that almost overwhelmed him at taking care of her. He was comfortable, as many men were not, with the gentle, nurturing side of himself, the side that had led him into pediatric medicine and showed itself every day in his work. But there was a difference in these feelings for Autumn. This was a tenderness mixed with respect, admiration, amusement, passion. Love. He'd never been in love before. He'd been waiting for Autumn, he thought whimsically, unable to resist looking at her for a moment before covering her lovely body with the soft T-shirt.

He tucked her under the covers, arranging her injured arm across her stomach. He winced at the angry red swelling around the stitches, his insides knotting as he pictured the accident. She could so easily have been killed or seriously injured. He didn't like the idea of her working in such a risky field. Construction workers were so often killed in falls or other work-related accidents. He wished…

No. Jeff sat quietly on the side of the bed, looking down at the woman he loved. She enjoyed her job, the challenges of working with her hands, just as he enjoyed his vocation. If she'd originally chosen to be an electrician as a form of rebellion against traditional roles, she'd stayed with it because she liked it. And he wouldn't make the mistake of trying to change her. There would be no faster way to lose her.

Besides, as he'd assured her repeatedly, he didn't want to change her. He loved her. If only he could make her believe him.

She didn't even stir when he kissed her. "I love you," he murmured, willing the words into her dreams. And then he stood, clearing his throat of emotion. "Well, Babs," he addressed the tiny poodle looking expectantly up at him from the floor. "Want to watch some TV?"

10

AUTUMN STIRRED, frowned and slowly opened her eyes. She had no idea what time it was. For that matter, she had no idea how she'd ended up in her bed when she distinctly remembered falling asleep on the couch.

She moved her injured arm and winced. *Jeff.* Lifting her head, she could hear the muted sound of the television coming from the other room. He hadn't left.

She dropped her head back down and moaned. God, she felt like an idiot. Sure, accidents like that happened every day, but not usually to her—not since she'd been a daredevil tomboy tumbling from one scrape into another. She was always so careful, determined that no one could accuse her of being unqualified for her job.

Her mouth tasted awful. She was hungry. And she needed to use the bathroom. She forced herself upright, flinching at the protest from jarred, sore muscles. She blinked when she realized that she was wearing only a white sleep shirt over her bikini panties. Jeff had undressed her, she realized, oddly embarrassed that he'd seen her so vulnerable without her knowledge. Her next thought was a self-reproachful question. How could she have slept through *that*?

A few minutes later she stood in the doorway to the bedroom and looked at the man sprawled comfortably on her couch watching TV with her dog curled on his knee. She'd run a brush through her hair in the bathroom, but she hadn't wanted to attempt putting on her robe over the sore, swollen arm. She couldn't help being a bit self-conscious standing in front of him in the thin, midthigh-

length cotton shirt, even though she knew he'd recentl
seen her in much less. As she had him.

"How're you feeling?" he asked, watching her closel
as she crossed the room to sit beside him.

"Better, I guess," she admitted. "My head doesn't hur
as badly now. I just feel so stupid."

He ran his knuckles lightly down her cheek. "Don't, Au
tumn. Everyone makes mistakes sometimes." He held ou
the hand he'd touched her with, displaying a thin whit
scar across the palm—a scar she'd noticed with curiosit
but had never gotten around to asking him about. "I di
that cleaning a fish after a fishing trip with Julian last sun
mer. Julian yelled at me the whole time he was sewing m
up. My patients all made fun of me for having to take car
of them with a bandage on my hand because I'd cut myse
with a knife. Pam told me I couldn't be trusted with any
thing sharp and threatened to take my medical bag awa
from me."

Autumn chuckled despite herself. "Gave you a har
time, did they?"

"Did they ever. Will the guys at work tease you whe
you go back?"

She grimaced. "My friends will. Those few who don
believe a woman should be an electrician will use this a
evidence of their sexist arguments."

"You didn't hurt yourself because you're a woman,
Jeff stated flatly. "You hurt yourself because you were mo
mentarily careless. I doubt there's one of them who hasn
done something similar at one time or another."

Autumn tilted her head and smiled at him. "Somehow
wasn't expecting this from you."

"Oh?" He looked surprised. "What were you expec
ing?"

"A lecture about how dangerous my work is," she an
swered promptly. "Maybe a tactful suggestion that I g
into another line."

Wearing his most innocent expression and fully dete
mined that she'd never know he'd briefly wished that ve

thing, Jeff shook his head reproachfully. "You should have known better."

"Mmm. Well, anyway, you've almost made up for coming across like a dictator about the pain pills."

He glanced at his watch. "Speaking of which, it's time for another dose. You slept for four hours."

"Jeff…" she wailed.

"Don't make me spoil your decent mood by having to play the dictator again," Jeff warned her with a smile. "That last dose will be wearing off any time now, and you'll be in pain again. There's no need for that."

"I hate taking drugs," she muttered, shifting the arm that was already beginning to throb, to her annoyance.

"This is just a mild painkiller," he answered soothingly. "You'll have to take them tomorrow, but after that you won't need them. Believe me, honey, I wouldn't insist that you take them if I thought they were bad for you. Are you hungry? Want me to warm up some soup?"

"I *am* hungry," she admitted, aware of the endearment and the warm glow that accompanied it. She spoke quickly. "And I'm thirsty. But I can get it."

"Take one step toward that kitchen and I'll really show you macho," Jeff told her humorously. "I'll bring you a tray. You can talk to Babs while I'm getting it. She's been worried about you." He deposited the drowsy dog on the couch beside Autumn and stood. He paused in the doorway to the kitchen, looking back apologetically. "Oh, I called you honey again, didn't I? Sorry, it just slipped out."

Autumn flushed and looked quickly down at Babs. "That's okay. I don't really dislike it all that much. I was just in a bad mood earlier."

She sensed his smile, though she could not make herself meet his eyes. "I'll get your dinner," Jeff said softly, wisely not commenting on her statement.

THE FIRST THING AUTUMN SAW when she woke the next morning was Jeff's smile. Her mind still foggy with the remnants of sleep, she decided that there was nothing she'd rather see first thing in the morning, though she had no intention of telling him that. "Have you been staring at me for very long?" she asked huskily, not sounding nearly as stern as she'd intended.

Head propped on one elbow, he looked down at her, his smile widening. "Awhile. You're beautiful when you're asleep. Did you know that? You're beautiful when you're awake, too."

She rolled her eyes and smothered a yawn. "I don't feel beautiful. I feel like—"

"Watch your mouth," he said quickly, teasingly. "Beautiful women shouldn't use such language."

"Now *that's* a sexist remark." Autumn tried to frown at him, an admittedly difficult task since he looked young and heart-stoppingly sexy with his dark hair tousled over his forehead, his eyes heavy-lidded, bare chest glistening in the sunlight streaming through the bedroom window. The shadow of his morning beard did not detract from the attractive picture—just the opposite, in fact. Her heart started a crazy tap dance, accompanied by the steadily increasing rhythm of her pulse.

"Sorry. How's your arm?" Jeff inquired solicitously.

She moved it experimentally. "Ouch."

"Sore, huh?"

"Yeah." She noticed that the sheet had slipped down around his hips, revealing the tops of low-slung blue briefs. She immediately forgot all about her arm.

"You should take one of your pain pills."

Autumn wondered if she'd imagined that his voice had gotten a bit hoarse. She studied him through her lashes. He seemed to be suddenly fascinated with the front of her T-shirt. The thin white T-shirt was stretched tightly across her chest by the position in which she was lying. She inhaled, pleased to note that his eyes immediately glazed.

She hadn't protested when he'd informed her the night before that he was going to spend the night, even though she'd known he was staying to take care of her if she

needed him. Although she'd firmly believed she was capable of taking care of herself, she'd allowed him to stay
quite simply because she hadn't wanted him to go. Last
night she hadn't felt like doing anything more than sleeping in his arms. This morning she was feeling much better.
She smiled slowly at him.

Jeff cleared his throat forcefully. "Stop looking at me
like that, Autumn Reed."

She reached out with her good arm and circled a tempting, flat brown nipple with the very tip of one finger. "Like
what, Jeff?" she asked with not-very-deceptive innocence.

"Autumn, you're injured, remember?"

Her finger trailed lower, following a thin line of hair to
the point where it disappeared beneath the sheet. "I'm not
dead, Jeff."

He caught her hand just as it was about to burrow beneath the sheet. "You're not making it easy for me to be
noble," he told her, and his voice was definitely hoarse.

"What makes you think I want you to be noble?" She
stroked his hair-roughened leg with one bare foot.

Jeff groaned and closed his eyes. "I sure hope you know
what you're doing, honey."

"I know exactly what I'm doing, *honey*," she murmured
wickedly, and leaned forward to kiss him, her hand escaping his to continue its exploration under the sheet.

"That you do, Autumn," Jeff muttered with a sharp in-
halation, willingly abandoning himself to her hungry caresses. And when she'd pushed him past the point of control, he returned the favor, always careful of her injury but
driving her without mercy to the boundaries of sanity. At
some point they crossed that line together, and the shared
madness was glorious.

"I wasn't going to do that," Jeff accused her when he'd
recovered. "You made me lose my chance to show you
how strong and considerate and self-sacrificing I can be."

Autumn chuckled weakly, still a bit dazed. "You keep
forgetting that I like you best when you're *not* perfect."

Something flickered across his face at the word "like,"

but it was carefully disguised. "Want some breakfast?" he asked.

"Don't you have to work today?"

He shook his head. "It's Thursday, remember? My day off. I've got my beeper with me, if they need me."

"You don't have to spend your day off waiting on me, Jeff. Really, I'm fine. As you should know by now."

"Yes, I know you're fine. But I'm still staying. I'm going to spoil you so thoroughly that you'll never want me to leave," he informed her smugly, climbing out of the bed and padding toward the bathroom.

Autumn watched him with a slight frown. That, she thought nervously, was exactly what she was afraid of. That she would never want him to leave.

Much later she was to realize how strange it was that she could so thoroughly enjoy a day at home with a sore, bruised forehead and a throbbing, stitched-up arm. She'd always hated being at all incapacitated, rarely took a sick day from work unless she was simply too ill to crawl out of bed. But then she'd never had Jeff to entertain her on a sick day before. If she wasn't careful, she thought some time during the afternoon, she was in danger of becoming a hypochondriac. As Jeff had promised, he'd thoroughly spoiled her.

He pampered her, he teased her, he kissed her repeatedly. He lost two games of chess to her, then soundly defeated her at Scrabble.

"A-n-t-i-c. Antic. Write down my points, Jeff."

"Great! I can finally use this *X*. X-e-r-a-n-t-i-c. Xerantic. That gives me—"

"Xerantic! There's no such word!"

"Of course there is," Jeff answered, looking insulted. "It means causing dryness."

She frowned skeptically at him, but he seemed completely serious. "Okay. I guess I'll believe you."

A moment later she protested again. "Now, come on, Jeff. Surely you're not going to try to convince me that 'xanthosis' is a real word."

Again the wounded look. "But it is."

"Oh, yeah? What does it mean?"

"Well, actually, it's a yellowish discoloration seen in some malignant tumors and degenerating tissues. 'Xanthous,' of course, meaning yellow and—"

"Never mind," Autumn sighed, staring glumly down at her own letters—she'd planned to spell "table" next. "I should have known better than to play Scrabble with a doctor."

Jeff gave her one of the wicked, piratical grins that always took her by surprise coming from him. "We could put this up and just play 'doctor.'"

Autumn glanced up through her lashes and dumped her tiles into the box. "I do like the way your mind works, Dr. Bradford."

"JEFF?" AUTUMN POKED at the man resting at her side as a sudden thought occurred to her.

"Mmm?" he mumbled without opening his eyes.

Clutching the sheet to her bare breasts, she struggled upright, wincing when her movements jarred her arm. "Wake up. I want to ask you something."

He sighed and rolled onto his back, one arm behind his head, his eyes finally open. "What?"

"What's the *E* for?"

He frowned, puzzled. "What's *what*?"

"The *E*. In your signature. E. Jefferson Bradford. It just occurred to me that I'm sleeping with a man whose first name I don't even know."

Jeff groaned. "This is the important question you just had to ask?"

"Yep." She smiled enticingly down at him. "What's your first name, Jeff?"

He rolled onto his side, turning his back to her. "I'm going to take a nap. Wake me in an hour, at six, and I'll make dinner for us."

"Jeff!" She grabbed his shoulder and pulled him onto his back again. "You haven't answered my question."

"I know. And I'm not going to."

"You won't tell me your first name?" she demanded indignantly. "Why not? You know all my names."

He gave her a bland smile and reached up to pat her cheek. "I'll tell you my first name on the day we get married."

"You'll...*what*?" Openmouthed, she stared down at him.

"You see, it's like this," he continued calmly. "I hate my first name. I never tell anyone my first name. Only members of my immediate family know what it is. I'll tell you when you're part of my immediate family."

And then he rolled over.

Autumn glared at the tanned width of his back, imagining all the painful things she could do to it. *This* was his idea of a marriage proposal? *This* from the man who'd courted her with flowers and candy and Valentines? Whatever happened to getting down on one knee and begging?

Not that she wanted him to propose, she assured herself hastily. She hadn't even gotten around yet to admitting that she loved him. She certainly wasn't ready to consider marriage. But he could have asked!

"I," she informed him coldly, "am going to take a shower. Enjoy your nap."

"Take a bath," he muttered in response. "And keep that arm dry."

She let out her breath in an irritated huff and slipped from the bed, deciding to take a very long bath.

The water had just stopped running in the bathroom when the telephone rang. "Jeff, would you get that?" Autumn called. "Tell whoever it is I'll call back later."

Jeff reached out for the receiver on the bedside table, propping himself against the pillows. He expected the caller to be Webb, checking on Autumn. "H'lo," he greeted, stifling a sleepy yawn.

There was a pause, and then a woman's voice asked hesitantly, "Is this Autumn Reed's number?"

"Yes, it is," Jeff replied, straightening and pushing a hand through his hair. "She can't come to the phone right now. Can I give her a message?"

"This is her sister, Spring. Your name wouldn't be Jeff, would it?"

Jeff lifted an eyebrow. "Yes, I'm Jeff Bradford. Has Autumn mentioned me?" he asked, pleased with the idea. He could never be sure with Autumn.

"Of course. You're the pediatrician she's been dating."

"That's right. And you're the pregnant optometrist," he said with a grin.

Spring laughed. "Well, yes, I guess I am. It's nice to meet you, Jeff. In a manner of speaking, of course."

"It's nice to meet you, too. Maybe we can do this in person someday soon."

"I'd like that. So how is my sister?"

Taking the question literally, Jeff told Spring about the accident, reassuring her that Autumn would be fine in a few days.

"This sounds so familiar." Spring sighed. "You wouldn't believe the number of times my parents had to rush her to the closest emergency room when she was a kid. She was always breaking something or cutting something or spraining something. Lucky for her that she doesn't scar badly or she'd look like a patchwork quilt."

Intrigued, Jeff cradled the receiver more comfortably against his ear. "Accident-prone, was she?"

"More accurately a daredevil. There wasn't anything she was afraid to try, especially if someone actually dared her. She'd climb trees, jump off roofs, ride unbroken horses, whatever took her fancy at the time. Daddy threatened to tie her up and keep her in a closet, only letting her out on a leash."

Jeff could picture Autumn as a redheaded tomboy, climbing trees and jumping off roofs. He was glad that Spring couldn't see his undoubtedly besotted grin as he turned his eyes toward the closed bathroom door. "Why does this not surprise me?"

"Did she tell you about the time she broke her hand?"

"I know she broke some bones, but she didn't tell me how she did it."

"Oh, well…" And Spring related the story with great relish, making Jeff laugh heartily.

"You're kidding!"

"No. Sure you still want to go out with her?"

Jeff sobered abruptly. "I want to marry her," he informed Autumn's sister, knowing that Autumn would strangle him if she knew he'd announced his intentions to her family. But he figured he needed all the allies he could get.

"Does she know?" was all Spring asked.

"She's getting the message."

"Good luck, Jeff. You've got your work cut out for you. She's scared to death of getting tied down like that."

"I don't intend to tie her down. I intend to set her free," Jeff stated unequivocally. He didn't explain that he meant to set Autumn free from her fears and insecurities, but Spring seemed to understand, anyway.

"Now I really can't wait to meet you. I plan to give you a big hug as soon as I see you," Spring told him with obvious approval.

"I'll look forward to it. I'll tell Autumn you called, Spring."

"Okay, thanks. Bye, Jeff."

Score one for his side, Jeff thought with a smile as he replaced the receiver. He'd known he'd like Autumn's family when she'd first told him about them. He was genuinely eager to meet them. Just as he'd become impatient to introduce Autumn to his own family.

Climbing out of the bed, he pulled on his briefs and jeans, leaving the button at the waist undone, and strolled into the bathroom.

Autumn was soaking as comfortably as possible in the hot water, her injured arm propped on the side of the tub. She lifted an eyebrow at him. "You said you were going to take a nap."

"I thought you might need help washing your back." He perched on the edge of the tub and smiled down at her, his eyes taking in every inch of the luscious body exposed to him through the clear water. "You look good wet."

She didn't quite blush, but Jeff sensed with amusement that she'd made an effort not to do so. No sophisticated flirt, his love, and he wouldn't have her any other way. "Can it," she muttered with her usual sweet charm.

Jeff laughed and lifted her right hand to his lips, licking a drop of water from her knuckles before kissing them, delighted when the gesture made her shiver. He caressed the hand, his thumbs tracing the faint ridges of once-broken bones he'd discovered on the day they'd met—almost four months earlier, he realized. "You never told me how you broke your hand."

Sternly lifting eyelids that had gone heavy, she straightened in the tub and pulled her hand from his. "I told you, it was an accident."

"You know what I'd bet? I'd bet you broke it punching somebody. Maybe you found a football jock twice your size picking on a scrawny kid and you walloped him one."

Autumn sighed deeply and reached for a towel. "You've been talking to one of my sisters. Which one called?"

Laughing, Jeff stood and helped her out of the tub. "Spring. Did you really try to break some kid's jaw?"

"Yes, I did," she answered reluctantly. "And I ended up breaking two bones in my hand. But it was worth it. He was an obnoxious bully."

"Guess you learned your lesson about taking on someone bigger than you."

"Nope. But I did learn how to throw a punch without breaking my hand," she answered sweetly. "Perhaps you should take that as a warning."

"You wouldn't hit me," he replied casually, wrapping her snugly in the oversized towel. "You love me."

"That doesn't mean I won't be inclined to deck you occasionally," she retorted unhesitatingly. "In fact, I—" She stopped, staring at him. He knew she had seen the hope that had flared to life in him at her words. "Dammit, Jeff!"

He lifted a hand to her damp, flushed cheek, almost afraid to breathe. "Do you love me, Autumn?"

"You pick the oddest times to get into these discussions. You could at least let me dry off and put some clothes on," she stalled.

"Do…you…love…me…Autumn?" he asked again, spacing the words deliberately.

"Yes!" she all but spat at him, her eyes narrowed furiously. "I love you, all right? Now if you'll excuse me, I'm going to get dressed." And she whirled and almost bolted from the bathroom, avoiding any actions or discussions related to her unwilling confession.

Jeff laughed quietly and ran an unsteady hand through his disheveled hair. He should have known, he thought bemusedly. He should have known Autumn would throw the words at him like a hand grenade, angry with him for forcing them out of her. But she'd said them and she meant them. She loved him.

His amusement faded abruptly. It still wasn't enough. There was still something she was holding back. He wished to heaven he knew what it was. And why couldn't he just settle for what she was willing to give?

He knew why. He wanted it all. As Spring had said, he had his work cut out for him.

Though Autumn clearly expected further discussion about the subject of her love for him, and just as clearly dreaded it, Jeff carefully made no reference to the scene in the bathroom. Instead, he cooked dinner and kept the conversation light and amusing as they ate, encouraging her to tell him more about her childhood with her sisters in rural Arkansas. After dinner they watched a television movie, and then he told her he had to go. "Sure you'll be okay tonight?"

"I'll be fine," she assured him. He wondered if he was imagining her reluctance to see him leave only because he wanted to see it. "Thanks for everything, Jeff."

"My pleasure. I'll always be here when you need me," he told her softly, dropping a kiss on her forehead.

He didn't miss her sudden stiffening. "Well, I could have managed just fine alone," she told him carefully. "But I enjoyed your company. And your cooking," she added with a weak smile.

"You're not planning to work tomorrow, are you?" Even to him his voice sounded suddenly strained, but she only looked quickly at him and shook her head.

"No, Webb told me to take off until Monday. Even then he probably won't let me do anything except serve as general gofer until my stitches are out."

"Good. I'll call you tomorrow, then."

"All right. Good night, Jeff."

"Good night, Autumn." He pulled her into his arms and kissed her lingeringly. "I love you," he whispered when he released her, and then he left hurriedly, while he could still make himself go.

So now he knew, he thought a long time later, staring into his pool as he sat beside it, unable to sleep. Now he knew what was missing. Autumn loved him, but she still refused to admit that she needed him. And until she did, they could never have the relationship he wanted them to have. There would always be a part of herself that she held back from him. She didn't trust him enough to allow herself to need him.

It hurt. It hurt a lot. Because he needed her so desperately, and he was terribly afraid that he would never really have her.

OUTWARDLY THEIR RELATIONSHIP changed little during the next two weeks. They spent their free time together, sometimes alone, sometimes with Jeff's friends or Autumn's. They attended the Jeremy Kane performance and were both caught up in the magic the skilled entertainer wove with his audience. Afterward they went to Jeff's house and made love, and their magic was even more powerful than Kane's.

But Jeff was still painfully conscious of the restraints between them. He couldn't stop himself from telling Autumn how much he loved her. He murmured the words when he kissed her good-night, spoke them into the telephone when he couldn't see her, gasped them in the throes of passion. At first she'd been hesitant to respond in kind, but as the days passed, it seemed to become easier for her. She could tell him she loved him. She would not tell him that she needed him.

It was the middle of March before Jeff finally convinced Autumn to go with him to Sarasota for a weekend with his family. It was his parent's thirty-fifth wedding anniversary, and their friends were giving them a small reception on Saturday evening. "How will you introduce me?" Autumn asked him warily.

"I'll tell everyone that you're the electrician I've been sleeping with," he returned without a beat.

"Jeff!"

He laughed. "Well, really, Autumn, how do you *think* I'm going to introduce you? I thought I'd tell everyone that your name is Autumn Reed. Does that meet with your approval?"

"I just don't want you to give your parents the wrong idea about us," she answered carefully. "It's…it's not like we're engaged or anything."

"Honey, just because I'm taking you to meet my parents doesn't mean they'll think we're engaged," he argued, though she fancied there was a bit of wistfulness behind his words.

"Then you've taken other women home to meet them?" She spoke lightly, trying to hide that she hated the very idea.

"Well, no, but—"

"So they *will* think I'm someone special to you."

"Autumn." He took her hands in his, staring patiently down at her. "My parents know all about you. They know that I'm crazy in love with you and have been since I met you in October. They know that I hope to spend the rest of my life with you. They also know that there is no formal engagement between us, so you needn't worry about that."

"You mean you told them—"

"I'm very close to my parents," Jeff interrupted firmly. "I don't keep important events in my life secret from them. I'd hardly keep quiet about you."

"Oh, Jeff, what am I going to do with you?" She sighed in resignation.

"I could answer that in detail," he answered slowly, his warm smile lighting his eyes, "or I could take it as rhetorical and go on to the next subject."

"You'd better take it as rhetorical."

"Consider it done. Will you go to Sarasota with me next weekend?"

"Yes, I'll go." She swallowed and tried to hide her attack of nerves behind bluff bravado. "But if you introduce me even once as 'the little woman'..." She let her voice trail off meaningfully.

He grinned. "How about 'my better half'?"

"You'd die."

"I'll keep that in mind." He pulled her into his arms. "I'll just call you the beautiful, fascinating, stubborn, capable, intriguing and oh-so-elusive woman that I love. How does that sound?"

She wrapped her arms around his neck. "Better just call me Autumn."

"Autumn," he murmured and kissed her. "Autumn." He kissed her again, longer this time. "Autumn... Autumn...Autumn."

"Jeff," she whispered after the last lingering kiss, and pulled his head back down to hers.

11

KATHLEEN BRADFORD WAS an attractive, fifty-eight-year-old woman who was still deeply in love with her handsome, sixty-year-old husband of thirty-five years. She also absolutely adored her only child, seeming to be unaware that her "child" was a thirty-three-year-old doctor. "Jeff, dear, are you sure I can't get you anything else to eat? You're not still hungry?"

"Thanks, Mom, but I can't eat another bite. Believe me, four eggs, six slices of bacon, half a cantaloupe and three slices of toast is a perfectly adequate breakfast." Jeff rolled his eyes comically at Autumn as he spoke fondly to the woman hovering over his chair.

His mother refilled his coffee cup for the third time, then dropped a kiss on his cheek. "Just let me know if you need anything else, you hear? What about you, Autumn? More bacon? Toast?"

"No, thank you, Mrs. Bradford, I'm fine." Autumn smiled a bit weakly at the woman with Jeff's blue eyes peering anxiously at her from beneath impeccably styled salt-and-pepper hair.

"Now, Autumn, I've told you to call me Kathleen. Mrs. Bradford is much too formal for family."

Autumn's smile grew weaker. "All right. Kathleen."

"Got any more of that fresh-squeezed orange juice, hon?" Charles Bradford asked, setting aside the morning newspaper he'd been scanning during breakfast, though it hadn't kept him from contributing occasionally to the lively conversation that had gone on between his wife and son. Autumn had been rather quiet during the meal, watching the interplay between the Bradfords, while she'd made every effort to be polite. She and Jeff had left Tampa early that morning to join his parents for breakfast on their anniversary morning, and they planned to stay through lunch the next day.

Kathleen bit her lip in obvious dismay at her husband's request. "No, we drank every drop. But I'll go make some more," she added hastily, hurrying toward the kitchen.

"That's okay, Kathleen. You don't have to—"

But she was already gone, her activities conveyed to them by a flurry of sound from the kitchen. Charles turned an amusingly wry smile at his son, who returned the look with a low laugh. "You've set her off again," Jeff accused his father.

"Guess so." Charles looked across the table at Autumn, clearly feeling it necessary to entertain his guest, though he seemed to be a somewhat shy man to whom casual conversation did not come easily. The successful businessman was lean and fit, darkly tanned, and Autumn could easily tell where Jeff had gotten his movie-screen handsome looks. Only the blue eyes had come from Kathleen; other than that, Jeff was the image of his hazel-eyed father. "How long have you been an electrician, Autumn?"

Autumn glanced quickly at Jeff, remembering the moment he'd asked her the same question. His smile told her that he, too, remembered. "Five years," she answered his father's question.

"You really like it?" Charles looked doubtful.

She smiled at him, amused by his expression. "Yes, sir, I really like it."

Charles shook his head once. "I never was any good with that kind of thing myself. The boy here's just like me. Not mechanical. Last time I tried to do anything electrical, just about electrocuted myself."

"The boy" grinned and added, "I did the same thing when I was trying to fix a television set once. Forgot to unplug it." He winced good-naturedly and added, "I haven't touched anything electrical since, other than to plug it in and turn it on or off."

Autumn laughed softly. "I've been shocked a few times," she admitted. "And to be honest, I *hate* to be shocked. Fortunately, I've never been badly hurt."

"So how long you planning to do this sort of thing?" Charles inquired curiously.

Autumn lifted a questioning eyebrow. "I beg your pardon?"

"The electrical work," Charles explained. "You planning to stay with it awhile longer, or is there something else you want to do?"

"I like my job," Autumn told him again. "I have another year before I can test for my master's license, and then maybe I'll start my own company someday. That won't be for several years, though."

Charles frowned, obviously trying to understand her. "But what if you were to marry, have children?" he asked with a sidelong glance at Jeff.

Jeff interceded quickly. "Dad, lots of wives and mothers work these days. Most of them, in fact. And not all for financial reasons. Many women work because they feel the need to establish their own identities outside the home."

"I never felt that way myself," Kathleen commented, entering the room with a full pitcher of fresh-squeezed juice. "I was perfectly content making a nice home for my husband and my son. And I was always busy in community activities," she continued with a smile at Autumn. "It's nice to stay involved in the community."

"Women used to think that was enough," Charles mused, glancing from Autumn to his wife as if comparing the two very different generations sitting at his breakfast table. "For thirty-five years Kathleen's been at my side, taking care of our home. She was there for Jeff when he came home from school, room mother for his classes, den mother for his Boy Scout troops. Yet I never doubted that she had her own identity."

"Now, Charles, this isn't the time for one of your discussions about the changing times," Kathleen reproved him indulgently. "You have women on the management staff of your own company, and you're known as an equal-opportunity employer. What was right for me isn't necessarily right for everyone, and neither of us is saying it should be."

"That's true," Charles confessed. Still, he couldn't seem to resist one more question on the subject to Autumn. "Did your mother work while you were growing up?"

"No, she didn't," Autumn admitted uncomfortably. "Except to help Daddy out with his store occasionally."

"Autumn's father owns a seed and feed store in Rose Bud, Arkansas," Jeff inserted, smoothly changing the subject. "That's close to Greer's Ferry Lake, Dad. Remember the time we went camping there with Uncle Dan and Aunt Josie?"

Charles nodded. "Good fishing lake. Beautiful scenery, too. My brother was career Air Force," he explained to Autumn. "Retired at the Little Rock Air Force Base in Jacksonville. He and his family liked it so well they stayed. Still live there."

"Jacksonville's not far from Rose Bud," Autumn commented, relieved that the topic had changed so easily and grateful to Jeff for engineering it. "Jeff told me he had family in Arkansas. Quite a few Air Force people end up staying when they're stationed there."

And then the conversation carried on for a time along those lines, contrasting the similarities and differences between Arkansas and Florida and the pros and cons of living in either state. But Autumn couldn't quite forget the earlier discussion, nor could she help but notice how diligently Kathleen Bradford waited on her "menfolk." Though Jeff seemed indulgently amused by his mother's attentions, and made no effort to encourage her, Autumn couldn't help wondering if he really enjoyed all that flattering attention.

After breakfast Kathleen refused to allow either Autumn or Jeff to help with the dishes but insisted that Jeff show Autumn around. Knowing of her fascination with the circus, Jeff took her to the thirty-eight-acre estate of the late John Ringling—of Ringling Brothers and Barnum & Bailey Circus fame—who, in 1927, had made Sarasota the winter headquarters for his circus. There they toured the Ringling Residence, a thirty-room mansion resembling a Venetian palace, completed in 1926 at a cost of one and a half million dollars. Hand in hand, they also toured the John and Mable Ringling Museum of Art, built in Italian Renaissance style and housing an impressive collection of fourteenth-to eighteenth-century art, and then—Autumn's favorite—the Museum of the Circus.

They had a wonderful time, neither of them referring to the briefly uncomfortable scene at the breakfast table. Autumn didn't know if Jeff avoided the subject because it bothered her or because he wasn't aware of how much it *had* bothered her.

They visited his parents again during the late afternoon, then went to the separate rooms they'd been assigned— without protest from Autumn, who wouldn't have expected to sleep with Jeff in her parents' home, either, despite her usual distaste for hypocrisy—to change for the anniversary party.

Autumn had bought a new dress for the occasion on a shopping trip with Emily, who'd also bought a new dress for a special date with her now-steady escort, Webb. Autumn's dress was a soft green, accenting her auburn hair and emerald eyes. The sleeves were long and the scooped neck quite modest, but still the garment managed to be seductive. Made of silk, it clung lovingly to her curves, making the most of her full breasts and tiny waist. She added black heels, then stared doubtfully into the full-length guest-room mirror, wondering if she'd made the right choice.

"You are so beautiful." Jeff's hoarse voice took her by surprise; she hadn't heard him come into the bedroom.

She turned and looked at him, tempted to echo his words as she took in his finely tailored dark suit that emphasized his muscular fitness so nicely. "You shouldn't be in here with the door closed," she told him with mock sternness, ordering her heart to stop fluttering so wildly. "You'll shock your mother."

"Then we won't tell her," he answered, stepping closer. "New dress?"

"Yes." She turned slowly for him. "Like it?"

"Very much." He slipped his arms around her. "And I love you."

Autumn's arms closed around his neck in a sudden rush of near desperation. "I love you, too, Jeff," she told him in a voice that surprised even her with its raw intensity.

"Autumn." He kissed her deeply, roughly, then held her a few inches away. "Is anything wrong?"

"No." She shook her head determinedly. "No, nothing's wrong. I just felt like telling you that I love you."

"I'm glad." His smile was spine-melting. "You don't say it enough."

"Don't I?" she asked without returning the smile.

Sensing that she'd meant the question seriously, he lifted one hand to her cheek, keeping the other arm around her to hold her close. "You could say it with every breath and I wouldn't hear it enough," he told her, his voice deep and so very sincere.

And then the hand on her cheek moved to bury itself in the glossy hair at the back of her head, his mouth coming down on hers with a hunger that never seemed to be abated, no matter how many times they were together. Autumn understood, since her own desire for him was as fresh and piercing as it had been from the first time he'd kissed her.

Long minutes later Jeff laughed raggedly under his breath and set her firmly away from him. "We'd better stop this or we *will* end up shocking my mother," he muttered regretfully. "Are you ready to go?"

"Give me a couple of minutes to repair my makeup and I'll join you downstairs," she answered unsteadily after swallowing to clear her throat.

He nodded, kissed her swiftly one more time, then left

her to scowl despairingly at the tousled, starry-eyed woman in the mirror.

Autumn's concerns about people misinterpreting her relationship with Jeff proved justified at the anniversary party held at a local country club, of which Jeff's parents were members. Jeff was well-known by his parents' friends, most of whom had known him since he was a toddler, and they'd apparently been hoping to see him married off for some time. Though he continued to introduce her quite correctly as "my friend, Autumn Reed," he might as well have added "the woman I love and want to marry," Autumn thought in exasperation. Something in his expression or his voice or his eyes when he said her name made people smile indulgently at her and all but pat her cheek with delight.

"So you're Jeff's little lady," one portly, red-nosed gentleman boomed loudly, making Autumn have to fight a wince. "It's about time that boy found himself a mate. And aren't you a pretty little thing?"

"It's so sweet to see the smile on Jeff's face when he looks at you," a blue-haired older woman told her later. "You make such a cute couple."

"You're an electrician?" one Junior League-type society matron exclaimed in near horror after a brief conversation with Autumn when Jeff had been pulled away by his father and another man. "At least you'll be able to get away from that when you marry Jeff. A doctor is such a nice catch, don't you agree?"

"How are you holding up, honey?" Jeff asked sympathetically as they grabbed an opportunity to converse with each other on the dance floor.

"Are you aware that, as we speak, two-thirds of the population of Sarasota is watching us dance with sickly sweet smiles on their faces?" Autumn demanded in low voiced frustration, holding on to her party smile with great effort. "I have been called 'little lady,' 'a pretty little thing' and 'dear girl.' I've been told that you and I make a 'cute couple' and that you're a 'nice catch.' I've heard about all the women who've 'set their caps' for you, and all the 'matchmaking mamas' who've wanted you to marry their daughters. I've been asked if I was aware of the demands made on a doctor's wife, and wasn't I glad that I wouldn't have to work at manual labor once I have you to support me. One woman even asked if twins run in my family."

"Well, do they?" he asked with a not-very-well-concealed smile.

Her answer was short, succinct and would have appalled all the little old ladies smiling so approvingly at her from around the room had they heard the murmured words. Jeff laughed aloud, causing those smiles to broaden. "So," he managed to say when he'd caught his breath, "how are you enjoying the party?"

In the same deadly quiet voice she told him exactly what he could do with his party and with his amusement, making him laugh again. "I can't resist this," he told her, then kissed her thoroughly, right in the middle of the dance floor, to the delight of their enthralled audience. "I love you," he told her when he released her mouth, making no effort to prevent anyone else from hearing him.

Fortunately for him, the dance ended just then—before Autumn could deliver the embarrassing and rather painful retribution that she was seriously considering. He wrapped an arm around her waist and led her to the buffet table to join his parents, effectively blocking any further conversation between them. For the rest of the evening they mingled, and Autumn was able to maintain her politely bland facade, never once revealing her true feelings as she had to Jeff on the dance floor. Though she seethed at his amused response to her complaints, she didn't know what she'd really expected from him. It was so easy for Jeff to shrug off other people's comments or attitudes, she thought almost resentfully. He was an exceptionally tolerant man, able to talk pleasantly to others despite differing viewpoints. But then again, no one had called him a "pretty little thing," she fumed.

"OKAY, AUTUMN. Let's talk about it. What's wrong?" Jeff demanded when they were alone in her apartment the next afternoon, having carried in Autumn's things from Jeff's car and retrieved Babs from Emily.

"Nothing's wrong, Jeff," she lied composedly, avoiding his eyes as she stroked the dog in her lap. "Did you miss me, Babs?" she murmured, trying to ignore Jeff's dissatisfaction with her answer. "Were you a good girl for Emily?"

Sighing audibly, Jeff lifted the dog from Autumn's lap, set her on the floor with an affectionate pat and settled firmly on the couch beside Autumn. "I'm not letting you change the subject this time," he informed her decisively. "You've pulled back from me emotionally again, and I want to know why. You can start by looking at me. I don't think you've really looked at me all day."

She kept her eyes trained steadily on her hands, laced in a white-knuckled grip in her lap. She'd known this confrontation was coming, but she hadn't been looking forward to it. She'd known it was inevitable since that kiss on the dance floor the evening before. It had been late when they'd returned to Jeff's parents' home, and there had been no chance for the two of them to be alone since, other than during a lingering good-night kiss before retiring to their separate beds. Autumn had carefully avoided his eyes through breakfast, church services and lunch with his parents and, claiming weariness from a night spent in unfamiliar surroundings, had feigned sleep during the drive back to Tampa. Jeff had allowed her to get away with the postponement efforts—until now. He would wait no longer for his explanation.

She'd made a decision during the long sleepless night in the guest bedroom of the Bradford home. She hadn't cried when she'd come to the painful conclusion, but she'd felt her heart twisting into knots in her chest. Still, she had to do it, she told herself relentlessly. It was the only decision she could make that was fair to both Jeff and her. "I think we should stop seeing each other, Jeff," she said, her voice entirely devoid of emotion.

He went very still beside her. "You think *what*?" he asked quietly.

"I'm sure you heard me," she replied, still looking down at her hands. Part of her mind wondered absently if her knuckles could get any whiter.

"Oh, I heard you," he agreed flatly. "I'm just not sure you really meant it."

"I meant it." She dipped her head a bit lower, her hair falling forward to partially hide her face. "There's no future for us, Jeff. If we keep seeing each other, one of us—or both of us—will be hurt. I'd like to avoid that."

"I'm sure you would." His voice held more sarcasm than she'd ever heard from him. She risked a quick glance at his face, then quickly turned her eyes back downward, not liking what she'd seen. "Want to tell me what precipitated this?" he asked with polite detachment. "I was under the assumption that we love each other. As a matter of fact, you told me only yesterday that you love me."

"I do love you, Jeff," Autumn whispered. She strengthened her voice. "But you've known all along that I wasn't looking for permanence. I told you that I wasn't cut out for marriage. I just can't be any man's 'little woman.'"

"That is utter garbage and you know it. Tell me, Autumn, what was it that caused this grand decision of yours? A few tactless remarks at the country club? Something my parents said at breakfast yesterday? Something *I* said?"

The hint of pain behind the bitterness went straight to her heart. She'd give anything not to hurt him. But, being Autumn, she reacted to her own pain and confusion by lashing out in anger. "Stop patronizing me, Jeff!" she snapped, jumping to her feet and finally turning to face him. "Stop acting like I don't know my own mind. This has been building for weeks. The weekend only convinced me of what I had to do."

"Suppose you elaborate a bit." His face was hard, his

jaw set ominously. She'd never seen him look quite so... intimidating.

"I'm feeling smothered again, Jeff," she told him in a rush of words. "Just like last time, with Steven." She had to look away from the expression that crossed his face when she compared him to her former fiancé. "I can't give you what you want, Jeff. I can't give up the independence that I've worked so hard to attain to try to make you happy."

"I have never," he told her concisely, rising to his feet, "asked you to give up anything. I want to marry you, Autumn, not chain you to a bed or a stove. I want us to share our lives with each other, not sacrifice our lives for each other. Is that so damn much to ask?"

"Yes!" she shouted. "It is! I don't know *how* to be a wife, Jeff! I don't know *how* to be a mother. Dammit, I don't even know how to be a lover. I only know how to be myself, Autumn Reed."

"That was all I ever wanted you to be." His voice was low, throbbing with pain.

"But how long would you be satisfied with that? How long would you be happy with a wife who wears coveralls and hard hats to work? Who sometimes comes home with bruises or cuts from work-related injuries? Whose friends all wear blue collars to their jobs? How long before you start asking me to behave like a prop er physician's wife, join the right clubs, cultivate the right friends? Give you the same kind of Ozzie-and Harriet-Nelson-Ward-and-June-Cleaver relationship your parents have?"

Autumn had once wondered if it was possible to make Jeff lose the temper he'd once warned her about. It was.

"How dare you?" he demanded, his hands falling ruthlessly onto her shoulders, his grip anything but gentle. His blue eyes were blazing, his handsome face set in white-mouthed fury. The fine tremor in his fingers let her know that he really wanted to shake her, hard, but he restrained himself. "Who the hell do you think you are to criticize my parents? And just what gives you the right to tell me what *I* want or need from a wife?"

He snatched his hands away from her as if he couldn't bear to touch her for another minute, shoving them violently into the pockets of his jeans. "All right, Autumn, if you want honesty, then you're going to get it. You are a spoiled, self-centered, immature, frightened child. You put on a big act of being sophisticated and liberated, when the truth is that you're a young woman from small-town Arkansas who hasn't got the guts to take emotional risks. You don't seem to be afraid of physical risks or physical pain, but you run like hell from any kind of mature, responsible relationship. Not because you don't want it, Autumn, but because you're too damn scared you can't handle it!"

Feeling the blood drain from her face at his words, Autumn gasped, furious at his unprecedented attack. "Why, you—"

Jeff kept on as if she hadn't made a sound. His jerky movements indicated just how little in control of himself he really was, despite his bitingly concise, low-voiced words. "You're not the liberated woman you want to be. You're chained to a lot of old fears and insecurities that trap you in a lonely, unfilled life, despite your claims that you're perfectly happy alone."

Wanting to lash out at him as he was at her, Autumn tried to interrupt, but he was on a roll, spurred on by sheer rage, and he wasn't finished.

"When I came along, I didn't try to change you. I love you exactly the way you are, stubborn and fiery and self-reliant and all. But you had to start looking for new excuses to break it off because you're still afraid to become deeply involved."

Though temper still edged his voice and hardened his face, his eyes suddenly looked sad. "So now you think you've found the perfect excuse. Not that I *have* tried to change you, but that I *may* try to change you at some nebulous point in the future. I've got to admit it's a great ac-

cusation, Autumn. One I can't disprove because I have
only my word that I would never want you to change
And that's not enough for you, is it?"

"No!" she almost screamed, then made a deliberate ef
fort to lower her voice and regain her tenuous self-contro
when it appeared that he was actually going to allow he
to say a few words. "Maybe you think now that you don'
want to change me, but how do you *know*? You coul
change your mind in a year or two years or five. How
could you possibly know that you won't?"

"I know because I know myself," he replied flatly. "Un
like you, I don't try to deceive myself or others about wha
I want, what I need. I love you now, just as I'll love you in
a year or two years or five. Or fifty. And you're willing to
just throw that love away because you're too scared to
take the risk that everything won't always be perfect. Too
selfish to be willing to make a few compromises to smooth
the way during the rough times."

His words hurt. Deeply. And they made her even an
grier. She wanted to hurt him as badly, but instead of the
insults that hovered on her tongue, a quiet question came
out. "You can say all these things about me and still claim
to love me?" she asked him, her voice strained, tight.

"I don't *claim* to love you. I do love you. Exactly the way
you are. And you're not perfect, Autumn. Neither of u
is." He pulled one hand out of his pocket to run a weary
hand through his hair. "I'm going to spell this out for you
one more time, and then I'm going to leave you to decid
once and for all what you want for us. I love you. I want to
marry you. I want to have children with you. I don't wan
to change you. If I wanted to be pampered and waited on
and catered to, I'd move back home to my mother. I lov
her deeply, but being treated like a five-year-old drives m
crazy. Why do you think I moved to Tampa? I can see m
parents when I want to, but I'm far enough away that I ca
live like a real grown-up the rest of the time.

"I was never looking for a wife who'd subjugate hersel
to me, Autumn. I want a mate, a partner. Someone t

stand beside me, not behind me. I want *you*, Autumn. Only you. I'm willing to make every sacrifice, every compromise I have to make to have you. But only if you're willing to do the same. You think about it. If you decide I'm worth the effort, you know where to find me.''

And then he kissed her, hard, not giving her a chance to respond even if she had wanted to. Almost blind with atavistic pain and fury, she jerked away from him. And he left her, standing in the middle of her living room floor and staring at the door he'd closed much too softly behind him.

Autumn spent the next hour throwing pillows, storming around the apartment in a temper tantrum. Remembering every terrible word he'd said, every slashing accusation.

"He's an idiot," she told Babs, pacing like a madwoman. "Everything he said was garbage. After all this time he doesn't even know me! But he sure as hell thinks he does!"

She paced and raged and muttered until the early hours of morning, when she finally threw herself onto her bed, physically and emotionally exhausted.

And then she cried. For a very long time.

SHE HADN'T KNOWN that anyone could hurt so much and for so long and still continue to function. The passage of almost three long weeks did nothing to assuage the pain of ending her relationship with Jeff. Webb's proud announcement that he was making Autumn foreman of a large, upcoming job should have made her happy. It brought her no joy at all. Only a dull ache because she had no one to tell her how proud he was of her accomplishment.

Webb's rather sheepish announcement a few days later that he and Emily were engaged almost destroyed her. She made a valiant effort to look happy for him. "I told you you were marriage bait," she said in a weak attempt at teasing.

"I guess you were right," he admitted with a grin, not looking at all chagrined at being proven wrong. "I was always against marriage in the past because I hadn't met Emily yet. I guess I was just waiting for her all along."

"You're absolutely sure that you want to do this?" Autumn asked him searchingly, envying his calm certainty.

"I'm absolutely sure," he answered without a moment's hesitation. "I love her, and I love Ryan, and I want to spend the rest of my life with them. So go ahead, Autumn. Make fun of me all you like."

"No," she whispered, her eyes filling with tears. Horrified, she tried to hold them back. She hadn't cried in front of anyone in more years than she could remember.

But Webb saw the tears and took her in his arms. "I'm sorry you're hurting, Autumn," he murmured, his voice deep with sympathy. "Isn't there anything I can do to help? Can't you and Jeff work out your problems somehow?"

"I drove him away," she said with a sob. "I took everything he offered and threw it away. And I'm afraid it's too late to get it back."

"It's not too late. It can't be. The man's in love with you, Autumn."

"He deserves someone better," she murmured, burying her face in Webb's comforting shoulder. "Someone who's not afraid to take risks," she added, remembering all those painful, heated, and oh-so-true accusations Jeff had made. Now she understood what Spring had meant that day in Little Rock. Spring had claimed to know her sister was in love because Autumn was worried about not being good enough for Jeff. Now Autumn understood.

Webb tried to talk to her further, offering again to help, but she drew back, wiping her eyes and forbidding him to mention the subject again or to contact Jeff. She apologized to him for casting a pall on his own happiness and forced herself to smile and talk about his wedding plans, trying to ignore the continuous pain the subject brought her. Webb wasn't satisfied, but he knew her well enough to accept that the subject was closed. Permanently.

12

On Sunday, three weeks after the day she'd sent Jeff away, Autumn took a long look at herself in the mirror and knew that she couldn't go on running. Perhaps she'd been quite content with her life prior to meeting Jeff. But she *had* met him and she'd fallen in love with him, and living without him was destroying her. So now it was time to decide exactly what it was that was keeping them apart, why she was afraid to share her life with him when she loved him so very much.

Need. It all came down to need. She was so afraid to admit that she needed him. But she did. She needed him desperately, and there was no way she could continue to deny that very obvious fact. Loving someone was one thing, but needing someone was terrifying. What happened if she needed someone who was no longer there for her?

On a sudden impulse she picked up her telephone and dialed Spring's number. She didn't even identify herself when Spring answered but blurted out a blunt question. "Spring, what would you do if something happened to Clay, or if he left you?"

Spring paused for a moment, then asked for clarification. "What would I do?"

"Yes. You have your career, you'll have your child in late July. Would those things be enough to make you happy if you lost Clay? I know this is weird, Spring, but humor me, will you?"

"They wouldn't be enough," Spring replied, making an effort to answer honestly. "I love my work and I'll love my child, but Clay is a part of me. Without him that part of me would die. Oh, I'm not saying that I would literally die,

though I might want to at times. I'm sure that life woul
go on, and perhaps I'd even find peace after a time. But I'
never be whole again. Do you understand that?"

"You need him," Autumn said with a sigh.

"Yes. I need him. I need him to make me laugh and kee
me from being too serious about life. To be there for m
when I need a hug or encouragement. To talk to abou
anything and everything that interests us. To make lov
with. And Clay needs me, too. For moral support whe
he's having a hard time getting through to one of his pa
tients, to give him an outlet for the fears and vulnerabil
ties that he hides from others behind his funny clothes an
quirky humor, to share the good times and the bad time
I don't spend time worrying about losing him, Autumn.
choose, instead, to treasure every moment I have wit
him."

"I don't want to need anyone," Autumn whispere
starkly. "I don't want to know that part of me will die if
lose that person."

Spring's laugh was brief, gentle, understanding. "W
don't choose to need, Sis. It's a part of living. When yo
love, you need." She paused, then asked carefully, "A
you and Jeff having problems?"

"We—I broke it off three weeks ago. I was afraid
make a commitment."

"I see. You were afraid that you needed him."

"Yes." The single syllable was painfully expressive.

"And do you love him any less now than you did thre
weeks ago? Does not seeing him take him out of you
heart or your mind?" Spring asked wisely.

"No." Autumn dropped her head and closed her eye
the receiver pressed close to her mouth. "No."

"Then you need him."

"Yes."

"The final decision is yours, of course, Autumn. I car
tell you what to do. But being afraid is such a paltry reaso
to throw away a chance for a lifetime of happiness, dor
you think?"

"I don't know," Autumn admitted after a pause. "I honestly don't know."

"You know," her older sister answered confidently, "you only have to admit it to yourself, Autumn."

"I have to go, Spring. Thanks, okay?"

"Anytime. I love you, Sis."

"I love you, too." Autumn replaced the receiver, then almost immediately lifted it back to her ear, her fingers moving over the buttons to punch another often-called number.

"Hi, Summer, it's Autumn. I want to ask you a question, and I want you to answer honestly without asking why I want to know, okay?"

"Okay," Summer agreed easily. "Shoot."

"What would your life be like without Derek?"

"Empty. Lonely. Frightening." Summer answered without even hesitating. "Any other questions?"

"You were happy enough before you met him. You had a great time with your parties and your friends. You didn't need anyone."

"Wrong. I needed Derek. I just didn't know it until I met him. I may have been happy before without him, but I wouldn't be now."

"But he's so strong, so self-contained. Doesn't it bother you to need someone who doesn't need you as much?"

"Who says Derek doesn't need me? He does, Autumn. As much as I need him. He says I bring sunshine into his life, keep him from being a stuffed shirt. He claims that he was never really happy before I came into his life. Personally, I don't intend to argue with him. I'd rather believe him. Now do you want to tell me what this is all about?"

Autumn smiled tremulously. "I'm in love, Summer, and I'm scared witless about it. I guess I was just hoping that those of you who've been there and survived could pass along a few pointers."

"You want my advice about love? Grab on to it and hang on to it with all your strength. Because when it comes right down to it, there's nothing in life that's more valu-

able. And it's too rare to pass up once you find it. Does that
make sense?"

"Oh, yes, it makes sense." Autumn pushed her hair out
of her face and sent a smile through the telephone lines to
her sister on the opposite side of the country. "I love you
Summer."

"I love you, too," Summer replied, surprised and
pleased with Autumn's infrequent expression of affection
"Let me know how this comes out, will you?"

"I will. Give Derek a kiss for me. I'll talk to you again
soon."

She spent the next hour on her couch, deep in thought
barely moving. Babs tried a few times to capture her atten
tion, then gave up and curled up at her feet for a nap. Au
tumn thought about women she knew who hadn't been
afraid of the risks—or if they had, they'd decided not to le
their fear keep them from reaching for their happiness
Autumn's mother had chosen to give up teaching to raise
her three daughters and sometimes help out in the store
Spring had combined a career in optometry with the re
sponsibilities of being a wife and mother. Summer would
finish her education soon and begin a new career but stil
looked forward to starting a family with her beloved, sup
portive husband. Jeff's mother seemed to truly enjoy tak
ing care of her husband and her son, when he would allow
her to do so. Jeff's friend, Pam, was a brilliant surgeon
whose love for her accountant husband and baby daugh
ter were evident to anyone who spent even a few minute
in her company.

Each of those diverse, intelligent women had deliber
ately chosen her path in life and had made whatever ad
justments necessary to follow that path. No one had tried
to tell Autumn that it was always easy, or that there hadn
been hard times, but all of them seemed content with thei
choices.

Autumn could marry Jeff and continue her career. H
wouldn't ask her to give up her work or her plans for th
future. He'd be right beside her, offering support whe

she wanted it, giving her freedom when she needed it. She finally allowed herself to acknowledge that it wasn't fear of losing her career or even her independence that had caused her to send him away. It was, after all, only a job.

So the crux of the problem was this need thing. And still she hadn't worked it all out. Some tiny detail was niggling at her, haunting her. Holding her back.

So deeply lost in thought was she that the telephone's strident ring made her jump and swear. She stared at it for a moment, wondering if it was Jeff. Just as she'd dreaded—and hoped—it would be Jeff every time someone had called during the past three weeks. "Hello?"

"Autumn? It's Pam Cochran."

Surprised, Autumn blinked and sat up straighter on the couch. "Hi, Pam, what can I do for you?"

"I'm calling about Jeff."

"Jeff?" Her heart suddenly stopped. "Is anything wrong? He's okay, isn't he?"

"No, he's not okay," Pam answered gravely, frightening Autumn even more. Her mind filled with all sorts of horrible possibilities as she broke into a cold sweat. And then Pam's words made her close her eyes in sheer relief. "He's miserable," Pam said flatly. "I've known him for a long time and I've never seen him suffer like this. What the hell is wrong with you?"

Light-headed with gratitude that nothing had happened to Jeff, Autumn chuckled weakly. "That's what I've been asking myself for a long time now, Pam."

"Look, I know this is none of my business, and he'd strangle me if he knew I was calling you, but I'm crazy about that guy and it's tearing me apart to see him this way. I'd stay out of it somehow if I hadn't seen the way you looked at him while y'all were together. I know you love him."

"Yes, Pam. I love him."

"So what's the problem? He needs you, Autumn. Why don't you go to him and put him out of his misery?"

He needs you.

Autumn promised Pam that she would make every ef
fort to mend the damage to her relationship with Jeff
thanked her for calling and ended the call as soon as she
could, her mind whirling with her revelation.

He needs you.

Clay needs me, too, Spring had said, not a trace of doubt
in her voice.

Derek needs me as much as I need him, Summer had confi
dently assured her confused younger sister.

He needs you, Pam had said.

And now Autumn knew why she'd been afraid. Wh
she was still afraid. But suddenly she knew she had to try
Because she loved and needed Jeff Bradford.

AUTUMN HOPPED NIMBLY out of her Fiero, tugging the brir
of her battered brown baseball cap low over her oversize
sunglasses to shade her face from the Sunday-afternoo
sun. Her auburn hair bounced defiantly around the shou
ders of her yellow knit top as she strode briskly toward th
front door of Jeff's house. She punched the doorbell with
slender, short-nailed finger, listening with satisfaction a
the bell chimed inside.

The man who answered the door was as beautiful a
ever, but three long, lonely weeks had left their mark o
his handsome face. For the first time since she'd met hir
almost six months earlier, Jeff Bradford looked every yea
of his age and more. There were lines around his blue eye
that had not been there before, a grim cast to the mout
that had always smiled so easily for her.

She had hurt him deeply.

"Autumn!" Even his voice was different when he u
tered her name, raw, hoarse, thick.

Autumn reached up to remove her sunglasses, revea
ing her eyes to him and hoping that he could read the lo
brimming in them. "I wouldn't blame you if you sent m
away," she told him quietly, her own voice rather wea
"But I'm praying that you won't."

His knuckles were white on the edge of the door. "I guess…that depends on why you're here."

"I'm here to tell you that I've done what you asked. I thought about us, about what I wanted for us. And I've decided that I want it all. That you're worth the risks," she told him boldly, her gaze locked with his. "Please tell me you haven't changed your mind."

His eyes closed for a moment, then opened to bore into her. "Come in." He stepped back to allow her to pass him, being very careful not to touch her as she walked by. She longed to reach out to him, but she hadn't expected him to make it that easy for her. She understood. He had to be sure this time that she wouldn't hurt him again.

In his den she pulled off her cap and dropped it and her sunglasses on a table before turning bravely to face him. "I love you, Jeff," she told him before he could say anything.

Something that might have been hope rippled across his drawn face, but still he hesitated. "And?"

"And…I need you," she told him steadily. "I need you so desperately. Won't you please give me another chance?"

In answer he opened his arms, his beautiful face lighting with the smile that she had craved for the past three unhappy weeks. Autumn flung herself into those welcoming arms, her own going tightly around his neck.

"I'm so sorry, Jeff. So very sorry. I was an idiot."

"Yes, you were," Jeff agreed lovingly, pressing kisses along the curve of her cheek. "I missed you so much. I was afraid that you would manage to put me out of your life for good, that you'd never allow yourself to admit that you needed me in any way."

"I need you in every way, darling. And I'm not afraid to admit it now." She smiled tremulously up at him, her fingers stroking the silky dark hair at the back of his neck.

His eyes flared. "You've never called me that before. I like it."

"I'm glad." She tugged his head down to hers, and at

last his mouth was on hers again. Their kiss was long and sweet and infinitely loving.

"Tell me why you were so afraid," Jeff urged her long minutes later, holding her close as they sat on his wood framed couch. "Tell me what made you change your mind."

Autumn cuddled closer to his shoulder, one hand around his waist, the other stroking his chest. Desire was there, just beneath the surface of their contentment, but for now they needed this time to hold each other and talk. Time to heal the wounds they'd inflicted on each other.

"I don't know if I can put it into words," she murmured thoughtfully, trying to compose an answer that would make him understand the turmoil she'd gone through during the months since she'd met him. She tilted her head back against his arm to look at him as she spoke. "At first I was afraid of having to give up the freedom I've earned by being independent. I wasn't sure what I'd have to give up to take on the new role you offered me."

"I understand up to that point." Jeff stroked her arm almost absently, fingers lingering at the pink scar left from her accident some two months earlier. "Sex roles are confusing and frustrating, particularly the ones that are obsolete and ridiculously restrictive. Believe me, I know."

Autumn lifted a questioning eyebrow.

"I was always a guy who liked little kids," he explained with a slight smile. "When I was in high school, playing football and doing other macho things, I was still a sucker for babies and toddlers. You never saw me without a few younger kids tagging at my heels, imitating everything I did, taking everything I said as gospel. I loved the adulation, of course," he admitted with gentle self-mockery, "but more than that, I was fascinated by the way their minds developed and interpreted things. And I couldn't stand it when one of them got hurt."

"So you became a pediatrician."

"Yeah. It's perfectly acceptable now for me to like kids, but at the time I took a lot of ribbing. The other guys my age couldn't understand my affection for the little yard-apes, as they called them. It was okay for teenage girls to like children, but not teenage boys."

"I hadn't thought of that," Autumn admitted, struck by his words. He *did* understand. At least as much as a man could understand a woman's rebellion against society's restrictions.

"What I *don't* understand," Jeff continued, "is why I brought out such panic in you. From the beginning I accepted your career and never made demands on you to change. Couldn't you tell that I wasn't a rigid traditionalist, despite my traditional upbringing? After all, your own background was pretty traditional, and look at the way you turned out."

"I know. I was using that for an excuse," Autumn confessed, hanging her head. "I didn't realize it until the past few weeks. I wasn't really afraid of loving you or of you trying to change me. I was afraid of needing you."

He nodded. "I figured that out after you hurt yourself and you were so careful to point out that you would have been just fine without me. Were you afraid that you'd grow to need me and I'd let you down?"

"That's it, I guess. At first, I thought my fear of need was another facet of the man-woman thing. You know, not wanting to be one of those clinging, dependent women who needs a strong, dependable man to make her whole, to center her life upon. And maybe that *was* part of it. But today I finally understood what I was really afraid of."

"Which was?" he asked, going very still.

She squirmed around on the couch until she was facing him directly. "Don't you see? I didn't want to need you because I couldn't imagine that you really needed me." She raised a hand to silence him when he would have spoken impetuously. "No, listen, Jeff. You're handsome, popular, a successful pediatrician. You have many friends, a close family, a beautiful home. You could have any woman you wanted with very little effort. You seemed completely at ease with yourself and your life, happy and content. I couldn't see you needing me the way I was beginning to need you because I couldn't see anything missing in your life, any void I could fill.''

Jeff had flushed uncomfortably at her matter-of-fact description of him. Now he shook his head in disbelief. ''Really, Autumn.''

She giggled a little at his embarrassment. ''Oh, Jeff, I didn't realize that I had such an inferiority complex until I met you. I couldn't understand what a man like you could see in a semigrown-up tomboy. I was terrified that, just about the time I allowed myself to admit my love and my need for you, you'd wise up and decide that I had nothing to offer you.''

''You *are* an idiot,'' Jeff told her in mock disgust, his gaze caressing her rueful face.

''I know that now. I've done a lot of thinking for the past few weeks. Today I started remembering a few times when you *did* need me. The time before Christmas when Julian paged you to tell you that the little girl with CF was dying. I didn't know how to reach out to you then, but I wanted to so badly. The time you lost the little boy in the car accident. The time you were up forty-eight hours straight and needed me to make dinner for us and then make sure you were allowed to sleep uninterrupted for eight full hours. The time your head hurt and I rubbed your temples for you. And I thought of all the many times I've needed you during the past few months and you were there for me. And I realized that *I* was the one who'd walked out. You'd allowed yourself to need me, and I wasn't there for you. I'm so very sorry, Jeff.''

The last words were spoken in a thin whisper. Autumn's eyes had filled with tears as she thought again of how deeply she'd hurt him, how deeply she'd hurt both of them with her insecurities. One of those tears escaped to trickle down her cheek. She swiped impatiently at it.

Jeff caught her close, shaken by the tears. He'd never seen her cry, he realized in near awe. She'd never allowed herself to be that vulnerable to him before. Now he knew that everything was really going to work out. She was offering him all of herself. Just as she already possessed all of him.

"I love you, Autumn. I love you so much. And God knows that I need you like I've never needed anything before. I've always needed you. Don't ever send me away again. Please."

"No," she murmured brokenly, her damp cheek pressed tightly to his. "Never again. Do we have to talk anymore now, Jeff?"

"No, honey. No more talk for now." He stood abruptly, his movements sure and smooth as he lifted her high in his arms. "Let me show you how much I love you. How much I need you."

"Yes," she answered trustingly, smiling through her tears. "Show me, darling."

And though both of them knew she was strong and healthy and fully capable of walking, he carried her to his bedroom as if she were a rare, precious treasure. And she allowed him to do so, and gloried in the gesture, because she felt the same way about him.

It took several minutes to shed their clothing because both of them were trembling so hard that their fingers were clumsy and awkward. Jeff swore beneath his breath, then laughed shakily when the zipper of her jeans refused to cooperate. "Maybe you'd better do this," he told her unsteadily.

"Maybe I'd better," she agreed in tender humor and swiftly removed her remaining garments. Then she held out her arms to the beautiful, strong, vulnerable man that she loved.

Jeff kissed her deeply, falling with her to the bed, his hands feverishly reacquainting themselves with the soft curves he'd missed so desperately during the past weeks, that he'd been so afraid he'd never hold in his arms again. His breathing was ragged, his heart thudding frantically, and he had to pause and take a long, deep breath in an attempt to regain control. He felt like a nervous teenager, overwhelmed by the depths of his needs and emotions. He wanted to go slowly, to love her with skill and patience, to take her again and again to ecstasy before allowing himself his own relief.

But then Autumn's hands were on him, caressing, demanding, and he groaned and drove himself deeply into her, fiercely welcoming her cry of pleasure. Skill and patience were abandoned, control willingly relinquished, and they loved each other with all the passion and hunger inside them. Kissing, arching, rolling, panting. Gasping out their love and their pleasure. And when they reached the point where neither could postpone their climax, they shuddered together, their delirious cries echoing from the evening-shadowed corners of the room.

And then there was silence, except for their gradually slowing breathing. The shadows lengthened, spreading like a warm, soft blanket over the glistening, damp bodies entwined in the middle of the big bed. Peace was a living, palpable entity in the quiet room, guarding the doors against the outside world until the recuperating lovers were ready to face it. Together.

A very long time later—hours? days? eons?—Jeff's voice inserted itself smoothly into the silence. "Marry me, Autumn."

She smiled into his shoulder and wrapped herself more tightly around him. "Yes."

Nothing more. He held her even closer, his cheek against her hair, and together they drifted into the restful sleep they'd both been denied during the past three lonely weeks, knowing they'd wake still wrapped in each other's arms.

Epilogue

"I NEVER THOUGHT I'd see this," Summer Anderson said with an incredulous shake of her head, her short, honey-brown hair accented with a spray of miniature flowers, her brilliant blue eyes accentuated by her deep blue brides-maid's dress.

"What makes *me* mad is that she had to let out the bod-ice of the dress," Spring agreed solemnly, the violet dress that matched her eyes styled to allow for her seven-month-plus pregnancy. She'd worn her silvery-blond hair up, and a spray of flowers identical to the ones Summer wore was clipped to one side. "Except for a slight differ-ence in length, mother's wedding gown fit *us* just fine."

"Don't pay any attention to them, honey. You look just beautiful," Lila Reed told her youngest daughter with a smile as she straightened the antique-lace wedding gown Autumn had just slipped into. The dress clung snugly to Autumn's nice curves and fell to just above her ankles. Its tea-length design had made it quite convenient for all three sisters, who ranged in height from Summer's scant five-feet-four to Spring's five-seven.

"I feel kind of strange," Autumn admitted, observing herself in the mirror of the Bradford's guest room. The woman who stared back at her was a pink-cheeked, dewy-eyed bride, her auburn hair twisted into a sleek roll adorned with flowers. She looked small and feminine in the delicate lace gown. Autumn thought longingly of her brown baseball cap and blue jeans.

She and Jeff had chosen to be married in the living room of his parents' Sarasota home on this Saturday afternoon in May. The guest list was small, somewhat to Kathleen's disappointment. Kathleen had wanted an enormous church wedding for her only son, to be attended by everyone she knew. Because the exchange of vows would be such a deeply private moment for Autumn, she hadn't been able to comply with that request, but they'd compromised with this intimate, very traditional ceremony to be followed by a reception at the country club where the Bradfords had celebrated their wedding anniversary a couple of months earlier. Jeff and Autumn had agreed to attend the reception, allow Kathleen to show them off a bit and then slip quietly away for a week-long honeymoon in the Bahamas, as neither of them could take off any longer than that from their jobs.

"Daddy's waiting for you in the hallway," Spring told Autumn, interrupting her bemused examination of her reflection. "He's been grumbling all day about having to go through this again, but he's really delighted that he's going to have the chance to give away his remaining daughter."

Autumn muttered something about "archaic, sexist traditions," but Spring only laughed and hugged her, careful not to muss her. "You look happy, Autumn. And Jeff is as wonderful as I'd expected him to be. I'm so glad you managed to work out your problems."

"Thanks, in part, to you," Autumn answered gratefully, returning the hug. "You were so patient with me when I called you in hysteria."

"You'd have made the right decision without me," Spring answered confidently. "But I was happy to help."

Autumn patted Spring's protruding stomach. "You've got yourself a terrific mother, kid," she informed her soon-to-be niece or nephew.

"You'll make a terrific mother yourself," Spring returned, hinting broadly.

"Yeah," Autumn agreed happily. "I think I will."

Summer stepped up to claim her own hug, and then it was time for the wedding to begin.

Her hand held snugly in the crook of her father's arm, Autumn paused in the doorway of the flower-bedecked living room, taking a deep breath that strained the already-snug bodice of her mother's wedding gown. Her eyes rapidly scanned the small crowd of witnesses, her heart swelling with affection for each one. Webb, Emily and Ryan, already looking like a family, though the adults hadn't yet exchanged their own vows. Bob and Pam Cochran and their tiny daughter, Pam looking as proud as if she'd been entirely responsible for the happy outcome of Jeff and Autumn's romance. Derek and Clay, smiling fondly at their youngest sister-in-law. Autumn's mother and Jeff's mother, sitting side by side and sharing a box of Kleenex.

Finally Autumn's eyes lifted to the makeshift altar, where Jeff waited patiently for her, flanked by her sisters on one side, his father and his partner Julian on the other, the minister standing just behind him. Seeing him standing there, darkly handsome in his pearl-gray suit, his ebony hair gleaming in the overhead lighting, his blue eyes glowing with love and happiness, Autumn remembered the words that had come to her mind the first time she'd set eyes on him that morning in October. A beautiful man. Now she knew that he was as beautiful on the inside as he was on the outside.

Her gaze locked with his, she stepped confidently forward, perfectly content with the roles she had chosen. Wife. Lover. Partner. Friend. Jeff smiled and held out his hand.

HOURS LATER Autumn walked out of their hotel-room bathroom, her hair loose around her shoulders, the clinging black nightgown—a never-before-worn birthday gift from Summer—swishing around her ankles. She caught her breath as Jeff turned to smile at her, wearing only the bottom to a pair of gray cotton pajamas. "So you really do wear cotton pajamas," she managed lightly, her eyes drinking in the sight of his gleaming, lamplight-bronzed chest.

"I haven't worn them much since I met you," he admitted with a husky chuckle. "They always seemed unnecessary on the nights we spent together."

"So why are you wearing them now?" she asked softly, one eyebrow lifted meaningfully.

He hesitated for a moment, seeming to consider her question, then grinned and shrugged. "The same reason you're wearing that luscious gown, I suppose. A mere formality. Come here, Autumn Reed-Bradford."

Autumn laughed and went into his arms. "I think we can do away with the hyphen. I don't mind sharing your name. Perhaps the custom is obsolete, but it does make things less confusing in the long run."

"I love you, Mrs. Bradford," Jeff told her unsteadily, pulling her closer.

"I love you, Dr. Bradford." She lifted her face for his kiss.

Jeff started to walk with her toward the bed, but Autumn held back, shaking her head firmly. "Oh, no. Not yet. There's something you have to tell me first."

He grinned, knowing exactly what she meant. "Elwood."

Autumn choked. "Elwood? Your first name is *Elwood*?"

"*Harvey* was Mother's favorite movie," he explained diffidently, his cheeks suspiciously warm.

Autumn laughed so hard that she had to hold her side. "I knew you reminded me of someone. Jimmy Stewart as Elwood P. Dowd," she managed to say with a gasp. "The consummate gentleman, unfailingly polite and considerate. Gentle, kind, sensitive. Just naturally perfect."

"I'm not a lush!" Jeff protested. "I hardly drink at all."

Autumn waved a dismissive hand. "That's not what I was talking about, and you know it."

"I knew this is the way you'd react. That's why I refused to tell you before you married me," Jeff muttered, his lips twitching with the smile he was trying to hold back.

"Oh, Jeff, I love you." She threw her arms around him, causing him to lose his balance and fall backward onto the bed, his arms closing around her to catch her to his chest.

"And I would have married you even if I'd known that your first name was Elwood. But don't you *dare* start talking to invisible rabbits!"

"I won't," he promised with a laugh, his hand going to the hem of her gown. In one smooth move he stripped the sexy garment off over her head, baring her to his exploration. The smile he gave her was anything but gentlemanly.

Delighted with the rare glimpse of the charming devil beneath his Southern gentleman exterior, Autumn abandoned herself willingly to her husband's lovemaking, eagerly returning the courtesy.

Harlequin is proud to introduce:

HEART OF THE WEST

...Where Every Man Has His Price!

Lost Springs Ranch was famous for turning young mavericks into good men. Word that the ranch was in financial trouble sent a herd of loyal bachelors stampeding back to Wyoming to put themselves on the auction block.

This is a brand-new 12-book continuity, which includes some of Harlequin's most talented authors.

Don't miss the first book, **Husband for Hire by Susan Wiggs.** It will be at your favorite retail outlet in July 1999.

HARLEQUIN®
Makes any time special™

If you enjoyed what you just read,
then we've got an offer you can't resist!

Take 2 bestselling
love stories FREE!

Plus get a FREE surprise gift!

Clip this page and mail it to Harlequin Reader Service®

IN U.S.A.	IN CANADA
3010 Walden Ave.	P.O. Box 609
P.O. Box 1867	Fort Erie, Ontario
Buffalo, N.Y. 14240-1867	L2A 5X3

YES! Please send me 2 free Harlequin Temptation® novels and my free surprise gift. Then send me 4 brand-new novels every month, which I will receive months before they're available in stores. In the U.S.A., bill me at the bargain price of $3.12 plus 25¢ delivery per book and applicable sales tax, if any*. In Canada, bill me at the bargain price of $3.57 plus 25¢ delivery per book and applicable taxes**. That's the complete price and a savings of over 10% off the cover prices—what a great deal! I understand that accepting the 2 free books and gift places me under no obligation ever to buy any books. I can always return a shipment and cancel at any time. Even if I never buy another book from Harlequin, the 2 free books and gift are mine to keep forever. So why not take us up on our invitation. You'll be glad you did!

142 HEN CNEV
342 HEN CNEW

Name	(PLEASE PRINT)	
Address	Apt.#	
City	State/Prov.	Zip/Postal Code

* Terms and prices subject to change without notice. Sales tax applicable in N.Y.
** Canadian residents will be charged applicable provincial taxes and GST.
  All orders subject to approval. Offer limited to one per household.
  ® are registered trademarks of Harlequin Enterprises Limited.

TEMP99   ©1998 Harlequin Enterprises Limited

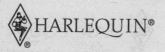